The Ashorne's Ingress

Seamus Eaton

Pumpkinwolf
Press

Copyright © 2018, by Seamus Eaton
Published in 2018 by Pumpkinwolf Press, Westchester, N.Y.

Cover Art & Design by Seamus Eaton
Cover Edit by M.H. Pasindu Lakshan
Map by Tânia Gomes, www.mystic-wings.com
Copy Editing by Kelly Cozy, booksidemanner.com

This is a work of fiction. Names, characters, places, and incidents either are the product of the author's imagination or are used fictitiously. Any resemblance to actual persons, living or dead, events, or locales is entirely coincidental.

Visit our website at **www.arbantales.com**

ISBN 978-0-972-1563-0-1

Printed in the United States of America

This book is dedicated to Dianne, Charley, and Teddy, without whom my life and work would mean nothing.

Author's note: If your eyes are as bad as mine,
take a look at a larger version of this map on **www.arbantales.com**

Welcome!

I offer an author's word to the reader, which is to say, not exactly a
conventional foreword, but more a moment of kindly advice...
There are appendices in the back of this novel that might prove somewhat
useful as one moves in and around the Environ that is Arba. Some of the
information held in the appendices will no doubt baffle and confound. A
good deal of it may in some small manner allay the nagging sense that one
is eavesdropping at a party at which everyone is speaking Squirrelese –
except you.
Have no fear. Dabble in the appendices, nod knowingly at their wisdom,
or don't, if you are more the "total immersion" kind of reader...(credit for
that phrase to my old German teacher Herr Kleinmann, who despite his
impenetrably Teutonic demeanor said, in my presence, two of the funniest
things I have ever heard. One involved coming down a chimney with a
"Guten Morgen" on Christmas morning; the other involved a Vice
Principal's toupee).

That segue aside, I very much hope the appendices help insofar as you
decide they can and do. I would like to point out one very particular item
as to prevent any confusion regarding some of the characters' ages.
A year on the planet OSM last fifty percent longer than ours here on earth.
And so a person who is sixteen years old in Arba would be closer to
twenty-four in Chicago or Kuala Lumpur.

Enjoy, and thank you for indulging me even I prepare to return the favor...

-    Seamus

Chapter 1
"Go jump in a river."

Place: Mount Kisco, NY
Date: August 8, 2020

"You were out!"

"He missed the tag!"

"The ball beat you, you didn't slide, and you crashed into him. You're out!"

"He dropped the ball!"

"He held on long enough!"

William Gentry heard the debate, but he wasn't really paying attention. He'd been knocked on his ass by the runner and was now looking, somewhat dazedly, for his glasses and cap. It was hard to find either without the glasses; he was groping around on hands and knees but having no luck.

Someone—and there was a small army of someones around him now—was almost guaranteed to step on the glasses and shatter them. His wife had told him to get the ones with the plastic lenses, but he hadn't listened, and he didn't have a backup pair with him. In fact, the ones that had just flown off his face in the collision had been the backup pair. The original pair he'd dropped in the driveway and run over with the car months before.

"How long did he hold on? He didn't hold on!" someone yelled. The runner.

"You're out! Get off the field or you're outta the game!" barked the ump.

A little blood from a cut over William's left eyebrow—probably from his frames being smashed into his flesh—dripped onto his arm.

"Ask him if he tagged me."

"No. You're out. Get off the field right now or you're outta the game."

William suddenly felt a little nauseous, dropped down on his belly, and then rolled over and took a deep, slow breath. He groped absentmindedly with his right hand for a few seconds, vainly searching for the glasses, and placed his left hand on his abdomen. No sharp pains, nothing broken. Probably nothing broken.

His right hand found his cap but not the glasses. He should've bought goggles with a strap, but he'd forgotten to do that. Didn't matter; the guy who'd run into him was huge enough to separate his head from his neck. Having goggles strapped on might've have meant having goggles permanently imbedded in his skull. This way, at least, he only bled and rolled, yet with his skull still marginally attached to his body.

He got up onto his knees, coughed, and wondered why no one was helping him look for the glasses. *Why would they?* he thought. *They just want to get on with the game.*

"Third base, you all right?" the ump asked him somewhat indifferently. Well, at least he asked. His teammates just stood around and stared from a safe distance. Assholes.

He glanced down and finally discovered the missing glasses, not two feet from where he was kneeling and still intact. "Yeah, thanks, I'm good."

He grabbed the glasses, put them back on, slapped some dirt off his pants, and got up. The world spun for a second, and he felt like puking. He shook off the feeling, and the game resumed.

A fly ball to left center ended the inning with the score six all.

This was the second playoff game for the Roundabout softball team of the New Castle adult "C" league, a 6:45 p.m. start. "C" league was for the old guys, the fat guys, the guys who could barely hit the ball out of the infield, and guys like him who could play pretty well but were prone to injury and so stayed away from the higher leagues with their screaming line drives and preening jocks and vicious competition. Most times, you could avoid injuries in this league if you played cautiously, and that appealed to him. The multiple health issues he was dealing with didn't need broken bones to compound them. Still, there were occasions where third base was as dangerous as an Alsatian trench circa 1917, minus the mustard gas, bullets, and shrapnel.

It was early August, the year of someone's lord 2020. His team had already lost one game in a double-elimination playoff. If they lost this one, that was it until next April. They weren't very good, at least on defense, so William expected them to lose, while at the same time holding on to the idea that he'd love to win every game and keep playing till Christmas.

Alsatian trenches and collisions aside, softball was a part of his life that made some kind of sense. At forty-six, recovering from two failed careers, first as an attorney and then as a teacher, most of his past and present didn't make much sense to him at all. Regrets, missed opportunities, bad choices, etc. At any given time, he had three or four minor conditions and one or two major ones, and he lived in fear of losing his health insurance. As a father, he felt like a perpetual schmuck, always trying but never getting it quite right. And as a husband, he felt like an ambassador from another galaxy, one in which long days of silence and tension were considered healthy, necessary, and compulsory. But once a week, he was a pretty good hitter who showed flashes of brilliance in the field — when he wasn't getting knocked on his ass.

"C'mon, guys, let's win this inning!" cried Carmen the Yeti, the co-captain and William's best friend on the team.

Two outs, bottom of the seventh, still a tie game. Runner on second. William was on deck.

And then he heard Michelle calling his name.

"Billy! Billy!"

It had to be his sister; she was the only one who still called him Billy. Where the hell was she? Everyone on his team was looking out at right field. He turned and looked out there too and saw Michelle running across the field to him.

Something was wrong. Really wrong.

He started running toward her and met her on the edge of the outfield grass. She was frantic, had clearly been crying, and was winded.

"Billy...Wanda...the kids..."

"What? What's happened? What?"

Then he saw the two cops walking onto the field from the parking lot.

It was a freak accident. That's what they always say about accidents that cost people their lives, isn't it? That's what they were telling him. Not just the once, no: everyone who came to the hospital, everyone who came to the funeral or called — hell, he even began to chant it himself, to them, to himself, in his sleep, in the shower. Freak accident — not a normal one, not a normal accident where no one dies and no one gets hurt and no one burns to death and everyone, except maybe the insurance adjusters, forgets it happened before they sit down for dinner. No, a freak accident has some additional mojo, a kind of super "hey, did you hear?" kick that normal accidents don't. And somehow "lethal" has, in the-unaffected-digesting-the-horrific language, morphed into "freak" — a word we use to make the thing we just heard that we just don't hear every day into something more amenable.

But "freak" is somehow more than "lethal" too, because it implies something rare, something special. So, lethal plus. New and improved lethal. Lethal 2.0.

The ground beneath the propane tank that serviced the Gentry home had been eroding unnoticed. The erosion had created a small sinkhole that tilted the tank. A kink in the copper pipe from the tank had caused a buildup in the line. Wanda had turned on the oven to make dinner for the kids.

The explosion killed her instantly.

The kids had been playing in the family room, separated from the oven by a fairly thick wall. The subsequent fire landed both of them in the ICU. A fireman from Chappaqua, maybe one of the guys William played softball against sometimes, had pulled both children out just before the roof gave way. The fireman was in the ICU too.

There was nothing left of the house.

There was nothing left of Wanda. Or at least, that's what they told him.

Part of the charm of the freak accident is relating the gory details, but it's usually considered bad form to report those details to those immediately affected by them.

He spent the night in a hospital hallway, still in his cleats, still wearing his dirty shirt and spare glasses. The small scrape above his eyebrow from the collision at third base started to burn and itch at some point. It had become infected; the next morning, a nurse insisted that he have doctor look at it.

He consented, if only to shut her up.

But the scrape was left unseen to and the doctor's ministrations never happened because Sylvester, his three-year-old son, died less than one minute after the nurse called the attending ER resident. His burns and the damage the smoke had done to his young lungs were too severe. Yancy, William's five-year-old daughter, was still in critical condition.

His son was dead.

His wife was dead.

His little girl was dying.

William didn't know. Anything. He couldn't think, couldn't even really see. People were talking to him, asking him questions. Michelle. Carmen from the team. Harold from the team. The guy who'd knocked him down at third. His father. When had his father driven up from Baltimore? How were the Orioles doing? Probably not too good: they never had any pitching, and in that division, you needed pitching.

Why did they never have any pitching?

In the seventies, they'd had pitching.

Someone brought him some clean clothes, and he changed in a room the nurse led him to. He drank some water. There was an update on Yancy at about 5:00 p.m.; she was going to live, but they couldn't say for how long. She was in surgery. They would keep him informed.

Surgery. Why? He tried but he couldn't remember.

His scrape was burning.

Someone put a bandage on it at some point.

They gave him something to eat. It tasted, not surprisingly, like death. He was not at all alarmed that he seemed to be very familiar with the taste of death. He knew how it smelled, how it tasted, how it felt. And he was good with that.

He took another bite.

He gagged, coughed, and then tried another bite to be sure he'd properly assessed the taste. Something very smug in him assured him he had.

They served fairly excellent food here at this hospital. *The cafeteria must be an amazing place*, he thought.

They gave — someone gave, always a someone, because though he was intimate with the sensorial delights and nuances of death now, faces seemed to be nothing but shapes and nuisances — him something to make him sleep. Maybe it was his dad; the hospital wouldn't have done that, not with insurance issues and their own asses always at the forefront of any decision. Water was tantamount to poison in the actuarial mind frame. They served death, but water was a no, and pills to the unadmitted…well, let's not even talk about the pills.

But he hadn't seen his father's face or heard his voice. No.

There is a house in New Orleans…

He hadn't slept for almost forty hours, but the pills did the trick, and death nodded its stinking, tasty approval. His dad was and wasn't there, so he went to sleep in a hospital bed one floor down from where his son had died and his little girl was dying.

They hadn't let him see either one.

Because of the freak accident thing.

Hey, did you hear about the oven that exploded and blew up that family over in Kisco?

Let me tell you, it was something…

And lord, you know, I'm one…

Just before he passed out, he remembered: no, he hadn't tagged the guy out.

It was a week later, two days after the funeral, when they came to him. He was sitting in his sister's yard in the dark, sipping a stale bottle of Guinness and listening to the crickets. Their song dragged him down with its easy, taunting pace, and each bug seemed to toss his soul across the flat, lost places of the world, where it was caught and held easily and interminably by another distant, sinister insect.

Yancy was still alive. She was hooked up to a machine to help her breathe. Only sixty percent of her skin had been burned.

"You are William."

And it's been the ruin of…

He didn't look up. People he scarcely knew or remembered had been approaching him all day with words of consolation and grief. He appreciated them doing so, but how could he tell them the bugs were playing volleyball with his soul, and the food in the hospital had tasted like rotted entrails, and the moon seemed to be spinning and twirling every night when it rose in places it shouldn't?

"We come to you with an offer. A request, in truth. And offer and a request."

Lord, you know, I'm one...

He stared numbly at his beer and breathed in. Something had been hurting, something neither physical nor emotional. A part of him he hadn't known he had. A new part? It hurt to breathe. "Thank you. Thanks for coming. My sister's inside. Have something to eat."

He turned his mind away from them and toward the problem of the Orioles' pitching staff. Why had they let so many good arms go over the years? Mussina. He was arguably a Hall of Famer. Angelos had plenty of money. He could afford a payroll, then and now. But sixty percent of his money was allotted to five players. Five players, sixty percent. That seemed a little lopsided. No, not anymore: Palmeiro and Ripken and Alomar were long gone. Palmeiro with his pointing finger, Ripken with his streak, Alomar with his spitting...and Brady Anderson with his freakish fifty homers and those sideburns...gone. Now it was Machado and Schoop and...no, they were gone too, weren't they?

They'd kept Yancy under so far. It was better for the recovery. He assumed it was better in the sense that a little girl who was suddenly conscious and who had been burned over sixty percent of her body would scream incessantly, braced by unthinkable agony, and no one wanted her to experience that, let alone experience her experiencing that.

They'd told him to go home and rest.

She was resting, so he should too.

Made sense.

In any case, he'd had to leave to bury Wanda and Sylvester. They were resting too.

He could come back, they said, tomorrow. Michelle and Dad had driven him home and to the funeral.

Closed caskets.

No choice there.

They'd offered the choice of cremation because the Gentrys hadn't had any plots.

William was steadfastly against burning his family a second time.

His dad handled the details while his sister led him to the car and gave him two Xanax.

They call the Rising Sun...

One of them, whoever they were, cleared his throat. "We would ask that you hear and consider our offer," he said.

"Please," the other one added.

William didn't answer.

"We know about your daughter. We know she will die unless we help her."

He looked up at them.

There were two of them. They were dressed in robes like monks, but the robes were a lightish color, maybe yellow or orange; it was difficult to say in the evening light. One was very short, almost childlike, and the other was about William's height, a little under six feet. Their faces were Asian in shape and feature but a very dark brown. The short one had a thick, untrimmed moustache that reached down to his chin. The other one wore a look of mild disgust; he owned the voice that had spoken first, the voice that had mentioned Yancy.

"You're not doctors," William said flatly.

"No."

"What are you? Born Agains?"

"We are ambassadors," said the short one. "We have come to make you an offer, and if you accept, we will intervene on your child's behalf."

"Ambassadors? What are you talking about? Ambassadors from where?"

"An answer to that question would require more time than you have," said the taller one. "Suffice it to say we have the ability to heal the girl in exchange for a service on your part."

"An ability? So you are doctors. Plastic surgeons? What? Burn specialists from…some monastery or something?"

"We are not doctors," said the taller one with a hint of impatience.

"I don't understand."

The shorter one touched his companion's arm, seemingly taking the lead in the conversation. "We are…devotees of an ancient practice, a practice with which you are doubtless unfamiliar…"

"I see. I get it. Mystics, huh?"

"In a sense."

"Who called you? Michelle?"

"No one called. We came here to speak to you. We know what you are."

"You know what I am? What I am? I'm a drunk on a lawn with no life left, and you're two crazies who have decided to join me. Have a fucking beer and shut up."

"We can help you."

"So, you're going to pray for Yancy and what, make her all better through the grace of some bullshitter of a God?"

"No."

"Then what? Who the fuck are you guys?"

The taller one spoke up again. "We are from Arba: it is a land far from here, on another world. As Utla said, we know who and what you are, Ashorne, and we will have your cooperation or your obedience. The choice is yours."

Feisty fucker, the tall one.

"What choice?"

"You can choose, when the time comes, to let the Arbans fail."

"What are you talking about?"

Utla threw a look at his irritated companion. "Apologies, please. B'mai doesn't agree that we should let you choose, but most of us believe it's essential that you do. Call it an interpretational schism."

"A what?" William was starting to get seriously annoyed.

"Again, we haven't the time to explain," said B'mai. "You will understand soon enough. If you comply with our conditions and allow the Arbans to fail —"

Utla interrupted him. "He means 'if you choose to help us,' then we can do more than simply save your daughter. We can make it as if none of this ever happened."

"This?"

B'mai looked William square in the face and smirked ever so slightly. "The deaths of your wife and son. The injury and inevitable death of your daughter."

"Really? You sure you don't want a beer? I'm having another."

"It is essential you understand: We are…sincere in our offer," said Utla.

"Okay then. Wait here." William regarded them both for a few seconds; they stared back at him, B'mai still with a look of disdain and that smirk on his face, Utla with an anxious, expectant expression.

William jumped up and half walked, half stumbled to the shed ten yards away. He yanked open the door and peered in, looking for something to swing. He found a crowbar and a posthole digger next to an old, broken freezer. He grabbed the crowbar and pulled, but it was stuck. He grabbed the digger.

Whirling around, he turned to face the two sonsofbitches who were interrupting his drinking.

They were gone.

He looked up at the house.

They couldn't have made it up there so fast. Had to have run into the woods.

He listened.

There was no sound coming from the woods.

"Come back, and I'll bust your friggin' heads open, the both of ya!" he yelled, but his adrenaline vanished. Within moments, he was fading back into his conversation with the bugs and the Oriole front office. He walked slowly back to his chair and dropped the digger on the grass.

Crazy fuckers.

On the chair, there was a piece of what looked to be parchment and a small brown triangle made of glass. He turned and took another look at the woods, and then he picked up what they'd left for him. Scrawled on the parchment in a strange and angular hand was a simple message:

> If you accept, and if you want her to live, you must dive into the water of a river at 2:17 a.m. on a night of no moon. Do not wear or bring anything of metal or stone. Carry nothing but the Germ of Reismyl — and carry the Germ you must, for the rest of your life.

He tossed the note aside. The triangle he held on to as he sat back down. "For the rest of my life. Huh." He lifted the triangle, stared at it a moment, and coughed. "So you're the Germ?"

And Lord, you know, I'm one...

He looked up at the sky and saw stars but no moon. He looked at his watch. It was just after nine. "No metal or stone. Guess that means I can bring my beer."

He sat there for a moment and sucked his teeth. The crickets crept up near him, listening, anticipating. He slapped his knee dramatically. "Well, of course. I would sink, right?" He rose and yelled, "Metal and stone would make me sink, right?" at the forest.

He took a sip of his beer. He cried a little. He pissed himself just a little, too, and plopped back down into his chair. The beer bottle fell out of his hand, hit the grass, and rolled a few inches.

Yancy was alive, for now. Wanda and Syl were not. Not ever again.

"Did those two trespassing monk bastards just tell me to go jump in a river?" he asked the crickets as he chuckled and wept and tried to take a sip of a beer that wasn't in his hand.

The crickets responded by grabbing hold of his soul ever so gently and tossing it back and forth to one another across the flat, lost places of the world.

Sometime about midnight, William climbed up the midportion of the steeply sloped lawn, a climb that seemed to take twenty minutes but in fact took two, and onto the deck. There were a few candles still lit on the table. Through the bay window he could see Michelle asleep on the couch, the TV flashing light all about the otherwise darkened room. Dad must've gone to bed. Michelle's husband, Frankie, had taken their kids over to his mother's, so Dad had probably retired in one of their rooms.

Or not.

"Bill…son, come inside."

The air was a little heavy, and the sound of approaching thunder warned of a storm.

"Thanks, Dad, no," William said as he sat down at the table and looked at a plate Michelle had left for him. There were mosquitoes on the watermelon. They were forming lines of battle based strictly on a sort of closely held secret regarding intricate mosquitoish affiliations.

"You need to rest."

"I know."

"Bill, I…I don't know what to say."

"Thanks for coming up, Dad."

"Whatever you need."

"I know. How's Baltimore?"

"Still there, I guess. Same stuff." Dad came over to Bill, sat down on the bench next to him, turned, and looked him square in the face. "I love you, son."

William didn't answer. He knew he loved his father too, but he couldn't think of why or of how to say that. He felt like he was in a tunnel, or in a closet, or high up in the sky, looking at his dad from a distance. He watched the man cry a few tears, felt him pat his hand, and saw him rise to go to bed. He thought his father said, "Why don't you go for a swim?" but Michelle didn't have a pool.

"What's that?"

"I sure am gonna miss them, Wanda and Syl. We all are."

"Yeah."

He sat at the table for a while and listened to the summer's evening wind. The mosquitoes had declared a general truce on the matter of the watermelon, and soon it was covered so thickly that only small spots of sickly pink were visible. The candlelight froze the swarm and then, to his eye, made it jump like an old-timey animation.

Jump, jump, stop, jump, stop. Jump. Freeze.

He looked at his watch. It was 1:43 a.m.

Too late to drive to the Hudson. Ossining was…too far, wasn't it?

Fuck yes, Ossining was too far. Fifteen minutes probably. Maybe a little less. Too far.

No, it wasn't.

Jump in a river. Jump in the river and defy the sixty percent, save the daughter, win the game, and make all the necessary corrections to the Orioles' roster. With the goggles on, of course, and the mosquito-infested watermelon divided up among all the hospital's guests. *I can see you, short round monk man, playing second next season, but the question is: Can you hit the off-speed stuff?*

A few weeks before, Wanda had been playing the piano. The kids were asleep, and she played with the soft pedal on. She loved to play show tunes but had recently learned something by Chopin because she thought William would like it. And he more than liked it. It sounded like a story to him, the story of something too sad and sweet to put to words, something elusively final, more memory than song. Nocturne no. 2 in E flat major. Something he'd somehow heard all his life, in the background, somewhere in his head. When had he first heard it? Where was he, what was he doing? And now Wanda was playing it for him, and how could he feel anything but love for someone who would do that, know to do that, when he'd never even told her how the song made him feel?

That night was the last time they'd made love. They'd made love and eaten chocolate donuts and fallen asleep listening to the rain.

He looked at his watch. It was 1:46 a.m.

Still too late to get in the car and drive to the Hudson and jump in a river.

Maybe. He wasn't sure. Why was he going to the river? Why would anyone drive to the Hudson at this hour? Watermelons, mosquitoes, line drives, Dad with a spatula flipping burgers on a gas grill that was always going to explode and kill everyone in Baltimore, everyone in Ossining, everyone falling asleep listening to the rain…

He got in the car and drove west along 133. The road was empty. The rain had missed them. He drove to Ossining, weaving.

He made it to the Metro North station by 2:08 a.m. He got out of the car and looked around. There were three cars in the parking lot. The bank of the Hudson was less than a hundred yards away. Chopin was smashing away at the inner wall of his skull.

"Jump in the river, save Yancy."

He opened the door and got out. He stood there looking at the streetlights reflecting off the big puddles in the parking lot.

"They can save her," he said to Chopin, to the crickets, to the Orioles' inept front office.

He took two steps from the car and then collapsed in a heap on the curb.

He started to sob.

When he stopped, finally stopped, he checked his watch. It was about 4:00 a.m.

He got back in his car and drove home.

The next day, August 22, happened to be Wanda's birthday. Strange day. Tough day. It became more difficult to bear when in the afternoon, at about 4:30 p.m., Yancy stopped breathing and didn't ever start again.

Chapter 2
"Sailing to Freme for peaches…"

Place: Tolii Nus Island, Arba Environ
Date: Boinage 16, AY 998

Leander Dossilea jumped down out of the skiff into the shallow waters of a very calm sea.

In full battle armor and unsure of his footing on the sand, he must've looked very imposing, however tentatively balanced, to anyone watching, yet he himself felt just then like laughing. He wasn't sure why.

The men would think me mad, he thought, *and even loyal men have a difficult time following a madman into battle, even when they themselves are mad. Which most of these are.*

That thought upped his impulse to laugh. Again, he refrained. Instead, he coughed and then stood and regarded the island before him, a mildly bemused but hardly insane look on his once-handsome face.

This is the last I'll have to deal with, and then it's home.

Wife, daughter, hall, friends, meat. The Cliffs.

Would that it were ever that simple.

He left his one-man captain's skiff to be secured to a reef by a crewman and then strode in toward the beach against the clear, warm waters of the departing tide.

Behind him, his men were doing the same with their six-man skiffs. The morning suns' light glittered and danced off their helms, the violets and pinks and greens flashing and blinding him momentarily.

The men's light armor hardly encumbered them. Like him — most often under his command — they'd landed this way on islands and shores hundreds of times.

The sight of an Aethrelean squadron marching out of the sea like an ancient army of immortal warriors born of the ocean's unknowable, immutable heart was a familiar one to all peoples in this part of the world. Friends rejoiced at the vision while foes fell as if they themselves were made only of sand, for the army to which Captain Leander Dossilea and the men he commanded forever belonged was the noblest and most battle-hardened fighting force in their world's tormented history.

They were conquerors, liberators, and warriors without peer.

Today we're here not to conquer, liberate, or make war, he mused. *This is about negotiation.*

But if we can't negotiate, we'll try something else, won't we?

Negotiation first. Those were his orders. He tried to firmly remind himself of this as he gained the beach, but the facts of the situation were tentatively held and easy to lose sight of, as facts so often are. Diplomacy was an art he relished but feared he'd never come close to mastering despite years of regular opportunity. Maybe it was mastery itself, in any capacity, that proved elusive

I'm a master of one thing and one thing only: not dying. And not allowing too many of those I lead to die.

The images of regrettable exceptions to that last phrase flashing briefly past his mind's eye, he turned to watch his men stomp out of the surf. It was his habit to do so whenever circumstances allowed. Something in the sight renewed in him the will to persist in his duty despite his roiling and increasingly troublesome doubts.

Often the beach march was the last pure aspect of a mission; stomping rarely required the intervention of diplomacy or the treacherous rigors of introspection and decision.

The last of the men lined up. They were all waiting for his orders.

What shall I tell them?

What the hell are we doing here?

It pained him to think they'd been sent by way of keeping them — of keeping *him* — occupied. He'd been sent on fool's errands before but never, to his recollection, one that was designed to brand him with the mark of the eternal fool.

Never one he had so willingly and knowingly submitted to, either.

He longed to be anywhere else. The Cliffs, Renikalar, Decone, Prementia, the far side of the world...

He sighed, nodded to the men to signal he'd be with them momentarily, and then carefully reviewed the muddled facts, what few there were, in his mind:

The Stavers are in the wrong and need to be corrected. The Saiblinor might not themselves be Aethrelean citizens, but they are long-invited guests of the realm, and Tolii Nus Island is a part, however small, of the Great Nation. Aethrelean law has been upheld here for over a century. The Stavers should vacate this place immediately and allow the Saiblinorans to carry on with their lives.

The Fourth Mandate Squadron was here to make certain the law would be upheld on this day, in this place, but there was the question of how far their commander could and would go to uphold it. Captain Dossilea had killed his own before, but never without a heavy price.

"Men assembled, Captain," barked Heop, his steady, barrel-chested markon.

"Very good."

"Scouts have returned."

"Tell me."

"The Sabbies are holed up in their village about two miles inland, loosely surrounded on three sides by the Staver brigade."

"How loosely?"

"Three hundred yards."

"Commander's name?"

"Rabishol, sir."

"Do we know him?"

"He served under Tamios Frendami at Menwaut last year, sir. This here is his first command."

"I see."

Menwaut: an unqualified disgrace and disaster. More than forty had been wrongfully slain in a dispute over seeds. Another two hundred had succumbed to malnutrition in the weeks that followed. And an absurdly callous motion on the floor of the Aethrelean Square to quarantine the island for ten years, a move that would have all but ensured the extermination of the Menwautians, had been narrowly defeated by the eastern Unchained caucus. A black day in Aethrelean governance, but one he felt confident would not be repeated; Sebastien Yallous's Extended Protection and Provision Act had passed, albeit not swiftly, and left little room for interpretation.

Tamios Frendami, he of the gap-toothed smile, huge inheritance, and multiple bastard children, had received by way of compromise an undeserved, no doubt much-boasted-over commendation.

He should have been fed to the sharks.

"And who's his right-hand man?" Leander asked.

"His markon is...we're not sure yet, sir."

"You need to know your mirror, Heop. In case there's a dance."

"I'll have that information shortly, sir." Heop turned and walked away toward the squadron proper. Another warrior strode up, this one much younger and possessed of an aquiline, sharp-eyed countenance.

So much like him, thought Leander. *Still.* "Lieutenant Wexshai. Tell me."

"Captain, you should also know that Rabishol is a cousin of Beir."

"Tha'it Beir, you mean, Lieutenant."

"Apologies. Tha'it Beir," said Wexshai, his disgust only slightly concealed. It was that expression that made him most resemble Shain. Or perhaps it was Shain who had resembled Wexshai. They'd been so very close, the three of them. Michael, Wexshai, and Shain. Brothers of the spirit.

Leander looked away, back out toward to the sea. He stayed that way for a full minute, willfully banishing the thoughts of his son from his mind and trying to focus on the task at hand.

"Sir?" asked Wexshai. "What are my orders?"

"Just wait, Lieutenant," said Heop as he rejoined them.

Leander sighed and shook his head. "Served under Tha'it Frendami, related to Tha'it Beir. He has a few interesting allies, this Commander Rabishol."

Is it too late to drown myself laughing? he wondered.

"That and a bowl of hoggy soup," grunted Heop.

Leander chuckled and then narrowed his eyes a moment and shook his head slightly. Heop stifled his humor.

"Well, be that as it may, our task is to head off hostile action and settle the dispute," said Leander. "We'll visit Captain...?"

"Marshal," said Heop.

"Really?" Leander smiled, but now it was his turn to show a small measure of disgust. "Then we'll visit Marshall Rabishol first. Remember, under no circumstances is anyone to engage his troops."

"And if they show aggression?" Heop smirked.

"They won't. This Rabishol, no matter his allies, can't be as big a fool as to blithely ignore the Code or to let his men do so."

"We've heard differently," said Heop evenly. "Stavers have already..."

"Yes, I know. I've heard what you've heard." Peod Barrens, where two Unchained were supposedly murdered by Stavers. "Do you believe it?"

Neither Heop nor Wexshai answered right away.

They don't have to, do they? he thought. *We all know what happened.*

"I don't know what to believe, sir," said Wexshai with a hint of bitterness in his tone.

"Aethrelean murdering Aethrelean?" Leander stopped and looked at them. "Neither do I." He paused and carefully straightened his belt. "Go in then, as always, expecting the Code to prevail."

"Very good, sir." Markon Heop turned to face the men and raised his arms.

"But, Heop..."

Heop waited, already knowing his commander's thoughts.

"Be ready for aggression."

"Always, sir."

Leander turned to Wexshai.

"I'm going to need you to do something here. It's a bit irregular."

"Captain."

"Go to the Saiblinor settlement. Find out who's in charge and tell him I want to meet with him. Be clear that we're here on their behalf."

"Legal rights?"

"Yes, use those words, and more than once. Invoke the Code, but only if you're having trouble."

"When should we expect you, sir?"

"Soon. It shouldn't take too long to find 'Marshal' Rabishol, spank him, and assess his stance and muscle. You'll see us coming, Wexshai."

"Very good, Captain."

Without delay or further words, Leander headed east toward the Staver brigade. This time, he didn't turn around to see if his men were behind him, nor did he speak. Silently, the men fell in and followed in the steps of their famous commander.

After about one hundred yards, he found a rough path that turned southeast. He looked at Heop, who shrugged and took the path.

Leander considered what he knew about this place. Tolii Nus was an unremarkable, sandy island that had been sporadically and temporarily inhabited by various races. Most had chosen not to stay, but the Saiblinor were not particular.

They could scarcely afford to be. Centuries of defeat had left them in a state where they were always in the market for unremarkable and thereby undisputed and relatively peaceful places to settle. Even in a reputedly democratic part of Arba, the victors gained the spoils while the likes of the Saiblinor scrounged for whatever was left.

The island was less than ten miles long and six across; except for a few small patches of tropical fruit trees and bamboo, it was covered mostly in coarse sand and bushes. The people made their living, such as it was, gathering mettlebracks—a variety of large oyster the shells of which could be, painstakingly, fired and strengthened for use in roofing, the crafting of household items such as bowls, and even light armor for archers, though most governments had long since stopped the production of such, particularly since the advent of the Crab armies. No doubt the economic impact of that decision had been devastating to these people, but as with every other catastrophe in their history, and there had been many, they'd learned to adapt and endure. They persisted in gathering mettlebracks. They made a lot of bowls.

There was little reason for the military to visit Tolii Nus. There was no outpost here, and the surrounding reef made it nearly impossible to approach with a craft larger than the skiffs Leander and his men had used. There was no harbor to speak of—just a few docks the locals used for fishing. The Staver brigade, which numbered over two hundred men, had gone through a lot of trouble to get to this impoverished little island. Leander wondered why, but he knew his wondering was a ruse. He was trying to blind himself to their true motivations.

As the squadron marched, the ground began to slope modestly upward. He turned and looked out at the sea and the sky above it, noticing a strange confluence of black clouds out past where their schooner, *Cliff's Awake*, and her sister runner, the swift and tested *Well's Time*, were anchored. A storm was coming, and at this time of year, that wasn't a fact to be ignored. "Weather, Heop."

"Sir."

"I was hoping we'd stay dry, is all."

"Been a rough season for squalls, Captain."

"Have five men find a suitable campsite and set us up. We may be here the night."

"Sir." Heop left his side for about a minute and then returned. "They're signaling the ship to send in more gear, sir."

"Very good." He turned and continued on the now widening path. Five minutes later, he was looking down at the Staver camp.

"Hold!" Three sentries wearing black chain mail and clearly laboring under its weight ambled forward with swords drawn.

Heop stepped forward and made a show of putting his hands out at his sides, palms down. "Fourth Mandate Squadron, Captain Leander Dossilea commanding, here on orders from the Chief of the Caucus," he announced loudly.

The Stavers didn't move.

"You men need to sheath those weapons, right now," barked Heop.

Still they didn't move.

Heop lowered his arms and smiled. "Come on now, boys. There isn't any need to get chippy."

"We're not to let anyone pass. If you're here officially, you've got papers," the closest Staver said.

"Papers? Well, let's see, we had papers, but they got all wet, doncha know?"

"No papers, no entry."

Leander stepped forward and removed his helm. "Markon Heop, I'm confident these good men are adherents of the Code and understand that in the absence of papers, or even in their presence, the word of a captain or tha'it is determinative. Lucky for us, I happen to be both."

The Stavers, unsure of what to do, held their positions for a moment more. Then they lowered their swords unsteadily.

Leander nodded once and strode right past them.

As he and the Fourth Mandate followed their commander past the deflated sentries, Heop said something about not having paper to wipe his ass with either; he noted the shame of that deficiency, given his pressing need to relieve himself just then.

The sentries had no reply.

The Fourth marched down into a small village of tents and Staver soldiers.

"Enough beige here to make a man think someone's been guzzling smekka," said Heop, not softly. A few of the Stavers turned to stare; two took a step in his direction. Heop shook his head, smiled, and nodded at Leander's back. Seeing the captain's insignia, they stopped where they were and just glared. Heop grinned at them and winked.

The guards at the entrance to the command tent were savvier types who immediately recognized Leander. They stood aside but did not open the flap for him. He ignored the slight and entered the tent. He paused for a moment as his eyes adjusted to the lower light, and the eyes and minds of those who beheld him adjusted to their new predicament vis-à-vis his presence. The men in the tent knew exactly who he was and why he was there. They stopped eating and stood up...all but one.

"Tha'it Dossilea!" said a smallish man in a clerk's uniform. "Frederick's times to you, many times, many times, yes!"

"And to you, Terwam Kesel," said Leander.

"Terwam? Well, thank you, thank you, sir, but I have not yet had the honor..." stammered Kesel.

"Then is it far overdue, good man."

"Thank you, oh yes..."

"To what to we owe the unbridled joy of this visit, Captain Dossilea?" said a thin blond man in a thick beige cloak. He was the man still seated, and he gave no indication of an intention to rise, present situation notwithstanding.

"You need to be standing, Rabishol," growled Heop from behind Leander.

Rabishol remained seated and smiled. "That's Marshall Rabishol, *Markon*."

"Please, Heop," said Leander. "I'm sure this is merely a matter of the marshal being unsure which protocol to follow under the current murky circumstances. Does he remain seated, assuming this to be a military meeting, and in the field no less, in which case his hard-won title outranks mine, or does he conclude instead that our gathering here today is one of diplomacy and governance, in which case my status as tha'it clearly outranks his as...well, a good citizen, shall we say?"

Rabishol reddened and slowly rose. "It makes no matter. We haven't any need of the Grand Fourth's heroic assistance here. Just some local shitbloods making trouble."

Leander gestured for all to sit back down, which they did, and then he sat down himself. "We aren't here to assist, Marshall. Only to observe and, of course, to talk."

"Talk?" said Rabishol in an amused and dubious voice.

"First, let me say I'm impressed that you were able to drag a war table in past the reef."

Kesel spoke up: "Oh, the Sabbies brought all our supplies in via fishing boat, Tha'it."

"Did they? Was that before or after they began to stir up such trouble as would require the attention of a full brigade?"

"Tha'it Janstrin Beir has ordered that this island be fully regimented," sneered Rabishol.

"For what purpose? There's nothing here," asked Heop.

"Correction, Markon: there will be nothing here, not after we remove the shitbloods and burn their disgusting shanties and all the sea filth they've collected."

Leander's eyes widened for only a moment. It was as he'd suspected, but he hadn't believed even Beir would ever give such an order. "You're removing the inhabitants, then?" he asked by way of making the situation absolutely clear to one and all. He didn't want any confusion down the road at the inquest.

One of Rabishol's subordinates, a markonite two with a harelip and eyes that looked at if someone had sprayed seawater in them, spoke up. "'Removing' is a gentle way of putting it, Tha'it, and not entirely accurate. Rather say 'discontinuing.'"

"On what grounds?" demanded Heop.

"As of this year, this island falls under the jurisdiction of the Beir Province, as per Yallous's pathetic Act."

Heop, never really an avid follower of the law and its limitlessly mutating nuances, looked at his commander. Leander simply nodded and rose. The Stavers clumsily and hastily rose as well, all except their leader, who had apparently decided that his earlier decision to rise might have been in error. Heop opened his mouth to reprimand the man, but Leander placed a hand on his shoulder that told him to stand down. Then he focused his eyes on the marshall's.

"Marshal Rabishol, Mr. Kesel, good commanders: thank you for seeing us. I need to file a return report for Minister Yallous and send it via messenger craft immediately. Good afternoon."

And with that, he turned and strode out of the tent.

"I don't understand, Captain. We're leaving?" asked Heop, hustling to keep up with his commander.

Leander shook his head and kept walking. "No. We're going to the Saiblinor settlement."

"What orders shall I give the men?"

"We're going to set up positions around the settlement until Wexshai and I can figure out a way to stop this madness. A legal way."

"And if there isn't one?"

"There will be. These people need our protection. The Stavers aren't here to deport them," said Leander, his jaw set with anger. "Beir has ordered an action."

"So I gathered."

"This is a bold and violent move. Rabishol wants blood, and plenty of it. The Saiblinorans are in a serious spot."

"Then they need our swords, not our words."

"Unlikely. Rabishol knows the Code. He won't bear arms against us; he'd be hung out to dry by any headman from Chralm Doanna to the Cliffs. The only way he might conceivably make a move is if he thought our presence here was unverifiable."

Heop paused a moment, clearly a little confused as the conversation drifted once again in the nuances of legality. "Then I'm glad Yallous knows we're here and that Rabishol knows he knows," he said.

Leander smirked. "Yallous knows no such thing. I told him we were sailing to Freme for peaches."

"Peaches? He'll know you were lying. The Fourth gets its peaches at Hukki Point, always has," said Heop. "Me, I don't even like the damn things. Bad for my delicate bowels."

"Yallous knows when we're doing something he doesn't want to know about."

"There was a time he loved peaches, if I recall correctly. And he loved knowing just about everything."

Leander replied, "So he did. But Musilia makes him very happy now and has for what…twenty years? And as for the other…who can say?"

Leander halted, turned around stiffly, and stared at the two sentries who were following them. The two men stopped, looked, and then turned around and walked away.

"I thought you said he sent us here," Heop said.

"Who?"

"Yallous."

"He did."

Heop grunted his lack of understanding and willingness to overlook any need to understand if it meant he might get to clobber some beige.

They strode north toward some of the larger tree patches. There was a small saltwater creek that ambled north–northeast, burbling and sighing over a bed of white stone and broken seashells. Crabs darted on the rocks, dancing away from the men as they approached.

They followed the creek toward the sea and within minutes spotted a series of scattered huts and barnlike structures. There was a heavy smell of manure and wet salt. A few of the huts had smoke rising from rough holes in the rooftops; the smoke smelled of burning fish that, when mixed with the manure and the salt, gave the air for an oddly pleasant aroma, a scent of the living. Leander thought momentarily of home and the Cliffs' stables near the sea.

Wexshai and an elderly Saiblinoran met them at the edge of the settlement. "Captain," Wexshai said, "this is Boss of the Creek Unji Maiter."

Leander smiled politely and only politely despite his impulse to chuckle. Saiblinoran titles were rarely uninteresting.

Maiter caught his smile and the suppressed chuckle; he smiled in return and held out a small, three-fingered hand. "You laugh maybe because it seems funny to have a boss in a place like this. Really, we don't need it, but I can't fish anymore, and I never made a bowl worth a damn, so they give me a name to make me feel useful. Worst decision they ever made: I am a hard boss, and I don't like it when people feel sorry for me."

Leander took the goatman's hand and shook it firmly. "Captain Leander Dossilea, commanding the Fourth Mandate Squadron. We need to talk, Maiter."

"Yes, and to eat, too. Will you join us for our midday meal, Captain?"

Leander smiled again, appreciating the other's open directness — the contrast to the attitudes he'd encountered earlier in the tent was not lost on him. "We would be honored to join you."

"Wise choice. No talk on empty bellies, eh, Captain!" affirmed Maiter with a soft slap on Leander's shoulder. He turned and shuffled toward the huts, urging them with a dramatic wave of his arm to follow him.

Heop poked Wexshai and muttered: "Sabbies have better manners than the pissing beige. They offered us not so much as a cup of dirty water, them."

"They have a lot on their minds, they do, Mr. Soldier," said Maiter as he led them into the settlement and toward an open pavilion made of driftwood and mettlebrack. "They are busy trying to think of how to spare themselves the trouble of moving so many. It would be easier, I think, for them to hack us up and throw us into the sea."

"How many are you here?" asked Leander.

"Two hundred and eleven, until maybe tomorrow sometime."

"What happens then?"

"My son's daughter is about to bring another into our family. Her fourth!"

"Congratulations," said Leander and Heop together. They glanced at each other, brows slightly furrowed at their choral moment.

"The number may drop back down to two hundred and eleven the moment the baby is born if it looks like the one we think it will look like. My son doesn't like him."

"Congratulations anyway."

"Thank you. Now come, sit. The fish and bread are almost ready."

Leander beckoned one of his troopers to his side. "Inform Michael he's to establish a rotating perimeter there, there, and there," he said, pointing vaguely. There wasn't any sign of confusion on the trooper's face. "Also, report at fifteen-minute intervals as to the marshal's movements."

The trooper nodded and left.

They sat at a long table, its benches a few inches too short for tall Aethrelean warriors and their legs. Several clay pitchers of water along with some small rough bowls for drinking sat before them. Over an oval fire pit in the middle of the floor, a few young Saiblinoran men worked, turning fish and some kind of vegetables on a spit. A delicate goatwoman, who was perhaps only a girl, brought forward a huge mettlebrack serving tray laid high with hardbread.

"Please, gentlemen, eat, eat," said Maiter. "Aliof, where is the salt oil? Bread without salt oil?"

The Saiblinoran girl moved jauntily but quickly on hooved legs to find the missing oil.

"You're being awfully kind to a bunch that is here, for all you know, to expel you from your homes," said Heop.

"Not at all, sir. Good friend Wexshai has already explained that you are here to stop those others from doing just that."

Leander looked at Wexshai. The dark young legal advisor turned his head away and tried to suppress a sheepish grin.

"Did he now?" said Leander. "Well, I can tell you that might be difficult. Unfortunately, the commander down there has clear legal authority to remove you."

Wexshai stopped grinning and snapped his face back toward the others. "Untrue. Yallous's Act returns this land to Beir jurisdiction, but they haven't any meaningful grounds for collective expulsion."

"They may not have the grounds, but they have the bodies," said Heop.

The Saiblinoran men placed large platters of sea salmon, eel, and shrimp on the table. The scent of hard red spice and pepper wafted up with the steam from the fish.

"And they have the grounds," said Leander. He knew the Act as well as anyone and had even helped Yallous to complete the final draft when the old man's illness had taken a turn for the worse. He had recovered, had Yallous, but of course no one knew how long that would last.

"Is there nothing you can do, then?" asked Maiter with the air of someone who suspected there was still much that could be done. "We are Aethrelean citizens, are we not?"

"Listen to the fisherman who dreamt he was an arbiter!" laughed Heop. *"Let us be to one another like brothers, and know that this above all else will bring the light!"*

"And the light is above all else, my brothers, or why else have we come?" answered Aliof as she placed another pitcher of salt oil before them. "Try this on the fish, if you please."

Leander looked at her face and then at his men. Not a one was unimpressed to find a Saiblinoran who could quote Frederick so easily. Heop clapped respectfully for her and for the words she had quoted. The others slapped the table in approbation.

Leander held up his hand, nodded to her, and turned to Wexshai. "Anything?" he asked. He knew there was. Wexshai was both brilliant and determined, if given on occasion to digression.

"That you are citizens — and clearly well-schooled citizens — is not in question. The issue lies in the degree to which all citizens are viewed as equal under the law of this particular province," said Wexshai with a frown on his face. He grabbed a handful of shrimp and dropped them on his plate. "But I'm sure there's something we're missing here, something commandmentary perhaps…an argument we might make about the soundness of the action…"

"You use such pretty language, Master Wexshai. I am content that you are on our side, I think," said Maiter. "Eat, everyone, don't be shy."

Heop cut a slab of eel for Leander and took the rest for himself. "Yes, it's very pretty language, Wexshai, and yes, we're all on your side, Maiter, but to whom would we make such an argument? The seagulls? They'd be more apt to listen than those morons in beige."

"Well, neither the marshal nor our tha'it has the right to adjudicate on Tolii Nus, to be sure; we'd need to appeal to…" Wexshai started to say. He stopped and laughed.

"Something?" Leander said casually, knowing his brilliant young friend had of course lighted upon a solution.

"Unji, do you own this land?" asked Wexshai.

"The island? We've been here for over one hundred years."

"It was granted to you, yes?"

"Yes, by Mark Oanime of Bas al Lowen. The story goes — "

"There it is," pronounced Wexshai. He stuffed two shrimp in his mouth and washed them down whole with a huge slug of water, almost choking and drowning himself all at once. He settled and then ripped off a large piece of hardbread and began to chew its corner.

"Wexshai, breathe," said Leander.

The young man paused, gasped again, coughed, and nodded. "Explain."

Wexshai swallowed and took another swig of water. "We

ourselves cannot legally interfere, but because this seems strictly to be a question of property rights — the land grant by Oanime must have been recorded at Renikalar — we can request that someone else be brought in to weigh the facts and rule on the matter. A neutral authority specializing in property disputes."

"But there aren't any such neutral authorities within three hundred miles."

"No, there aren't. The closest one would be found in Renikalar itself."

They all stopped eating and looked at him.

He'd found the loophole.

Michael Pulami, reconnaissance and navigation master of the Fourth and the fraternal twin brother of Wexshai, came to the edge of the dining pavilion but did not enter. Leander noticed him at once and rose. Heop rose as well. Michael's chiseled face wore an assuring expression.

"Please, gentlemen, finish your meals and then see Heop for your positional assignments," said Leander. "Rotate your men in here and see they get something to eat. Use our rations; we don't want to empty the local larders."

"We have plenty, Captain, and you are welcome to it!" said Maiter.

Leander glanced at him. "Then I thank you, sir, for your hospitality. Heop, no one sleeps tonight. No shifts."

Wexshai left the table and went to his brother alongside Leander and Heop. "Relief from the ship?" he asked.

"Youssef's crew have already been signaled," answered Michael. "They'll be on the beach in less than an hour."

Leander patted Michael's back and steered him outside, Heop and Wexshai falling in behind them. "Tell me what I need to know," Leander said.

"The Stavers have armed themselves fully and seem to be waiting for nightfall."

"Weapons?"

"They were attempting to assemble one huvet sling, but it didn't appear to be going well. They have no firestone in any case; it would have been too difficult to transport without getting it wet."

"Doesn't mean they didn't try, the bastards," said Heop.

"Right. Let's assume they get the sling working and managed some rock from their frigate, just to be on the safe side," said Leander.

Michael nodded.

"Are your men in position?" Leander asked.

He nodded again and said, "And the ten at our camp."

"Good. We're sending Wexshai and Famish in to explain the situation to the marshal. Famish will do his drunk thing; at that time, take out the sling and whatever rock."

"They'll retaliate."

"Maybe. Without a big weapon and clear tactical advantage, I don't think even Rabishol is stupid enough to move ahead in the dark, despite his numbers."

"He knows who we are."

"You bet your ass he does," snarled Heop.

"Yes, I'd bet my ass he does," said Leander, "and tonight I'm also betting our reputations will do more damage than our swords. Michael, I want you to get word to Youssef; he's to request a property arbiter from Renikalar. Send the *Well's Time* with a skeleton crew."

Michael looked at him oddly but didn't comment upon the order.

"I know, it will take weeks before the man gets here," said Leander. "We're counting on it."

The day was coming to a close.

The orders had been followed out and the men positioned according to the plan. Leander and those of his command who were not otherwise occupied waited, somewhat removed from their newly made decoy camp, for things to play out. Wexshai and Famish had returned from their visit to Rabishol, convinced that hostilities were not necessarily inevitable but clearly being considered.

Thereafter, nothing went as planned.

Trilesti lingered in the sky for about an hour after her sister had disappeared. Still no word from the Stavers. The sky was still glowing with a dark violet hue when they heard the first explosion.

The ground shook beneath them.

The first was followed by at least a dozen more. Some came from the south and the Staver encampment. Some came from the Saiblinoran settlement. And there were at least two from the direction of the Fourth's decoy camp.

The twilight sky filled with a hideous black smoke.

From their watch in the dunes, they could see a massive black hole where their decoy camp had been. They could hear screams from the direction of the Saiblinoran settlement.

Leander started in that direction. Heop joined him without hesitation. He signaled the rest to stay back.

They scuttled and scurried among the dunes, the full mile or so back to the settlement.

The place was a wall of fire. There were no screams, and nothing was moving but the flames.

Heop looked about, a bewildered expression on his face. "What in the hell happened?"

Leander stared and shook his head.

"Let's get out of sight, Captain. Whatever did this isn't gone."

But it was gone, whatever it had been. There were no more explosions. They made their way back and waited, pinned in their hiding places, aware that concealment had spared their lives. They waited through the night and didn't stir until Ponasa rose. Nothing else happened. It was over.

At dawn, what was left of the Fourth Mandate Squadron searched the entire island, sifting through burning rubble and corpses that were no more than ash. The sand near each of the attacks had turned to black glass in some places. There were no traces of tents, structures, or equipment, or any people of any race. Even the creek was gone, seared off the island like a leech off a leg.

They were alone.

Leander's inner circle had survived relatively unscathed. Wexshai had a burn on his back and Youssef, who'd come ashore leading the now-dead replacements — twenty-one in all — had broken his wrist when he'd been knocked off a small sand cliff. The skin on his face was red. Michael and Heop were present but shaken.

Leander tried to wrap his head around that: two soldiers who had fought by his side for over a decade were shaken. The attack had been just that swift, just that brutal.

They'd never seen anything like it.

Before the suns set, Leander ordered them to reassume the positions they'd had on the night of the attack. They hid and they watched and they listened.

Nothing.

It was over three weeks before *Well's Time* returned on its now completely meaningless errand.

Her crew found less than half the squadron still alive: only those who had been on watch had gone unnoticed — or ignored — and untouched by the aggressor. The survivors confirmed what anyone viewing the island might have suspected: every Saiblinoran was dead, as was every Staver.

There was also no sign whatsoever of *Cliff's Awake* nor of any enemy vessel. Leander and his men assumed their ship had been sunk straightaway by whatever had bombarded the island, and they took it as a good sign that the enemy had withdrawn. The remainder of the Fourth had gone out looking for any sign of a battle in their skiffs, but the sea was devoid of both vessel and debris. There was no trace of any encounter: no ships, no debris, no footprints on the beach, no anything. It was as if they'd never been there.

Who did this, and what was the purpose? wondered Leander. It made no sense. Unless it did.

He stopped himself from thinking any more about it. There'd be time enough for that, and he feared that time would be upon them quite quickly.

"Who is in charge here? Where is Tha'it Leander Dossilea?" The property arbiter sounded more terrified than indignant, though he did his Aethrelean best to mask both emotions.

"His walk from the beach must've been eye-opening," Heop said flatly.

"Here," said Leander. He was sitting drinking some water from a large shell.

"Captain, what happened?" asked the arbiter, sounding far more awed than officious.

Leander couldn't blame him. Half his squad, gone. "We don't know."

"Where are the settlers? Where are the Stavers?" the arbiter asked, growing more confused and anxious. "I was sent to answer a question of law..."

"All but those you see here and a few of our men gathering food on the other side of this island are dead."

"Dead?"

"I'm sorry to have made you come all this way, Arbiter..."

"Arotrhis. Ketnice Arotrhis. What happened?" he asked again. The situation was clearly not within his range of expected challenges, but again, Leander could not hold the man accountable.

"We've no idea. There was an attack in the night, the very night I sent word to retrieve you. We've been here almost a month, with very little food and water. Only the fish and the rain kept us alive."

"I see," said Arotrhis, clearly not seeing at all.

"In any case, it's not safe here. We're leaving."

"As you wish. And I fear...I am sorry to...I should tell you, rather digressively, good Tha'it, that you've been recalled to Renikalar. Or perhaps given all this, not so sorry."

"Recalled? Why?"

Arotrhis was glancing about, perhaps wondering if the men before him had somehow done this. His awed expression was quickly evolving into one of terror.

"Arbiter, why have we been recalled?" Leander repeated.

Arotrhis collected himself and looked straight at Leander and then straight at the ground. "Janstrin Beir has called a Full Session of the

Square. It seems three districts have held independent votes, and there's been a momentous alteration…"

"Which three?"

"Foam March, the Lingler Forest, and Stestipha."

Leander stood quite still.

So it's happened.

Bad timing. Very bad timing.

"Of course, Command will want a full report of this…whatever this was," Arotrhis said awkwardly.

Heop answered: "He said we don't know what it was. Don't infer anything."

"I've inferred nothing, of course," said Arotrhis, whose terrified eyes said otherwise. He was trapped on a little island with a group who might very well have murdered an entire brigade and all the settlers as well.

Leander shook his head. "Get everyone to the ships. Ship. Send two men to find Michael and tell him and the others we're leaving," he said.

He started walking back toward the path to the beach. Heop caught up to him.

"What is it, sir? What's happened?"

"I believe the Stavers have just taken control of the Great Aethrelean Nation."

Chapter 3
"Boasts of unmatchable oddness"

Place: Island city of Pashka, kingdom of Pherriuskata, Arba Environ
Date: Boinage 21, AY 998

"I haven't time to consider all the angles, Lon. I'm a very busy duke, you know, one of the busiest in history, if Jemein the Reader is to be believed."

The summer wind from the Naipek Sound, unencumbered by any structure because none in this city were as high as Tower of Faler Mussan, slapped at them with a bold easterly fierceness. Two servants scurried about, trying to keep the lunch accoutrement from flying off to points unknown in the vast city below.

"The Reader is indeed most learned," Grewea replied with a flat tone. He shifted his backside in the notably uncomfortable palace chair that had been brought up to the deck for his comfort. The shift helped not at all.

Over a dozen centuries on this planet had rendered him nothing if not a somewhat broken, prickly bearded old skeleton, draped in the foolish purple-and-green robes of his current tiresome office. Still, he was many times the greater man when compared to the gyrating buffoon before him. The leader of over seven million, at the last rough count, and yet unable to properly shave or brush his hair or even to instruct someone to do it for him. Duke Estau Velliok indeed. This man should have been fed to something in the Garden long ago.

"Really? Nonsense. The man's a moron. Or so I thought. And I thought you agreed. Am I wrong? Oh, Great Advisor, tell me what I think, do." The duke smiled darkly and waved his glass at an attendant who quickly stepped forward and filled it.

Grewea stared at him for just a moment, wondering how he'd allowed this man to ascend to such a position. The duke was malleable, as his father had been, but he was also a perpetual nuisance, a thing that needed his hand held and his disheveled head stroked, as his father most assuredly had not been. Neither had his father been so damned fat. "One doesn't tell a duke what to think," Grewea said.

"Why not?"

"Primarily because a duke," he responded with a small smile, "should have his own thoughts, and plenty of them. And most of those should be shrewd, vicious, and productive."

"Most, not all?"

"No, not all."

"Why not?"

Grewea raised his eyebrows and curled his mouth down in an attempt at a matter-of-fact expression. "A man has to piss and eat and fuck, doesn't he? One doesn't need shrewd or vicious thoughts to acc-omplish any of those."

Duke Velliok laughed loudly, perhaps too loudly, signaling both his amusement with and his hatred of his companion. "Please, whatever it is you're doing with your face, don't. Four's sake, stop before I choke!"

Grewea altered his facial expression and offered something more familiar: still, cold, serpentine hatred, barely masked and utterly potent.

"Better, thank you. And to answer your question, I just don't know. Some of my more memorable dalliances have been rife with viciousness. And of course, pissing, eating, and fucking all need to be productive, at the least."

"But to make them productive, one needn't necessarily have productive thoughts. One need simply act," said Grewea.

"Are we still talking about bodily functions here, or have we moved on?"

"Don't hemorrhage yourself, but I just caught the faint scent of something shrewd about that question."

The duke stopped laughing; it was now his turn to raise eyebrows. He waited, staring intently at his companion. When Grewea did not speak, he said, "I think it better that you now say more. So say more."

"I haven't the energy, not today," Grewea offered with a tired smirk.

"Having a tough time of it? I expect that will happen more and more as you approach your—what is it, eightieth year?"

Grewea didn't answer. He gazed blankly down at the city, a thousand issues and complications pressing for his attention from within, and waited for the man he truly believed was the prince of all morons — and given the vast number of morons he'd known in his long, much longer than eighty-year life, that was a pitiful title to bestow—to finish pretending he knew what this meeting was really all about. The alternative, and one he momentarily considered but rejected, was to wave a finger at the fool and cast him over the side. Wouldn't it be something to watch that awful mauve dress jacket flap in the wind as it and its contents plunged some four hundred feet into the Rosen Square?

Wouldn't be the first time someone had taken that plunge.

The duke interrupted Grewea's contemplation of his murder. "He—the aforementioned Reader—knows enough to rightly state that I am absolutely besieged by expectations, duties, and all the other trappings of rulership. I cannot even find the time to properly scheme; I have to rely on you entirely to do that for me. You are among the shrewdest, most vicious, and subsequently exquisitely productive men to ever advise a holder of this burdensome title."

Grewea sighed. His forefinger twitched. "Besieged or not, you must nonetheless make the time to think this through." He put aside his homicidal thoughts and considered the effort it no doubt required for this cherub-faced royal mule to do something as complicated as think. He frowned.

"Must I? Oh, stop it with the frowning and the sighing." Duke Velliok popped a small purple pastry in his mouth and chewed it slowly. "Delicious. That Pastorine talks too much, but, my, is he useful in the kitchen." He picked up another pastry, this one white with yellow stripes, and regarded it with deceptively nonchalant eyes. The duke was really quite passionate about food. Passionate enough to have required four strong men to carry him up the many stairs that led to this heralded vantage point.

Perhaps Grewea would need to use both forefingers, if it came to that...

"Does this look like the Erris Tarbiz flag to you? These are supposed to look like the flags of dead nations, but I thought the Erris Tarbiz flag was yellow with white stripes."

Duke Velliok put the pastry back down on the plate and waved away the old servant who'd been standing there, holding a tray of delicacies despite the presence of a large round table right before them. "Enough of these, Weru. Let's have the supper now. And the cheese. You know, old man, my navy has brought me cheese from Prement."

Grewea sighed once again and suppressed a shrewd, vicious impulse to incinerate this blob who was once again wasting his valuable time. The magick might bring the Scourge Ravagers, but it would be worth the battle to see this idiot burn like a dying star.

He gazed down over the Wondrous City of Pashka, the Jeweled Eye, at its sparkling fountains and its seemingly infinite towers and statues and peoples. What a mess, what a glorious, unmanageable, unseemly, and enviable mess. Peopled by nothing but the spoiled, the decadent, the ignorant, and the scheming, the whole of them worth next to nothing.

Decades of peace had proven nothing but the usefulness of a damn good bloody war now and again.

They two, the duke and the grandmaster of the Mer Ponx — among other things — were seated on the observation deck of the highest tower of all. There was none higher in all of Arba; Duke Velliok's father had seen to that. Even that ugly thing at the Scar couldn't compare, though it had proven on occasion to be far more useful.

Velliok belched and then seemed to nod off. Grewea politely tapped on the table, whereupon the voluminous duke stirred, belched again, and reached for his glass.

They were there to make decisions. Or more accurately, for Velliok to be quietly shoved aside, as was custom, while Grewea decided the fate of the Triumvirate and its seven million citizens...as well as that of a few other places and their many citizens. He wasn't much moved by the gravity of his role, particularly as it compared to the compulsion to murder his lunch companion. He'd seen dukes come and go. He'd seen citizens perish by the tens of thousands. He'd played major roles in many of those occurrences, and though the appearance of passivity was a skill he'd mastered long ago, he often let others see his cards as a reminder to them — and to him — that he was very much a player and never just an observer.

Duke Velliok turned so he could still see the city, or at least the southern ports and markets, but also face to some degree his ancient advisor, a man he no doubt trusted about as far as he could have thrown the entire Wondrous City of Pashka. Grewea chuckled at the thought and imagined he himself being tossed over the side. Of course, he'd plenty of ways to stop that happening; he wondered also what this poor fat fool would think to learn that the "old man" had taken that plunge several times, voluntarily and discreetly, just to see what it felt like.

Did it feel like falling from a plane? From an aerothrope? From a spacecraft? He'd concluded that, as with most things, the answer was yes...and no.

"Let me ask you, Grewea. Have you thought it through?"

"Yes."

"You have debated it within that hideous circle of yours?"

"Yes."

"Then why do you come to me?"

"You know why: it is the law."

Velliok smiled and turned once again to watch the passing of a particularly large caravan far below. Weru and two lesser servants returned with several crowded trays of supper, which they quietly placed on the table. The servants nodded respectfully and left, Weru practically shoving the other two back whence they'd come. "The law. Yes, of course, forgive me. The law. What I meant was: What is it you expect I'll do? Agree with you?"

"I have no expectations except that you, as the Thirty-seventh Duke of Pherriuskata, Minister of the Schau Edicts of Elevation, and sovereign ruler of all Arba, consider the matter carefully and wisely and choose a course of action that will lead to the continuation of our most precious way of life."

"You want me to agree with you."

"Absolutely."

Velliok stood up. He teetered a bit but soon found his balance. He ambled away from the table, down to the railing.

After a moment, seeing that today's game would require a hint more relish than was typical, Grewea rose from his uncomfortable chair and followed him. They walked along the deck's edge and then stopped and stood at the stone rail looking out over Lake Iale. Here, high on the Faler Mussan in a late afternoon, on a day that bore no particular importance — particularly if one downplayed the true reason for the lunch and all the decisions that should spring from it — they watched the comings and goings of the lake in silence. They did this for two, maybe three minutes, and then Velliok seemed to decide to do exactly what he was essentially being told to do, which was to decide, or be told to decide on, the horrible fate of an entire nation.

"Do you know when I was a boy I used to come up here in the middle of the night?" the duke said.

Grewea listened. Here was this fat man, once a fat boy, who stood before him, knowing and not caring that he would be unyieldingly apathetic to the duke's childhood sins. Why then did he feel the need to prod Grewea's apathy? Was it to let him know that while on some level he was every bit the puppet his government — and most of his subjects — made him out to be, he could still push a party to a place where it became necessary, though incidentally so, to indulge him? He likely found it typically drove such parties to distraction, and it was within such pockets of carefully crafted distraction he had discovered a gift for the casual extraction of puzzle pieces.

Or so he thought. Grewea had long ago impressed this puzzle paradigm upon him as a means of control, though the fat fool had since forgotten the origins of this habit in which he took so much vain pride.

It was a little sad…and more than a little pathetic.

But it was, as were most things Grewea did, necessary.

"Did you?" asked Grewea, his voice taking on the intended weariness of the listener who believes he is about to be asked, without any right of refusal, to waste a fair chunk of his time.

"Yes. Often. With no wind deflection and no protection."

"That was bold of you."

"No, it wasn't. It was idiotic. I wasn't a bright child, you may be surprised to learn. It was only through years of rigorous study and intense devotion that I achieved the mediocre intellect that today affords me the power and savvy to rule our great and trembling union."

I was the one who ensured your idiocy by steering your education toward the useless and the absurd, thought Grewea. *You don't remember my having been your teacher because you truly mastered idiocy, something even my designs couldn't have completely predicted.* "I recall you being something of a young scholar," he said.

"A lie, spread by my ashamed and compulsively untruthful father. But as I was saying, only an idiot would come up here without protection. Or a bold man, as you say. Over the two centuries since it was built, this tower has proven most lethal to the bold and the idiotic alike. The winds up here have blown at least seven full-grown adults off and to their deaths."

"And one Challowian."

"Yes, and one Challowian. You know how heavy they are, I expect. Give even me a run for the money. Just imagine the wind that did that poor fellow in."

"History isn't quite clear on how the poor dragonman found his way to the streets below." Again, his finger twitched.

"Yes, that much is certain. But what is in question, what is of particular intrigue, most particularly in certain old houses on the Isle, is…why in fact did he choose to embark on his vertical journey?"

"I wouldn't know."

"Really? I thought you were up here at the time."

"Was I?"

"That's what they say."

"Do they? Well, then, perhaps I was. But that was very long ago, and an old man cannot be expected to remember every little incident, can he?"

"It wasn't so little to the dragonmen. As I recall, they went to war over Hju's death."

"Your recall fails you here, my friend. They only considered war."

"I see. Yes, maybe I did hear something about that…"

"They reconsidered after a pointed letter from your great-grandfather."

"Ah, yes. The famous Rurstmeyer Letter. So you do remember." Grewea said nothing.

"And do you remember delivering it?"

"I do indeed. I'm not that old."

"Odd claim for a…for someone so well worn as yourself, someone possessing such a keen yet selective memory."

"You only say that because you've never met anyone quite like me. Or don't remember if you have or haven't, at least."

"Are there others?"

"If there were, their boasts of unmatchable oddness would surely put mine to shame."

"Then here's hoping there are no others. You, my friend, are quite enough to manage."

And now he's thinking I foolishly believe I manage him, Velliok ruminated as Grewea gently listened. *Maybe I could end up doing just that, if I keep ahead of his expectations and suppositions. But no. I cannot afford to believe it, not for even an instant. He will see right through me. This one manages himself and plays puppeteer with all those who stumble or charge or sneak into his web. And I am very much in his web.*

Grewea, having glanced for a moment at Velliok's thoughts, recoiled ever so slightly from the direct exposure to such a surprisingly disciplined mind. He smiled at the realization that the conversations Velliok had with himself were far more compelling than any he had with parties that did not live in his skull.

He wondered why he'd done it, the thought-reading, for it was no easy thing to see into another's mind, and it cost him much effort to do it successfully while not accidentally killing or driving the object mad. It was a power he rarely used, a power he even vaguely feared, for it was always possible an unknown mind could overwhelm or otherwise damage him.

And then he realized he hadn't used it. It had used him.

The thought disturbed him greatly.

"What's with the frowning, my friend? It's extreme today, even for you," said the duke as he ambled back toward the table and lunch.

The servant, Weru, brought to the table bubbled glasses of Ignataus Blood, a platter of giant lakeprawns, and a huge bowl of the blackened Ialish crowderfish the duke had earlier demanded of his harried staff. Crowderfish was flaky and therefore nearly impossible to blacken, even for a Pastorine cook, and lakeprawns were out of season.

The duke poked at the fish on his plate and then waved to Weru. "This is too well done. Let's try again, hmm?"

The servant made off hastily with the plate.

Velliok sat a moment with his eyes closed and once again gave the appearance of a man on the verge of a nap. Grewea was used to it. The duke believed he had long ago learned to feign such sleepy contrivances in the interest of gaining conversational leverage. It sometimes irritated those in his company and served to make them easier prey for the duke's silken-trap mind; more often had almost no effect. But at least it bought the duke time to collect his thoughts, and such time could never be overvalued.

Or so he thought. In fact, his little naps had been designed by Grewea to allow himself time to focus on more pressing matters even while "engaged" in ducal discourse.

Velliok snapped his eyes open, no doubt hoping to catch his adversary napping, and asked a rather profound question: "And so what is your plan when the Vo'ixtavracci decide they're not satisfied with having the Aethreleans supply their needs?"

Finally, thought Grewea: the point.

"The Aethreleans, even after the likely civil war, will number in the hundreds of thousands, perhaps even more than a million," he answered.

"And yet the Vo'ixtavracci are still the Great Takers, are they not? They have never been renowned for their diplomacy, nor for their adherence to treaties."

"They agreed to the Gift. That was diplomatic, some would say. Very much so."

"Ha!" Velliok laughed mirthlessly. "The Gift, my dear Grewea, was blackmail, a Taking of the highest order. We have purchased our threadbare independence with the blood of our populace for over three hundred years now."

"I am aware."

"'We will take, or you will give.' Isn't that how it goes?"

"It was the other way around, I'm quite sure, but yes. We now, however, know more about them than ever before," replied Grewea.

"Do we?"

"Yes."

"How's that?"

Grewea gestured at the Fassan Garden that accented the center of the observation deck. "Please, may we stroll again, my duke? My old legs grow stiff if I sit for too long."

Velliok looked momentarily put upon — he did so enjoy a meal — but then he nodded, rose slowly to his feet, and stretched a bit. Grewea followed suit. They made their way to a series of vined trellises wound with roses, morning glories, and beige-and-crimson Prementian hornflowers.

"All this walking. I shall have to schedule a second supper," chortled Velliok.

Grewea ignored the jest. "You know of the Redeemers and their missions."

"Of course."

"The Redeemers comprise only a small portion of our information network."

"But the best portion, if common wisdom is to be believed."

"The point is debatable, but common wisdom is sometimes accurate despite itself."

"'The people, the people. What to do with all the people,'" Velliok quoted.

"'One must ultimately elect utility over compassion,'" came the reply.

"What would we do without Max and Kalor?" sighed the duke as he stifled a manufactured yawn.

"Probably spend less time trading bloated quotes and more time making essential decisions."

"Quite."

Weru appeared with another tray and more glasses.

"And yet quotations and sayings are so much more, shall we say, 'invigoratingly detached' than the lies they are sadly called upon to adorn and even, we of all people must admit, to disguise." Velliok turned his attention to the tray and delicately wrapped his fingers around the stem of a twisted flute glass speckled with silver and violet. He waved Weru away. "So you've sent spies into Vo'ixtavracci environs," he said as he lifted the Ignataus Blood to his lips.

"'Spies' is such a hateful word, my duke. In the vein of your most eloquent phrasing of our sad linguistic dilemma, let us add to our abuse of quotes an abuse of euphemism and think more along the lines of 'observers.'"

"One man's observer is the same man's spy. How many and how good?"

"The best, as you say," Grewea said matter-of-factly. "Scores of them in every corner of the Vo'ixtavracci Empire. Very keen, very observant, and quite numerous."

"Though not as numerous, I suspect, as when you first sent them out to snatch from the world what they could."

"There have been casualties, of course. Sacrifices."

"Main courses, you mean. We should have had them poison themselves and extend the courtesy to their consumers."

"The Vo'ix have ever proven extremely resistant to whatever poisons we have tried, alas. Those dear observers, once at table, had by then achieved all they could, their learned service at an undeserved end."

"No doubt. And what, pray tell, had they learned?"

"That the Empire is not now what it once was."

"I see." Velliok drained his glass. From across the balcony, Weru once again came scuttling forward to refill it. Having done so, he scuttled away. A moment later, he returned to the table with a new plate of crowderfish, set it down graciously, and scuttled away again, but not before subtly verifying that the duke had seen him and the plate both. "So you've learned that the rumors about a Vo'ixtavracci collapse aren't quite as false as most wise men would have deemed. All men, all things on the OS Maeketel, have needs, and so all by extension have weaknesses, even the big, bad meaties."

"I would concur with you there, my duke."

"And so now you believe we can rid ourselves of a political complication by making a deal with the devil, confident that the devil, somewhat weakened of late, will be held in check once he's let in the house?"

"There is something else you may not know about the current Vo'ixtavracci situation, my duke."

"And what is that? Their hearts have softened and their taste for human flesh has faded mercifully away?"

"While their empire is in truth eroding, it is by no means collapsing. Nevertheless, they find themselves at war."

"This was ever so, ever the rumor. It's the primary theory behind why they haven't shown to collect their last two…Gifts."

"It is the reason," said Grewea.

"Explain."

"They are not only at war, they are losing."

"Losing? To whom?"

"We are not sure. Some power on the other side of the world. Some race we haven't seen. They call them the Pwaklon."

Velliok drained his glass again and stood, staring out over Lake Iale. Grewea felt compelled to peek again at Velliok's thoughts, but this time he did so of his own volition.

Why? Because he needed to know exactly how the duke was taking this information. And he needed to confirm his suspicions. Velliok was savoring the rare flavor of the wine and feeling the sensation of blood quickening his pulse. It, combined with this promising news about their ancient, exploitative bane, excited him, yet he did his best to take hold of himself and hide his reaction.

Grewea was satisfied. This man was a fool, but he was still Grewea's fool and not one who belonged to the Vo'ix.

Weru came forward once more, new bottle in hand, and this time the Duke waved him off and said, "And these Pwaklon are…a race that can defeat the Vo'ixtavracci?"

"So it would seem. So they claim."

"You've met with them?"

"Indirectly, yes."

"And you believe them?"

"I believe no one, Duke Velliok. I simply see that the great Vo'ixtavracci Empire needs reinforcements, supplies, and sustenance, all in large quantities, or their empire's greatness might more than simply lessen, and very soon…"

"You're saying they could altogether fall?"

"Anything is possible."

"Are you proposing…?"

"Yes."

"Both ends. And we sit blithely in the middle, offering comfort and counsel. And meat."

"Sitting strategically, I would rather say," said Grewea.

"You play a dangerous game with all our lives, old man."

"My young friend, I never enter into a game I don't expect to have already won."

"You've made the deal?"

"Yes. Pending your approval."

Velliok snorted at this. "And the Vo'ixtavracci?" he said, popping a small tart into his mouth.

"Have agreed to visit Aethrelius."

Chewing the tart with relish and doing his best to look uninterested, Velliok asked, "When?"

"Within the year."

"That soon?"

"Perhaps sooner. As I said, they have needs."

"Four deliver us."

"Well, as you wish…but I can state with confidence that the Gift the Vo'ixtavracci take from Aethrelius will be the last one they ever take from Arba."

"The Aethreleans, gone. The rhetoric, the chest-thumping, the damn Mandate…gone."

"And with the Vo'ixtavracci sated and indefinitely preoccupied, our little Tri will essentially rule unopposed."

"You have thought it through."

"Yes."

"The Mudarrisi?"

"It seems the honorable Aethreleans resent their dependence on Jamoian assistance, so much so that they're prepared to terminate relations."

"How did you manage that?"

"I? I did nothing. The spark cannot be blamed for the dryness of the wood."

"Yes, well, that spark had better hold its secrets close. Don't want these asses in the Sheel getting wind of your incidental efforts."

Grewea gave no answer. He was growing impatient with having to maintain this facade.

"What do you make of this Proving business?" The duke reached for another tart but instead grabbed a massive lakeprawn, which he promptly shoved into his mouth. He chewed, swallowed, and continued: "The Holymen tell me their congregations are working themselves up to a lather."

"You and I decided long ago the Proving was a tale told by an idiot. Or three idiots, to be precise."

"Those Books! I should have had every copy burned thirty years ago."

"Thirty years ago, you weren't in power."

"But I had my father's ear. And more importantly, my mother's."

"Oh, how I do miss her, the dear woman."

Velliok cast him a look. "Well, you can always spend time with her if you miss her so."

"It's not the same."

"No, I suppose not. She's so very quiet these days." He chuckled to himself and reached for a bit of the blackened fish. He stabbed a forkful, glanced at it with a sharp eye, and then popped it into his mouth. "Ah, yes! Perfect. Have some of this fish, Grewea. It was caught only an hour ago, and the cook's done it right this time."

"Fish doesn't agree with me, my duke. I now eat only soft, sweetened grains."

"Do you? How uncharacteristically herbivorous."

"We all make our concessions to age."

"Some of us prefer to make the age concede to us."

"The few and the lucky."

"Yes, I suppose so."

They sat in silence for a few minutes more, both knowing that there was one more item to discuss, each content to let the other believe it was of little importance to him.

It was the duke who blinked. "And the Wilds? Vincent Bleuss?"

"Oh, I think you needn't trouble your head over poor Vincent and his valiant efforts, my duke."

"You have that in hand too?"

Grewea smiled blackly.

"I know of your history with Vincent, Grewea. Do your best not to martyr the man."

"My history is irrelevant. It is our future that preoccupies me day and night."

"A prosperous, glorious future indeed."

Velliok pushed his plate away with a dramatic sigh.

"The Jamoi still might have something to say about all this," he said. "We have only a small understanding of their policies. And there won't be a second fortuitous Chewing to follow the first. The Vo'ixtavracci will not—cannot—touch them, not in their own country."

"I have something in mind for the Jamoi as well, Velliok. Two things, in fact. Neither is pleasant."

"Pity."

"A prosperous and glorious future is a grand wish, but it should not and cannot remain a wish. It must either come to pass or be rendered an impossibility," Grewea said, rising slowly and then adjusting his hideous robe.

"And whatever you have in mind for the Jamoi…?"

"Will foreclose on the possibility of impossibility, my duke."

"For the good of all?"

"For the good of all."

Chapter 4
"You've heard something…
or are you just being prophetic?"

Place: Vaprosta in the new nation of Chrestikos,
western coast of the Arban continent
Date: Boinage 38, AY 998

Suashi stood in the center of her wooden sea hut and began to pray.

"Blessed Three, tell me now who I can be, tell me now what I must do, tell me now how I might die for you, tell me now how I might live for you."

Her hair was filthy. Her face was filthy. Her feet were filthy. Each time they'd come to her and offered her water, soaps, and oils, she'd turned them away. The last time, she'd shoved the first one down back into the others; she could hear them cursing as they stumbled their way back down the vigil tower's steps and out onto the beach. It amused her for a moment to hear such pious characters spewing curses like Pebbuskan sailors.

The push had accomplished something: they had not returned, and for that at least she was grateful. Filthy, but grateful.

But ensuring her solitude ensured little else.

This isn't working. This is not working. What am I doing here?

The wind blew out two of her candles. She re-lit them and then took three small triangular pieces of gold from her pocket and placed them on a reddish, cylindrical altar to her left. Taking a deep breath, she closed her eyes and sang the words.

"Naipek wrote: 'He will land in shadow, he will embrace the empty, he will be lost among us, he will die before he lives, and his name is Ashorne.'"

She touched her forehead with her fingers for a moment and then lowered her arms to her sides. Breathing deeply again, she removed a small flask from her pocket and placed it gently on another altar, identical to the first in all but color, to her right. "Frulla wrote: 'He will have no children, he will burn a city, he will save the first wise child, the Last Dreamer will find him, and her twin he will slay.'" The flask tipped over; its contents dripped down the altar's dark-green sides.

The wind howled and blew hard through the hut's small, west-facing opening. Out there in the dark, the Decone Ocean's waves whispered and slapped. The stilts and struts of the hut were well placed, but the hut rocked a bit nonetheless.

Part of her wished the winds would whip harder, hard enough to snap the stilts and struts and haul her out into the ocean that legend said stretched all the way around the world. Perhaps she'd circumvent the entire planet and wash up in Jamoi or Grellgorot or even Aethrelius. How ironic would that be?

Her candles blew out again, and again she relit them. She glanced out the window opening, wondering how anyone ever got through a whole ritual in this damn hut with winds like that.

Those winds: born of places so far west no one ever spoke or knew of them, ceaselessly. The Decone was both humbling and everlasting, blasting this land, this coast, this holy place…

Blasting me, or trying to, keeping me from finding whatever it is I'm looking for, keeping me from remembering what to do and why this isn't working…and why only my capacity to contradict myself, no cause for celebration, is a source of refuge for me.

What must I do? What am I looking for?

What have I forgotten?

The froth on the ocean's waves sparkled as the light from Branaedes, the Silver Giver, the moon of boundless, impossible temptation, bounced and danced, seeming somehow to celebrate its current nearness to its wicked larger sibling, this terribly damaged place she and so many others called "home."

At least the tides were tame, relatively speaking. The Brother was not in season.

She hesitated in the performance of the blessed ceremony for a moment when she saw the bright moon's full image reflecting off the ocean's troubled surface. The naked beauty of the sight made her suddenly ashamed — the flickering of countless silver-and-white lights upon the roiling waves, like a million candles lighting up a world in dire need of even one — and that feeling intensified, consumed her, forced her to wrestle with the impulse to eschew the pointless completion of her so-called holy ablution and simply go for a very long swim.

She stopped.

She took a breath.

She forced down her fear and ignored her disgust.

Say it, do it, finish it. Maybe this time…say it.

"Tristan said: 'He will be a slave, he will be a soldier, he will fly and crawl, he will deliver the Fourth, and the Fourth will Prove.'" She placed a slip of parchment for the Scholar on His rightfully centered altar, the one colored silver and blue. Had it not been he who had bridged the gap between Naipek's harsh justice and Frulla's wide embrace with cogent reason and diligent argument? Yes, that was his legacy, those were his teachings: learn, focus, teach, grow.

Tristan will help me see this through. He has to, for without him and

without what only he and his fellow Three could provide, I'm lost. We're lost.
Lost is a place I don't like to be.
Lost is a state I will never accept for these people. My people.
All of Arba.

She placed both of her hands on her belly just below her navel and repeated the last four words.

"The Fourth will Prove."

The wind blew hard once more but somehow let the candles be this time.

And so began her nightly meditation on the seventeenth night of purification. She stood there, her hands on her belly, her breathing slow and deep. But despite her efforts, her fears, and her inner declarations of unmitigated devotion, such as they were, it wasn't working. She knew this and didn't hide from the knowledge. The lie she'd been told was as powerful now as ever, but its power had turned her faith of so long into an enemy she could neither see nor resist. She took a deeper breath. The weeping began now, as it had for the past sixteen days. Was it the hunger? She had many times gone longer periods without food. The last pangs had left her after the fourth day.

If I starve, I don't have to do this anymore. If I starve, they can find someone else to save them. No, that's not true; that's not what I want. I don't think it is. No, it isn't. This is all nothing, but in the nothing, there's something. It's this ritual that plagues me, this ritual with its mumbling and candles and remorse.

She glanced at the altar and gave it a kick; she slapped one of the golden triangles off the altar and onto the floor.

"This is all shit," she hissed. But there was still a low music in her head, and it was good. *I still love the music, and maybe that means something. Even without a full and joyous three, a drum for Naipek, a voice for Frulla, and a Watersean flute for Tristan, I almost always have Pao's baritone to harmonize with me...my awkward alto chants that sound like a bird on a spit...but he's not here, not in this place.*

She missed him then, but only for a moment. He was never far, and his absence was not her problem, not here and now.

I'm not going to find it. I've lost it, and I cannot find it. They've left me, they know me for the lie I am, and now all that was to be is a poison cup.

Her hands were still on her abdomen, and she felt it tremble as she wept. She pulled her hands away with a start, as if she'd felt a sudden fire, but only the depth of her guilt had caused her action. "Forgive me, Fourth, I meant no slight. I know one such as you can have little use for a child of lies and the schemes of low deceivers...but please, I beg of you some mercy: I did not know, I did not know, I did not know..." She sank to her knees and wept more, repeating her empty denial, feeling the cloak of her unearned shame descend upon her. It pressed her to the floor and into another dreamless, fitful sleep.

She woke just before Trilesti's rise. It was over. There was no more to say or do. She had tried and failed, and whatever she decided to do next would be, for better or worse, entirely up to her. The Three had offered her neither guidance nor comfort.

Removing her cloak and her small ceremonial accoutrement, she readied for the day ahead. A day outside of this place.

She took herself down the stairs and toward the beach. A soft, violet sunlight played on the sand as Trilesti soundlessly whispered the new day's secrets to any who would listen. Soon, her sister would emerge and bathe all Arba in her brilliant whiteness, but for perhaps an hour more, the canvas was the Violet One's to paint.

Suashi frowned that such celestial subtleties distracted her even now, despite her massive failure. She took a certain satisfaction in accepting that her own foolish tribulations meant nothing to bodies so vast and distant, but that vastness and distance accented, too, the futility of her own life in such a way as to make her shame more real and more alive than her very breath.

She was unworthy. The heavens knew it, she knew it, and she suspected the people knew it.

But being unworthy didn't render one without options. An argument could be made that the unworthy were the most important players of all, for they had it within them to belie expectations. They had it within them to snatch improbable victory; they just had to be damn good and damn lucky to do so.

She was good; she knew that. Luck was another matter still, but none of it would make a difference if she couldn't make her decision and make it stick.

She shook her head and scoffed at her musings. Gazing at oceans and beaches alight with the fire of heavenly orbs was for fools and dreamers who had lost their way and forgotten the gifts of the Burden. Was that her? *Probably yes*, she thought. And the gazing was not the only symptom of foolishness that held her in its purposeless grasp. Her hunger had returned, far too soon for one whose goal was purification, devotion, and awakening to the Path. Her shame welled up again; this time, she snarled at it and forced it back down. There were only so many times she was willing to apologize for playing the fool, and she decided that, come what may, the last time had come and gone.

Her plan would be hers and hers alone. She thought about that a moment and realized: she could live with that. The Three could kiss her ass.

Paomaintanna met her at the southernmost dock, the one where all the spinsters came to throw their baskets into the ocean. He was sitting there, his feet dangling, his long black hair tied in a double braid, staring into the water. His back was covered in sand like he'd been napping or rolling on the beach. There were no spinsters in sight.

"I hear it's easier to catch fish if you use a net or a pole," she said coming up behind him. She reached down and began to brush the sand off of him. "Or are you waiting for a wife?"

"A wife? No need. And don't believe everything you hear. I've heard the same things said of you, but there's no net that could hold you, or at least that's been my experience. And as for poles...I wouldn't even think it. There isn't a man on the whole coast who would."

"I just came from the vigil. Be kind."

"No food, no drink, no smoke, no sex...seventeen days. What would constitute 'kind' in this moment?"

"Food and drink to start. Maybe smoke afterward."

"And the sex?"

"Your pole belongs to another."

"Huh. And she keeps it in her pouch. I haven't seen it since Miaki was born."

"I guess you either need to steal the pouch or spend more time at home."

"I'm afraid of home. I would steal the pouch, and the pole inside it, if a man can actually ever steal his own property, but what good would it do me? Your father seems to have taken my testicles."

"A vision I could have done without."

"Apologies."

"People have taken too much from you, old friend."

"I don't care. It's all safer with them, anyway. I lose everything." Pao rose and patted her shoulder twice. "You look well. Thin, but well. Did you find anything?"

"Nothing."

"Okay. We go anyway?"

"We go anyway."

"When?"

She didn't answer that question. She knew the answer was "soon," but she needed time. A few days, a week. Maybe just enough time to forget all this, grab a boat, and head off out into the vast sea to find the K'nevar Environ where the fish could talk and there were no damn humans like her and the fools who wanted her to save them.

They walked together off the dock and toward the town. Several barefoot fishermen strolled by them, dragging the day's catch. They were laughing and drinking from short brown bottles.In the distance, there came the sound of hammering and yelling. Pao glanced that way and waved a casual hand toward the yards. "Your father's doing a nice job with the boats."

"Ships."

"What did I say?"

"I think when they're that big, you have to call them ships."

"Well, they're big, that's for sure, and there must be a dozen of them now."

"It won't be enough," she said.

"It won't be, you're right, but who says he'll stop at a dozen? He's got more lumber coming down the river all the time. My people are complaining."

"Really? Your people? Imagine my shock."

"My people are good at heart," he said. "Simple people, you know. They eat and they fuck and they dance. They just want to know how much of their forest you transplants are planning on ripping down."

"I don't know. How much transplant coin can your simple people spend?"

"They don't spend it. That's the problem. They throw it into the river when they pray."

"And the fish eat it and swim downstream, and now I know why you were staring into the water. That's a slow way to get rich, brother."

"Especially without a pole to fish with."

He was plugging her for information, as usual, and she knew she should give it to him, but if she did, he'd feel he had to tell the Ailo-shut leaders, particularly Akanouava. He'd make a case of how a son tells his father all the important things, and she'd make a case of how a daughter keeps her father's secrets, and they'd both get drunk and probably end up making love and forgetting the whole thing, secure in the knowledge that the nations of Chrestikos-by-the-Sea and the Ailo-shut people weren't relying on them to swap, bargain for, or steal state secrets to ensure survival. Or at least, not one another's secrets.

The Triumvirate was fair game, but sadly, or maybe not so sadly, neither Pao nor Suashi could claim Duke Velliok as a father or even a distant cousin. For those secrets, they had to work. And pay.

They made their way through the narrow, seashell-covered streets of Vaprosta, not quite a city but still the only true town in the very young nation of Chrestikos. Suashi rarely spent time here anymore, though she would like to, she thought as she noted a row of new cottages and shops being erected. The place was much bigger than it had been when she'd first come here as a girl, but it still held the same salty-aired, inviting charm it always had. New people made their way to this city her father had named for his long-dead sister, and no matter who they'd been before they came, they never took long to embrace the ways of their newfound and long-sought refuge.

It was the way her father wanted it, the way he'd planned and envisioned it when he'd set out from Aethrelius all those years ago. He'd passed through the great gate of Chralm Doanna with no more than forty of his countrymen, yet when he'd reached the western coast of Arba months later, more than two thousand brave souls reached it with him. She herself hadn't been there, but she'd often heard the stories of those first weeks on the beach, and even now it warmed her heart to hear them again. Chrestikos was a good place in a very bad world, and she should know, because she'd seen plenty of that bad world firsthand.

"Bread and meat, or bread and fish?" Pao asked.

"I don't like to break a fast with meat. Upsets my stomach."

"Fish, then. Schmidt's or Dwivedi's?"

"Dwivedi's. Schmidt doesn't change the water in his shrimp tank."

"Ever?"

"I don't think he knows how."

"There's good protein in shrimp shit."

"I get enough protein out on the trail: rabbit, squirrel, rabbit, squirrel...and I want some good rice."

"Chandyo makes the best rice."

"No wives, not right now. I'm not willing to walk all the way across town just to have her hit me with the evil eye."

"She's hitting you right now anyway."

"Probably, but I feel it less with a few miles between us."

"Dwivedi's, then."

They wound their way through the market. It always opened at dawn but never really got busy until a little later in the morning. Vaprostans typically preferred to shop in a crowd; it gave them a sense of community to rub elbows, so they often waited till they were sure the markets would be packed. *Strange custom*, she thought. In the Tri, crowds were considered a nuisance, and shopping was more a battle than a pleasure, despite the dissembling demeanor of the shoppers.

She preferred the Chrestikot way.

They reached Dwivedi's, a small, hut-like structure separate from the row of shops. Pao picked a table outside but as far from the street and the other occupied tables as he could find. There weren't many other customers; everyone was perusing the shops or fishing or sleeping or building. There was always lots of building going on here.

Three young mothers were sitting twenty feet away, drinking tea and giggling and cooing at one another's infants. Suashi looked at them a moment, thinking nothing but doing so purposely. The mothers, seeing her look, smiled at her and waved. She tried to smile back but managed only a nod.

"You could do that," said Pao as they sat down. "Babies."

Suashi shook her head once. "Could, but won't."

"Things are different now."

"Not so different. I know, but they don't," she said, gesturing at the market crowd.

"They don't care."

"They care."

"Yes, they do, but you know they would understand."

She thought about that and realized that he was right. Chrestikotes weren't Wildeans; they had little use for prophetic dreams, sham or not. She glanced at the mothers again. "Not yet."

"When?"

"I think we've got too much to do."

"About that…" he started, but then Dwivedi's son, Alukko, sauntered up and smiled.

"Hello, both! Hello and good morning. Fish and rice?"

"And a little salt beer, Alukko, please…"

"We have only sweet beer today," said the boy with a look of slight shame but an even more intense smile. His face looked somewhat pinched.

Suashi smiled back and nodded. "Okay, two sweet beers, but small ones, please…you know this one."

"Me? I don't like a sweet beer. None for me," Pao protested lightly.

"Then bring him a well water."

"No, no. Give me the beer; I'll suffer through it."

Alukko left to get the beer and food. Suashi closed her eyes a moment and listened to the sounds of her home. Someone was yelling about the price of rainbowbacks, someone else was yelling back. Two carpenters were using a very long saw to cut planks. A gremfi was snorting its annoyance at the number of blackflies it had attracted. Young children were playing and laughing as they tried to trick the sugar merchant, Lixue, into giving them free samples. The fat, bubbly old woman always fell for the "tricks" — she'd been falling for them for as many years as there'd been a market, and her laugh was a loud and true as ever.

"Will you miss it?" Pao asked.

"Always. But I don't really belong here anymore."

"So you've said, many times. But if not here, then where?"

She smiled at him and shook her head. *I've got to tell him. He*

*probably already knows, but he needs to hear it from me to make me feel like I
know what I'm doing, so I've got to tell him.* "The Ashorne is almost here."

"You've heard something, or are you just being prophetic?"

"The slaver will be grabbing him very soon now. If we paid him
enough. You never know with these people."

"How do you know all this?"

"My father forwarded my mail to the tower."

"Isn't that missing the whole point of the tower? No food, but you
get mail?"

"Maybe. No, not really. I went to the vigil to get some guidance on
this very matter, didn't I? But the point now is: he's coming. We've got to
go."

"And you still want to see her?"

"No, I don't. But we have to. They have their spies too, and they'll
know somehow he's coming. Just like you."

Pao grunted. "Maybe they'll send someone else."

"No, it's got to be me."

"And when you refuse?"

"They'll send someone else. But they'll send him to the City of
Tents, and if all went right, that's not where we're headed."

Their food arrived. Suashi dove in. The fish tasted good going
down, and she was eating too fast, but the smells of the market and the
eateries had quietly teased up her hunger as she'd sat there, and now she
could do little to control the impulse to stuff herself full. Fasting might be
the pious way to purify the body, but breaking the fast was the sweetest
part of the ritual.

She ordered a second helping when she was through with the first,
but when it came she set about eating it at a more restrained pace.

Making yourself sick won't get you out of this, Suashi, she thought.
Take your time and enjoy it. It's back to rabbits and squirrels soon enough.

When she was through, Pao, who had been watching her with
mild amusement, put some coins on the table and rose. "There's something
I want to ask you," he said. "Can I walk with you to your father's?"

"Who says I want to see him?"

"Me. You won't leave without a conversation."

"You're right," she admitted. "But I'm not going to tell him when
we're going. He'll want to send me with an army."

"And me."

"No, not you. He doesn't like you."

"I don't blame him. I get his daughter drunk and take her to faraway lands."

"It's not the drink he minds, or the travel. He prefers his grand-
children not be fathered by a man who already has too many wives."

"I have one wife. Here. The others are in the Wilds. They don't count."

"The others are still alive, so they count."

"He knows?"

"He knows."

They left Dwivedi's and headed north toward the fort. Her father, Vincent Bleuss, would be there. Or if he wasn't there, he'd be at what he called the "government yards," overseeing the building of his precious ships. Not everyone believed in the Proving, but Vincent Bleuss was a man who favored bold preparation. When all was said and done, he expected his fleet to contain more than fifty massive vessels, each capable of carrying over four hundred Chrestikotes. Combined with the hundreds of smaller boats, skiffs, and refitted shabbaks the nation already boasted, it should be enough to get his people away from Arba if and when the time came.

But to where, he'd not yet told her. She was certain it was because he wasn't sure. The Decone was a vast ocean bordered by another vast ocean to the west—an environ to which very few had ever sailed. Decone itself had but few islands and many dangers in its dark and violent waters. And the Prementians had made it clear, thanks to perpetual invasions and raids by the Triumvirate Navy and its Juks Xi Ren pets, that no humans were welcome in their environ. Vincent would have ships, but ships filled with civilians, not soldiers. He could not hope to conquer territory for a new settlement.

It would never come to that, she knew. She believed with all her heart that she would find the Ashorne, and he in turn would find the Proving Fourth. It was the reason for her journey, the reason for her very life, and though the forest bitch had lied to her about her role in the Unburdening of All, she nonetheless clung to her faith in faith. She would find him, and Arba would be spared.

As they neared the fort's south gate, Pao stopped and put his hand on her shoulder. "Your father came to me while you were in the vigil."

"He did?" She was definitely surprised. Though she would never tell Pao, her father truly detested him. Vincent often knew more than was good for him, and so he knew all about Paomaintanna's troubles with the Biblists. It was something she knew he did not understand—in fact refused to understand—so for him to seek out Pao for any reason was more than a little unusual.

"He knows what you're going to do, but more than that, he suspects there are dangers…beyond what we might expect."

"Who is he worried about?"

"He wouldn't say. And as usual, I have no idea where he's getting his information. But 'there are forces in play in this drama that are not of our kind.' His words, not mine."

"Interesting. What did he suggest?"

"He suggested we skip the trip and get on a boat."

"Ship."

"Ship."

"You know what?"

"What?"

"Forget my father. Let's just go."

"Yes."

"But not yet."

"Not yet."

Chapter 5
Not like the Puddy Tat I tawt I taw…

Place: The Wierson Psychiatric Center, Peekskill, NY
Date: December 2020

There was snow tonight, and that was good, because it was almost Christmas.

Or he thought it was almost Christmas. Yes, it was. There was some tinsel in the hallway, hanging arbitrarily on the posters. In the nurses' office, a very small white tree with small red lights and a huge Star of David on top sat on someone's desk, evidentially an exercise in compromise.

But there should be snow on Christmas, shouldn't there? He knew there should. Or he knew people thought there should, other people, people who weren't here, people who used to be here. Or wherever they were when he knew them. Still knew.

People liked snow on Christmas.

Snow angels, fallen angels, no angels. No people.

Fireplaces. Chestnuts roasting. Everything roasting.

Everything burning.

There were some things he tried hard not to forget. *No luck with that*, he thought, the memories liberally beating the shit out of him. Her smile. His crayons. Her tiny dresses. His toys being chewed by the dogs. Hers not.

What had happened with the dogs?

Were they dead too?

Why had they always chewed his toys but not hers?

Other things, the things he wanted to remember, he couldn't be sure if he were actually remembering or just imagining. Either way, not so much luck. They came, he saw, they shit on him.

And some things he remembered without trying to. Snow was one of those, but there were the other things, things not quite as pleasant to recall, that forced their way into his thoughts and gave him dreams he believed might be visions of a place he'd love to run to so he could die there. Die quickly, again and again and in the worst ways imaginable. He'd tried to set himself on fire a few times in recent memory, for sure, but he couldn't really say with certainty, so whatever.

They'd never give him access to fire here, would they?

No. He hadn't tried to set himself on fire.

Why would he do that?

His stuff: Worse than anyone had ever experienced? The game was afoot, the studio audience leaned forward, the cameras rolled. Yes. Definitely. He sat back coolly and awarded himself that prize. His story was the worst. Wait, what was the story? Someone had died. He was pretty sure someone had died. The people in the audience grinned at him like hungry, sympathetic jackals. Jackals with plans.

But like Rodney'd once said, he hadn't yet met everyone and certainly hadn't asked anyone, so how could he know who besides him might have or might not have experienced something worse? The jackals didn't say.

He knew the dreams were the worst things he'd experienced. Though he could scarcely remember them, every morning in his neat little white bed he woke up screaming with the sheets and his pajamas soaked through. He had the pneumonia to prove it, he had the medicine to counteract the pneumonia that proved it, and neither was worth a damn.

Tell us your story. C'mon, tell it again.

The host wanted more. The jackals wanted more. The cameras were rolling.

They'd brought him an eggnog to go with his not-so-terrible turkey meatloaf dinner, a special treat to celebrate and toast with. Eggnog was a Christmas drink. Nothing in it, of course. No rum, no brandy, not in this place. Nothing to wash away the taste of not-so-terrible turkey. But with all the sedatives and MAOI inhibitors and the nasty stuff they called olanzapine (but his fellow patients called the "Heebie-Jeebie Shakes"), who needed booze to get a party started?

During his rare lucid moments, William sometimes reflected on the notion that, no matter his problems before he'd come here, the treatment was a hurricane with a tornado and a blizzard on the side. Wowza. And slam bang, his chin said to the floor more than once.

Four months of contemplating this and bouncing off the floor had generated in him a certain certainty. And if losing his family to a freak explosion had pushed him to the edge — and during moments when he was in possession of any of the narrative and enough of the details to go with it, he freely admitted it had — the Wierson Psychiatric Center for the Treatment and Care of the Mentally and Emotionally Challenged and the bugs who love them had kicked his ass right off it.

Adeste fideles, Laeti triumphantes…

And what's more, the turkey dinners, which they seemed to serve every other night, regardless of the holiday spirit, the snow, and the fucking unspiked eggnog, were evil. Not so evil as eggnog without booze, but he abhorred apples-and-oranges argumentation.

Everything here sucked.

The jackals wouldn't say either way.

His, the worst. The turkey also, the worst.

Fall on your knees, oh hear the angel voices...

Most nights and most days and everything in between, he was either openly weeping (without feeling anything like sadness or indeed anything like anything), or sitting there cackling (because he wanted to strangle everyone in the place and thought it was hysterical that they didn't know it), or pacing the halls and counting things (because counting things is the only beauty there is). A true madman, to be sure, a caricature of the most pitiful ilk. A counter, a scrivener staring at a wall, a mumbling fart that used to be human.

Yes, counting was a thing to do, and counting things or appearing to do so was best of all. They of course all thought he was counting things, but really he was just counting. Beautifully. You know, in the abstract. It gave him something to do, and misleading them gave him someone to fuck with while he planned his mass stranglings emotionlessly.

Without someone to fuck with, there is no life.

Sometimes he did something other than count, but there were decks of cards to play with, balls to throw, a big room with mats in it to stretch or roll on, music to listen to, and plenty of arts and crafts to do. They took his arts and crafts privileges away when he squeezed two whole bottles of Elmer's glue into his ears, nose, and mouth.

He couldn't help it, not really. Something about seeing crayons and little wooden scissors and figures of sailboats and dinosaurs and fruit you could cut out had reminded him of something he didn't want to be a part of. They'd stopped him right before he could put the glue in his eyes.

After he got out of the infirmary — they'd had to do two small operations to dig the hardened glue out of his nasal cavity and ear canals — he spent most of his time walking around counting or rolling on the mats. The movement seemed to help, even more than the drugs, he thought, but his doctors (he had three or four of them, depending on if that woman with the smelly purple smock was a doctor) disagreed.

It didn't matter. Let them drug him up; he offered no argument. He had nowhere to go, and sometimes the drugs gave him fantastic dreams. Preludes, of course, to the horrific ones, but fantastic nonetheless: tits and baseball and guitars and forests where it never rained. Sometimes the drugs did nothing: no dreams, but that made the nights when he had the good dreams even better. So the drugs were good for something, maybe more than something, He was still around to debate the point, which he suspected was the goal. Their goal, not his.

And then, right after the first candle was lit for Chanukah, he stopped counting and started to just relax. He still went to the mats, but he mostly just lay on them and hummed to himself. Sometimes he tossed a ball up, lying on his back, but his coordination was for shit, and that ball reminded him of the game where his sister came and told him…told him. So the meds were working, but balls and little wooden scissors and now moving and tomorrow something else were all being eliminated from his repertoire, one by one, and so what?

So it was almost Christmas Day, and he was sitting there watching the television with his uneaten but actually pretty tasty dinner in front of him and his gutless eggnog in his hand. They were showing the History Channel, a special program devoted to the origin of the New Year's Eve holiday.

He learned something new that night. Okay, so maybe it wasn't so new. He kind of thought it was something he'd already known but forgotten. It was new to the context, which was in itself something new, and doesn't a new context reinvent us, in a sense? Or at least, doesn't such a development afford us the ability to do those things for ourselves?

In Germany, they call New Year's Eve "Sylvester." Not just Germany, but also Austria, France, Israel, Poland, Switzerland, Italy, the Czech Republic, and Croatia. Even in Luxembourg, that's what they called New Year's Eve. They all called it Sylvester. Not like the Puddy Tat I tawt I taw, mind you, or like Rocky Balboa. No. They called it that because of the saint, a pope named Sylvester who died on the thirty-first of December a long time ago. The year 335.

William questioned whether or not that was true. Did they have popes all the way back then? Who knew? Were there books that survived that long? Cave paintings? Monolithic megaliths or massive mile-long pictographs only the most discerning and solidly tenured could discern? The legend said that this Pope Sylvester had slain a dragon. Not on New Year's Eve, on some other day. And now they called New Year's Eve "Sylvester" in Europe. And in Israel. He wondered about that. Some of those people in Israel had come from Europe, anyway, right, so they must have brought the name with them. But people came to North America from Europe, and we called it "New Year's Eve," so what happened to Sylvester here?

He decided to blame it on England. Maybe it was a whole dragon-slayer rivalry thing. After all, George is just another guy if Sly did it too, and after all, they use Georgie's name to knight people, and there's that symmetry — bada bum, bada bang, bada schlimazel, you're a knight — to worry about and what business did a pope have slaying a dragon? Or was it THE dragon he'd slain, and if he had, why didn't THE dragon stay down?

Daddy, what's a dragon?

And he tried not to think about his Sylvester, who would never see England or Croatia or Switzerland or Israel or a dragon. He could not think about him. He could think of nothing else. Sylvester on Halloween in a *Toy Story* outfit. Sylvester taking a nap in a pile of stuffed animals. Sylvester kissing his mama. Sylvester punching his sister. Sylvester with chocolate all over his face.

And then he thought about, could not stop thinking about, a photo of all three of them, one he'd brought into his drawing class to sketch. He could only see the sketch now, in his mind, and not the photo, and not the faces as they had been but as they were in the drawing. They didn't look like themselves, Sylvester and Wanda and Yancy. Their heads were too big and their eyes were too big and those heads would never fit on passport photographs and you couldn't use a sketch for a passport — could you? — and without a passport, no Austria or Italy or Israel or Switzerland, no Germany where they called New Year's Eve "Sylvester" and they dressed up like Woody from *Toy Story* and everyone in Europe took afternoon naps in piles of stuffed animals and kissed their mamas and punched their sisters good-bye while they waited for dinner and eggnog and a fresh, new year of dragons and schlimazel and goddamn turkey meatloaf.

After you get what you want you don't want it,
If I gave you the moon, you'd grow tired of it soon…
    Redeemer our Lord the Redeemer he redeems he offers redemption and forgiveness and love and understanding but at what price? Just for the asking, just for the picking, just…

We are expected to sin we are expected to do wrong we are expected to make massive mistakes. We are the sun and moon and wild, distracted desert lizards of our own delectable landscapes, and I am the rainforest who needs to be more than they all believe I am. THE dragon is a schlimazel with sugar on top dancing in the streets of Heidelberg or Jerusalem, watched from ancient walls above by the biggest bunch of do-nothing fuckwads in all eternity.

Merry fucking Christmas.

Early the next day, probably near dawn but who could tell with all this snow, deep, crisp, and even, all about, the tepid color of the last dragon's piss after he choked out his final serpentine utterance (*A goddamn pope did this to me?*), he opened the door.

The snow was falling, more thickly now than at dinnertime, general all over New York state, falling and swiftly falling and burning its way through the clouds and frelling up the world as he knew it. He stood staring at it, watching it fall past the lights on the top of the building, watching it swirl in the wind. The wind was strong, and it made the snow dance and whip in a wild, blinding way, and he stood there in the hallway with the door open and watched it. He and the bunch of fuckwads, who were, it was said, always watching. The jackals never sleep.

But everyone else was asleep. There wasn't really anyone to stop him. He could go, if he chose. He really could. But he'd been here before, maybe a dozen times, maybe more. He was farther along than he usually got. He'd only opened the door twice before; most times, he'd just stop in the hall and stare for a while at the knob until he got hungry or had to pee.

What stopped him, when he stopped, which he always had? The meds? The turkey? Fear of the fuckwads, who might in fact take umbrage with the title he'd bestowed upon them and might very well be watching from the courtyard's trees and the roof of the little chapel that sat up on a hill, not adjacent to but instead quite separate from the facility at which he had, for four months, been an honored, turkey-chomping, glue-guzzling guest?

Or was it the door, the locked-tight steel door that stood between him and his immolative destiny, that gave him pause?

It wasn't locked. It should be; it should be locked tight like all the doors and windows in this place. Not this time, no. Nor was there a camera in this hallway, or if there was one somewhere hidden where he couldn't see it, there wasn't anybody watching it. Or if someone was, that someone didn't seem to care what William did. Maybe that someone had even left the door unlocked for him. Maybe that someone wanted to help him leave. Maybe that someone just didn't want him around anymore. Pope Sly and his masterful Fuckwaddy Minions — maybe they all wanted William to go jump in a river.

And there *was* a river. He'd heard them talking about it, and he remembered crossing it when they'd brought him here. He'd been in the back seat of the car, looking out the window, not knowing or caring where they were going, listening to the man on the radio talk about oil prices. That was in September.

Wanda and he had been married in September. They had the wedding at their house. That was three days before 9/11. They had three days of postvow bliss but no honeymoon. They couldn't afford a honeymoon, and William had just started teaching business law and composition at Huniper College. Then, 9/11.

On 9/12, after a light breakfast, Wanda had said, "That's probably the worst thing that will ever happen to us."

She meant the whole world, he thought.

And them. She meant them too.

There was a river, and it wasn't far, but which direction should he take?

Now that he'd opened the door and was fairly sure he wasn't going to close it again like he had those other times, he had to pick a direction. After the fence.

And there is something on the other side of the fence – but I need the right direction.

Why?

Because it's New Year's Eve.

You don't have a watch.

Nitpicky.

You don't have wings.

Nitpicky.

There might be dragons.

God, I hope so.

The snow started blowing into the hall and in his face and hair. It was nasty cold, and he had no coat and no shoes.

He took a step. Then another. Then he was in the yard, moving toward the fence, moving toward the big fir tree next to the fence. He couldn't see much, but he knew where he was. He reached out and felt the tree anyway, just to be sure.

Yes. Tree. Good.

He looked up into the trees to see if they were watching.

In sin and error pining...

He'd sat, now and again, or pretty much every day for centuries, for hours and stared at this tree. During fresh air times, which lasted up until the snows came, or so he'd been told. The lower limbs were ten feet above the ground, but up past that, the limbs were a spoked ladder that climbed at least one hundred feet in the air.

The fence itself couldn't be more than twenty.

Ten feet tall if it were an inch, I tell ya.

And the jackals leaned in, wanting more.

So he jumped. It was hard to jump like that in the snow. He missed the limb he was going for five times. Six. Seven. He fell on his ass.

He sat on his ass.

In the snow. He sat on his ass and stared up through the spokes.

While shepherds watch are keeping, keeping, keeping...

The wind was whipping harder now, but the snow was letting up a bit. He was very cold. His robe and pajamas were soaked.

He sat there, soaked, half frozen, and stared up through the spokes.

"Will, are you coming? The kids are in the car."

"One minute. Lemme just..."

"I'm gonna go out and put on the air conditioning..."

"Okay. I'll...okay."

He was trying to fit some old tools into a bin down in the basement, tools he hadn't used in years. It'd taken him an hour because he kept stopping and thinking about what projects he could do with such-and-such piece if he ever got the time. He'd always wanted to learn how to use the router. You could make good furniture if you knew how to use a router. You could make a pool table. Or maybe not. But lots of things.

"Will, are you coming?"

That was a trip to…where? Her sister's house. A day with the family. The boredom was mind numbing, but at least his usual anxieties failed to follow him into the protected, boring space of his in-laws' world. The kids had a good time playing Go Fish with their cousins. The dogs slept at his feet in the yard and woke up to snatch the occasional unfinished hot dog. Sylvester was big on taking one bite from anything and leaving it to its fate. Silly Syl. He didn't know what a fish was or how one could actually go, but he loved to play anyway. He loved to take only one bite.

William pondered the idea that Sylvester and the dogs had a good thing worked out between them, and while he pondered this and similar notions, his usual anxieties remained on the outskirts of his mind, watching, not quite in the picture. For now.

"Did you have a good time?"
"Well, you know…no. But it wasn't so bad."
"No, it was okay this time."

He lowered his head to look at the tree trunk more carefully. And then he saw it: the broken branch.

It was much lower than all the branches, a gnarled stump sticking out about three inches from the trunk. It was only three feet off the ground. Had he noticed this before and forgotten it? Someone must've come along with a chainsaw at some point, long ago, and chopped off all the lower branches. All but this piece of one.

Probably didn't want to bust the blade on all the thick knots.

That must've been it.

But he'd stared at the tree for hours and that lower branch, that stump…it hadn't been there. He would have noticed. He was sure he would have noticed.

Well, it's there now, said the jackals in unison.

And the host smiled. And the music blared.

And he remembered his plan.

Run at the tree and jump. Land one foot on the broken, knotted branch. Stick up your arms and let your momentum swing them up to the first branch of the ladder.

Easy peasy.

No: it was a Terrible Plan, but it was all the olanzapine had allowed him to come up with.

Do it, the jackals cried.

Do it, Pope Sylvester demanded.

Do it, the dragon chuckled with its last dying breath.

He stood up. He backed slowly away from the tree, his feet nearly numb from the wet and the cold. He took a deep breath, thought about that arrangement his son had made with his dogs again, thought about why Grady Little elected to leave Pedro in, and why would he care, he hated the Red Sox, and almost forgot completely where he was and what he was doing, but then ran straight at the tree and jumped…

A few minutes later, he was at the bank of the river. It was closer than he'd imagined and so far away. *Listen to me, honey dear…something's wrong with you, I fear…* The moon—there was a moon—and the clouds it touched and tinged with pale but fungible hope and the lights of the interstate, illuminated the scene well enough, and what with all the glowing snow— reflecting saying wanting telling knowing but not telling—he could make out where the shore ended and the water began.

He could make out.

He walked. More. And then more.

Through that glowing snow. To where it ended, it and its shore and its glow. The water was dark and moving swiftly. He himself was mutinous, deadly, gone. Nothing watched him. The snow had stopped, but the wind was now strong enough that he had to fight to keep his balance. There was a rabbit sitting under a bush, just watching him. But nothing else. Nothing else watched him.

Promises are mine to give you.

He stood at the shore and looked at his watch.

Yes. He had a watch. In his pocket. On his wrist. On the mantle at home over the fireplace.

Mine to give.

He had some time.

Chapter 6
Why would they come?

Place: The Windgiver Sea, a few miles off
the northern coast of Xatumka, Arba Environ
Date: Boinage 40, AY 998

They were screaming below. He'd set them on fire, and they were screaming.

They were trying to get out, but the hold hatch held fast, and they burned. The night was hard with storm, and the Windgiver Sea's winds hammered the ship, feeding the flames as they whipped across the deck and into the hold. The rains were no match for the fire.

Baks Mu, first mate of the *Ho Matsuni*, stood tall at the helm and ignored the screams, the storm, the fire, and even his own blinding rage. The ship was burning all around him, and the heat was drying his sleek reptilian skin to the point where he had trouble breathing, yet he held the wheel firmly and stared forward into the night.

The flames hadn't yet touched the masts, but the sails were ablaze. The wind was getting stronger, pounding at him, and it took all his substantial strength to stand fast.

Where am I going? he asked himself.

There's nowhere.

Only here.

Should I head in?

No.

The *Ho Matsuni* would reach land soon enough, if it held together that long, or at least get him close enough to swim to shore, but could he bring these things near the shore with him?

They were burning, but what if they got out?

He could not allow that.

Like all Juks Xi Ren, he was an excellent swimmer. He doubted the things burning in the hold could even tread water. But they didn't need to swim. They could fly; he'd seen it.

But could they fly when charred?

A few long minutes passed. He steered his dying ship into the night, toward nowhere, maybe even in a circle—it was difficult to discern with all the smoke and flames and wind. He stared around him at the once-beautiful craft that was now a floating tomb, a burning husk upon which dozens of his shipmates—his countrymen—had been slaughtered.

He ignored the screams. They were not the cries of the Juks Xi Ren, not the cries of his friends. No.

The cries belonged to *them*.

Yes, they were still alive, these attackers, still trying to get out of the hold. A claw came through the charring wood of the deck; Baks left the wheel for a moment and rolled a huge barrel of ballast sand onto the claw. The snap of its bones filled him with a wild but brief sense of pleasure, and then the grim purpose of his ship's final journey weighed down upon him once more. He kicked the claw and returned to the business of the wheel.

His goal now was to oversee the sinking of his ship with all hands —and all the uninvited—sinking with it.

So he sailed. Soon, when the sails had burned to ash and the masts started to snap and fall, he and the vessel simply drifted and spun and heaved according to the whims of the waves.

He would miss his wife and daughters.

He would miss the rare times they'd had together on Challow's Isle.

And he would miss the seas and sailing and life among his brothers.

He stood, hands still on the wheel, though he was sure he'd long since lost control of the ship. He was not where he'd expected to be. The outpost island, its signal light flickering on the starry horizon, was maybe two miles off, much closer to the shore than he'd hoped. The helm was indeed useless, the rudder unresponsive, and the drift of the waves was guiding the ship entirely now. The ship was bound to run aground.

He waited, leaning into the wind, and he thought.

What is to be done? All I need do now is make sure nothing gets off the ship.

He released the wheel and grabbed an enormous scimitar from a rack of weapons. *If they free themselves from the hold, I'll greet their skulls with this,* he thought.

And then he saw a shadow from behind him.

"Who are they?"

Baks spun like a snake and almost lashed out at the voice, but then he saw who had spoken.

Vidra Tal, the captain of the *Ho Matsuni*. Or what was left of him. His left arm was missing, his left leg bent unnaturally. He leaned on the scuttlebutt and breathed heavily.

"I don't know, Captain," said Baks.

"You need to go."

"But they are…we cannot let them escape."

"They're not going anywhere. You trapped them…and I will finish them. But you need to go."

"Sir, how will you…?"

The captain glanced down at a satchel he had slung over his

shoulder. "I will end this."

Baks was quite sure he knew what was in the satchel. Explosives. Forbidden by the Pesil Acu, but Vidral was clearly unconcerned with any but the most immediate consequences right now.

"I'll stay with you, sir, keep them down," Baks shouted over the wind.

"Unnecessary. What you must do is swim and speak. Tell them what happened here."

"They won't listen."

"They will. Go to our home and speak."

"I cannot believe — "

"Go!" commanded the captain; the very act of doing so almost seemed to drain him of whatever life was left in him. "Swim," he whispered as he nodded toward the shore.

Baks Mu clasped the captain's shoulder, stared at him momentarily, and then silently turned away and dove off the ship into the dark sea.

He swam to the shore.

As he did so, as he found the rhythm of the water and moved effortlessly through it in the manner of his kind, the images of what had occurred returned to him, flashing through his mind like streaks of lightning crashing over waves.

He'd locked them all down there where he'd found them: there were at least a dozen, maybe more, and they were all down there, looking for something. He'd pitched barrels of oil into the hold and, as their dead eyes stared up at him through the grate, pushed burning torches down at them. They'd caught and extinguished the first two, but the third had hit the floor.

They should all have been dead within minutes, but they weren't.

Why were they still screaming? Why were they alive?

They couldn't get out.

He knew that, along with them, his own crew would also burn. But they were dead or past saving. Those things had been tearing them to pieces, eating them, toying with those who remained barely alive. His fire had granted his friends and fellow crew the mercy they deserved. In a few minutes it would gain them vengeance as well. Perhaps if the fire couldn't kill these things, the sea would.

As he swam, the storm passed.

He paused for a moment to regard the catastrophe he had just escaped.

There was no moon, but there were also no clouds to obscure the brilliant starlight — only the vicious wind of the Windgiver Sea taking wild, whispering note of the passing of so many proud Juks Xi Ren lakeservants. The seas glittered fully, and the light that bounced off them was more than enough for him to see that there was no trace whatsoever of the other two ships in the *Ho Matsuni's* party. No running lights, no torches. They were gone.

As impossible as it seemed, they were completely gone.

He swam for the shore, the young memory of the attack flashing in his mind.

He'd been in the water, hanging from a strong rope, dragging behind the *Ho Matsuni*, when they'd attacked. He'd seen them board the ship from midair. At first, they'd seemed like large black birds, the hush of their approach like a cold, invisible wind. They lighted upon the deck silently.

He'd seen the attack. His crew was relaxed, most of them asleep or sitting quietly at their posts. The two in the masts, Yalo and Strun Hao, had fallen in pieces from their perches along with shredded pieces of sail.

Why hadn't he joined in, why hadn't he fought with them?

The Felsorad ritual.

No, it wasn't the Felsorad.

He swam away from his burning ship, his captain, his friends and their deaths. His mind was cold, his warrior's default mind-set serving to save him once more from his own sense of doubt.

Was it his weakness, his lack of discipline, his descent into the ways of the humans that had crippled his vigilance? Had he chosen the wrong moment to honor his son? Could there be a wrong moment to do such a thing? The sea had been calm, the journey uneventful...and then this.

He'd tried to break free, to quicken the exit from the ceremony, but there was nothing for it. He'd only become himself again when it was too late to help anyone.

So he did what he could. He'd toppled the last three remaining barrels of oil and, without a glance at the fire, taken the wheel and headed landward.

The sea grew rougher as he swam; another storm was moving in. He'd spent almost as much of his life swimming as walking, and he welcomed the choppy edge the water provided. It calmed him to focus on the rhythm of the swim. And it would make him more difficult to spot if the others — the ones who had attacked the two other ships, as he assumed they must have — came looking for him.

Why would they come?

They would see the burning ship and understand that someone

had interfered with their design. Someone who might still be alive.

Or maybe they didn't care. Maybe they'd gotten what they wanted and were on their way back to whatever hell had spawned them.

He reached the shore in under an hour. Hiding among the jagged rocks of the northern coast, he stared out at the sea. He could see nothing of the disaster that had befallen them and no sign of any pursuer. And now it was left to him to make his way back to Camedua and find answers to what had happened. Or to answer for the destruction of three ships, which was the more likely outcome.

Lightning cracked the sky as the storm returned, much more intense this time. He made his way along the shore toward what looked to be an unlit lighthouse. Perhaps there'd be some food there, or at least a map. The thought of stumbling around, trying to find a road south, was neither a pleasant nor a promising one. The rain and the swim had renewed his strength, but being on land, as always, made him uncomfortable, and he wasn't sure where he was.

He gained the empty lighthouse and crept around it. Though it was custom to provide food and shelter to any sailor in need, most often the unspoken truth specified the sailor in need be one of the provider's own species. So it was with men – and it was no different with his own people. He'd seen more than one man pitched over the side into the sea and at least one beaten to death with his own arms by Juks Xi Ren he considered gentle friends.

He himself thought and felt otherwise about men, but he did so in the privacy of his own heart. These were not the times to offer a dissenting opinion. The Triumvirate's treatment of his race had always been terrible, but of late it had worsened, and the Juks had taken notice.

There was no one in the lighthouse, and it was not locked. Inside there was little of any use: no food, no wine, no way to make a fire. It didn't matter: he wasn't hungry, he needed to keep a clear head, and a fire would only bring his enemies down upon him, if indeed they were still interested in finding him.

He sat down on a low table and closed his eyes a moment to listen and to think. The voice of the sea and the chorus of the storm cleared his mind a bit.

What had they been looking for?

Had they found it?

His best course of action, he knew, was to head back to Challow's Isle and seek an audience with the leaders of his people. They would not stand idly by once they heard his story, law and treaties be damned. The Juks Xi Ren were neither pets nor servants, and the Triumvirate land shits were not in command, not of them.

He felt a little colder inside as he tried to sell that lie to himself.

The truth, and he knew it, was that he was probably very much alone now. And with so much to answer for, his life would surely be forfeit.

His brief time steering the dying craft, however, had afforded him the opportunity to contemplate his own inevitable and likely violent end. It wasn't the first time for such a contemplation, either. He chuckled to himself.

I'll go to Camedua and take what they give me. And maybe give something back.

Chapter 7
A game she called
"distal contemplation."

Place: Island city of Pashka, in the kingdom of Pherriuskata, Arba Environ
Date: Boinage 43, AY 998

Petrecia Celeranet looked out the window and saw a small fleet of sailing ships headed out of the bay to lands far away.

At least, she imagined they might be headed out to faraway lands. More likely they were bound to Quintish to deliver dresses or pots or politicians and to acquire grain or cured meats or wine…and politicians.

What did it matter? They were going somewhere. She stayed here. In Pashka. Always.

She acknowledged, in a not so very rare and original moment yet with a weak burst of insight, that she had just lied to herself. Again. It wouldn't be the last time, or even the last time this morning. She was going somewhere, and very soon. A great feast. It was an honor to be invited, although not as great an honor as it would have been to be invited elsewhere. But where she was going and how they were getting there…she was doing her best to put all that out of her mind. Any ship would be preferred. Four be damned, it would be better to swim.

Particularly if swimming meant drowning.

But there was no ship, and one didn't swim Lake Iale, not even if one were Challowian.

Or did they swim there? Yes, of course, they did. Those people were practically fish themselves.

She had no ship waiting for her. No, the next day, she and her beloved husband — the mystifyingly self-satisfied, insufficiently endowed Rodolpho Canamow of the Anhariq Measured Fields, lord of whatever he thought he was lord of, and member of the Triumvirate Body — were taking the Mansdrelam to Castle Motatinfo for the Low Feast of Trantuse.

She had begged him not to take her. Not directly — that kind of simpering appeal would not have been well received — but in subtle ways that got her message across without endangering her cheekbones.

Rodolpho had, of course, ignored her. She was going, and there was to be no discussion. Still, and to his credit, he hadn't struck her. He could be very kind, he could, despite the busyness of his schedule and the incessant demands, whatever those were, of his position.

So she was going with him. Despite her horror and revulsion, they wouldn't be taking a ship.

The Mansdrelam awaited them.

"Which of these dresses do you prefer, ma'am?" her woman, Synthyea, asked her.

Petrecia turned and regarded the three that were spread out on her bed. "I don't know, Synthyea. You pick one," she said. "I have to think about a mask."

"Not the flowerbird?" Synthyea asked with a slight note of surprise in her voice.

"I don't know. Perhaps not. What else is there? What haven't I worn?"

"Well, other than the bird, you've got...let's see. There's a sea tortoise, a Miranquellan wobo bear—that's a nice one from home, no?—and there's the leopard. That's one you've never worn."

"A leopard? I didn't know I owned a leopard mask. Where did it come from?"

"I'm not sure. I think you've always had it. I assumed it was also from your home."

"There are no leopards in...well, maybe there used to be. Yes, I think there were..."

"Want to try it on?"

Petrecia considered it for a moment. Something different, something to take her mind off...yes. "Very well, let's try it on. Can't hurt to make an effort. Who was it that said, 'These precious pursuits must be given due time and warmth'?"

"I'm sure I couldn't say, ma'am."

"Sure you could. It was Hua Tsetang, wasn't it?"

"I'm not sure I know who that is, ma'am."

Which was a lie. Who didn't know who Tsetang was? But Petrecia thought nothing of it. She lived her life, always, as if everyone were lying to her. Because with one or two possible exceptions, everyone was.

She had turned thirty-three years old not too long ago and could no longer remember a time when anyone had told her the truth. Nor could she remember a time when she'd cared.

All she cared about now was finding the right time and place to die.

She dined alone that night. Rodolpho was with the Triumvirate Body, or maybe with Duke Velliok, or he was fucking himself silly in a Moloa Boulevard pleasure house. Or all three. Maybe the Body and the duke joined him in his stupid dalliances. For all the governing they did or didn't do, it would explain a lot.

"I'm quite sure Lord Canamow will be here shortly," the manservant, Braun, said after apologetically delivering each course of her meal. Once he added, "Affairs of state can't keep a man away from his lady indefinitely."

She smiled at him and asked, "Would you care to place a wager on that, Braun?"

He raised his eyebrows and looked trapped, but she immediately took pity on him and covered with, "I'm sure you're quite right; he'll be along any minute now…" while patting him on his arm.

Braun retreated with a mixed look of relief and consternation. She couldn't blame him. She'd broken the unspoken rule: Never call a thing what it is. Never even hint that you know what it is.

The next morning, her husband had still not returned, but she didn't much mind. She preferred when he wasn't around. It allowed her time to read — something women were, officially and ridiculously, discouraged if not forbidden from doing in the Tri — and to spend his money — something women of this particular part of the Tri often excelled at and were very much encouraged to excel at. Spending spoke of quality.

"And we all crave quality, don't we?" Petrecia muttered to herself, bitterly quoting any one of a hundred stupid women she knew.

Merchants visited the house as they did every day after breakfast. Petrecia bought a few rugs, a coolaght of wine (more than any three households would need for a year, but Rodolpho had such a thirst), some shoes, two sculptures of dancing children (her idea of being a little clever), and a collection of fruits from her homeland that were almost certainly rotten inside but which nonetheless gave her a moment of reflective pleasure.

The Y&T slavers came, as they always did, and tried, but she'd have none of it, as usual. "No, thank you, and please don't come again: we have all the help we need here," she told them for the thousandth time. Why did they keep coming back? She guessed at an answer: they were hoping to come on a day when Rodolpho would be home. He would buy.

But they were hoping in vain. If he had been home, he would certainly have been up in his chambers, passed out or busy imagining he was once again fucking Elzbieta.

Dear Elzbieta. Her friend, her rival, her confidant.

Her replacement.

Well, at least they'd agreed on slavery. Elzbieta was from Aethrelius. They kept no slaves there.

On the other hand, they'd thrown her out, the Aethreleans had, for breaking one (or maybe it was a few) of their precious commandments. Or so she'd implied. Elzbieta was by no means an open book, and she was as skilled a liar as any trueborn Pherriuskatan. For all Petrecia knew, Rodolpho had bought her in Arbana or from Pebbuskan pirates on one of his so-called diplomatic holidays to Mariendo. She'd appeared out of thin air years ago, just after Petrecia had confessed to her husband for the last time that she wasn't pregnant…again.

And Rodolpho had murdered his lovely Aethrelean five years later.

Her body had disappeared back into the thin air from whence it had materialized.

Petrecia put the now-dead Second Wife out of her mind and tried some of the rotten fruit. Terrible. She told Braun to have it hauled out to the garden and used as mulch.

"Are you sure?" he asked, dubiously regarding the massive pile.

She ignored his second-guessing, so he ambled away, mumbling something about informing Hobknot, the ancient gardener. She imagined the two of them trying to tug the pile of dead fruit outside; it made her smile. Somehow she was sure the pile would end up falling on one of them.

Ah, to be buried alive by rotten citrus! What Miranquellan could resist such a death?

She made a mental note and noted also that she was once again lying to herself about her capacity for ending this broken life of hers.

Her husband came home sometime in the midafternoon. Synthyea informed her of his arrival.

"Very good. Thank you."

"Is there a message for him, ma'am?"

"No. No message. I suppose we should start to think about getting dressed, though. What time are we due at the—" She caught herself, unable to say its name, the horrible device that would transport them. "What time do we need to leave?"

"The twenty-sixth hour, ma'am, is when you are due to arrive."

"Here or there?"

"Ma'am?"

"Are we due in Motatinfo at that time, or at the place the name of which neither of us can mention?"

Synthyea looked at the floor and mumbled something.

Petrecia sighed and waved her away, saying, "It's all right. Don't worry about it. It'll be fine."

"Forgive me, but I don't think you believe that, ma'am," Synthyea said as she turned and fled the room.

And she was right.

Petrecia hated the very idea of the Mansdrelam. It was an abomination, the purported usefulness of which had rendered it to some an acceptable evil and to others a device that filled them with the thrill of powerful privilege. No matter what view one took of the thing, there was no denying one singular fact: it took lives to make it work. It always had, and it always would, and as long as there were people who weren't at all troubled by the cost, that wouldn't matter.

And few seemed troubled by the cost.

She herself had never used it. The question had never come up. They had no Mansdrelam in Mont du Grace — they never had — and she had only been the one time to Hunberg, on her journey eleven years ago down from Miranquella.

Rodolpho used the Mansdrelam. It wasn't to his liking either, she could tell, or she hoped she could tell, but he did what he needed to do to maintain his position and increase his chances to climb. Sometimes that meant travel. Sometimes it meant immediacy.

Yet he didn't enjoy it, she was sure. At least she could say that in his favor. He was often cruel and stupid and selfish — in fact, he was always cruel and selfish but admittedly not often stupid — but he valued human life. All life, as far as she could tell, but it was difficult to tell. Their interactions with other races were so infrequent. An occasional Slau merchant, with slits for nostrils and four-fingered hands, or a Challowian naval officer with massive, semireptilian body and resonating voice, or a Brull trader, monstrous and silent and who breathed quite loudly, were their dinner guests, but those instances were quite rare, and always there were a dozen or more humans between her and the more exotic invitees. She'd never actually spoken to any of them. One time, in Mont du Grace, she'd met a Prementian, or dreamt she had, but that was very long ago. Rodolpho had laughed at her when she'd told him about that.

"They never come south, my dear. They hate us all and would rather we stayed very far from their precious homeland. I suspect they have a rude awakening coming at some point."

Threats. Always threats, subtle and otherwise. That's how it was with the Tri. Threats and lies and lies about threats and threatening lies.

She thought of the places these others came from and how things would be there. She'd often wondered how life would be for her in Aethrelius, in Prement, or even Jamoi. Ha! The very thought of her in any of those places made her chuckle. No mask, no merchants after breakfast, no endless stupid balls and fests to attend? What would she do, who would she be?

The answer always choked her, chuckling down with its blunt power:

Nothing. No one. Never.

****

"These festivals are a drain on the senses."

Rodolpho was bored. Or at least pretending to be bored. It was the perfect excuse to become angry.

They were waiting in line behind twelve other, more important couples. The onlookers were jostling and pressing against the ropes on either side, and the soldiers who'd drawn the task of keeping the whole mess in order were beginning to get irritated.

"Look at them. You'd think these little mice had never witnessed a procession before," he said to Petrecia. His balding head was showing quite prominently beneath his tilted and unfashionable hat.

She glanced at him and suppressed a giggle. She could scarcely hear him over all the noise, and she did her very best to look like someone who couldn't make out a word he was saying. He was oblivious. Too concerned with who was here and seeing him on this queue.

Petrecia was playing a game, a game she called "distal contemplation." She'd seen it in a book, one she was sure Rodolpho would have made her eat if he ever realized it was in his collection and that she'd read it.

Truth was, she'd read it three times.

The game worked this way: What she could hear, she ignored. And she'd feed him little assurances that had nothing to do with whatever he'd said, or just stare blankly at him, or occasionally hum an indecipherable response.

The goal of the game was, over the course of years, to drive the husband quite mad. According to the book, the technique worked extraordinarily well with a husband who possessed a temperament such as Rodolpho's: prone to anger, prone to self-doubt, prone to a terrible penchant for overrating his own savvy.

In an extension of the game, she likewise ignored the crowd and its odd attempts to share in a life it could never know. It was said the people were poor, the people were envious, the people were, in the end, perpetually and fatally just one small moment from a very long walk to Rash al Brek and the Takers.

Though she felt for them, today she wasn't concerned about them. Let them be envious; it was safer than being included in the process that awaited the fools in the queue.

Maybe they'd take the Walk tomorrow, but as no one had in a hundred years, she assumed not. And she was glad for them. The Takers were long gone, and these people, the crowd, were the lucky ones: they would probably be alive tomorrow. Others wouldn't be so lucky.

She decided to distract herself — an essential component of the game — by noticing the dresses Lady Umda and the Fifth Rendlet's new wife had donned. Such exquisite material. Such unique and flowing colors: Lady Umda's a fine cream, the wife's a soft, swirling violet. Where did their leadwomen lay hands on such material, and why hadn't hers? She'd have to punish Synthyea a little. She smiled slightly; Synthyea so loved a good punishment.

Petrecia blushed when she considered how much she enjoyed punishing Synthyea.

It was working, this trick of hers, this distal contemplation. Thinking of other things shielded her from the now. And Rodolpho was becoming agitated.

The line moved a bit. Rodolpho subtly pulled her arm just enough to make it ache.

"My love, you are smiling at something, hmm? But not about what I said, I'm sure." He squeezed the arm a bit. "I'm hurt that you've chosen not to listen again, Pet. I was just waxing poetic about the behavior of our beloved local rodent population, and you weren't paying me a lick of attention," he whispered in her ear. "Haven't I told you time and time again how that wounds me?"

You have indeed. She smiled at him brightly and said, "I'm sorry, love, what was it you were saying? Mice something? Oh, look. The line is moving…"

There were a few instances in the world of the Pherriuskatan elite where the concept of the pecking order was set aside; the queue to utilize the Mansdrelam Exchange was not one of those. In fact, there was quite a bit of pomp and privilege connected to the device, and there was an official whose sole function in life was to form and break and manipulate the queue according to the applicants' social status. The Mansdrelam Man at Pashka Exchange was a tall, wiry fellow given to slow, dramatic sweeps of the arms and harshly nasal pronunciation of titles. His mask was gray with maroon etchings, denoting his unmistakable call of service to the duchy. He wore a wig in the old style, neatly arranged, and a long black silk jacket adorned with Baybish morning glories, some white and some a deep, rich violet-maroon that almost matched his simple bureaucratic mask.

"Look at him. Fop. Idiot," muttered Rodolpho. "That wig looks like an old beheaded cat that fell into a keg of Kisstari cider. And he's wearing a mask. It's in very poor taste."

"I'm sorry, whose wig?"

"Was it necessary to wear that brooch, Pet? I adore your father, I do, but the man understands nothing about anything, especially the Songs of Adornment. Has he even ever read them, let alone memorized them?"

"My father cannot read, Dolphie. You know that, love."

"The hell he can't. Don't start with me tonight, *love*."

"Dolphie, this brooch was a gift from Papa's sister Hanziella, meant to be worn at all occasions, in all weathers, and in whatever company."

"It's ugly, and it offends me."

"It probably feels similarly about you, but alas, it has no means by which to voice its complaint."

"Tread carefully, little bitch. There won't be a crowd forever."

"No, but wouldn't it be nice if there were? You could perform your manly acts for all Arba to see. You might give the Reestenfal a rival, such would be the public adoration heaped upon you!"

"Why, your mouth is in rare form tonight. I will take that into consideration when we settle in our sweet lovers' chamber tonight. Or perhaps this is all an act, hmm? Are we trying to tamp down our noble objections to this form of transportation? You know Naipek and Frulla did as we are doing."

"You don't know that. And I'm not being noble just because I despise this savagery."

"Sure you are. Fine, noble Pet of the fine noble Celeranet family of simpering ass-kissers, nobly standing in ineffectual defense of our fine Mansdrelam volunteers."

She pulled her arm away, furious, and snapped, "Perhaps you should volunteer in their stead. I'd be more than willing to transport in that case."

His look was dark, and he gave no reply.

She wasn't sure if she'd overdone it. She knew what he liked and how to keep him enticed and confused, but there was a line, and it was forever shifting. *I might have just crossed it*, she thought. His tone this evening seemed more threatening than enticed. *I'll have to work at the ball to see he becomes too drunk to exchange threatening for something more...visceral.*

Given what she was about to do and what she was about to take part in, she hoped he would beat her bloody, right here and now. But at least she'd registered her objection, however powerlessly. And at least she'd never been made to do this before.

The line was moving steadily. The crowd, sensing the end of the little event, was pressing in even harder now. Somewhere, a quartet of wind instruments contended with a throatsinger's attempt at an old seasonal ballad. Ahead, the crumbling entrance to the ancient Mansdrelam Temple yawned like an old but hungry lion at a dance for young lambs.

The couple in front of them were called.

"Why are we going to this thing? No one goes to the Low Feast of Trantuse anymore. And why in Motatinfo, for Four's sake?"

"People do go, Dolphie. At least, those who aren't invited to the High Feast go. Motatinfo, this year, is the refuge of society's overlooked."

He absorbed the insult. His grip on her relaxed. He smiled, but not at her. "Finest Trantuse, the time for humble fare, our blessed season of decisions small and large, Pet. Let us decide, together in spirit, to make this a blessedly tolerable if not altogether enjoyable journey." He looked her full in the face. His eyes were not smiling.

"Lord Rodolpho Canamow of the Anhariq Measured Fields, and his bride, the Lady Petrecia Celeranet of Mont du Grace."

Together and without any hesitation—for hesitation might give the gossips something to titter and gnash about—husband and First Wife stepped through the temple's door. Behind them, the crowd clapped and hooted.

There was a dark tunnel of about twenty feet before them; at its end, another official, this one short and thick, dressed similarly to the Mansdrelam Man but without the adorning flowers, beckoned to them stiffly and unnecessarily. They walked toward him with a slow, dignified gait.

"Please, step onto the lift and, if you please, hold the center rail firmly during the drop," said the Mansdrelam assistant.

Rodolpho and Petrecia stepped onto the platform before them but pretended not to have heard him about the rail. There was a loud series of clicks, and the platform began to descend.

"You know, I must speak to Jaik about the recent quality of our linens," Rodolpho said.

"Oh?"

"I discovered, just yesterday, a stained sheet on one of my beds." She said nothing.

"We can't have Jaik faltering in his duties. I may have to have him replaced."

Still she said nothing.

"Or perhaps I could simply do the right thing and have him burn such sheets after their use."

"Perhaps," she managed. "Or perhaps Jaik can find a way to turn such sheets into a festival garment for you, something to wear at the next High Feast you're not invited to."

He clutched her arm and pulled her close. His hawk's mask pressed against her leopard's, and underneath the mask his eyes were wide with rage. "Or perhaps I can have him burn those sheets after all, with something bloody but still very much alive wrapped in them."

She knew the game was up. Rodolpho was nothing if not a sore loser; the points she'd scored here would cost her. She turned her head from him; after a moment, he released her.

They rode down slowly together, into the darkness, toward the heart of the Mansdrelam Temple. Neither spoke for the final two minutes the lift took to reach the bottom.

"Please, step into the chamber and to the left."

The chamber was dimly lit, with only two small sconces on each wall. To their right, a series of many small cages, each large enough for two humans to hunch together on their knees, lined the temple wall. Most of the cages were empty, but one held a small old woman and what looked to be a blind, hairless child. The woman was staring at the floor, weeping; the child sightlessly gazed at them through the bars of the cage.

Petrecia began to shake.

On the floor in the center of the room was a circular dip containing a shimmering, silvery liquid. Surrounding the dip was a railing with two breaks for entry. A third official, this one wearing an identical mask to those of the first two but otherwise dressed in the rolling yellow-orange robes of his magickal order, indicated with a gesture that they should proceed.

"If you please, step into the pool and close your eyes. Please be aware: the process is much more comfortable if you also are able to hold your breath."

"This isn't the first time we've done this, Magicker."

"Magickus, my lord. As it pleases you."

Rodolpho walked forward with practiced nonchalance. Petrecia followed, her legs heavy. This was in fact his forty-second time, her first. They entered the pool. They closed their eyes.

"I really will be speaking to Jaik. There are other matters for us to discuss. And to decide upon," said Rodolpho.

The process began, and a steady, icy sensation crept up Petrecia's body. It climbed up to her neck. It would happen momentarily, and then they would be in Motatinfo.

She knew she shouldn't, but she had a sudden impulse to open her eyes.

She ignored the impulse and held her breath. A great swell of sorrow rose up in her.

Someone was about to die so she could go to a party.

Chapter 8
"No Reismyl. Absolutely not."

Place: The Landing Point, kingdom of Arbana, Arba Environ
Date: Boinage 44, AY 998

For a very long time, it was very dark.

For weeks, it was dark.

For years.

Forever.

The cold of the river's waters stayed with him throughout. Cold and dark, dark and cold, and empty, and having no thoughts and dreaming of things he couldn't quite see or hear or in any way recognize. Faces. Objects. Events. Places. He saw them and knew them as things he had known but beyond that, nothing. And then he wasn't even sure he'd known them, and the things he dreamt of started to go away, leaving him only the cold and the darkness and the quiet.

It got very quiet in his mind.

And he thought that then: that in his mind it had become very quiet. But he had no understanding of what a mind might be, or why that word would be before him, or who he himself that had these thoughts might be, or why…and then he abandoned thought and just became a silent witness to all that was cold and dark and quiet and without thought.

And he forgot time, and it forgot him.

He didn't care. He didn't mind. He didn't know.

He knew nothing, he thought nothing, he was nothing.

But he was aware. He was alive and present enough to be aware. Not to compare, not to reflect or ponder or lament or rage or want or intend or understand or know…but aware of all that was there before him. And that there were things that weren't.

Aware of the cold.

Aware of the complete absence of light.

Aware of infinite time and now.

"Hioem' rulik navvka, perst!"

There came a sound. It was deafening, here in the eternal quiet, and it was unyielding…and it came again.

"Hioem' rulik navvka, perst!"

He felt something. It was…it hurt.

There was pain, and he remembered pain then, and he didn't like it.

And then there was more pain, and the sound once more.

"Perst! Perst fu awer! Hioem' rulik navvka! Perst!"

He opened his eyes and for a moment was amazed that he had eyes to open, and that he knew what they were and what they did. And the light hurt him. And then the other pain, again. And once more.

He was lying down on a bed. No, it was hard, more like a table. There was someone in front of him. Something. A man with the head of a...of something he knew...had known.

A cougar. Like a cougar.

He remembered seeing photos of cougars.

And then, more pain.

Cougar Man was striking him, hard. They were in a small, dark room, the walls of which looked to be wattles and clay. Or was it a cave? William couldn't tell. And Cougar Man was hitting him. Repeatedly.

He flinched away from his assailant and tried to get up and walk.

He fell down; that hurt too.

"Pili naavka, perst gu'wa to!"

Another blow, and then he was yanked up onto his feet.

There was a second voice, lower, softer, and then he felt a sharp pain in his...back? His head? No: his neck.

He heard screaming and laughter, and he knew he was making some of those sounds. There was a smack, this one to his face. And another.

Pain, such pain. Again, a smack.

And just like that, he remembered.

He remembered who he was...what he had done, where he had been...and them.

They were gone. They were dead.

He was dead.

He'd drowned in the river.

Why was he here now?

Where was his family?

They were dead.

No, they were...they were.

Dead.

He remembered, but he didn't understand. His awareness groped for understanding, a reason for what he could now remember. His memories lay before his mind's eye like scattered books and photos and debris, a senseless heap that should mean something to him but did not.

"You need to listen, human. Now."

He turned and saw Cougar Man. Next to him was a short, stout woman in a dirty gray smock, holding a syringe.

"He is not listening," Cougar Man said.

"Give him a minute," said the other.

"He is Mindless."

"Maybe. But we've already had more than twenty from this crop — twenty of twenty-three, mind you. You wanna tell Strak this is number twenty-one?"

William blinked a few times. "You...you gave me a shot?" he asked. "I'm allergic to penicillin and levaquin."

The words coming out of him made him start. They sounded strange, alien. He hadn't spoken in centuries, he hadn't made words for eons, and language was an enemy, for with it came thought, and thought brought him pain — this much he also remembered.

"Well, Four be damned. It worked," said the stout woman, glancing at the syringe. "He's got an accent, though."

"It's a shit batch. Strak gets a kickback," said Cougar Man.

"Don't let him hear you say that," said a new voice, this one deep and melodic.

"Strak! We've got a keeper for you," said the stout woman.

"Do you? Pella, my dearest, don't tease me now! You know I hate disappointment," said the owner of the third voice, a large man they called Strak. "Okay, say something for me, Entrant. Tell me, who won your last war?"

William, feeling dizzy and exhausted now, turned slowly to look at Strak. He was definitely big: a burly man with a goatee moustache, hands the size of toasters, and a UCLA baseball cap. He had drawn his face up close to William's. Very close.

"I like your hat," said William.

"Hahahahaha...he likes my hat. Okay, then. If you like it, tell me please: What do its symbols mean?"

William stared at the hat again, not seeing any symbols or anything else but the four letters. *He must mean the letters. Why wouldn't he call them letters?*

Strak's eyes were wide and expectant. He was nodding slightly in what seemed to be an encouraging gesture.

"University of California, Los Angeles?" guessed William, assuming he was right but not sure he knew exactly what game they were playing.

Strak burst out laughing and punched William in the chest hard enough to knock him back down onto the table, which brought a fresh round of guffaws from not only Strak but his two subordinates.

"Correct!" shouted Strak. "We have a keeper!"

William did not know what he meant by that. He felt momentarily ashamed, and then hopeful, and then he felt a sensation when he reflected upon those feelings.

The sensation was...amusement.

He was amused to be feeling anything at all.

Given that he had somehow survived suicide by drowning, floated for however long in silent darkness, and woken up to find himself in the company of, among others, a man with the head of a cougar and another with hands the size of toasters, he found it funny that the thing he'd suddenly and arbitrarily been most concerned about was what this Strak meant by the word "keeper."

After you get what you want, you don't want it...

"Why is he smiling? Hey, why are you smiling? Something is funny?" asked Cougar Man.

"Spoke too soon. Mindless," said Pella.

Strak grabbed William by the jaw and bellowed, "No smiling. Idiot Mindless Ones smile. Let me see a keen look. Do it! Now!"

William stared hard at him, but not because of the command. The man's grip was like a wood clamp on his face, and it hurt. And William was feeling something else now, something more...he was angry. And getting angrier.

Strak laughed and released him. "There's a good boy. Rage! Keep that up, my little friend. Rage will keep you alive, it will, and also, it will keep you out of Yanz, eh? Yes!"

"Yanz is full. It's Tritto this month," said Pella.

"Tritto? Don't you just love Dakaj? What a season. All the gifts, the unexpected gifts, plus the drinking."

"And the caterwauling and the speeches and the taxes," mumbled Pella, shaking her head.

"Never mind those. We get to go to Tritto!" Strak laughed.

"We've got at least twenty Mindless, boss."

"Twenty. And two not?"

"Three."

"Three. Time was, there'd be thirty."

"Been a long time, boss," said Pella.

Strak seemed momentarily lost in thought. He raised one eyebrow and touched his cap. "UCLA! What a place, huh? Beaches and basketball, right?" He laughed. "Oh, no matter. I have a lover in Tritto. A few, in fact. I'll begin packing."

"And what do we do with him?"

"Don't start, Pella my dear."

"We have to. You remember the last time."

"Yes, dammit, I remember the last time. But this one is different. No Reismyl. Absolutely not. We can...can we do the trick with the agilios and get him out, yes?"

"They have sniffers. They'll know."

"They'll know we used agilios, but it has all kinds of applications, doesn't it? Of course it does," Strak said, almost pleadingly.

Cougar Man weighed in. "Not here it doesn't. They're on to that trick, boss."

"Shit."

"What's the problem? He seems clean," said Cougar Man as he jabbed two fingers into William's side. William sat up and slid off the table away from him.

Strak waved Cougar Man away. "Let him be." Strak put his face close to William's again. "'Seems' is not good enough, Misle. I need him alive."

"I could go through with him," said Misle the Cougar Man.

"Misle, you would do that? For me?" Strak clapped Misle on the back and grinned. "Tell me more."

"No more to tell. I could see him through. Done it before."

"Have you? Of course you have. Okay. Sold. Do it."

Misle went to William and took him by the arm. "I'll feed him first, then bring him to the weapons room. You know how to fight, you?" Misle asked William.

William looked at him quizzically.

"Do you know how to fight?" Misle repeated, this time more curtly.

"I've fired a rifle at a range a few times but never at a person," William answered, remembering that this answer was accurate. Or was the Cougar Man talking about arguing? William had been to law school. He knew how to argue. But he wouldn't call it fighting, per se...

"No guns here. Never guns," said Misle.

"I took aikido a few years ago," William said, attempting to be helpful. "Studied it for two months till I broke my wrist."

Misle frowned at him, shook his catlike head, and pulled him toward the door.

Pella, looking anxious, spoke up: "Can I ask why we're risking Misle on this?"

"I told you: I need this one alive," Strak said flatly.

"But why this one?" Pella persisted. William saw her throw a look of concerned affection at the Cougar Man, who stopped pulling him and waited for Strak's reply.

"Someone wants him. Someone's paid a lot for him, and I need him alive," said Strak.

"More than the Grehmann Block, they've paid?"

"Much more."

Pella looked puzzled and intrigued. "Three ways?" she asked.

"Quarter share for each of you if he lives. Nothing if he dies," said Strak.

"What's so special about this one?" asked Misle.

Strak smiled broadly. "The buyer paid so much, I forgot to ask."

Misle led William out of the room and down a long corridor lined with cells. The cells were filled with people, all of whom were staring blankly at the walls or at one another or at the hall. None made eye contact. None moved much except maybe to sway back and forth.

"What's wrong with those people?" he asked Misle.

"Mindless."

"What does that mean?"

"Means they all of them had a rough trip, is what it means," said Misle, throwing him a look that seemed to say "no more questions."

But William had another question. Dozens, in fact. *Where are we? What is this place? What are you? Why am I alive? What language was being spoken at me? What do you want from me?*

He chose an easy one to start. "Where are we going?"

"To feed you. And to pick a weapon for you."

"A weapon for what?"

"You want to live, don't you?"

William hesitated, the irony of the question not lost on him. He was quite sure he was undecided, but he nonetheless nodded in the affirmative.

"This is the only way that happens," said Misle.

They came to an iron door, and Misle knocked. A small peep hatch opened to reveal a large nose, a beard, and some very bad teeth. "How many?" came the gruff answer from behind the door.

"Two. Me and one," Misle said.

"Who's me?"

"You know who I am," Misle growled, clearly a bit anxious himself.

"Not if I don't see your money, I don't."

"It's for Strak," Misle said.

"Let's see Strak's money then," said Bad Teeth.

Misle reached into his vest pocket and pulled out a small pouch. He held it before the peep.

"That's a small bag there. Pass it through."

Misle did as he was asked.

"All right, you can come. And I ain't gonna ask you why you're coming with him."

"That's what the money's for, Thriz. No asking, you. Just opening."

"Don't get smart."

Misle did not reply. The door swung open, and in they went, he and William. He dragged William through the room to another door; this one opened without challenge. There were a table and several benches in this next room. "Sit there."

William sat.

Misle went to a counter by the wall and opened a few cabinets. William was reminded of a kitchen; not the kitchen at home, no, not that one…because something had happened there, something he didn't remember, didn't want to remember, something he could never remember, would not allow…it blew up.

Yes, that's it. Kitchen blew up. All hands lost. Film at eleven.

"You all right?" Misle said, dropping a small loaf of brown bread in front of him. "There's no soup, but here's water." He placed a mug down on the table and pushed it toward William.

William glanced once more at the cabinets and then turned his eyes away from them and started eating and drinking.

"Still can't tell if you're Mindless or what. You're like…a half-breed or something. Or were you just dumb on Earth?"

"I had my moments."

"I'll bet."

William chewed while Misle tapped his foot nervously on the floor. The Cougar Man was salivating slightly; water dripped from his fangs, and one of his eyes leaked badly. "So…we're not on Earth?" William asked.

"You're not all that dumb after all, are you?"

No, I'm just dead, and this is hell, or whatever hellish dream takes over after you die, William thought. He wondered if madness—and he'd been aware of how mad he'd gone even as he'd watched himself falling further and further into it, he was sure of that—stayed with you in the next life. Then it occurred to him that he'd made a significant discovery for all humankind: there was an afterlife!

Too bad I'm sitting here eating shitty pumpernickel bread with a guy who looks like a sick alley cat, about to fight a battle of some kind to save my ass here in the afterlife. No phones, no Internet: no way to tell the world about my glorious discovery.

Fuck me.

"Listen, I know this is all mad shit for you right now," said Misle. "Put it out of your head. What you need to know now is: if you don't fight like a demon for the next few hours, you're going to die…for good. No third chances."

So I did die.

Why would I want a third chance?

Is there any more of this shitty pumpernickel?

He finished up, had one more mug of water, and stood, implying to his delightful companion that he was ready to fight for his second life. It occurred to him to ask if Misle himself had received eight extra chances at life—being, you know, a kitty—but he decided the question wouldn't be perceived as being sufficiently on point.

"Ready to die?" Misle asked him.

William shrugged.

They strode through another unlocked door and found themselves in a large courtyard. It was surrounded by a stone wall, and in the center of the courtyard was what looked to be a stone crypt.

But neither the wall nor the crypt was what caught William's eye.

No, he instead looked up at the sky and the two suns that looked back down at him. One appeared almost violet in color, while the other seemed a rich, full orange. Neither was nearly as bright as the sun he knew.

"Stop staring at the sky. When they're both up there like that, they'll blind you unless you're a Slau," said Misle as he pushed William toward the stone crypt.

"But..."

"You ain't a Slau, are you? Let's get this over with."

Suddenly there came a tremendous crack of thunder, and then another, and another. The wind kicked up, and it began to pour.

"Where did that come from?" William asked, astounded even in his state at the abrupt shift in weather.

"Happens. Landing Point's crazy like that. Something about the mechanism, is what they say. Keep moving unless you want to eat a lightning bolt!"

And then as if on cue, the lightning came, hitting the tops of buildings, the ground, everything. Misle pulled William hard toward the crypt. When they reached the crypt, which was really just a big, solid, rectangular box made of stone and some kind of metal, Misle pounded on the door.

After a moment, the door opened. There was a tall, thin man behind it who smiled at them with a set of sharpened teeth. "Going in again, Misle? That's good. I think it's hungry."

"Is it? Too bad. It's not getting fed today, Esut, you skinny little parasite."

"Your insults can't hide your terror, Linosian. Usual wager?" chuckled Esut.

"Why not? Always brightens my day to take your money," said Misle as he pushed past the gatekeeper. William, his eyes readjusting to being inside again, followed, watched closely by Esut. He could still hear the booming of the thunder behind them.

"You picked a particularly tasty partner today. Not fat but somehow...delicate."

"See you tonight. Have my money ready," said Misle as he led William down a winding flight of impossibly high stairs.

"She pays if you die, right?" called Esut. "She knows?"

"She knows," Misle called back up the stairs without turning around.

"Four's blessings to you!"

"Fuck off."

William noticed a kind of elevator device in the center of the spiral staircase. Misle saw him glancing at it.

"Believe me, you don't want to take that down. Esut has broken many a man's legs in hopes of an easy feeding. Better we walk down."

After a while, when they seemed to William to have gotten no closer to the bottom, he became overwhelmed, not by fear but by the impatience of a man who wants to abandon his dream and wake up. "May I ask you what it is we're doing now?"

"We're going to meet the Reismyl."

"That clears things up."

"The Reismyl is a massive, multiheaded reptile that determines whether or not you get to live."

William decided to play along. He couldn't think of a reason not to. "How does it determine that?"

"Not sure. I think it smells you."

"Why me?"

"Not just you. Any Entrant who isn't Mindless has to face the test of the Reismyl."

"Why?"

"It's the law."

"Oh."

"Look, it's bad for business, and there's ways around it, but they're on to those now, and so this has to be done. Don't worry: I've been through here before; I'll get you through. I've got a few allies in the maze."

This was making less and less sense, even in a mad world where Cougar Men fed you pumpernickel and barbarians wore college caps. The sensation of wanting to wake up was palpable in William, and yet he resisted it. He wondered why for a moment and quickly understood that, laughably, he was curious as to how all this would play out.

He'd never seen a huge multiheaded reptile before, and even if he had, he was quite sure it would have been safely contained on a DVR disk.

He certainly had never seen one that would smell him to determine whether or not he lived. He wondered why he wasn't scared shitless; he remembered being not all that brave back in the real world.

Maybe it was because he was dead.

"You'll need to choose a weapon when we get to the bottom. I suggest a spear," said Misle.

"Why a spear?"

"To stave off the others."

"Others? There are others?"

"Not everyone who comes down here comes out again, even if they live. Sometimes they come down here and hide in the maze and never face the Reismyl. Sometimes when they do that, the Pesil Acu changes them, gives them a new race. Don't ask me why. Sometimes the change comes even if you face the Reismyl. Hey, bright side is, I think you'd look good as a Slau."

"I don't want to be rude, but I need to confess something to you."

"What's that?"

"I've pretty much had no idea what the fuck you've been talking about since I met you."

"Don't worry. If we get through this, you'll have plenty of time to brush up. When you're not running for your life or taking it up the ass."

"I'll contain my excitement for now," William said, convinced that at any moment, the cold, quiet darkness would reclaim him and dispel all this foolishness.

They reached the bottom, where several tunnels led in different directions. There was a large stack of medieval-looking weapons, some of them familiar, most of them not, and almost all of them rusted.

"What a pile of shit. Wait, here: this spear is okay. Try it," Misle said, plucking a long spear out of the pile and handing it to William. "How does it feel?" Misle asked, watching him.

Our family learned to love him
To our hearts he was endeared
But now they're gone in mourning
'Cause poor Fido's disappeared

"I like it. I feel like I could kill a thousand Rash-mells!" William pronounced.

"Idiot. You don't kill the Reismyl. It kills you. Or it doesn't."

"My bad. I feel like I could kill...others!"

Misle stared at him a moment and shook his head. "I guess Mindless really isn't the worst thing a body could be coming out of the Trip. You're a true lunatic, my friend. Lucky me. Now let's go in."

And with that, Misle led the way down one of the tunnels.

In the next hour, William's assumptions and perceptions about what was real and the very nature of terror were changed so utterly it was as if he'd been living in a cardboard box from the time of his birth till the moment he followed Misle down that tunnel into the caverns below.

He never saw the Reismyl, but he felt its breath and heard its echoing whispers. He saw Misle torn to pieces not ten feet from where he stood…but it happened so fast, all he could claim to have actually seen was a flash of gray and red, again and again. He hid in the shadows, in the nook of a cave, but he couldn't get his whole body in despite a frantic amount of writhing and shoving.

He wasn't afraid to die, he'd never been afraid to die, not even when he was alive, and yet this experience wasn't about death. It was about terror, about how much of it one person could stand. The Cougar Man hadn't died right away. He had begged for help, for mercy…and none had come. William could do nothing. Misle's body seemed to disintegrate before him.

And so why was he alive? He wasn't hidden, he couldn't see, his guide had been maimed, and yet he lived.

Why?

He heard it again. The breath. He felt it. It wasn't hot. It was…damp, almost chilly.

And then it was gone.

And when it was gone, they came. The others.

They too were of a nightmare, a collection of creatures with horns and goat faces and wolf heads and frog-like heads and missing limbs and single eyes in foreheads that were impossibly huge. They rushed at him, some with swords but most with clubs or fists, and they beat him badly, screaming in his face the whole time, demanding something, but he knew not what. He could only make out one word: Ashorne.

He had no idea what that meant.

He didn't want to know.

He wanted to go home and have a beer and eat mesquite chicken or fat shrimp off the grill, he wanted to field a ground ball and make a throw without incident, he wanted to talk to his father about how cold this winter would be…

Instead, he was dragged by his feet by this crazed horde, kicked and beaten and once or twice stabbed. He passed out. They woke him by touching a torch to his arm. He passed out again, and they shoved his head in filthy water and held it there until he saw the darkness again and forgot, for a time, who he was or if he was. Then there was a fight, a battle of some sort. Shouting, lots of shouting. He passed out again, the only thought in his mind was the vain hope that even in death, one can have terrible dreams.

William was lying on a table, staring up at a dim ceiling. He glanced around at the room.

There were half a dozen of them — not the ones who'd beaten him, the ones who'd beaten them and helped him. He sat up and rubbed the back of his head where he'd taken a few blows. His vision was iffy.

"Who are you?" asked the one called Samson, who looked something like a goat with one horn and rabbit ears. "Talk to me. Are you human or are you Arban?"

"I'm sorry, I don't understand what you're asking."

"No doubt, no doubt. Listen, you've got nothing to worry about. We've got you."

William rolled off the table and puked on the floor. After a minute, he finished puking — he could see chunks of pumpernickel bread amid the little pools of blood that had come out — and he tried to stand up. "Nothing to worry about? I saw something that looked like a dragon with dozens of heads eat a man — a cougar man — right in front of me. His name was Misle, the man. I still don't know why it didn't eat me. Why didn't it eat me? It looked at me. It was close. Three heads were so close I could smell their breath and see flesh dangling from their teeth. Their eyes were a hideous yellow green and…I didn't move. I couldn't move. The heads were fast, faster than me, faster than the man I saw devoured. So fast…"

He'd started to tremble with intense fear during his ramble, and now he found it difficult to draw breath.

"Slow yourself, my friend. Just try to breathe," said Samson. "If it came that close, it smelled you, and it let you live. You passed its test."

"Well, that's a relief, but after that those…those things came at me and attacked…why?"

"That's just what Pef and his boys do. Probably would've eaten you if we hadn't come along."

William looked around the room somewhat dazedly. "And you won't?"

"Won't what?" asked Samson.

"Eat me."

"Hells no, boy! We saved you to sell you. Back to Strak. He's paying very well for your safe return."

"Why?"

"Don't know, don't care. Oh, and by the way, the answer you want to give to that question is 'Arban.' Don't let anyone hear you say that other word, not outside this maze."

William had no idea what Samson was on about, but he didn't

care. He didn't like this place. Whether it was heaven or hell or somewhere in between, it sucked worse than anything Dante ever described. He hadn't been here long, but he was sure he was going to have a postmortem nervous breakdown, if it weren't already well under way.

"We have to get you out of here now. No time to waste. Pef's coming back for sure, and he's got more on his side than we have on ours."

"Whatever you say," said William. "Lead on."

Chapter 9
"And we love the law,
and we honor it in every way!"

Place: Castle Motatinfo in the Kingdom of Arbana, Arba Environ
Date: Quattrenim 1, AY 998

They entered the Grehmann Hall.

What Petrecia saw reaffirmed in her mind that the Low Feast was the best — and the worst — of all. Her eyes scanned the room; her senses were laughably overwhelmed.

Fashionable citizens from every corner of Arba bustled here and there. Their masks were spectacular and horrifying and wild. Piles of meat and cheese and fruit and cakes stood like delicious mountains about the room. There were banners of all the major and minor districts spread throughout, with the flag of the Triumvirate dwarfing them all.

That flag. Ugly, multicolored rag that it was. It hung from the central chandelier rather obnoxiously, she thought, but secretly the spectacle of her adopted nation's dominance filled her with a sort of unapologetic pride. And that pride became, almost instantly, shame.

Candles of every color filled sconces, but on the hundreds of tables — each for four, always for four — were candles of the richest orange imaginable. Trantuse was a flowery god, if nothing else. He was known for his revels, his wit, and his supreme sense of excess.

He would have been quite comfortable here in the hall. Balkac and Druthec Grehmann had gone above and beyond. This would most certainly be a night to remember.

Most of the ladies' masks were more than likely not from their day-to-day stock but rather had been designed specifically and frantically for this strange, complicated occasion. And what strange, complicated masks they were! Birds and lizards and dragons and fish and crabs and antelope and horses and lions and foxes and sharks. Masks that honored the four seasons; the skies; Birth, Youth, Wisdom and Death; the Proving, the Nulling, the Harvest, and the Scourge Ravagers. North, South, East, and West were present. Masks of famous figures: there a Ki Ang, here a Burned K'tain, there a Kalor Bromata…she spotted three Scarlet Owls (the ancient symbol of Arin Sheel) on three recognizable heads from Hunberg, two Four Tower'd crowns (tastelessly denoting Kold the Creator) on two old women from Weapons Guild money, and even a few Reismyls, masks so heavy the wearers' heads had to be supported with elaborate trusses.

Those had to be worn by some Landing Point broker's wives. The Reismyl was a ridiculous choice for a feast. There was nothing wrong with trying to represent one's region, but regional pride had its limits.

This being the Year of Orferio the Wicked, many rears sported plush, thick black double tails as well. The ubiquitous presence of the Garden Cat was a good excuse for getting one's dark side up, and Petrecia had every intention of doing just that.

"We should find our table and offer our wagers, Pet," Rodolpho said cheerfully, his earlier ire chased away somewhat by the spectacle before him. "Unless this poor feast is too trivial for you?"

"Oh, Dolphie: you know I love a good low time, no matter how passionately I protest," she cooed in her most practiced pout.

He grimaced and shoved her a little. "That's enough. We'll get back to our talk later, but here and now, act the good Pherriuskatan wife."

"Willing and able?"

"Obedient and silent."

"Not a chance, love."

She smiled despite herself and regarded her confederates. The women around her were just as masked as she; and like her, they were hardly of a silent breed, whatever their origins. Pherriuskata demanded, above all else, decorum from its female citizens, but decorum, Petrecia had found, was a direct function of the context.

Yes, at a feast such as this one, one was inclined to be anything but silent, husbands' specifications be damned. No, here and now it was time for all the colorful birds to sing, especially those who had been forever stripped of color and denied its particular delights. And the singing was expected to give way to sounds more extreme as the night progressed.

They made their way through the crowd, Rodolpho jerkily dipping his head this way and that, his hawk's beak seeming to poke and scrape at each nod's recipient. Petrecia took note of who was there and who was not. She wondered if the High Feast, taking place this year in Quintish at the palace of the great Overbaron Covo di Rienta-Chu, was anywhere as raucous as the scene in this place. Four bands were playing in the four different corners of the room, and musikers wandered about randomly offering their own voices and witty observations. At times, all the music seemed to flow together in one great echoic symphony; at others, the cacophony of their contending notes and rhythms was almost too much to bear. It was just as it was supposed to be: a festival of diverse and warring elements struggling—and failing—to find their way into harmony. Trantuse had been a master of, if nothing else, nonsensically garbled horse manure. Why he was celebrated was beyond Petrecia's understanding. Harmony was something only children believed in, and failure to achieve it was as obvious as death.

"Here we are," said Rodolpho as he stopped and regarded his table's strategical position. "Excellent spot, wouldn't you say, Pet?"

Indeed, the table was situated almost directly in the center of the room, a place of relative honor only thirty feet or so distant from the pending event that would bring the night's festivities to a crescendo: the Last Dance. Druthec Grehmann, the self-titled King of Motatinfo, and his son, the notorious and stumpy Balkac Grehmann, were seated not twenty feet away. She glanced their way and noticed their wives were in a virtual stupor, each sitting before massive, half-empty bottles of something quite dark. Brull wine, perhaps? Illegal in the Tri, but very potent, very good, and so very expensive. Those things that were very expensive by their very natures oftentimes rendered the question of legality illegitimate. Brull wine was such a thing. And the Ladies Grehmann looked as if any concern for law, legitimacy, or even gravity had long since failed to distract them.

"I wonder who will be joining us tonight, Pet?"

"I couldn't say. Your spies offered no help there?"

"My spies have better things to do than waste time on trivialities like dinner pairings."

"Meaning they tried and found out nothing."

"It doesn't matter; the reason we —"

"Well, the blessings of that most Orange of Orange Wonders, the Good and the Glowing Trantuse, on the both of you!"

It was old Jakob Duhnx who stood before them, waving a small orange Trantuse puppet on a stick like a child at a street fair.

"Jakob, you silly old scoundrel!" chirped Petrecia despite herself, relieved to see her uncle.

"How wonderful to be paired with the ambitious Lord Canamow and his astonishingly beautiful wife!" the old man cried with a sardonic twinkle in his eye.

"Now how would you know anything about my beauty, Uncle?"

"Or my ambitions?" asked Rodolpho with a cunning but sincere grin.

"I've seen you, young Petrecia, without that sly leopard on your face! Without any mask at all, to be sure!"

"Jakob Duhnx! You'll give scandal to the poor thing!" chided a shrill female voice from behind the High Master of Jewelers, who continued unabashedly:

"Hush, wife of mine! And now, Rodolpho, my good man, even the squirrels and waters are aware of your ambitions! More strength to you, I say: we need smart fellows like you whispering in the duke's ear."

"My whispers and my wife's true visage are none of your concern, you lunatic. Pass me that bottle then..." Canamow answered as he rose to shake the old man's hand.

"A thousand pardons, a thousand pardons! Blame the wine! Blame the music! Blame the Aethreleans, if you must blame someone!" Duhnx laughed as he turned to face his owl-masked wife and offer her a seat. "Where's the graffalman? Off smoking his own burden?"

"Patience, man! You'll graffal plenty tonight, I've no doubt! Good wine?" Rodolpho said, gesturing with the bottle.

"Pure piss. And it's taken three bottles to make that determination," Jakob confessed.

"You've been here a while..."

"No more than an hour. Travel always makes me thirsty."

Hanziella Duhnx pushed her husband aside and moved in to embrace her niece. "He's already pounding on the door of madness, my dear...pay him no mind!" she said as she found her seat. "Rodolpho, rein him in!"

Rodolpho shrugged in mock helplessness and plopped down in his chair.

"Uncle, why the Aethreleans?" asked Petrecia laughing and pulling out her own seat.

"What's that, dear?" Jakob asked over a musiker who was blasting a gumhorn into the ear of someone at the next table.

"The Aethreleans. Why blame them?"

"Why not?" asked Rodolpho as he sat down and poured himself a glass of something green. He regarded a platter of soft yellow loaves that was on the table, picked one up, measured its weight, and chucked it at the head of the gumhorn player.

Hanziella put in, "I'm the last one to defend the righteous mongrels, but surely the Aethreleans have had nothing to do with my poor husband's base lapse in judgment, Rodolpho! Seen her indeed!"

"On the contrary, dear Hanziella. When one finds oneself in the awkward situation of having no one to blame, one must always do one's best to hastily manufacture a culprit. It has ever been the Triumvirate way, has it not, and so it becomes by default my way!" chuckled Jakob.

"Kold's Curse on the Aethreleans!" laughed Rodolpho.

The women echoed him with a giggle. "Kold's Curse on the Aethreleans!"

"Quite right!" said a new voice.

Petrecia turned to regard its owner: Grewea Lon himself, Duke Velliok's highest advisor and Core of the Mind. A gnarled thing he was, with a small, stiff white beard and no moustache. He wore no mask; his ancient, twisted face itself was more than mask enough.

Rodolpho jumped up at once and offered his stammered greeting. "Oh, um, uh, Core Lon! A distinct honor to see you here, sir!"

"Thank you, Lord Canamow, for that most eloquent welcome. And Trantuse's blessings on you all."

All returned the greeting but with a somewhat curtailed enthusiasm, a fact not missed by a bemused-looking Grewea, who chuckled at them, his crooked teeth showing, and shook his head. "And if at some point tonight you would find a few minutes for me, Rodolpho, I would be very much obliged," Grewea said with a voice that precluded the capacity for anything resembling thankfulness.

"Of course, sir, of course! Shall I find you or…"

"My man Sh'arnau will visit you."

Rodolpho got suddenly very still. The table and those within ear-shot went quiet as well.

"To bring you to me for our discussion," clarified Grewea. "When the time comes."

"Very good, sir. I shall look for him."

"No need. He'll find you."

"Yes…well, till later, then."

"By all means, enjoy yourselves. Ladies." Grewea nodded, again showing his teeth, and then turned and headed off toward the Grehmann table.

There was silence for about ten seconds, and then Hanziella broke it with a loud, musical laugh.

"Whatever are you laughing at?" asked Petrecia.

"The power of names, my dear, the power of names!"

"I don't think it's so funny," muttered Jakob. "That Thicknomite shouldn't be anywhere near this hall tonight, let alone in it."

"Jakob is sore because Grewea's man cost him some money."

"Some money? Woman, is one hundred thousand barb just 'some money' to you? Just how were you women of Mont du Grace raised? In gold cribs and silver skirts?"

Petrecia was going to follow up about what Sh'arnau had done to poor Uncle Jakob, but he seemed to lose interest in the subject when a platter of steaming goose tarts and mettlebrack claws was placed before him.

"Ah, the appetizer! Top notch, this Grehmann! Does everything well!"

"You don't always say as much when the monthly shipment arrives."

"Please, Hanziella. I'm trying to enjoy the feast. I had a ship waylaid by pirates on the lake, I had four shops ransacked by the North-erners this month alone, and the prices, oh the prices: they're higher than at any time since my father was alive. Can we make this the last mention of business and just eat?"

"Surely. My apologies. Let's."

"I mean it, I do. Let's not talk for another instant about anything to do with business. I want to have myself a time. And to that end, business is a closed subject!" declared a not atypically pouty Jakob.

They all began to eat in contented silence but with a distinct sense of urgency, as if they expected the food to be somehow yanked away at any moment. After a few bites, Petrecia put her hand on her uncle's forearm, leaned in toward him, and asked in a somewhat raised, jovial voice, her mouth still stuffed with mettlebrack: "So, Uncle Jakob, I've been wondering: How's business?"

The others burst out laughing. Jakob jabbed his niece in the ribs with a claw and laughed too, the sweet white meat spraying out his mouth and onto whatever and whoever.

The meal went on for hours, and the guests made their best efforts to eradicate any vestige of the burdensome selves and concerns they'd brought along. They did this with wine, graffal, liquor, and, between courses or sometimes during them, sexshots from Wrangun.

There were delicacies from every corner of the Triumvirate to assist them in that endeavor: wines from the Dying Plains of Xatumka, meats from the flats of lower Slauland, spirits from as far away as Abeilon and Saiblinor, and plenty of illegal Wilds graffal to thicken the air and empty the minds. Wrangun provided the orgasms; there were doubtless hundreds of flushed faces beneath the many masks.

The men ate and ate and vomited and then ate again. They smoked and drank until they cried or toppled or slept. There were fistfights and duels all around. Such fine fellows as they were, it was horrifying to witness them reduced to damaged animals in disheveled wigs and soiled masks. Again.

"We every one of us ought to feed ourselves to the Reismyl. What a sorry, stupid lot we are," cried Jakob as he yanked the cork from another bottle and spilled half its contents on an oblivious passerby in a raccoon mask.

"Ha! There you go again, Jakob, including me in a club to which I've no wish to belong!" belched Rodolpho.

"You're just like the rest of us!"

"Drunk?"

"No."

"Stoned?"

"No. Decadent! Unrepentant! Immoral!" cackled Jakob as he dropped the bottle and grabbed the massive breasts of the server wandering by. She favored him with a quick hand on his crotch. He nodded vigorously as she whispered something in his ear.

"Ha!" cried Rodolpho. "I suppose your speech's end will have to wait."

"I suppose it shall…" chuckled Jakob as he rose to his feet. He stumbled, turned, and vomited once more into a nearby bucket — or almost into it — and was led by his scarf toward one of the side parlors.

"Well, I shall not wait for it!" Laughing, Rodolpho slammed his head down onto the table and passed out, his forehead bleeding.

Petrecia and Hanziella watched all this but hardly paid their husbands any mind. They too ate and smoked and drank, but not nearly at the pace their sorry husbands had set. It was a woman's duty to monitor her companion, comfort him, and revive him when necessary. And to make as big a fool out of him as his unsteady consciousness might allow.

"I believe your noble husband is bowing out," observed Hanziella. "A bit early, even for him, don't you think?"

"He's not asleep. He's preparing his next charge at the spits."

"Looks dead to me."

"Hanziella, you say the nicest things to me. But he'd never die before the Last Dance."

"Never say never, my dear. Anything's subject to change. And that man is *out*."

"Dolphie, are you asleep, dear? Hand me my beige box, would you, Auntie? Dolphie? Come now, you've already been slapped up three times, and you know what too many does to your temper." She picked up a mug of tepid water (mixed with a little incidental vomit) and dumped it over the back of his head.

He did not move.

"All right, then, open wide, my dear, because here comes dreaded Number Four!"

Guests at nearby tables stopped what they were doing momentarily to watch. Number Four was always very unpredictable and usually quite entertaining.

Petrecia grabbed Rodolpho's hair at the back of his head, yanked his head up, and shoved the beige box under his nose. She let go of his hair. His face smashed down into the box.

Seconds passed. The guests leaned in.

Rodolpho twitched a few times and leapt up, his eyes wild, the veins in his throat popping. He looked around in a rage. Grabbing a two-pronged fork, he lunged at an old man at the next table who had made the mistake of giggling. The fork penetrated the old man's shoulder just as Rodolpho chomped down and bit into his neck.

The old man's screams were drowned out by the roars of laughter from the crowd. Men were laughing so hard they were drooling. The women were howling and pointing, and some even threw things at the old man and Rodolpho. Lumps of something like greasy pudding were flying through the air. A bottle connected with the old man's ear.

Rodolpho released the man, who then stumbled backward and collapsed on a pile of discarded bones. The crowd ate it up. Three women scurried over to the old man and kicked him viciously as he attempted to gain his footing and escape the bone pile. The old man laughed so hard at this that he shit himself. The stench was awful, and the crowd beat him even more furiously in response.

Rodolpho's chin and mouth were covered in blood. His crazed eyes regarded the laughing crowd and suddenly softened. He started laughing as well, but only for a moment, and then he was still. He was completely and utterly sober and awake.

"The medical magick of Pir Choss's lower division, at your service, my husband."

"That was the Third?"

"The Fourth."

"Really? What time is it?"

"I expect it is time for you to learn how to count. You know, even noblemen and aspiring rulers sometimes have to fall back on the most basic of skills."

"Bitch. Have yourself a sexshot. Give me that bottle."

"I've had two already. And do you mean this bottle...or this one...or this?" she asked as she tipped over a series of empties.

"Where's the server? Damned server keeps disappearing. And why would you give me a Fourth?"

"Oh, come, Rodolpho, don't be sore," tsked Hanziella. "The Dance begins in less than an hour, and if anyone had seen you sleeping, you'd be in it, not watching it."

"They wouldn't dare," he intoned with an attempt at a glare that fell short of the mark.

"Weren't you paying attention when Grehmann's freak made his little speech? 'This is Arbana, and we do our festivals just a little differently.'"

"Give me the bottle."

"Canamow." A deep, rumbling voice.

"Yes?" said Rodolpho huffily. He turned to see a massive, wolf-headed Thicknomite standing behind him and instantly paled despite his altered state.

"Grewea Lon wishes an audience."

"I see. Yes, of course."

Petrecia was about to make a crack about how fortuitous her administration of the disintoxicant had been, but the mere presence of Sh'arnau the Slayer urged her to hold her tongue. Her husband rose, nodded to her and Hanziella, and left with the Thicknomite.

Hanziella sighed. "That poor creature."

"Which?"

"Sh'arnau."

"You're joking?"

"No. It's really quite a sad story, from what I hear."

"Sad and bloody and horrible. He's a murderer, a thousand times over."

"No doubt. But he is something more, or so they say. Oh, never mind," said Hanziella, dismissing the subject and raising a new one. "It does seem your beloved spouse is moving up in the world a bit, if that cracked crow wants an audience with him and requests it so publicly."

"I wouldn't know. His business is his own."

"Well, take it from me, Grewea Lon doesn't play any game that doesn't either greatly reward or quietly destroy the players. Let's hope Rodolpho comes back to us after their little chat."

"Yes. Let's," Petrecia deadpanned.

They both burst out laughing again, cackling until Hanziella started gasping for air.

Rodolpho did return, and when he did, he was a man deep in thought.

Hanziella had gone off to mingle and find some fresh air. Petrecia rose when she saw her husband, but only halfway out of her seat and more out of a sudden understanding that something of weight had occurred: Rodolpho was never, ever deep in thought.

"Everything well?" she asked.

"Yes." He sat down beside her but didn't reach for a glass or a bite.

"What did he want?"

"Want? Nothing, really."

"I don't understand."

"He didn't want anything. He had some information for me, is all."

"That sounds...that's a little odd, no?"

"How so?"

"Grewea Lon isn't known to just pluck random persons from random tables at random feasts to offer up random pieces of information. What did he say?"

"Never mind what he said."

"It certainly turned you out, didn't it?"

"Where's Jakob?"

"Fucking somewhere. Or probably lying on a floor half-naked believing he's fucked."

"Yes, well."

Rodolpho brooded a short while. But then, at clock's stroke that marked the start of thirty-one, the Sad Singers of Calmy entered the room, bellowing in their famous bass Dubaku's "Harbinger of Maja's Dying Dance" — a song Petrecia was sure had never been intended by its composer to be used for such a vulgar purpose, written as it had been to conclude an opera and highlight the selfless achievements of its heroine's short but eventful life — and bulling their way through the crowd toward the center of the room. The crowd, or at least those in the crowd who could still function on their own power, moved aside while the singers strode forward, waving their arms slowly to emphasize the metaphorical burden of their short but impactful journey: it was time for the Last Dance.

Grehmann's freak, a vile cross between a man, a Slau, and something from the Garden that might at one time have been able to fly but now was only able to flap its black, sinewy, and malformed wings, jumped up on a table and cried, "Dancers! Be SILENT!"

And the crowd, to their inebriated credit and with only a few glaring exceptions, shut up and listened.

"Tonight, something special! You're in Motatinfo now, my fine people, where we celebrate in the old way, where we believe a Round-about in honor of such a — what shall we say — capricious god as Trantuse should embrace the spirit of that most holy of deities, in the old way, in the dark way, in the way of blood, yes, but also in the way of second, and final, death."

The crowd hesitated. Petrecia wasn't sure she'd heard him right. Looking around, she could see she wasn't the only one. Had he said "second death"? But he must be joking or introducing a riddle. Such a thing was not permitted; it wasn't just against the law, it was…had been…implicitly shunned for centuries. It wasn't joked about, and it wasn't played with, no matter how differently they thought they did things in Arbana. The freak was talking nonsense.

But then he continued: "Good people, fine people, hear me now! We all know the law, we know the words of the Oldest Ones, and who better among us than our beloved King Balkac Grehmann, who knows and worships the Words as none other? And we love the law, and we honor it in every way! We honor it most by knowing it, and we keep it by knowing it well…and yet tonight is not just any night but a night in celebration of Trantuse the Lawless, Trantuse the Soultaker, Trantuse the Merciless and the Unyielding. The law provides for its own sweet, and fleeting, absence.

"Tonight, the Last Dance will see some souls taken, and the law grants us every right to honor our god in this fashion. You will behold second deaths!"

All around the room, among the shocked faces, heads bobbed as the many arbiters and several Brown Men in attendance saw the legal truth in what the freak had said. Some seemed as shocked as the rest, but most quickly resigned themselves to the truth of the thing.

Petrecia had never understood the law half as well as someone of her station should, but she thought at least she understood the evil inherent in a second death. Would Grehmann and his people be so rash as to provide one as…entertainment?

"Come, my good ones. There is no need to release the spirit of unbridled merriment and delight and invite in her stead the grim visage of regret and doubt! Here now, there is simisola for one and all!"

A roar rose up as the crowd again expressed shock; this time, however, the shock came in the form of wolfish expectancy and greed, for simisola was without question the finest narcotic in the known world. It came from Ma'erya, a full two environs away, where it was harvested by that place's dying race from the eggs of the most dangerous species on the OS-Maeketel. An ounce of simisola was worth a fine house and a staff, and a pound could buy an army or a fleet. If the Grehmanns truly had enough of it here to indulge the entire crowd, the presentation might just be the grandest show of wealth in recorded history. The power derived from the ownership of two million slaves and most of the Triumvirate's food supply, now that the Northerners had wrecked Xatumka, was on full display here tonight.

There was a crazed howl and the playing of three discordant notes on a bass serpent, and then dozens of tall, beautiful, and gracefully emaciated women emerged from curtained doorways along the walls of the hall. They carried large yellow-and-purple baskets made of some kind of thinly wrought metal. Circling the tables, they dropped small yellow-and-purple packages, wrapped of course in orange ribbon, all around them. The partygoers grabbed and dove for the packages. One of the women had her basket ripped from her arms. Another was tackled and went down under a pile of writhing bodies. The guests were grabbing the packages and chewing right through the wrappers and ribbons.

"Please, good people, please—there is plenty for all!" the freak cackled above the din, though his gargoylian expression said he wouldn't have minded if a few of the good people were trampled to death in the stampede.

The Sad Singers cut in with another chorus of their song. Then, from high above in the rafters, a massive cage, held in place by ropes the ends of which were secured by four hairless frenecoots, was slowly lowered toward the floor in the hall's center. The crowd, seeing this new and unexpected spectacle, settled down a bit while chomping on chunks of the party favor.

"And now, good people, the Dance. Who among you will call the Dance's cadence? Who among you will guide the music and bring our boundless celebration to its time-honored conclusion?"

"What's the Dance? Tell us the Dance!" cried voices from around the hall.

"Why, it's a surprise! Don't spoil it! We've dealt with the tedious legalities and distributed the desserts! Who is ready to play? Who is ready to Dance?"

No one volunteered.

Petrecia's eyes scanned the room. This was a critical moment, a unique and electrifying time for the ambitious and the bold, when fame could be grabbed by the handful and held tightly for years to come.

No one moved. They were afraid. Despite the drugs, they didn't trust Druthec Grehmann and didn't want to be played for the fool or worse. And if no one came forward, tradition held that Grehmann himself must. She turned to looked at his table and saw him sitting there, his eyes half-closed, moving not a muscle.

And then Rodolpho stepped forward.

There were four of them in the cage. None of them appeared to be older than four or five, and each one was fast asleep. Their mothers and fathers were brought forward and seated on benches outside the cage. In the center of the cage, sitting there obedient and silent, was a monster the likes of which Petrecia had never seen, a huge thing so horrible to behold that she nearly lost her urine when they uncovered the cage. Even the thirty or so Crabs who surrounded the cage, crouched and at the ready with their long Qiang spears, looked unnerved to be there.

"Seated before you on the benches, these fine citizens of Tritto are, all eight of them, Entrants. Sweet stories, theirs, of how they found one another and fell in love. Earth itself never knew stories to rival theirs.

"And there in the cage before you sit the dear, dear products of that love. Tonight, these citizens will be asked by our Last Dancemaster, Lord Rodolpho Canamow, to make a choice. Each pair can elect, as a loving couple, to enter the cage and exchange their lives for their child's. Or they can remain without and watch their child dance. The creature in the center has no preference as to its meals, but we do: either both parents enter, or neither may."

The crowd, now fully under the effects of the delicious simisola and the moment's sinister intrigue, leaned forward. Petrecia, who had foregone the drug, looked about, hoping someone would object to this hateful distortion. She was all in favor of a little off-color fun and even a fair amount of violence when the night called for more excitement, but this was too much. Did those poor people even know what they were being asked to do?

She saw doubt in some of the eyes that met hers, but most eyes were greedily or sluggishly fixed on the Dance.

One of the parents near the cage stood up. He was light of skin and fair of hair, the kind of man rarely seen in this world. He turned to face the crowd, a wild, frightened look in his eyes.

"What the fuck is wrong with you people? What gives you the right to do this? Answer me, you sick fucks! That's our son in there with that thing! He's three years old!" He tried to get through the Crabs at someone in the crowd but was thrown back. He lay there a moment and rose, crying and shaking his head. "This is a sick-ass shit hole of a world. I hope all you assholes burn in hell."

And then he grabbed his wife's hand; trembling, they walked to the cage. The wife turned to the crowd and said, "I hope Jesus will forgive you."

Rodolpho met them at the gate, key in hand. He unlocked the gate and stepped back.

The Sad Singers began to hum.

The doomed parents put their hands on the gate, kissed, and opened up the entrance to the cage. Before entering, the woman turned and said, "May Jesus Christ forgive you all. Take care of our son."

They went to their boy and shook him awake. The man led him to the gate, pushed him through, and watched as Rodolpho shut and locked it. He then turned around and went to stand next to his wife.

What followed was so brutal that not even the worst of the crowd responded with anything but silent shock. Within seconds, the boy's parents were torn to pieces.

When all was said and done, three of the four sets of parents sacrificed themselves for their children. The fourth mother could not convince her husband to go, and so they lived and watched as the horrible thing in the cage ended their daughter's life, along with the lives of the six other adults. There was little left to recognize of any of them.

Throughout, the Sad Singers bellowed and hummed, hummed and bellowed.

Six people lost their souls, for as everyone knew, an Entrant who takes his life a second time forfeits that ethereal item for all eternity, no matter the reason. And these six probably hadn't understood that. She felt herself hoping that they had, that they had understood completely and chosen to save their children anyway. It couldn't be true that someone who would do that would be damned.

The last couple was led out of the hall, the wife screaming, the husband's head bowed in a shame that would never fade. The three freshly orphaned children stood next to the cage sobbing, alongside the freak, who now looked slightly less enthusiastic about the Dance over which he had thus far presided.

The Last Dancer was then asked to decide upon the fates of the remaining children.

"What say ye, Rodolpho of Canamow? Shall it be mercy and back to the rigors of Tritto for these three, or shall we let them have a go with our friend in the cage?"

Back into the cage? But their parents had just died to save them, thought Petrecia. She rose and tried to push her way to where her husband was seated.

Rodolpho stood up. He listened to the crowd, which had again found its voice, with a blank expression on his face. They had seen blood, but it seemed they had not seen enough. "Put them in, put them in!" they cried.

"Entrants' scum!"

"Put them in!"

"Give them back to Jesus!"

There was no sport in this: the Second Deaths were done, and these children had been rightly spared. But she saw Rodolpho's face as he listened to the drugged-up, crazed crowd of the Triumvirate's elite...and knew right away what he would do. She pushed but couldn't get near him; she shouted at him to stop, but it was too late, for he had already turned toward the gate, the key raised in his hand.

And in keeping with tradition, the freak himself led the children into the cage and stayed there till the festivities, in all their dark delight, were through. In the end, his enthusiasm dimmed fully, but there was something in his eyes that looked like peace.

Chapter 10
"I got lucky."

Place: Beene Street Holding Facility, Camedua Town, kingdom of Xatumka
Date: Quattrenim 3, AY 998

Baks Mu sat down on the stone and crossed his legs in front of him.

The shackles made it difficult to move his arms, so crossing his legs almost made him pitch backward. He growled in annoyance. The arbiters glanced at him, exchanged some whispers, and then looked back down at the papers they'd been examining.

Three days of this nonsense with the shackles and the glancing and the whispers was starting to make his blood simmer. He'd been advised to hold his temper and play along, but he'd never been very good at biding his time.

Vod Pamitter, renowned special advisor to both the Brown Men and to the Xatumkan seat, stood and bowed ever so slightly to those several interested parties who now sat in the modest hearing room. A human of middle age whose only notable feature was his perpetually glowering dark eyes, he loved an audience, or so Baks had heard. Perhaps it was his unimpressive appearance that had inspired in him an unnatural need for attention. Pamitter had proven thus far as slippery and officious as his reputation allowed. That did not bode well for the case of one Baks Mu, former second-in-command of the *Ho Matsuni*.

The final die was not yet cast, however. While Baks himself had never had the pleasure of being the focus of such a proceeding, he felt confident he'd be able to turn the situation around. How best to bend the focus away from the loss of a few ships and toward the nature of the attack? So far, no one seemed concerned about the attackers.

He found that troubling, to say the least.

He looked around the well-lit hearing room, with its tables and its rows of chairs and its ridiculous chandelier, and he wondered when or if this charade would reveal its purpose. His immediate hunch was that it would not.

He yawned loudly and in such a way that all of his substantial Challowian teeth were displayed for the gallery.

Pamitter cleared his throat, shuffled some papers, and then began to read aloud:

"This hearing concerns the events of the night of 40 Boinage, Arban Year 998, on the Windgiver Sea, twenty miles north of the northern coast," he announced needlessly. "The accused will now tell this body exactly what occurred that night on the *Ho Matsuni*."

"Again?" snorted Baks.

"Yes, why not? Indulge us, Captain," said Pamitter as he took his seat and signaled the servant for more wine. "Tell us again, because your story gets more and more fascinating each time you bring it forth."

"My story hasn't changed. There is only one story. You know what I saw and heard. You know what I did."

"Yes, we do. Let's see: This time, why don't you first tell us why you and you alone escaped death, Baks Mu? You haven't yet said, despite the many unaltered tellings."

"Is my officer under suspicion, here, Pamitter?" asked Laen Shi, Baks's wise and somewhat pungent-smelling representative, a full co-mmander in the navy of the Juks Xi Ren. A close family friend and a capable proponent of the law but hardly one who would be able to negotiate past this bunch's crafty inquiries. Shi expected the game to be fair, always. It was a wonder he was still alive. And yet there were times he was at least as formidable as he was aromatic.

"Yes, of course. If, however, he answers my questions truthfully and clearly and satisfactorily, that might change," stated Pamitter.

"If he says he doesn't know what happened, I can see no reason to doubt him."

"Perhaps. But doubt is my stock in trade, Laen Shi, so I wonder if you might indulge me a bit longer before we all come to the inevitable conclusion that Baks Mu is without blame and above reproach? After all, ships have burned and Juks have died, have they not?

Laen Shi stared blankly at the inquisitor, seemingly unable to muster a response. Neither point could be argued.

"Excellent," Pamitter continued. "I think it's clear that an officer with the experience and knowledge of the one we have before us tonight should have, at the least, more complete speculation to offer as we try to unravel this mystery."

Shi found his voice in protocol. "Speculation? You don't want speculation. You want payment. The Challowian Navy does not guarantee safe passage of any merchant vessel, regardless of the cargo, nor do we compensate merchants who've lost cargo, ships, or personnel. You know our policy."

"Indeed. Your policy is very fair—for you. But don't worry: I'm not looking for restitution from your people, Laen Shi. Not yet, anyway. We're here to deal with the immediate fact that, in addition to your Challowian ship, two triple-masted Fellows Seas and Lake vessels, the *Elean Val* and the *Moresso*, both of which you'd been commissioned to escort and protect, were completely lost on the night in question, along with all hands and all cargo. What the Guild does want now—and is more than entitled to, both legally and ethically—are answers and explanations, your policies be damned."

Laen Shi spread his hands in a gesture of helplessness and astonishment and then smirked, perhaps to indicate he was neither helpless nor astonished. "What more can he tell you here and now that he hasn't already dictated to your investigators? Vod Pamitter, if you please. It was dark. There was no moon. All three ships came under attack by an unseen, unfamiliar foe. Within minutes, the battle was over, and no one was left alive."

"No one but Baks," said Pamitter flatly.

"And the things he trapped in the ship's hull."

"Yes, the 'things.' And what about them? What were they?"

"Unknown," answered Shi truthfully. In point of fact, no one here on either side had yet offered even a theory as to who or what the attackers might have been.

"Please tell us why, if they killed everyone else on all three ships and destroyed all trace of the vessels and their cargo, did these 'things' decide to leave Baks Mu alive?" asked Pamitter with a bite in his voice.

Shi shrugged. "Baks was performing the Felsorad ritual in honor of his son's First Day."

"The what?" Pamitter asked. Before Shi could reply, Pamitter turned to a gray, stoic gentleman on his left and whispered something to him. The other man nodded twice. Pamitter looked back at the Juks Xi Ren on the stand before him. "Please, Mu: explain to us once more what this Felsorad is."

"You know what it is. I've told you several times," answered Baks. His shackles were becoming very uncomfortable.

"Have you? Forgive me. My thirst for knowledge of your cultural particulars is virtually unquenchable, and why wouldn't it be? If you please, indulge me just once more."

"It's in the record, plainly and clearly, is it not?" protested Shi.

"It may very well be, but I would hardly call anything about his report 'plain' or 'clear.' And records notwithstanding, he will answer whatever questions this court puts to him, won't you, Baks Mu?" asked Pamitter.

A moment passed.

"I will not," Baks said.

Pamitter stared at Baks coolly for a few moments and then stood up and started to collect his papers. "Then I see no reason to continue. Guardsmen, take…"

Shi motioned to Baks and nodded. Permission had been given.

Baks cleared his throat and spoke: "The Felsorad is our ritual for honoring family. We each must tempt or mock death in a way most fitting and most available. As my son, Bu Shua, was born in the ocean aboard a sinking ship, I honored him by climbing down to the hull of the *Ho Matsuni* and dropping myself into the waves."

Pamitter sat back down. "So when this enemy attacked, you were in the water?"

"You do not have to explain yourself any further, Baks! A Juks's business is his own!" cried Shi.

Baks understood the ruse. *Give them something, but give them nothing.* They couldn't work around cultural nuances they didn't understand without violating all kinds of agreements and rules. "But I would prefer to, Commander, if I might have your permission," Baks said.

"You may not. The arbiter is being unreasonable," answered Shi.

"Let the lakeservant speak, Shi!" said Pamitter. "Unless of course some part of the tale is…something you'd prefer us not to hear?"

Shi sighed and sat down. "The tale is irrelevant. Again. You can listen to it a thousand times, you may put it to note and sing it while you sail the world searching for the hot, dead waters of K'nevar. Irrelevant and inadmissible. You know our code regarding outsider review of any seabound event or process."

Pamitter sat down as well. "Your code. Your policy. Your ways. Yes, we know all about your stipulations for provision of seagoing protection, Shi. We've all been held hostage by them for, what is it, centuries now?"

"For centuries of protection and guidance."

"In whatever limited forms the Juks were inclined to provide."

"It was ever a fair exchange."

"Yes, well, again, I would question that. Fairness is often painfully subjective, wouldn't you agree? I would also question the need to invoke so pliable and self-serving a term as 'fairness.'"

"You are coming dangerously close to reprimand, Pamitter," warned Shi in a low voice.

"I am not a member of your Liam, Shi, and therefore not subject to your petty reprimands."

"And yet I can recommend to your superiors that they hit you with a punishment so cutting it would remind you, without doubt, of your place. Shall I do so?"

Pamitter glared but said nothing. Baks was sure he understood all too well the game of leverage, and in this instance, he didn't have a winning hand. Pamitter raised his hands slightly as if to concede the point.

"Our policies stand," Laen Shi said, resuming control of the hearing. "We will conduct our own internal inquiry into this matter. Might I remind you that we lost twenty-five Challowian sailors in this battle and that we have at least as much at stake as you who lost…what? Grain, veaffer, and some seeds! Or was there something more, something we weren't told about?"

Pamitter's momentary withdrawal ended. "Who's overstepping now, Laen Shi? Discussion of the particulars of our cargo is a violation of every agreement between you and the Triumvirate. You still serve that great entity, as far as I know. So unless you can convince the Mer Ponx to give you access to the Mansdrelam, and I wouldn't hold my breath there, your losses are yours to bear. And though I grieve for you, I cannot concern myself with nonhuman fatalities."

"I grieve too, Vod Pamitter, for the imminent but long-overdue dissolution of those agreements. We are neither grease for the wheels of your transactions nor fodder for your commerce. We are not the wind for your sails, human," Laen Shi said, clearly getting angry as he let slip the offensive word.

Pamitter, perhaps sensing a ruse toward distraction, did not take the bait. "Yet your wind is as plentiful as ever, Shi. I will take the matter to my fellow Brown Men, and there will be a further hearing. For now, we will hold Baks Mu."

"But you cannot—" protested Shi.

"We can, and we will. Do you not know the law? Have a care, Shi, or I shall go to *your* superiors and explain your attempts to interfere with due process."

"You'd be making a grave mistake," Shi said, again in a warning tone but this time less convincingly.

"When will you learn, you fat, unhappy lizard, that in this place, here and now, you are the servants? I've never heard your people referred to as the 'lake*masters*,' have you? No? Two cargo ships are gone, and it was your people's responsibility to ensure their safety. They didn't do their job, and their employer is both unwilling and unable to cover the losses. And your sole survivor? Well, his story just doesn't hold water. We Brown Men will ponder the facts and his fate, and if there's any justice in the world, he'll go to Bi Prison."

"He's going home," Shi said.

Pamitter ignored the interjection. The advisor at his side leaned in once more and whispered something else to him. Pamitter started, shook his head, and started to rise. The advisor grabbed his arm and stared at him intently, whereupon Pamitter sat back down and, with a somewhat ashen expression, reluctantly pursued a new line of inquiry.

"Regarding the creatures that attacked you. You say they descended onto the *Ho Matsuni*, is that correct? They flew?"

"Yes," replied Baks.

"Do you realize what you have implied here?"

Shi stood up. "He's implied nothing. He's related the facts of the story, and I see no reason why this proceeding shouldn't come to an immediate end. Release him."

"Release him? Not a chance. With all that the facts he's related imply? I hesitate to raise this question at all, because the implications of its possible answers are both daunting and unprecedented, but here we are, facts in hand, and so I must ask: Were the creatures who attacked your ship Visshilla?"

There was an immediate air of disquiet in the room from both human and Challowian alike.

Pamitter continued: "Because as we all know, the Visshilla do not permit flight by any other creatures except for perhaps birds and bats. They never have, not in all of Arban history going back to before Watersea. So you see, your experience aboard that ill-fated ship can only point to one of two realities: either something that flies has decided to completely dismiss the Visshilla prohibition on flight, or else it was the Visshilla themselves who attacked you."

"The Visshilla have never committed such an act," cried Shi. "They defend the high places; they do not attack ships!"

"I agree," said Pamitter. "That has been the case for almost a thousand years. And yet we have Baks Mu's own testimony to reconcile. Something doesn't fit, and as I said, the implications are most grave."

The issue hung in the air for all to consider. The implications were indeed devastating. A change in or challenge to Visshilla policy would simply wreck the known order in Arba. Ships, caravans, cities, forts, villages, fields, islands — in theory, none would be safe.

And there was the inevitable question of collusion. Someone or something might be working with the Visshilla. It was an unprecedented and terrifying thought.

"I have a final query for our brave sailor here. Sort of a blend of my earlier questions, if you please. Baks Mu, how exactly did you manage to destroy a host of silent, powerful foes singlehandedly while these selfsame creatures vanquished your entire crew and the crews of two other ships within minutes? How did you manage to trap them all in the hull so easily?"

Baks Mu glanced at Laen Shi to gauge his position on a response, but the old Juks Xi Ren just stood there with his head slightly bowed, looking as if he were deep in thought. Baks looked up at Pamitter and said as straightforwardly as he could:

"I got lucky."

"So it would seem. If I were you, I should hope my luck holds up just while longer. As they say in Pherriuskata, 'Bi is the place where the lucky and the bold go to die.'"

In his cell, there was a small wading pool and a low table. The single sitting stone was worn and uncomfortable.

Baks stretched his arms upward and scraped his claws lightly against the ceiling. His back was still hurting from when he'd pinned the bars on the hull hatch.

He'd been in the cell for over four hours. Laen Shi was still negotiating his release, which was not a foregone conclusion. The Guild had no authority to hold him longer than one full day, and he'd been taken into custody early that morning, so under ordinary circumstances, he'd shortly be freed. But the Brown Men could order him held indefinitely.

They probably already had.

Circumstances were not ordinary, not by any stretch of the imagination. Ships were lost all the time: the seas surrounding Arba were vast and filled with dangers both known and mysterious. Payment was normally the salve that healed wounds and gave compensation to the families of those who were lost. This, however, was all something very mysterious indeed.

Whatever those ships had been carrying had been more important than Pamitter had admitted to. He was under strain to find someone to blame or a lead to follow; that much was clear. Someone was putting pressure on him, probably the someone who had wanted that cargo delivered safely and securely. But what item of such value could they have been transporting from Abeilon? Hell, the beer wasn't even all that good, and the meat was mediocre at best. There were occasional archeological finds, even on Abeilon, but something extraordinary would itself have been placed on his ship for security purposes, assuming it had extraordinary value.

Something about this made no sense to him, but he was not surprised at that. So often, this life, his orders, his people's arrangement with the Tri made no sense whatsoever, but still he gathered, he sailed, he delivered. The only thing that did make sense was the sea. How far he had sailed, how long, and how many wonderful and terrible things had he seen? He knew he had done terrible things, unforgivable things, all in the name of retaining his ship and his sub-captaincy. The life he loved.

Now that was all over. They would condemn him for sure. Maybe he shouldn't have reported to the Guild. By law, he was required to, but that law pertained to merchant transactions and military escorts, not to hostile engagements, lost ships, and lost crews. He could have gone directly to the Li Poam Tascut naval command, but he'd wanted the Guild members to know right away about their loss of life. He'd sent a messenger to the Tascut.

Laen Shi entered his cell. "They're sending you to Pashka."

"What for?"

"Further testimony."

"I don't want to go to Pashka."

"Understood. And if your tale hadn't included the detail of aerial assault, you wouldn't be. But what you witnessed — not the hijacking or destruction of a ship, but the way it was accomplished — they'll want to hear about that firsthand."

"Are you sure this isn't about the cargo?"

"What? No. Maybe. Not sure, really. The things that attacked you were after something beyond beer and fruit. But the Visshilla question — that has got to be answered."

"Have I been tried?"

"You have. In a sense. The Brown Men have found you guilty of at least thirty crimes. All of those will likely vanish if I pay the right people. But you have to go to Pashka and tell your story."

"They're afraid."

"Without question. Terrified."

Chapter 11
Where had all the great ones gone?

Place: The Violet Halls, Sheel's Keep,
island city of Pashka, kingdom of Pherriuskata
Date: Quattrenim 4, AY 998

"There's been a troubling rise in the use of magick in our united Trium-virate nations, my friends. Make no mistake: Xatumka, Arbana, and Pherriuskata are all three equally vexed by this development. I've called the seven of you to sit with me today because something needs to be done about it."

Cra Savanie, the snarling, perpetually displeased senior advisor to Duke Velliok and the very epitome of Triumvirate scheming, had called the Mind Session to order. After a few moments, the conversations around the room subsided, and the respective parties turned their attention to the day's chair.

"What we are to do about it is the question. As well, we have a guest, a Mindman Emeritus, our former Core, whom we are honored to welcome…the esteemed and venerable Grewea Lon."

There was a mild tapping of tables, a gesture of reserved, if not required, respect.

"We also welcome once more our former member Druthec Grehmann, here one assumes to oversee the delicate assumption of his seat on and responsibilities to this venerable enclave by his son Balkac," added Savanie with as little enthusiasm as a body could muster. "Now who will help us begin today…?"

There was an initial hard silence, then some shifting in chairs.

Governor of the West Simon Rurstmeyer spoke up first, his white double moustaches shaking with his head. "I've heard these idiotic rumors myself. They're nothing to get worked up about. My people tell me only one in ten thousand is born with a color these days, and those are identified by our neutered Spectrum friends and shuffled off to the Jamoi bitch kingdom or executed, just as they have been for centuries."

"Where are your people getting their data, Governor?" asked Savanie. "Our sources tell us the problem is much worse than that."

"What are we talking about here, people? A few fires, a few thefts?" chuckled Trelk van Underrac of Arbana. He had the stiff bearing of an old soldier and the entitled countenance of someone for whom wealth is a given. "Is this really what we were called here to discuss?"

Thrsea Machaul, the shriveled, ferret-headed Fra Lwang of the Mer Ponx, said, "Savanie is correct. The problem is worse than you know.

My Mer Ponx have been falling over themselves trying to place Ravagers at the right locations. The rogue magickers, however many they are, keep moving from place to place and causing trouble. They destroyed an entire row of containers set for shipment from Quintish," he lamented. "The barons are very unhappy, particularly Andre."

Everyone in the room turned to look at Marcin Popov, the barons' representative in the Mind. He favored them with no more than a pregnant silence. His round face was a blank, his bald head completely still.

"No matter. The barons, particularly Andre, are always very unhappy," chuckled van Underrac. "But if this bothers them so, let them pay for some Ravagers of their own. Maybe theirs would actually be able to, you know, ravage."

"What are you implying, sir?" demanded Machaul.

Van Underrac shook his finger at the magicker. "Only that whatever you keep in those cages of yours can hardly be said to be effective sniffers and eliminators. If we're really having yet another problem with these so-called rogue magickers — and what does this make, the third or fourth time since we authorized a new collection, to the tune of some five hundred thousand barb? -- perhaps it's time someone did your job for you."

"You know as well as I that the ships to Decone are often lost; few return with useful specimens. Few return at all, in point of fact," said Machaul with a hint of bitterness.

"If so few return, perhaps you and your order should find passage next time. I'd just as soon be done with you."

"Gentlemen, please. There isn't any need to squabble. The duke is more than willing to help with this problem...and with the expenses that finding a solution will doubtless generate," said Cra Savanie. "He understands the infection that is magick better than most."

"What are you proposing, Cra?" asked Rurstmeyer.

"What else?" shrugged van Underrac.

"Not the release of the Watlier's stock?" said Machaul.

"Why not? They're hungry, and what's better, they're free," said van Underrac, with a clear emphasis on his final word.

"Free is nice. We like free," rumbled Balkac Grehmann. He had seemed to be asleep up until this point.

Machaul stood up more quickly than one might expect he could and shouted, "You cannot be serious! Those wretched, undisciplined things cannot and will not make any distinctions, and this you know quite well. They would come after anyone who practiced, anyone at all."

"Worried, Machaul?" asked van Underrac.

Machaul sat back down and fixed a hateful eye on the Arbanan.

Savanie raised his eyebrows and scowled slightly at them both.

"Perhaps that's the point, Machaul. The duke is of the opinion that while infrequent magick is good, no magick is better. He suggests that your order — which, let's face it, is really more about herbs and potions than true color, even in the Highest Seasons — might be better off focusing its special efforts and renowned intelligence on the development of industry and technology. For example, this coal engine everyone at Pastori University is so excited about."

"Coal engines? You speak to me of coal engines and herbs, after the many services we've provided you over the years?" shouted Machaul.

"Yes, and electric lights. You've had some success there, no?" Rurstmeyer shouted back.

"Gentlemen, calm yourselves," said Cra Savanie, trying to regain the room. "The age of magick may be very much near its natural end, but that end has not yet arrived. The Mer Ponx will persist, I will convince the duke to hold his stock for the time being, and we will find a way to deal with the rogues that is more amenable to all parties. It's one of the reasons we're gathered here in this timeless hall, after all."

Popov cleared his throat and spoke up. "And what, pray tell, are the other reasons? Are there a myriad of other disasters we need to attend to?"

"Not a myriad," answered Grewea. "Just two."

Eight faces wearing expressions ranging from placid expectancy to outright panic turned to Grewea. He let them wait a moment or two; then, having other more important matters to attend to, he let them have it. But first, he needed to draw Theodore Oxenhaft into the conversation.

The chubby scholar had been sitting there the entire time with a slightly bemused look on his face. He'd been reading something while pretending to listen, or listening while pretending to read something — it was difficult to be sure. Passivity was not his strong suit, and so it was necessary that he be pulled in, and not on his own terms.

"Theodore, you've been very quiet over there. Is whatever that is more interesting than the highest affairs of this auspicious and mindful council?" Grewea softly chided.

Oxenhaft looked up and smiled. "Oh, no, no. Do go on. I was very much enjoying the conversation."

"Any thoughts thus far?" asked Savanie.

"Um...no. None that I need or wish to share. Though I wish you all well with this magick problem. And I will surely weigh in should I feel the need to do so." Oxenhaft was one who subscribed to reason and learning and therefore dismissed, as best he could in a world where magick played a role, however small, all things magickal. Except perhaps for one.

"Very good," Grewea intoned. "We eagerly await your

commentary." He stood up slowly and looked at the faces of the so-called Mind. He found them to be nothing more than a collective pile of faintly stinking manure. Where had all the great ones gone? Gone, they were indeed: dead these many centuries. There had been some, in those years, who could have helped him now — ones who would have seen the wisdom of his efforts and even offered key insights. Few, but some. All gone.

Rurstmeyer spoke up. "Well, then, Lon, what is it? What's troubling you?"

Grewea broke away from his thoughts and addressed the room. "Let us leave this pressing magickal concern for a moment and turn our attention elsewhere. As you all must now know, there is trouble brewing in Aethrelius. If left to their own design, they might take eons to resolve their difficulties, but Duke Velliok and I have something more…expeditious in mind."

"You plan to involve us in their domestic affairs? Why?" asked Rurstmeyer, who almost certainly knew very well why.

"They are on the verge of a civil war, or at the very least, a paradigm shift the likes of which they have not seen in decades, if ever."

"I say, let them have their civil war, and when it's done, we'll offer the victors entry into the Body. As a lower part, naturally," said van Underrac.

"A reauthored Quadrate?" huffed Rurstmeyer. "I won't support that."

"Neither will the barons," said Popov with a shake of his head.

"Certainly the Aethreleans can't believe they're relevant any longer," said Thrsea Machaul. "The Hallowed Undertaking is a distant memory. The Renewal didn't take, and the Commandments are more ceremony than actual law. Those fools are like spring wolves fighting over last fall's deer carcass."

Rurstmeyer cleared his throat and adopted a lecturing tone. "I'm sure there are some that do still feel as if they're relevant. I'm sure whichever side emerges victorious will take its triumph as a sure sign that its interpretation of those cretinous Commandments is alive and well and deserving its blood-earned mandate."

"Well, that won't do," said Savanie. "Not at all."

The table fell silent. They were waiting on Grewea to speak. After a long moment, he did.

"No, it won't do, you are correct, Cra Savanie. But that's how they'll puzzle it out…unless we first puzzle it out for them," he said. "We intend to introduce something…new into the mix. Or something very old, depending on your point of view."

"You seriously mean to offer them entry? I'd sooner see the Slau legitimized," joked Rurstmeyer.

"No, not entry," said Grewea. "I believe our plans for them should be somewhat more definitive. And conclusive."

"What are you suggesting? War?" asked van Underrac.

"I think we all know what he's suggesting. We've all heard the rumors, though one can scarcely believe even the Great and Feared Grewea Lon would be bold enough to do it," said Oxenhaft. He peered at Grewea, watching him carefully.

So it's as I suspected, thought Grewea. *The university scholar is going to confuse values with perspective.*

Machaul coughed and shook his head vigorously. "I contend it's madness. There's no sane reason to consider it."

"Why?" Lon asked.

"History tells us not to upset the balance."

Druthec Grehmann spoke: "Is there really any need for such drastic measures? Why meddle with their affairs at all? If the Stavers win the Aethrelean civil war, they'll stay where they are and leave us be."

"I don't believe that, and neither do you," Popov said.

Druthec ignored him. "And if the Unchained take the day, they'll be so busy keeping order in that superior land of theirs they won't have time to think about expanding the mandate, not for a very long time."

The faces around the table seemed to relax. And it had taken a Grehmann's insight, of all things, to make that happen.

But Grewea wasn't finished. "Your assumptions are troubling in their logic."

"How so?" huffed Druthec.

"The Unchained cannot win, first of all. We've seen to that. And the Stavers have only stayed as long as they have in Aethrelius because the Unchained had great support among the people in our lands. That is all about to change."

"What have you done, Lon?" asked Theodore Oxenhaft. "Or is the better question, do you know what you've done?"

"Long ago, they openly declared their disgust with our ways. They left us and set out to find a land that was free, to author a new, superior land, but they have finally reached the same conclusion our ancestors understood when the Kis were running the show: nothing is free in Arba. And there is always a bigger fish," said Grewea.

There was a cautious murmur of assent in the chamber.

"What then, dear Grewea Lon, would you suggest we do about the Aethreleans?" asked Theodore.

"Tell us plainly," said Savanie. He seemed very ill at ease.

Druthec snorted. "It's the worst-kept secret in the Triumvirate, Lon. We know your intentions."

"Yes, we do, Druthec, but I want him to say it out loud. I want there to be no misunderstanding down the line about who said what here today, nor about who agreed with him," said Theodore.

Everyone looked at Grewea Lon.

He said: "The Vo'ixtavracci. We have arranged for the Vo'ixtavracci to take their Gift...from Aethrelius."

The chamber was absolutely silent. Thinking a thing is one thing, but saying it aloud gives it life, gives it opportunities to actualize, gives it the right to be.

"Then it's true! The Vo'ixtavracci? You can't be serious!" exclaimed Machaul.

"I am."

"The Vo'ixtavracci will not deal with us. They consider us food," said Druthec.

"Bad food, it would seem: they haven't even shown up here for...fifty years, is it?" asked Rurstmeyer. "Or is it a hundred?"

Grewea tsked at him. "Come, Simon. You know exactly how long it's been. And I know why they haven't come. But we summoned them, we offered this deal, they will come. And Aethrelius won't trouble us anymore."

"Let's say we were to agree to this insanity," said Savanie. "The Vo'ixtavracci long ago were turned aside by Frederick and his allies, and though the Sword is long lost, they remember — of this there can be no doubt. And the Mudarrisi and Jamoi are still very much a factor."

"The Mudarrisi are strong in their magick," added Balkac, smiling and nodding.

Grewea noticed not for the first time how embarrassingly unintelligent the slaver-prince was. What would it have meant were he to ever assume control of Motatinfo, as was intended? Thank the Waln that would now never come to pass. "The Mudarrisi will very soon find themselves and their assistance quite unwelcome in the Great Nation," he said. "The people are even now deciding that the foreign wielders of color have long overstayed their invitation."

"They would be fools to believe that," said Machaul.

"Then fools they are," agreed Grewea with a small smile. "When left to decide for themselves, the people, any people, are almost guaranteed to run straight into certain catastrophe. The Aethreleans, it seems, are no exception."

"And when the Jamoi's pets leave them..." said Rurstmeyer, clearly feigning discomfort at the scheme. Another idiot in the mix.

"Aethrelius is an open field, waiting to be tilled."

"Their army —"

"Hasn't got a chance," stated Grewea.

Savanie was shaking his head. "They'll all...every one of them will be slaughtered."

"I expect so. Some of the women might be kept alive for breeding purposes."

"You're mad," barked Druthec, waving he hand dismissively.

"Yes, perhaps," said Grewea. "Debatable point, truly. If you like, I will come to your cell to discuss it."

"My cell? I think not." said the elder Grehmann, his face the picture of indignation.

"And I think so. That is, if you fail to vote for my measure, Druthec Grehmann."

"Explain yourself."

Grewea said, "Good council members, worthies of the Mind, hear me: I have already gleaned ducal approval for this measure and acted upon it. Our beloved Duke Velliok has concluded that this arrangement with the Vo'ixtavracci is of such critical importance to the sovereignty of this state that I have been granted the power to arrest and detain any council member, citizen, or elite blowhard animal that opposes it."

"On what grounds?" cried Savanie.

"We must, in these times, speak with one voice and act with one will. Dissension has its place in times of peace and sloth, but we stand now on the brink of an extraordinary time, a time of strife, change, and expanded possibilities. Such moments by their nature will brook no democratic gibberish from anyone, including the luminaries who sit here today at this exquisite but unfashionable slab. Duke Velliok believes it his destiny to unite the peoples of Arba and lead them into a new millennium. He believes also, and with this belief I agree, that this council — both Body and Mind — has become a complete pain in the ass. Actually, I have long believed it, but he has just recently come around to share my point of view. So, your choice is simple: support our proposal, or get used to life in a small, dark, unheated cell. Unless you prefer Bi, the welcoming mouth of which is ever wide open."

They sat there, the Mind did, in stunned silence. Rurstmeyer rose and spoke:

"I cannot support this madness. You're manipulating an entire nation toward its doom because…because…well, it's not clear, is it? You're murdering a country, and you haven't said why."

"Haven't I?"

"No, you have not."

"Imagine that." Grewea looked at Rurstmeyer until he sat back down, slowly, and shut his mouth.

When no one raised the subject of the second issue he'd hinted at, he decided, in the interest of bringing this stupidity to a close, he'd better spoon-feed them:

"And as to the other matter I'd like to offer for your consideration, we have evidence that the Proving…the Prophesies, the Fourth, the entire matter…is actually, in a manner of speaking, true. Therefore, we need to decide on a policy."

"Are you going to sit there and pretend you haven't already decided on one and that you require our input or approval?" asked van Underrac.

"I am not pretending anything at all, Trelk. I really do need and welcome your suggestions. You are, after all, humans — forgive me, Arbans-- and I, as some of you have probably known for some time, am not. A Purging would affect your kind much more than it would me. And my kind are all long since dead, or so they tell me, so they're not much a factor here, are they?"

Grewea watched their faces. Five of them were still in shock over what he'd said about Aethrelius. Only two, Savanie and Oxenhaft, seemed themselves, and Savanie was very much struggling to maintain his mask.

Oxenhaft on the other hand was already making plans, he could see that. And so he'd have to be dealt with. Preferably in a manner brutal enough to send a message to any other voices inclined to object, here or wherever else in Arba they might be. Or maybe there was another way…

Having delivered his message, Grewea rose and strode to the door. He stopped and reconsidered for a moment. Yes, he should say something in conclusion.

"I see that perhaps we all need some time to digest what's been said here today. Let's meet again in, say, three days' time to discuss this Proving business and put also to rest the matters of magick and Aethrelean tumult. Agreed?"

Sh'arnau was waiting for him in the hallway, his thick, wolfish head lit strangely by the secret hall's lone torch.

Grewea said, "Well, my friend, that went as planned. We'll have to keep an eye on them, of course."

"I'll see to it."

"As I knew you would," said Grewea as he walked toward the stairs that led up to the street.

Grewea sat alone in one of his many hidden domiciles and sipped a cup of honeyed tea. The tea was flavored with a special ingredient, one he didn't much care for but very much needed.

He stared into the fire and thought for a moment about the fate that awaited the Aethreleans. He wondered if the Vo'ix would honor the arrangement they'd made. He expected they would not, and he wasn't at all concerned. In fact, he was counting on their natural appetites to make their decisions for them.

Would that be enough, or were there further steps to take?

He put down the tea, leaned back in his chair and closed his eyes.

It took a bit longer tonight than it normally did, but soon enough, he found himself there.

"You must come in and sit down, Grandfather. Your soup is getting cold, and so is the wind. Why must you sit out here when the fire is so warm inside?"

He was sitting at the edge of a small stone patio, staring aimlessly at the reflection of a thick grove of pine trees. The small mountain lake rippled as the wind skirted over its surface, and the trees he saw on it seemed to be thinking of losing their true form and disappearing from his sight. It disturbed him a little; the message pecked at him like some dying but defiant bird. He slowly stood and turned away from the bird and its irrelevant message, turned toward the voice that had beckoned him.

"You love to stare at that old lake, and though I know it's beautiful, I need you to spend at least as much time playing with me!" cried Jerold. He held a basket of small maroon squash, and something about their color and their odd, spiral-twisted shapes reminded Grewea of a thing he'd seen a very long time ago. He gazed at the boy's face and smiled.

"Very well, here I come, here I come," said Grewea as he took Jerold's extended free hand and allowed himself to be led into the cottage. "It's time for the biscuits, then? Who made them, Elu or the little Turtle?"

"Elu? Grandpa, you know she can't bake anything! She's only two!" cried the indignant Turtle, who'd been hiding behind the door, waiting for her grandfather to enter.

"Only two? And how old, pray tell, does that make you?"

The Turtle held up four fingers, then added another, then put one back down and seemed to settle on the four.

"Are you already that old?" asked Grewea, smiling at the little girl he called Turtle.

"I am! I am four!" cried Turtle, holding up three more fingers.

"Then I suppose you're the perfect age to bake biscuits! And I am famished!"

Inside the cottage, he looked about. The pottery, the burning cook fire, the small wooden table...it was nothing he'd ever really known. But he'd been among them for so long, these humans, and were his kind really so different, was what they wanted so different? No.

Or yes.

The vision dissolved; he blinked twice and then reached again for his tea.

"Time to rest, old man," he said aloud to himself.

Tomorrow they would head up to Hunberg via ducal schooner. He hated that boat, and he hated the lake and the weather and the waves. There'd been nothing like them where he came from.

He wondered if there was anything left of where he'd come from.

They wouldn't tell him, even if he asked. Not unless they could somehow calculate the effects of telling him and wager upon whatever crooked numbers they conjured.

And he wasn't the sort to give satisfaction to sorts like them.

He tilted his head to one side and fell fast asleep.

Chapter 12
Maybe rodents ate butter and biscuits…

Place: Camedua, kingdom of Xatumka
Date: Quattrenim 7, AY 998

Gossie Fundra emptied the remainder of the second wine bottle into his glass. Or was it the third? He couldn't recall, and he didn't care. The goals were to get drunk fast and to be fully drunk and to stay drunk indefinitely. Forgetting how to count was one of the benefits of pursuing these goals, all of which he was coming admirably close to achieving.

The letter was still on the desk, beneath a plate of barely touched meats and cheeses. He hadn't had much of an appetite after reading it, and food tended to interfere with the goals of getting drunk fast, fully, and indefinitely. Stupid letter. He had only read it the once — or was it twice? — and had gotten, according to plan, quite drunk since doing so, in an attempt to ignore the letter and enjoy his untouched meal.

Stupid letter. Its words usurped his every thought.

Gossie looked around the room, a rented flat above a tavern named "Shen's" that smelled like dead fish and charred animal, and tried to center his thoughts. What a shit hole. Why were they always shit holes? He used to live better.

When was that?

He belched loudly, pushed the plate aside, and, after a quick internal debate about the merits of sticking one's head up one's arse, had another look. It took him a moment to focus.

> *Sir:*
> *The cargo ships* **Elean Val** *and* **Moresso** *have been lost at sea. The Challowian vessel charged with their protection was also destroyed. There is but a single survivor; he is in custody and is being held by Trades and Guilds in our Beene Street facility. He has had an initial hearing and awaits now the judgment of the Brown Men.*
> *Our regrets for your trouble in this matter are of course most grave and we therefore undertake in this form to make you whole as per our lawful and unimpeachably enforceable agreement. Your recompense will come in the form of seventeen hundred T&G credits and twelve months' suspended docking fees, as per your membership and contractual arrangements. Please be aware that though suit may be brought against the Challowian Navy and the Juks Xi Ren Protectorate, such measures are to be considered formalities only.*

*Your presence and testimony is required at the Brown Men
hearing, scheduled for Naipta, Quattrenim 13, Year 998, at the
start of the fourteenth hour.*

*Regards and regrets,
M'ushon Fre Smythe, North Ports Overseer and First
Exchanger, TG 4th*

Seventeen hundred credits. An insult. A vile insult. A blatant display of unmitigated arrogance and stupidity designed to not only strip
him of his property rights and standing as a trader but to also fracture his
very being at its core. T&G had been waiting a long time to fuck him, and
now he was sure they were congratulating one another on their good luck.
He half wondered if they'd sunk the ships themselves, but no: they were
far too greedy and far too cowardly.

Ha. Piss on them. Piss on them and their greed and their
cowardice and their stupid Brown Men hearing.

And yet seventeen hundred, though a vicious kick in the testicles
to be sure, might somehow be enough to buy him safe passage out of
Camedua before someone had him killed. And someone would want to
have him killed; on that point there could be no debate. Not that that
notion wasn't perpetually true in one form or fashion when applied to his
often off-the-cuff existence, governed as it was by loosely held and fascin-
atingly malleable standards, but in the here and now, the danger was
certainly more immediate than on a typical Gossie day, and what's more,
he was having a little difficulty thinking of an angle. He blamed the wine.
He blamed his advancing age, his physician (who he had not seen in decades), and his barber (who he'd seen yesterday or the day before for a
barely satisfactory trimming of his ample beard and graying mop).

He tried to focus.

*If I could bargain the credits into barbs, that would be a good start. Yes.
That's it.*

He was sure he could, or reasonably sure, or maybe just hopeful.
He still had contacts here, though most of them had died or moved on.

Hells with that, huh? Camedua used to be his town, damn it.
Didn't it? Still was!

Probably not, no.

Until last month, he hadn't been here since…Cronelle…995? 994?
And before then, just a few scams, albeit brilliant ones, with the Hookel
gang in the early eighties…

He got up and paced the floor a bit, steadying himself on the few
pieces of furniture that adorned the shit hole. He lost his balance, reeled,

and plopped down into a chair. Something snapped in the chair, and he felt something sharp jabbing into his buttocks. Shifting, he focused once more on the problem at hand.

It was really just a question of where to go and who to bribe. It was also a question of who knew what and who was working for whom. And how to get out of town and when and in which direction.

So there were a few questions.

And of course, he had to act quickly because these days they — whoever "they" were in any given scenario — seemed too often to know what only he should. No doubt there was a trick or two they hadn't anticipated and wouldn't, but at the moment those tricks were eluding him.

He suspected he was getting tired of the whole damned game. How long had it been?

It both saddened and amused him that he couldn't state with any certainty how old he was. He chuckled then, tears of mirth and fleeting insight coming to his eyes. Then he coughed and rose.

What to do, what to do. And what the hell had happened to those ships? All hands and cargo lost, with a Juks escort on those seas? A child in its own nursery in the middle of some Pherriuskatan palace would have been more at risk. The story didn't add up, or hadn't been told in full. (Then again, when had any story, ever, in the whole history of stories?) And this both annoyed and excited him. A good mystery was mother's milk to him, for good mysteries were always ripe for exploitation: someone would pay, someone would need answers or reasons or a way out of something, or into something, or both.

Right now, unfortunately, that someone was him. He needed an in to his out and was having the most difficult time figuring it all out. Again. This used to be easy, right? Or had he always sailed by the seat of his ass?

He sat there ruminating slowly, and much to his own surprise he actually dozed off a few times. Again, he blamed the wine. And his age. And the Juks Xi Ren and the Brown Men and the damn T&G.

Snapping out of it, he thought that action without a plan was just as like to get him killed as waiting here, asleep, would…but beyond the credit for cash move, what could he do?

How much had he borrowed to finance this venture? One hundred thousand barb? More?

He was ruined as a shipper. That was a given, but he'd been ruined before. Many times, in fact; he was very good at being ruined and even better at rising from the ashes. Nor was this the first time his business ventures had put his life at risk. In fact, he preferred when business ventures headed straight for the cliff, with the butter and the biscuits tumbling all jump and flutter about the cart and the rodents hot on one's tail. It got the blood pumping and the mind bubbling.

This time was a little different. Very different, he admitted glumly. It wasn't just a matter of paying the money back: he was far more concerned with the party whose cargo he'd lost. They were obsessive, and they were everywhere. And they'd warned him just how serious they were about prompt and discreet delivery. As if they'd needed to. Fucking maniacs. Bad for business, that bunch. Bad for a lot of things. What had possessed him to take on their offer?

Boredom. Damn him if it wasn't boredom. All this brown market shifting of crates and sacks around in the dark, getting paid a fraction of what he could be making elsewhere, wherever elsewhere was (he couldn't be bothered with specifics), and drinking himself into a near stupor every night at whatever pub would have him and give him credit had turned his mind to jelly. This apparent mistake he'd made was, to his way of thinking, his mind kicking him in the ass: *time's come for a new venue, Gossie, you fat old swindler*. Got to get out of this town. Maybe work the Wilds…or Motatinfo. Would they still be looking for him in Motatinfo?

His mind, keen as it could be and independent of his many self-defeating impulses as it reliably was, held him to a certain elevated standard. Recognizing its independence, he often referred to it (though never out loud) as "Mr. Mhetlonac." And right at this moment, it was time for the both of them to figure a way out of this fiasco.

He kicked himself for the hundredth time for choosing to do business with T&G and the Siddiquis and those other things, whatever they were. He should have known better. He did know better, dammit, but there'd been *so much* money involved, he thought just this once it'd work out. His better instincts had told him to back away, but he had a lifetime's habit of completely ignoring his better instincts (the honorable, nagging Mr. Mhetlonac) in favor of his wild but arguably calculated impulses…and so far, he'd done okay for himself.

Not today. He should have reacted sooner, but things here had been so good for so long: fifteen, twenty ships from the north, and oh, the money! And he'd thought this time they, the good things, might stay that way. Instead, he'd spent nearly every penny and now was in profoundly deep shit.

Gossie, you got soft, he thought. *Better lay off the desserts for now. And maybe the wine.*

Mr. Mhetlonac just grunted.

"Oh, shut up, you!" Gossie grunted back.

So: What to do about the Siddiquis? The Camedua merchant family owned the bastards who'd sent this letter. They'd have already sent someone to find him. That someone was probably downstairs right now. It very much surprised him, come to think of it, that the lad who'd dropped off the letter itself hadn't also brought an axe with which to split open his skull. The kid had accepted his tip, smiled, and taken off. Maybe he didn't know. Maybe rodents ate butter and biscuits with kerchiefs around their necks too.

Gossie dropped the hated letter to the floor and spat some wine at it. Why had they bothered wasting the paper? The law might find the letter or even have received a copy of their own from interested parties and then have an official reason to clear T&G of any wrongdoing, but the Brown Men were in bed with them and knew how the game was played, so who was the letter intended to fool? Waste of good paper, that. He spat on it again.

Yes, they'd be coming for him. He held out little hope that he could both give them the slip and take with him all his hard-earned and useful stuff: A decent painting. A crate of pelts from the Brull border. Two cases of Miranquellan port. Several dozen books he knew a pseudoscholar in Pashka would pay top dollar for. Or was that man in Pebbusku now?

Still, there were ways to make himself scarce. There were always ways to do that; he'd invented most of them on the fly here and there and despite his lessened physical skills. There was a time he could (and did) dive off a church steeple into a raging river, swim a mile, and steal three horses all the while carrying his loot on his back or in his teeth. He still had an admirable bags of tricks with which to baffle, annoy, and foil any pursuers, and he had hard-earned and useful supplies—coins, clothes, weapons, maps, trinkets, antiques, bottles, disguises—in hideouts in cities and towns from here to Aethrelius. A lifetime of perpetual and necessary motion had informed his choice of many baskets over one, eggs being what they were.

Nothing here was particularly precious, but still he hated leaving his belongings behind. The painting of the Blutkirche he'd purchased just last week. Oh, fuck all—it was worth something, but it was ugly as sin. He'd leave it and everything else for Shen, and maybe someday he could come back and get a fraction of the value back. Doubtful, but maybe.

He picked up another bottle, popped the cork, and took a long pull.

"Now that is some very good port," he said, staring for a moment at the label. "Maybe I should move my ass to Miranquella and become an exporter." He took another pull, decided the port wasn't all that good after all, and muttered, "Maybe not."

He'd have to forget about the insult of the "credits" for now. He'd pay back Trades and Guilds in spades, particularly that serpentine piece of shit, M'ushon Smythe, when the time was right. That was for later, but for now…he needed to get to the river, and he needed to do it soon.

His kingdom for a steeple from which to dive!

The next sound he heard told him he should have already done whatever it was he needed to do. There was a hard knock at the door, three raps in succession.

He froze. Or, as drunk as he was, tried to freeze and failed. He wobbled silently.

"Gossie? Gossie Fundra? You in there?"

More knocking followed. What were they, smashing the door with a boulder? He plucked a small flask out of his waistcoat pocket and regarded it with regret.

I was getting good and hammered, he thought, his head shaking.

"Gossie?" Another voice spoke up. It was Shen, the half-blind old innkeep, his current landlord, and the world's worst bartender, soon to be — one way or the other — quite a bit richer. "Wake up. There's some men here to see you."

Some men to see me, huh? More likely some men to break both of my arms and drag me to that cesspool Smythe had so casually referred to as the "Beene Street facility." Facility, my ass, he thought. *That place is a butcher shop.* Sad but true: if they grabbed him, being dragged there was the best he could hope for.

How'd they get here so soon? It might have had something to do with his nodding off, he admitted, chuckling despite himself.

He shook the small flask of lifewine so to stir up its sedimentary ingredients and then chugged down every last drop of its contents. Time to get serious.

The effects were almost instantaneous as his drunkenness was replaced by a jolting buzz of clarity.

Unfortunately, that gave his overactive inner Mhetlonac a chance to up its nagging.

He glanced about, a plan forming.

The drunken haze had fallen away completely. The lifewine was working its way through his veins, and he took note of how exhausted he must have been to be feeling now such profound effects from the potion.

Yes, he was getting old. Fine. But it was time to think — and act — young.

"Open up, Fundra, right now."

That wasn't Shen's voice. He wondered how many there were.

So, the plan: He was on the second floor, and the narrow window was, given his girth, too small to slither out of. He'd have to fight his way out or surrender. Not much of a choice. Well, really, there was a choice: he'd had a trapdoor quietly cut and installed behind the mirror; it led out onto the roof. Mhetlonac's idea, about which he might never hear the end. But where was the fun in just disappearing?

Besides, he wanted to have a look at the meat the Siddiquis had sent; he needed to know just how badly they wanted him dead, and the look of the knockers would answer that question. He thought he recognized one of the voices as belonging to someone who owed him money. A pig named Nattle or Mattle or something. Boy was here to play a round of "kill the noteholder."

Gossie walked to the mirror, considered its trapdoor for a moment, and then put on the best besotted expression he could muster. He stared a few seconds at himself, adjusting the look. Then he sat back down at the table, knocked a wine bottle over loudly with his left hand, and grabbed the hilt of his rapier with the right. He put his head on the table and waited.

He didn't have to wait long.

They broke the door open and burst into the room. There were only two of them, plus Shen, unless the footfalls lied.

"There he is, the sot. What do we do?"

"What do you mean, what do we do? We take him with us."

"You have an order for that action?" Shen was not a man typically concerned with legal particulars, but he'd known Gossie a long time and enjoyed the regular rent and extra fees for privacy that Gossie paid him.

"We have no order, and we need none. This man's life is forfeit."

"You can't..." Shen said.

"Hallo!" Gossie cried, leaping and drawing.

His ploy had worked; he had them both dead to rights. The man before him, a thick fellow with a leather vest and an unkempt beard, he quickly stabbed through the throat. Nattle or Mattle — the one facing Shen — didn't react soon enough to the fact that the targeted sot was armed, on the move, and full of lifewine. He parried the first blow but not the second, and he too fell, clutching his throat.

Gossie checked Nattle-or-Mattle's purse; it was empty. The dead man bore the markings of the T&G on his tunic, but he had no papers.

"You didn't need to kill them, Gossie," whimpered Shen.

"Like hell I didn't."

"And you're robbin' them too?"

"Just him. And there's nothing to rob. Man's broke." Gossie stood up and stared closely at Shen. "You've been fair with me, and that's no lie. All the stuff in here, you can have most of it, but I want the painting and the books put in storage."

"You're coming back?"

"I always come back."

"Which painting?"

"You know which painting." Gossie grabbed a small bag, threw a few things into it, and then turned back to Shen. "Have you got any money?"

"Me? What, on me? Sure, I've got…"

Gossie smacked him hard on the side of the head, but not hard enough to cause any real damage. "They'll want to know if you tried to stop me. Believe me, you want them to think you did."

Shen was wincing and rubbing his head. "But did you have to hit me?"

Gossie grabbed a second satchel from a wall hook. "No, to be sure, there are other ways to avert suspicion. I could have stabbed you through the eye; they'd feel sure of your loyalties then."

"You're joking."

"Am I? You really could use a good eye-stabbing, Shen. Maybe it would restore whatever sight you've lost to time and the drink."

"It was the sickness done it."

"Nonetheless, the offer to stab out your eye stands." Gossie looked around to see what else he might take with him. Not much, he quickly concluded.

"But we're friends!" cried Shen.

"Friends? A friend would have told them I was out or that he'd never even heard of me."

"It wouldn't have worked. They knew you were here. And they knew I knew."

"Spies. Gotta hate 'em."

"I thought you was a spy."

"That, Shen, my bumbling would-be friend, is probably why I am so oft filled with unmitigated self-loathing." He put his hand on the doorknob and listened a moment. "Remember, I always come back, so stick to ground, or here's praying the sky-cullin' shitwings don't pick you up and drop you from the heavens!"

And with that, Gossie Fundra hurried from the room, not entirely sure what his next move should be but loving every second of the action. He made his way to the back stairs that led to the kitchen, the larder, and the little dock that serviced both. They'd be watching all the exits; still, he thought he'd heard…yes. Shen's sons were loading the old beer barrels down the chute. "Hold up, there, boys…I've a favor to ask."

He slipped a fat coin into each of their right hands and put a finger to his lips. "No questions, not a sound, and by all means, say nothing to your father…"

He popped the top off a barrel, got in—it was a tight squeeze, a fact he blamed on Shen's wife's excellent stargazy pie—and signaled them to seal the barrel.

"Drop me in with the rest, boys, and don't give it another thought."

Moments later, he felt himself falling and then splashing into the water. With any luck, the watchers hadn't figured on anyone going out with the empties and weren't watching the waterway. The brewery flatboat would tie him on with all the other barrels and drag him the two miles to Swinler House.

It was a gamble, to be sure, and one he'd probably read about in some happy storybook somewhere long ago. Most of these barrels were old and often sprung leaks. More than one had surely sunk to the Camie's bed or even floated downriver and out to sea. If he'd picked a bad barrel, some poor fisherman in Bikita Badru or maybe even Narth Downs might be pulling his rotted corpse out of this sorry excuse for a craft in a week or two.

To his relief, he stayed afloat and made it to the brewery intact and relatively dry. He heard the grunts as the dockhands unhooked his barrel and tried to get hold of it. When he was up on the landing and the lid was off, he popped out like a clown entertaining at a low wedding.

"There we are, and a fine ride, too. Sorry, boys, but I noticed a few fine drops of the Swinnie at the bottom as they were closing 'er up, so I dove in to salvage 'em…and was sealed in before I knew what was where. Worth every bump and turn, it was, and gave me quite a thirst for more, so I'll be off to buy a flask at your counter now. G'day."

The dockhands stood there, mouths agape, as this balding, bearded, girthy figure climbed out, removed his satchels, and went on his way.

Chapter 13
"I've just got a few questions."

Place: On a road, kingdom of Arbana
Date: Quattrenim 14, AY 998

The man lay face down in the dirt at the side of the road. He had vomited and was breathing very rapidly.

Cvuklon knelt next to him with a canteen of water in his hand. His uncle watched from the side, wearing a sour expression and chewing nuts.

"He is not well, Uncle," Cvuklon said, his vestigial gills wheezing from the effort as he tried to find a way to give the man some water.

"No, he is not. Leave him," Grivtel chided. "Lunch is over. We need to keep moving, and we're wasting time and water." He'd been sitting on his thick, short horse, chewing the nuts and occasionally popping a salted rice ball into his mouth. He licked his fingers, spitting out pieces of nut.

"It's only a little water. And a little time."

"My water, my time. Who are you talking to?"

Cvuklon ignored the rhetorical foolishness. He gently flipped the man onto his back, lifted his head a bit, and tilted the canteen to his lips. The poor man drank nothing. The water trickled down his chin and onto his chest.

"He looks dead. Leave him. And stop glancing at my food. You don't need to get any fatter, and these are mine." He popped another rice ball in his mouth.

"But he is not dead...and he has value," said Cvuklon, giving up his attempt to force water into the man.

"Value? What value does he have?" Grivtel barked, bits of rice flying from his wide, somewhat amphibian mouth. "A single Mindless One has no value, not when I have two hundred others in this train."

"I...I am not sure he is Mindless."

"No? You're not sure? Look at him. Just look at him!" Grivtel said, rolling his eyes and shaking his head. "He doesn't even know how to walk or how to drink water. He lies in his own vomit, staring at the bright sky, not giving one shit about my precious water or my valuable time." He threw a rice ball at the man on the ground for emphasis. It struck the middle of his target's face. "He is not dead. No, he is worse than dead!"

Cvuklon stooped and brushed the rice away. "But I have seen his eyes...his 'staring eyes,' as you call them, aren't dark like a Mindless One's should be. They move. He sees the sky he stares at!"

"Eyes! What do I care of eyes? He doesn't speak or even moan. He breathes like a dying rabbit. And what do you know of these matters, who is Mindless and who not? You are fat, like a phlobalor who shoves its head into the trough and suffocates on its food. Your face is so fat you can scarcely see. Eyes, he says!"

"Uncle, please..."

"Please what? Shut up, fat phlobalor. You want this Mindless meat to come along? Put him on your gremfi and walk. But if he falls off or causes me even one more second of delay or one more drop of water, I leave him here. And you, if you say another word."

"Thank you, Uncle."

"Shut up, you fat thing."

Cvuklon watched his uncle ride slowly away toward the head of the train. He heard him barking commands at this one and that, mostly irrelevancies and redundancies aimed at achieving a greater measure of control over the slaves in his charge. No one responded directly; few even glanced at him save the one or two key subordinates who had long since grown numb to the routine but nonetheless played along by lazily cracking whips and echoing barks.

The train began to crawl forward grudgingly. Such was the life on the road from Motatinfo to Oak Harbor, or from Oak Harbor to Rash al Brek, or from any slave market to the next: a lot of barking and crawling, and most of it strikingly lazy and sad but also, inevitably, forward moving. A bad life, to be sure. Bad for the slavers, worse for the slaves, worst for the Mindless Ones.

Cvuklon thought he'd almost rather be left here, not moving, not listening, not being told to shut up again.

He looked down at the man lying by the side of the road. He knelt next to him and whispered, "Please, you must get up. The train is leaving, and if you lie there, my uncle will certainly have you beaten or dragged."

He sat the man up and used a small scarf to wipe some of the vomit away from his face. "Can you hear me?" he asked.

The man's eyes blinked open and closed a few times, then shut tight against the glare of Ponasa despite having just stared at the sky. The man seemed to be awakening from a trance. Or almost awakening. "Leave me," he said in a scratchy, parched voice. "Leave me here."

"Not possible," said Cvuklon. "I promised to see you safely to your friends, and this I will do."

"I have no friends. Not here," the man grunted almost inaudibly.

"No, not here. But somewhere, which is where we are going, you and I."

"Nowhere."

"That isn't true. You will see. Now, sit up...yes." Cvuklon helped him to a sitting position.

"Really, thank you, really, but please, just go, just let me be," said the man.

Cvuklon squatted beside him and offered him the rag to clean his face. "Please do not argue," he said as he grabbed him, not unkindly, by the arm and began to pull. "You don't have to walk anymore; you can ride…"

"Oh, c'mon, would ya just go away and leave me be!" the man growled angrily.

Cvuklon started, alarmed slightly by his charge's sudden energy. "Enough of that. Let me help you. There are very good reasons for me to keep you alive, not the least of which is that doing so will help to keep *me* alive."

"What are you talking…who are you?"

Cvuklon put his shoulder under the man's arm and hoisted. This was getting more and more difficult, and his uncle would turn his head at any moment to assess his poor fat nephew's progress, of which so far there was very little. Always the tests. Everything was a test, and all the tests were rigged against him. But he knew the game well.

At this moment in this time, the game was simple: get moving and wait for an opportunity.

"I'm a friend. Please, just stand up and get on."

The man allowed himself to be helped to his feet and then onto the gremfi. His human height made it impossible to fit his feet in the stirrups, so he slumped onto the stumpy mount's neck and let his feet rest on the ground. Cvuklon pulled a few straps and retightened them so the stirrups would be long enough to accommodate the man's feet. "There. Now you ride."

"I can't breathe – air feels a little thick."

"That's the agilios powder; your body is forcing it out. It won't last long."

"The what powder?"

"Something they gave you back at the camp. The place we acquired you. Do you not remember?"

The man thought a moment and then gave up and shook his head.

"It doesn't matter. Just hold on and try to be still," Cvuklon said.

The train had almost moved past them entirely, and the two Arbanan mercenaries taking up the rear were making urgent, annoyed gestures a dozen feet behind them.

"And we go," said Cvuklon, clapping his hands twice near the gremfi's left ear.

He started walking next to the ambling steed and was easily able to match its pace. Though fat, he was not nearly the helpless animal his uncle made him out to be. In fact, there was much his uncle either didn't know or would never believe about him. "Fat" didn't begin to cover all he was, though he had to admit to a certain undeniable extra about his person. The extra made the unknown easier to pull off. Due to his girth, they never saw him coming. Or going.

Cvuklon frowned, recognizing faintly the amount of trouble he'd gotten himself into. He enjoyed his secret little deals and maneuvers, but somehow this was way beyond what he'd ever imagined he'd do. It both thrilled and sickened him.

He glanced at the man who was the source of his anxiety and tried to smile. "Rest, my friend. We have a little time before we take the next step."

Disaster averted, Cvuklon began to hum a dancing tune he had once heard coming from a tent in the Landing Point. It was not a new song, and he had never truly enjoyed it, but for some reason, this version of it…sung by three women in a strange blend of harmonies without a melody…had been playing in his head on and off since that night.

After about an hour, the man lifted his head and cleared his throat. Cvuklon drew nearer to him to listen.

"That thing…your uncle…wanted to leave me," the man said. He was bouncing softly as the gremfi carefully picked its way along the road.

"No, he was just acting big in front of his people. He would never simply leave a living slave, even a Mindless One, and lose the chance at even the smallest profit. But he would have beaten you, or more likely had you beaten, for the benefit of his…obedient audience." Cvuklon thought he saw a small grin on the man's face for a moment. "You are feeling better, then?" he asked.

"A little. I'm nauseous," said the man, his face still grinning.

"What is funny?"

"Nothing. I…nothing, I just…never mind. I'm going to try to sleep," said the man.

"No, wait," said Cvuklon. "Stay awake if you can; it's better for you after the powder. Take deep breaths too. Yes, like that. Now tell me: you wanted to say something…tell me."

"I've just got a few questions."

"So?"

The man cleared his throat a bit, hesitated, and then asked, "What are you?"

"What am I? Do you mean who am I?"

"No, not really. No."

"You confuse me, sir."

"Join the club, we have hats," said the man.

"The club?"

"Never mind. Who are you, then?

"I am Cvuklon, a young, intelligent Slau from Tadills."

"What's a Slau?"

"We are…I am a Slau."

"Okay. And you say you're intelligent?"

"Yes, I am."

"Okay."

"You had another question?"

"Yeah, but after that first answer, I don't know if I can handle a second."

"May I ask your name, then?"

"Sure. I'm William. Bill. Billy. Or I was. Before all this."

"What do you mean 'all this'?"

"This place. Everything. You. That other thing."

"My uncle."

"Yeah, that."

"What about us?"

"I don't know. I've gone nuts is all, completely nuts. And I'm probably dead or in a coma, and I thought heaven…even hell…would be different."

"Ah."

"Ah?"

"I think I understand why you are confused now." Then it was true. But if it was, then what in the world had Cvuklon gotten himself into? And more importantly, what could he do to get out of it?

"You do?"

"Yes, but I am not at all sure I could or should explain it to you."

"No? Why not?"

"I am not at all qualified."

"I don't understand."

"You have come through from your place to ours. To our world, our home."

"What?"

"Never mind. Please, I don't know how to do this. Dalter didn't tell me you were…"

"You don't know how to do what?"

"Indoctrinate an Entrant."

"Come again?"

"Talk to you and make you understand where you are and what this place is."

"What? Listen, I just want some answers…"

"Please, don't speak too loudly or too often. We should really stop talking altogether. If my uncle hears that you are anything but what he believes you to be — a Mindless One slated for delivery to the harbor — he will begin to ask questions. Questions I am not sure I could convincingly answer."

"I don't care. I want…"

Cvuklon quickly reached up and put his palm against the side of William's head. He pressed a soft, black agilios flower there and then withdrew his hand. The flower dissolved into powder within seconds.

William looked at him, twitched twice, and then slowly passed out on the gremfi. Cvuklon made sure his straps were secure so he wouldn't fall out of the seat; he poked the steed, and they both got back in step with the caravan. The flower wasn't as potent as the powder, but it would work well enough to prevent any further complications and questions. Now was not the time for those.

It had been two days since Dalter Bubussa had approached him with the hurried request.

"Please, you must take this man to my brother in Carthage. For your own safety and his, you must pretend he is Mindless. I have given him something to assist with the maintenance of the façade. First, go to Wukneesh and see Clara Pyan-wu…"

Bad luck, really. Just because Cvuklon had attended a meeting, a meeting Dalter had dragged him to and then left him at — alone among some very dubious-looking strangers — he had been drafted to undertake a very urgent and very dangerous mission. He did not love his job or for that matter his uncle, but he was not inclined to abandon both for the sake of a whispered mandate and a few ideas he scarcely understood. Oh, that stupid meeting! Oh, stupid, stupid Cvuklon! He was in deep now, and he could see no way out. Someone might be looking for this man!

Still, there was something to all this…something different and interesting and new. It was exciting, and very little about his life was either new or exciting, not since his father had died and Cvuklon's two remaining brothers, both of whom were much older than him and hated him bitterly for reasons they never bothered to explain, had decided his time at the school and the money it took to keep him there were ill spent.

So for over a year now, he'd been on loan to his uncle Grivtel, collecting mostly Mindless slaves from the Landing Point or Yanz or Tritto and delivering them to Oak Harbor and Carthage and, once or twice, all the way to Pashka. Boring journeys all, with little to distract but the occasional impotent raid by bandits or broken Crabs. The latter were horrible to behold but, like most other would-be aggressors on the highways and roads, easily repelled. Most of the time, anyway.

Once, they had almost made the journey up into the mountains to Pir Choss…but the winter snows had come, the pass had been blocked, and they'd lost nearly the whole stock to an ice storm. Uncle Grivtel hadn't been happy about that; he had seemed to blame the storm and the loss both on Cvuklon and on anyone else in his employ. The whining and chastising had gone on for months. One learned to block out the sound of Grivtel's voice.

Cvuklon had been relieved not to have to go to Pir Choss. One heard things, unpleasant things, about that place and the man for which it had been named. Typically, the people met up with the caravans on the Southern Road to buy, and that was more than fine with Cvuklon. One couldn't always count on a storm to block the pass.

His birthday had passed and gone unacknowledged. The Slau never made much of birthdays in any case, but Cvuklon recalled fondly when both his parents were alive: they would bake lemon cakes and sing funny songs on one another's birthdays. His brothers were long gone even then; they had gone to fight in the Thicknomy Wars, which never seemed to end and never seemed to matter except to the families of the thousands of dead soldiers who'd fought for reasons no one could ever recall with any certainty. No one complained. Cvuklon never understood why. He'd lost three of his brothers without ever understanding why.

He spent a good deal of time speculating about that and about why his living brothers hated him and about why there was so much close-minded idiocy in the world. There were times he imagined himself travelling to Hunberg, becoming a scholar in earnest, and writing a book filled with these and other contemplations. For now, though, he walked the slaver roads.

He was fat, but with the healthy lime-green complexion and bright orange-yellow eyes of a strong Slau youth. His reptilian head was perhaps a bit a knobby at the crown, and his jowls were thick and dark, but he had it on good authority that as he ventured deeper into manhood, both of those unfortunate flaws would correct themselves. He still had all his own teeth, which was more than he could say for his brothers. Actually, Hneock, Strevkla, and Butrok still had their teeth, Cvuklon presumed, but they were buried with them somewhere in the scarred Hills of Wild Winter, perhaps frozen in those same, stupid, mocking smiles they used to flash at Cvuklon just before they delivered another senseless, furious beating. Oh, how they howled and laughed at his cries of pain.

Beating Cvuklon had always been his brothers' favorite sport, a sport whose newest enthusiast was Uncle Grivtel.

"Your Mindless pet has fallen asleep. It seems riding agrees with him."

Cvuklon looked up to see his cousin, Hasalk, grinning down at him.

"You should have left him. Father will be blaming you for

delaying the train."

"I have delayed nothing, Hassie. And this man is…ill. I have administered some treatment; he will heal."

"You have done what? I think your fat has seeped into your brains, Cvuk. You think you're a healer?"

"No, I…"

"No one can cure Mindlessness. Pir Choss himself could not do it. But you, my fat, slow, cowardly cousin, you have cured a Mindless One of his 'illness'? Ha!"

"I didn't mean that. I meant he may be Mindless, but he is also ill."

"Then he's not worth the trouble."

"I say he is."

"The coward with a heart is twice a coward indeed."

"I am not a coward."

"Yes, you are."

"Okay, maybe I am. But I am a living coward, the only living coward my parents left in this world."

"Too bad for them."

"Hassie? I need to tell you something."

"What? Tell me, then…what?" Hassie demanded with a snort.

But Cvuklon just shook his head. "Never mind. It can wait."

He'd waited until night, when all the slaves and most of the guards were asleep. Then he went to a particularly lazy guard named Wesse, who was dozing off near the back end of the caravan, and tapped him on the shoulder.

"What…oh, you. What do you want, Fat One?"

"Well, I would like you to stop calling me 'Fat One,' but that is not why I'm here."

"You're not supposed to bother the nightguard, you know. There could be raiders about."

"I don't think so. Uncle has paid his protection money to the Gumundurs; no one will come tonight," said Cvuklon.

"The Gumundurs aren't as tough as they make themselves out to be. There are other things out here that raid, you know, and some that just want to eat you."

"Maybe, maybe. But let me tell you why I'm here. I cannot sleep; I have indigestion, and it's keeping me awake."

"You have indigestion? Is that a new feeling for you?" chuckled Wesse.

"Laugh, but you will be crying if I fart."

"Then go away and fart somewhere else."

"I could do that. Or, if you prefer, I could keep the watch, and you could go get some rest."

Cvuklon couldn't have made a sweeter offer to Wesse. If Wesse could sleep twenty-nine hours a day, he would do it. He eyed Cvuklon suspiciously for a few seconds and then laughed.

"Very well, Fat. Maybe for an hour or so. Have you got any wine?"

Wesse's second-favorite pastime, Cvuklon knew, was slugging down wine. "As a matter of fact, I have some right here. I was going to sit and drink it if you let me take your watch, but I suppose I could part with it..."

Wesse grabbed the wineskin with a grunt and ambled off toward the guard tents. "You remember to tell your uncle you ordered me off the watch. That's what I'm gonna tell him. Don't eat too much," he grunted over his shoulder.

After Wesse had gone, Cvuklon waited about an hour. He sat and watched the dark, moonless hills, and his mind wandered for a time to the idea that there were bad things out there, things other than raiders. Of course, there were—everyone who worked the long highways of Arba knew it. There were campfire stories, some of them quite horrible, about the things that preyed on travelers and merchants. Were any of them true?

He could not say, but he did remember a time, once when he was young and travelling with not only his uncle but with his brothers and father as well, when they'd come across something terrible on the Southern Road. It was the remains of a small caravan; the people and animals had been torn apart. There were limbs and heads everywhere but no torsos to be seen. And the strangest thing of all was that the cargo was completely untouched. Of course, his father and uncle saw the opportunity and snatched most of what was valuable, but they didn't linger long, and there were no stories by the fire for the remainder of the trip.

It was very late when he stirred from his macabre reverie and turned his attention to the business at hand. He had to leave here, tonight, with the Entrant named William. He had to get him to Carthage and wash his hands of him. With any luck, he could concoct a story about having been abducted in the night by raiders and a matching story about his escape, and he could come back to his uncle's caravan with little fanfare except perhaps a beating designed to teach him the profitlessness of getting abducted.

Chapter 14
The figure she saw

Place: The Glaring Cliffs, northeastern shore of Aethrelius, Arba Environ
Date: Quattrenim 14, AY 998

The waves crashed against the seawall far below.

Frainle Dossilea squinted her eyes against Trilesti's late-afternoon brightness. She could make out a single figure walking along the wall, away from her vantage point atop the family tower. The person's path turned up among the stones, and he — or she — was gone. Waiting another moment, Frainle watched to see if the figure would appear again on the southerly stairs, but it didn't happen.

The sentries didn't typically walk the wall; they watched it from stations on the ridge above. She wondered who it had been and why the sentries hadn't taken action. No one was allowed down there without special permission; that had been the policy for decades.

It had to be a sentry.

Or maybe it was a Delariun spy, one of those mysterious fishmen who could swim hundreds of miles without surfacing, come to take her from her father and mother. Was she a hostage worth having? Of course. Worth swimming across an ocean for? Probably not. So maybe the spy wasn't a spy at all; maybe he — or she — was someone who'd watched her from a ship way out on the horizon and desired only a moment with her, or a smile, or more…and would not be denied, and now, having landed on the forbidden beach and climbed onto the wall, risked everything for the moment or the smile. Or more.

Maybe not. Romantics were always the most disappointing suitors; she'd learned that the hard way, more than once, till the lesson had stuck. She smiled a bit at the thought of a love-starved sailor anyway.

Never mind all that. It probably was just some sentry checking the beach for anything worth scavenging — the wages the government paid these men were a pittance, that much she knew, and sometimes good things washed up on the shore, things a man could sell or keep, or so the saying went. Maybe someone was just having a stroll or a piss.

Frainle felt a sense of slight satisfaction in knowing she would probably never know. In a life she secretly — or perhaps openly, given her mother's telling exasperation — rued as oppressively predictable, a little innocuous mystery now and again was mother's milk to her.

She knelt over her sketchbook and tried to recall what the image of the spy-sailor-strolling-pissing-soldier had looked like. The wind was whipping, though, as it often did during the latter part of the summer, and the paper in her hand fluttered too wildly to control. She set it down and placed a stone on it to keep it from flying away. After sketching a few rough lines, she leaned back, closed her eyes, and then, after finding the image in her head, reopened them to assess what she'd done. Not bad, she thought. Not good either, but a start. And now she felt a bit irritated that her model had disappeared, innocuous mystery be damned.

Father will be back soon. The thought dispelled her irritation. It had been some time since he'd been home, and when he'd disappeared for so long on Tolii Nus, she had begun to truly worry. But there'd been word from him earlier in the day, and the whole of the Glaring Cliffs was anticipating his return now. The keep's inhabitants were of mixed mood, for some of the squadron had died on that island, and though they were all relieved their friends, brothers, and captain were coming home, there were many who were only now beginning to wrestle with their grief.

The Fourth Mandate Squadron was heading to Renikalar for a Square assembly, but that would not take long. Her father would see to that. It never took him very long to grab hold of the diplomats and dissenters and set them right. He detested the duty, she was sure. One day, she'd trick him into admitting it. Maybe.

Her mother had smiled a little at the good news and placed her hand on her belly, as if to somehow relay the news to Frainle's baby brother. Frainle herself had spent the better part of the day deciding which dress to wear, even though she knew her father wouldn't care if she were covered in mud. He'd pick her up and spin her and laugh aloud to see her again. He'd tell her how big she'd become, even though she, now a young woman, had long since stopped growing, and maybe give her a gift — something strange like the shell of a thing that no longer lived in these seas, or something sweet from a chocolatier in Renikalar, or a colorfully painted book from the Tri. She loved when he brought her books, even ones that came from the Tri.

Especially ones that came from the Tri, she admitted to herself. Too many of the keep's books were about war and military tactics and heroes of the Aethrelean Nation. She'd read all those, many times, but it was books about art and romance and the wild places in the world she truly craved. She loved illustrations and paintings, and she longed to visit the museums of Pashka and Hunberg and Mariendo, where the artists painted in the streets among the merchants and the winemakers.

Her father would embrace her, she knew, and hold her close and talk to her and listen to everything she had to tell him. He always had, and he always would. But then he would turn to his wife and his unborn son, and his dear daughter would be somewhat forgotten.

No, that wasn't fair. Not forgotten; never forgotten. He loved her, and he was devoted to her mother, but he'd only ever adored one of his family members, and that one was gone from them. And he had never forgiven himself for that. They all knew, but never said, that this new baby would be a boy, and this boy would help to lessen her father's sorrow.

The wind caught her hair and whipped it around her face, blinding her for an instant. The papers beneath the rock danced and flapped wildly. *Wanting to go somewhere*, she thought, *maybe out to sea, or maybe to the Tri to become part of someone's colorful book…or far away to a land of fish-spies and disappointing lovers.*

None of it was true, of course. Her father's now-legendary sorrow was a lie. Leander Dossilea was a good man but also and too often a blind fool, and his single-minded devotion to his country was enough to drive any who knew and loved him to madness. She knew what he believed; she knew despite her mother's insistence to the contrary that he had reconciled the death of his firstborn with the hallowed and unyielding precepts of the almighty Code. Shain had died serving Aethrelius, and it was a good death. So Leander had said, and so he believed, and any insistence that he bore an unhealable pain within him that his proud reconciliation couldn't assuage was a lie.

And that was the way it had to be for a captain, a tha'it, and a believer. His duties demanded such interpretations, he had told her, had told them all in his own way.

Shain's death had served Aethrelius.

Leander accepted this and loved Aethrelius all the more for it.

Frainle would never forgive Aethrelius. Or her father. Or Shain.

She thought of Shain for a moment now, and hot tears welled up in her eyes.

Foolish girl! No! she thought harshly as she squashed the emotion. *No more.*

Leander Dossilea could not allow himself to grieve or suffer. Or maybe he hadn't the capacity; it was difficult to say. So his daughter had grieved and suffered for him. Or for Shain, at least. Always for Shain. Her father loved her for it, in his way and for the duty she seemed more than willing to perform. Or so she thought; again, it was difficult to know for sure. Leander was a closed man, a living legend who had little time for explanations and confidences, at least with her.

And while she loved him, she also hated him for how and who he was: his private nature, his expectations, his misplaced appreciation, and his legend. Or so she sometimes feared.

But was hate too strong a word? Perhaps. Perhaps it was simply the wrong word, for she felt very little for or against her father, for the actual person she believed him to be, and her laugh when he picked her up and twirled her around after months of being away on some pointless mission or political counsel was a necessary disguise for her growing apathy.

Frainle, at least, knew the truth, and she kept it close to her, wrapped away like a young thing that might die if the wind were to blow too freely against it. Once she'd craved her father's love, of course, and she had sometimes hated Shain for the way that love had been so freely given him. Yet here, now, she cradled her dark suspicions and hid from the bottomless paradox to which they led her: that in order to win that love for herself, she too would have to give all she had for the sake of their dying country — and what she had would never be enough, and what she might give was not hers to offer.

Aethrelius accepted only the most dearly got — and given — gifts.

Aethrelius demanded of her people all they could give her.

Frainle could not win, and she could not follow Shain, and she had no idea who she was supposed to be.

Her father would love the new baby with all his soul, that she knew, at least until it was of an age to die on some ship somewhere for no valuable reason. She felt twinges of envy despite herself; they blended awkwardly with her disdain, like two competing predators gnawing at the same barren skeleton. Shame rose up quickly and, with a night sky's all-consuming presence, blanketed and stilled both envy and disdain. Being so familiar with shame, almost intimately so, Frainle dismissed all three emotions of a moment and got back to work.

She'd sketch the horizon and the sea. Again. She'd done it a thousand times, ten thousand times, but she never got tired of it, and though she felt more for color than for almost any other thing she knew, both living and conceptual, she never, ever used color in her art. No, it was instead light that drew her up to this tower day after day: its soft and powerful settling in the clouds above, its flickering trickery and brilliance on the waves below. Each season, each hour in the day, offered unique expressions of its elusive and maddening splendor, and she was compelled sometimes simply to gaze out and watch it do what it did so well and so reliably.

The baby, the baby, the baby. It was difficult to watch her parents doting over a child who wasn't her. *Ridiculous! I'm not a child.* In truth, she was secretly proud of her mother for being able to conceive a new child at her age; Baeselle Dossilea was by no means young. Still, this baby! After all this time, and at this odd time in history when so much might potentially change and for the worse.

Frainle would love the baby too, and she would help him understand as he grew that there were paths other than Shain's. Yes, she would make sure to do that. Aethrelius would not take another brother from her, no matter her father's designs or flaws. Aethrelius could keep its demands and be damned.

Pinning the paper down with her elbows and forgetting, for the moment, baby, light, and sea, she drew a quick series of dark, thick lines with her charcoal. Had she caught the essence of the figure on the wall? Who was he, really? A guard? Someone who missed his family, doubtless. Though most of the Glaring Cliffs' brigade were permanent residents — or, at least, men who now called this place home — too many young Aethrelean men were rotated through here and made to stand watch on the cold seawalls or the rocky, empty roadways. She'd fallen in the privacy of her heart for at least a half a dozen of them since she was very young; now she wished they'd just stop coming altogether. Who were they? Each had entered service as someone, sure, but service stole his identity and replaced it with longing. She'd seen them arrive and watched them change, all change, and become what Aethrelius needed them to be. Believers. Or at least, pretenders.

And so they stood and watched nothing, nothing but the ocean: no enemy had dared attack these shores since the Twelfth (and last) Delariun Empire still sailed that wild ocean and ruled the Scattered Islands. Their eyes watched the emptiness, and their minds…what went on in their minds? Were they hoping for something, anything to sail toward them, an enemy fleet perhaps, or some ghastly thing far astray from its Garden? Were they hoping to go home, to live out their lives on some farm or fisher's skiff, or were they content to stand there, empty, and watch?

Were their eyes watching her?

She thought again about her father. How long had it been this time? A full season or maybe more. Tolii Nus had been a nightmare, but no, it wasn't just that place or that incident that had kept him away. There had always been a Tolii Nus to tempt him and keep him away.

And there were other considerations that plagued both her family and her nation. So much trouble there was these days with the Stavers and their petty ways. She sighed in relief to think they were nowhere to be seen here at the Cliffs. The closest Staver was leagues away in Chalp, and even there they seemed to know their place. Hateful, scheming dissenters. That's what her mother called them, when she acknowledged their existence at all. She'd known more than a few Stavers in Renikalar. There was rumor she'd even loved one once, but Frainle didn't believe it. Baeselle lived for Leander, just as he lived for Aethrelius.

"Frain, up you up there?"

She smiled to hear Enimuat's voice. He wouldn't come out of the stairwell; he was dreadfully afraid of heights. "No, I've gone down to get ready for supper."

"So you're not actually up there sketching?" he asked playfully but with a trill in his voice.

"What else did you hope I would be doing?"

"I don't know, but I just wanted to believe my friend wasn't mad enough to risk her life for a charcoal drawing."

"The lowliest art is worth a life, is it not written?"

"Yes, it is, by a pompous idiot who, despite his idiocy, knew better than to write two hundred feet above the ocean's shore and its extremely unforgiving rocks."

"Be kind to the rocks. They're beautiful."

"Yes, but also unforgiving. Ask the mussels."

"I will, if you ask the gulls. Now come out here and tell me what you think of my drawing!"

"No, absolutely no! Come down; it's time for supper now."

"Supper? I don't eat supper; you know that!"

"You will tonight. Your mother's sent me to fetch you."

"Has she? Well, then you'd better do so."

"No!"

"Not even for my mother?"

"I..."

"For the sake of perpetuated art, then?"

Enimuat was terrified of heights. Frainle was determined that he should not be.

"Art or word or mother, yes, and yes again, but more so yes to discussing these things where the wind can't bear me down and smash me against those shit-strewn rocks!"

"Your red would add variety to their whiteness, Eni, my love! You would be the grandest mussel of all, for a few seconds at least, and the gulls would sing your praises for generations! Come out here, you coward, if you want to debate the merits of art and the written word!" she laughed.

Enimuat crept forward and poked his head out of the opening. "Coward, is it? Well, let me just say that in truth, I don't wish to debate those merits at all; such a task is beyond one as knee-deep in other arts as myself. I leave it to the scholars of Hunberg to decide which is the greatest art, and as far as I know, none of them would advocate being blown off a tower to one's death in the pursuit of either the art or the decision...please, by all means, abandon your lunatic's errand and come down!"

"I will if you come up and kiss me."

"Kiss you?"

"Yes."

"You're serious?" he said as doubt, fear, and wonder wrestled for control of his heart. Like every other young man within fifty miles of the Glaring Cliffs who could claim the use of healthy eyes and other parts, he'd wanted her from the first moment he'd seen her.

"You'll have to come up to find out."

Eyes closed, Enimuat sighed and then slid his feet forward to risk his life for the promised kiss. He stood there trembling as she sneaked by him and scurried down the stairs.

She was waiting for him ten minutes later when he finally came down, red faced and shaking. "Did you fall asleep up there, or were you admiring the view in defiance of the wind?" she asked.

He slumped against the wall and sank into a crouch. "It took me a full minute to figure out what had happened, and then I had to get up the courage to find the stairs again."

"Well, you were very brave to have come out there the way you did. You must have really wanted that kiss." She puckered her lips playfully.

He said nothing and looked horribly unkissable at the moment. The color had disappeared from his cheeks, and he seemed about to vomit.

She took pity on him. "I'll tell you what: if you'll come sailing with me, I'll give you not one kiss but three!"

"I wish..." he began before giving in to a wild burst of the sudden shivers as his pent-up anxiety got the best of him. Frainle took him in her arms and clutched him close.

"Yes? What is it you wish? Come on, Eni, the day's wasting..."

His shaking eased off, and he found his voice. "I wish I could believe you."

"Ah, but you can! Come with me and see!" She laughed, released him, and ran down the steps and toward the small open lift that would bear her down to the wall, the shore, and the docks.

He didn't follow her this time. Maybe he'd fainted on the stairs.

Poor Eni. So brave in the classroom, so daunted by the physical world.

The lift jerked and shook, but she wasn't afraid. On the contrary, she felt somehow free, fantasizing that it would shake and shatter and that she would become a gull or an eagle or a Visshilla and fly to all the places she'd dreamt of.

You're a little crazy, aren't you, Frain? Shain used to say when he was teasing.

Her answer she still withheld.

She lowered herself down to the wall; the figure upon which she'd earlier fixed her attention had not reappeared. She stood for a moment and stared at the sea, and then she turned and climbed the stairs that led to the keep and her mother's supper.

She entered the dining hall late.

They were all there, some thirty of her fellow Aethreleans, mostly military and diplomatic personnel already well into their meals and debates. Her mother sat at the end of the table, chewing slowly and looking a little sleepy.

The men all dropped their spoons, put down their chalices, and stood up out of respect until Frainle reached her seat. She nodded to them and smiled. They returned the nod and the smile both and then sat down and resumed their feasting.

Ignoring the sour expression on her great-aunt Venla's face, Frainle winked at her mother and reached for the wine.

"Not until you've prayed, child," corrected Venla with a hard tone.

"Have I missed the prayer?" asked Frainle, knowing she had and knowing she'd intended to.

"You missed the prayer, the Recounting, and the first course, yes, dear," said Venla. "But you can make amends for some of that by offering us a prayer now."

"Very well, then: a prayer." Frainle stood dramatically — whereupon all the men stood once again — and intoned loudly:
Renik's blessing on the feast,
We're the lords of all the least,
Have we nothing in defeats,
I hope we all eat rotted beets.

She sat down, poured herself some wine, and took in the mixed reviews of her poem. The few younger soldiers present were smiling and even giggling a bit; the older fellows were stone faced and clearly not amused. They all sat down rather tentatively, as if they were not quite sure she wouldn't pop up with a second and equally lowbrow verse.

Others had reactions as well. Her great-aunt looked ready to shit out a dragon. Eni, who was seated directly across from her, was red-faced and bug eyed. Pliask the Mudarrisi had a slightly bemused expression on his face, but his eyes said his mind was elsewhere. Graig Fredobbil, he of the raging Staver sympathies, glared at her but also smiled a thin and somewhat secretive smile, lascivious but also quietly boastful. Of what, she couldn't say and didn't care.

When had he arrived? Who had asked him here? How badly did he need that smile slapped off his birdlike face? She'd been wrong earlier when she'd assumed there wasn't a Staver within miles of her home. There was one at this table.

Her mother seemed not to have heard her. Baeselle's eyes gazed dully at the far wall; she seemed to be having trouble keeping them open at all. Frainle put down her wine, pushed back her chair, and rose. This time the gentlemen, after offering her a collectively wary glance, kept their seats.

"Mother, are you...how are you feeling?" she asked as she headed around to where her mother sat.

Baeselle broke from her half-stupor enough to offer a half-smile.

"Has no one here noticed that my mother is ill?" exclaimed Frainle.

Venla stood and waved to a nursemaid, who was standing dutifully near the kitchen entrance. "Well, yes, of course. Let's get her to a couch. Excuse us, gentlemen."

Frainle helped the nursemaid, Thusear, guide her mother out of the hall and to a nearby sitting chamber. "There you are, Mother," she said. "Better?"

"Some...thirsty," said Baeselle as she began to fall asleep in earnest.

"Can you please get her some water?" Frainle said, turning to Thusear. "And where is Dr. Sadneesh?"

"The physician's been called for, miss, and here's some water." Thusear handed her a cup of ice water and stood there, waiting with pitcher in hand. The nursemaid's face wore an expression of genuine concern; here at least was someone who loved her mother and not her mother's status as wife to her father.

Baeselle's eyes popped open. She drank a cup of water, then another, and tried to rise.

"Slowly, Mother, slowly. You're not well..."

"I'm fine." Baeselle stood, brushing away all helping hands. "Now what kind of prayer was that, Frainle? I'm sure your father would not have found it at all amusing. No, not a word. Let's go back and try it again, shall we?"

Just like her mother. Not wanting to correct her daughter in front of the other diners, she'd staged a spell and grabbed a private word.

It wasn't so much that she couldn't stand to see Frainle embarrassed, although she must have believed Frainle's conduct in and of itself was oftentimes its own punishment; no, it was more that she was firm in the belief that her family, the bearers of her husband's name, should put forth the best possible face at each and every moment, most especially in front of the men under her husband's command. These men were serious, and serious patriots, and it wouldn't due to have Frainle mock them and their stalwart patriotic convictions to their faces, if at all.

Frainle knew all this about her mother and yet tested her again and again. It was a game they played, a sort of distracting entertainment they engaged in day after day, perhaps to burn away the boredom that marked their lives here.

Having returned to the table, where they were met with courteous nods and even a salute or two, they continued the charade at which her mother was so much more adept than her. As it wouldn't have been appropriate to offer a new prayer just at that moment — the timing would have certainly marked it as having been commanded or at least strongly suggested — Frainle waited until after the main meal to stand and make a remarkably snappy and even slightly sincere toast to her father and the good men of the Fourth Mandate Squadron, wherever they were. She wished them a safe journey home, lamented the loss of life that they had incurred on the now-hated and infamous little island, and, with the watery accent and diction of the original Aethreleans, finished with the Freedom Prayer, in which almost everyone at the table joined her.

And no one blinked, giggled, or corrected. Her mother smiled and began to pick at the dessert torte she'd just been served.

The lid was back on the pot, as Eni might say.

He seemed to have recovered nicely from his earlier brush with death and a kiss. He was constantly schooling her in the art of keeping one's head down and averting suspicion, something she found odd given that he never did much for anyone to get suspicious about. And then, not for the first time, she considered that maybe he did and was just that good at practicing what he preached. Certainly the Mudarrisi were teaching him something in those lessons, though what that might be he never even hinted at. He wasn't permitted to.

The meal had ended, and the men were rising and excusing themselves. Before any of them were able to get away, however, Fredobbil, the Staver sympathizer, tapped a spoon on the table and spoke.

"Gentlemen, ladies, please, if I might have a word before we break, I would be most grateful."

He looked down to the end of the table where Baeselle sat studying him with a cool expression. After a long moment, she nodded.

"Thank you, Lady Dossilea, and thank you, dear guests and family. A particular thanks to Leander and Baeselle's lovely and spirited daughter for her moving rendition of the Freedom Prayer.

"We live in the eye of the storm, we Aethreleans, but that is nothing new. For as long as this great nation has forged its path of decency and democracy and righteousness, we all have understood that whatever is worth having is worth sacrifice.

"And what sacrifice is now being asked of us, and what reward shall we have for having made it, my friends? The time is nigh — no, the time is long overdue — when Aethrelius should be returned to the possession of true and pure Aethreleans! Time for the foreign filth to get out!"

Fredobbil was shouting now, slurring his words somewhat. The men around the table stared darkly at him, barely able to contain their disdain for his Staver ideology. They understood what he and his fellow

Stavers desired: the expulsion of all foreigners from these lands.

Frainle knew what that meant. The Mudarrisi would be forced to leave. And though few here truly believed that those borrowed magickers performed anything but a ceremonial service to the Aethrelean Nation, there were those who feared their removal might invite invasion. The protective storm spells had long held many a would-be conqueror in check, or so it was said. So few had challenged that belief of late; it was impossible to be certain of its validity.

But the Mudarrisi had been with them and among them for so long that they were as Aethrelean, to her mind, as anyone she knew. Wexshai served at her father's side. Old Pliask had served with her grandfather and his father as well. And even poor Enimuat was studying the arts in the hope of somehow contributing to the collective good of the people.

How could they expel their own?

What kind of people were these Stavers to make such definitive distinctions?

They needed to be taught some manners.

She got up from her seat at the table, poured herself a full glass of wine, and walked around to where Fredobbil was still making his hateful speech.

She planted herself in front of him, raised her glass, and shouted:

"This nation welcomes all who embrace the Commandments; this nation repels all those who do not! And the Commandments are ours to defend!"

Fredobbil stared at her. He opened his mouth to reply, and she splashed her full glass of wine right into his mouth, crying, "Time for YOU to get out, Staver!"

Everyone in the room sprang to their feet and cheered for her.

Everyone except her mother, who was instead pointing four guards in Fredobbil's direction. They grabbed him as he coughed and wheezed and dragged him out of the dining hall.

The men were still cheering.

The daughter of their tha'it had just shown what it truly meant to be Aethrelean.

And she'd almost drowned a Staver in wine.

She slept well that night, her heart bursting with pride over what she had done. But she dreamt not of patriotic outbursts or the silencing of hateful partisans. Instead, she saw a figure on the wall, moving closer to her, watching her in her tower even as she watched him.

Chapter 15
"His offer is sincere."

Place: City of Hunberg on Lake Iale, kingdom of Xatumka, Arba Environ
Date: Quattrenim 18, AY 998

The door to the chamber opened.

Hatitorp Manhoui paused a moment, glanced back over his shoulder at the street and the night, and slipped into the chamber.

From the shadows, Sh'arnau watched him carefully. He was crafty, this Hatitorp, and quicker than one might expect of a Quintian of so many years.

Not quick enough to avoid what was coming, though. There would be no help for him now, no escape to the Gapa Islands. His paid passage to that distant hiding place would go unredeemed. He had entered his last chamber and seen his last night sky.

Grewea Lon sat there behind his large desk, a desk that over time Sh'arnau had seen grow from a mere hunk of wood to a place of severe judgment. It was covered in books, papers, trinkets, and vials—each of them no doubt linked somehow to death, deceit, and some terrible plan or other. Grewea was renowned for his merciless involvements and for his terrible plans. Children wept at the sound of his name, it was said, and while that probably wasn't true, it was undeniably true that men of power throughout Arba shit their pants on hearing he'd summoned them.

No, Grewea was not just an old man wise in the ways of politics and commerce, as he sometimes jokingly claimed he was. He was a thing of nightmares. Sh'arnau had played a bitter role in promoting that reputation, and it was a reputation built on actual horrors, not on tales. How many had died to inspire the quivering and the shitting that were now a matter of course?

How many had died at Sh'arnau's hands in the service of Grewea Lon?

Sh'arnau didn't know. Thousands, maybe. It had been so very long, his service to this creature. So long he could not now remember the beginning.

He was sure Grewea didn't much care. The old one was concerned only with the particulars of his private and meticulously calculated intentions, and he was intolerant of anything that distracted him from the same.

And this fool, Hatitorp, had tried to trick him. That qualified as something distracting. A willful attempt to distract. Unwise.

Why had he done that? He was a fool, but he was an informed fool who knew with whom he was dealing. He'd chosen to throw away his life; no other outcome could have come to pass in these circumstances. But why? Sh'arnau felt a moment of pity for a man who could be so victimized by his own greed and stupidity. The Gapa Islands were no cure for a man's own flaws, no place to start fresh when you'd tried to screw over the most dangerous man in the environ. Not that Hatitorp would ever get a chance to understand that firsthand, but still it amazed Sh'arnau how suicidally shortsighted so many otherwise resourceful people could be.

At least Sh'arnau wouldn't have to chase him to Gapa now and waste his time on the water. He found Lake Iale less than inviting, and always had. His home environ had known no lakes.

His home world he could no longer clearly recall. *Trees. There had been trees.*

Two massive black candles burned at the corners of the desk; their holders were shaped like human hands. Hatitorp stared at first one flame and then the other. Was he hoping to blind himself to the inevitable, or had the flames and his predicament mesmerized him into a sort of waking trance of self-delusion wherein his mistakes were conveniently erased? There was a slight smile on his face, as if he were expecting to be rewarded for a job well done. Idiot.

Sh'arnau's disgust with the fool got the better of him; he growled low, but it was enough to reveal his presence in the shadows to Hatitorp's left. The fool's smile disappeared.

"You are sure you were not followed?" asked Grewea, without looking at Hatitorp.

"Yes. Quite sure, yes."

"Close the door."

Hatitorp did as he was told.

"You came the way I told you to, yes, and circled the grounds four times, ever watchful?"

"I'm sorry, I should have…I'm sorry."

"No matter, Hatitorp."

"Sir?"

"Would you like a cup of wine?"

"Why…no, sir, no. I'm fine."

"Are you? How fine can you be when you refuse to share a cup of Wevelor's Finest? Or have you sampled it before and found it wanting?"

"I've…never had the pleasure, sir. I thought…"

"Yes?"

"The Finest is thought to be no more. How did you…?"

"How did I come across a bottle?"

"Yes."

"I didn't. Sh'arnau here came across a full ship's hold worth, not one month ago if I'm not mistaken. Or am I? Was it one or two, Sh'arnau?"

Sh'arnau stepped from the shadows and revealed his full wolfish Thicknomite self. He slid to a position immediately behind Hatitorp, who turned and saw a creature a full three heads taller than him, its eyes glowing a sickly, glazed yellow, its breath rank and smelling of old blood. Sh'arnau ignored the man's reaction; he'd seen it countless times before and had long since become apathetic to the knowledge that it was he who could invoke such abject terror in even a hardened cutthroat.

Hatitorp, playing his part effortlessly, pissed himself. Grewea glanced at both the man and the Thicknomite; Sh'arnau understood he was to take a step back, and so he did. Grewea then rose and poured the unfortunate and terrified man a cup of the wine. He pushed it slowly across the desk toward him. "Here you are. Replenish your inner waters."

Hatitorp quivered and balked but then bravely reached out with a trembling hand and grasped the cup. He glanced behind him at Sh'arnau, who favored him with a small, fanged smile. Hatitorp turned his head away and stood there, shaking and clutching the cup.

"Are you not...not drinking?" he asked Grewea.

"You see, Sh'arnau? Contrary to what you told me, he is very keen, very observant. No, my friend Hatitorp, I am not drinking. I lost the taste for it long before you were born, I must admit."

Sh'arnau wished it were done with, this business. He hated to watch Grewea play with his prey, though he had to admit that, inevitably, the play produced at least some useful piece of information or other. There was method here, not just madness.

"So, let us talk, hmm?" said Grewea, sitting back down in his chair. "You believe you were perhaps followed, Undercambist Manhoui, blessed son of the Four Manhoui, dear old Hatitorp of Fester Quay. Perhaps you wanted to be, and perhaps that's why you failed to approach in the prescribed manner. Perhaps that's even why you forgot to close the door. Were you expecting someone else?"

"No, no."

"Perhaps you invited someone else?"

"I would never presume, sir, please, to invite someone to another man's house."

"And is that what I am to you? Just another man, just another payday?"

"No, sir, no. You are the great Grewea Lon, counsel to the duke ...Fra Chiang of the Mer Ponx!"

"Fra Chiang?" Grewea chuckled. "That's one I haven't heard in a while."

"Please, sir, I was not followed."

"You don't sound confident enough. Sh'arnau, does he sound

confident?"

Sh'arnau shook his head and then made ready, mildly surprised that the interview would be ending so abruptly.

"Ask him why," said Grewea Lon.

Sh'arnau put his hands on Hatitorp's shoulders. The cup of wine fell to the floor.

Grewea coughed and chuckled. "I suppose you're right. The Finest isn't so fine as all that. Reputation undeserved, shall we say?"

"Wait. Stop, please. I am confident I was not followed!" cried Hatitorp.

"Why?"

"Because whoever it is who might have been following me —"

"Or having you followed."

"Or having me followed…"

"Yes, go on," said Grewea as he rose and jauntily made his way over to where Hatitorp was standing. "Lord Thusollus?"

"Yes, Thusollus…or Vaces, or Druthec…"

"Druthec?" asked Grewea in mock surprise. "Druthec Grehmann?"

"Yes, but never mind about him, sir, please…whoever might have thought to follow me also thinks I am working for him."

"Them, you mean."

"Yes, yes. Them."

"Or just 'him' perhaps."

"Him."

"Which is it? Them or him?"

"What?"

"Oh, Hatitorp!" Grewea chided. "It's getting late, and your story is implausible, which leads me to believe you were followed. Or not. Either way, you've come with no information. How do I know this? Because if you had found the information I was looking for, you'd have kept it for yourself, and my man, who was following you, would have had to steal or otherwise take it from you sometime later tonight, perhaps as you were looking to sell it to your friends in the Broken Mind before you boarded your ship to the Gapas."

"I don't understand, sir."

"No? Then let me put it more simply for you: Your presence is a clear indication that you are of no further use to me."

"Lord Grewea, please, I have no friends in the —"

"Sh'arnau."

Sh'arnau ripped Hatitorp's head off his neck.

He caught the body before it fell and gently placed both head and body side by side on the floor. He growled low and sharp once, and within seconds a small, hunched figure emerged from a thin door on the far wall. The figure grabbed Hatitorp's remains and pulled them back to the thin door and through it. A small puddle of blood, mixed now with a bit of Wevelor's Finest, was all that remained to indicate Hatitorp Manhoui's life had ended.

Grewea walked behind his desk and sat down. He reached up to stroke his wiry, unflattering beard, held his hand there for a moment, and forgot to complete the gesture. He reached instead for a black book on the desk in front of him.

"It seems you were right and I was wrong, Sh'arnau. Hatitorp wasn't very useful after all."

He opened the book but didn't look at it. Sh'arnau waited.

"Unless you consider that he did almost exactly what we needed him to. Druthec's people are watching?"

Sh'arnau nodded. There were three; he'd spotted two of them easily. The third was more skilled, but Sh'arnau had seen him on the roof on a nearby shoe merchant's warehouse.

Grewea closed the book, stood, and gave a slight, joyless grin. He came around the desk, placed a hand on Sh'arnau's arm, and walked him toward the door. "That makes me...happy, Sh'arnau. Do I look happy?"

Sh'arnau didn't look at him. It wasn't wise to look at Grewea when he was in this kind of mood. On the surface it might seem playful, but playfulness had nothing to do with it. And while Sh'arnau did not know fear, he did know sorrow, and Grewea could inspire sorrow like none other.

The old man started to speak and then paused a moment, his eyes shifting slowly from left to right and back. He was thinking, and that was a terrible thing to witness, even for one who'd served him for so very long and seen the full range of his wrath.

"Very well. We'll go to the source. Let them follow you. Go and find Oxenhaft. Do what it is you do. Do it quietly, if you'll forgive me my penchant for unnecessary and redundant utterances. I am old. Perhaps you can let them watch you do it, but if you do, make sure they're seen and you're not. Once that's done, my friend, I have one final task for you, and then we can agree to finally end your service."

The Thicknomite stared at Grewea, wide eyed and suddenly even more disconcerted than witnessing his employer's contemplations had left him. He did not understand, and he didn't believe.

Grewea caught the look and chided him much as he had Hatitorp. "Come, Sh'arnau. Are you so surprised? Enough is enough. We've kept you far too long, far longer than we promised we would. If you do this one little thing for me, you can at long last go and be with them."

Sh'arnau stood stone still. Could this be...true? Grewea was not fond of jests, even when in such a "playful" mood...but if this were not a jest, then...

"Go on now, get to it," said Grewea. "And for what it's worth, I thank you."

He turned and walked back to his desk without another word.

Puzzled though he was, Sh'arnau did as he was told and made his way through the wet, narrow streets of Hunberg toward the university. Another Daetelle storm had brought the lake into those streets three days before, and its cool, late-summer waters were just this evening sufficiently receded to allow foot traffic. True to Xatumkan tradition, or at least to Hunberg habit, an impromptu Cleansing Festival had been declared by Makeiron Hall, and the people were stumbling and twitching like marionettes tied to mainsails as they bounced from tavern to tavern.

None of this mattered to Sh'arnau. He was more concerned with luring Druthec Grehmann's men along and doing his duty before they could do something clumsy that would interfere with his objective.

He was certain they were Druthec's men. Neither Lord Thusollus nor Vaces of Trades and Guilds had the stomach or the resources to go up against Grewea, even on the sly. Not that Grewea would let Thusollus or Vaces off the hook; their names had been mentioned, and so their deaths were imminent.

Druthec was another matter. A former Mindman. A soon-to-be-indebted-to-Grewea-for-life former Mindman. Why had he decided to butt heads with Grewea? Or had he? His son was supposed to be the fool, not him.

Tonight, following Sh'arnau, there were indeed three: one a magicker, most likely of the Broken Mind, one a soldier, and a third who was elusive and skilled, probably only discernible because the other two were slowing him down. That one might at least provide a few engaging moments. The other two he'd prefer to dispatch immediately, but he had his orders: someone had to watch it happen.

Sh'arnau led them up into the Highnight District, past the crumbling taverns and the filthy brothels and the madcap outdoor performances. There were small street fires lit everywhere, a dozen per block at least, and the drunken revelers were doing their best to act as if the lake really had cleansed their stinking part of the world, all the while mucking up the job with their vomit and discarded beer tins.

Stupid tradition, that. Xatumkan idiots. There was only one way to cleanse anything. Sh'arnau didn't know much, not anymore, but he knew that. One of the drunks bumped into him, looked up, and grinned. Sh'arnau dragged him into an alley and pinned him against a wall. And yet, the man, so drunk that he could barely see, continued to grin, so

Sh'arnau dropped him and continued on his way.

He imagined the Broken Mind who was following him trying to interrogate the man to learn what they had discussed. The thought brought a slight smile to his face.

He paused on a corner just long enough to ensure he'd be properly followed, although he was sure the stealthy one hadn't bothered with the drunken decoy.

There was one tavern, the Seventh Westerly Inn, he favored. He led his tail away from Highnight's core and toward the Vostliki District, where the homes were deceivingly quiet and the streets empty. At the edge of the Reveler's Delight, where one could view the humbly guised palaces of baron-thieves and statesmen and military power brokers as they rose among the dark, cobbled hills, sat the Seventh.

It was in this place he found the comfort of being among those who understood power, its varied forms, and its consistently complicated nature. He was neither overly feared nor overly respected here; to the others who patronized this place, he was just another very dangerous Arban, a brother who, like them, had tacitly agreed this place was neutral ground.

He entered and approached his usual place at the far corner of the bar. A tall man in the purple cloak of the House of Cruakle, the banker's guild, was in his seat. The bartender, a Mariendan with a missing ear for whom Sh'arnau had little use, rapped his knuckles twice on the bar in front of the banker. The man stiffened slightly and then calmly took his drink, tilted his head in deference to Sh'arnau, and went to find another seat.

"Is he here?" asked Sh'arnau as he sat.

"No," came the bartender's gruff reply. "But soon. Drink?"

"Manafla. Cold."

"Bottle?"

"Two."

The bartender nodded and left to get the bottles. There were some behind the bar, but the better stuff was kept downstairs in the cold cellars. Sh'arnau paid extra for those, but still he smelled the bartender's resentment for being made to go down and grope around in the dark for them. The bartender was a lazy piece of shit and always had been, but he knew how to keep his resentment and anything he happened to overhear to himself. Discretion was valued highly in places such as the Seventh, and his practice of it was no doubt the only reason this particular lazy shit was still alive.

The common room was nearly full but not loud as one would expect given the number of warm — and cold — bodies. There was no music of any kind. Smoke was thick in the place, always, but as usual it smelled not of frantish but of luven tobacco and greunes, both of which were very expensive, very illegal, and very pleasant to most noses. To Sh'arnau, the smoke smelled like shit, seaweed, and rot, but that's what most things smelled like to him unless he was somewhere far away from the cities.

There were women, but they were more ornamental and less obtrusive than they would be at the pubs down in the lower streets. None had ever bothered him save for one, and she was no longer in Hunberg, as far as he knew. He could still smell her scent in the room, as if she'd just walked past him. He wondered idly if she was alive somewhere. A woman could do well for herself down on the lake in the Pebbusku, even with just the one arm…

The bartender returned and placed the drinks on the bar.

"Two bottles. And he just got here. Came up from below, went right upstairs to the open room."

Sh'arnau grabbed the bottles and acknowledged the information with a mild toast. "Then I shall take my refreshment upstairs."

"He asked if you were here yet. He seems a little jumpy."

"I have no doubt."

Before going, he drank down half a bottle of the thick black liquid, a brew that few others in this city could even sip without vomiting or even possibly dying, and then he belched and drank the other half. "This manafla is old," he said, flashing a fanged, yellow smile at the Mariendan.

"My…apologies."

Sh'arnau dropped the empty bottle on the bar and headed to the stairs. It was not lost on the bartender that he had not paid.

He had not intended it to be.

"Sh'arnau."

The voice reached out from the darkness of the room like a whisper. There were only two walls up here on what had once been a corner room on the third floor of the Seventh. A disagreement several years ago had rendered the once-cozy room open to the night air.

"Seastinoa," Sh'arnau said as he peered into the darkest corner. "Are you brooding, sleeping, or drinking?"

"None of the above. I am here to eat. And of course, I know why you're here," came the reply. A flame ignited, and a candle was lit on the corner table.

"I doubt it," Sh'arnau growled as he looked for a chair. He found one and plopped down at the table.

"That shriveled magickal whoremaster has sent you to kill Theodore Oxenhaft. You're here to sound me out on the matter."

Sh'arnau took a long swig from his inadequate manafla and regarded the squat Brull with cold yellow eyes. The creature was dressed in black, as always, and looking a little frayed around the edges. What little hair he had left on his hoglike head was white now. There was a dinner before him, but he had not touched it.

Sh'arnau finished off his second bottle, wiped his mouth, and leaned across the table, putting his face mere inches from the Brull's. "Someday, Seastinoa, you will have to tell me how it is you know what you know."

"And someday I will," said Seastinoa, leaning in closer to Sh'arnau's face. "And on that day, you will also tell me how it is you don't know all you don't, including how to wash your formidable teeth."

"I can tell you now. I remain focused on the present and on the target. And I prefer the smell of my breath to be...memorable."

"The mark of an excellent slave and of a slovenly beast."

"The mark of an excellent killer and a deadly beast."

"Yes. And you are both, are you not, my old friend?" Seastinoa leaned back. He lifted a small bowl with both hands, took a sip of the light-red liquid within, and added, "Or may I say, without causing offense, all four: slave, slovenly, killer, deadly?"

"If you must, you may," said Sh'arnau as he too leaned back.

They shared a mirthless chuckle, each keeping a close watch on the other. Seastinoa reached down to the floor and produced two more bottles of manafla. "I took the liberty."

"I thank you," Sh'arnau said as he pulled the cork out of one of the bottles and drank. "This isn't what they serve here."

"No good?"

"Much better. Unless there's poison in it."

"No poison. I'm more interested in getting paid than in watching you twitch and gyrate on the floor while I eat. Old friend."

Sh'arnau drank some more and stared out at the Xatumkan capital. He hated this city. He'd spent decades in and around it, and during that time his hatred of it had grown incrementally, but he wasn't sure why. "Is that what we are, Seastinoa? Old friends?"

"We have a long, shared history. We've saved one another's lives once or twice. We've fought on the same side a dozen times."

"And on opposite sides more often than that."

The Brull belched and then thumped his chest twice with the side of his fist. "True enough. But today, in this place, we emphasize the sharing, the saving, and the fighting side-by-side, and conclude that, for the moment, we are...friends."

"Agreed." Sh'arnau raised his bottle in salute, and the other raised his bowl. "So tell me again, friend. Why am I here?"

"You want to know if you should do it."

"Yes."

"You want to know why Grewea has finally agreed to free you."

"Go on."

"You want to know if his offer is sincere. And you want to know what task could mean so much to him that it would warrant releasing you after so many centuries."

Sh'arnau finished the bottle and stared at Seastinoa, who began to pick at his plate of fried oysters and clams. He reached over, grabbed a handful of the Brull's meal, and threw it into his mouth. "You have answers?" he asked his friend, for whose delays and games he had less use than for the torn remains of the disgusting clams in his teeth.

"What are you offering?"

"What would you like?" Sh'arnau grabbed more of the other's dinner despite his dislike of the stuff. His eating was more about compulsion than pleasure: a Thicknomite needed frequent feedings. A weakness, to be sure, and not one he had fully mastered despite centuries of earnest attempts.

"Another plate of clams and oysters, I think."

"Done. Anything else?"

"Let me think about it."

"Very well," said Sh'arnau. He knew enough not to press on this point. "Tell me."

"You want to know now, or shall I give you a more thorough answer via courier? Your choice," Seastinoa chirped. "Now will cost you more."

"My task is expected to be completed tonight. Tell me."

Seastinoa shoved the last handful of seafood into his wide, round, gray face. He chewed for a few moments, swallowed, and let out a barely audible belch. "His offer is sincere. You should do what he asks because...there is no other way for you. Grewea himself must choose to release you."

"What is it he wants of me?"

"He wants you to find something, something very old...older perhaps than you. Something very powerful — an object. Something that might not even exist except in tales."

"What object?"

"This I do not see."

"But you are sure about the rest?"

"Absolutely. Do what he asks, and he will free you."

Sh'arnau rose and started for the door.

"Wait. There is something else."

Sh'arnau stopped but did not turn around. He had expected this, for with Seastinoa, there was always a further condition, tacked on for not only the sake of playful, Brullish intrigue but also expense. Each word would cost, and so he was surprised to hear only four:

"Do not kill Oxenhaft."

"What? Why not?"

"Oxenhaft must live. If you or anyone else kills him, you will never be free."

"I don't understand."

"Neither do I. But you know how this works: understanding is not a prerequisite to sight, nor is it a guaranteed effect."

"Grewea was clear in his demand —"

"I know. But you were having doubts when you came in here. I have only confirmed them for you," the Brull said with a slight smile. He seemed very much to enjoy his client's discomfort; it was rare he had Sh'arnau at a disadvantage, and he wasn't going to let the moment pass unexploited.

"I have never disobeyed him."

"Tonight, you must."

Sh'arnau turned to face Seastinoa. "And if I don't?"

The Brull took a small sip from his bowl and looked away.

"I see," said Sh'arnau.

"There is one more thing you need to know. No charge for this."

"I'm not sure I want to hear any more from you tonight."

"Nor I from you, but our desires are like farts near a fire, are they not?"

"What is it, then?"

"Someone is watching. Someone even I can't see."

Sh'arnau was not at all surprised by this information. He'd felt something odd even while following that idiot from Fester Quay. It was a feeling he'd felt before. "Masters?" he asked, knowing the answer.

"I cannot say."

"How interesting." And then he added, "I assume you know I was followed here."

"Grehmann's people. Yes. Broken Mind."

"Watch out for them."

"It's not me they want, but I appreciate the warning."

Sh'arnau stood up, nodded to Seastinoa, and went downstairs. "Bring two more plates of whatever he was eating up to him. And get some better manafla," he barked at the bartender as he threw a small bag of coins on the bar.

Sh'arnau turned and left the barroom. This time, he descended the stairs to the lower exit so as not to make things too easy for his tail.

He felt slightly more puzzled than he'd been before the meeting, not at all a common perspective for him. The Brull had never misled him, not in over twelve decades, not even when they'd nearly killed each other — twice — and yet this information was difficult to reconcile. How could he expect Grewea to honor any promise if he failed to carry out his orders tonight?

Killing Oxenhaft was no trivial task; the man was a member of the Mind and possibly the most famous individual in Xatumka, if not all of Arba. The grandson of one of the Four. The head of the university. Grewea would know Sh'arnau had broken ranks if Oxenhaft saw the morning.

So what then was the game? Leverage? Impossible: no one got the better of Grewea, ever. Sh'arnau had served him for almost three hundred years, and no one ever had.

Yet of all the nights in all those three hundred years, this one was most assuredly the oddest.

He exited the Seventh and, making sure his tail picked him up again, continued on his way.

An hour later, after stopping a few more times to take in some music and drink bad beer — the low taverns never offered manafla — Sh'arnau climbed his way up and out of Highnight. He came to Raja's Wall and paused for a moment to admire its decaying design. Porous and neglected, broken by centuries of endless wind and absent attention, it nonetheless stood vigilant and thick with memory.

He strode along a gravel path that wove through dead grass and dead shrubs. The sounds of music and laughter wafted up and mixed with that of the wind. He turned and looked out at the lake. Two ships coming in by night: a Challowian from the west and some merchant vessel inching its way toward the harbor. Now that the storm had passed, the lake was calm enough to sail at night. If you chose to sail. He rarely did. He hated the water and always would.

He hopped over another, less renowned wall into the Garden of Waiting, where once the wives of the Last Quadrate Armada had set up a vigil in expectation of their men returning from the Lake War's final battle. But those ships had sailed away and were lost somewhere for reasons no history had recorded and no person living now knew.

Sh'arnau had known, but as with so many memories, he'd chosen to let that knowledge go. Some said the ghosts of those wives still sat and waited for men long dead who had never returned and never would. Perhaps they were waiting for him to provide them with the answers and comfort they sought. If so, they waited in vain.

Sh'arnau knew other ghosts who were waiting, persons he'd tried to forget but could not after countless attempts and near-limitless anguish. Those ghosts had been waiting much, much longer than even those in this rotting park. He had no answers for them either.

But he often found that despite himself, he still had questions.

He turned to look once more out over the city and the lake. He lit his pipe and watched. The Challowian vessel had turned south, away from the city.

The city was afire with cries of false salvation; the lake was as calm as a friend who came for dinner and stories of wealth but left your cupboard exhausted, your purse no fuller, and your wife pregnant. The lake was a thief and a liar. Anyone who thought differently was a victim trapped in a fool's vest.

But what was he if not that? Grewea would not tolerate anything but obedience. Theodore Oxenhaft needed to die. None of this made any sense to Sh'arnau, and he found himself beginning to mistrust Seastinoa. Who had gotten to him? Was that even really Seastinoa he'd spoken to? Even with centuries of exposure to magick and its effects, Sh'arnau was never quite sure when it was in play and to what degree. It was the single most irritating thing about his job.

He sat for a while, pondering his situation. He only moved again when he was sure his pursuers had spotted him.

He left the Garden and traced along a very steep wall until he found the east-facing Quality Steps. He had only to climb them, to pass through the university gate and ask for Oxenhaft, and it would be done. Simple.

It had been so long. But it was true, and he could feel it was true: Grewea was not deceiving him. After three centuries of service, three centuries of murder and war and disgrace, he would finally be going to them. He wondered: Would they remember him? Would they know his face after all this time? Would they remember what he'd done and why? He knew that even after so many years and so much distance between them, they still might not have forgiven him. They might very well hate him. It was a chance he had long been willing to take, if only to look upon their faces for one moment.

He found he could not move.

So long, so long. Waiting. Yes, like the wives in the Garden, he had waited. And now his wait was over.

And he could not move.

Oxenhaft? Who was Oxenhaft to him? A holy man, but not holy to Sh'arnau. If the fools who worshipped in the churches of ONOF hadn't thought to protect this man, this son of a son of a god, or a saint, or whatever that Tristan had been, they deserved to see him die.

Oxenhaft must die. And he would make that happen. He would destroy the man and find the object Grewea desired and then finally embrace the death that had so long eluded him.

He heard something behind him.

"You there. You work for Grewea, yes?"

Sh'arnau stared at Druthec's Broken Mind magicker coldly.

"We know why you are here," the man continued. He was a thin reed of a man in a bluish-gray robe, and he had a mildly insane look about him — not unusual for a man of his order.

"And why are you here?" asked Sh'arnau, his voice neutral.

"Only to observe and to make certain the job is done," said a soldier who stepped forward and joined his magickal companion.

Sh'arnau noted the man's light crossbow, his scimitar and red leather. "One of F'nios's boys, huh? You're a long way from home."

"So are you," said the soldier.

Sh'arnau looked at him. "Agreed." He wondered where the third man was. "So tell me this," he said. "Why does Druthec want him dead?"

"Druthec's desires are complicated and not of your concern. Oxenhaft must die," barked the magicker.

Sh'arnau gave a slight shrug and said, "True of all of us, or most of us, unless I've been mistaken all these years." The irony of his words stung him, but only momentarily.

The soldier and the magicker stood before him, no doubt trying to determine his mind. Sh'arnau wasn't in any hurry and hadn't decided yet what exactly he should do, so he stood there too and did not move. The winds kicked up, and the flames flickered in the street lamps.

"We were wondering why you've been taking your time getting up here. Was it something the Brull said to you?" the soldier asked, breaking the silence.

"I was enjoying the festival."

"Indeed. The Time. But what of Oxenhaft?" asked the Broken Mind magicker.

"I have decided not to."

"Not to? Not to what? Grewea Lon holds your essence, does he not? Have you really a choice in this matter?" cried the magicker.

"He holds my essence, yes, but there are limits to that power."

"Indeed, Sh'arnau of the Northern Plains, there are. Sh'arnau of the Xereshon as well, no? And Malliorelum's Bane? How many names have you garnered during your service to Grewea Lon and his hateful ilk? How many did you serve before him, and how many names did they bestow upon you?"

Sh'arnau offered the so-called magicker a blank stare and then turned back toward the lake.

"You are what you are, Sh'arnau," said the soldier firmly. "Do what it is you came to do. We will not interfere."

"And if I refuse?"

"You will not!" said the Broken Mind.

"I may."

"Why?"

"I'm not at liberty to say. You can, of course, try to force an answer from me."

"We have a contingency plan. Do you?" asked the Broken Mind.

"I confess, I do not. I so rarely require one," growled Sh'arnau, who despite himself was beginning to find this conversation almost interesting.

"Then step aside and let us do your duty," said F'nios's man.

"Not my duty. Never my duty."

"Forgive me. I misspoke."

"Why are you really here?" Sh'arnau asked. "I know it's not for observation, nor are you anyone's contingency plan. Grewea has complete faith in my abilities."

"Not tonight, he doesn't. Please...step aside," said the soldier.

Sh'arnau did. He let them pass, the magicker, the soldier, and then the third, who suddenly slipped out from a nearby alley. He was an assassin from Patrick's Essentials. Sh'arnau had had dealings with his kind before, long ago, on Fan Pell; they'd used scents to block his olfactory sense. This one had done the same.

Tricky bastard.

And now he knew what he was up against.

He swung his mace at the head of the passing assassin. The mace didn't hit the mark, but it did knock the parrying Essential back down the steps.

"What are you doing?" cried the magicker, his throat already taking on the deep whisper of his magick. "You cannot strive against the...no!"

Sh'arnau threw a dagger that buried itself deep into the magicker's forehead.

The soldier had turned and was in midswing with a halberd, but Sh'arnau ducked and then crushed the man's skull with the speed of a striking serpent, instantly killing him.

Something whisked through the air and clipped Sh'arnau's snout.

He knew without turning around that the Essential would have witnessed the deaths of his party and disappeared. It wasn't the assassins' way to confront foes head on, particularly foes as thoroughly tested in battle as Sh'arnau. The dart was more to cover the retreat than to invite further trouble.

He clutched at his snout and felt a little wetness. Blood. No poison, or at least none that would affect him. Perhaps. Time would tell.

He looked up. Something was moving high above: two cloaked figures peering down from up on the university wall. They were watching him, just as Seastinoa had told him they would.

Would they be pleased at his decision? Did they know what it had cost him? They could go fuck themselves, meddling pieces of dung that they were.

He started back down the hill but turned toward the lake and then back around when he reached Raja's Wall. There was something he needed to do before reporting back to Grewea, and he had little time.

Chapter 16
Unexpected, but not determinative.

Place: Lake Iale, just west of Hunberg, kingdom of Xatumka, Arba Environ
Date: Quattrenim 19, AY 998

"Who are you?" asked the thrashing, whining thing in the bag.

"My name is Sh'arnau. Be quiet."

"Sh'arnau, the Rage of Thicknom?"

"Yes."

The bag was silent for a moment. Sh'arnau held it on his shoulder and noted how heavy it was. He watched the lake and waited for their boat to round the pier.

"Why have you brought me here? If you're going to kill me —"

"Just be still for now. We have a long journey ahead, and there is still danger."

"Danger? What danger? Where are we going?"

"There are people who want you dead. We're going where they won't find you."

The bag seemed to weigh this information. Its contents stopped thrashing, and all Sh'arnau could hear was some labored breathing.

"Can I get out of this bag?"

Sh'arnau stopped and considered this. There was no one near to see them. And as long as he could get the man to stop talking and breathe more normally, no one would hear them either.

He decided the best way to get the bag to shut up and calm down was to answer his questions and then, if he wouldn't agree to be still, to make him pass out from pain. He opened the bag; out crawled his famous and powerful charge, looking neither famous nor powerful.

Theodore Oxenhaft stood slowly and brushed himself off. His underclothes were disheveled, his face and tight beard covered in sweat. He regarded Sh'arnau cursorily and nodded to him. "Thank you. For saving my life. I'll take my robes back now. And my shoes."

Sh'arnau returned the nod. "No robes. No shoes. Had to use them. And no need to thank me."

"You did save me, yes?"

"I did."

"How? And why?" asked Theodore as he looked about him, no doubt trying to determine where he was and if it were possible to escape.

"I pushed you off the Seer's Walk."

"That was you?"

"Yes."

"But you obviously did something other than just push me, because clearly I didn't die…"

"Yes, obviously."

"I fell into some kind of a net, correct?"

"I had to make it seem as if you had been killed."

"So one now assumes. But why?"

"It was the only way to save you."

"Understood. Save me from…whom?"

"From me." The boat came into view. "There's our ride."

"Our ride! Of course," cried Theodore sarcastically. "And where are we going, or don't I get to ask that? Never mind! It doesn't matter. I can't get on a boat."

"I understand."

"Do you?"

"If I never saw another boat in my life, I would be glad of it. But right now, we need to get you someplace where everyone isn't trying to kill you."

"Including you?"

"No, I'm done killing you."

"You make almost no sense. And I still can't get on a boat."

The plan to placate the man by answering his questions was looking less and less viable with each moment. Sh'arnau took him by the arm and guided him firmly toward the pier. There was very little wind, but he could smell rain on the way. More rain.

Theodore resisted the walk but was no match for Sh'arnau. "I know you. You're Grewea's man. His famously lethal Thicknomite."

"None other."

"We've seen each other before. At the Mind meetings."

"Twice. He usually doesn't require me in Pashka."

"He sent you to stage my death?"

"No. He sent me to kill you."

"But you didn't. Why?"

"I don't know."

"Still not making much sense, you."

"I'm making just enough sense to afford you one more day of breathing," said Sh'arnau as he took hold of the rope the boatman threw toward the dock.

"I need to get back to the university," stated Theodore flatly. Here was a man used to having his needs attended to. *He's going to have to get used to something else,* thought Sh'arnau.

"That's not possible now. We're leaving," he said.

Theodore pulled away from him and stood there, somewhat imperiously despite his lack of clothing. "No, we're not. Let me ask you:

Do you have any idea what would happen if I just disappeared on some boat with…with you?"

"I just told you I faked your death," Sh'arnau said. "Going back is not an option."

"Until when? Surely this farce must have an end game…"

"It does. You're dead. No going back from dead."

"You mean, ever? I can never go back — is what you're saying?"

"You can never go back. Correct."

"That's insane."

"That's the price. And right now I'm trying to decide where it is you can go without ever being seen. We can't run forever."

Theodore, though clearly distressed, seemed for a moment to exude something like sympathy for his kidnapper. "You really didn't think this through, did you?"

"No, I didn't. There wasn't time. Would you prefer I let you die?"

Alarm bells were sounding in the distance. The university guards, such as they were, would be out in force; by now, they would have discovered what Sh'arnau had left for them.

"No. I'd prefer to live. On my own terms. Let me go."

"I cannot."

"So I'm a prisoner?"

"Not unless you need to be."

"But I've got to…there's someone waiting — "

"Whatever you had planned, it's no longer relevant. Once again, let me explain, and for the last time: if you want to live, we need everyone to believe you're dead."

"The only way they'll believe that is if they find my body."

"They already have."

Sh'arnau guided Theodore on board and down into the hold. He handed him a large black cloak, some knickers, and some sandals. Theodore regarded the garments with something like dismay and indignation, but after a moment, he quietly slipped into them.

The boat left the dock, and they settled in for the journey, each unhappy to be on board but for entirely different reasons. After a while, the Thicknomite gave the scholar some bread and water and a few pieces of dried melon. The food, the drink, and the sitting seemed to have a calming effect on Theodore. He was suddenly quite contemplative, almost sedate compared to how he'd been minutes before. His breathing had slowed considerably as well.

Sh'arnau was impressed by the man's apparent self-control. He seemed to have accepted, at least for the moment, the reality of his situation and seemed resigned not to waste any more energy railing against it.

They sat in silence for a while longer. Sh'arnau didn't for a moment believe he'd heard the last of Theodore's objections, but for now they both just sat listening to the wind, the water, and the creak of the boat as it made its way to the next point in their new journey.

A while later, Sh'arnau left the shocked man to his doubtlessly frenzied contemplations and climbed up to the deck of the small craft.

Having stopped only to quickly pick up his passengers, Derric, a wiry old man who was quite possibly the most gutless human in Xatumka, a fact that didn't negate his willingless to do just about anything for barbs, was piloting the ship along the coast, away from the city, keeping just within sight of the shore. He regarded the uncomfortable look on his lethal employer's face. "Still not very fond of boats, are you?" he asked.

Sh'arnau snarled, "Boats are fine. When they're in dry dock."

"Listen, I don't know who you've got down there, but someone's looking for him. There were lights and skiffs circling like buzzards around there five minutes after we kicked off."

"Were we followed?"

"No, I don't think so."

"I doubt we will be."

"Because...?"

"Because whoever's looking for him in the water will be told to call off the search by those who've recently found him. He'll be just recognizable enough for the poorly observant to conclude the man they're looking for is dead." Sh'arnau was almost certain he believed the ruse himself. "Put ashore at the Riles; my men there will pay you once we're gone."

Derric didn't miss the mention of the "men" — but it wasn't as if Sh'arnau needed anything but the weight of his own terrible reputation to command obedience from the Derrics of the world. The prospect of having to deal with mere men was no doubt more comforting than threatening. Derric always seemed much more at ease when his business with Sh'arnau was through. That wasn't unusual in Sh'arnau's experience. Most people felt better when he wasn't around. He took no offense.

"No rush. I know you're good for it. Let me ask you: If so many are looking for the person in my hold, what chance do you give me of surviving the night?" the boatman asked.

"Don't worry, friend. You keep your mouth and eyes shut, as always, and you'll get paid and be on your way, as always." Knowing men tended to take him literally at the most inopportune times, Sh'arnau added, "Well, don't close your eyes, but don't see anything you shouldn't."

"Will do. Or won't do," was Derric's attempt at a comical reply.

Sh'arnau ignored him. He turned away and headed toward the bow. It was a cool night, and the recent storm had left behind some ragged wind and chilling dampness. Rain was still pending, but that wouldn't affect their journey.

He sat on the deck and crossed his legs in front on him. He rubbed his snout where the Essential's dart had grazed him. It burned. The dart had probably been poisoned, sure. Being what he was, Sh'arnau could usually only be annoyed by poison. Thicknomites as old as he (Had there ever been one as old as he? Probably not on this world, and he'd been so young when he'd been taken from his own that he now remembered next to nothing about it) were vulnerable to several kinds of attack but not to poison. Still, the effects of this particular one were proving more lastingly annoying than he'd believed they would. And as he was fond of remind- ing others, anything can die, even the oldest Thicknomite on the OS Maeketel.

Looking up at the dark sky, he considered his options. Dying was definitely one of them, although it was not his first choice. The others weren't so alluring either.

Now that he had Theodore Oxenhaft, he had to figure out what to do with him. Grewea's spies were everywhere. Oxenhaft's own people and the Triumvirate buffoons would assume he'd been murdered — Sh'arnau had timed his move to ensure there were at least a half a dozen witness- es — but without a clearly identifiable body to confirm the story, Grewea would remain suspicious and unsatisfied. Eventually, the truth would out.

Sh'arnau would have to report within the hour in any case.

What was particularly troubling was that he'd said too much to Druthec's men. Was it overconfidence or the pending sojourn into forbidden territory that had opened his mouth so widely and so foolishly? The one who got away, the Essential, might have heard what he'd said to the magicker. He might have heard, and he might tell. Someone. He might also be a Redeemer spy. It didn't seem to make sense that Grewea would have an Essential working for Druthec and then spying on both Druthec and Sh'arnau, but then, it made perfect sense. Grewea's spies were every- where, and his mind worked like an incomprehensible machine.

Sh'arnau had to proceed with the assumption that Grewea knew exactly what he'd done. But he still had to go to him and receive his final instructions. He still had to hope somehow that Grewea was willing and able to free him. If not, Oxenhaft was his leverage. If Grewea wanted him dead, he'd have to agree to terms.

And it had to be that way. Grewea had promised him a hundred times before that he would be released. Each time, Sh'arnau had, against all reason and experience, believed him. This time, he had the advantage; this time, he would force the monster's hand. And he'd do his best to forget Seastinoa's warning.

The hard, black water of the lake slapped against the boat's hull. They weren't moving fast enough. Sh'arnau looked up and saw that Derric wasn't at the wheel. He got up and headed toward the hold.

"That's Fat Teddy down there," Derric said.

"Yes."

"What are you doing with him?"

"You don't need to know."

"Yes, I do. He's a Mindman and the head of the school…we can't—"

"You were paid to provide a few hours' safe passage. Nothing more."

"No…this is too much. They'll find me…those wizards, or the Essentials."

"No one knows of your involvement."

"I'll tell them. I have to. No amount of money could—"

Sh'arnau ran his thinstick through Derric's throat.

He cut the body a few times to make it bleed and then pitched it into the water. The lake's watery greed would handle the rest, but now he'd have to have one of his men get rid of the boat. Unexpected, but not determinative. The critical part of his plan—what plan there was, anyway—involved getting Theodore out of Wauni and either into the Sapphire Forest or somewhere far north. He hadn't decided which yet. For now, Fat Teddy would stay hidden.

But now he had a more pressing question: Who would steer this boat?

He went below to rouse Theodore, who at least had the courtesy to display mild amusement at the irony of being asked to actively participate in his own abduction. Sh'arnau in turn was not at all shocked to hear Theodore claim he was an excellent sailor. "Not much time for sailing when your face is buried in books, I'd think," Sh'arnau remarked with doubt in his voice.

"You would think so, wouldn't you? But no, I wasn't always just a scholar. When I was a young man, I even served in the navy for a short time."

"The church let you do that?"

Theodore shrugged and then made his way up out of the cabin onto the deck. Sh'arnau followed. "They didn't know, not at first. I joined under an assumed name," Theodore said as he took hold of the wheel. "Saw the whole of Lake Iale and beyond. Miranquella, Grellgorot, Aethrelius, Bno Suj…I even spent a few days in Wrangun. Tell me please, in which direction shall I steer this noble vessel?"

"Do you see those blue lights there? Steer us toward those."

Theodore turned their craft toward the shore and the lights. "Do you miss it? Wrangun?" Theodore asked as he turned the wheel slightly and put them on course.

"What makes you think I've ever been there?" Sh'arnau was not particularly interested in having a discussion about himself.

"Other than for the obvious?"

"I've never gone."

"But if you're not from there…are you telling me you came directly from Uo?"

"Indirectly. Yes. A long time ago."

"I should say." Theodore paused and seem to think for a moment. "Tell me you weren't with the Horde?"

"I was."

Theodore coughed and shook his head. "Forgive me. I had no idea your people could live so long."

"They can't. I did."

"Apparently. I must tell you, I am genuinely fascinated," said Theodore, coughing again.

"I don't care. We're here. Put this damn boat in."

They put ashore. Three of Sh'arnau's men approached them and began tying off the boat.

"Take this thing out into the lake and sink it," Sh'arnau growled.

Without a word, one of the three stepped aboard and made the boat ready to head back out. The other two untied the bow and aft lines they'd just secured. One of them whistled, and two more men stepped out from behind a tree grove on the shore. They came out, secured a small rowboat to the aft of the late Derric's craft, and then stepped back while the first three headed out onto the lake to make good on Sh'arnau's command.

Theodore looked to be completely exhausted, as if he might pass out. His calm self-control seemed to have suddenly dissipated, and his attempts to regain it were less than convincing.

Sh'arnau gripped his shoulders and looked hard into his eyes. "Are you all right?" he asked.

"Not really. That trip…and the fall…who are you…why?"

"You look sick."

"I…am…sick."

"It will pass. The lake wasn't that rough tonight."

"It's not seasickness, not just, anyway. I have Plaetithon's."

"Plaetithon's? I didn't know that," Sh'arnau said, watching the man's face for lies.

"Few do. We kept it a close secret at the university. Not even my father knew."

"Your father doesn't have the resources I do. Damn it. You're not lying, are you?"

"No. Believe me, this is something no one could fake." He bent over slightly and then heaved out the contents of his stomach. Sh'arnau could smell blood.

"Can you travel?"

"Travel...where? I can't..."

"I told you, we can't stay near Hunberg if you want to live."

"I need to rest, or I'll die anyway."

Sh'arnau thought a moment and then nodded. "We can't stay here long."

"A short while should be all I need," Theodore rasped. He coughed a few times and then asked, "Do you have...is there any Quintish viahrta root?"

Sh'arnau motioned to one of his men, a reedy-looking man in battered greenish lake garb. "We've got roots at the Sincere, no?" Sh'arnau asked.

"Not sure," said the man. "We should. Thimi keeps that place stocked, but he's been down at the Bents since his woman — "

"Quintish viahrta, now!" Sh'arnau cut in. Turning to Theodore, he asked, "How much?"

"I need to make the tea, maybe two or three pints..."

"There's that fishing village," said the reedy man. "About a half hour west, in Mattan."

"Mattan is more like an hour from here," said Sh'arnau. "Nowhere closer?"

The man shook his head and looked at the floor.

Sh'arnau took Theodore's face in his claws and shook him a little. "You need to ride about an hour. Can you do that?"

"No. No, I cannot," Theodore answered groggily.

"Is there somewhere else, somewhere local?" Sh'arnau asked the man.

"This time of night? Doubt it. Riles ain't got much. Maybe over in Mattan."

"You said that, Pedram. Mattan is too far, damn it..."

"No, sorry, I meant Molish...Molish, not Mattan. Molish'll have something!"

"How long?"

"Twenty minutes there, twenty back. Five more if the place is open, ten if it's not."

"Go," Sh'arnau said, grabbing the man's arm. "And you know what happens if he dies."

Pedram nodded, terrified, and sprinted away toward the stable.

Sh'arnau looked down at Theodore, who was now wheezing and sitting on the ground. How could he have missed this? Moving a sick man in secret was twice as difficult as moving a healthy one. "Is there anything else that can help you get by until Pedram returns?"

"Water. And rest."

"Tret, get him inside."

The other man moved next to Theodore and knelt. "Is this, uh, platey-thing…is it catching?"

"Only if we mate."

Tret raised his eyebrows momentarily and then began to help Theodore to his feet. "I hope you won't be insulted if I pass," said Tret.

"On which? The mating or the catching?" Theodore chuckled between coughs.

"Both, beggin' yer pardon."

Sh'arnau watched them approach the small fisher's cabin at the other end of the dock. Then he sat down, closed his eyes, and listened to the night.

He could hear Oxenhaft wheezing and coughing and Tret grunting a bit under the weight of his charge's lean. The wind was steady through the trees, and the water lapped against the pylons and the lakewall. A whestibird called out from somewhere off in the pine grove that lined the east–west road. And the fading thud of Pedram's horse's hooves was the only other sound from that road. The few fisherhouses in the Riles were either shut down tight for the night or unoccupied altogether, their owners somewhere out on the vast lake angling or bootlegging or snoring in their small cabins, their bellies filled with raw salmon and Kisstari liquor.

Good. He, his captive, and his men were, so far, alone.

Why hadn't the scholar mentioned his disease? What would it gain him to die? Nothing.

Then why…ah. Of course. Theodore wasn't a fool. He was attempting to slow them down so…what? So his men from the university could find them. But how, given the precautions he must now assume Sh'arnau had taken, did he expect that to happen? Who would have been able to track them from the wall to the shore out onto the lake and then here?

It didn't matter. Fat Teddy was expecting someone, someone who would save him from the grip of the Thicknomite Terror. Someone formidable.

Sh'arnau found a position on the roof and waited.

He didn't have to wait long.

There were six of them. Tri soldiers. Battle hardened, or at least, they looked the part.

Their fatal mistake was not knowing who they were up against. Or rather, assuming that whoever they were up against wouldn't be up to dealing with their apparently battle-hardened selves.

Sh'arnau kept one of them alive, the youngest of the bunch, because young, lower-ranked foot soldiers were often terrified or brazen enough to offer answers, even to questions he wouldn't think to ask. And he was genuinely curious about how they'd been able to locate Fat Teddy so directly.

Unfortunately for him, the youngest also turned out to be the head of this unit: Commander Distrel Muertiva, born in the Measured Fields on the fourteenth of Feschille, trained at the Trink, assigned eleven months ago to the Hunberg University guard to keep an eye on Theodore. He enjoyed rabbit, the Slaver Trials, Miranquellan wine (but not the older vintages), and well-muscled young men. Under Sh'arnau's gentle guidance, he confessed more about himself than anyone would ever care to know or remember.

What he was unable to confess was the one thing Sh'arnau really needed to know. Either he never had a clue how they'd tracked their prey, or the shock of having his right arm pulled off had somehow relieved him of any access he might otherwise have had to that information. Sh'arnau couldn't be sure. The unit had simply been told where to go to find Oxenhaft, but what remained a mystery was: Who'd done the telling?

Commander Muertiva bled out within minutes. No more rabbit for him.

Sh'arnau went into the cottage and nodded to Tret to go outside.

"Your little unit has found you," Sh'arnau said to an even more groggy Theodore.

"My what?"

"If I were you, I'd dispense with the feigned ignorance. It might get you killed, and I really wouldn't want to see that happen."

Theodore opened his eyes and regarded the Thicknomite. "Where are they?"

"Outside."

"Dead or alive?"

"Very much dead."

Theodore sighed and shook his head. He tried to stand up but immediately reconsidered. "I knew their commander's mother. A distant cousin of mine. I have to send word."

"No, you don't. What you have to do is answer me now. No lies."

"Very well."

"The Plaetithon's is real?"

"It is."

"Is it lethal?"

Theodore hesitated. "Rarely," he admitted.

"How did your cousin's child find us?"

"I don't know."

Sh'arnau stepped closer to Theodore. "I'll ask you again, but only once more. Before you answer, please understand that while I've got my reasons for not killing you, there's no reason I can't hurt you. Badly."

Theodore threw him a look of impatient disgust. "Imagine my shock at hearing a threat upon my person," he said, scowling. "This being the first time, you'll have to walk me through it. How should I respond?"

Sh'arnau grabbed his throat and squeezed just a little. "How did they track you?"

"They didn't. They tracked you," Theodore wheezed.

"Explain."

"They were tipped off that you might be coming for me."

"Me, specifically?"

"Yes."

"By whom?"

"I think you already know the answer to that question."

"But...why would he..." Sh'arnau released his grip on Theodore's throat and took one step back. None of this was making any sense.

Theodore rubbed his throat and coughed a few more times. "I have no idea. Perhaps he wanted you to know he was watching. Perhaps he has a plan within a plan you're not aware of. I suspect with him that's always true, yes? The important question to consider is this: If he sent you to kill me but knew you wouldn't, why did he send you at all? If he wanted me to live, why send you at all?"

"He wanted it to seem as if you had been killed," said Sh'arnau.

"It would seem so."

"But why?"

Theodore looked deflated and exhausted, and he didn't look like he was faking either. "We have more questions than answers, my friend. And our lives depend on how we deal with both. For now, I'd like that tea you promised. Plaetithon's may not be lethal, but it is very, very uncomfortable, and I think your man has just returned to us. Or Grewea has sent another emissary on horseback to kill us."

"You'll get your tea," said Sh'arnau. But what he didn't say was that Theodore, if his story held, might also have known that Sh'arnau would be coming for him — and yet he'd done nothing to avoid his fate.

The man clearly believed he was twice as clever as he needed to be to fool the Thicknomite. Sh'arnau decided right then to let him keep believing that until such time as the story sufficiently unfolded. In an odd way, there was something almost comforting in all this mystery. After so many years of performing tasks almost by rote, it was almost a pleasure to be, at last and at least, somewhat confounded.

Chapter 17
"What's with the whistles?"

Place: On the road to Wukneesh, kingdom of Arbana, Arba Environ
Date: Quattrenim 20, AY 998

"My people are leaving here."

"Which people? Your family?" asked William.

"No, no. Not just my family. All the Slau. They…we…are leaving Arba."

"Why?"

"We are not from here," replied Cvuklon. "Nobody is, really, but we are not the race that belongs here now. That distinction belongs to your people. For what it's worth."

"Ain't worth much, huh?"

"Time, you perhaps don't know, is short. For all of us."

"I don't understand. Is there something wrong?"

"Have you heard the term 'Proving,' William?"

"I've heard it, yeah. I can't claim to be able to tell you what it refers to, though."

"Ha-ha. Few can, my friend, although every person you meet seems to have a unique, fascinating, and entirely groundless opinion on the matter. This world is peopled by idiots."

William regarded the chuckling Slau for a moment and asked, "That so?"

"Oh, yes. It is so."

"Which? The part about everyone being an idiot or the part about no one knowing what this Proving really means?"

"Both, of course. And when I say everyone, I include myself. I am perhaps the biggest idiot of them all, if my calculations are correct." Cvuklon chuckled again and took a swig of water. He offered the flask to William, who gladly grabbed and drained it.

"Don't know what it is about this damn place that makes me so thirsty all the time."

"I don't know. Maybe it's the two suns. I understand the world you come from only has one."

"Yup. One. And your planet?"

"This is my planet. I was born here, William. As were most of the people you will meet here. Only a few are taken from off-world each year, and most of those die."

"Tell me about it."

They rode in silence for a while. The day was actually quite cool.

Autumn was coming, or so it seemed to William. He hadn't been here long, but somehow the seasons seemed a bit different from those he was used to on Earth. Different, like just about everything else.

Cvuklon had told him they were headed to south to Wukneesh, the grandest city in the Arbanan hills, or at least a place where Cvuklon had relatives more sympathetic than his uncle. He hadn't said much more about it, but William liked the kid and was in no shape to make alternate plans. It seemed everywhere he'd been in Arba so far--at least those parts he could even vaguely recall--had brought him nothing but lousy luck and worse pain, so sticking with someone who treated him civilly, answered his questions, and fed him didn't seem so bad.

The hill country here reminded him of a part of Texas he'd once seen on a visit to a college buddy in San Antonio. The vegetation was very different — Arbana, which he now understood was just a region, as opposed to Arba, which was the name of the whole environ, whatever that was, was no Texas climate-wise — but the granite and limestone sticking up through the tight, gnarled patches of grass rendered these hills somehow familiar to his eyes. He'd never been, but he imagined this might be how certain regions in Pakistan or western Canada might look. It took him a moment to admit to himself, for the thousandth time since he'd arrived here, that those were the kinds of places he'd never see again, not on Earth. But these hills, here, were almost...peaceful.

After a while, he asked, "So what do you think? About this Proving, I mean."

"Me? I think it's real. My people have seen it in action several times. We Slau failed to Prove over four thousand years ago. No one remembers why or how. Just that most of us died, and those who didn't were those who had been wise enough to flee."

"To where?"

"Everywhere. Anywhere. No one knows for sure, of course, but it's assumed that our kind our scattered over the whole planet."

"And now you live here. Some of you."

"Yes, for almost seven hundred years. We Slau here in Arba call ourselves 'the Unwalien.' It means...'forever seeking' or 'lost for eternity' or something dramatic like that. My Slauween is terrible. Don't tell any-one."

"Your secret is safe with me," William said, having no idea who Cvuklon thought he might tell. He smiled at that. He liked the kid and was getting used to the more froggy aspects of his otherwise cheerful face. "Long time, seven hundred years. Must be tough to have to pack up and leave after so long a time."

"Yes, it is," Cvuklon said, "but it's something my people have done often enough to become accustomed to it, if one can become accustomed to moving an entire race thousands of miles to a new and most likely unwelcoming place. In any case, it would be...unpleasant if we decided otherwise."

"Forever not seeking anymore, huh?"

"Exactly."

"Where will you go this time?" William asked.

"That is an interesting question. Many things have changed in the last seven centuries. And given that we have run from the Nulling of so many other races so many times — as well as our own — we are running out of places to run to. But we have a place in mind."

"The Nulling of...what do you mean?"

"If a race fails to Prove, they are erased from their place."

"What do you mean, 'erased'?"

"None are left alive within the environ."

"My God! Who would do such a thing?"

"God indeed, William. Maybe that one. Actually, no one is sure. Or if anyone knows, he isn't saying."

"And let me see if I understand: you're saying this Proving...your people are fleeing Arba because this thing is supposed to happen soon?"

"Yes. In just about two years, at the end of the millennia, it happens. 'Every race gets its thousand,' or so it is said."

"What year is it?"

"The year 999 is soon to begin. Two more years, and it is over. You came to this place at the wrong time, my friend."

"No shit. Story of my life."

"Ha. Mine as well, mine as well," said Cvuklon as he nodded in agreement and then shook his head in apparent despair.

William thought for a while about this new information. Maybe it wasn't such a bad thing. He'd died and gone to hell, but hell was ending. Or maybe it wasn't. He laughed despite himself to think even death had left him with no clue as to what was really happening around him. "Is there anything that might prevent this...to prevent it?" he asked Cvuklon.

"Well, yes, there is always the chance that you humans will Prove."

"How much of a chance?"

"We have never seen it happen."

"Never?"

"No. No one Proves. You either flee or you die."

"Terrific."

"Maybe you can come with us."

"With you?"

"Yes, and my family. We are currently planning on taking a ship to Decone and maybe finding a place to live in Prement. The Prementians'

Proving isn't for another four hundred years, and they are a hospitable people. To some, that is. But my father wants to go to the desert where no one lives."

"Why?"

"He believes the Vo'ixtavracci will take Prement soon. Or at least, their war will find its way to Prement. Many Slau agree with him. For a very long time, we Unwalien have mostly stuck together as a people, traveling from place to place, but I'm afraid that might not be possible now. Our people might split up over this debate."

"Who are the Voxtavaratchee?"

"Vo'ixtavracci. I'm sorry, William. I have horrified your fledgling mind enough for one afternoon, and we need to get back on the road in any case."

"Pretty bad, huh?"

"Worse even than the Nulling, if you can believe that."

"What could be worse than being erased?"

"Being consumed."

That night they made camp among a few small limestone formations just off the road. The chill in the air begged them to make a fire, but they were concerned about bandits, so they refrained. Cvuklon set about preparing a light, cold meal. William fed the gremfi small brown roots. The animal looked at him dolefully, and William felt a stab.

Sylvester.

He'd loved those books. Pooh. Piglet.

Eeyore.

He held out another root and patted the gremfi's long, donkey-like skull.

"Well, if your ears weren't so much like an elephant's, I guess you would be Eeyore, wouldn't you, pal?" he asked the deliberately chewing beast. "Mind if I call you Eeyore? Or would you prefer Dumbo?" He glanced at the back of the animal to check its gender. "I've heard him call you 'she' once or twice, so maybe Eeyore isn't the right choice. How 'bout...Eeyora?"

The gremfi stopped chewing and turned its head left, staring off into the darkness. Then William heard the noise.

The precaution they'd taken with the fire, though sound, soon proved pointless. While they ate their evening meal, it became apparent fairly quickly that bandits had already spotted them and were whistling back and forth.

"I wonder: Will they have the courtesy to wait until we are through eating?" Cvuklon said, a small trill of nervousness in his voice.

"What's with the whistles?" William asked.

Cvuklon came over, patted Eeyora a few times on the neck and then whispered something in her ear. She immediately settled down and accepted the handful of roots he offered her. "It's a thing they do, these so-called bandits. They believe they're being crafty, sounding like nightbirds. But they, like so many, as I explained, are idiots. The birds they are imitating have been extinct for over one hundred years. They all died from some funny disease that made their feathers fall off."

"That doesn't sound so funny."

"Forgive me, yes, you are right. But the sight of them...anyway, there are limericks about the poor vamana bird that are...amusing."

"They sound like they're getting closer."

"Yes. But don't worry. We have nothing they want. They'll harass us a bit, maybe take our food, and move on."

"Not your first rodeo?"

"I'm sorry?"

"Um...you've been through this before, huh?"

"Of course. This...rodeo...is a regular occurrence on the slave roads, especially for those who don't travel with protection, but sometimes for the protected as well. Come, eat something before they take it all."

It didn't take long for the bandits to give up the whistling and approach the camp. Three of them strolled in and sat down as if they were long-expected friends.

"Pleasant evening," said the tallest one.

"Pleasant evening to you," Cvuklon replied, nodding to them.

"What's that you're eatin'?" asked another bandit, this one missing an arm and wearing a cloak that was a few sizes too big for him.

"Just some dried fish and bread. A few sweet roots. Not much."

"It's a chilly night. Why no fire?" asked the tall one.

Cvuklon smiled as best he could and held out his hands in a placating manner. "I think you know why. But now you're here. Come, have some fish and pleasant conversation."

"Don't he talk?" said the bandit who hadn't yet said anything as he pointed at William.

"Not much, I'm afraid. He's a Mindless One, so he isn't much for conversation. Bread?"

"We already ate," said the tall one, who seemed to be the leader. "Mindless, huh? His eyes look awful bright for that. Where'd you find him?"

"My uncle—perhaps you know him, Grivtel—he purchased him at the Tent City."

"Did he?" replied the man as he grabbed a piece of fish, chewed it, and spit it out. "That's some shit fish you got there, Slau boy."

"It's not for everyone. Do you know my uncle?"

"I've never heard the name." It was a lie. Every bandit and slaver between here and Bno Suj knew Grivtel's name. He'd outnegotiated, outplayed, and outright cheated most of them.

The bandit who'd pointed at William spoke out again. "Gribble's the slug that tricked Vensol out of those horses last winter."

"You're sure?" asked the apparent bandit leader, such as he was.

"Gribble. Yes. That was his name. Eleven horses. Tricked him with some garbage about the law. Vensol was fumin', he was."

"Is that true, sluggy? Your uncle a tricky slug?" the tall one asked softly as he looked out into the night.

"There's no need for rude talk. And as for this alleged deal, I wouldn't know. I wasn't present."

"Well, my friend Foplu here was," he said, gesturing to the third bandit, "and that's what he said happened. I guess what I'm saying is, you owe us. More than shit fish and conversation." The tall one stood up; his companions placed their hands on their weapons. "Well, I expect you know what's next."

"You want something, of course, as a tribute, but unfortunately other than the fish and conversation, we don't have much."

"You've got him."

"He's not for sale."

"Did I say we were interested in buying? You must have misheard me. We're more the taking sort, we are."

"You have no right under the slaver's law."

Out came the weapons.

Cvuklon's small knife stayed sheathed.

"We have every right. Eleven horses for one Mindless One? Shit. You're lucky we don't take you too."

"The law forbids the enslavement of Slau. It also forbids the appropriation of slaves without a proper and clear display of right and currency. I expect you know what the penalty is, yes?"

The man without the arm shifted uncomfortably. "Sinhag," he said to the tall one, "maybe we should listen to him."

"We're taking what he's got."

"No, we shouldn't. Not like this. I can't lose my other arm, brother."

"You're not losing another arm, Hak," said Sinhag.

And now I know their names, these idiots, thought Cvuklon. If they took William, he'd have an argument to make before the Bigs. If they didn't kill him first. It wasn't much, but it gave him a moment's comfort.

Foplu slid over to the other two and whispered something to Sinhag. Sinhag nodded, gestured at William a few times, and asked Foplu, "You're sure?" twice.

When the whisper conference was over, the three bandits adopted a placid stance.

"Okay, seems like we've had a slight misunderstanding. We've decided to go get the proof you're asking for so we can then collect what's owed. Where are you headed?"

"They have to be going to Wukneesh," said Foplu.

Sinhag nodded. "Is that right? You headed to Wukneesh?"

Cvuklon didn't see any point in denying it. He had to go there in any case, and maybe he could get help from Dalter Bubussa's contact. "Yes. Wukneesh. I have family there," he lied.

"And isn't family a pleasant thing to have?" asked Sinhag. "I lost all mine years ago. The war you slugs keep having with the catheads took them."

"I'm sorry," said Cvuklon.

"Yeah. Me too," answered Sinhag. "Well, we're leaving you now, but when you get to Wukneesh, stick around. Don't disappear with our property, slug."

Cvuklon decided to ask. "And you are?"

"We're with the Gumundurs. Have a good night."

And with that, the three bandits left them alone.

Not seeing a reason not to, Cvuklon went about building a nice, warm fire. As he did so, he muttered, "Don't worry," to William often enough to ensure the man would soon be very worried, if he had any idea what was at stake. Cvuklon chuckled despite the situation as he acknowledged that he himself had no idea what was at stake. Despite his superior intellect and unmatchable cunning, he was really just a puppet, and it made him extremely uncomfortable.

"You think we'll see them in Wuck Knees?" asked William.

"Wukneesh. And I don't know. I thought they were fairly ordinary bandits except for that Foplu. Normally when I invoke my uncle's name or drop hints about the slaver's law, these types take a little fish and disappear back into the hills. These seemed fairly certain about their claim, and they were too specific about our plans—and theirs—for my liking."

"But that's not all."

"No."

"Spit it out."

"They claim to be Gumundurs. This is a very organized and formidable group of bandits; they mostly deal in soldier-slaves for the Highway and specimens for Pir Choss."

"You believe them?"

"Maybe. They mentioned a man named Vensol, and he is known to me. This is not a group we want to have trouble with."

"You think your uncle screwed them?"

"If that means what I think it means, yes, he probably did."

"Not good?"

"No, not good. The Gumundurs don't take kindly to being… screwed, and Vensol hates my uncle. Still, I highly doubt they'll be able to acquire the requisite proof, and even if they do, we'll be long gone from Wukneesh, I think."

"Maybe we shouldn't go there at all. Why give them what they want?"

Cvuklon just shook his head and stared at his newly made fire. "Don't be concerned. Please. I will think of something."

They slept a few hours and were headed back down the road before either sun peeked above the horizon. Neither said much. Cvuklon was lost in thought and a little bit run down. *He probably isn't used to all this running*, William thought.

He himself was having trouble physically. The effects of the evil leaf had worn off, or so Cvuklon had promised, but William was still exhausted and in pain. The days here were much longer than those on Earth; they seemed to go on forever. And William had been a teacher whose major physical challenges in life were the occasional ski slope, sprint to first base, or heavy load to the curb on garbage night. He wasn't in bad shape, but hiking hills and long dirt roads was more than a match for him.

At least they had good weather. In fact, it had been balmy ever since the hellacious weather he'd experienced just after he'd left the Landing Point in those nasty chains and that odd purple skullcap. Cvuklon told him the summer season, what they called Daetel around here, would be ending soon.

"And then after dark winter, we have Chairo. Cool air, leaves changing…you have this back on…where you come from?

"We do. We call it autumn." William didn't ask what "dark winter" was. He wasn't in the mood for any more depressing information.

He'd always enjoyed autumn. He and Wanda each had a birthday in September, and they'd also been married outside on their lawn in that same month. They'd done the wedding themselves to save money. The money had gone to home improvements. When they had a home. When there was an October and a Wanda.

In autumn there had been pumpkins and costumes and apples and cider and children, always children…and the dogs, and walks among the leaves, and the raking and the children jumping in the leaves…

The pain of loss was still very much with him, though not every minute of every waking hour like it had been in the hospital. He was thankful for that because he was starting to be able to think a little more clearly about what was going on around him.

He wondered why that was. Why was it "still very much with him" yet not driving him further and further into madness? What had the trip to Arba cost him? What had it done to him?

As for his family, in his mind he could still see their faces and hear their voices, but both the faces and the voices were somewhat distorted. They were not gone, but they were going, and the thought horrified him. He'd died, he was sure of it…but then where were they? Why hadn't he joined them?

And then the thought occurred to him.

Maybe they were here.

Maybe they'd come through and were somehow in Arba.

That thought, as he strode alongside Cvuklon and Eeyora in the strange autumn air, made him double over in physical agony. How could he find them? How would he protect them? Sylvester and Yancy and Wanda, alone, here, in this insane, vicious place. Had they come through the Landing Point? Had they survived that nightmare? How could they? How could children survive that?

And yet some had. He'd seen them. He was sure he'd seen them.

"Are you all right, my friend?" asked Cvuklon.

"Yes, all right. I am. Fine," William answered, thinking: *I have to get back there. I have to get to the Landing Point and find them. I have to leave this kid and figure out where I am and somehow make it back there.*

That afternoon, they reached Wukneesh.

To William's eye, it was not a great city, or really a city at all, but then he hadn't seen settlements of any kind other than the Tents and the small town around the Landing Point, and while the former had been impressively sprawling, it was hardly Manhattan. This, by comparison, was scarcely a village.

The people here were a mix of Pumcat, Slau, humans, and a whole bunch of races William might have seen at the Tents but couldn't name. Cvuklon led them through the several narrow streets, asking the occasional Slau about a cottage. Everyone knew which cottage he meant, or assured him they did, but each one pointed him in a fruitless direction.

"I don't understand it. This place isn't all that big," said William as they went down yet another path that led pretty much nowhere. "How could a cottage hide here?"

"It isn't hiding. But these people are misleading us because they've been told to."

"Who told you to come here?"

"Dalter Bubussa."

"That guy? And you're just going along with it? Jesus."

"No, don't say that!" Cvuklon hissed.

"What?" William asked, taking aback by the Slau's sudden anger.

"What you just said. That began with 'je'...don't!"

"Why?"

"Because that is a word that will get even you killed, Ashorne," a woman's voice whispered behind them.

They turned to see a small, gray-haired woman with a walking stick grimacing at them. "Here in Arba, Earth's religions are not to be spoken of," she said.

"You're the one we're supposed to meet? You are Clara?" Cvuklon asked.

The old woman turned and started walking away. Over her shoulder, she said, "Maybe. Maybe not. But come back to the cottage, and we'll talk a while. You can decide then who was supposed to meet who — and who I am to you."

Chapter 18
Through inclusion, through tolerance, through faith…

Place: Renikalar, the capital city of the Great Aethrelean Nation,
Aethrelius, Arba Environ
Date: Quattrenim 22, AY 998

"Janstrin Beir, what is the true focus of your ambition?"

Czackus Hall fell silent as the question hung in the air. The flickering of a thousand candles was all that was heard.

Leander stood at his place at the Unchained's First Table and waited, his look of practiced patience masking the mounting rage he now felt. After a full minute of silence, one of Beir's new allies spoke:

"Tha'it Beir, don't answer that question. It isn't legitimate, and it isn't respectful."

Another minute's pause elapsed, during which time Leander began to wonder if Beir had somehow gone deaf. If not, his impersonation of a deaf man was impressive.

Eventually, Janstrin Beir, tha'it of Deer Vale Province and newly elected chief of the Caucus, rose slowly from his chair and said, "No, it is neither legitimate nor respectful, and thank you, Minister Pou'esi, but I will answer the question, if for no other reason than to humor the vanquished."

He's put on weight, too. Deaf and fat now, is it? thought Leander.

Beir looked squarely at Leander Dossilea and walked around the edge of his own party's first table, never taking his eyes off the man who had questioned him. He strode almost bouncily to the center of the hall; once there, he began to laugh.

"Something is funny, Beir?" asked Killinad Furain of Greater Bay.

Beir continued to laugh for a few moments and then calmed to a chuckle. He stopped chuckling and just stood there, with a broad smile on his lips, still staring at Leander. "Yes, Furain, something is funny. Why else would I be laughing?"

"I find your lack of respect disconcerting," said Furain.

Beir raised one finger to his small, pointed beard in a mock show of contemplation. "Well, to be sure, there is a shortage of respect under this venerated ceiling this evening. But let's cut to the quick. Answers were requested and promised.

"First, I'll answer your question, Furain. What I find funny is this: it occurred to me, as I sat over there and listened for — what's it been, four hours? Five? As you once-unassailable, still-righteous windbags struggled to make some kind of argument to delay or even head off the inevitable result of these proceedings, it occurred to me that you haven't the slightest idea what you're doing. The position in which last week's Full Session left you is so utterly unfamiliar to all of you that you have utterly no idea how to act. Well, I'll tell you how to act, because like everyone else sitting on that side of the room, year after year after year, I've gotten a lot of practice.

"First, you need to make a lot of noise about how absolutely unfair everything that's happened here — the calling, the vote, the appeal — has been from top to bottom. That part you've done very well at, I should think, very well indeed, particularly for novices. I commend you."

The tension in the room was palpable. No one was interested in hearing what anyone else might say, and violence was only held at bay by the timeworn practice of restraint through convention. Such practices had been earned over the many years, and the bill for their status here today had been paid in blood.

"Second, and here's where you're starting to have trouble: you need to begin to realize and even to accept that the structure of our procedural laws and government don't offer the slightest chance that the seemingly horrible and unthinkable results you see before you now can ever be overturned, not by you, not by the judiciary, not by Renik himself were he to stumble through those big old doors right now with a flask in one hand and that faerie-tale dirk in the other.

"Lastly, you need now to simply shut up and listen, just the way we've been told for five decades to shut up and listen, and you need to do it without insult, without protest, and without in any way unlawfully or discommandmentarily interfering in the rightful, destined, efficacious functioning of this auspicious Square."

He paused a moment and passed his eyes slowly over the faces of those at the Unchained Tables, finally lighting on Leander's. And then he smiled and said: "You lost, gentlemen. Brace yourselves or recuse yourselves, but you lost. Act accordingly."

Beir laughed once again and started to return to his seat, but then he stopped and looked once again at Leander. "And as for my ambition and its true focus, Dossilea, I think I've made that quite clear throughout the recent campaign and debates. My focus is on returning this Great Aethrelean Nation to greatness. My focus is on purging the debris from our streets, our schools, our markets and, yes, our military so that each and every true and good Aethrelean receives what they are entitled by birthright to receive: food, shelter, comfort, protection, and education.

"My brothers and I believe Aethrelius has been stolen in the night from the Aethreleans. We intend to get her back and to punish the bastards who've taken her!"

The side of the room belonging to the Stavers erupted with

applause. Beir tipped his head and returned to his seat.

Leander stood up and slowly walked to the spot where Beir had delivered his answers. It was time for him to respond, to say what needed to be said in the here and now. His country might have been usurped by madmen, but he and his allies must be heard, if only to put the opposition on notice. The fight was not over.

When they saw him, the Stavers abruptly stopped applauding and began to hiss. By contrast, each representative of the Unchained stood, one by one, and remained standing, silently, as they waited for Leander to speak.

"Aethreleans, my friends, my colleagues…why is there an Aethrelius? Why do we do what we do? Why are we what we are? Is there truly an Aethrelean way of life, an ideology that can be clearly defined and reliably fixed in times of doubt and conflict, yet adaptable and wise enough to encourage honorable expansion of both its most cherished principles and our perpetually necessitated interpretation of them? Who are we, and what do we believe, and why? What did Renik believe? What did Frederick believe? Are the Commandments they authored timeless mandates, ideas intended to weather change and storm and emerge un-altered and strong, or are they tools designed to shape a tomorrow the challenges of which few of us can accurately predict or imagine?

"And who is an Aethrelean? What does he look like? What does he believe, what does he hold dear? Those who came east so long ago were of many races and every color…some were not even human, some had beliefs and appetites and preferences and habits and histories so repulsive to the others that few ever spoke plainly of these things in mixed company…and yet, they all came east, and they were all, when the Good Work was done, Aethreleans.

All shed blood to gain this land. All shed blood to defend it. Whose hands did more work than his brother's? Who built our country? Our canals, our aqueducts, our docks, our towns, our fortresses? Only the men of Lingler? Only the folk of Stestipha or Bvay or Jensenom?

"No. This nation was created by the many and varied peoples, linked not by a shared past or shared genetics or even a shared set of religious beliefs but by a desire to build something better than what they'd known before. It was faith in this new nation that bound them together and gave them the will and freedom to persist and thrive. It was a careful, persistent examination and judicious, tolerant application of our Commandments that many times kept our varied peoples from all manner of conflict. Including, on more than one desperate occasion, civil war.

"Our people have since the founding of this country invested their mutual, collective faith in the idea that fairness and inclusion and freedom would be available to all who desired them. Many came to find those things, which were offered them freely, though the price for their acquisition was not cheap. New Aethreleans, whatever their origin and wherever their settlement, have always accepted eagerly the need to help perpetuate both this nation and the principles on which it was founded. 'New Aethreleans' is a curious term, in fact, because at one point or other in this great nation's history, we were indeed all new. Before Renik, there was no Aethrelius. He was the first. Should he have said, when crops failed and plagues ravaged the populace, that all others should be shouldered with the blame for those maladies and so be exported or even murdered to return his new nation to glory and prosperity? Should Renik have stood alone as the sole original Aethrelean?

"No. He would not have done that. He believed in the unimpeachable power of cooperation and faith. He believed in law and work and comradery. It is our great fortune that many extraordinary men and women who followed him in leading this country to its present status as the one truly free place in all Arba shared his beliefs. They guided us, but we followed their lead. We did so together, through inclusion, through tolerance, through faith.

"You now have the power. For many years, you Stavers — the party whose very name invokes the need to repel rather than embrace — have longed for this day, and though I may never understand why it has come, it has arrived. I ask you now to pause a moment and consider what I've said here today. I ask you to understand the true history of this country. It has ever been a history of interdependence, of inclusion, of new strengths through new combinations and additions. If you turn your backs now on those principles, you will usher in the end of our culture, for you will have robbed it of its greatest strength: diversity. We are the better for all of us being one.

"And if you somehow follow through with your suspected intention to focus your ire first and foremost on the Mudarrisi, who have for centuries helped ensure the safety of this nation, you may indeed forfeit all our lives for the sake of a misguided impulse."

Leander turned and walked back to his seat. When he sat, every member of his party sat with him.

Beir rose, clapping his hands together slowly and once again laughing. "I'm always warmed to hear the slanted, righteous rhetoric of a bastion of the glorious and eternal Unchained, particularly in this chamber, where so many oratorical wonders have echoed from corner to corner and out every window to the waiting, eager ears in the plaza below. How brilliant Cornus Wie was to have designed this place for such maximum and far-reaching effect. Its domes can, through mere yet mighty augmentation, transmute even the blackest of lies or the most eerily silent of omissions into resounding and unquestionable truth. We here and all below have heard the majestic intonations of good Leander Dossilea, captain, warrior, governor, husband, father…and fool."

There was now a murmur of discontent from the Unchained side of the room.

"Yes, fool, I said, and fool I meant, if he attempts in any way to convince us of this sham he calls 'inclusion.' Commandmentary? Diverse? Nonsense. Or did you forget, Leander, and would you imply by your omission that we too have forgotten or would forget, how this country came to be? Whose lands were these before we came? I'll tell you, I'll tell you all, just to be sure we're clear on this point: Aethrelius once belonged entirely to the creatures we now call Saiblinorans. Once, this place was Abtrinora. You all know the name.

"We took this land from those creatures by force and without mercy. They had no strength, no beliefs, no enlightened sense of judiciously orchestrated freedom and comfort: they were animals. And we killed them, most of them. We did so because history had rendered a ruling: it was time for their culture to submit to our own. And so it did.

"Most died. Some remained, and most who did were removed and resettled on the rock that is Saiblinor. Those first Aethreleans never indicated any regret for what they'd done. They never apologized to the Abtrinorans. They did what was in their rights to do. Genocide? Hardly. Today the descendants of the Abtrinorans are everywhere – in the Teeth, in the lands of the Slau, in Arbana, and even, they say, in Jamoi. They hold a privileged position in Pir Choss – most there live better than Duke Velliok himself, they say.

"And do you know what I say? Good for them. The animals have had their day. But the time for whatever charity our ancestors once thought proper to extend them is over. They and all the other visitors who have poisoned our culture must be made to go. They don't make us stronger, and they don't make us more unified. What they do is drain our resources, stink up our cities, and put our women and children ill at ease. They must go, and so they will. And somehow, Leander Dossilea, we will have to hold our trembling nation together without their great contributions to our diversity.

"And as for the poor Mudarrisi, well, let's leave my 'suspected intention' alone for the nonce, shall we?"

An attendant entered and bowed. "I am sorry, my lords, and do beg for the interruption, but Minister Yallous is requesting Tha'it Dossilea's presence," he said.

"What is it then, Retoue?" asked Leander of the attendant.

"Again, I apologize, but the physicians are indicating the minister has only…has a very short time before he is taken."

Leander rose and left the hall.

He was there, in a small bed—fitting for a man his size, a man who had never stood more than chest high to most men in the room and yet had led armies larger than the population of all Renikalar. There was a strong fire going in each of the room's two fireplaces. Above the bed was a very large painting, a depiction of the Two Brothers and their Son, and its subtle colors and shadows seemed to render the scene somehow a natural extension of the bedchamber.

Candles burned low around the room, useless in their efforts with the fires so high. Yallous himself looked nearly spent, almost an empty thing, a misplaced gnome that someone had forgotten to feed for a very long time. His eyes were no longer bright; the medicines the men from Pir Choss had administered seemed to dull him to the point of near silence and absence, but his smile was just as it had ever been: welcoming, true, and unreadable. "So, you're here," he said to Leander.

"I am."

"Tolii Nus?"

"Not good."

"I heard." The old man wiggled a bit and slowly sat himself up. Leander made to help him, but a small shake of Yallous's head told him help wasn't wanted.

"I assume you know about the vote," said Leander, hoping the answer was "no."

"I am sick, not dead. Not yet." Yallous looked from right to left and then over to the other side of the room. "Could you…there is some water on that stand…yes."

Leander poured a cup of lukewarm water into a small mug with a handle that looked like a sea dragon. He knelt next to the bed and handed it to his old teacher. "It isn't cold."

"Hmm. Yes, good, thank you," Yallous said, sipping from the cup. "Not supposed to be…cold water increases the pain tenfold…though I can tell you, it's so hot in here it's almost worth it."

Leander rose and found a stool against the far wall. He carried it to the bedside and sat down. He watched the old man sip his water, and he closed his eyes. He was tired, and seeing his friend this way was, on top of everything else, almost too much to bear.

"Am I that hideous that you cannot look upon me?" Yallous coughed with soft bemusement. "Very well. Let us sit, eyes closed, and pray. Or at least, nap. You look like you could use it."

Leander didn't answer, and Yallous fell silent.

They sat that way for an hour or so, just as they'd often done after lessons back at the Cliffs when this strange and powerful man had taken on a ten-year-old Leander as his student. How many lessons had there been, and how many arguments, and how many battles had they fought together through the years? Leander tried to recall and couldn't. His capacity to count had been usurped by other numbers: the number of essential votes that had been stolen, the number of years they'd held off the madness, the number of dead that lay now and forever on — or in — that useless island.

He opened his eyes and tried to smile at his old friend. "Remember, Yallous, when we knew what to do and were strong enough to do it?"

The old man chuckled softly and then coughed twice. "The Brull. The Creli Monshua," he said.

"The Stestipha Containment."

"The Containment. Yes. I remember, my friend. We knew what to do."

"We were all we were supposed to be. Protectors, facilitators, peacemakers —"

"Yes."

They each fell silent again, but eyes open this time, Leander half gazing at the painting, Yallous quietly looking down at his damp nightshirt and waiting for his friend to continue. When he didn't, Yallous prodded: "And now?"

"Now." Leander stared harder at the painting: at the keep, at the fields of dead grass, and the three dead warriors resting with their backs against the Battrishea pine. The tree's massive, twisted trunk seemed somehow to be repelling them, tilting their bodies in such a way that at any moment they might each topple over and roll back down the hill they had so deliberately climbed. Above them, looking down with an absent, cold expression, a young child hid behind a cluster of pinecones and needles, its feet and fingers scarcely visible, its wise, threatening eyes nearly lidded but expectant and even sinister. "Now I fear we're lost. Now I fear the Aethrelius I loved and defended..."

"Is less than it was?" asked Yallous.

"Yes."

"And you don't know what to do."

"I know what I could do but not what I should."

"You cannot challenge the vote," stated Yallous. "It would undermine the process so fully as to destroy it."

"But what is the worth of a process that has betrayed its own nature? A process that has under the guise of legitimacy ceded power to the Stavers?"

"The process remains true. It was never intended to preordain results, only to provide opportunity."

Leander looked at the old man with a question in his eyes. "What opportunity is there now?"

"You can leave here."

"Leave? And go where? The Stavers cannot govern this land. With what they plan to do, the government will fall—"

"Then it falls." Yallous shrugged.

"I cannot let that happen."

"Aethrelius is more than a place, Leander."

"Yes, this much is certain. And yet, it is also a place."

"The place itself is incidental. Aethrelius is—has always been—a noble idea."

"I know it."

"Then you know the Aethrelean idea will not perish, not from this crisis or any other. What we believe here we can believe somewhere else."

"A new country?"

"Why not? This old country has been fading away for years, as surely as I now fade. The Stavers are but a symptom of an ideological disease…for which I fear there is no cure."

"I cannot abandon this place," said Leander flatly.

"If you do not, there will be war."

"We've averted war before."

"True. But always we had the people behind us. Most of them."

"I cannot believe the people want war."

"The people don't know what they want, Leander, not anymore. They can no longer understand the argument for remaining separate and apart. They want what the Three Thieves have, but they don't understand what they'd have to give up to get it."

"Where, Yallous? Where would we go?"

"Where indeed. That was Renik's second question."

"What was his first?"

"'Why?'"

There was a knock at the door. A Saiblinoran with a tray opened the door halfway and peeked in. "I'm sorry. Shall I…?" said the nursemaid.

"Please, let me," said Leander. He took the tray from her and placed it on the stand.

"Tha'it, sir, only a little longer, please," the nursemaid said. "He needs his rest."

"What he needs is a seaworthy skiff loaded with thatch and oil somewhere off the Mouth," coughed Yallous.

"Thank you, mistress," said Leander as he gently closed the door. He sat down beside the bed and thought for a moment. His eyes wandered again to the painting, but he quickly closed them and lowered his head. "I know what you're suggesting. We've spoken about this before. I cannot go to him."

"I'm not sure I understand why. I know why you felt that way then, but why still?"

"Nothing has changed. He abandoned us in our time of need."

"Perhaps, but that isn't why you've chosen to foreclose on the idea altogether."

"I know what I believe, but I expect you have a different reason in mind."

"You are too much like him. It's part of the reason you find yourself in the current predicament. I would also say it's an essential determiner of our current national predicament."

"How so?"

"He would have stayed had you asked him."

"He would have gone regardless. Vincent only ever followed Vincent, and once his mind was settled, there was no force that could stir or change it."

"I know differently."

"How so?"

"I know because he told me. And I believed him."

"He was always very good at making people believe him."

"Except for you, Leander. Except for you."

Leander stood and walked to the window. Below, he could see the plaza; the place was still mobbed. The people weren't sure if the Calling was over and were probably unsure of what any of it meant for the future of their country. The Unchained and their political predecessors had ruled Aethrelius peacefully and profitably for most of the last century. Did they truly believe that the recent troubles were reason enough to throw caution to the wind and give the reins to those madmen?

Leander finally said, "You want me to leave."

"Not just you."

"Of course not, but…are you suggesting a Second Wildean Hadj? Impossible."

"The fact that it's so named suggests otherwise."

"My father was half-mad and completely deluded on the finer points of law, but he was also larger than life."

"Undeniably."

"I am not my father. I could not lead these people — half of all Aethreleans — elsewhere."

"It wouldn't be half. My heart tells me that, even under optimal conditions, only a handful would go. Maybe one hundred thousand, maybe less. Fewer than half of those would survive the journey."

"Be it thousands or less than ten, I would not go."

"If you choose not to, they will likely die."

"Who? All the Unchained? All the would-be pilgrims? Who?"

"I fear the toll will be unimaginable."

"What are you saying? Janstrin Beir wouldn't dare...there will be no civil war."

"I'm not talking about civil war, my friend." Yallous gestured for Leander to help him sit up. He swung his legs over the edge of the bed and rested his feet on the floor.

"You shouldn't. The medicines..."

The old man waved him off and then, slowly but with more stamina than one would expect from a man mere hours from death, he stood up. He looked Leander in the eye. "I stopped taking those days ago when I knew you'd be coming."

"The pain...it must be tearing you apart."

"The pain isn't so bad, really. It reminds me quite unerringly that I am still alive. I don't expect ghosts feel like they're burning up alive." He put his hand on Leander's shoulder. "Leander, you do understand the real purpose behind Beir's push against the foreign born, yes?"

"He hates Saiblinorans. He hates Slau. He hates Brull. He hates anything that doesn't look like him."

"So he would have us believe, but there is something else at work here. Did you know Beir was raised by a Saiblinoran woman?"

"What?"

"His father was killed in a minor campaign against the Brull, killed by his own mercenary troops, the Upper Pherriuskatans our government long ago contracted out for political reasons. His mother, the Reyna of Deer Vale, as she was once called, had a nervous breakdown and was unable to care for her three children. The older two were sent to foster with military relations, but the youngest, our Janstrin, was until the age of nine raised and cared for by a 'Sabbie.'"

"I don't understand."

Yallous abruptly sat back down on the bed. He took three deep breaths and continued: "It's difficult to fathom that over two hundred thousand people might be used as a decoy, but I suspect that's what's going on here. You see, the real target of the head Staver's ire and actions is none other than the Mudarrisi."

"The Mudarrisi? But why?" Leander asked, though he'd long suspected he knew the answer to that question.

"There can only be one reason, for the Mudarrisi have only ever provided one service."

"The Jamoi magick."

"The Jamoi magick. Or the Geer magick. History isn't clear there, and it doesn't matter."

"Beir wants them gone."

"He has convinced himself, it seems, that the reason for the Mudarrisi presence is no longer pressing. Most of the people, perhaps even yourself, quietly share this view. We pay these guests an extraordinary sum to keep them here providing the magickal protection they always have. But no one has seen or heard of a Vo'ixtavracci attack here for many years. They've even stopped collecting their horrifying Gift from the Thieves. Some believe — though how one dares believe such a thing is beyond me — they no longer exist. Such things happen to races in this strange and unforgiving world. Quite frequently, in fact."

"I've heard this rumor, yet one would be a fool to believe it. The Vo'ixtavracci have reigned and roamed for a thousand years..."

"Longer than that."

"But why would Beir take such an enormous risk? Surely rumor and public scuttlebutt haven't so completely robbed him of his sanity."

"No, whatever else he is, he is quite sane. And he never does anything out of passion. Our friend is an actor, of course, but beneath the actor is a clever, patient, needful politician. A man who would, perhaps, be king." Yallous let his words hang in the air for a few moments, and then he asked: "So how would getting rid of the Mudarrisi serve him? Forget him. He's not the point. Ask yourself instead this question: What if he's wrong? What if the Vo'ixtavracci are out there, waiting to strike..."

Leander turned. He knelt and looked deeply into Yallous's face. "What are you not telling me? What do you know?"

"I know very little. I suspect a great deal more. But what I do know is that Janstrin Beir has been receiving some strange visitors these last few months."

"What kind of visitors?"

"Redeemers."

"How do you know this?"

"Quite simple. Janstrin told me."

"He told you? Why would he do that?"

"I have given that question a great deal of thought. I have come to the conclusion that, arrogance and ambition and charade aside, he is terrified."

"Beir? Of what?"

"He has made himself a deal, Leander, and found himself in a situation he cannot possibly hope to survive. He has, to serve his own designs, inadvertently sold his country. He has no grounds through which to retract."

"If this is true, he should have just ended his own life."

"It wouldn't matter. In fact, it would make things easier for those who have deceived him. Their next puppet wouldn't be play-acting: Beir's subordinates are all howling in blissful ignorance."

"Why has he told only you?"

"If he'd told anyone else, what is going to happen would have already happened."

"Which is?"

"The end of our civilization."

"The Vo'ixtavracci."

"They are coming, Leander. It is now a given. They are coming to destroy us."

Chapter 19
Felterson's Shoe or the Last Spoon
of Countess Cha Rettinbotter

Place: Northern Xatumka, Arba Environ
Date: Quattrenim 33, AY 998

"You go to your death, my friend."

"Perhaps."

"Not perhaps. They will not listen. They will arrest you. They will almost certainly execute you."

Xian Lo Fui, humble Timesinger, and old Wolsa, the most assertive if not the wisest of that order, were seated beneath the gnarled vines of the Westview Garden, sipping their cups of bitter tea. The morning, as most mornings were in this part of the world, was warm and windy.

"Doubtful. There are few left who would remember me and fewer still who would remember what happened," said Xian.

He wanted to placate his friend and elder but frankly had much more pressing things on his mind. The fact of his journey was a given; what he needed to wrap his head around were actionable tenets of its purpose. He was willing to make whatever sacrifice was necessary, but one had to be certain the sacrifice would not be made in vain. Results were a must.

But which results?

Wolsa replied, "There are more than a few. And then there is him. He has the most to gain by silencing you. And do not doubt it: he remembers everything."

"We were friends, Wolsa. Or something akin to friends. And he could have done me in long ago if he were that concerned about the possibility of my meddling in his myriad affairs."

"Perhaps you're on his list of concerns."

"Perhaps, but if so, it's a very long and poorly attended to list, and I sit near the bottom. I'm telling you, the man bears me no ill will. No more than he bears himself, leastwise."

Wolsa grunted and shook his head. Xian smiled at him faintly and took out his pipe. He offered some tobacco to his companion, but the other just shook his head again.

"I suspect the ill will he bears himself is substantial. And you were never friends, Xian. You were allies. At best."

"Sometimes there is little difference."

"Sometimes there is all the difference in the world. Alliances end when the common purpose of the interested parties dissolves or is otherwise satisfied."

"And friendships?"

"Friendships are their own common purpose."

Xian chuckled and took a puff. "Then perhaps you are right after all: we were never friends. But our alliance was a strong one, and there remains the common purpose of keeping our shame buried. The shame has never dissolved, I'm afraid. That fact will win out in the end."

"You're certain of that?"

"Reasonably. If I am wrong, I am wrong. It is worth the risk. The task I have before me is worth the risk."

"That's arguable. For the sake of us all and for your sake in particular, I hope you are right," said Wolsa as he shifted his old body a bit. The low wooden bench he sat on was clearly making him uncomfortable.

Xian did not point this out, however, knowing as he did how much pride the old man had in his habit of eschewing niceties. They both, to be sure, hated bitter tea, but somehow it seemed more orderly and vigilant for them to choose it over wine or sweet tea. Such were the foolish gestures of those who hoped their discipline would reconstitute their relevance. "This time, I believe I am right, Wolsa."

"You believe. Maybe we believe. But they never will. He never will."

"Never mind the duke. He's not the problem; the Mind is. And Theodore will believe me..."

"Theodore? Nonsense. That's the weakest part of your plan by far, and your plan on the whole is astonishingly weak one for a man with such a keen mind to have authored."

"Thank you for your confidence," replied Xian. "It's very encouraging. But Theodore will back me, rest assured. I just have to convince him. Shouldn't be too difficult; he does, after all, have a calendar."

"You won't convince that bloated fool of anything, calendars notwithstanding, except perhaps of the need to order more of our wine. But if you do, and if he does agree to help, will that be enough?" asked the old man.

"More than enough. Scandals aside, he still holds great sway with both Mind and Body. And also with his own order, despite recent difficulties. His pedigree ensures his status and always will."

"Always? Blasphemous words for a Timesinger, my friend. I should have you removed along with all three of your belongings."

"Two. I gave the Prementian shell to Gustav," Xian confessed as he poured a bit more tea for them both. The winds off the ocean, he noticed, had a sudden slight chill to them. Calendars indeed.

"Did you now? After two decades he finally wore you down."

"He did."

"Good for him. Nothing in return?"

"He wrote me a ballad."

"Please, do not sing it for me! My old ears are very sensitive."

They shared a light laugh. Wolsa looked sleepy, but his eyes remained open and alert. "Teddy's status is not in dispute, but there are other considerations. We cannot know how the approach of Proving has affected the Tri," he said.

"Probably not at all. To them, the Proving is a joke couched in a myth. To most of them, anyway," Xian said with a hint of irritation.

"Point taken."

Xian lifted his teacup, winced at Wolsa to indicate his requisite hatred of the tea, and said, "We can and do know that the Mind is never without an agenda. Our information has to impact them in such a way that it disturbs their schemes and plans."

"Are you listening to yourself?" chided Wolsa. "Now you, at the ripe age of—how old are you anyway?—now you're going to challenge the plans of the Mind! Such arrogance! You've been mending books too long; you've forgotten the brutal lessons of life among your fellow Arbans."

"I understand your fears, I do. And I have not forgotten, I assure you. But I have to do this. I have to try." Xian stared wistfully out at the sea, wondering if anything he was saying here bore any resemblance to the truth. He was both moved and disturbed by the idea that it might.

Odd sensation, that. What was it? Ah, yes: fear.

He smiled to himself. He'd thought himself beyond fear, and it was interesting to suddenly discover he was not. What else would he discover, he wondered, as he journeyed south and east? "I have to atone, Wolsa. The bill has come due."

Wolsa tried to comfort him. "What happened…that was not your choice, Xian. You need to let it go." He yawned and shifted again in his seat.

Xian sat silently for a while, listening to the wind and watching his old friend nod off.

You know it was, and you fear me and my past despite your assertions and advice, and so you are completely willing to let me go and let me die, if it comes to that. And you believe in none of this, do you, my friend? The Proving, the Four, the Ashorne. Nonsense, you've said a thousand times. I can't blame you. Legends and hints and warnings are not the sort of things on which one banks the survival of a civilization, thought Xian.

Wolsa stirred.

"You are tired, Wolsa. Why don't you rest? Or shall I…?" said Xian as gestured at the teapot.

His offer to pour was softly rebuffed. "More than my fill I've had, thank you," said Wolsa, now looking very tired and somewhat troubled. Xian could tell that despite his misgivings, Wolsa truly wanted him to forego this doomed mission. Perhaps after all the years and the talks and the teas, something like affection for one another had taken hold.

Not perhaps, no. It had. This man was his brother.

Xian put down the pot and nodded to the novice who was attending them. The boy came and took the tea tray away. "Please, a small pillow for Master Wolsa's head," Xian said to the boy.

"Nonsense," murmured Wolsa, "I'm not at all tired."

The pillow was brought and placed in a corner of the bench in such a way that Wolsa could lean into it, head propped but body still semiupright. It would allow him the dignity of falling asleep midsentence while maintaining the illusion of engagement.

Xian spoke to him low. "I have tried to let it go, my dear old friend. But I find that no matter how earnestly I devote myself to that end, the knowledge of what I was and what I did…well, it refuses steadfastly to let *me* go."

"Have you not found peace and comfort here with us?" Wolsa said in a near whisper. His eyelids were fluttering.

"You know that I have. But peace and comfort are not enough. I must do what I can to make amends."

"But if no one remembers and no one knows, what will it matter?"

"I am not sure. I have only my intentions and my knowledge to guide me. What others choose and do, I cannot determine. But I must try." He bowed to his friend and then stood straight, regarded him, and embraced him. "Take care of yourself, Wolsa Vettunik. I am forever in your debt for all that you've done for me."

The old man opened his eyes momentarily, and they were both sharp and kind. "No debts, my friend. All you owe me is your safe return."

Xian nodded, knowing without doubt it was a debt he would never repay. He left his old friend to nap in a world that was not yet vanquished, not yet lost.

The next morning, Xian Lo Fui left Ashkinda.

He wasn't alone. Several others of the order were headed down along the ocean to Fort Dilan for supplies and trade, and he'd arranged to tag along with them. He'd neglected to say why; being Timesingers, they took the hint and didn't ask.

This was not unusual. Theirs was a somewhat paradoxical order, given to practiced habits and inherent inclinations that bespoke of a very deliberate balance between curiosity and patience. They understood that, oftentimes, answers came to those who did not ask and even because they did not ask.

He could nonetheless sense their curiosity, and so he told them, when they arrived at the fort, that he would not be returning to Ashkinda with them. Two of them immediately volunteered to accompany him to wherever it was he was going. And that bespoke of an unfortunate development that had, for some time now, plagued the order: Timesingers were not trusted, and often that led to them being the targets of unpleasant actions. Arbans imagined history to be a danger, and no one loves the purveyors of danger, however imagined. There had even been serious discussion among the order to adopt a rule that no Timesinger should ever travel alone. But the rule had yet not passed, owing to a regrettable need for lengthy deliberation before adoption. Xian wasn't willing to bring another brother, however well-intentioned, on a journey that would almost certainly end in death, so he politely and firmly refused the offer of assistance. He stayed one night with them at a low inn at the fort, listened to a few stories and shared one or two, and in the morning when they headed back north, he went east. Alone.

For days, he rode his gremfi along the edge of the cliff on the High Visshilla Pass and reflected on his friend Wolsa's objections. A firm late-summer wind, its tendrils hinting of autumn's arrival, whipped at his face and made his eyes water.

Traipsing along the ocean's familiar shore down to Fort Dilan from Ashkinda with a few others of his order had been a small but, he realized, somewhat unwelcome distraction. They were good sorts, and part of him, in truth, would have been glad of their indefinite company. Still, he'd been privately eager for his long journey to begin in earnest. This was his quest and his alone.

Old fool I am, he thought. *Might be easier to just pitch myself down off the pass and leave this damned environ to its fate. Surely I've done enough damage for one man?*

He stifled those thoughts and tried to focus on something more productive. How long had it been since he'd traveled this way? A decade or more. The precarious path to Havenor and points east was just as he remembered: barren, windy, and utterly boring. He wondered idly if he'd made a mistake refusing the brothers' offer of company. Better to be bored together, no? It wasn't as if he would have needed to drag them all the way to Pashka, he chuckled to himself.

Solitude was best, he admitted with a pang of guilt for the selfish thoughts he'd just entertained. There was nothing to distract him here on the pass, and that worked well, because his mind needed time to parse through the necessary tasks and probable troubles ahead.

The math of the thing was elusive and tricky.

Old Wolsa wasn't wrong. He just wasn't in possession of all the facts. And he didn't know Duke Velliok.

Of course, Xian himself wasn't in possession of all the facts either. He was playing a hunch. Or several. What he'd found in the texts, the evidence concerning the Noble Four and the Proving, combined with recent events and even a taste of coincidence and paradox, he couldn't sit on or ignore. Wolsa had agreed to that, at least, but he'd been more in favor of sending messages to the various heads of state even while admitting those messages would surely be tossed into the closest fire pit or read aloud at a feast for a laugh.

The gremfi snorted and stopped. She hesitated a moment, sniffed a few times, and then continued.

Xian's plan hinged mostly on his belief that he could get the duke to listen to him.

It was not a belief grounded in cogent reason. He and Velliok had a history only the two of them knew and understood. They'd done what they'd done for what were, in theory, good reasons at the time, but history has a way of sapping the good from any justification and rendering the best of intentions nothing short of criminal, does it not? When all is said and done, one is left with only the cold recitation of what occurred. Historians — and these days, Timesingers were little more than that — are free to contemplate the whens and hows, but few if any care enough to collate the subtext and truly understand the whys.

He rode the long, high rock road. The past rode with him.

What else could we have done?

The Malliorelum were a threat to humankind. To the way of life humans had finally arrived at after centuries of slaughter and suffering and terrible mistakes. Or so they'd argued.

Maybe we were wrong.

They'd chosen, the best of them — or the Vellioks had chosen, anyway — and that was that. What had begun as a debate had quickly morphed into genocide.

None of it could be helped now. Amends, maybe. Atonement, at least. But for now, this journey, today, the one he had undertaken, was what was necessary and possible. It had always been necessary, but he wondered: Had it also always been possible?

Maybe it was. And maybe it was always going to be how things played out. And the reasons were the same.

He hoped in his heart the results wouldn't be nearly as horrific and brutal. There'd been far too much horror and brutality in these lands.

He'd chosen the path because there was a brother in Narth Downs who might be of some assistance to him. Bjarni Malaji was a reputedly very strange man with an oddly poetic name who'd been politely ordered to leave Ashkinda decades ago under circumstances few understood or discussed. Banishment, or at least mandated relocation, was extremely uncommon for the order, and the general feeling was the less said about it, the better. Malaji was, however, also the foremost living authority on the lore of the Proving.

Xian was certain that although most Timesingers would flatly deny it, Malaji knew more about the Proving than all of them, or anyone, put together. That he was a curmudgeonly, exiled drunkard given to telling elaborate lies was beside the point. He never lied about the Proving, as far as Xian had ever been able to tell — many late nights spent reading and checking Malaji's writings had convinced him of that, thought he'd never once met the man — and whatever else he might be, in this instance he'd be an invaluable resource.

Xian was mildly concerned that he'd written to Malaji a month before but still hadn't heard back. The man was even older than Wolsa, though, so delayed responses were not cause for severe alarm. Malaji would have some answers. Or at least, better clues, Xian hoped.

After the Downs, he would head to Mak and, with any luck, gain an escort. Without an official escort, he'd have almost no chance to petition the Body for audience. And without admission to the Body, he wouldn't get near Velliok, the man he had to speak to.

Below, Xian could see the rough beginnings of the Broken Flats as they crawled from, or fell into, depending upon one's race and interpretation of legend, the Carata Chasm. The mule-like, reddish-gray gremfi scarcely seemed to notice the precarious nature of the path before her. She ambled forward and somewhat side to side, as if asleep. Xian had long since learned to trust these animals, so sure were their footing and awareness both. After a long glance down at the chasm, he set aside his fear of a fall and recovered his thoughts.

Of course, Wolsa and the others were right, which was to say they were right about the little they knew: it would be difficult to convince the Body to listen to Xian. This was one of the few points on which he and the others had agreed, but the Body didn't matter anymore, and even the Body knew that. But they, all one hundred and eleven of them, were the gatekeepers.

The Mind was where the power lay. So it was the Body, then Duke Velliok, then, if Xian convinced them both of the need, a frank presentation to the Mind.

His fellows were right to fret. These were dangerous times, with unrest in nearly every corner of Arba. Not the optimal conditions for presenting a case that the world was about to end for all of them.

The Timesingers all understood their own precarious position vis-à-vis Arba's ruling congress and its canny, savage members. It had been a very long time since any Timesinger had been welcome in the Violet Halls or the Watlier, longer still since the Body or its betters had sought that order's wise counsel. Historians were frowned upon in a world with such a brutal and sinister history. The truth of a thing was often the most direct path to the grave. Those in power, unsurprisingly, were very much in favor of controlling perceptions.

And so the Timesingers had been reduced to mere curiosities, called upon rarely when some lordling sought to impress his guests with some trumped-up scavenger hunt for a rumored artifact like Felterson's Shoe or the Last Spoon of Countess Cha Rettinbotter. The subtext in the absence of official and meaningful participation was clear: *We don't want to know, and you aren't allowed to tell. Anything to anyone.*

This situation was different.

Or so Xian would argue. If they gave him the chance. If any of them had an interest in following the crumbs and clues to the inevitable conclusion he and a handful of his brothers had reached.

A small hawk circled above him, crying out at the morning sky.

Xian checked to be sure it was indeed a hawk. One could not be too careful this high up in the mountains, most especially here on the pass. Here there was always someone else watching.

Truth to tell, the Timesingers were more than comfortable with the restrained and now time-honored arrangement they shared with, or had had imposed on them by, the Body. Timesinging did not lend itself to glory or dispute. Those who felt the calling to remember, to learn, and to never again forget inevitably found their way northwest to the temple by the sea. Having made the journey, they invariably abandoned their pasts for new lives. Ironic, that: the need to abandon one's history in search of wider historical truths.

They studied. They wrote. They debated quietly among themselves. They revisited the facts and sifted through the rumors. They learned for the world and remembered for the world.

Yet even as they devoted their lives to remembering, the world did its best to forget them. They died without being marked by any pilgrimage or ceremony or return to the places that were once their homes. Xian was one of the very few who had even travelled east of Fort Dilan, let alone to Pherriuskata, during his summoned life. Timesingers didn't often travel. There were some, like Jemein the Reader, who were scattered about the known world, and they collected what information they could and sent it back to Ashkinda to be contemplated and catalogued, but they were fewer and fewer.

Like most of the others in his order, Xian hadn't always called Ashkinda his home. Ashkinda was a home one typically found later in life, after the mistakes and sorrow of a lifetime had narrowed down the definition of a home and made one yearn for something closer to a refuge. Most of the Timesingers were either old or very old.

And Ashkinda welcomed them. With her soft sea winds, her black beaches, and her gnarled, stalwart pine forests, she sat through time and gave them comfort.

The gremfi snorted again, twice, and then another three times, which for her was the equivalent of screaming and bucking. She also stopped dead in her tracks.

Xian stirred from his musings and glanced about. Nothing. He was reluctant to look where he must — up — for rarely did the mountain peaks reveal anything one wanted to see. He tugged softly on the gremfi's reins and bade her to go on. She refused.

He turned his head to the left, toward the mountains, and tilted it so his eyes could glance sideways up the slopes. Still nothing.

Too much nothing.

As he'd assumed, he was being watched.

The question as to who was doing the watching wasn't a puzzling one. When one travelled along the mountains in Arba, any mountains at all, observation by a distant, curious party was standard fare. The party in question had ruled the sky and the mountains since before there'd been an Arba, perhaps before there'd even been mountains.

The Visshilla suffered to let most weary travelers coaxing gremfis or pulling carts pass. Few told stories of Visshilla aggression, and fewer recalled a time when a Visshilla had even been seen up close. One saw them, if at all, from a distance, circling high above in the clouds or lighting upon a heavenly cliff. As long as one adhered to the rules, one had nothing to fear. Not from the Visshilla.

And it was so very easy to follow the rules:

The sky belongs to them.
The peaks are their home.
The sky belongs to them.
Flight is theirs alone.
The sky belongs to them.
Climb and die, fly and fall.
The sky belongs to them,
And they see all.

Xian looked back down at the path and urged the animal forward. She hesitated and then grudgingly complied with a quick, nervous snort.

He considered the rule about climbing and wondered, not for the first time, how very close to breaking it those who traversed this lonely pass actually came. Certainly if he tried to dismount and follow one of the many nearly dry, steep stream beds up toward its source, there might be trouble waiting for him.

He had once considered that very notion when another steed of his had gone mad from poisonous wounds inflicted by bandits. She'd tumbled into the chasm, taking his water, his food, and his wounded companion, Yaderfa, with her.

Without the water, he had almost died, but he had understood then as now that to pursue water here meant certain death in any case.

Climb and die, the Xatumkan freefarmers warned their children. *Fly and fall.*

Not even the Brull in their mountain caves and keeps were known to violate these rules.

But as the gremfi ambled along, now seemingly free of her earlier concerns, Xian knew he did not need to climb to die. Death was ever at his shoulder and had been since the Velliok Action and that distant, angry evening when they'd murdered Glea Siven.

And as for falling, well, he believed he'd probably fallen further and longer than any man alive, and were he honest with himself, which before breakfast he often was, he would admit he was falling still.

So now, he rode. He must try. He owed those debts, debts so great no deed or bounty could ever repay them. And yet, here was something, something he could do, to set this sorry, doomed world on a better path. Or at least a path not quite as tragic.

His observer must have been satisfied regarding the nature of his journey and its toothless direction, for the gremfi did not snort again. He urged her onward — unnecessarily, for it was now she who determined the pace.

About a week later, he reached Havenor and was met with the news that Theodore Oxenhaft had been murdered in Hunberg.

The news shook him.

He hadn't really known Oxenhaft — they'd met twice before, once at a Triumvirate state celebration and once at an ONOF conference on Mariendo — but he'd read much of what the man had written and had often defended his perspectives in discussions with his brothers. Oxenhaft was the descendant of the legendary Tristan Oxenhaft, the third of the Noble Four upon whose deeds, lives, and teachings Arba's predominant faith was founded. His pedigree aside, he was a brilliant scholar and a man of intensely progressive political attitudes.

The murderer had not been caught, nor was anyone under suspicion at the time of the two-week-old report Xian read at Havenor.

Neither had a body been found; however, there was enough blood — a substantial amount — and a finger, albeit only one — at the scene. The collective evidence undeniably pointed in one and only one direction.

But why? And why now?

Xian sat at a small table in a typically sparse Xatumkan inn, sipped a new wine, and considered the possibilities. Clearly Oxenhaft had a thousand enemies; anyone of his stature and position would even if he hadn't the unique effect on the tenets of religious discourse and practice the only living descendant of a Noble One would. Yet there was something ominous about the timing, particularly when juxtaposed with all that Xian knew about the precarious times in which they all now found themselves.

"They say something ate him, that one. Must've had an appetite to eat that fat bastard."

A drunken farmer missing most of his teeth was leaning over Xian's shoulder, smiling at his own joke. Seeing that Xian wasn't amused, the drunk shrugged, belched, and stumbled away.

Xian grimaced slightly, reminded viscerally of just how ill-informed and callous the average Arban tended to be. And yet there was something about the man's observation that struck a chord…

Xian remained in Havenor for two nights, taking time to restock, find passage with a small caravan heading east to Fort Ram and the Downs, and write a letter to a friend in Hunberg that he would mail when they reached Ram.

During the week that followed, he amended and rewrote and edited and rethought that letter countless times in his mind and then on paper. He asked, he theorized, he reasoned, and he wondered on that paper, and ultimately, his mind settled on one clear course of action.

When he arrived in Fort Ram, he threw the letter in the first fire pit he saw.

He was old enough to know letters of that kind should not be mailed. Writing them was one thing, but burning them was almost always the wisest course of subsequent action. In years past, he'd seen several men tortured and executed based on letters they'd written. In the case of at least two, the letters had been severely — most severely — misread.

He stayed one night in Fort Ram. Now that Theodore was dead, his plans had to change. He'd lost a potential ally in his fight to convince the Body and Mind that what he'd learned was worth listening to and acting upon. A very important ally. Irreplaceable? That was arguable, but it could not be denied that having Theodore at his side would have increased his chances of success manifold.

He had to build his case. He had to talk to Malaji.

But five days later, when he reached Narth Downs, he found that Bjarni Malaji was no longer there. He'd been gone for months.

He'd lived alone and kept to himself, so information about his departure was sparse. Not one person could account for his whereabouts. He'd left most of his things and simply disappeared in the early part of the summer. Someone said he'd left in the month of Boinage; someone else remembered he'd left the month before, in Ceou. No one was sure.

It was puzzling but given the degree to which he'd been marginalized, it was not so unusual that a man like Malaji would head off to some other part of the world without informing anyone about his plans. Still, he was very old. What could have called him away or compelled him to travel so suddenly at his age?

There were no answers to be had in Narth Downs. Xian had been traveling hard and was very much in need of some rest. He decided to stay put for a while and think. Eventually, he would go on to Pashka and whatever waited for him there. He had time. Not much, but enough.

There would be plenty of caravans on which to book passage from Narth Downs to Quintish and Lake Iale. He'd have to sell his gremfi, but he could always buy her back when he returned. If he returned.

So he rested his body. His head, filled with questions, found little respite. The death of Theodore was extraordinary, the disappearance of Malalji was merely odd, but the juxtaposition of the two events, given the importance of each man to Xian's current undertaking, seemed horrifically coincidental, a wild expression of terrible luck.

Being a Timesinger, Xian believed in neither coincidence nor luck, though he did, when circumstance demanded, acknowledge the roles each often played in the unfolding of events.

This was not such a circumstance, he knew. No, someone was working against him. More likely, someone had an agenda that ran afoul of his own.

He wondered if he'd be allowed to get anywhere near Pashka to tell his story.

Chapter 20
I don't know anything right now.

Place: Glaring Cliffs, Aethrelius
Date: Quattrenim 27, AY 998

There were five Aethrelean warships out there. Frainle could see them well because they were all five burning.

"What the hell's going on?" Eni yelled as he woke.

"We're under attack," she told him, not believing her own words.

But they were true. From her little sailboat, *Sunray*, they watched it happen.

One ship had turned and was headed their way, back toward the Cliffs. The other four were fully ablaze. From this distance Frainle couldn't tell for sure, but she thought she could make out men trying to escape the flames by rowboat. One rowboat, full of men, seemed to be dangling off the side of the ship. There were screams now, rising above the wind.

"We need to go. Right now," Eni said.

Frainle grabbed *Sunray*'s tiller and began a starboard tack. There wasn't much wind, but what there was, she made good use of. She turned the quick little boat around in just a few moments.

They were less than half a mile from the battle. Too close.

"We've got a good wind," she lied to Eni. "We're far enough from them."

"Good, good. We should make it, then," he stammered back at her.

She could see he was becoming wildly uncomfortable in the way he sometimes did when his emotions overran his reason, yet she could not focus on her friend right now. There was a very good chance they were both about to die, and it enraged her.

Turning her head, she watched the ship that had been running explode. Something massive had hit the deck, something that was itself burning with wild blue flames.

"What are they?" Eni cried.

"I don't know."

"Can we outrun them?"

"I hope so. Stop asking questions and let me do this!"

Behind them, she could barely make out on the dark sea what looked to be a hundred — no, a thousand ships. Or what must have been ships, but of a size she'd never imagined possible, each half the size of Cliffs' Keep itself.

They were under attack by a thousand floating keeps. And above and around each of those keeps, swarms of flying...somethings.

She knew they were all going to die. It was a certainty.

Frainle hated certainties, particularly ones that were imposed upon her. She gnashed her teeth and gripped the tiller even harder.

The alarm bells in the keep's watchtowers were ringing. They'd seen the fires; they knew something was wrong. But had they seen the enemy fleet? Doubtful. She'd barely seen it herself out there in the dark amid the smoke. At the very least, she needed to warn her people of the seriousness of the attack.

To do that, she had to get close enough to the shore to light the requisite signal fire. But was it…was it a purple flame or a green one?

She couldn't remember. She should remember, but she couldn't.

Then Eni said, "We have to light the green flame…we need to warn them!"

Eni might be a bundle of nerves, she thought, *but thank Renik and Frederick and every other ik for his beautiful, knowing brain.*

She was putting some distance between their boat and the battle, but not as much as she'd first hoped to. *Sunray* was making good time; the wind was now a bit stronger, and she was coming in hard and fast as they moved toward the shore. Frainle prayed she'd missed the reef; bottoming out right now would seal their fate.

Her prayers were in vain. They hit the bottom, and she felt the hull tear.

Stupid.

"Look in the cabin, Eni! Are we taking on water? Look!"

Eni jumped up and ran for the door. She knew what he'd say before he said it; she was already feeling *Sunray* lag to the starboard side.

"Some, yes, but not a lot."

"What's a lot?"

"It's coming in but not gushing."

Frainle jumped down from the tiller and looked for herself. "We're not going to make it."

"What? What do we do?"

She climbed back up to the tiller and stared hard at the shore and the inlet.

"We still have to warn the towers. That's our duty now. Hold the tiller. Straight, hold it straight…"

Eni did as he was told while she dug around in a small wooden box near his feet. "But do we have…what are you going to do?" he asked. "Let me do that. I can't steer this thing!"

She pulled a small flask out of the box and emptied its contents onto the water behind them. Lighting up her cap with a flint, she grimaced a moment and flung it out onto the oil. The water behind *Sunray* burst into green flames.

Within seconds, the tower bells were ringing more feverishly. The Cliffs now knew an attack was imminent.

Given what had happened to the warships, Frainle wasn't sure it would matter, but at least they knew. At least they could assess the threat and evacuate if it came to that.

Over four thousand people occupied the keep and its surrounding village.

"We'll be sunk in a minute or two," she told Eni. She was almost calm when she said it, though her mind, like the water and the ships behind them, was afire.

"Frain, if this thing sinks, what do we do, swim in? I can't do that."

"Neither can I, not like this. It's too far, and they're coming up too fast behind us."

"What then?"

"The guard's coming. They'll come and get us."

And they were. A guard boat, rowed by four strong men, met them about halfway between the reef and the Inlet Gate. Good timing, too, because *Sunray*'s cabin was almost completely filled by this point.

"You have to swim to us!" cried Mannler, the guard chief. "You have to clear the reef!"

Eni blanched and stood stone still.

"Eni, just jump in. You can stay afloat, I've seen you. I'll pull you to them!" she cried.

He didn't move, so after a moment, she pushed him in.

And then she did as she'd promised. She grabbed him with one arm and began to swim toward their rescuers.

The guards had thrown out several ropes to help her. She got hold of one and looped it under Eni's left arm. He flailed a bit but stopped when he felt himself being pulled toward safety.

Once near the guard boat, Frainle looked back toward the ocean and winced, trying to glimpse the attacking fleet. But the enemy seemed to have stopped altogether. Perhaps they'd detected the reef somehow — it ran in patches out as far as a mile from the shore — or perhaps, Frainle thought with a sick feeling, they were waiting.

But what were they waiting for?

"Get on, get on," cried Mannler, "we've got to get moving!"

Frainle pulled herself on board with Mannler's help while two of the others grabbed Eni. He was shivering and twitching a bit, but he turned to her and managed a smile. "She was a great little boat, your *Ray*. I'm so sorry you lost her," Eni said.

Frainle smiled back as best she could, but she was far too frightened to offer him much comfort or thanks.

The men turned the guard boat back toward the shore and rowed hard.

She was a great little boat, yes, she thought, *and more than that, a gift, but she's gone.* She glanced out at the slowly approaching enemy ships. Now they were completely visible, and seemed impervious to the reef somehow. They were enormous, and countless, and her heart sank knowing that the certainty she'd defied was truly inevitable.

And then it happened. Massive burning objects were flung from those ships, thousands of them, all at once. They flew high over the guard boat and against and over the seawatch wall.

The sky rained flame, and the night was alight with horror. The noise was deafening as explosions rang and rock tumbled into the water. One of the towers that flanked the gate was shorn in half. Two others were completely obliterated at their bases, and the screams of the men in those towers punctuated the din as they pitched down onto the rocks and into the sea.

Mannler ignored it all and steered his stubborn craft forward toward the closed gate. When they were almost there, he yelled, "You two are gonna have to swim for it; use the Shark Hole…they know you're coming."

"What about you?" Frainle yelled back.

"I'll follow."

Frainle grabbed Eni's arm and pulled him. He hesitated for just a second at the prospect of more swimming, but then he jumped with her, landing awkwardly in the water, just as a pile of stones hit the aft section of the guard boat. Mannler was flung about fifty feet in the air and then landed in the water headfirst. He did not resurface.

And so they swam, Frainle pulling her friend, for the Shark Hole, not knowing if they would at any second be crushed or drowned.

But by some small miracle, neither happened. The Hole was open, though there was no one there waiting for them. They climbed up the small ladder leading to an inner hall, found the stairs, and were soon outside and on the Seapath.

When they got to the split that led either down to the docks or up to the keep, Frainle chose the upward path.

Eni grabbed her arm. "What are you doing? You can't go that way!"

"I need to get back to the keep. My mother…"

But he was right. Fire and rock flew through the air, and they could hear the screams of the dying all around, especially from the direction of the keep and the village.

"Please, Eni…I have to see…" She tried to pull away from him.

So they climbed up a bit. From a concealed place on a rear subwall that was part of the original old fort, they stood stunned at the sudden deluge of agony that had descended upon their home. The keep was almost completely gone; the village was burning. They saw no one alive.

A burning stone landed a few feet from them and exploded, setting Enimuat's cloak on fire. She pulled it off him and tossed it aside.

It sounded for a moment like there was some fighting in the north section closer to the keep, or where that part of the keep had stood, but they couldn't see anything through all the smoke and flames.

And then they heard three tremendous blasts, as if from some unthinkably loud horn, and those blasts came from inland, from the southwest. Turning around, ears ringing, Frainle saw the things she had heard about in tales but never believed were real.

But here they were.

What could only have been Vo'ixtavracci were approaching from inland, cutting off any chance of an escape via the roads.

The town and the keep were surrounded.

The Great Takers, the Eaters of Men, had come.

They were leading what appeared to be legions of huge men made of stone. They were at least a mile or more away, but their size made them seem incredibly close.

Monsters had come to destroy them.

She cried. She sank to the ground in horror.

The Glaring Cliffs were completely surrounded. There was nowhere to run to.

Enimuat just stood there beside her, but he wasn't looking at the horde or the enemy ships. He saw all that, he saw what she saw, he must, but he was looking at something else. Looking frantic, he kept scanning about for something, kept fighting to keep control and see something...some way out, maybe...

She watched him, and she tried to look with him, but her eyes were wet with smoke and tears, and she saw nothing but fire and death.

"Frain, the catacombs!" Enimuat cried. He pulled up by her arm and pointed down along the wall to a small path.

She didn't understand at first but then realized what he was suggesting. "We won't make it," she said.

"We will!" he answered, yanking her arm as he headed for the path. "We must!"

"We'll be trapped if we go in there."

"And we'll be killed if we stay here. Look around — there's no other way!"

And she did look, just once more, but there was nothing left to see. The fire from the ships had destroyed her home, the creatures coming from the southwest were smashing and killing. Thousands were dying, and she could do nothing to stop it.

Enimuat pulled at her arm again and she, having no reason not to, followed. They ran together down the path to the hidden entrance in the cliffside.

They saw no one, not an Aethrelean, not an enemy, on the way. She realized that yes, they could get to the catacombs, but once they were in, what then? Die among the dead?

"We'll be trapped!" she said again, hesitating.

"No, we won't. Hurry." He pulled her arm again and turned toward the dim opening, a hundred paces from where they'd been having some wine hours before.

The fires were spreading, and already burning debris was toppling near where he wanted them to go. He dodged around one pile, gently guiding her, and then pressed against the wall to shimmy past another. They reached the opening and the stairs inside that led down into the darkness.

"You have to trust me, Frain," said Eni. "There is a way, a secret way," he said as they hurried down the stairs.

"Eni, I don't want to be captured by these things," she said. "I'd rather face them and die than hide and wait for them to kill us anyway."

"Surrender, and they will not just kill you. They will eat you. But I wouldn't let that happen, Frain, and you know that."

I don't know anything right now, she thought as she followed him down. She was too terrified to argue and too shocked at what had happened to their home to wonder for more than a fleeting moment where he'd found this burst of courage. They were still alive so far, and that was all she knew. His words did little to comfort her, but he had a direction and she had none.

She didn't want to be eaten.

She followed him.

After a few minutes of climbing down the stairs, he grabbed a torch and a flint from a shelf on the wall. He didn't light the torch. They pressed forward until there was just about no more natural light from the stairs behind them. Only then did he strike the flint and illuminate the old stairwell.

She looked down and gasped at the narrowness of the stairs. They were made of wood and stone, but most of the wood had long since rotted away. "Can we make it down these?" Frainle asked, her voice a raspy whisper.

"Just stick close to the wall and step on the stones. We'll be fine," answered Eni. Seeing the doubt in her eyes, he added, "I do it all the time, Frain!"

Had she not been so fearful of what was destroying the Cliffs, she might never have attempted to descend these broken, rotted steps. The irony of which of them was now afraid of heights did not escape her despite the moment's raging urgency. Nonetheless, descend they did, very carefully, for maybe another ten minutes, until they reached the bottom and the entrance to a narrow hall.

"What's down that way? Tombs?" she asked as she peered down the dark hall.

"Yes, among other things. Hurry," he said as he led them in.

The hall was narrow and damp and still. The air was rank with mold and the stench of leakage from sea storms. Enimuat led them deep into the catacombs. For what seemed an eternity, they half ran, half stumbled along twisted halls and down crumbling stairways. Once, she fell and hurt her knee badly. For a moment or two, she wasn't able to put any weight on it. He made to carry her, but she tested the knee and pronounced it "only a scratch." She was lying. It hurt like hell, but with hell at their backs, she could live with the pain. And there was no way Eni, who was a half a head shorter than her and no heavier, could have carried her more than ten steps—and surely not down any.

"We're almost there," he whispered to her more than once.

And then, they were there. Or at least she thought they must be: he'd stopped, and there was a pensive, searching expression on his face. He put his hand on the wall in front of him, and it began, ever so slightly, to glow.

The glow took her aback. She'd heard about magick but rarely seen it—the Mudarrisi weren't inclined to entertain and preferred to do their protection magick on the sly. She felt a twinge of sorrow, realizing that the protection magick was, like everything else, gone.

This was how the Vo'ix had come, she knew. And she knew something else: somehow, the Stavers had doomed her home and, in all likelihood, their country.

She hated them all.

Eni was running his hand all over the wall, searching, probing.

"What are you doing?" she whispered, panting from both pain and exhaustion. Something might have burned her—she felt a pain in her midback--or maybe it'd just been the nasty, stifling heat that had surrounded them during the attack. "Is this something you need to be doing right now? Let's go!"

"No. Wait," he said, his hands now skimming along the wall in small circles.

"Wait for what?"

"Just wait."

"Eni, how do you know about this place?"

"Part of my training. Please be quiet."

She stared at the back of his head and began to understand what this was all about. Magick. Eni hadn't been studying weather patterns and seasonal effects on fishermen's harvests after all. He'd been honest with her all along, and she hadn't believed him. He had a color.

But her surprise was false, she had to admit. Deep down, she'd known all along what he was and what he'd been doing with the Mudarrisi. And she was sure her parents knew too, but if they'd known and allowed it to go on, they must have believed Enimuat training as a magicker was an idea worth supporting. Frainle herself had chosen not to pry, or rather, to wait until Eni came clean about what he was learning.

Frainle hoped her parents were right. And she believed him now: he had a color, and perhaps was even already a magicker or something close to it. *Pray to Renik he's a good one*, she thought. The things that were pursuing them had destroyed most of the Glaring Cliffs in what had seemed like minutes. They couldn't be beaten or even briefly checked by force of arms; perhaps magick was the only answer…if there was an answer.

Now Eni was pushing at the wall, then feeling along its edges, then pushing more. "It's here, Frain. Just a moment more."

"What is it you're looking for?"

"A key. Or maybe not. Sometimes I can open this without the key, if I just bump it in the right place."

Kneeling down, she began to search for something that resembled a key. Maybe it had fallen…

"No, no; it wouldn't be on the floor; it's always up high, or stuck to the edges somewhere," he said, grunting a bit with the effort of the magick he was attempting.

She stood up and felt around the wall and the edges of its rough, wet stones.

He saw what she was doing and asked, "Anything?"

She shook her head and kept looking.

They heard the voices from far off. Or at least they seemed like voices: deep, low, grumbling voices that echoed down the hall toward them.

Someone was down here with them. Someone was looking for them. Frainle thought she could feel the hall getting warmer as the owners of the voices approached. Yes, it was getting warmer. *How did those damn things find us so quickly? Or was it someone else?*

No, it was them.

They were coming.

"Where's the damn key?" Eni hissed as he frantically felt around the edges of the wall. There looked to be a stone door there, maybe, but if it were there, it had no hinges and no obvious places to grab, pull, or push.

She backed up against the far wall. "Show me where you bump."

"Ah, well, here…or sometimes here," he said, pointing at two different spots.

"Both at the same time, or just either one? You're sure it's opened without the key?"

"Yes, both…both spots at once is best…but…slamming it won't help. There's some kind of old locking mechanism that has to be jarred in just the right way, or it won't budge."

The sounds of their pursuers were growing louder, and the heat was becoming unbearable.

"Just let me try," she cried, not caring who heard her.

He glanced at her and nodded, and then he stepped aside.

Frainle ran and jumped into a flying dropkick, slamming both feet onto the wall in exactly the spots he'd pointed out. She fell to the floor with a grunt.

With a snap, the door popped open.

"Hurry…" he said, helping her to her feet and urging her inside.

They entered a cavernous room with a very tall ceiling and dozens of crumbling, ancient statues of things that didn't look at all human. Eni pushed the door closed behind them, and she heard the locks snap back into place.

"What is that?" she asked, staring up at strange spiral horns that angled down from the ceiling. The cavern was concentric; all the horns seemed to be pointed toward one spot on the floor.

"It's a Mansdrelam Temple," Eni said, hurrying toward the center of the room.

"Who built it?" she asked, following him but still looking up.

"Watch your step!" he said as he stopped her from tripping over a series of small decorative stones that stuck up out of the floor. "Don't you study history anymore?"

"Not if I can help it."

He chuckled despite the situation, and she felt momentarily soothed by the inevitability of what would ordinarily be a massive lecture on some obscure topic.

"So who built it?" she asked to prolong the illusion.

"I don't know. I'm not sure anyone does."

"How could this be down here without anyone knowing about it?"

Eni was searching about again, this time stooping to look at various stones on the floor and reading or trying to read their inscriptions. "They know. My teacher knew, at least, and I'm sure your father and some of the others."

"But how come I've never heard about it?"

"Aethreleans don't go in for this type of thing. This is all about magick, Frain, very old magick, and our people left that kind of thing behind long ago."

There was the sound of metal smashing on rock.

"They're going to find a way through that door; I think they saw us go through...so whatever you're going to do..." she said.

"I know. Here's the one...yes." He put his hand on a stone and coughed violently once, then again. The stone began to glow like the wall had. "Let's go."

"Go where?"

He led her to the center of the temple, to the small, dry, circular dip in the middle of the floor. Other than for a small altar a dozen paces or so from the circle, there was nothing else near the dip. She looked up and saw that all the spiral horns were pointed at the spot where she was now standing.

"Don't move, not at all. Don't even talk. And close your eyes."

She stood there and did what he asked, but she opened her eyes right away to see what he was up to.

He was standing at the altar with his hands on its sides.

"What are you doing?"

"Please, don't speak. I've never done this before, and I can't really be sure —" He let out a huge breath and seemed to double over in pain.

"Eni?"

He straightened back up and placed his hands on the altar again. "Frainle, no matter where you go, they will be looking for you. You cannot let them find you. Wait for your father to come for you."

"What do you mean? You're coming with me."

"I can't. It's just how this works. If it works. When you get where you're going, get out and hide. It may take a long time for Leander to find you."

"Eni, no! You can't stay here! We have to get out together!"

"No, Frain. There's no way now for that to happen. Don't worry about me. I have a few tricks I can try. Maybe they won't find me."

But she could tell he was lying. He was a terrible liar. It was one of his finest qualities.

"No! Please..." She tried to walk toward him, but something held her there. Her body began to tingle. Her head hurt.

"Frain! You have to close your eyes! Please!"

She could see him beginning to die. He looked like he was melting. He was trying to say something, but there wasn't enough left of him to say it.

Her tears were so thick she didn't know if her eyes were shut. She squeezed them and cried, "My friend, please...I love you...please..."

Chapter 21
He missed her mouth and kissed her eye.

Place: Tent City, kingdom of Arbana, Arba Environ
Date: Quattrenim 27, AY 998

She watched as they chopped off the head of a man. And then another, and then a third.

She and Dalter were at the back of the crowd, inches away from the entrance. "We need to go, my dove. Now," he whispered in her ear. There was no mistaking the message in his otherwise kindly voice: they were in danger.

It should be easy enough for them to back away and make their way to their own tents.

Easy, she thought, as long as no one noticed them leaving or had reason to want to prevent her master from leaving. Hadn't they all been told to stand and watch?

The axe was raised above a fourth neck. Just as it came down, Dalter Bubussa backed out of the grand tent, pulling her. They hurried away.

They passed a few guards, one of whom gave them a curious look...but nothing more than a look. He wouldn't stop them; he was known to Dalter and had often done business of one kind or another with him. A slight shake of the head was all it took to tell the man that now was not the time for conversation or inquiry. When another guard turned to look at Dalter and then to regard Ftuu in the way men usually did, the first took him by the arm and whispered something in his ear. Dalter was free to go on his way, his beautiful attendant in tow.

When they reached the living tent, Hara and Justella were there, sitting and waiting. Dalter bent over and took a minute to catch his breath; he was too fat, and he knew it. After almost hyperventilating both from the effort of their flight and the fear of what he and Ftuu had just witnessed, he told them what they had to do. "You need to leave. All of you. Tonight."

"Leave?" Hara asked, her mouth agape.

"Gather your things."

Justella, ever obedient, left the tent to collect her things.

"But where should we go?" asked Hara, not moving. She rubbed his right arm rapidly and pressed her hard Yanzian body up against him, a worried expression on her scarred face. Her scars wrinkled with concern, making them somehow more pronounced and angry.

Ftuu put her hand on Hara's forearm, attempting to comfort her.

As always, she did not speak, but she regarded Hara warmly and with understanding.

Hara smacked her in the face.

"None of that!" Dalter said, pushing Hara aside. "I'll have none of that now!" He smiled at Ftuu and then turned away and poured himself a goblet of sweet milk.

"But...where should we go?" Hara repeated.

"I don't care. Go west, there are places to hide in the west. In the forest."

"The forest?" whined Hara, clutching at his arm.

"Yes, the Wilds, woman...the Wilds!"

"But the Wilds are so far away, Master..."

"Then go east, yes, forget west, go east: to the Teeth, to Pir Choss...they might take you in at Pir Choss."

"What is Pir Choss?"

"Damn you, woman, you know what Pir Choss is...the people of medicine, the ones who fixed your arm two years ago..."

"They are nasty beasts, those ones!" Hara hissed. "They wanted me to come with them, they said —"

"Then go south! Let the Slau put you to use, or the Pumcat!"

"Please, Master, explain. What is 'Pumcat'? Why are you sending us away?"

"Listen to me, and please listen to me well. Do it now, do it right now, my sweet doves! If you do not flee this instant, you will all be killed!"

"But you can protect us."

"I cannot. I am sorry, I cannot. Not this time."

"Why?"

"Why? I have asked myself that. I blame my many foolish choices, but I leave you to draw your own conclusions, if you are lucky enough to get someplace where such contemplations and the time they require are available."

"Come with us!" cried Hara.

"Would that I could, dear ones. I cannot, and you must believe me. Our time together is over. My life is over, Hara. They are coming for me, and if they find you here with me, they will kill you."

Ftuu stood aside and stared at the scene. She had no idea why Dalter was so distressed — they'd seen a few beheadings before, although never so many at once — and his reaction was frightening her. She didn't want to leave him, and she didn't want to go anywhere with Hara.

"I don't understand, Master: why would they want to kill us?" whimpered Hara.

Dalter stopped and thought, but only for a moment. Then he shrugged. "Why does anyone kill anyone? They are evil. They want something. Someone took payment from someone or worse, tried to help someone." He sighed and slapped his forehead. "I shouldn't have done that. Stupid man!"

"Who did you help? Who?"

"It doesn't matter. Here, here: take this, take these barbs, take these jewels — it isn't much but — no, no. Put it in this pack. Yes, like that! Now pick a direction and run! You have food?"

"Food? I've eaten…"

Ftuu shook her head. She had not eaten or could not remember in the moment if she had.

"Doves, you need food for the journey! No, forget the food: just go!"

Hara grabbed his arms and thrust herself at him. "I'm not going anywhere, Master, please. My place is by your side!"

"Hara! Stop and listen! If they cannot learn what they want to know from me, and even if they can, they will want to question everyone who worked for me, everyone around me. My sons. The slow riders. You."

"But…please, can we just talk about this? Please!" she whined.

Dalter stopped what he was doing and focused on her face. His features softened for a moment. "Okay, okay, you're right. Yes. We'll talk. First, though, go into my small tent and fetch some food — all the food you can carry. For you and Justella and Ftuu. Go, quickly now!"

"You said forget the food!"

"Go and get it!"

Hara did as she was told.

The frazzled old slaver turned to Ftuu and looked longingly at her. "Good-bye, my soft love, my Pebbuskan delight, my silent flower of the finest bloom!" He reached out to her, and she gently resisted his embrace. He smiled in spite of himself. "If I were capable of such a thing as love, it would have been with you. It would have been all for you, beautiful Ftuu…"

He produced a small box from within his cloak and pressed it into her hand. He pulled her close and whispered in her ear:

"This is all I have to give you. Forget Hara: she will only get you killed. Lose her immediately. Leave before she returns. Justella is smart; she will find her own way. Or take her with you if you must. Find your way east and south to Carthage. Cross the Vinatuat River and Southern Road, carefully now, and look for Cvuklon the Slau. You remember him: the chubby thing, the one who reads, him with the crazy uncle. From the Summering Markets."

Ftuu nodded.

Dalter pulled at a bulging pouch hanging from his belt. He loosened the strings and dipped two of his fingers deeply into the pouch.

"With any luck, he will at some point in the near future find his way to the Ferrela Fout, a small, ugly Carthagian inn. I sent him there to deliver something to my brother, Nuadac, not very long ago. Cvuklon, bless his young, stupid heart, never travels in a straight line. Always distracted by his quest for a good meal. I love that boy." Dalter flashed a small smile. "Go there and find him. If he's not there, wait for him. My brother will help you. I hope. No, he will. He will."

The fingers, covered in Thicknomite red dust, came out of the pouch. Dalter regarded the amount with something like resignation and then shoved both fingers way up his nose, breathing in sharply. "I have told you of my brother, yes? Oh, don't make that face. He's not as bad as I made him out to be; every story needs a villain, and Nua just fits the part. Fine, he fits it far too well. Family is family." He pulled out a small envelope with a letter in it; on the letter was the name of the inn — Ferrela Fout — and a tiny sketch of a small fountain. "His wife's family owns the inn. He himself works with eyes, you know. He helps people see. Or he used to. No more. He trained at Pir Choss…he can do as much as you will need, and more, until you find Cvuklon…if you find Cvuklon." He turned to her, closed his eyes, and bent to kiss her, but she turned away again. He missed her mouth and kissed her eye.

"It will be very difficult to reach him; Carthage is not close. Travel in the dark, make yourself invisible…stay clear of any travelers, especially big parties, or you will find that there are masters in this world not quite as susceptible to your beauty as me."

He stopped for a second and looked as if he were about to belch. Ftuu watched him take a deep, slow breath and then gasp for more air.

"But do not lose sight of the road, whatever you do. And when you find Cvuklon, show him — but do not, whatever you do, give him — the box I just gave you. Show that only to him, and to…"

Hara reentered the room and stopped when she saw their embrace. Justella entered right behind her.

"Jamoi," he whispered to Ftuu.

"I have the food," Hara announced poutily. "I filled my pack."

Justella added, "I have clothes. And a few more small jewels to spend…"

Dalter gave Ftuu one last small hug. He kissed her on each cheek and on her forehead and then backed away, his eyes afraid, his nose slightly bloody. He turned to Hara and Justella and embraced them curtly, nodding to each as he let go. "All of you: get out of this camp, and find somewhere to hide! Go!"

He reached down into a chest by the door and withdrew a large, curved knife. He held it up and gave it a careful look; he then sighed and shook his head. "What am I doing? Would someone tell me please?"

Without looking again at them, he turned and scurried out of the tent, glancing left and then right and deciding on the left.

Ftuu, Justella, and Hara were left standing there.

Hara turned to the other two, trembling with fear. Justella started to weep. Ftuu stared at Hara with a question in her eyes.

"I don't know. I do not know. What should we do? Without Master, how will we live?" Hara sat down and also began to weep. "What did he just say to you? What did he whisper?"

Outside, there was shouting and the sound of hoofs coming from somewhere in the camp.

Justella wiped her eyes and peeked outside. She turned to the others, gave a small shrug, and left the tents, taking her pack with her.

"Where is she going? Why is she taking our things?" cried Hara.

Ftuu knelt, hugged her, and tried to pull her to her feet.

Hara refused to move. "No, no! We cannot! We would be punished by Master, or perhaps by…by someone else. We cannot go."

Ftuu gestured intensely toward the back flap of the tent.

"We cannot, Ftuu!" cried Hara.

The shouting outside was getting louder.

Ftuu grabbed for Hara's pack.

"What are you doing? No! This is mine!" Hara screamed. She rose and hissed at Ftuu, mad with fear. "You can't have this, and you're not going to run! I'll give you to them, to the ones who are looking for the master! You're his little whore, you know all his secrets!" She slapped Ftuu in the mouth and laughed hysterically. "Still can't talk? Little liar…I've seen you, talking with the slow riders, late at night, and more than talking…I know all about you. I know you're pregnant, little whore —" Another slap, but this one missed.

Ftuu stepped forward and hit Hara with her palm, right between the eyes. Hara dropped like a stone. Dalter had paid for her to learn how to do that, or at least, he thought he had — she'd had such skills from long ago, a time she could not remember, and his "investment" might now save her life — if only she could get out of here.

Hara would give them nothing but a story. Maybe, if the story was enough, they'd let her live. Ftuu couldn't worry about Hara, though. It was time to leave.

She yanked the pack off Hara's shoulder, slung it onto her own, and slipped over to the rear flap. Hara lay on the floor in a ball, weeping openly.

Ftuu saw no one outside, but very nearby there was the scream of a man being beaten. And voices — strange, scratchy voices that sounded like branches on stone.

She crept out of the tent and headed away from the scream and the voices.

Ftuu made her way between the storage tents. Some were so tightly pitched to the ones at their backs she had to slither very carefully to avoid falling into a tent wall. Twice she tripped and fell on stakes. The second time knocked the wind out of her and left her with a deep, painful bruise on her ribs.

As she neared the southern edge of the camp, she realized she had no idea where she was headed. Even if she got out of the camp, which was doubtful given the shouts and screams that came from every direction, there was nothing but low brush country for miles around.

She reached the edge, and there were no more tents to hide behind. Twenty paces stood between her and the brush beyond the camp.

There were voices ahead. They were already searching the brush. They were searching the tents too.

"Here, here. Hide here."

An old woman with a shawl was calling to her from a rear opening in a tent she'd just passed.

"Quickly!"

Ftuu did not recognize the old woman, but she had no choice: there was nowhere else to hide, and they were almost upon her.

She slipped into the tent past the woman. It was very dark inside — she realized she'd almost walked right into a large crate. She turned to go back out, but the woman firmly took her arm. "You can't go back that way; they will find you."

Ftuu looked at her quizzically.

"They are looking for you," said the woman, "but I can fool them. They've already searched this tent, even this crate. Don't worry. They'll soon believe you found a way out and into the hills. Get in!"

Ftuu did it. She climbed in and squatted down. The old woman looked in at her from over the top, and then she climbed in also.

"Good, good. Now be still and wait..." The woman closed the top of the crate and then reached through a hole and pulled at an old tarp that smelled like something dead. Ftuu saw what she was doing and reached through to grab also. Working together, they partially covered the crate.

They squatted next to each other and waited.

Soon, there were voices. Through the gaps in the crate, Ftuu could make out the main opening of the tent and two dark figures. She watched them move, very slowly, almost unnaturally, and it made her shiver. They seemed to pause for a moment, but then there was a loud howl from elsewhere in the camp and with that, they moved away.

"Them's what's looking for you. You'll want to steer clear of them, trust me," whispered her sudden ally.

Ftuu glanced at her and then back at where the figures had stood.

"What are they? Well, maybe they're servants of the Mind, or maybe the Slau, but that's not the truth of it, I thinks. Let's just stay quiet, and then I'll show you something."

They crouched on the floor of the crate and waited. They stayed that way for maybe an hour, maybe more. The dark figures had not returned, but the old woman had shaken her head each time Ftuu had made to rise.

At some point the woman decided the time was right; she flung open the crate and jumped out. Ftuu followed her lead.

"We have to go," whispered the old woman. "It's not safe here." She started pulling Ftuu's arm and leading her toward the exit.

Ftuu hesitated.

"C'mon, girl! What I need to show you's in the next tent. Be quick!"

They crept up to the main flap where they'd seen the dark ones, but now there was nothing, not even the sound of soldiers searching or calling out. The camp was deathly still. The old woman turned to her and put a finger to her lips, a redundant gesture in Ftuu's case.

They slipped across to another tent, one that looked identical to the one they'd just left. Inside were three large crates and two small ones.

"In there, yes, there…" the old woman said as she led Ftuu to one of the smaller crates. "Get in there. And good luck."

Ftuu threw her a puzzled look that became slightly panicked when she realized the woman was shoving her into a crate and sealing it behind her. She pressed her face against the wood and peeked through.

"The floor, dear, the floor! Poke at it!" whispered the old woman. Then she slinked out of the tent.

Ftuu felt around the base of the crate. Nothing but wood. What had she expected to find? She was trapped, and they were looking for her. She kicked her heel on the crate floor. Something shifted. The slat cracked a little and then fell through. *To where?* she wondered.

There was a hole beneath the crate, maybe eighteen inches in diameter.

She peeked into the hole and then shoved her arm into it.

There was a tunnel. She couldn't tell how far it went, but it seemed to be heading toward the edge of the camp.

This was a way out.

And she had to get away, to anywhere, far away. She knew this to be true.

She knew they were not only after Dalter.

They were after her.

They were after her child.

She wanted to stay, to find Dalter and even Hara and make sure they were well, but something assured her they would never be well again. She had never seen Dalter with such fear in his eyes. He'd worn the look of a man who was resigned to dying with no chance at reprieve. She shivered to think what those dark creatures might have done to him. Why were they here? Who had Dalter helped, and how had helping someone led to this?

What did they want with her child?

Ftuu slithered into the tunnel and then began to crawl, very slowly and carefully.

She slipped down into a dry, sandy gully. Its height allowed her to run in a low crouch. At first, she seemed to be circling the camp, but then the gully turned away from the noises and the lights and began to bring her deeper into the night's darkness and closer to the hills.

She was terrified that there would be soldiers in the brush, but there were none. Maybe they'd given up. Or maybe they were waiting, watching for anything that moved.

She lay there for a moment in the gully, catching her breath. The crawl through the tunnel had almost suffocated her, and she was very thirsty. She was covered in mud from head to foot.

There was suddenly a tremendous light in the sky over the camp, bright as midday.

Screams filled the night air, screams of something she'd never heard before. She felt very cold. High above, something was circling and screaming and...looking for her. Something was flying, and that alone was cause for fear, because anything that could so openly defy the Visshilla must be both dangerous and insane.

She was out in the open; anything above could easily spot her in this light. Fear froze her in place. She felt very much like crying, then very much like vomiting.

Ftuu realized the mud that caked her body must be making her blend into the gully's soil.

And then the light went out and the screaming stopped.

She got up and ran.

A minute later, the light was back, but far behind her. The flying thing was searching the brush.

She ran faster. She ran so hard she found it difficult to breathe. She stumbled many times over rocks and into gullies small and large. Her shoulder was smashed, her right knee was on fire, and her bruised ribs ached with every breath she took. She could barely see where she was going. Still, she ran.

She didn't stop running until she could no longer see the light from the camp, or any light at all save the stars. Miles passed, or what seemed like miles, and she reached the top of a hill overlooking a dark little valley. There was a sound of trickling water. She took a step, tripped, and rolled down the hill into the valley. Breathing heavily, scared out of her mind, she lay there and listened. Again, the sound of water, but nothing else, not even wind.

When she found the strength to move again, it was morning.

She guessed at which direction was east. She willed herself to move. She was still caked in mud, but it had dried and was flaking off her as she walked.

But she didn't go far.

As afraid as she might be, it still didn't make sense for her to be on the road.

No one was about. No one seemed to be looking for her. But that could not be true. Someone was looking. She would need to stay hidden.

She found a small cluster of pine trees and broken old branches.

With her hands, she dug a shallow hole, something to lie in, something to hide as much of her as was possible. This wasn't anything she was used to, not by any means, but fear drove her to action, however inconsequential that action might on the surface seem, and she dug.

She dug until her fingers bled.

When she could dig no more, she lay down in her hole, pulled branches over herself and quietly waited for nightfall.

After a short while, as exhausted as she was, she fell asleep praying she would wake up.

Chapter 22
"And Trilesti traverses the sky more quickly than Ponesa..."

Place: Aethrelius, Arba Environ
Date: Quattrenim 28, AY 998

Their captain was leading them home.

They'd departed mere hours after Yallous was in the ground. The weather reports from the sea were terrible, so Leander had reluctantly opted to leave *Well's Time* in the hands of its skeleton crew at the Khampier and travel by horseback up the Battrishean Road to the Cliffs. He'd led them north, away from Renikalar and its fresh stink and its suicidal leader and its fate. The journey would take ten days under normal circumstances, but as they were anxious to get home, they were pushing to do it in eight.

But they never truly made it home.

Not to the home they remembered.

On the fifth day, a farmer on a horse that wasn't his own galloped past them, yelling something about everything burning. Leander's men laughed at him and told him to sober up, but Leander wasn't sure the man was drunk. He was covered head to toe in soot, and his eyes were not glassy but crazed. Still, his babblings, most of which were incomprehensible, were quite mad. He went on his way still yelling, the men still laughing at him.

They didn't laugh long.

On the sixth day out of Renikalar, they met a mob of people, some of them from the Cliffs, who were fleeing for their lives. Gretus, a kind old Saiblinoran who tended to the keep's stock of wild deer, was among them, one arm badly burned and poorly wrapped. Despite his injury, he ran to Leander as soon as he saw him

Leander reined his horse, dismounted, and made to embrace his old friend. Gretus winced at the contact; he was more badly hurt than he appeared to be.

"Gretus, what is happening?"

"You've had no word, Captain?"

"Nothing. We're six days out of Renikalar, and we're heading for home."

"You cannot do that, not now. The place is gone, Captain: burned. I fear we all must flee south..."

"Burned? By whom?" Leander asked, his pulse quickening, his anger flaring. He did not have to ask this man who'd attacked. He knew. It was happening now, and his family was in danger, maybe even dead.

"I don't know, sir. They came in the night. They burned everything. Ships, houses, the keep, the stables…I was out on an errand for the lady; I tried to make it back to her and to poor Frainle, but there was no way: the fires were everywhere. I fled with a few villagers, and more have joined us along the way."

Heop came forward: "Sir, we should press forward. Perhaps —"

"Do NOT! You must NOT do that!" shouted the near-delirious Saiblinoran. "I tell you, there is nothing left!"

Leander nodded to one of his regiment medics, who came to his side at once. "Thom, see that this man's wounds are tended to. Michael, take all but four of the men and escort these people back down south."

Michael stepped toward Leander. "Back to the capital, sir?" he said with a slight trace of doubt in his tone.

"What? No, no. I suppose not. But stay inland. Send them to the lake, and wait for us there at Banterkam. Or, no — Midpath. Camp outside Midpath, give them all food and shelter. Wexshai? Where is Wexshai?"

"Here, sir."

"You ride to Renikalar and tell those fools what's coming. And if you can get a message to them any other way and sooner, do it."

"Your permission, sir?"

"Yes, dammit, you have it." This wasn't the time to debate about magick, and he was betting the Stavers would at least understand that much. He wondered for a moment if Beir had seen this coming, had wanted the Vo'ix to…but that couldn't be true. The man was an ass, but was he insane?

His men went about carrying out their orders. Within minutes, most of them were already heading south, having surrounded the fleeing villagers with a vanguard formation, double thick in the rear. Michael had pulled Gretus up onto his mount; the man could scarcely walk at this point. Wexshai had sped off with his man, Daris, ahead of the mob, but they would only race as far as was necessary to gain some privacy. Magick must still be used guardedly, and these poor people had already received shock enough to last them a lifetime, however long that might now be.

Heop, Famish, and Lyknore were with Leander, waiting intently on his orders.

"We ride north to confirm there are no survivors and to reconnoiter this enemy, whoever they are," he said in a low but firm voice. "We ride to see if our families and our home survived this madness."

"I'm sure ol' Gretus was just up in a lather, Captain," said Heop. "No way our boys didn't beat them off."

Lyknore chimed in, "That's right, Captain. The Buzzard wouldn't have given 'em an inch, not even if they got a good shot or two in firstways!"

Leander smiled slightly at their confidence but could not share in their optimism. Not wanting to dispel it either, he said nothing; he simply turned his mount back onto the road and headed for whatever remained of his home.

He needn't have bothered. Two days later, after a near-nonstop charge from where they'd met the mob, they reached the Cliffs. From a ridge above the Piell, he and his men stared down at a sea of burnt and burning country. The entire plateau, as far as they could see in every direction but south, was black. They descended and tried to proceed, but the road itself was so hot the horses would not tread upon it; when the men tried to walk instead, they found it was impossible.

"What could do this?" wondered Heop aloud.

"Something we've already faced, I think, but have not yet seen," answered Leander.

"Tolii Nus," stated Heop grimly.

But that had been an island, Leander thought, *one small island.* This was...hundreds and hundreds of acres. Thousands. Far off in the distance to the north, he imagined he could see tiny columns of smoke rising from the earth's blackened edge. Was that the Cliffs?

"What do we do, Captain?" asked Famish.

Leander stared out north for a moment and then answered him. "We turn around and join the rest of the squadron at Midpath."

"And the Cliffs?"

"We'll regroup, commandeer a fleet, and go around by sea."

Heop agreed, "That's right. Bastards can't have burned that."

They turned around and road south until nightfall. They camped along a small shale cliff face and made no fire — not because, Leander thought, they were worried about discovery or pursuit but perhaps because they'd already seen too much burnt to endure the sight again in whatever amount.

They slept in shifts, two hours on, four off, till morning. Leander wasn't in any desperate hurry to get back to Renikalar. Part of him wondered if there would be a Renikalar to get back to. He doubted the enemy would head as far in as Midpath, at least not right away; after all, once they'd destroyed the High, the Khampier, and the Cliffs, the capital was all but fallen.

But where were the bastards now? They'd burned the Cliffs and then...what, retreated back to the sea? Where were they?

He didn't say any of this to his men. He didn't say anything at all to them, except perhaps "yes" when asked if he wanted a second piece of bread with the morning's meal of cheese and dried meat. There wasn't much to discuss, and there was a small thought germinating in his head, a reaction perhaps to the presumed deaths of his family and destruction of his home. He found himself thinking not of Baeselle and Frainle but instead of Shain, his brave and shortsighted, handsome and happy son. How old would he have been by now? Leander's head was too filled with smoke and sadness, too clouded by vague elements that would let him neither think nor act in any full capacity...and he could not figure out what age Shain would be had he lived to die at the Cliffs with his mother and sister.

And still the small thought, more a disturbance in his unavailable mind, persisted in making itself known at a vexing and unwelcome time. It denied him sleep and, as they rode toward Midpath and what they hoped they would find there, it asked a question of him he wasn't willing to answer or even consider. Yet. And it was the qualifying "yet," he knew, that empowered the thought to maintain its current small but ominous course.

Having seen his home, he'd succumbed to the thought's inevitable will, and it had taken hold of him.

There was, it was known to all Aethreleans, the story of a weapon that, long ago, had been used by several of the greatest warriors ever to walk the soil of Aethrelius to vanquish foes untold, including the Vo'ixtavracci. This weapon was known as Mosta Nom, the Sword of Endings. It was "forged" or otherwise created in 479 and wielded by Renik, who may or may not have forged it, to defeat K'olowinyad the Creator, a murderous wizard (or scientist, depending on which history one was reading; Leander had read them all). There were no exact surviving records of how the thing itself was created, what the nature of its power was, or even what form it actually took. To this day, scholars in Hunberg, Carthage, and Pashka still debated the question of whether Mosta Nom was an actual sword or instead something that one, for lack of a more precise term, analogized to a sword.

What was known was that in 664, Frederick Czackus, the Aethrelean who led the Revolution, helped author the nation's Commandments, and actualized the split from the Quadrate, had somehow found the Sword and used it to attack and defeat the Vo'ix themselves.

Again, history was stingy with facts, particularly where the fate of the Sword after Frederick was concerned. Some believed it had been stolen; some believed Frederick, as the story went, had thrown it into the sea just before he died; others believed a man like Frederick would never have been foolhardy enough to voluntarily deprive his nation of a relic so valuable to its perpetuated existence. The question became moot upon the alliance with the Jamoian Mudarrisi, whose magick, until a few days ago, had kept a repeat invasion by the Gift Takers at bay. And yet in the minds of Aethreleans everywhere, the legend of Mosta Nom persisted.

Many believed it would always return to protect them.

Many believed it was somehow with them, watching over the Great Nation, guiding the people in subtle ways few dared to try to comprehend or question.

Leander didn't know what to believe. He'd assumed it was mostly nonsense, a story to tell children and young warriors who needed a reason to keep watch and march and train — all this despite the fact that his mother was obsessed with the object and had scarcely gone three days during his youth without mentioning it and hinting that it "would be a spectacular and princely enterprise for him to pursue," meaning that she believed he should devote his life to finding it.

He generally adopted the policy, more and more as he grew older, of doing what his father did and ignoring the obsession of his mother. Most of the people they knew, both military and civilian, regarded her as insane. She was not, after all, a native of their country, and her propensity to shout to any and all who would listen that magick was the salvation of all peoples everywhere and that the greatest magick resided not in the Proving but in the Sword of Endings, solidified public opinion rather neatly.

Theresta Dossilea, the Mad Lady of the Cliffs. He loved her still, years after her passing, but to say he had never shared her obsession or her certainty that a role in the Sword's legend was his to play was an understatement of the most severe kind. He liked a good story as much as the next man, but he did not put stock in stories: he trusted in his men, his steel, and his command abilities. And his mother had been, without a doubt, quite mad.

But the Vo'ix were here now; the Vo'ix had certainly killed his family and destroyed his home. And if the reports of the destruction and what he'd seen on the Piell were any clear indication, the Aethreleans would have no way of contending with them. It was conceivable that every man, woman, and child in the Great Nation could perish.

Maybe what they needed was a little madness.

Maybe his mother had been right all along.

"Captain, we're approaching the fork."

Leander stirred from his musings and looked up. "Yes, of course."

"Are we still bound for Midpath?"

"You are. Go and collect the men. I will ride forward to Renikalar and speak to the Square."

Heop growled a bit but refrained from questioning the order and the idea behind it. "Very good, Captain, although I'd feel better if you weren't going alone."

Leander smiled. It was a sad smile he offered his friend and fellow warrior, but it was the most reassuring he could offer. "Heop, what's ahead of me is nothing compared to what's behind me. And this has to be done."

"Don't let them take you alive, sir," said Famish.

"I prefer they not take me at all!" Leander managed with a chuckle.

And with that, he turned south and left them.

Renikalar was a tortured beehive awash with frenetic activity.

He'd seen as much when he'd entered the city, but not for long. He was taken into custody and jailed immediately on the vague charge of impeding military action. This for demanding an audience with Janstrin Beir.

That evening, he sat in the jail and listened through the window to the sounds of an army mustering and a people in panic. They were right to panic, he thought, but there wasn't much point to the mustering. They didn't stand a chance against the assault that was coming.

He wasn't in the jail alone. There were a few old men, three women, and a child. All looked badly traumatized; some were wounded. There were burns on the child's back and arms. Still, she was alive.

He wondered if she were better off that way or not, given what was likely in store for the living.

I shouldn't think that way, he corrected himself. *What happened up north doesn't have to happen here. Perhaps the rockmen can't attack that way on land; maybe they need to hurl their hell from the deck of ships.*

"And Trilesti traverses the sky more quickly than Ponesa," he muttered to himself sardonically, "and I'd be faster on foot than on the back of a Garden dragon."

The child looked up at him and whispered, "Are there dragons here? Is that what burned Anbet?"

"Who is Anbet, child?"

"My baby sister. She likes to cry a lot, but she's not here now."

He tried to smile and comfort her, but he found all he could do was wince. His tongue felt thick in his mouth, a symptom of too little sleep and too little water. The child looked away.

So this is to be my fate: sitting in a jail with wounded oldsters and children, waiting to find out that my theory about the rockmen is nonsense.

Beir was a fool, he'd always been, but was he mad? It had been he who had championed the movement to expel the foreigners, he and his kind who had ended the relationship with the Mudarrisi. Why? He knew as well as anyone that the Takers were not a thing of myth but instead a very real threat from history not too far gone. Why would he sell out his country? Why would he leave the people so vulnerable? His life's ambition has always been to overthrow the Unchained and rule Aethrelius with the help of his fellow fools. Why would he let her die?

Leander closed his eyes and tried to think more clearly. It wasn't easy; his jailers had given him quite a beating. He winced again. *My skull might be fractured. That will make burning to death easier to take, I should think.*

And how did the Vo'ix know to attack now, so soon after the Stavers had taken power?

Someone told them. Someone's been working with them.

Who?

Who stood to gain by the complete obliteration of everything Aethrelean? Not even the Tri could make that claim, because with the Takers here and the Great Nation's military gone — not that it had proven itself in any way effective against the attack so far — the Tri itself was ripe for the picking.

None of this makes any sense.

Maybe the crack to the skull has robbed me of reason, he thought. *Or maybe it was the death of all I hold dear. Maybe it's the doom of my country. Or maybe I'm already dead and reason holds no worth in what comes after.*

He put his head down on the floor and fell asleep, but not before the thought that had been harassing him harassed him once more. He thought of the Sword and what a thing it would be if he could find it...

"Captain?"

Heop was shaking his shoulder.

"Captain, wake up. We're taking you out of here."

"You're not taking him anywhere, Chainer: Janstrin Beir is taking him and sending him and you on the coward's path."

Leander opened his eyes and saw Heop grab the guard by the throat. Half a dozen Staver men pointed their weapons at Heop's head.

"Say another word, my sad little Staver friend, and I will pull your throat right out of your neck."

"Heop," said Leander softly, "mind the child."

"Always wanted some, sir, never had the time. My boss ran me ragged — no opportunity for even the briefest shag."

Leander smiled and made to stand up. Addressing the Staver whose throat was in peril, he asked, "Is Janstrin Beir ready at last to speak to me himself, Lieutenant?"

Heop released the throat and took a step back. The other guards backed away a bit but did not lower their weapons.

Rubbing his neck, the lieutenant hoarsely replied, "You're to be tried in the public square as cowards and deserters, and then exiled...probably to Chralm Doanna."

Chralm Doanna? The commander there, Cedril sa Mino, would

hardly imprison him, unless dinner at the First Keep's table was considered a kind of imprisonment, which on occasion it had felt like. God, that man could talk.

"Very well," said Leander. "Lead on."

The public square had a name, though the Staver lieutenant had failed to use it. It was called Aidan's Square, and it had been so named for Leander's paternal grandfather, Aidan Bjarn Dossilea.

Leander was sure that it would now be renamed — if someone could stop running and screaming long enough to think of a name and put together a ceremony. Perhaps they could call it "We Let in Hell" Square. Maybe not. It was likely the Stavers wouldn't be doing the renaming in any case. He tried to conjure up some harsh-sounding Vo'ix name, for if anyone were truly going to be a position to effect a new name, it would certainly be the Vo'ix, but his command of their language, if one could call it "command," was limited to three words, only one of which he was sure he knew the meaning.

There was no one in the Square when he arrived, not even an arbiter to pronounce sentence. So they waited: Leander, his twenty-five or so remaining men who had apparently come or been collected while he sat in prison, and the guards who had escorted them, whose numbers had swelled to twelve along the way but now stood at six. The other six had run off to help with the fortification of the city's walls.

"What do you think they'll do with us, sir? Send us to Chralm Doanna?" asked Wexshai, his face a mask of calm.

"We've violated Beir's fucking pronouncement, so they have to do something," said Heop.

The Staver lieutenant puffed himself up a bit and stepped forward. "Keep quiet," he commanded. Leander noticed his step had taken him no closer to Heop.

In the distance, he could hear deep, resonating explosions. Rockmen.

My theory was wrong, he admitted to himself. *They're able to hurl that fire on land as well. Disappointing.*

He wondered how long the city had. A day? Two? Hours?

Presently, two dignitaries, Stavers that Leander recognized but whose names he couldn't recall, scurried into the Square. One of them carried a parchment which he then read aloud. He was out of breath from his scurrying, so he sounded less than official.

"The eminent Janstrin Beir — legal and sound head of the Square — has decreed that the Fourth Mandate Squadron will be escorted to Chralm Doanna, far from the fight for our dear freedom and liberties, disgraced by cowardice, publically denounced as discommandmentary, and denied the right to assist in the defense of this country we hold so dear."

Heop started to say something, but Leander shook his head and stopped him.

"When the war is over and the Great Nation is once again victorious, having upheld all that is just, eternal, and above all, commandmentary, the Fourth Mandate Squadron may be permitted to return to their homes, stripped of all rank and privilege, pending the will of the eminent Janstrin Beir. Commander Cedril sa Mino of Chralm Doanna will detain the squadron until that time arrives. Sentence to be carried out immediately. Please sign, Capt — Mr. Dossilea."

Leander signed. It was done.

They left the city as Trilesti rose.

There were forty-two of them: Leander, Wexshai, Michael, Youssef, Heop, Famish, Lyknore, twenty-three soldiers of the Fourth including Thom and Daris, and twelve Aethrelean High Guardsmen loyal to Leander and his party, most of whom had also been sentenced to temporary imprisonment.

At the Free Men Gate on the Lake of the True, the Fourth stood aside while at least four thousand strong Deer Vale men with poleaxes and crossbows marched through.

"Olin's Keep must be emptied. The Deer Vale and its surrounding towns can't have held many more men than these," said Michael. "Beir's left his mother's home unguarded."

"It is as I feared. The governors are responding without question to the letter of the law; they are keeping for themselves only a handful of men with which to maintain local government," Leander said.

"This is lunacy. What will these Staver shits do if the city is taken or placed under indefinite siege?"

"If that happens, then Aethrelius is done," said Youssef.

"But if he stays within the walls, what else could happen?" asked Michael.

"He will not stay behind the walls. He will lead Aethrelius out to meet its foe," said Leander. "Beir is many things, perhaps even mad, but a coward he is not."

"If he does what you're suggesting, he will surely fall," said Michael flatly. "Why would he do such a thing against this foe? The walls offer protection enough, but..."

"They have not seen what we have seen. Never have we faced such a threat. Did you believe the Cliffs would ever fall? Do you believe it now, even after witnessing it, the ferocity of it, the finality of it?"

Leander's questions hung in the air as they watched the brave legions making their way to their beloved Aethrelean capital.

The last of the Deer Vale's best had passed them by, and the gate was now clear to pass. Leander's men urged their horses through and headed down the sloped highway with the city at their backs.

Below, the Chinunam Plains were a tapestry of farms and homes and well-tilled fields and long yellow stretches where a horse could run for more than two days without the trouble of swamp or root. The bright, full light of a double dawn lit the plains for as far as the eye could see, and the roofs in the towns seemed to glow with both welcome and defiance. Seen from such a vantage point, with the towers of Renik's bold city gracing the horizon like an unyielding guardian and thousands of acres of the earth's bounty cradling the places where the people lived and worked with unassuming but equally unyielding pride, Aethrelius looked peaceful and strong, captured in a shining, eternal moment of indefinitely renewed promise.

Leander smiled despite himself. *This is my country, and these are my people.*

I will find a way to save them.
I will find the Sword.

The Bellindor Highway was packed with travelers heading west, away from the approaching war. Checkpoints had been set up to validate travelers' rights and to ensure that no military personnel were taking the opportunity to escort their families to safety. Troops had been designated for that purpose, though it was clear that few believed in the efficacy of the escorts, preferring instead to be attended to by their own. Being Aethreleans, they nonetheless succumbed to law and to their eventual placement in temporary camps that had already been established in four small towns a day's journey west of the city. Yet Leander noticed plainly that none were glad of the arrangement. "These are people who are very much used to having a say in their fate," he said to Heop.

"They'll have to put up with this for a bit, I suppose, but we'll right the ship for 'em soon, sir," answered Heop, who while never naïve was forever invested in his own rough brand of hope.

Throughout their journey west, they passed hundreds of soldiers on the highway heading east toward Renikalar to join in its defense. Men had been called from every district and township throughout Aethrelius that wasn't already engaged in — or lost to — battle. Leander's party saluted each group that passed them and noted there was no fear in their eyes.

"Look at them. So bold. They have no understanding of what they march to face," muttered Youssef to Leander.

"No, they do not," said Michael. "But the question is not whether their faces would wear the same expressions were their foe more known to them. The question is: Would they still be marching?"

Heop growled, "They're Aethreleans. They would march into the Vo'ixtavracci Environ itself if it were so commanded."

"'Obedience to one's commander is only as prudent as the commander is wise,'" Youssef said.

"Quoting Frederick won't help these men," Leander said. "They have need of Frederick himself, I'm afraid."

"And if you are successful, Captain, they may yet have him," Wexshai whispered to his commander.

Leander had confided in him and only him what he'd been contemplating and what he intended to do. The others, even Michael and especially Heop, were military men who hadn't time for legends and quests for long-lost mythical items.

Wexshai understood these things. Wexshai had been trained in magick.

But Leander would tell the others as well when the opportunity arose. Each man must be afforded the right to make his own choice in this matter. For all Leander knew, finding the Sword might take months or even years. And if it didn't exist anymore...but he stopped himself from contemplating that possibility, mostly because it wasn't, in his mind, an option.

The debate raged inside him. The Sword was a myth, an annoying ideal used by his mother to get him to eat his vegetables and do his chores. It was a fairy tale Aethreleans told themselves to ward against the fictional dread that came with theorizing that one day, the Stavers might chase all the Mudarrisi away. No one believed in the Sword, no one gave a shit about the Sword: it was a symbol of everything Aethrelean that had been allowed to rot and fade and crumble. Like the Aethrelean ideals of Renik and Frederick and Benjamin Feespeaker, the Sword was all but forgotten. And soon, there would be few left alive to regret the mistake.

They'd ride west for perhaps thirteen days, depending on the weather. Aethrelius was a big country, and they'd never got around to building a better system of transport. It had never seemed necessary, and there was always a stubborn need to eschew anything that could be perceived as mimicking the Tri.

That stubbornness might be their undoing in the here and now, Leander thought.

There were, initially, few travelers on the highway in the west. For the nonce, life along that road seemed placid in the various towns and villages, almost as if nothing were happening that was out of the ordinary. The men from these places were mostly gone, but otherwise the residents seemed to be carrying on with their lives.

Perhaps the Vo'ix wouldn't come. Perhaps they'd taken enough from the Cliffs and its sister forts along the coast. Perhaps Renikalar would not fall and their stay at Chralm Doanna would be brief.

Leander rode along silently and played rounds of "perhaps" with himself.

He suffered heavy losses with each round.

But there was a round remaining he would not lose.

Chapter 23
Looking to harm.

Place: A road south of Tent City and north of Wukneesh, kingdom of
Arbana, Arba Environ
Date: Late Quattrenim, AY 998

"My dove, have you ever heard of the Jamoi?"

Ftuu shook her head.

"The Jamoi are a people who live far from here, in the south where
the hard snows fall in winter and the fields are full in spring. They are
women, mostly. Or maybe all of them are women, I don't know. I only
know what I've heard.

"It is said they never turn away a woman looking for shelter, a
home, or even a purpose. They are reputedly very skilled at imbuing the
purposeless with purpose. Some raise eyebrows at this; me, I tend not to
judge."

She poured him some wine and strolled back across to him. He
pulled back the covers in an inviting gesture.

"It is also said that they are a race of nasty, spiteful, magick-
wielding bitches bent on exacting revenge on everything with a penis for
wrongs done a very long time ago by people with penises. Bad people, if
history is to be believed. Or perhaps that history is still happening in certain parts of our beloved environ. I couldn't say. I suppose it's all a matter
of perspective."

He took the cup of wine from her, sampled it, and favored her
with a broad smile. "Apricot?"

She nodded and returned his smile and then climbed into the bed
and nestled up against his ample body.

"In truth, I myself have thought it wise throughout my career to
avoid visiting Jamoi. As it happens, I am quite fond of my penis." He
sighed a bit as she took hold of him. "So, apparently, are you."

Later, when they were through, he lay there in satisfied repose.
She stroked his long salt-and-pepper locks and with her head on his
regrettably bloated belly, listened to him speak as he sipped some more of
the apricot nectar wine. She loved to hear him speak to her, though oftentimes she believed she missed his point.

Perhaps there were times when he wasn't bothering to make one.

Not tonight, however.

"I believe a woman of your unbelievable beauty might one day
find peace and safety among these Jamoi. I believe they might welcome
you and help you to become...well, who can say? Someday, you know, the

things I do and the people I do them to...well, they might catch up with me. Not might. Will."

He sighed and shook his head, looking very sorrowfully at her in a way he'd never had before. His looks were often somewhat sad, as if he had much to tell but had decided not to. Here and now, his look said something more.

"I haven't been very good, which I don't care much about, but over the years, I also stopped being very careful. Ah, Ftuu, you should have known me in my younger days. I was so, so careful and also, so very good. Mostly good. I got the best of every bargain and gave the worst to every simpering would-be cheat. But today...I am not what I was."

He sighed again, this time with a pitiful flair that seemed to instantly disgust him. She knew he was wondering if he still knew how to be sincere, even to her, for he had asked that question aloud many times. He drained his glass and set it aside, and then he gave her his best genuinely delighted smile. "This really is excellent. You chose this?"

She nodded and smiled.

"You have learned so much, so very much. And you've taught me a thing or two, no?" He reached down to pull her tighter to him. "You are without doubt the most beautiful woman in all Arba. A face that could begin a war, and a body...well..."

She nuzzled his chest and began to nibble at his soft, chubby neck.

"Ah yes, yes...no, no, wait, Ftuu, please..." He gently pushed her away. "Please, my dove, my silent love. There is something I need to tell you."

She stopped and looked up at him. The point was coming.

"There is someone coming, maybe tomorrow, maybe next week...I do not know. They are coming, and I'm afraid I will not live to see them go."

She wasn't understanding him, not fully, not yet. He often spoke flamboyantly and with a decidedly dramatic flavor, but there was something different about the tone he used now. He seemed to be...afraid.

"A few months ago, I made a deal. I made a deal to find someone, someone who would come through the Point, and spirit him away. And you remember him, right? I plucked him from the freshly Taken not six weeks ago. Bought him from that imbecile, Strak. A pitiful thing, he was. No mind to speak of." He shook his head as he described the man and then laughed out loud. His laugh soon faded. "This pitiful one was big trouble, but how could I have known that? There had been no signs. Or maybe there were and I missed them.

"Ah, dove, it's the sort of deal I've made a thousand times, ten thousand times before. I am a fleshbroker, am I not? A dealer in 'fresh talent,' a merchant who trucks in only the best...but I erred in my calculations. I thought he'd been selected to become someone's amusing pet, but there is nothing amusing about him, it seems."

He stood up, put his slippers on, and slowly walked to the brazier, where he held out his hands and absentmindedly rubbed them together. She watched him and wondered where his odd confession was heading.

"He is apparently someone of great value, although to whom I cannot say because I do not know. But they want him, and now he is gone and...they know we had him here for a bit. How do they know? We've been betrayed, of course. But by whom? I am at a loss there. Someone close, someone we know...someone who watched us. They saw us with this man and pieced together the puzzle and betrayed us. Betrayed me. Not you. Me."

She gazed at him and could feel his terror. And she wanted to hurt them, whoever they were.

"But when they come for me, that will be the end. And I will no longer be able to hide you from the world, my most beautiful bird. They know who I am, Ftuu, they know who I am. I don't know how they know, but they've been asking for me, this much is certain. And now, they come. It is now a question of when, not if."

She came to him and took his arm. She made gestures to indicate he should leave this place.

"Flee? Well, yes, of course. Don't think for a moment I've stayed here by choice. But what happens from here on out I have calculated, and the results are not pretty. These — people — who are coming, well...they would find me no matter where I fled. I have run before and come out wearing most of my own skin, but this time...as I said, I have erred. It was, I'm both happy and sad to say, an inevitable result of the life I've led."

He rose from the bed and led her to a small object, no more than a foot high, that was hidden under a red cloth on one of his tables.

"Please, I have something to give you. Something you will need in the times to come."

Funny how she could never recall what had been in the box.

Two weeks later, his fears had come to pass. He was likely dead, and she was on the run.

Ftuu slept the day in a small ditch alongside a wide road. Her bedding was a collection of broken fir branches and brambles. The odd speech, her last real interaction with Dalter Bubussa, her longtime master and lover, came back to her in fits and starts.

Sometime in the afternoon, she awoke. She listened, waited, listened again. She crawled a few feet from where she'd been sleeping, pulled down her pants, and relieved herself. For the third time in the last three hours, she noted unhappily. She pulled her pants back up and crawled back to her spot.

There was a little dried fruit, some kind of cured meat, and some olives in Hara's pack. Hara, whom she had never liked but for whom she now felt a swell of terrible pity. Was she dead? Probably.

Ftuu devoured almost everything, realizing that she hadn't eaten since the afternoon before. It wasn't much, but it pushed back her hunger and, for a few minutes, lessened her fear. After she ate, she fell back into a restless half sleep.

She woke to the sound of thundering hooves. She froze and listened, her breath held, expecting to be caught and dragged back to the camp. But the hooves were come and gone in under a minute, and she exhaled slowly and soundlessly.

She had never, to her recollection, ever spoken to Dalter. She rarely spoke to anyone, in fact. She had long ago learned that she felt somehow safer when silent, and she had never made any serious effort at changing that. It was better to be silent; it was better to listen. She had never understood why she felt so, but for as long as she could remember, it had been her way.

She remembered the man Dalter had spoken about, the pitiful one. She had known him in the camp and had even cared for him. Dalter had forgotten that. He scarcely noticed much of what she did, and he rarely remembered most of what he asked of her. That had been best for both of them. Until now, perhaps.

Dalter had asked her to tend to this man, this Entrant, and to bathe him well and watch him very closely. Of course, she'd slept with him— he'd hardly been conscious, but it was always a part of what "tending" meant, so she'd gently urged him despite his state. She wondered now if she shouldn't have, if maybe that wasn't what had been requested of her. It was confusing but not unusual: Dalter lived by hints and innuendo; she lived by guessing. The man had scarcely responded to her touch, but he had responded enough that she had had to drink the tea the next morning.

The tea had not worked, she now knew.

Still, while Dalter's request had been in no way unique, it was, when she considered it now, somewhat unusual given that this man hadn't been a business interest or a fellow slaver or friend. And the next day, the man was gone, and Dalter hadn't mentioned him again until a few nights before he'd commanded her to run for her life.

No, Dalter hadn't mentioned the man, but he hadn't forgotten him. And he knew that she knew exactly who he'd been worried about the night he told her to flee. Dalter had lain with her dozens of times, but never once had she become pregnant. And she wasn't a fool. She and the strange, broken man had been brought together for a reason. Dalter had his reasons. He'd tried to explain them to her, but there hadn't been time.

That was it.

She was no fool, but she had too faulty a memory. When was all that? Two months ago? Three weeks?

Or maybe it was just last night.

She couldn't be sure. She was exhausted, and her sleep had been so strange, so irregular.

There was something wrong with her. She hoped it was with her and not…with her child.

But she felt that it was neither.

There was something else, someone else, watching…closely.

The sensation both terrified and excited her, but she could not say why. She had no words or thoughts…and then there were moments when she suddenly had too many thoughts, and too many words…which wasn't like her at all.

The suns had gone down, but there was a lingering violet tint to the darkening sky. The stars were coming out, and the sight of them lifted her spirits. Wily old Dalter had taught her a little about how to tell one's direction by looking at the stars. She wasn't very good at it, but she was fairly sure that east was within her power to find. And she would travel east, if she ever got up the courage to leave her ditch and cross the road.

Along with a brother in Carthage, Dalter had once mentioned having a dear friend, a physician, at Pir Choss. Not his brother; he had trained there, yes, but there was another…

That place was one of medicine and healing, she knew. She had heard stories of soldiers who had been healed of terrible wounds and even a few thought dead who had been brought back by the healers of that mysterious place. She had once seen a group of Pir Choss physicians when they'd been camped close to Yohemu on a buying sojourn. Strange, blinking creatures, the ones she'd seen, accompanied by a Saiblinoran goatman in a wild and threatening-looking costume. They'd healed a dying woman who'd just birthed a baby.

She remembered they'd taken the baby — as payment, it was said, for the life of the mother.

But this physician friend of Dalter's had twice come and saved his life, once when he suffered fever and another time when he'd been nearly trampled to death by a small herd of Rouks pullers.

Carthage seemed a risky place, and she had never liked the stories she'd heard about Dalter's brother. Pir Choss seemed perhaps safer, but would they know if she herself was with child, and would they demand her child as payment for food and shelter? She could not know the answer, but she was afraid. She would not allow that.

Where else could she go? East to the mountains, to those Teeth, and then where?

She walked east, following a small trail that paralleled the road, and thought about the Jamoi.

Who were they? Why did they hate men? What were they, and why had he spoken about them to her just before he disappeared forever? Were they women she could find a home with or magick-wielding witches who would judge and hate her, as so many women had before?

What she understood from Dalter's hints and questions was this: yes, she might very well find a home among them.

A home among women who were not afraid of men. A country of women.

Was such a thing possible?

Her legs hurt. Her feet hurt. She had not truly bathed in days, and she stank.

The most beautiful woman in Arba, as Dalter often assured her she was, felt as terrible as she assumed she looked. But she didn't care, had never cared, about what she looked like. Mirrors she avoided and always had. She lived inside herself mostly and did her best to deflect the attentions of all but her protector. Many a man had gone away hurt and angry. A few had tried to harm her, and one had succeeded, several years ago. Dalter had dealt with him.

And now, there was no one to look, no one to want her, no one to deflect, and so her appearance would not matter. Or so she told herself.

But she recognized her own lie. She was sure of nothing except that there were those out there who would be capable of harming her. And not just those who were pursuing her.

She crossed the river right before reaching the road. She'd had to swim it, but she'd always known how to swim and swim well. Dalter had found that amusing, how she became his "little fish" rather than his "little dove" so readily whenever a pool or lake was within reach of the camp.

The current had been strong but not so strong that it had pulled her very far. It ran to the north, and that wasn't where she wanted to go, so she'd fought hard to reach the other side.

How wide had it been? How long had she swum? She couldn't say. She'd almost passed out on the bank but decided she'd better rally herself and make for some hiding place. A while later, she saw the road and felt the fear…but then spotted the ditch and the bramble and the small parallel path.

She had no idea how far she'd come or where she was, but she was sure Tent City was far away now. They would come, if they came, on horses…and they would track her. No distance she might have travelled in the night — or was it nights? — would have been enough to ensure her safety. And now, they'd had a lot of time to look for her. If they were looking.

She didn't know why, but she was sure they were.

Looking to harm.

She wondered how she could lose track of the passage of time yet know for a certainty she was being desperately hunted.

There was a small place along the path that had a rock ring for a fire. She stopped there because the ground was level and soft in a few places and she needed to sleep. She ate a little dried bread and some fruit. After so much walking, the rest and the food were very welcome.

She missed their tent and its comfortable bed and the glow of the decorative candles. Thinking about those things made her heart hurt a bit but also helped her quell the incessant terror that had accompanied her on this wicked flight. She fell asleep.

Wake.

A voice in her dreams was telling her to get up. She was still so very tired and so comfortable. She ignored it.

Wake.

The voice insisted. She did not do as she was told, but she answered sleepily: *No.*

Zeni, you must wake!

Who? Why?

Thieves have found you.

What?

Five thieves.

She opened her eyes, and there they were. Five men grinning down at her, one of them holding a torch.

"She's a pretty one."

"She is at that. You've got a good eye, Barli."

"Always have, always have."

"She ain't got much. Nothing here to borrow."

"Oh, I don't know about that. Seems there's plenty here to borrow."

She tried to stand; one of them pushed her back down.

"Probably easier if you stay down there, pretty."

She closed her eyes and knew one thing was true: they meant to harm her. And in harming her, they would probably harm her child. She could not allow that. She would not allow that.

Zeni…I can help you.

How?

I can make these men go away.

How?

Shall I make them go away?

She felt hands on her, felt them grabbing her ankles and heard her dress tearing. Then there was a man on top of her.

Shall I make them go away?

"Hold her still, would ya?"

"Stop movin', you!"

Something hit her hard in the head. She saw light for just a moment and then passed out.

She dreamt of a dock filled with fishermen and sailors. Playing among them were two other children, a boy and a girl, laughing and eating shrimp and hopping onto boats while the fishermen laughed and waved and gave them things, shiny things like shells and coins and trinkets from the sea.

She was giggling when she woke up.

And then she remembered where she was and stopped giggling.

Ponasa had begun to rise. She'd slept a long time.

Her head hurt a little.

Looking around, she gasped.

There were five dead men stacked not twenty feet from her.

In front of the stack were five satchels and a small pile of weapons.

How had this happened? She did not understand. They'd been on her, holding her, and one of them must have hit her…but this? Had someone else come, had someone saved her? Who? And where was he now?

She got up and stumbled. Her head was hurting more now, and she was dizzy from having stood too fast.

She looked at the stack of dead men. She did not feel sorry for them. She'd seen their kind many times before, usually from a distance. They were of a cowardly sort, and they didn't dare bother her in the City of Tents where everyone knew who she was with. Dalter was a kindly man with her, but he brooked no fools in his dealings with others and would not tolerate any man who sent anything but wistful admiration her way.

She glanced at the satchels and thought of going through them to see if there might be anything of use. She decided against it. Gathering her few belongings, she started back along the narrow path that she hoped was heading toward Wukneesh. Or some other point south; she hadn't decided on any destination. Just south. She found herself wobbling slightly; the world before her was unsteady and pitched slightly to the left…

They have currency.

The voice was back. It was real, or it was real to her; she couldn't be certain which.

As before, she spoke to it in her mind. *Who are you?*
They have currency. You will need that to survive.
Answer me please: Who are you?
I am Alwaud'wah.
What are you?
A chassariete.
A what?
I can protect you. Take the currency. You will need it.
What are you?
A chassariete.
What is that?
I will help Zeni.
Who is Zeni?
You are Zeni. Take the currency.

She did not understand what was happening. This thing inside her, this spirit, was not answering her questions. She did, however, see the sense in taking the money the thieves had been carrying. Was the spirit trying to help her? Perhaps.

She took the coins and jammed them into her pack by the fistful.
She had what she needed.
The rest she would figure out later.

Chapter 24
"Goodnight, ladies, and enjoy the sea air!"

Place: Camedua and points south, kingdom of Xatumka, Arba Environ
Date: Quattrenim 29, AY 998

For two weeks after his escape from the inn, he hid.

He had to get out of Camedua, but he knew they knew that and would be watching. So he hid.

It hadn't taken him long to figure out where he'd be able to hole up. Veter Iocole, along with his entire household, was away on a buying mission in Mariendo. Veter had hidden stores beneath the cellars of his mansion on the Jamestone Quay, as well as a few very well-hidden tunnels under the hidden stores. Most were flooded, some were not, and those that weren't flooded were perfect for smuggling anything that wouldn't be affected by too much moisture. Veter called those tunnels "the Alligator's Belly" — and not without good reason.

He'd no idea Gossie knew about them. And up till now, it hadn't mattered that he did. What use had Gossie of flooded tunnels? Now, however, there was a clear need, and Gossie found himself living like a fat, wet gator by torchlight: drinking some very good whiskey, eating handfuls of seaweed, and reflecting on his ridiculously precarious situation.

As he'd floated along in his barrel, he knew he'd fooled them. They'd be coming after him, of course, with the full fury of a Brull horde. Not the T&G: they weren't all that thorough, and they preferred to wait and catch those who'd cheated or betrayed them down the road a spell. They were patient, like an old house cat who takes his naps by a mousehole. The trick, he'd long ago learned, was to never emerge from any particular hole twice.

No, the ones he was concerned about were those who'd bought and paid for the cargo — they hadn't seemed at all the type that would write off a loss. It very much bothered him that, despite his many sources of information and rumor, he still wasn't entirely sure who they were and what they really wanted out of all this. He wasn't used to not knowing, not in the slightest. He liked to see all the angles and understand the players inside and out before proceeding. Typically. Not this time. Why not?

Greed. Age. Arrogance. Drunkenness.

Yes, yes, yes, yes.

Still, he couldn't shake the feeling that there was something else at work here. Some kind of impulse…a cloudiness of judgment, a spark of imprudent bravado of the kind he'd long ago abandoned for sounder and more layered practices. From the start, from that very first meeting two months ago, he'd felt somehow younger, a man who could see the thing through with all the impunity and deftness of a Pengyou Ren, which he, despite his admittedly overdeveloped sense of self-flattery, certainly was not. He could throw a punch, but scaling walls and clinging to ceiling beams was not his style. Nor had it ever been, he confessed to himself and whichever gators might be eavesdropping.

Even that business at the inn, pretending to be asleep when they broke into his room. He was handy with a blade, but he could have easily ended up bleeding out on the floor or chained to the wall in a Beene Street cell. He'd had the out: his trapdoor. Why hadn't he taken it?

Why indeed.

The plain truth of it was, he just wasn't acting like himself.

But the question was: Why?

And there was something else troubling him: What could one crazy old woman be worth in the scheme of things? Who was she?

She was an unusual bit of contraband, but it sure wasn't the first time he'd been a party to the clandestine transport of a person. He'd been the go-to smuggler for pleasure-seeking Pherriuskatan fat cats for more than a decade, ferrying hedonistic, drugged-up, spoiled brats back and forth between Pashka and all the Eastern Islands. They didn't call Fan Ni Dok the Devil's Mask for no reason. He'd made quite a bundle there, so he wasn't inclined to judge. Nor was he inclined to return.

This old woman was somehow different. Those things that were after him were sinister, and for some reason they wanted her, and badly. She meant something to them, or to someone. Oddly, she seemed to be aware of that but for some reason played along. Or didn't care. And she'd almost died for it.

Almost.

He would have patted himself on the back for that move, but his arms were cramped and twisted as he sat, stuffed in his barrel, and ruminated. His ruminations were terribly inconclusive, but he had other concerns at the moment.

After emerging so triumphantly from his makeshift transport, he'd eased through the massive tasting room of the brewery and out the side door. The Jamestone Quay was the next one over. He'd quickly found the hidden entrance to Veter's tunnels and into the Belly but was never at any moment completely confident he was safe.

Two whole weeks he waited. Twenty-two damned days.

And that was all he could take. He was running out of seaweed and blacking out from way too much whiskey. Once or twice, he was certain an actual alligator had joined him in his hiding place, but that might also have been a symptom of the whiskey.

"You can't stay down here forever, Gossie," he burbled to himself.

"If they haven't found you yet, they've stopped looking."

He didn't believe that for a second, but he hadn't fled the inn to end up a fat, drunk corpse in a smuggler's cave, so he collected himself and swam the length of the flooded tunnels back to the entrance, praying he was wrong about having spotted a gator.

Once he'd gained the surface and dried off a bit, he made his way stealthily back up the quay. He stopped behind a stack of barrels and quickly reversed his tunic and donned a hood he'd kept in his pocket. Everything was wet. He bent low, adopted a slight limp, and slipped out into the night's foot traffic. Shuffling quietly down onto the avenue, he glanced about. No one seemed to have taken any note of him.

Good so far. Here in the land of the drunks and the dockhands, one chubby waddler such as himself was unlikely to draw attention; he played the part well, naturally, but he had his doubts about the ease of his escape from Shen's. If the ones that were after him were any good — no, that wasn't it: clearly they were good, but were they as good as he suspected they were? — they'd be on him at any moment.

He was sure the idiots who'd come to his room had been a smokescreen. No, this game was a bit more layered, but at least he'd won round one.

As he went along, he was careful to stumble into a crate or trip on a stray rope here and there. People glanced at him but no one stared, and this was as it should be. Still, his left hand rested comfortably on his dirk; in the other, he palmed a small pouch of something he liked to keep plenty of in the event of emergencies and untoward encounters. Cost plenty, but he never regretted the expense; the stuff was far too useful.

He bumped into two Chop Pointers sporting the full purple regalia and then bowed to both and chirped a barely audible, "Very slow, fairly full" to them. They laughed at his application of the old sailor's greeting — "I think you have that backward, old man!" — and went on their way.

What more should he know about that tricky, crazy old hag? he wondered. Come from Thesseline, indeed! Idiot. He'd offered her some lifewine just to shut her up and clean her up a bit, but after a tiny sip, she'd refused it outright, saying, "You can call it whatever you like; that's not my recipe, fattie! Give me a workshop and an hour, and I'll show you the good stuff!"

Now what in the twelve hells of Namus had that meant? Recipe? For what? Stupid old woman.

After he'd handed her over to the Juks — or handed someone over, anyway — he'd hit an Abeilonish pub and thought more about her comment. A half-dozen short drinks in, he'd come to postulate that maybe, just maybe, this rude hag had somehow come up with or come across — likely stolen, he thought — a way to improve on lifewine. As far as he knew, it all still came from Carthage, and the recipe was guarded by what might as well have been an army of dragons, but it wasn't beyond the pale of reason that someone might have somehow figured out a way to make it more potent or cheaper or both.

Upon further reflection and four more drinks, these not so short, he'd dismissed the thought as ridiculous; the one making the claim was no doubt a dozen kinds of mad…and yet someone was paying to move her and keep her safe.

Or, he thought now, someone had; it just hadn't worked out so well. Bitch was probably fish food now. Or so they thought.

But if that's what they thought, why were they after him?

As far as they knew, he'd done his job and knew only what they knew: she'd gone down in the attack.

Except that she hadn't.

And maybe they weren't happy with that because…maybe they were the ones who'd attacked. *Which means they knew she hadn't been on any of those ships.*

Dammit.

None of that mattered in the moment, not if they caught up with him and did to him what they'd done to those three crews. Who cuts through two dozen Juks Xi Ren like that? It was unheard of; no navy he knew, save one, would even be bold enough to try. And those things weren't part of this equation, Four be thanked. Those things hadn't been seen in a very long time.

He strode along, his mind teeming. Someone — a few someones — he'd trusted for a very long time had grabbed the hag before she'd boarded the ship. They had her holed up in a place he'd told them to keep to themselves. Someone else had murdered all hands — including a full crew of dragonmen — and scuttled the ships. He was in no position to sit and wonder why or how or to do anything about it. The mystery would have to remain a mystery, even if it had cost him damn near everything he had left. The priority of the moment was getting out of town and lying low somewhere while he figured out how to resurrect his life.

At least he had the woman.

She was probably the key to tomorrow, but the getting out part would be enough to chew today. And they would be closing in on him. Anyone who had the resources to do what they'd done to those ships had the resources to find one fat old man stumbling around in a port town pretending to be drunk.

And now he was being followed.

That was quick, he thought. *Must have half the town working for them.*

He strode off the quay and ducked into a suitably dim alley. It was a dead end with only one locked door as an option for exodus. Someone was bound to come down that alley at any moment, and the results for old Gossie would be most unpleasant, he had no doubt. The barrel trick had delayed them awhile, but they'd picked up his trail.

He had not expected them to do so with such daunting efficiency.

He had no illusions about why they wanted him, and now he almost wished he could give it to them. It might well have been his only way out. Too late for that. He was sure his pursuers weren't the types to fall for the old "I don't have her here, but I can bring you to her" ruse.

He opened the door with a flash of a small copper pick and a moment of jiggling the lock. On the other side of the door he found a room with a few chests, a small desk, a bureau, a dozen or so sacks, and stairs that seemed to lead up to a second floor. Some light from the quay spilled in from the room's one small window. It would have to do. He found himself a spot in the dark corner behind the bureau and waited.

He didn't wait long.

Something yanked open the door, slowly entered the room, and sniffed. Cloaked, and not human, not with that stink: rot and the sea and something like musk. Its face was not visible, but the form itself was hunched, almost twisted. Gossie glanced at the powder he held at the ready. Probably a waste to use it here; the stuff didn't always work on nonhumans. He admitted sadly to himself that if this was one of the things that had attacked the ships and murdered the Juks, he was going to die.

But he wasn't yet ready to die.

He had a hand or two to play yet.

The creature sniffed the stairs and then turned toward Gossie's position behind the bureau. "Fundra," it rasped. "Where is she?"

Definitely not the powder for this one, thought Gossie. What else then? He stuffed the powder into his waistcoat and, with his other hand, pulled from out of his pants pocket a very small twig-like item, a good luck charm he'd been holding on to for a very long time.

"This had better work," he muttered to himself. He imagined he should pray but couldn't think of anything suitable, so instead he coughed once and then stepped right out into the room with his arms wide open and a big smile on his face.

He was less than ten feet from the creature. It looked at him with glowing purplish eyes and repeated its demand. "Where is she?"

"Where is who, my sinister foreign friend?"

"Frulla of Carthage. We require her."

Frulla of Carthage? What was this thing on about? "I'm afraid your requirements are quite a few centuries off, good crooked beastie…that one's been dead since before even I started in this business. Not to put too fine a point on it, but that's quite a while indeed."

"Give her to us."

They think I have Frulla of Carthage. What the hell? Insane things. Unless...the old woman? But how? "I'm afraid she's not mine to give."

"Oh, but she is. We will know what you know."

"I've told you what I know, and that's all of nothing."

The thing was still for a moment, and then it twitched and dove at him, claws extending from its cloak. Gossie darted aside and then jumped back behind the bureau as he raised the hand holding the twig and winced.

If this doesn't work, he thought, *I'll never get a chance to strangle the lout who sold it to me...*

But it did work, and very well. His attacker threw the bureau aside and lunged at him again. Instantly, the twig left Gossie's hand and exploded into a nest of writhing, black, viny arms that wrapped themselves around the creature. The nest contracted and squeezed and choked while the thing inside its embrace thrashed in an attempt to break free.

He'd been told the Twine of C'nai could not be broken by any living thing and that very soon after being engaged, the Twine would crush and consume its prey without fail. Gossie stood and watched the process, but his curiosity had always played second fiddle to his instinct for survival, and the creature in the twine was putting up a very violent fight, so a moment was all he allowed. He exited the room and ran back up the alley, slamming the door on the indignant, mad screeches behind him.

He ran up to the main thoroughfare and quickly hailed a carriage. He bought passage and instructed the driver to head out of town with all due haste.

The driver sensed his vehemence; he would have had to have been dead not to. The cab itself had not been empty when he'd jumped in, but the two elderly women within hastily made their way out the carriage door. They'd seen something in his face and heard enough in his terrified tone, he was sure, to make them fear for their own safety. And they weren't wrong there.

"Goodnight, ladies, and enjoy the sea air! Blessings to you both!" he called as he flipped a small satchel of coins to the driver.

Within minutes they were heading out of Camedua and south down the Blackbear Road at a speed he hoped nothing that might be following them could match. He had, after all, just spent his only Twine, and his dirk was no match for anything but drunks and amateurs.

The thing he'd just faced off against was neither. And he was sure that somehow it had survived the Twine.

After about twenty minutes, he called for the driver to stop the carriage. He offered another satchel of coin and so bought one of the horses (for about twice the going price; this was by no means the time to haggle and besides, he'd stolen the poor driver's purse during the ride, managing to make a small profit on the trip).

He mounted the horse, bade the driver a good night, and headed south into farm country with all due haste.

He didn't stop until late that night.

When his horse could at last go no farther without a rest and his own uncooperative bladder was begging for relief, he stopped. He led the horse into a small grove of apple trees. Among them was a pond, and the horse drank deep while Gossie relieved himself.

He picked a few apples and ate. The horse, he saw, was staring at him, so he held out an apple to her, and then another. They stood and chewed apples together and for a moment, Gossie felt whole, or something close to it.

Where to go now? He had no map, but he put himself about fifty miles southeast of Camedua. Not even halfway down the Blackbear Road. Mak was still at least four hours away on a fresh mount, and his hardly qualified: the animal looked ready to drop.

It was quiet here, a good place to stop and think and collect himself. Or it would be if he had any idea about the capabilities and limitations of the creatures that pursued him. Had he put enough distance between himself and them? He doubted it. He thought about his predicament and came to a sad conclusion. If they believed he had who they thought he had — as insane as that was — they'd be looking for him everywhere: Bikita Badru, Mak, Narth Downs…and on this road.

The questions he then considered were: How many of them were there, how quickly had they picked up his trail (if they had, which he had to concede was a near certainty), and how hot was their pursuit?

The answers, at the moment, were irrelevant. It couldn't be helped: a rest was mandatory. His horse was done for the night. And so was he. All-night hell's bells flights down dark passes were for younger, thinner men. And he'd had nothing to eat or drink since this had all begun.

He dismounted, tied the horse to a tree, and went about looking for something besides apples to eat. Mushrooms, maybe. He had no luck, though.

What were they on about, these slithering, hissing things? Frulla of Carthage? His knowledge of ancient history was sketchy, to be sure, but every child in Arba knew that Frulla had travelled north to the Thesseline Environ and then disappeared over six hundred years ago. End of story.

Or was it? His knowledge of religion, past, present, or apocalyptic, was even less complete than his knowledge of ancient history.

What nonsense. What idiocy. This was just another expression of Proving Madness, albeit one with a bizarre and unfortunately lethal twist.

Still, if someone believed the woman he'd saved was in fact Frulla, that might mean a payday. A very rewarding payday, perhaps.

What to do? And how to do it?

He might have a job to do, something with his cousin in Pherriuskata, but not till later in the month, and it wouldn't do to show up early: too many people knew him in that town, masks or no, and too many of those had trained pet magickasses scoping out men in his profession. No, the less time spent in Pherriuskata, the better. He knelt beside the horse and drank his fill, and then he sat and had a smoke and gazed up for a bit at the stars.

No answers came to him, but there was no urgency. He'd cleared Camedua and gained the beginnings of farming country and all the anonymity it could provide.

"Ha." He chuckled despite himself. "You used to be much better at lying to yourself, old boy."

He'd find no better cover in Mak, that was obvious. If they could find him hiding in a random building in the bustling, stinking port town of Camedua after he'd ridden a wine barrel down the river, hid in the Alligator Belly for twenty-two stinking days, and donned one of his most trusted disguises, they could find him in a small trading town. Or probably in the biggest city in Arba. Or on Branaedes itself.

It was only a matter of time with these things.

He needed to do something they wouldn't anticipate, to go somewhere they couldn't follow. Not knowing much about them, it was difficult to imagine what and where…

Into Maelor's Country, toward the farmers' little rebellion? The fighting and mayhem might provide cover. It would probably also provide him with an ugly death in the crossfire. War zones were not his forte.

Where to go, where to go?

This he contemplated as he and his mount ate many more apples.

A short while later, he chanced a peek back at the road. From behind a maple grove, he spotted the lights of a small farmhouse. *Why not?*

The owners, two old brothers who looked to be north of at least sixty, were more than happy to take him in for the night given the gold he pushed into their palms (half of what he'd taken from the carriageman, which rendered the wild journey momentarily profitless). They offered him a room, but he made an excuse about his mount being skittish in new places without his company and so went to sleep instead in the barn. Not that he wouldn't have preferred a nice, warm bed, but he had a sad suspicion that a full night's sleep and a leisurely breakfast were not in the cards for him. And besides, why put these good people in danger?

Before nodding off, he smeared himself with three different kinds of manure — the worst being that of a young gremfi — and buried himself in the hay in the corner of his horse's stall.

Let's see them sniff their way through that, he thought as he began to fall asleep.

Within the hour, he woke up, startled. Had he heard something?

No. There was nothing. But he was now awake and alert. He collected himself and thought again about his pursuers' uncanny tracking skills. *They found me amid all those wonderful seaside aromas. They'll find me here amid the horseshit.*

He stood up, sniffed himself, and rolled his eyes. The horses and cows in the barn were all staring at him. "Yes, I know, but it seemed like a good idea a little while ago."

He removed his saddle from the horse he'd ridden and put it on one of the others, this one a tall black gelding. "You don't mind getting out to see a bit of the world, do you? Apologies for the stench, but somehow I expect you won't mind."

The horse whinnied; he took that for an affirmative reply. Gossie pulled out his very light purse, withdrew a few silver barb from it, and placed them on a shelf next to the barn door. He hopped up on the horse, nodded to his former steed, and headed back into the night.

The Blackbear Road was still. No moonlight, no wind, no sounds of any kind. Were they here? He couldn't be sure. In any case, the road was bound to be unsafe. Still, he had little choice. The woods were thick, and there were no alternate paths. Or were there?

He heard a cry from the north. A bird? Was it them?

Or was he being paranoid?

No. Maybe.

The question returned to him, in fact had never left him: *Where to go, Gossie?*

He still needed to find a place where they wouldn't be able to track him.

Where would that be?

He turned to his left and regarded the darkness. Gnarled trees for several miles, no doubt, and then…the mountains of Brull country. And to the southeast, the Midforest.

For all he knew, the Brull were the ones behind this attack. Sneaky, evil bastards, the lot of them. Wouldn't put it past them to enter a contract with whatever was chasing him. They'd love to corner the market on lifewine too, those piggy beasts.

No, that wasn't the way.

The Midforest? Lunacy to enter there. Sure, he'd elude his

pursuers, but he'd almost certainly never get out.

He needed something daring, something extraordinary.

A jump to a completely different part of the world.

A Mansdrelam.

That meant Quintish, and he doubted he'd make it all the way south to Quintish.

But there was another option…an old gate…where was that? Somewhere in Maelor's Country, from way before there ever was a Maelor, he was sure. Still functional?

He'd never used a Mansdrelam, not willingly, and he'd told himself the one time he'd been forced through one that he'd die before doing it again. And he'd meant it — still meant it. But he was, if nothing else, a resourceful man, a man who prided himself on finding ways to work around problems of practicality, context, or even ethics.

He could and would use a Mansdrelam gate if it would save his life.

And the life spent to operate the thing?

He knew very well what to do about that. There was a solution, one that would likely be to the benefit of all relevant parties. And the thing pursuing him would never see it coming. Trouble was, he really had only a vague idea about where the gate was and only a faint recollection about how he might use it.

Both of these facts were massive obstacles to his escaping the current predicament alive. Firstly, if he was correct, the gate was nowhere near his present position. It was, or once had been, somewhere near the Oliver Woods — some two hundred miles from here. His spirits sank. Yes, that's where it was.

Unless he could literally learn to fly — which was not impossible in his experience but extremely ill advised owing to the shitwing Visshilla — there was simply no way to be sure of traversing such a distance without his enemies eventually catching up to him. On top of that, if the stories about the *Ho Matsuni* were true, his enemies actually could fly — and they didn't seem to fear the shitwings.

Secondly, without an exacting ability to recall and perform the necessary rites, he could end up dead, half dead, or dead smack in the middle of some Vo'ix environ halfway around the planet, sitting on a dinner platter covered in sea salt.

As clean an escape as the use of a gate seemed in theory to offer, he had to admit to himself it was simply an impossibility, or so near to being an impossibility that his best option at present was to put it out of his mind. No, he needed another solution: a place to run, a place to hide, a place to disappear for a time that didn't offer whiskey and seaweed as the only options on the menu.

At some point, he also had to make his way back to the alleged Frulla or at least get word to those who had her. He had to get to the bottom of whatever was happening. He was used to being in mortal danger; he'd spent his life as a thief, a rogue, a trickster, and a liar, no matter the affable flavors he applied, but this current situation? It was intolerably unfamiliar to his experiential grasp, however vast he might have in more innocent times — meaning twenty-two days ago — believed that grasp to be.

He sighed heavily and shook his head. It was unavoidable. He knew what he had to do and where he had to go.

The Cturrom Road.

The Midforest.

Which meant he had to deal with *them* again.

He accepted it. It was his only way out, the only path that offered him a chance to get through this mess and come out in one piece. Maybe.

An hour later, he came to a small opening in the dark pines on his left. He'd gone far enough south to avoid the mountains of the Brull and was now staring at a path that would wind its way down, he hoped, to the Cturrom.

He dismounted, smiled to the horse as he patted its neck, and removed the few things he had: a tiny pack of handy sundries and little satchel of food he'd been given by the farming brothers. The horse looked at him and then seemed to nod in understanding; it turned and headed slowly back north toward the farmhouse and the safety of its barn.

Gossie envied the horse, for even as it took those steps toward comfort and the known, he himself strode quietly into the abyss.

Chapter 25
"I am not your enemy."

Place: Eshe, kingdom of Xatumka, Arba Environ
Date: Quattrenim 29, AY 998

"You are Aethrelean."

"Yes."

"You told my friends that you were the daughter of Leander Dossilea, high captain of the Glaring Cliffs, the champion of Believers everywhere," said the old man in front of her.

She didn't remember saying that. She didn't remember saying anything. "That's Vincent Bleuss you're speaking of," Frainle replied.

"She speaks!" someone cried.

"What did you say, girl?" said another voice.

"My father Leander is not the champion. Just the captain...of the Ciffs," she said, the mention of that place flooding her mind with images of flames and death.

"Hush, Soham!" said the voice before her. "Yes, perhaps we speak of Vincent of Chrestikos, child. Yet your father is also a champion and a believer, is he not?"

"Yes. He is both."

"And he fights for those who cannot fight for themselves?"

Frainle searched for any irony in his tone and decided there was none; he could not be aware of his question's implications.

"Yes, he does," she said with cautious defiance. "And I am not a child."

She had gone through the Mansdrelam as she watched Enimuat die. A rush of cold air, a stumble in the dark over something—no, someone—and they'd grabbed her. She'd screamed, but she didn't know why; it was a scream that had little to do with where she now was, wherever she was. She'd started screaming in the catacombs as the magick had seemed to swallow and freeze her, and then here, wherever here was, her scream had ended, but not before someone had heard her and taken her—and someone else—into immediate custody.

For several days she waited, alone, tied up and gagged in a wagon. She heard the strangely accented voices of her captors just outside the wagon but was unable to make out what they were saying save for a few words. What she did know was that they were not discussing her. These people were at war with someone. Had she escaped one fight and landed in the middle of another?

It didn't matter. None of it. She slept when she could, which was rarely, and when she dreamt, she saw fire. And when she was awake, she saw fire.

Her mother. Her friends. The guardsmen, the sea watchers, the villagers, the cooks, the stable hands, the maids who did the laundry and raised the turkeys and collected the eggs from the hens, and…Eni.

All gone.

All burned.

Her home was gone.

And she saw fire. She saw fire but felt nothing.

And she could not think.

They fed her and gave her water, but they wouldn't let her talk. It made no difference to her. She had little to say. But one thought, one small ray of hope, went through her head amid the visions of fire:

It wasn't the Vo'ix who captured me. It wasn't the Vo'ix who captured me.

For that, at least, she was grateful.

But everyone else she'd known was dead, and her gratitude was swallowed by a bitter pain she could scarcely endure.

Eni hadn't followed her. He'd died too, but not in fire. The Mansdrelam had taken him. Or maybe it hadn't. What she knew for a certainty was that he hadn't followed before they'd led her away to this meadow where she was being questioned. There was someone else, another prisoner, a man with a hood over his head.

He was not Eni.

She was here now, not there, not burning. She had lived, or so she suspected, and was now a captive of what looked to be an army of farmers and villagers, standing before a small bonfire and facing questions delivered by a very old but very determined-looking man. The summer stars were familiar, but the land was not; there was no trace of the ocean's scent on the wind, and its absence unnerved her greatly.

"And how have you come here?" the old man asked her.

She stared at him. She understood him despite his odd, thick accent, but she had nothing to say.

"This girl is an imbecile. She doesn't understand your words," someone said from behind the old man.

The old man shook his head. "She's no imbecile. She's in shock."

"Or acting like she's in shock. She's a spy."

The old man came closer to her and asked her again, in a very gentle voice, "How have you come here?"

"Here?" she answered. "I'm afraid I don't know where I am."

"That doesn't seem to be the truth," he said, regarding her with sad, tired eyes.

"It is."

"How could you not know where you are?" demanded a tall man with a thin moustache and a scythe in his hand. "Herdas, she is lying. She is a Triumvirate spy. Look at her clothes."

"If she is lying, we will know soon enough, David," answered Herdas. "Tell me, daughter of Leander, why are you here, and how have you come here? And why did we find you in the company of a known mercenary, a man who's so often in the employ of our enemy?" He pulled the hood off her fellow prisoner. He was a rough-looking, handsome man. He blinked a few times and then looked at her, smiled, and shrugged. "Young woman, please explain yourself," insisted Herdas.

She stared at Herdas as best she could.

The situation was beyond her. Who were these people, what did they want?

Inside her, everything was burning.

She tried to remain silent and ignore the ones who surrounded her. She tried to leave them to believe whatever they wanted to believe and do whatever they needed to do. She had survived the attack on the Cliffs, but something of her was still there, still with them, still burning, and that part didn't care about these stupid farmers with their questions and accusations and accents.

She stared at their fire.

"Nothing. She's insane. Maybe a Mindless One, or something that escaped from the pleasure houses," David said with disgust.

"Or a spy," said the one called Soham. "Execute her. We can't keep a prisoner."

"We don't execute people," barked Herdas. "Not even spies, Soham. Enough of that talk."

"You can bet she'd execute any one of us given the chance!" spat Soham.

A raging debate kicked up among them.

Frainle didn't bother to listen, but she did understand, from a certain internal distance, what was at stake: her life. And in that moment, she realized she valued that life. And she realized why.

There was something she needed to do. She didn't know how or when she would do it, but there was no question, no doubt whatsoever in her mind:

I need to kill the Vo'ix.

So she had to live, and she had to convince these people to let her live. She had to tell them something and hope for the best. They weren't Vo'ix, but they weren't Aethreleans either. Aethreleans, even Stavers, would have released her immediately upon learning her name. And they would have believed it was her name. No, she'd travelled somewhere. Far to the west. Xatumka.

"I have come this far seeking my father," she said, playing her cards as close to the vest as she dared. The crowd went silent on hearing her speak. "And I have no idea who that man is," she added, pointing at the man who'd worn the hood.

"Your father, here? Why would you look for him so far from his — and your — homeland?" asked Herdas.

"I don't know why I'm here, specifically — what I mean to say is I know why I've travelled, or rather been sent, but…I had no say in my destination."

"How so?" asked the old man incredulously.

The cards she'd been trying to play so close were now tumbling from her grasp, and she saw the people around her getting anxious, shifting and frowning.

"You're not being very clear, young lady, or very honest, I think," said Herdas.

"She's a liar. Let's hang her and good ol' Stephan straight away and be done with it," cried David.

Frainle had no choice. She lifted her chin, eyed the crowd, and played her hand: "I have travelled here by magick."

There was a murmur among the crowd. Some of them began to yell, some backed away fearfully, but Herdas raised his hands and quieted them.

"Whose magick? Your own?" asked another man, a short, stout fellow with muttonchops and a white staff.

"The magick of…a dear friend. A friend who died so that I might live."

"We grieve for your friend with you, then," said Herdas. "Don't we, good Northerners?" he said to the crowd, but more directly to the tall man and the stout fellow.

"So we do," said David, though his look conveyed neither sympathy nor compassion.

"So you claim to have used the ancient transport, which in and of itself is a crime punishable by death in these lands. And what was so important about your journey that your friend himself needed to die to see it succeed?" asked Herdas.

"As I said, I am here to find my father."

"Why would you be seeking him here? Or rather, why would your devoted friend have sent you here, so far from Aethrelius?"

"I am not sure. He was afraid, and he was new to the magick — that much is so. This is where I was sent. I had no choice in the matter, and there wasn't time for explanations."

The stout fellow spoke up. "Why no choice, and no knowledge of your destination? I would have thought such a magickal undertaking would require at least the most basic of information to be imparted, considering the nature of the spell. Are we to believe this novice magicker was able to induce the Mansdrelam to work without having the wherewithal to determine its parameters?"

"Fair questions, Soham, fair questions!" someone cried.

"What's her answer?"

"No more lies!"

This was going nowhere. Clearly, confessing to Eni's magick and sacrifice had the reverse effect of what she'd hoped for, which was sympathy and maybe a touch of awe. These people might put her to death if she didn't win them over quickly. She glanced around and saw there was no chance to escape; she also noticed a very bemused look on the face of her fellow captive, the man they had called Stephan.

Soham, a thick, broad man with a long brown beard that was tied off into three tails, walked toward Frainle, scowled at her, and then turned to face the crowd. "She won't tell us anything but stories about heroes and magick because the reason for her presence here is clear: she's a spy, working with Stephan there, sent by those Tri bastards to ascertain our strength, our numbers, and the depth of our resolve. Hang her."

Several people pushed forward to grab Frainle. She yelled at them, "No, wait!" but they kept coming.

Herdas stepped between her and the mob and held up his hands.

"There is no rush, here, Northerners! We are not Tri animals who decide a person's fate before a fair hearing and time to consider are rendered! You know this, you believe this. Now please, let's hear her!" He turned to Frainle and said: "You'd better make your next words count, child."

What else could she do or say? She knew but scarcely believed it herself, and if they'd found her name and her mode of transport difficult to accept, they'd surely hang her for the final piece of information she had to offer.

She offered it anyway.

"We were under attack. My friend did all he could to save me…and to give me a chance to live and to act. He was trying to do something, anything, to save me!"

"Under attack by whom?" David asked her.

"You would not believe me if I told you. But you must know the Glaring Cliffs have fallen, and so the whole of Aethrelius is threatened. And my father, if he isn't already dead somewhere, is now on a quest to find the Sword of Endings."

She believed what she was saying. She had no way of knowing if it were true, but she knew in that moment she had no choice but to believe it.

Herdas regarded her not unkindly and then came close to her and stared into her eyes. "He told you this?"

"My grandmother did." It was a lie but only very small step from the truth. She was thankful she'd made a habit of eavesdropping as a child. She'd heard so much she didn't understand, and she knew her father had ever been reluctant to embrace the legend of the Sword, but she also knew his heart and his capacity for doing whatever was needed to protect his homeland.

"And you know that he has left Aethrelius?" he asked.

"No, I don't: how could I? I only know that was his plan and the promise he made to my mother. If he survived, I am certain he headed west, or soon will."

"But what of his duties in your country?" cried David. "Leander Dossilea would not abandon his land!"

The crowd murmured in assent. "She's lying!" someone said, and others repeated the sentiment angrily.

She ignored their anger and focused on David's question. So her country's doctrine had spread as far as this distant land. How ironic for these men and women to be going to war believing in something that was, quite literally, doomed.

"As I said, Aethrelius cannot help but fall now," she intoned. "The enemy destroyed our keep, which has guarded the eastern coast of our country for hundreds of years, in minutes. Everyone died, everyone but me, or I hope they did, because those that might have lived…I cannot bear to imagine. Believe me, or don't, but there is no hope without the Sword."

Soham sputtered, "The Great Aethrelean Nation, gone? The Eastern Keep fallen? This cannot be. What foe is so great as — "

She spoke in as firm and clear a voice as she could muster:

"The Vo'ixtavracci have come."

For a few moments, there was complete silence.

Then David spoke up, but with something like a note of doubt in his voice. "The Vo'ixtavracci? Surely not! Good Northerners, how can we stand here and listen to these outlandish lies! We need to hang these spies and march!"

"They are not lies," came another voice. "I too have heard tell of the attack on Aethrelius."

"Stephan, hold your tongue. We'll get to you in a bit," growled David.

Herdas dipped his head and ran his hand over his sparse hair. He looked strong but also weary. "Why would the daughter of the greatest warrior of our generation lie?" he asked, his eyes rising to meet hers.

"I am not lying."

"You must be, Frainle Natchalef Dossilea, or whoever you are," said David. "Everyone knows the Vo'ixtavracci are a myth. A stupid myth at that, designed to frighten the people, created by the Mind and its lackeys to keep us from questioning their hateful practices. Giants who eat people...a lie."

"No. I wish it were so. My home is destroyed. My dear friend is dead. My people are dead or dying or worse. I have seen it with my own eyes. Believe what you wish."

"We believe little of what we are told. Our enemies are masters of lies," said David.

"I am not your enemy."

Herdas gazed at her thoughtfully. "No, I do not believe you are," he said. "You haven't asked us for anything but understanding, and your story, though incredible and terrible, rings true in the telling. And yet I still don't understand why you were sent here."

"I came to escape a war."

"And yet having come here, you have traded one war for another." He thought a moment and then smiled sadly. "Forgive us. Trust is as precious as a sea of lifewine, especially in these troubled times. If you say it is so, we will believe you. But you may come to wish you'd stayed home."

"There is nothing to forgive. In your shoes, I would think my report the words of a madwoman. But the Vo'ixtavracci are real, and they are here...in Aethrelius. In Arba."

There was a further murmur in the crowd. Frainle could hear some of the elders excitedly trying to explain to those who'd never heard the stories what the Vo'ixtavracci were. She turned away from the crowd; she could not bear to watch the abject horror that came into the expressions of the listeners as they absorbed the dread descriptions.

"People, people, listen now," called out Herdas. "Let us disperse for the evening meal. Please, everyone go back to the encampment and eat hearty of what you've brought! If the man or woman next to you has nothing, then do what we do: share your get, offer comfort to a stranger. There are three oxen being roasted by the main tent, so all can eat. Trouble your minds not with tales of giants and distant lands. We have a just fight to fight on the morrow!"

The people, Frainle noticed, were clearly comforted by the suddenly steady and jovial countenance of the man who was without doubt their leader, his wearied and aged countenance notwithstanding. They turned and headed to a village of tents, still talking but with firmer resolve in their expressions. She had scared them, but only for a moment. She wondered whether that was a good thing.

"Come, Frainle Dossilea, come with me. We can eat and talk some more," said Herdas. "And please, no more talk of what you've seen and know to my people…they have about all they can handle before them, perhaps more."

He took her arm and led her to the south side of the camp. Three guards, David, and Soham followed closely. When they reached a large tent about ten yards from the roasting pits, Herdas entered, leading Frainle, followed by Soham. David tried to follow, but Herdas shook his head. The younger man withdrew with a scowl.

"He seems not to trust me," Frainle said.

"He trusts no one, least of all me," sighed Herdas. "But he's a good worker and, as it turns out, a fine fighter. You'll have to forgive his demeanor; he lost his wife and two daughters near Fort Dilan several months ago."

"Your enemy kills families? It's that bad?"

"No, it's worse. And I fear that, one way or another, Eshe and Maelor's Country, the Xatumkan farms and fields we love so dearly, will never again be as they once were. Too much has happened here: too much death, too much fire, too much hunger."

"Too much Triumvirate."

"Yes, especially that, yes," he said with a long sigh. "But let me ask you more about your tale. Are you sure Aethrelius has fallen? Is there nothing to be done?"

"Not by the Stavers and the fools that follow them. But I'm not sure even the combined might of all our forces could have defeated this foe. Perhaps nothing can."

"What of the magick that defended your lands? For centuries it was said…"

"That's all done with. The Stavers started expelling the Mudarrisi, who for so long were our guests and protectors, just after they took power. The fools believed it was beneath them to accept the aid of foreigners, even ones who had lived for generations among us."

"An attitude they regret today, no doubt. But what of your father…does he truly seek the Sword of Endings? Might there not then be a hope?"

"He believes there is."

"The Sword itself is believed to be a myth or, if it were ever real, a thing long since lost to the maw of time."

"My father knows both the myth and the history well. His mother spent a lifetime studying them both, for she believed it was his destiny to find it."

"Theresta was wise, it is said, and strong. She was born near to here, in Dalleo Winds, or so the story goes."

"The story is true. That part, at least. My grandmother was an enigma beyond compare. Strong and wise, yes. Also true," she agreed.

"But wisdom and strength cannot make the unreal real. Only magick can do that."

"Not even magick can do that."

"Then how?"

"My father will seek a man, a Timesinger, who knows of the Sword's fate...and location." *Or he will if he's alive, mobile, and able. He has to.*

"Truly? The Timesingers are known throughout this land for little else but their hidden, digging ways."

"So it is in Aethrelius as well, though we had none of their order in our land."

"Then why believe them?"

"I do not know. I only know Leander Dossilea seeks Mosta Nom, the Sword of Endings, so that he can vanquish the invaders and unite our divided land. And he believes he can find it."

"Can he, though? So many have sought the Sword throughout the centuries. One wonders if even a man as formidable as he can succeed where they have failed."

"I wonder too."

"But you suspect he may succeed?"

She didn't answer right away. She couldn't. She hadn't yet decided what she herself believed. When she did speak, her words were guarded. "Perhaps. I cannot say. I do know he will spend his life trying."

Herdas must have noticed her hesitation, but he did not comment upon it. He was watching her, not unkindly. "I've no doubt of that," he said. "And yet, I've seen...lives spent on less precious objects. I am afraid, Frainle of Aethrelius, that we can offer you nothing here, save perhaps some soup and a blanket to sleep on. We Northerners are now at war with the Triumvirate."

"Why? Xatumka has been at peace...for a very long time, isn't that so? This land has ever been the breadbasket of the Tri."

"It was, yes, until several months ago. Peace never lasts, though, not anywhere. The poor crop seasons have been too many and the demands of the governor too harsh. The people could bear it no more. They spoke out, they argued, they were arrested. When others protested the arrests, they were slain. Hundreds of us were imprisoned or murdered." He bowed his head. "We cannot afford to sit by and simply tend our fields now. Bread cannot bake while blood spills. Now, we fight."

"And how goes the fight?" Frainle asked him earnestly.

Herdas looked at her, but his eyes were seeing something far off, something he'd seen perhaps too much or too little of — she could not be sure. "We are almost beaten. What you've seen here, along with some who've gathered in Yi Shu — we are all that are left. They've burned our homes, they've butchered our families, and they've brought in slaves to sow the fields. The Northerners, like your people, are a dying breed."

A young woman in a gray tunic, her hair tied back in a single ponytail, a small axe in her belt, entered with three plates of food.

Soham spoke for the first time since entering the tent. "Ah, some roasted ox. Come, Aethrelean girl: we eat, then we tie you to a tree and deliberate on what to do with you. Fair enough?"

As long as "tying to a tree" wasn't a local phrase meaning "hanging from a tree," she thought so, and said to him, "Yes, and thank you. Thank you for taking time to hear me out and consider my words."

Soham stabbed a piece of meat and, without glancing at her, replied, "If your words are true, we may yet all regret not heeding them."

David had tied them to each other and to an oak tree. After a few moments of struggling in vain, they'd settled down and tried to listen to what the Northerners were discussing, but they had no luck because the men were too far up the hill.

"We're in trouble if that David wins the day," Stephan growled.

"Then I think we'll be fine. Herdas seems to have things in hand."

"You're probably right. But these people don't take kindly to people popping unannounced into their fight for untaxed potatoes. They think you're a spy and a liar."

"They'll listen to Herdas."

"I doubt it. They think he's a fool who gives soup and meat to spies and liars."

"They seem to respect him."

"They do, I'm sure, but that doesn't mean they'll follow his recommendations concerning what to do with you. People do funny things when they're afraid, and funnier things when their blood's up."

"Sometimes people surprise you."

"Yes, that's true. For example, you surprised me."

"How so?"

"You saw that what you were saying was scaring the hell out of these farmers, but you kept saying it anyway. Don't you know what the truth is worth around here?"

"Truth is golden in every corner of Arba."

"Ha! Well, of course it is. And that is why you're tied to a tree while they debate, among other things, what to do with you."

"You are tied to the tree as well."

"Yes, but in my case, there is no debate. There isn't a man up there, save maybe Herdas, who isn't completely convinced I'm a louse who deserves the noose."

"Are you?"

"Yes. But not in the sense they think."

"I don't understand."

"I am a spy, usually, and more, but I wasn't spying on them. I was, to tell you the truth, only napping. In the wrong place, as it turns out."

"That was you in the old temple? The body I tripped over?"

"Yes, I was that body."

"Sorry."

"Don't mention it. Just promise me, in the future, you'll assess the situation and then scream. I had a pretty good hiding space there."

"How good a hiding space could it have been? You were snoring."

"Maybe, but not as loudly as you were screaming."

"Sorry."

They sat for a while and listened but could hear only the wind and the occasional word.

"You really aren't like these others," she said.

"You're right about that."

"You remind me of someone."

He turned awkwardly and looked at her. "Who?"

"Don't take this as anything but a loose comparison. You remind me, in some way, of my father," she said, looking away.

"I'm honored."

"You should be."

"No, truly. I've heard he's a great man. A true warrior, deadly as the Reckoning. That's what I've heard, anyway."

"Much of what you've heard is true, I'm sure, and just as much false."

"He is not great?"

"No, he is. Of course he is. He is…more than great." She turned to him. "And less."

"'Greatness is a rough tale to tell, and its depth changes with each teller.'"

"You've read the *Book of Naipek*?"

"The others as well. You're surprised?"

"No, not at all…well, yes. You don't seem the sort."

"I'm not the sort. But I can read, and I have read the Books."

"And what guidance have you found in them, if any?"

"I've found neither guidance nor answers. But I didn't read them for such lofty rewards."

"Then why read them at all?"

"I was learning to read, and where I was at the time…well, they were the only books I was allowed to touch."

She laughed. "Truly? You were raised in a Noble home?"

"That surprises you as well?"

"Yes."

"Where should I have been raised?"

"I don't know. Somewhere far away, the Wilds, maybe. Maybe somewhere not even in Arba."

"I wasn't raised anywhere. And the house where I learned to read, as a young man, was not my own. But it had many books, so it wasn't strictly a Noble home, but the people who owned it were...good to me."

"If there were many books, why in the world would you have chosen those to read?"

"I prefer to read outside...more privacy. The Noble Books were just the only ones I was allowed to take out of the house."

"Why?"

"My friend had several copies and even gave me my own set. The other books he had were precious to him, and rare. He had books of history and even of magick."

"Magick? History? Did you live among the Mer Ponx?"

"No. He was a farmer."

"A farmer with a heretical library...and a fool for a friend."

"Why a fool?"

"Caught with magickal books in the Tri, especially magickal books under the same roof as Noble ones, and your lives would have been forfeit."

"I didn't get caught. Neither did he, as far as I know. And who said my home was in the Tri?"

"Was it? I mean, you're here now, and your accent..."

"Yes. For a time it was, yes."

"It moved?"

"I did."

"Why?"

He looked at her again and then turned his head slowly away and stared out into the night. "It was time to leave."

The look on his face was one of slight, wincing pain. She understood; there was something he hadn't yet dealt with, something he'd chosen to live with and never face. Or maybe, she thought with a slight smile, he was just sitting on a rock.

"What kind of books did you read?" he asked in a low voice.

"What?"

"I'm guessing you studied the Nobles if you can recognize *Naipek* quotes, but I doubt that's where your learning stopped."

"Well, don't tell anyone, but I never finished *Frulla* or *Naipek*. I tend to retain things, useless things, lyrical things. My mother said my greatest gift was curiosity. I read a lot."

"Was she right? Or do you have other gifts?"

"She was right a long time ago. She was right before my brother died."

"And after he died?"

"I suppose I became more…focused. And less."

"Focused on what?"

"Art and war."

"Interesting mix."

"Can be. I read about war and spent most of my free time drawing, painting, sculpting…"

"I'd like to see your work."

"Might be difficult. I'm quite sure it's all ash now."

"Well, in that case maybe you can find a way to apply some of your other passion to your life's condition."

"Yes. Perhaps. I'd like that."

"Tell me, what books on war did you read? *The Retractor? Mariendo Compact?* Maybe some of your father's writings, if he wrote?"

"I read everything."

They fell silent for a while. Frainle sat and listened to the debate on the hilltop. Though the wind had died down, she still couldn't make out many words, but the voices themselves were very anxious and argumentative. She closed her eyes and let her thoughts drift, but they brought her back, as they incessantly had since she'd fled Aethrelius, to the attack on the Cliffs.

"Aethrelean…you might want to stay awake for what's to come."

She opened her eyes and said softly, "I wasn't sleeping. I was thinking."

He poured himself some beer. "Good of them to leave this. Being bound to a tree with a beautiful woman is thirsty work. Not sure how I'm supposed to drink it with my arms pinned in like this, but the gesture was a civil one, don't you think?" He looked at her and gestured with the bottle.

"No, thank you."

He nodded and twisted himself to take an awkward pull. He relaxed, smacked his lips, and smiled at her. "Sorry, you looked sleepy, with your eyes closed and all. And thirsty."

"'Look if you like what you see,' my mother often says." She was in fact very tired, she admitted to herself. *Why wouldn't I be?* She propped her head against the tree stump, trying to bunch up the hood of her cloak to use as a pillow.

"Smart woman, your mother, even if she was half-wrong about your curiosity." He chuckled. "Sleep, then. I'll wake you when they come. A nap won't change the outcome."

"I'm not sure I can sleep, not now, not after all that's happened. Not with all that's happening now."

"No, I suppose not. But you'll need to be rested for what's to come."

"You mean for what happens after they finish fighting with each other up there."

"Yes."

"What will happen?" she asked.

"Not sure. One of two things, I suppose. Either they'll come back down the hill under an agreement, or they won't. If they don't agree, they have to kill us. If they do agree, they might agree to kill us. Or they may agree to hide us or even bring us to the Oliver Woods."

"Doesn't sound like we have much of a chance."

"We don't."

"So why don't you look more worried?"

"I suppose it's because I know something you don't."

"Which is?"

"They now have something bigger than us to worry about."

"What do you mean?"

"Look down there, to the southeast…no, there, yes. Can you make out that small column of —"

"Torches. Yes, I see them."

"That is a regiment of Triumvirate soldiers — Caratans — probably led by a dozen Knights of ONOF. They're coming to kill our friends on the hill."

"What about us?"

"I'm sure their standing orders are to slay anyone within the enemy camp. That means me, and it means you…unless you tell them who you are, I suppose."

"Should I? Maybe I can save us both…"

"No, you can't. They won't recognize you, I'm sure, but on the chance that you are who you say you are, they'll take you with them and hand you over to some very nasty people."

"What should we do?"

"What can we do? We're each tied to a very big tree with very strong rope."

"Should I scream again?" she asked him, her voice dripping with sarcasm.

"Well, if that column gets much closer and our hosts haven't noticed it, it might be worth a try. But first, let's see if we can't knock some sense into our hosts," Stephan said as he stood up. The rope slid down off him, and he grinned at her. "Coming?"

Chapter 26
It gave him more time
to contemplate his own stupidity…

Place: Carthage, kingdom of Arbana, Arba Environ
Date: Quattrenim 30, AY 998

He reached Carthage not long after losing William.

At first, he'd tried to follow the Gumundurs, but they'd seen him and fired about a thousand arrows his way. They were terrible shots, but then they'd come running to collect their arrows, and he'd had to hide. By the time he thought it was safe to poke his head up, they were gone.

Why had William volunteered to go with them?

Was he insane? Clearly not. Did he not understand what they were?

Cvuklon made his way along the shore of the Other Sea, what the people here called "Lequoia Lake" in honor of some princess who'd once saved them, to Carthage. Even pushing, which meant practically dragging Eeyora, it took almost a week. And every day, every minute it seemed, she kept looking around for William.

"Sorry, girl. He won't be coming. Not today. Maybe soon."

How would he explain what had happened? A fire that had killed a dozen people, losing the letter of transit for his "property" to a gang of ferocious Brull thieves, an attack from the Vo'ix?

He was not above telling whatever lie he could to avoid being held accountable for what was actually true, and anything was better than a confession that he'd let them take William without so much as a threat or an attempt to win him back.

For all his conviction that he was surrounded by fools whom he could readily outthink, he was now the greatest fool of all.

Would whoever was waiting for him be angry? Probably. Short of getting William to the cottage in Wukneesh, and that had proven pointless, he hadn't done what was asked of him. What would Dalter Bubussa say? Would he be at his brother's house, waiting and tsking and shaking his moustaches in disappointment? No, he wouldn't have come, but he would hear of this catastrophe, and then the moustaches would shake.

None of it mattered now. William was gone. The Gumundurs had taken him, fair and square according to the slaver law, and there was nothing Cvuklon could do about it.

But the people who wanted William, the ones he was supposed to meet…maybe they could do something about it. He knew, or he thought he knew, where the Gumundurs had taken him: to the Measured Fields, to sell him into one of the Road vans that made the run from Chralm Doanna to Motatinfo. Not a pleasant prospect but not an unfamiliar one, not to him. He'd dealt with the Road maggots and their masters plenty.

Life on the Road was very tricky, though, for a soldier-slave, and very dangerous. Whatever else he was, William was no fighter. Cvuklon had to find him and get him out of there. He had to get help.

His meeting had been set for Quattrenim 36 at the Ferrela Fout in Carthage. Those were the arrangements. And he'd made it there early. To the city.

There was, of course, a layer or two of stealth and secrecy built in to the whole operation. For example, he had no idea who he was meeting or even what they planned to do with William once they had him

He could guess why: these people were very enamored of secrets, and rightfully so. Stealing and transporting an Entrant was a serious crime that warranted substantial punishment. Stealing and transporting an Entrant that might or might not be essential to the fate of the entire environ…the punishment there would be unimaginable.

And he was too young to die. On top of which, he really wanted to know. He wanted to answers to all the questions he had about William, even the ones he didn't know how to begin framing in his mind. He needed the world to make some kind of sense.

If there was even a chance that this Entrant, this man from Earth, as unremarkable as he seemed to be, could save the lives of quite literally millions of people, Cvuklon had to know why anyone would stop him from attempting to do so.

But someone was very keen on doing exactly that.

He thought about it more carefully: if the environ failed to Prove, all life in it would be eliminated, and then eventually, who could say when, another Primary Species would be placed there. Or that was what history had to say on the matter.

Of course, history was very porous, very mutable and subjective. But even given that, it seemed the only reason any being had to thwart a species' chance to Prove was to gain the environ for itself. And that made no sense because it wasn't like the place would become an empty house. The new residents would be forthcoming at some point—and until then, the environ would likely be uninhabitable.

Round and round he went in his mind to the point where he had tied himself in knots.

He reminded himself: he was five days early. It was Quattrenim 30. He'd lost track on the road in his desperate hurry, but here he was. His early arrival, however, gave him no comfort. If anything, it gave him more time to contemplate his own stupidity and the impossible math surrounding the fate of this environ.

Rather than give him a sign or person to look for, which Dalter hadn't, the plan was probably for someone to be on the lookout for a particularly stout Slau and a gangly human slave at the Fout. Trouble was, despite his formidable ability to forever maintain his stoutness, he no longer had the human.

Would they spot him anyway? Probably. Maybe. Maybe he could ask Dalter's brother. He wasn't sure if Nuadac Bubussa was in on it, whatever "it" was, but he was sure he could lay a bag of barbs on him and get him to help. Assuming he could help. Cvuklon couldn't know. What a horrible position to be in. What he did know was that he'd never met someone who wasn't willing to bend over backward for a bag of barbs. There was always a first time, though, for the gremfi to ride the Slau, his uncle was fond of saying.

There was no saying giving a bag to every able-bodied individual in Carthage would make one bit of difference. He wasn't even sure what he'd be bribing them for. *Excuse me, I'm supposed to meet someone to hand over someone to that someone for a reason I cannot reveal because I was never told. Here's some coins. Help?*

He'd had to pay ten barb just to enter the city, and the gate guards took half of his food, his best blanket, and his flute. They gave the flute back when it wouldn't make any noise, not understanding that a Slau flute could really only be played by a Slau. As if he were the first Slau they'd ever swindled and legally robbed at their stupid gate.

They couldn't play his flute, so they handed it to him as if they were giving him a holiday gift.

"Thank you. You know, I don't think it's you. I'm fairly sure only Slau can play it."

Whereupon they took the flute back and threw it in their fire.

"Now no one can play it. Whatja think a that, slug?"

He wasn't paying attention. His mind was going at full tilt, and now he was questioning his assumption. He wasn't sure if what he'd told them was completely true: he'd never seen another race, other than the humans at the gate, try to play one. Maybe the Juks Xi Ren or the Brull could play a whole symphony on the thing.

Either way, he was down to the twenty barb he'd hidden in his belly sack, plus a bad blanket and half of one meal. And in his own mind, he was babbling, trying to figure out everything and pretty much coming up with no answers. It was a wonder he remembered to breathe.

There was no sense in making a direct line to the Fout; he had to think first about what he was going to say to his contacts, should he be lucky enough to even make contact. He still had no idea who they were or what they might be able to do, but he was out of options, unless he turned around and went to the Road himself.

He wondered for the hundredth time: Why had William volunteered to go with them? He knew where they were going.

And then it hit him: *he knew where they were going!*

He shuddered at the thought and kept walking, taking turns here and there and keeping away from the Southern Gate District, where he knew the inn was.

The thought, however, kept recurring to him. Without William, he was just as likely to be killed by these contacts as aided. And who knew what they wanted William for, anyway? Maybe Dalter had sold the Entrant to the highest bidder for who knew what purpose.

Maybe the buyer was from Pir Choss, where the physicians had ducal permission to experiment on patients in any way they deemed necessary to their research. Cvuklon had been around long enough to have heard the stories. Even his uncle refused to go anywhere near the place, profit be damned.

But why would these people not want to investigate this whole idea of the Ashorne? People had believed this legend and legends like it for centuries. Surely a fact finding was in order. Unless…unless…and back around his mind went.

He was being a coward, wasn't he? Telling himself tales of Pir Choss and failed Provings and maybe rescuing someone from Road van servitude singlehandedly…ridiculous! His best bet was to gain — or buy — allies. He could come up with a plan, but the extra time to consider had reminded him of something that was both a shameful flaw and, para-doxically, a quality that had saved his life more than once: he was terrible at execution. And that was because he was even worse at drawing an actionable conclusion. Indecisiveness was his bane.

It was a small miracle he'd gotten as far as he had, with or without his "cargo."

Night was coming on, and he needed a place to sleep.

He decided no new plan was going to spring into his mind.

It was time to chance the Ferrela Fout.

"You know my brother?" asked Nuadac Bubussa.

"Yes, yes, I do…I have met him many times in the Tent City."

"Work for a slaver, do you?"

Cvuklon didn't like to be questioned so directly by someone he'd just met, but he'd started this by walking into the man's establishment. "I did, for a while. A year or so. My uncle's."

"Well, that kind of work is bad business, I always told my brother. Better to get out young; he stayed in, and he'll never get out now. Haven't even seen him in years. How is he?"

"He is well."

"Good."

"Has there been anyone…has anyone been asking for me?"

"For you?"

"Yes, I was thinking maybe…"

"No, no one asking for a…what'd you say your name was again?"

"Cvuklon."

"Suvukalan…got it. Well, no, like I said. It's been slow around here, and the wife is ready to eat my head 'cause of it. We've only had three customers over the last month. None of them asked for a Suvukalan, though."

"Any of them…anything out of the ordinary about any of them?" Cvuklon asked.

"No, not really. Known them all for years. Merchants. Cheap as hell, had to fight them to pay the bill, but that's nothing new."

Having nothing to go by, Cvuklon decided he should probably just wait. "I guess I'll take a room. And maybe you can ask around, see if there have been any unfamiliar characters about."

"Unfamiliar, huh? That's not much to go by."

"Dalter didn't tell me much. Just said to come here."

"All right, I'll keep my ears open. Barb a night for the room, 'cause you know my brother."

"Thank you."

"You can eat with me and the wife tonight too, but I'm sorry, we don't have any of that cold stuff your people like, so you'll have to make do with a simple Carthie dinner."

Nuadac Bubussa showed him to his room, patted him on the shoulder, and left him to his thoughts.

Cvuklon, standing there next to the bed, was filled with a sort of hopeless dread. His mission was a failure, and he was sure whoever might come for him, if anyone did, was going to be unhappy with his incompetence. And so he was once again in a position to contemplate the incompetence that seemed to follow him from road to town, from gremfi to bed, without fail. Maybe his uncle was right about him. Maybe he was just a fat child with nothing to offer the world but his fanciful notions and blundering stupidity.

But maybe not. He sat down on the bed and thought about what he should do.

In a very short while, he fell sound asleep.

In the morning, he went down, and Nuadac offered him some breakfast.

"Missed you last night. Wife was looking forward to complaining to you about me, she was. Sorry, bread and boiled eggs just now, but I can hail down a street vendor who might have something you'd prefer, if you like."

Nuadac, Cvuklon noted, was very unlike his brother in some ways, and yet he could see some strong similarities in how they carried themselves and how they treated people they liked. Or maybe they just were in the habit of pretending they liked everyone in order to gain some kind of advantage. Either way, Cvuklon appreciated the kindness.

A street vendor did venture by, and Nuadac bought some iced fulmadun, enough to feed a whole Slau family for a week. "Guess I got extra. You look like a man with an appetite," Nuadac said. "I'll join you, if you don't mind. I'll have the eggs, though."

Cvuklon certainly did not mind, so the two sat down and ate some breakfast together.

"I was thinking about what you asked me—about the unusual characters. This city sees plenty of them come and go, this particular square more so because we have our gate right here."

"I imagine you see all kinds. Plenty of my people, Pumcat, Thicknomites."

"All true, all true."

"But you're saying...there was someone of note?"

"Not at all, not really. A week or so ago, I did notice a particularly beautiful woman, alone, sitting now and then at the fountain."

"A whore?"

"I don't think so. Not a local one, anyway. She looked...like she was waiting for someone. And she was with child."

Cvuklon nodded with polite interest, but his mind was beginning to drift. A pregnant human woman, however beautiful Nuadac might have found her, was of little interest to him. Still, it was pleasant to sit and listen to this man. He hadn't Dalter's way with words, but he was somehow just as charming.

When they were through with their meal, Cvuklon thanked his host and set out to take a small stroll around the square. He was hoping perhaps to be noticed by...someone. Or to notice something himself. His stroll was, however, entirely uneventful.

"Out there looking for the beautiful mother-to-be, were you?" Nuadac joked when he returned to the Fout.

Cvuklon tried to smile but failed and instead just nodded.

"Who knows, maybe you're the father, hmm?"

The Slau said, "I am rarely so lucky," and then, somewhat numbly, handed Nuadac a five-barb coin.

"Five nights will get you a sixth for free, my friend. Come down and join us later. Wife still wants to complain about me to you, yes she does!" Nuadac called after Cvuklon as he climbed the stairs to his room.

His head was churning. He unlocked his room, went in, and sat on the bed. Undressing himself, he began to cry. Then he stopped crying, lay down, and realized he was still completely exhausted. He tried to stay awake and think but found he could not.

He did not wake up until the following afternoon.

And when he woke, there was a knife at his throat.

"Get up, slug."

Not a great start to a conversation, thought Cvuklon.

"You were supposed to come here with someone."

"Yes, well…yes. And you are?"

The knife pressed closer to his throat, and he winced a bit.

"Who I am is someone who, like you, was entrusted to do a job. Unlike you, I am trying to do that job. You've rendered my efforts pointless."

"My apologies. He was…taken from me. Who are you?"

"I'm not going to tell you my name, so stop asking."

"You are a woman. A human woman."

"Very impressive. You have ears. Or whatever those are."

"Aural holes."

"This is not the time for jokes, slug. Get up and get dressed."

"We're going somewhere?"

"You're going to take me to where the Ashorne and you parted ways. Then I'm going to pick up the trail and follow him."

"And what happens to me?"

"Maybe I'll stick this knife into one of your aural holes. Let's not concern ourselves with the future right now, though. Get dressed and meet me downstairs. Try to run, and I will slice you open."

She left him alone in the room.

He grabbed his cloak and tunic and began to dress himself. *What to do, what to do?* His assailant had sounded more worried and put out than threatening. She was clearly under a good deal of pressure to deliver results, that much he could discern from her posturing. He had no doubt she could make good on her threats, but it was also almost certainly true that she needed him.

The trouble was, he knew exactly how to find William. And he knew exactly what would happen to them both if they did. He wasn't concerned about the fate of his assailant, but he himself did not want to end up in Yanz, Tritto, or the feeding trough of some freakish work animal somewhere along the road.

He decided to lie to the assailant, to tell her William had been abducted and brought south down the Trace. Maybe that would give him time to break away and get back to his own country.

It was a terrible plan that relied entirely on his physical stealth and prowess, both of which were borderline pathetic. Lying to her might be a massive mistake, but telling her the truth would mean heading up to the Qi Dao Lu and, without doubt, being captured and worse.

He changed his mind about lying to her.

All this time, he'd been operating in the dark with no one to trust or to talk to. Dalter had told him next to nothing. William knew nothing except that he'd woken up from death to find himself trapped in a terrible place that to his mind was worse than death. Dalter's brother knew nothing. And he himself had not been contacted by anyone to tell him how to proceed now that disaster had befallen his mission.

Until she appeared with a knife at his throat, no one had been willing or able to give him any answers. Maybe no one had any to give. But he suspected strongly she might.

Was there any doubt that she was the contact he'd been waiting for?

He decided to tell her the truth.

"Leaving, huh? Shame. If you're headed south, mind yourself on the Trace. It ain't safe like it used to be," said Nuadac as Cvuklon made his way out the front door into the square. "Your friend is outside waiting for you. She pretty? Her face is covered. Shy, I guess. Or Pherriuskatan, which means you've got a load of trouble coming your way!"

Cvuklon shrugged. "I'm not sure what she is, but...I've got to go."

Nuadac smiled. "Say no more. Come back whenever. You're still paid up for a few more nights, you are."

Cvuklon shook his hand and gave him a smile. "I'll be back. I still haven't heard your wife's complaints. And thank you, Nuadac," he said warmly. "It was a pleasure."

He stepped out into the square.

"Let's take a walk, you and I."

She was behind him. He glanced at her and saw her face was still covered. She was short, shorter even than him, and her knife was nowhere to be seen.

"There are a few things I need to tell you," he said.

"I'm sure there are."

They strode east, down toward the shore of the Other Sea, moving in silence for about twenty minutes. The early-afternoon streets of Carthage were bustling with life: students running here and there, merchants pushing and arranging carts, fishermen hauling loads of lobster and sea bass and elephant fish to the various trading grounds and open markets, and citizens of every race going about their business in a generally urgent-but-sane manner.

Cvuklon envied them. Their lives seemed so certain, so unassailably self-contained. Nothing like his life with his uncle, crawling along dusty roads through ugly hills to uglier places. And nothing like his life since his uncle: stumbling and scurrying from place to place like a gremfi without nostrils.

Eeyora. What would happen to her?

Nuadac would probably sell her. Or maybe not.

Cvuklon felt a pang of sadness. He'd had her for over a year; she was a good beast and loyal.

"Stop here."

He stopped. They were at the top of a very steep, winding staircase that led to a shore path. "There's no need to be so hostile. I am very willing to help."

"I don't care about your willingness. All I need is information, not help," she said, starting down the stairs and gesturing to him to follow.

"I'll tell you whatever I know."

"Talk," commanded his companion.

He told her what had happened. What Dalter had asked him to do, what William was like, how the Gumundurs had taken him away, and what they had likely done with him.

"You're saying these Gumundurs...they have no idea who he is?"

"*He* doesn't have any idea who he is. Neither do I."

"Dalter didn't tell you?"

"I'm not sure Dalter knew. I think he was paid to find William at the Landing Point and somehow get him down to Carthage." Cvuklon wasn't lying, not now, not enitirely. There wasn't much reason to. And he had a hunch this woman, whoever she was, wasn't his enemy. Although he did not doubt she was capable with her ever-present blade, she seemed to be trying to sound far more threatening than she was.

"Paid by whom?"

"I don't know."

"We have to find him. We can't let him die," she said. Cvuklon could feel her sincerity and urgency. This woman was not his enemy.

"I was very afraid that you would say that. But if we pursue him, just the two of us, we will be the ones who die. And I'm also afraid there's a very good chance he's already dead."

"We need to know. We need to find out where he is and if he's still alive."

"I understand."

"You're saying he volunteered to go with the Gumundurs, even though he knew what they planned to do with him? Why would he do that?" she asked.

"I've been giving that some thought, and I think perhaps I have an answer."

"Don't be shy, my friend. Let's have it."

"I believe he might be trying to get back to the Landing Point."

"Why the hell would anyone ever want to go back there?"

"Because he believes his family is there."

"Are they?"

"No. I don't know. I hope for his sake they are not."

"But he thinks they are?"

"Yes, I think so."

"But you don't know?"

"It's a guess."

"You're not much help, are you?"

"Not usually, no."

"How are you in a fight?"

"The same. Not much help."

"Well, you're coming with me anyway. Maybe someone who tries to stick or shoot me will nail you instead."

"So I'm to be your what, shield?" asked Cvuklon.

"Think of it as dying for a Noble cause."

"I would rather live. Let me go home. To Slauland."

"Sorry. I need you."

"Why?"

"You know what he looks like. I don't want to search for weeks and grab the wrong man, do I?"

"I see your point."

"Excellent. Ready?"

"I had a nice bed at that inn."

"I saw it. You asking for something?"

"What? No. I'm just saying it was nice to get a couple nights' peaceful sleep. I expect they'll be my last for some time."

"If you don't help me save this man, trust me: no one in Arba has many nights left to sleep, peacefully or otherwise."

"I don't understand."

"William is the Ashorne. He's the key to Arba's Proving."

Cvuklon could not believe what he had just heard. He'd suspected, he'd mused, but he hadn't let himself believe it. Not entirely.

The Ashorne.

The one the verses were about. The one who would "make the Fourth." That Ashorne. Cvuklon had been travelling with him for weeks. And he'd just let him go...with the Gumundurs.

His stomach began to hurt.

He followed the woman, wondering if there would ever come a day where he wouldn't be such a colossal idiot.

Chapter 27
Its subsequent sweet deterioration

Place: Pashka, kingdom of Pherriuskata, Arba Environ
Date: Quattrenim 33, AY 998

The afternoon was hot and damp, and the Rosen Square teemed with the frenzied activity of buying, selling, browsing, and preening. Howled arguments, songs of price, prayers to random and generally ineffectual gods, and screams of feigned pleasure punctuated the churning and jostling. The smells alone were enough to drive a person mad with hunger, nausea, or smoke-induced delusion, and the bodies pressed against one another like the wild root system of a forest whose trees' thirst could never be quenched.

This cacophonous commercial assault demarked without doubt a typical day in the ancient city's Grand Market. Today, however, a typical Pashkan day's capricious passion was augmented by the presence of the elite, who appeared but twice a month, if that. They made a telling impact when they did, with fortunes and time to spend on everything from wines to furs to gadgets to perfumes.

Here and there, merchants argued, laughed, pushed, shoved, and cursed. Some were beating others with fists, satchels, or, in the case of one irate baker, a hard loaf of bread, to gain favored positions on the Row of Plenty. Two were even killed while arguing over whose cart belonged on a particular corner; they stabbed each other simultaneously, both dying with expressions of bemused disbelief on their faces — and, after a moment's hesitation on the part of the thrilled onlookers, had their wares hungrily absorbed into the stock of other, less impulsive members of their class.

None seemed to grieve their passing, Petrecia noted.

Yes, wealth was out in force, purchasing and drinking and posing, the women in their masks and flowing, bright-colored clothes, the men in white, gray, or powder-blue chitons smoking long pipes and walking in tight groups behind their scattered, aggressively spending women, and the armies of servants and attendants struggling to keep up while bearing the many whimsically acquired items of their respective employers and owners. The parade of the monied pushed forward at the pace of a rock rolling uphill whilst the sea of greed and need before them roiled with an energy that cascaded in an almost threatening manner.

Not only the Row of Plenty but all the nearby streets of the market were packed with merchants from far and wide, their booths overflowing with pottery and paintings, fruits and silks, trinkets and bottles, live animals performing tricks and dead ones roasting over hot coals. Acrobats tumbled and poemsmen performed, and on every corner except the one that had featured the stabbing was a different singer with a different version of what often sounded very much like the same hackneyed song. So it always was on most days in the Pherriuskatan island capital, the greatest city in the known world, but during the weeks following a festival with the elite about, the effect could take one's breath away.

Or make one sick to her stomach, which was how Petrecia now felt.

But she wasn't prepared to blame the festival or the merchants or her friends' insatiable need to throw away coin on unhealthy delicacies and forgettable trophies. No, she'd have felt just as troubled sitting in her own chambers, alone, staring out at the night sky and listening to the wind.

It had been three weeks since the scene at Motatinfo, but still she could feel her skin crawl each time she looked at her husband. She had disliked him before — their marriage had long been a loveless lie, without doubt — but now there was nothing left. Nothing left of her she could share with him, nothing he could give or offer her that would ever bridge the gap between them. Not now.

Not after the Dance at that Feast.

Not after the deaths of those children.

What he had done…what he had volunteered to do. Had he known? Had Grewea ordered him to…but why would that be? No, she was sure of it: Rodolpho had made his own choice.

And she hated him for it.

And she hated herself for her disgusting hypocrisy. She had known what was in store, or had known about the disregard for life and the ever-inventive penchant for excessive cruelty that demarked these feasts and this horrible culture from which one could scarcely shield one-self. She was not innocent. She was very much a part of everything she saw around her. She was no different.

She knew all this, and she did nothing, nothing but ignore the vicious sickness that pervaded her world like a writhing, clutching, poisonous smoke. She saw but did nothing.

She was not innocent.

"Would you like a tea, ma'am?" asked Synthyea. Petrecia turned to her woman, barely having heard what was asked, and shook her head slightly. Synthyea smiled prettily and backed away, rejoining the ranks of the trailing servants and attendants.

Among Petrecia's contemporaries and alongside her one true friend, Fernanda — who at least didn't spend all her waking moments thinking of ways to make her one true friend a social pariah just for fun, which is what passed for a true friend in this part of the world but not, Petrecia knew, many others — she felt as close to safe and happy as she was able to here in this city of agony and decisions. But then again, safety and happiness were relative terms, and as for other places, she knew very little because she'd never visited them, was forbidden to read about them, and was not really inclined to know anyway — she thought she might somehow put the happenings at Motatinfo out of her mind for an afternoon.

That was proving impossible. For whatever reason, an irrepressible feeling of horror was eating her from within. The screams of the children, the screams of the six parents who had died for love, even the screams of the hideous Dancemaster and, in the end, the monstrosity that had provided so much entertainment for the guests. It had proved too unmanageable and so needed to be killed by the Crabs. It too had screamed.

No one was safe. Nothing was sacred.

She heard them still. Now. Weeks later. More so, even. Why, she could not say. And the sounds were not in the back of her mind, no. She heard them as if they were happening right now, right here in Rosen Square, as if the cage and the creature and the Dancemaster and the children and the parents were dying amid the carts and the musikers and the greed, dying again, dying unnoticed.

She glanced around, glad of the mask that hid her desperate expression, glad of the surrounding chaos in which her upended countenance was unnoticeably lost. She spun for a moment until her eyes lighted upon the thing she hated more than herself.

He was there, walking behind her with his lapdogs and colleagues, laughing over some trivial and challenge-less victory or other, and she stared at him for a moment, seeing in him nothing but bestial disdain for anything that wasn't him. She saw not a killer but a monster.

She saw herself taking his arm two days after the Trantuse Feast, re-entering the Mansdrelam with him, and walking away from him while he called to her again and again.

He had called until she'd finally come.

What choice had she?

She found her eyes darting toward the various alleyways and side streets, searching with a helplessly vague bravado for a means to escape him. Not that she ever would, she admitted to herself as she often offhandedly did, but today felt different. Today she felt the weight of what she was admitting.

She would never be free of him.

For better or worse, her fate and life were bound to his. She'd known that forever meant forever the moment she'd agreed years ago to leave dear Miranquella and come to this bizarre town, a place that seemed so full of life and wonder on the surface but had quickly proven to be nothing short of wretched and diseased.

A man with three monkeys on his head and shoulders jumped in front of her, all four of them chattering the usual something about the best price in all the Tri, all smiling with yellowing teeth and flicking tongues…

Her attendants beat the man and the monkeys without being asked to do so.

Beaten, they ran, but they didn't run far; she could still hear the monkey seller chattering his line about price from somewhere in the crowd.

"Monkeys from Miranquella! Come and see, come and watch them dance and play!"

Monkeys from Miranquella indeed.

She'd been from there, once, though she no longer remembered ever knowing how to dance or play. She'd been sold and no longer remembered why.

Of course, she hadn't in those youthful moments known that her husband-to-be would favor the killing of children as entertainment. She hadn't had any idea that such things truly happened anywhere but the darkest places of the world, and of the darkest places in the world she'd known next to nothing. That hadn't changed much, not in the years between her wedding and the Low Feast, this despite the hints and facts and whispers and laughter over atrocities she told herself time and again she must have misinterpreted or misheard. What she saw on the streets she dismissed as willfully farcical rather than grimly symptomatic. Tricks of the merchants—that wasn't real blood, those weren't real cries.

She was in some sense content and, with the sense of self-delusion only the circumstantially solipsistic and defiant can conjure, content to keep it that way. It served to mask the realization that she had virtually no power to effect change of any kind.

At the time she'd left her home, she'd been a child herself, overwhelmed by the attention his courtship had visited upon her and by the pressures her own people had applied in the interest not of her happiness but, as she gradually came to admit and then forget, of their nation's freshly sanctioned perpetuity.

The truth and its subsequent sweet deterioration had long since come along to dissuade her of any but the most remote romantic notions, and yet she still on occasion felt he somehow needed her and that her choice to become his bride had resulted in a union that was something more than simply mutually beneficial, her ever-growing hatred of him notwithstanding. Those rare occasions did not include the semiregular beatings he gave her on nights his self-doubt threatened to overthrow his seemingly limitless bluster.

She glanced at another alley and at her attendants, who were beating another merchant and laughing at him because he'd shit himself. They were not looking at her.

If she were to flee, where would she go? The very thought was remarkable in its striking capacity to alienate her from herself. Go? She'd adjusted her expectations even as she'd become addicted to the near-unlimited splendor that was afforded her by this complicated life. She loved Rosen Square of a Quattrenim, even in the unbearable heat: the beautiful bodies, the game of who watched whom, the fabrics and wines and gifts and trinkets and performers and speeches and shows and dances. She loved the festivals and the subtleties and the lies and the flirting, though in that last diversion she never took part: Rodolpho had made it plain that such sport was closed for his Mont du Grace prize.

No, for Petrecia Celeranet, former monkey of Miranquella and now bride in a gilded hell, going was tantamount to sprouting wings, and she had a near-pathological fear of heights—she'd worked very hard to make sure of that—so what good would wings ever do her?

She'd stopped looking for alleys a long time ago.

What use had a sold monkey for such things?

"Oh, see there, Petrecia: the Calawaki aged cheeses are finally here!" sulked Fernanda Ji Norva to her left. "And George is complaining I'm getting too chubby again…oh, maybe just a taste!"

Fernanda, resplendent in her newly wrought Ponasa mask, shuffled her ample self toward the Xatumkan wagons and held up a single finger to the closest merchant. From a short distance, her husband scolded her with a vicious whistle, but Fernanda only blushed, laughed, and took the cheese the merchant had quickly wrapped for her. She came back to Petrecia and giggled. "Want some?"

"I want all of it, but I fear that George is not the only one who complains," Petrecia replied.

"Still correcting you, is he?"

"He is, but not with the same verve he once had."

"I know a man who knows a man who knows a Brull, you know."

"So you've told me. And while the idea sometimes warms my heart, I'm afraid my courage is not what it once was."

"Beatings have a funny way of doing that," said Fernanda as she shoved in a chunk of cheese.

"Oh, hush, and let me taste that!" said Petrecia, ignoring the opening.

Fernanda did as she was told, and they giggled as they ate the forbidden delicacy. "I feel myself getting fatter by the nibble!" Fernanda declared with mock exasperation.

"I see it, I see it!" laughed Petrecia. And she made herself somehow believe, just for a moment, she really could. That the laughter, for that moment, was real. Some small part of her was able to slip out from under her malaise and breathe and make fun and laugh with her friend. She felt like a prisoner who'd spotted a cloud from her cell window, and the sensation was more than welcome given her current, more sullen contemplations.

The sensation was bordered on disturbing.

Dumb monkey, get back in the cage, she thought she heard a merchant cry.

Fernanda chuckled, and then her eyes went wide and she spit out the cheese.

"Not to your liking?" laughed Petrecia.

Her friend, between spitting more and wiping her mouth with a big purple cloth, managed to cough out, "The worst cheese I've ever...how come you're not...?"

"Oh, it's not so bad," answered Petrecia even as she felt a slightly uncomfortable heave in her belly.

Fernanda grabbed one of her attendants and pointed at the cheese stall; in moments, the cheesemonger was on the ground, begging for his life through broken teeth. Fernanda frowned but then smiled and giggled, and the man rose, attempting to giggle and live.

The women's walk continued. "Tell me, Petti...is she still bothering you about the dress?" asked Fernanda.

"What? Oh, no...hasn't mentioned it in weeks. I think she saw the subject was annoying her prince, so she let it go."

"I'm sure it still eats at her."

"I'm sure."

"Second Wives. What can you do?"

"Well, I've considered trading places with her. Might mean fewer bruises."

"But you'd miss all that sex."

"Maybe, but I'm sure I could find nightly ways to fill up that minute or two."

They laughed again at Rodolpho's expense. And this laugh wasn't like spotting a cloud. It felt more like spitting in the food of the jailer when his back was turned.

This was her favorite kind of laughter—complicated mirth with bite, with an edge that said maybe she hadn't yet played all her cards and maybe those wings were yet sproutable. But in truth, she balked at its expression, mostly because she wasn't unaware of its truly biteless nature and of how bitter she'd become in the knowledge of that fact to the detriment of all other emotions. She was a ghost within herself, and she lived daily with the sickening realization that she'd volunteered to become that ghost. She'd done everything she could to end her own life without actually dying. All in vain.

She could have told her father, "No."

But she'd wanted to say, "Yes," somehow just to spite everyone who wanted and needed her to say yes. She'd wielded her own fate as a weapon in youth's uninformed, blind rebellion…and she had paid the price.

Collusion in one's own demise is never a pretty thing, sang the musikers. She knew herself so well now, and she relied on the only discernible direction in her life: her unimpeded plunge toward unthinkable, collusive ugliness.

It was a wonder she'd not yet gouged out her own eyes.

Those eyes lighted upon a booth of terrible art. There were many such booths, and in her mind, they should have all been banned or burned long ago. It was one thing to sell bad cheese, but to sell bad paintings? Even in a world this deformed, it seemed above and beyond to do so.

Someone here, somewhere, would be selling Elzbieta's paintings, she suspected. And unlike most of the ham-handed works of so-called art in these booths, her paintings would sell, and for handsome prices.

Elzbieta had been gifted, so gifted in fact that Rodolpho, renowned and passionate patron of the arts that he was, had often threatened to have all her materials thrown into the sea if she so much as displeased him. She'd rarely displeased him in any case, so attentive and intuitive was she to his needs, so his threats were understood by all to be unabashedly grounded in envy. Petrecia was shocked he'd allowed her works to be seen, let alone sold; she assumed he derived some vicarious pride from the attention they received. It was said even Duke Velliok had not one but two of her lakescapes hanging in his halls.

Second wives indeed.

Fernanda was playfully haggling with a Mariendan over some violet silk dress that wouldn't have fit over her leg. The Mariendan's propensity for flattery was being taxed to the extreme, and Fernanda was enjoying immensely the degree to which she made the man squirm. Petrecia wondered, not for the first time, if she herself understood the meaning of the term "true friend." Fernanda was something of a brute, however affable and giggly she might appear.

Petrecia left her with the Mariendan and wandered off toward one of the dozens of seashell-shaped fish ponds on the edge of the square. Her feet were hot and sore from all the walking; Rodolpho had insisted she wear heels that were best reserved for the ballroom or bedroom.

There were two young boys dangling their sandaled feet in the pond, laughing and joking. She thought the fish might be nipping at their toes. Leaning over to see the fish, she was surprised to find a group of tiny purple turtles, swimming back and forth, brushing their bumpy shells against the boys' feet. She watched and listened and almost smiled.

More uncommon sensations. Wings and smiles and conscience.

She suddenly felt anxious and sad. She moved hurriedly away from the pond.

She hadn't known before she married Rodolpho that she couldn't bear children. How could she? How would anyone? After a year of trying to get her with child, he'd sent her to a physician who'd trained at Pir Choss. The results were inconclusive; the physician wanted to send her south to Pir Choss itself for further tests and a possible procedure, as he called it. She'd begged Rodolpho not to send her there. Pir Choss was not a place you went if you ever wanted to return whole. The stories she'd heard were too horrific and too many to chance a visit. Wasn't there anything else they could do?

There was. A Second Wife. Pherriuskatan law allowed a man to take another wife as long as the first gave her permission. The First Wife, whose permission was a given, would remain a wife — nothing could change that — but she might sometimes be relieved of some of her marital duties, including those practiced in the bedroom. She would, however, always be required to attend her husband in other matters — functions, festivals, travel, and the maintenance of his household accounts and staff, if he had either. The Second Wife could come too or substitute for the First if all were in agreement. Or if the husband commanded it.

This arrangement was very common. It was even more common when a First Wife was barren, but it wasn't entirely about siring children. It was about men wanting more than one wife and wives having no say in the matter. Some men, but only the most wealthy, took a Third and a Fourth Wife; who else could afford so much shopping?

Rodolpho had wasted no time finding — some said, buying — Elzbieta, an artisan whose work he'd admired on trips to the Grandeis Hold, where she was a distant cousin of the dervinth himself. He'd brought her back to Pashka less than two weeks after gaining approval from the proper authorities. She was pregnant one month later. He had three children by her: all girls, to his disappointment. His disdain for Elzbieta had grown to match his disdain for his increasingly despised First Wife.

Then, not long after the birth of the third daughter, something changed. Rodolpho, bucking official custom but following customary practice to a fault, brought the wives together, perhaps out of a twisted desire to see the two diametrically opposed women tear each other to shreds. Later, though, he came to very much desire the attentions of his wives together.

This went on for almost a week. He then succumbed to the obvious fact of his weakness as a lover. His sad inability to satisfy one woman became a source of bitter rage when faced with the daunting task of satisfying two. He took to watching them, then to beating them, and then one night he left them alone and never returned to the bed.

The women, as people facing the same strife will do, developed a bond. At first it was primarily sexual, but soon it grew into a true but secret friendship. They met, they talked, they shared. Petrecia did fall in something like love with Elzbieta, and she was nearly sure that Elzbieta felt similarly toward her. Unbeknownst to their husband, Petrecia began to help her friend and lover to care for the children, who were at that time very young. And because Elzbieta showed an interest, Petrecia also taught Elzbieta how to do figures and understand the financial and practical elements of running a Pashkan household.

Elzbieta in turn taught Petrecia how to paint.

This, both knew, was a very dangerous and very illegal thing to do. Petrecia, though she never discussed it and had never heard anyone mention it since she'd come to Pashka, had been born with a color. Women with color were either executed or, if they were lucky, found by the Spectrum and sent to be with their own kind in Jamoi. Her father, Lord Jorge Celeranet, had done all he could to avoid either of those fates for her. He'd cut a deal with the Mer Ponx to let her live. It hadn't cost him much: only Dalivia Island and half the rights to his thousands of acres of orange, lemon, and olive groves.

And even then, after such a massive sacrifice, she was not allowed to stay in Miranquella indefinitely: it was agreed that when she came of age, she'd be married off to someone who lived much closer to the seat of Mer Ponx power in Arbana so they could use her or at least keep a close eye on her.

In a way, she knew she had her genetics to blame for her marriage's coming to be, and perhaps also for its emptiness. But without either, she would never have met Elzbieta, and she would have never developed her love affair with color or with Elzbieta herself.

That was all over now. Elzbieta had died. Something had gone wrong inside her head, and her body had begun to shake, and her eyes went blind. She was gone now, long gone, and the children had been sent away to schools in Hunberg and Carthage. The paints and canvasses and brushes had all been burned, and whatever Petrecia had felt stirring within her—a passion for color, a passion for expression, a passion for the love of another—had vanished within those flames and the flames of her almost unendurable sorrow.

And now, years later, she was alone. She confided in Fernanda, but mostly there was nothing to confide. She'd never told Fernanda about

Elzbieta and their life together. She hadn't told anyone, and now it was like she had a secret that had once kept her alive but which she now could barely remember herself. All that was left was an unmistakable ache.

She walked away from the boys and their dangling feet, saddened to distraction by her remembrance of her dead friend, and stumbled right into an old woman in a ruby cloak. The woman was keen of eye but did not look at her angrily. Rather, there was a sense of recognition in the way she regarded Petrecia.

"I beg your pardon. Please, allow me to account for my foolish misstep," said the old woman with the manners of a well-bred Pashkan.

"Don't think of it; the fault was mine," responded Petrecia reflexively.

"Please, walk with me a while, and let's share the day and company," said the woman.

Petrecia did what was asked of her. She went with this person for a walk. She did not know why she went or for how long. When she returned to Fernanda and the shopping, though, no one commented upon her absence.

And she had no idea what she and the woman had spoken about.

All Petrecia could remember was her name:

Aschare.

Chapter 28
"Why in Four's names did you bring me here?"

Place: Atuut Mountains, Arba Environ
Date: Quattrenim 33, AY 998

"They're coming for you, old man. You know that, don't you?"

Gossie hadn't been twenty minutes into the Midforest and now, this.

All around him, Brull warriors. A band of about twenty. His fortunes had not improved.

"You boys are taking a chance being in here, no?" he said to them, knowing a bit about their history with the Tromontieri.

"As are you, old man," chuckled one of the Brull.

"Well, that point's arguable — I've had ups and downs in this strange and unique part of the world, to be sure — but you'd have to admit, the ones that dwell here aren't very fond of your kind. And that's putting it mildly," answered Gossie with a wistful smile. He'd no idea what these chaps were about, but it seemed — for the moment at least — their intervention had upped his chances of surviving the day.

"True enough, true enough. But as you see, we are here, risking our lives. You have to come with us."

"Risking your lives? What, for me? Why?"

"You have a choice to make: come with us or die."

"That's not much of a choice."

"Best offer you're going to get today, old man. Those things that were looking for you in Camedua? They're not more than a mile off, and they're coming."

"Something tells me the Tromontieri won't like that."

"Maybe. But maybe not. Who knows what motivates those creepy beasts? What I can tell you for a certainty is despite your claim, ups and downs and whatnot, the Tromontieri don't care what happens to you. We do."

"Is that so?" Gossie asked, somewhat bemused at the idea in spite of his precarious situation.

"It is."

"I am genuinely confused. I can tell you're trying to be truthful, but I'm not sure what part of what you're saying is a lie."

"Not my concern. Come with us before we all get killed."

Gossie wasn't lying. He still really had no idea what was going on. The Brull were no friends of his, although to his recollection he'd never screwed them over in any major or memorable way. It was without doubt odd that a bunch of them would be here, in the Midforest, trying to save him.

More than odd: impossible. Someone had sent them…but who?

He wasn't surprised that whatever had come after him in Camedua hadn't truly lost his trail, flooded caves and stinking barns notwithstanding. Whatever they were, they were something he hadn't a clue how to contend with…and now, this development.

Without another word, the Brull collectively turned northeast and started marching toward their mountains. They snorted softly through piglike snouts but made few other noises. Impressive, given their girth and heavily armored appearance.

Gossie followed them, saying to the one who seemed to be the leader, "Well, it's not like I had better plans, and if they're really coming for me, I'll have better odds dealing with them if you're around."

But not much better, he thought. The Brull were tough fighters and had a little magick they could use in a pinch. The things that were pursuing him — he assumed there were more than just the one he'd entwined, but maybe he was flattering himself — were not merely tough fighters. They were lethal monsters who could slaughter Challowians and fly. Or maybe they were. He still hadn't decided if the thing he'd fought in Camedua was one of whatever had destroyed the ships. He hadn't seen it fly, and he hadn't seen the ambush of the dragonmen either.

"By the way, what's with the 'old man' shit?" Gossie asked the leader.

"Term of respect," came the reply. "Now keep quiet till we're out of this forest."

Gossie did as he was told. It wasn't like he had a choice: the jogging pace the Brull kept was enough to suck the wind out of him and render him barely able to keep up. After just over two excruciating hours, during which they scarcely paused to drink some water once or twice, they reached the edge of the forest and stopped for a genuine rest.

"They're still after us," said the Brull leader calmly. "But they're slowing down."

"They don't want to follow us where we're going, nossir," said another Brull, this one missing an ear. The others grunted and snorted their assent.

"I've seen these things in action, and I've heard about what they did on the Windgiver Sea. I wouldn't think they'd be intimidated by mountains — or, and please forgive me as I mean no disrespect — you," Gossie said. He was huffing and puffing, still unable to catch his breath after the trying run.

"We know what they did on the Windgiver Sea. But the Challowians didn't see them coming: they flew out of the dark and jumped them," said the leader. "Once we're in the mountains, they haven't a chance."

Gossie still had his doubts about who was chasing whom and if they were in fact the same things that sank those ships, but those he kept to himself. He wondered how the Brull knew what had happened to the Juks Xi Ren. Someone must have fed them information, and that information could only have come from…the only survivor of the attack. Baks something. The one at the hearings. Maybe Gossie should have attended after all.

And if you had, you'd be dead, he thought. *Dead, instead of traipsing into Brull country for reasons unknown.*

Again, reasons unknown. Ever since he'd become involved with this whole business, he'd been three steps behind and living in the dark.

He decided right then and there that needed to change.

"So you know who attacked the *Ho Matsuni*?" he asked.

"No."

"Then how do you know what happened there?"

"We were told."

"And you trust this information?"

"Yes."

"Who gave it to you?"

The leader smiled and snorted twice. "You'll find that out soon enough, I suppose. Don't be too anxious is my advice."

"I see. So whoever this is…up in your mountains, hmm?"

"No."

"Then why are we going that way?"

"There's something you need to do."

"Something *I* need to do?"

"Something only you can do, or so we've been told."

"I'm intrigued and probably flattered, but really I think you've got the wrong man here."

"No, we don't. No more questions for now. We've got to keep moving."

"Okay, keep your secrets, but please, indulge me a moment more, if you would…"

"What is it?"

"What do I call you?"

That got a double snort as reply.

They headed north for another hour. The Atuut Mountains rose before them, impossibly high and snowcapped and darkly mysterious, a part of the world few Arbans ever visited. These were the mountains into which the Gri Na Leus had fled after their defeat by the combined armies of the midkingdoms and Aethrelius in the early 600s. Not so different, Gossie assumed, from the barren, sun-baked mountain ranges of the Namus Environ from whence they'd come. Perhaps a shade cooler.

Upon their defeat in Arba, rather than return home to face the new carnivorous residents, the Gri Na Leus had compromised and kept these mountains for themselves. Nobody else wanted them anyway, so the claim and the arrangement stuck.

What they'd done in those mountains was anyone's guess. But over the centuries, the rare merchants or wanderers who'd come to trade with those who now called themselves "the Brull" — which meant *the disgraced* or *the defeated* or some such thing — reported that there was now a modest civilization of caves and small forts and rock-enclosed settlements scattered throughout the range. The Brull had survived, but they were not an industrious race of builders, nor were they particularly innovative. They were plunderers and thieves, and without anything to plunder or steal, theirs was a limited albeit stubbornly perpetuated existence.

Gossie noticed, as they made their way deeper into the mountains, that the small settlements looked threadbare and woefully underdeveloped. And yet, they had enough to make do, and had for centuries. A paradox, to be sure. What had allowed them to persist for so long?

Could it have been stubbornness alone? Doubtful.

He squashed his curiosity and focused on what it would take for Gossie to persist a while longer. He prided himself on a certain stubbornness in that regard as well.

"I wonder if you'd like to tell me how much farther we need to go. As you mentioned a dozen or so times, I am getting old, and these types of forced marches I find a tad too challenging," he said to Bavish, the leader of the band.

Bavish gave his now standard double-snort. "We're almost there."

"And when we get there, you'll tell me what all this is about?"

"When we get there, I don't think we'll have to."

It was an odd reply that didn't inspire Gossie with anything like comfort. He was curious, to be sure, but curiosity wasn't the trait that led to profit or purpose, or so they said. "Well, I hope whatever's waiting there includes a soft chair, a cool flagon, and maybe even some salted meat."

"We've got stone chairs, old man, but the rest you'll get. And more. Just do your job, and everything will work out jolly for you," said Bavish.

My job? So they do know who I am. They must've been looking for me.

No, they were waiting *for me. Why does everyone seem to know what's going on but me?*

Just before nightfall, they arrived at a settlement, located at the base of one of the stone mountains, that featured at its center a large cave. It was drizzling slightly, and there were puffs of mist all about the houses and the small shops and the rock structures whose purpose was unclear. A large fire burned near the front of the cave. Over it turned several large carcasses, probably elk or moose, and around it sat dozens of elderly Brull. Most of them were likely centuries old, he guessed, knowing that the former residents of Namus were reputedly a long-lived people when they weren't getting butchered by the Vo'ix or the once-and-future Quadrate. He nodded to them politely, and a few of them snorted greetings, or what he liked to think were greetings, back to him.

Bavish indicated he should sit. "We brought you here because there's something we need to show you."

Gossie gratefully accepted the chance to sit, hard and cold as the seat was. He wondered if he would ever have the strength to get up again. "Okay. Why do you have to show it to me?"

"You're the man we were told to show it to," said Bavish flatly.

"And who are you taking orders from?"

"No matter how many ways you ask me that question, old man, my answer will remain the same: you don't need to know that yet."

"So I should just be patient and follow orders too, huh?"

"That's usually for the best given who and what is in play, yes."

Gossie wanted to punch Bavish right in the snout. He checked the impulse because not all the spits over the fire were occupied, and given that they were strong enough to hold an elk or moose, he was sure they could also hold up his substantial frame.

Bavish was perceptive enough to recognize his charge's frustration. "Listen, old man, I know you're not used to this type of thing. Just be patient and do what you need to, and it'll all be done."

"Will it? Okay. And what do I get out of it, hmm? Other than some much-needed exercise and a visit to this mysterious chunk of our glorious environ?" Gossie asked sweetly.

"You get a leg bone," Bavish said as he rose to greet a young Brull who strode up to them with a plate full of meat, "or whichever other piece you fancy off this plate. You get as much cold mountain water as you can drink." Another Brull, this one a female, approached them with two huge stone drinking bowls. Gossie also rose, gingerly and with great effort. He took his bowl, bowed as best he could in thanks to her, and then after a moment, snorted. The girl laughed and walked away.

"And you get to live. Or have you already forgotten about the unpleasant beings that were tracking you?" Bavish said as he lifted a bone, snorted his approval, and, plopping down with the plate beside him, began to eat.

Gossie was starved, so he too grabbed some meat, plopped, and ate. Then he grabbed more meat. He drank and ate for a while, sitting there with Bavish, and had to admit that as abductions went, this one wasn't too terrible.

Afterward, they sat there in silence, recovering from both the run and the meal. Gossie felt sleepy. *All this mountain air and jogging is way more than I'm used to*, he thought. *Back in Camedua, I'd have been into my second bottle of wine by now, sitting there staring at my stuff and worrying who was going to swindle me next.*

Here, at least, he was out making new friends, he wasn't drunk, and he was pretty sure of who was looking not to swindle him but to end him. What he wasn't sure of was: Had his Brull escort been skilled enough to evade them and throw them off his scent? These fellows, as decent as they seemed to be despite their race's reputation, stank like a Xatumkan cow farm.

Bavish rose. "Ready to do your job?"

"What, now?"

"When else?"

"Old man, resting?"

"Enough rest. Come with me, do the job, and then we'll see."

"We'll see what?"

"About finding your old human ass a place to sleep."

"Human? I thought we were eschewing insults."

"Sorry. Old habit," said Bavish. "My granddad didn't like your kind much. Called you 'humans' because he knew how much you all hate that word."

"Don't think twice about it. Gupta was a moron, and we can't none of us help where we come from, can we, sandpiggy?"

Bavish snorted in laughter. "No, I don't suppose we can, Arban."

"Then lead on, my good Brull," answered Gossie with a smile. "And let's see to this job."

"Wait here a moment." Bavish walked over to the elders by the fire and spoke to them a bit. They seemed to be listening to him and ignoring him all at once. All Gossie could tell for sure was that there were many, many snorts, most of them of the sad, slow, wheezing variety.

After a few minutes, Bavish came back with three of the elders in tow. "We've got to go into the cave. Not too deep. They tried to pull it out a bit so you could take a look in better light, but they couldn't move it."

"Couldn't move what?" Gossie asked.

Bavish didn't answer. The five of them made their way into the dimly lit cave and toward its rear area. The pace was deliberate, but Gossie, his legs aching, didn't mind.

When they got to the rear of the cave, Bavish pushed on a certain spot on the wall. After a moment, that portion of the wall moved inward, revealing an entrance. The Brull walked through it. Gossie followed.

Once inside, it was difficult to see. There were no torches on the walls, but there were some glowworms living in their crevasses. Gossie could barely make out the Brull in front of him. He walked gingerly, feeling along with his feet by almost sliding them down the passage. *Maybe Brull can see by glowworm, but I can't*, he thought. *I hope they're not going through all this trouble just to push me down some dark, subterranean hole...*

And then, there was light.

Not much of it, but enough so Gossie could see what was in the room they entered. The Brull stood aside so he could get a good look.

"This is why you brought me here? A stolen sarcophagus?" he asked as he moved toward it. It had to be stolen, he knew, because the markings on it were clearly those of the Boi Na Empire — the first true Arban civilization. And this was not just any sarcophagus, even a cursory glance told him. No, this was final resting place of a royal.

"We did not steal it. We acquired it during the time of our rule," said one of the elder Brull.

"Hmm, yes, okay. You were in power for, what, a year? I'm not judging, but why would you remove this from...where?"

"The Bulin Arc," said the elder.

"The Bulin Arc...really? Well, maybe back then it wasn't as...well guarded as it is now."

"It was. And though we had help, many died removing this thing from that place," said another elder.

"I don't doubt it," Gossie said as he ran his hands over the massive burial piece. "But again, why would you take this? It has no jewels on it — not anymore, in any case, and these types of coffins weren't typically decorated with jewels or rare metals. I don't see what other value it might have had. Riches inside, maybe?"

"Your kind often don't see what's staring you in the face," snorted the third elder.

Gossie couldn't disagree. Clearly this piece had been stolen a very long time ago and hadn't been moved in almost as long a time. It was practically molded to the floor. "Well, I see it, right in front of my face, and I have to tell you, I'm still at a loss as to why you would have brought me all the way up here to show it to me. I'm not a Timesinger or a dealer in ancient artifacts, and I'm certainly no grave robber."

"We robbed nothing, Fundra. My people took this to protect it," said Bavish. "And recent developments have proven they were right to do so."

"What recent developments?"

"Knock on the sarcophagus."

"Knock? Why? Is there something inside?"

"Yes. Knock on it."

Gossie was in no real position to argue, but this situation was becoming truly moronic. And yet, they had saved his life, and they had fed him, and no one here looked like they were joking. "Very well," he said.

He knocked.

Nothing.

He knocked again.

"I don't understand why I'm —"

Something knocked back to him from inside the sarcophagus. Three times, then after a pause, a fourth and fifth time.

Despite himself, Gossie took two quick steps back.

"Now you understand."

"Um, no, now I don't understand even more than I didn't understand a minute ago. Who's in there?"

"Can't you read the inscription?"

As best he could from where he now stood, Gossie looked more closely at the Boi Na symbols but was at a loss to translate. "No, I cannot. Can you?"

"No, not anymore. But we know what they say in any case. The knowledge has been passed down for many centuries."

"And?"

"And there's no reason to reveal that to you."

"Excellent. Brilliant. Why in Four's names did you bring me here, then?"

All four Brull snorted loud and hard at once and kept snorting, clearly amused by his response.

"I'm very gratified to be a source of amusement for you. Who have you got sealed up in this thing? My mother?"

"We haven't got anyone sealed up in there, no. Whoever is in there was put there long ago, and not by us," said Bavish. "You were not brought here to amuse us, Fundra, nor does it matter that you cannot read the inscriptions that all of us here have had memorized since we were children. No, you were brought here for one reason and one reason alone."

"And at long last, that is...?"

"We need you to open it."

And now he understood. They — or whoever was pulling their strings — knew he was a thief and a safecracker, and they weren't able to open the sarcophagus themselves. So maybe, just maybe, there was actually a rich treasure in there, a pile of jewels and gold and spell books and ornate bric-a-brac to make children and widows weep. But if that were the case, why had they waited so long, and how was the bric-a-brac pounding on the inside of the container?

No, they weren't after riches, these Brull.

There was more at stake than that.

He looked closely at the sarcophagus as his hosts watched him and snorted in soft, expectant huffs and wheezes.

And one thing became immediately clear to Gossie Fundra: he had absolutely no idea how to open the thing.

It was going to be a long night.

Hours later, after trying almost every trick he knew, he'd failed to do for them what they'd asked him to do. And he hadn't a clue what else he could try.

What was extremely unnerving was the fact that whatever was inside was clearly getting jumpy. It must have heard the noises outside its housing and sensed the possibility of release. Now, it wanted out.

Try as he might, however, Gossie simply could not oblige. He hadn't got his tools with him — those had likely been confiscated by whoever had ransacked his lair back at Shen's — but the Brull had given him some fine thieving equipment in any case, so that wasn't the trouble. There were no clues written on the sarcophagus itself, just a bunch of pronouncements about the Ki emperors and the Golden Age of Thiote and a little about the Medlites' discovery of magick. Bavish had gone over, ad nauseam, each inscription with him. Nothing.

He'd even tried, until they stopped him, bashing on the side of the thing with an iron-bound club, but he did far more damage to his own arm and shoulder than he did to the container. More to the point, he didn't even make a scratch in the thing. Despite its ancient appearance, it was made of a damn strong material. Not quite metal, not quite stone. Really very impressive in its own right. Maybe worth something to someone too, just for the materials.

It had been made clear to Gossie that this cave was his place of residence until the sarcophagus was open. Having no other options, he lay down on the floor to clear his head and immediately fell fast asleep.

When he woke up, he was alone.

Well, that wasn't entirely true. The Brull were all gone, but there was someone else in the room with him.

Someone he couldn't see.

Whoever it was whispered to him:

"He will land in shadow, he will embrace the empty, he will be lost among us, he will die before he lives, and his name is Ashorne."

Gossie froze and listened.

The words were repeated, and then again. The speaker was somewhere on the opposite side of the room, beyond the sarcophagus. The voice was raspy but clear.

"He will live in shadow. He will embrace the empty. He will be lost among us. He will die before he lives…"

Gossie knew those words. He'd heard them before. Where? He tried to remember. A poem…a performance somewhere? Yes, surely that, but this was…no. A place long ago. With his mother.

The church.

The Church of Our Noble Four.

Those were the words written by Ki Naipek, the First of Four.

But why was he hearing them now, in this place?

He turned and regarded the sarcophagus and saw what he knew he would.

The sarcophagus was open.

"Is…is someone there?" Gossie whispered.

"He is the Ashorne," came the susurrating reply.

"He is? Well, yes. Of course he is, yes," Gossie stammered. He wasn't sure what to do; he wasn't even sure if he were fully awake or not. He stood and screwed up his courage enough to approach the voice. He took a few steps and listened. He could hear no breath, but there was definitely someone there. Or was the voice in his head? "I'm coming over to talk to you, face-to-face…is that…may I do that?"

There was no reply.

Gossie inched closer to where he thought the speaker must be. There wasn't much light on that side of the room. The glowworms had gone dormant for the most part, and the torch flame was weak. "My name is Gossie, and…may I ask yours?"

He reached the other side of the room, the corner he hadn't been able to see due to his vantage point and the position of the sarcophagus.

What he saw then was a childlike, shriveled figure, almost skeletal but with small, bright yellow eyes, lying there wrapped in tatters. It was impossible to tell if this were a man or woman, but it seemed Arban in race, and it was definitely alive, although just barely. It was so frail it looked to be made of flower petals that had been left to hang in netting for several seasons, and he feared to touch it let it turn to dust.

"May I…may I help?" Gossie whispered.

The figure did not speak, but with what face it did have, it looked up at him, smiled, and nodded.

Gossie sat down next to him, for now he saw that the figure was male, and held out his hand. The frail man reached out slowly and took it, and the two of them stayed that way, hand in hand, not speaking, for however long it took for the Brull elders to return.

And when they returned, Gossie was astonished to find he'd been doing something he was extremely unaccustomed to doing.

He was weeping.

"I don't understand what that was," Gossie said to Bavish outside.

"I don't either. Don't let it trouble your mind, Arban," Bavish answered.

"Who is that?" Gossie asked. His exasperation was evident, or at least he hoped it was because he was even more confused now than when they'd led him into that cave.

"I don't know," said Bavish with a curtness that suggested he knew damn well who it was.

"What will they do with him?"

"I don't know that either."

"Well, allow me to compliment you on your stonewalling skills. May I leave now? I have a life to get back to."

"Yes, you can go. In the morning. Assuming you were heading south and not looking to take up residence in the Midforest when we found you, we'll escort you along the eastern border down into Pherriuskata."

"No jogging this time, I hope."

"No jogging."

"I have a friend among the Vied-Bronste I'd like to visit."

"We can get you close to that estate. Close enough, anyway."

"Thank you. And really, thank you for saving my life. I'm usually a one-man show when it comes to that particular action."

"My pleasure."

Gossie hesitated. "You really can't tell me what's going on?"

"It's not my place to do so. But I can tell you, answers are forthcoming. And more tasks, I would assume."

"Didn't I do the job you called me for?"

Bavish snorted. "Well, yes, I suppose you did. But it wasn't me who called you."

"Still not going to tell me who, then, huh?"

"Can't."

"Well, let me make you an offer: if you ever find you need to make some extra on the side, or you get tired of the mountain air and want to live the wild life my sort does, I could use a Brull with your talents. Look me up."

"Us sandpiggies don't do so well in the Tri."

"Not usually, no, but I've known a few. You know a Brull named Seastinoa?"

Bavish snorted loud and long. "Yeah, I know that one, you could say that."

"He lives a good life down in Hunberg."

"So you say."

Gossie nodded, having made his pitch, and asked, "Which way to a bed?"

Bavish snorted loud and long again and clapped Gossie on the back. "This way, my friend, this way…" and then led him to a small stone hut and a good night's sleep.

But Gossie didn't drift off right away. When he closed his eyes, he heard the soft voice whispering the Noble words…and they left him with a haunting question:

Who had opened that sarcophagus?

Chapter 29
A staggered defense…

Place: Eshe, kingdom of Xatumka, Arba Environ
Date: Quattrenim 35, AY 998

"They're outnumbered about three to one," Stephan estimated.

From their hiding place, Frainle could make out at least ten Northerners, including Herdas, David, and Soham.

"We should help them," whispered Frainle. "Or maybe you'd prefer to run?"

"This isn't our fight," replied Stephan. "But there's nowhere to run to. The main part of the regiment is down in the valley, but there are scouts all around to cut off escape, I'm sure. And I can't think of how to help these farmers, except maybe to convince them to surrender."

"Is that a good idea? Do they…does the Tri accept surrender?"

"Yes, of course: it's good business, what with the ransoms and all. They do a brisk business in slave labor too, and the entrances are always open at Yanz and Tritto."

Frainle grimaced. "The exits, not so much. Not much of an option, surrendering."

"No," Stephan admitted.

"So what do we do to help?" she asked, suspecting she was grasping at straws. What could two people do in the face of a regiment of Triumvirate soldiers?

There was the sound of a single rider galloping up to the Northerners. A small man on a chestnut mare pulled up to them and hopped down.

"They've sent someone up to talk," said the rider as he handed his reins to David and stooped to the water bucket for a drink. The other men were silent, perhaps waiting for this rider to say something else, but he drank, put the ladle back in the bucket, and offered nothing more.

Herdas approached him and put his hands on his shoulders. "Where is he, Ratner?" he asked.

"We've got him down by the path," Ratner said. He reached for the ladle again and, after gulping down some more water and dousing his brow and the back of his neck, he added, "You want him up here?"

"Please."

Ratner stood and whistled in three sharp, successive tones. From somewhere off in the distance, a similar whistle answered.

"Do you mind if I stay? This one's big, and a bit of a twitcher. Wouldn't want him gettin' out of hand," Ratner said.

"You're one of us now, horseman, I told you that. You've every right to stay; you don't need my permission," said Herdas.

Ratner nodded and stood to the side, his right hand on his dirk.

Presently, a large, scowling Caratan soldier, his black and whites — the standard ringed mail and tunic of his kind — evident by the light of the campfire, was led into their midst by three husky and alert Northerners.

Ratner drew his dirk and stepped forward, getting right in the Caratan's face. "All right, you, speak up."

The Caratan stared at Ratner in surprise, trying to hide his fear. "Which of you is in charge?" he asked, arrogantly but with a quiver in his voice.

Herdas said, "You can speak to everyone here as equals."

The Caratan scoffed. "Equals. Well, if you say so." He cleared his throat and, in a loud, nasally voice, said, "Commander Julian Attard of the Caratan Third Army out of Vamoul Downs sends word that you and your people are to surrender at first light. Any attempt by any person in this encampment to leave here will be considered a violation of the offer to surrender and will result in an all-out attack upon your persons."

David looked amused despite the situation. "By what right does your commander order us to surrender? What is the charge?"

"This assembly of armed combatants is unlawful as per the Triumvirate Allocational Guidelines. More so, Governor Simon Rurstmeyer, he of both Body and Mind, whose power is directly derived from His Eminence Duke Estau Erik Velliok, has declared any citizen of these northern provinces who bears arms against his lawful and loyal armies to have voided his or her citizenry and be subject to such punishments as the aforementioned guidelines provide."

"That was a mouthful," Ratner cooed. "How long did it take you learn it all, Caratan queen?"

Herdas silenced him and addressed the soldier: "What evidence do you have that any of these people has borne arms against you?"

"You do so now and have done so for months. There are almost one hundred persons in this camp, most of whom have been conducting an ongoing and illegal war against their rightful government."

"So we've already been judged, and are to be punished, without trial, without a hearing, without any application of potential mitigation?"

The man sneered slightly and glared at Herdas. "According to both governor and duke, you are outlaws. Outlaw pigs don't get trials, and the only mitigation you'll get if you don't comply is hot iron."

Ratner slapped the soldier hard in the face. "Then you won't mind if I do this?" He slapped him again. "And this?" He stuck his dirk into the man's eye. "And this?"

"Ratner, please!" Herdas cried.

"What's the difference?" Ratner answered as the soldier fell to the ground twitching and kicking, blood spurting out of his skull. "You heard him. We're all dead or worse, bound for Yanz."

"Then why was he here? Why bother at all?" asked Soham.

Ratner laughed. "They wanted to save themselves a fight. Fuck them."

"We need to make it to the woods," David said. "Fight our way through."

"No, we should just break the group up," said Soham as he searched the body of the dying soldier. "We have a better chance if we head in separate directions."

"What, and give up?" snarled Ratner. "No. Not after everything that's happened, not after so many lives. We've lost too much to run."

"He's right," muttered David, and then louder: "He's right. We have to fight them."

Herdas shook his head. "Would you waste more lives, see more of us die? Look down there, Ratner. That's not an eight-man platoon we can ambush: there are at least two hundred Caratan fighters down there."

Soham said low, "What chance do we have against that many?"

"We've got almost a hundred of our own…and we have the higher ground," said David.

"We've got maybe fifty fighters," said Soham, wagging a finger at David, "and most of them are farmers and craftsmen who've never served in the military. The other fifty are boys, old men, women. We should leave here now, scatter, and try to make it to our people in Yi Shu, while those bastards are still down there and not charging up the hill."

"And how many of us would never see Yi Shu?" asked David.

"Not as many as would never see it if we meet them head on," Soham said.

Frainle listened to all this and couldn't help but wince. Back at the Cliffs, every man had an opinion, to be sure, but there was always someone in charge, and though there was sometimes an open debate about how to proceed, it was always clear that the man in charge would make the decision. Here, it seemed, there were no decision makers. It was mayhem.

Stephan tapped her on the shoulder and then nodded toward the group. She looked at him quizzically, not sure of what he was indicating.

"Good time to make an entrance, methinks!" he said with a grin.

He stepped out of the shadows, his arms open, his hands spread wide. "Gentlemen, a word please. The way I see it, it's more than likely you're already surrounded," Stephan announced.

Swords were drawn. Ratner leapt toward Stephan and almost stabbed him, but Herdas cried, "Wait!"

Stephan slid around Ratner, hammered his arms down with a blow, and took his dirk right out of his hands. Four others advanced on Stephan, and he brandished the dirk at them, a grin on his face. "I'm ready when you are," he said as he smiled and twirled the dirk in such a way that it made all those around him watch its dance.

"Why aren't you tied to that tree?" Soham asked, his old fingers notching an arrow.

"I got tired of resting," Stephan said. "And the beer was atrocious. I thought you farmers would make better beer."

"Grab him and hold him," cried David.

He's going to get himself killed, Frainle thought, and then, not knowing what else to do, she too walked out of the bushes.

"Wait," she said to them, her empty hands held open and wide as Stephan's had been. "This man has some knowing. Let's all calm down and just listen a minute."

"She's loose too? Get a hold of her —" cried Soham.

Two men grabbed her by the arms, but not roughly.

Stephan was still holding the dirk, but seeing her, he shrugged and flipped it onto the ground at Ratner's feet. Ratner looked at her untrustingly and then nodded to her and retrieved his weapon.

The prisoners safely contained for the nonce, Herdas spoke to Frainle: "Young woman, why should we listen to Stephan? Do you know that he worked for these men, these Caratans?"

Frainle wasn't surprised, given what little she knew about Stephan. "I didn't know that, but I suspect his involvement with them might, in that case, prove more useful than detrimental to your cause."

"He's a traitor and a spy!" cried Soham.

"Spy? Traitor? None such, my friends. I've worked for them, yes, but I've worked for some of you too, or had you forgotten?" Stephan said.

David said, "I hadn't forgotten. But I remember also that you were nowhere to be seen at Tiero when they came. How is it they knew we were there? And where were you when they came?"

"I don't remember. I imagine I was in a pub somewhere, spending your money."

"You should have stayed," said David, a sharp note of bitterness in his tone.

"You hadn't paid me to live out my life with you. You paid me to get you to Tiero, and I did."

"My wife and children died there."

Stephan looked at him carefully. "And for that, David Abadjide, I am deeply sorry, but they did not die because of me."

There was silence for a moment.

Herdas stepped forward. "He knows that. Don't you, David?

Braima died...your family died because of men like that one," he said, gesturing at the now-dead Caratan on the ground. "Stephan could not have saved them."

"No, but the question is: Did he lead the Caratans to Tiero?" said Ratner.

"Why would he do that?" Herdas asked.

"Why else? Barbs," spat Soham.

"No. No, I don't believe that. And neither do you," stated Herdas. "I suggest you say something here and now, Stephan, to convince my fellows you're not their enemy. They'd already decided to hang you, you know. Lucky for you, the Caratans arrived."

"Yes, I feel lucky. Now I can die by the sword or a trampling instead of the noose," answered Stephan. He took a deep breath and sighed. "Listen, there's no way I can convince you of anything, not if you already believe I'm a spy and a traitor. But what I can say is this: I never once scouted any of your villages or movements for the Tri. Nothing I ever did for them ever led to a single Northern death."

"That's horseshit!" cried Ratner.

"No, it's not," said David. "It's not. Stephan scouted thieving parties for the Brown Men, and I'm sure he sometimes led the wrong people to the right caravan, but he never sold out his own people."

"A minute ago you were sure he'd helped them when they butchered your family!" said Soham.

"I was trying to put him on the defensive, trying to get him to lie," David answered.

"Well, it worked. Man hasn't spoken a word of truth since he walked out of those bushes," Ratner said.

Stephan chuckled and turned to Ratner. "Hey, you. You're really very ugly. True or not true?"

The bickering continued for a while after that.

Frainle wondered what she was doing there, and she began to feel faint, as if somehow the stress and the fear and the magick that had moved her from one land to another was suddenly demanding of her a price. She needed sleep, or at least a long, deep pull of lifewine.

"May I sit?" she asked in a soft voice. Herdas nodded to the two who were holding her, and they let her slump to the ground. Someone brought a small stump-stool onto which they hoisted her.

Stephan stood there a moment, just looking at her. He seemed to be considering something. Then he spoke.

"For what it's worth, I have some knowing that might have, under different circumstances, been helpful, yes," he said. "And whether or not you trust me, I know this terrain, and like a few — too few — of you, how to skirmish. But there's a whole regiment of Triumvirate Caratans out there.

They knew where you were, so they have scouts, and they knew how many you were, so they can count. Counting, you'd be wise to acknowledge, is an underrated skill in warfare."

Ratner scoffed. "That much we know. Have you anything to offer? Or maybe you two are the reason they know so much."

"Maybe. But then why did you find us tangled up in the Old Temple, bumbling around like two drunk otters?" asked Stephan.

"Maybe you were fucking," said Ratner.

"So we scouted you, went back to deliver our information, and then snuck back among you to fuck and get caught?" laughed Stephan.

David waved his hands in frustration. "Enough of this. Do you know anything that might help us here, now, or not?" he asked.

Stephan looked at him, sighed, and said, "I do not."

"Very well," Soham said. "Take them back up and this time chain them to that tree —"

"I wasn't finished," Stephan said. "I do not know how to help you here and now...but she might." He pointed at Frainle and smiled.

Frainle just gazed at him in disbelief. What was he up to? He knew nothing about her, and she knew nothing about these people and their enemy. She tried to stand but was too weary, so she just shook her head a little at him to try to shut him up.

But he didn't shut up. "You have among you a daughter of this generation's greatest soldier, a woman who's read more about war and tactics than all of us combined, and you don't even bother to ask her opinion of the situation?"

The Northerners turned and began to regard her with something like hopeful interest.

"We assumed...she's little more than a child!" Herdas said.

"Well, you were wrong to assume," said Stephan with a grin. He turned to Frainle and beckoned her forward. "Tell them what you know, Aethrelean."

Frainle hesitated a moment, but then, looking around at all these brave but clearly terrified people, she understood that they desperately needed help, maybe even hers.

She felt herself trying to maintain focus on their need and on the present situation. She knew that if she disengaged, even for the fleetest of moments, all that was waiting for her inside was a vision of fire and death. She heard no scream because at the Cliffs, there'd been none to hear; she'd heard only the thunderous crashes of whatever fiery hell the enemy was raining down on them. No, that wasn't right: there'd been one to hear, at the end.

Eni.

That was there and then, she insisted inside. Here, now, there was something else, something like purpose, something that was anything but the torment of those last few moments at the Cliffs. She had to help these people, if only to help herself.

But what help could she be? She'd never fought in a war, never applied anything she'd read. She'd only read all those books to hold on to Shain, to keep his memory alive; much of what she'd studied she hadn't understood at all.

But some of it…some of it was elementary, some of it must be useful in the here and now. She searched her mind and then lighted upon something…yes, that might work. She stood up, uneasily but not so the others would notice her discomfort. "I'll need a map."

They found a map and laid it out on the ground before her.

"This shows this region for…how far in each direction?"

"You've got about, say, twenty-five hundred square miles there," said David. He pointed at a spot with a stick. "We're here. The western part of Maelor's Country."

"May I?" Frainle asked, gesturing at his stick.

He handed to her, and she began to silently take the measure of the map by tracing across it from point to point with the stick. After a few minutes, she began to describe her thoughts to them.

"The first thing we need to do is locate whatever sentries they've posted to the west. They shouldn't be too hard to spot; they don't seem to expect much of a fight from you. And after a long march north, they're probably banking on getting a little sleep and just accepting your surrender in the morning, unless maybe they get really angry when their man here doesn't return."

Ratner looked down at the ground sheepishly and snorted.

"Have you got any excellent night hunters?" Frainle continued. "I mean men who are virtually silent in the dark?"

"Of course. Demarr and Sinhag," said Herdas.

"How good are they?"

"They've killed wolves, and Sinhag once fought a trearlinket," said David.

"Really? And he's still with us?" said Stephan.

"Most of him. He lost a hand and an ear that night," David replied.

Frainle interrupted. "Send those two west to scout the locations for any sentries or guard posts. Send each one with three strong young bowmen. It's absolutely essential that none of the sentries break free and report back."

"Why? What difference would it make? They know we're here. We can't all run without them knowing," said Herdas.

"We're not all going to run. Some of us will stay here."

"Who volunteers for that?" asked Ratner.

Stephan smiled. "I do.

Frainle looked up at him. "Good. Yes. And you'll need about ten men to stay with you."

"Noble of you, Stephan Takacs," said Ratner. "But how do we know you won't just wave a flag and surrender our men to the Caratans?"

"You don't. You really have to take anything I say now on faith, because your alternatives are to run and die or stay, fight, and die," said Stephan. "What you should understand is that my alternatives are identical to your own. And her plan is a good one. Listen to her."

They turned their attention back to Frainle.

"So if he stays, what do the rest of us do?" asked Soham.

"We head west, quietly, and make for this place," she said, pointing at the map. "Calawak Pass."

Soham snorted with disgust. "The Pass? That's a dead end. Why the hell would we go there?"

"Because doing so might just save your lives," she answered.

Stephan seemed to see what she was suggesting and why. "It's true, for the most part: it is a dead end, but it's also an excellent defensible position. You said you have more people out there, at Yi Shu and…where else?"

"Just Yi Shu. About two hundred, a third of whom are fighters."

Frainle said, "Once the enemy sentries have been removed, send a rider to Yi Shu. Tell them to head for Calawak."

"This is madness," said Soham, waving fingers at everyone and no one. "You're trying to get us all in one indefensible place; it'll be easy for the Caratans to slaughter us."

Frainle shook her head and explained, "No, it won't. By the time they get to Calawak, they'll be too exhausted and stretched too thin. We're going to use an old technique against them, and hopefully they'll be too cocky to see what we're doing."

"What are you suggesting?" asked David.

"A staggered defense. Between here and Calawak, about twelve miles, it looks like there's nothing but hills. Is that the case?"

Herdas nodded.

"We set up four — no, five positions including this one — and engage them," Frainle said.

"Engage *them*?" asked David disbelievingly.

"Yes. Engage with about ten men, and then retreat to the next position."

"You want us to engage but give up ground?" Soham asked.

"Yes, exactly. Don't just give it up, though: make them earn it each time. Use the hills to keep them guessing as to how many of us there are at each point. It would help to have a few of our riders harassing their flanks as well, distracting from the retreats."

"We've got a few good riders, that's for sure, and horses that can handle hills as well," said a tall man in the rear.

"That's good...?" She looked at him inquiringly.

"Marlon."

"That's what we need, Marlon. Then we engage, hold ground for a while, harass, retreat, all the way to Calawak."

Ratner gestured at the map. "Let's say we get all the way there without most of us getting six arrows in the back. What do we do when they've got us boxed in at the pass?"

"We lure them in," said Stephan. "I see where she's going. From the elevated positions, we can strike at what's left of them, and then your people at Yi Shu can close in from behind."

Herdas stepped forward and stared at the map for about a minute. The others stood back and let him take his time, she noticed. Maybe she'd been wrong, and one man did make the final decisions around here. She wasn't surprised to find Herdas was that one man.

"Sounds like it might work," he finally said to no one in particular. "It's better than staying here and getting slaughtered when they charge up this hill in the morning, and it's better than a ticket to Yanz. But how do we get them into the pass?"

"Some of us will have to go in first, lure them in, fight from the ground."

"Bait, huh? Whoever does that will be killed for sure."

"Maybe, but it's the only way to make them chase us in."

Stephan pointed at the rear part of the pass. "This section collapsed a long time ago, that's why the road through here was abandoned, but there are plenty of caves and crevices where the bait can hide and wait and drive the enemy mad."

"You've been there?" Frainle asked Stephan.

"Hell, I spent four nights in there hiding from...well, hiding."

"Then I guess you'd have no problem leading the bait?" she asked him.

"No, no problem, but that assumes I make it all the way back. This plan's a good one, but they're going to get some of us, you can count on that. If they get me, you'll need someone else to lead the men into the pass."

Frainle thought for a moment. "If they get you, I'll go."

"You?" Soham shook his head and crossed over to her, a newfound respect in his expression that was tempered by something slightly patronizing...or was that genuine concern? "You may be a fine strategist for a young girl, but you're no warrior, Aethrelean or not. Let David go."

David shook his head. "No, I need to be up front with the defenders, pulling back. I may not make it either."

There was a moment of silence. The wind was picking up, and the Northerners' makeshift banner was flapping more violently now. Soham looked at her and then glanced down at the ground.

"So, me then," Frainle said

They all stood there looking at her for a moment. Some of them were studying the map with grave expressions. They weren't yet convinced. She was.

"Listen, I know it's madness, really, but it's the best I can come up with. From what you've said, they haven't got much in the way of cavalry, and the terrain should give what horses they do have fits. Against infantry, this kind of thing can work. It worked at Tahmores for Alex Furain, it worked at the Holy Three in Delariun for my father…and he did it on the water with a small fleet. I'm not saying it's perfect—we might all die anyway—but it's worth trying, no?"

When no one spoke, she thought to say more but decided to wait. War strategies were something she understood, but these men, however well intended, seemed to need a moment to digest and decide.

After a minute of silence, David said low, "Maybe. Yes, I think yes."

All eyes turned to Herdas, who nodded in agreement.

Stephan clapped his hands once. "Good. How many bowmen do we have? Good ones?"

"Maybe…two dozen. A few less," said Ratner.

"All right. Ten of them stay with me and David and fire on the Caratans with pitch. The rest go with you and take up positions along the way, covering our retreat. We'll need every arrow you've got."

"Every arrow? What do we use at Calawak?"

"Stones. Climb the cliffs and hurl stones. There are plenty of pieces of shale there that will cut a man in half if dropped from the right height."

"You want us to climb in the dark?"

"Those who can't climb can hide. Trilesti should be making an appearance at just about the time you reach the pass; her dim light will help with the ascent. That assumes no resting, because once the other one's up, we'll lose the shadows and any stealth advantage we've got. Remember, once Ponesta begins to rise, your people up top have to lie low. If anyone's spotted, the Caratans will know something's up."

"Is everyone in agreement? David? Soham?" asked Herdas.

Frainle felt a slight surge in her blood, a blend of fear and excitement she'd not felt in a very long time, and maybe never in quite this way. This was her plan and, for better or worse, she was the one who was leading these men, these strangers who were fighting for their lives and homes and families. "Okay, send out Sinhag and Demarr. Gather the other archers and bring them here. Stir the camp, but this above all things: silence and do not, I repeat, do not break camp. Appearances are essential here."

The men began to move, to put the plan in action. She added, "Take only weapons and a little food and leave the tents and whatever else. We need them to believe we're still here when the fighting begins."

And so it went. Her plan worked.

Herdas and Soham both died, as did eleven of their people, including Marlon and two of his horsemen. Ratner was injured, but not so severely that he didn't kill seventeen Caratans on his own. He was an absolutely ferocious fighter, as was Stephan.

David and Stephan seemed, through all the fighting and the retreating, to reach an understanding, the kind only a mutual fight for survival can perhaps provide.

And most importantly, most of the Northerners were safe and alive.

In the end, their staggered retreat exhausted the Caratans, who though seasoned soldiers were ill prepared for a pursuit that would ultimately last over seven hours. The reinforcements from Yi Shu arrived a bit late but in more than enough time to attack the Caratans from the rear and spare all but one of the men — and the woman — who had entered the pass as bait.

Several dozen of the Tri soldiers, including Commander Julian Attard, fled south, while thirty found themselves surrounded and those quickly surrendered. Having disarmed them and with no viable means of holding prisoners, the Northerners sent the captured enemy troops south as well, holding only two officers in the hopes of gaining some intelligence from them.

By default and due to the deaths of Herdas and Soham, the latter quite slowly and painfully, Frainle and Stephan, on the strength of the victory, had gone within the span of the day from being tied to a tree to the de facto leaders of a movement to which neither of them belonged. Stephan seemed indifferent. Frainle, who recognized quite clearly that she had been somewhat battle drunk, was just grateful to have something to fight for, something to believe in, and something that wasn't fire.

But when she slept, she burned.

When she slept, they all burned.

And there was but one small scream.

Chapter 30
"We don't fear that future,
because it will never come to pass."

Place: The Graviss Glen, Wilds of southwest Arba, Arba Environ
Date: Quattrenim 38, AY 998

"In the terrible nations, they shall have him: Our protector, our savior, our long-awaited deliverer. Alone, in their hands, he will surely die."

The old woman spat and whirled and then faced the sky and began to gyrate wildly like she was being attacked by some invisible assailant. She stopped suddenly, raised her arms, and spread her hands. Staring deeply into the massive fire before her, she let out a low moan that increased in pitch and volume till her many listeners cringed at the sound. She held the note for what seemed an eternity and then abruptly fell silent.

She knelt to the ground. An attendant brought her a roughhewn cup and then backed away. Bringing it slowly up to her lips, the old woman sipped and then moaned once more, low and sad. She jumped to her feet. The fire rose higher; she spat into it and cried out in a voice like a hawk descending on its prey:

"Alackanna do benasta, qui gastu, ke gastar!"

The crowd in the center of the Graviss Glen, numbering in the hundreds, had themselves been nearly silent until then, spellbound as they were by this elaborate and time-honored performance by their most revered priestess. Now, in response to her violently shrieked words, they began to shout and to call out to her and to one another: "Tell us, tell us…what must we do? What will happen?"

She hissed at them sharply, threw down her cup in a rage, and threw her body down onto the ground and lay there, unmoving. The people drew back and ceased their cries. The only sounds were the desperate, sharp popping of the ceremonial bonfire and the wild whisper from the windblown firs.

The old woman stood, hissed, and fell silent again. She dropped once more, this time to her knees. She folded her hands beneath her stomach, bent as if in pain, and wept.

Several minutes passed.

No one moved.

Finally, a pale young woman wrapped in a dark cloak stepped forward and stood behind the old one.

"What is your wish, Pu'arinya?" she asked. "What have you seen?"

The old woman did not lift her head, but she spoke loudly so all could hear.

"Suashi Dao Bleuss, Daughter of the Wilds, One of Whom Many Dreamt, you will go to these terrible nations. You will walk their broken, hateful avenues, you will taste of their foul food and their foul drink and their foul ways. You will search in the stinking pits of servitude and the high halls of unabashed excess and their so-called Mansions of Devotion."

She suddenly rose and raised her withered face to stare into the younger woman's. The wind was all one could hear for a long moment, and then she cried in her hawk's voice:

"You will find the Ashorne."

The crowd exploded in cries and cheers.

The young woman turned and walked away towards the edge of the glen. The people fell silent as they strained to hear Suashi's response.

And after a moment's pause, she gave it.

"This I cannot do. This I will not do."

They would not like that answer, she knew. And they didn't. There was murmuring and shouting and cursing. A baby started howling, then another and then a third. Something was thrown and landed near the fire: a Book. She could not tell which one from where she stood.

The Pu'arinya sank to her knees once again, her hands linked behind her with her arms straight as if she were yoked and being forced to the ground, an expression of unlimited agony on her leathery face.

"You can, Suashi! You must! The word of the Pu'arinya is law!" cried a fat older man sitting on a stump near the edge of the glen.

"Your law, Hustel. I was not born in this forest. I am not subject to your laws, your accords, or the whims of your faith. I will not go," said Suashi calmly.

"But if he is not found, we are all doomed!" yelled another woman from the crowd.

"I don't believe that. Few here do," said Suashi.

Again there were cries of protest and a great discontented murmuring. The people were unhappy and yet, some — the brave and the reticent, thought she — were nodding in agreement.

"Please, then, tell us: What *do* you believe? If the Noble Four are a myth, and the Ashorne will never come, what will happen?" asked Hustel.

Suashi walked a few steps back toward the fire and then turned and regarded the people slowly. All eyes were on her.

"The Ingress of the Ashorne is a story, nothing more. That there would be one who would find him, and even the Three who preceded him, our so-called greatest citizens, is untrue."

The crowd was largely silent. They knew she was referring to herself now, refuting her own part in this legend, in their beliefs.

"And the Proving?" Hustel asked in an almost matter-of-fact tone.

"A lie told long ago by an emperor who treated his subjects like insects," Suashi answered.

This got a response from the people. She wondered if she would leave here alive.

Hustel rose and came face-to-face with her. "Suashi Bleuss, do you believe then in nothing?" He was selling it; she had to give him that.

"No, Hustel of Red Hill. There are things I believe in. Freedom. Equality. Justice."

"Where is the justice in a Proving that fails because no one tried? What do freedom and equality mean in a dead world?" implored Hustel.

"Freedom and equality are alive and well in Chrestikos, and justice cannot prevail until we all accept that the Proving is a lie," she said.

"Blasphemer! Betrayer!" cried Pu'arinya, rising once more.

"Name me what you will. I betray only your image of me — an image that is false."

"No one is betraying anyone," said Hustel. "Poor Suashi simply does not understand the urgency of her…calling. We must make her understand."

"There is no means by which you could make me understand this situation any differently," said the young woman.

"There are means. If you believe otherwise, it is because you've been away from here, from your people, for far too long."

"Threats, good Hustel?" she said, turning away from him. "Are you become no better than the leaders of these so-called terrible nations to which you would send me? Perhaps in the old way, such threats had their uses, for it was better to believe in something false and come together than to cling to partial truths and die apart. But that was then, and those days are gone. There is something better now."

"There is nothing better!" the Pu'arinya cried.

"You know that isn't true. You also know they're coming. And when they come, teacher, will you trade your truth for theirs to survive? Will you fight them or embrace them?"

Suashi Bleuss addressed the crowd around her. "What say you, Wildeans? Duke Velliok has not forgotten you. He has not forgotten how you welcomed and sheltered his enemy. He despises your freedoms and covets your forests. Someday soon, the Triumvirate's Noble army will march toward you and claim these woods for its hungry, mad leader and his rotting Body. They will come, and they will burn this glen to the ground."

"They will not! In our forest, they must obey our law!" cried Hustel.

"They care nothing for Wildean ways. Neither do they care about the Proving or the Noble Four or the Ashorne, though those beliefs are alleged to be the very foundation of their corrupt and decaying society. They mock them openly in their courts, their festivals, and their homes! The Four are dead in the Tri. Its citizens are mad, and in their madness they know but one truth: to be what they are, the bill must be paid, and all the bills of tomorrow. They see you and all the common people of Arba as nothing more than fungible meat. Should the Forum ever agree to their terms—or even if you choose to fight—your deaths and the deaths of your children—via enslavement, via persecution, via starvation—would surely follow. These creatures are indeed terrible, and they will destroy this place, your home, as they did their own. They will take from you until you have nothing but your lives to give. And then they will take those too. Would you die a Gift or live free?

"I am returning to Vaprosta. There my father waits for me, and for all of you. There we will continue to build and strengthen our young nation, a place where the Triumvirate and the duke and the primate and the herald and the hateful magickers and violent fools who serve them have no power over us. In Chrestikos, no one fears a march to Rash al Brek. No one wears a mask. No one is slain or sent to Bi Prison for her beliefs or for crimes she did not commit. Can the Forum offer you the same assurances, the same future? For fifteen years, Vincent has proven as good as his word. That word has been heard in the pastures of Xatumka and on the waves of Lake Iale. Even in the still, frozen moors of Slau and the blooded hills of Thicknomy, even in the wretched hells that are Yanz and Tritto, the vision of freedom germinates and thrives.

"I've come here tonight to extend his promise to you: join us, come west with me, and begin again. For the sake of your families, for the sake of your values and your very lives, join us. We will not fail you."

The Pu'arinya pointed a bony finger at Suashi, crying, "Your words are strong ones, but your promises are lies, and even your false father cannot defend against the holy fate that awaits us…just as you cannot avoid your role in it."

"That fate is the lie. The Four are a lie. This world may fall, and we with it, but though oppression and lawlessness and the whims of an unchecked Elite may bring us to our knees, no foolish legend our grandfathers had near forgotten long before they grew old will convince me to help you," said Suashi, "And there is nothing false about my father, witch."

Suashi stood and listened to the murmuring of the crowd.

"Wildeans, consider well what I've said here tonight. I invite you all to come with me, to join us at Chrestikos in friendship and solidarity, but know this: I will not do this thing you ask of me. And I cannot save you, not that way. No one can."

Suashi bowed to them and then found a stump and sat down. The crowd was silent but for a few murmurs.

Hustel stood and strode to the middle of the glen. He chuckled, shook his head, and addressed the crowd. "You all know the story. She has been raised from a child to do this thing, to find this one man who might save all of Arba, all of us, all of you. She was found, sickly and alone by the Salora, and it was our people—you, the good peoples of the Wilds—who dreamt of her, gave her all she would ever need, and taught her of her holy destiny. She has been protected, trained, guided—all for one purpose! Are we going to let her toss that purpose aside, now, when the time is almost near?"

"No!" yelled some in the crowd.

"She believes she's found a home and a new purpose and so has abandoned the beliefs and fate that were like her very blood and air for twenty years…all for Vincent Bleuss. Vincent, a man who, when the needs of his people were dearest, fled Aethrelius and left it to its fate. Today, if the rumors are to be believed, that country faces ruination from civil war."

"Vincent did not cause that," said Suashi.

"No, but he might have prevented it, just as you might prevent something far, far worse. And this future you warn us of, this imagined invasion by the Triumvirate—we don't fear that future, because it will never come to pass. Without a successful Proving, no one in Arba will survive, not your friends in Chrestikos, and not your precious father. We need you to help us. Don't run away now, Suashi. Don't abandon us as your father abandoned Aethrelius."

There was near silence in the glen.

"I came here to honor traditional understanding between us, and in hearing you, I have done so. I have offered you all that is mine to give. There is nothing more I owe you," said Suashi. "I leave tomorrow after first meal."

The old woman walked toward her, eyes cold with rage.

"If you refuse to fulfill this destiny, to seek the one called by the Known Noble Three 'the Ashorne,' to guide the faithful of the Wilds and all Arba to a future in which the Unknown Fourth comes forward and delivers us, then you doom us all."

Suashi walked away.

The Pu'arinya spat. "You are no longer a Daughter of the Wilds."

"You spit far too often."

"And if you are not a Daughter, Suashi Bleuss, you are an enemy. You and your father and your so-called bastion of new freedom. Enemies all. And Wildeans know what to do with an enemy."

There was stunned silence in the crowd. Some yelled assent to the Pu'arinya's last statement, but most waited, breath held, to hear Suashi's response.

"You would do well to reconsider that threat, old woman."

The Pu'arinya turned her face away slowly and stared off into the night. Suashi shook her head, sighed, and then faced the crowd. "I leave in the morning."

She left them in their holy glen, knowing they were wondering what to do in the face of a future they could not possibly understand. She strode away past the crowds and down toward the small streets of Wildberry District. No one followed her. No one from the crowd, at least.

She had lied to them. She had tried to strike fear into their hearts, break them down, and offer them hope all at once. She had done it to save them.

It hadn't worked.

She hadn't expected it to, but maybe she'd fooled the ones her show was really intended to fool. They could report back that she was no longer a threat to them, and that might give her a little time...

There was a slight drizzle that somehow seemed to shroud the small fires and lamps of Graviss Glen in mist, and the homes in the district were dark. Everyone had been at the meeting.

She neared her small, borrowed cabin. Twice she spotted persons trying not to be noticed, persons who had been instructed to wait and watch for her. There were more, she was sure, keeping track of her movements, and they would have to be dealt with eventually, but for now she was content to let them believe they'd done their jobs.

In the cabin, a one-room affair hewn from elder pine, she let out a deep, uneasy breath. She'd entered without letting a third clumsy watcher across the path know she'd seen him, but resisting the urge to walk up and slap him had been challenging. Removing her cloak, she listened for a still moment to the sounds of the forest night as they sifted in slowly through her room's sole window. Those sounds, the wind through the trees, the murmur of families ending their days, and the soft song of the many wooden wind chimes that hung throughout this place, brought her back, for a long moment, to a time that soothed her.

She poured herself a mug of water and drank. The mug was rough in her hand, made by the cabin owner's youngest daughter from the knot of some fallen tree, misshapen but balanced as she set it back down on the table. She considered the care with which the girl had fashioned the mug; it was impressive handiwork for a girl of only six.

He was late. There wasn't much time to spare, but first, before she left this conflicted, beautiful place, they needed to talk. She sat down on the floor and waited. Outside, the rains of Iobus began to fall in earnest. The water on the thatched roof added to the night's subtle chorus sounds like sighing, restless horses.

A short while later, there was a knock.

"Please, come."

The door opened, and Hustel entered. His large, round, balding head was drenched in rain and sweat. Under one arm, he carried a small bundle wrapped in canvas. "May I speak with you?" he said somewhat loudly.

"Of course," she said, stepping aside and waving her arm less than invitingly.

Hustel looked around. "Small cabin," he said as he removed his wet cloak and hung it on the door.

"I need no bigger," she said. She sat back down on the floor and crossed her legs.

"I'm afraid I cannot join you on the floor. My back..."

"I know, teacher. Please, sit, and say what I know you must."

His face took on a gentler expression, and his shoulders dipped slightly as he said: "No, Suashi, my role in that farce has ended. They can't really hear us in here, not with this rain and not if we keep our voices down. I come to you now as a dear old friend, not as adversary in a glen debate." He sat down on the room's only chair.

"There are things in this world that can hear a bug sneeze."

"True enough."

"You argued well tonight."

"As did you."

"Thank you."

"I mean you no compliment, Suashi — you may have changed the course of Arban history with your words. Without a clear path before them, it's not at all clear what these Wildeans will do, but one thing is certain. They never take kindly to being told what to do. Or to being refused in a matter such as this."

"You know I haven't refused."

"I do. And I also know that if they knew that, you'd be as good as dead, and you'd certainly never find the Ashorne. There'd be a wall of Crabs five hundred miles long blocking the way, and five spies behind every tree, on every road, and at every table."

"They have to go to Chrestikos. War is coming, those Crabs are on the march, and after that — "

"War they've seen. War they can handle, or think they can. But a Nulling...I'm afraid they fear it, but not nearly enough."

"They've seen war, sure, but nothing of the kind Velliok will bring to their doorsteps. My father will have to come. It's only a matter of time."

"Time isn't something we have in great supply."

"There won't be a Nulling. I will find the Ashorne, and then the Fourth."

"I believe you will. Yes, I believe that," Hustel said with a hopeful yet small smile.

Suashi tried to smile back but managed only a nod. She looked out the window into the night.

Hustel sighed. "If we could only tell them the truth. These faithful Wildeans deserve that much. They're a good people."

"You still consider yourself an outsider, after all these years?" she said, knowing he did but never understanding why.

"No, of course not. And yes, always. This is not my home."

"And yet you stand for them."

"The Pu'arinya's gone completely mad. And there's no one else they'll even listen to without shouting down. Too many tribes in these damned woods."

"It has to be you. Lead them," she urged him.

He shrugged. "There is no other who can, or so they mistakenly believe."

"They could do worse."

"And they could do better. They could have you." He gave her an imploring look.

"You knew how this would end before you called me here."

"Yes. But I suppose I still maintained some hope that these well-meaning, good people would find their sense and listen."

"Some did."

"Some, but not enough. You know these woods and these folk as well as anyone. Nothing unites them better than a common, voted-upon purpose. Majority rules, even if the majority has gone mad."

"They believe in the Proving. Still."

"Yes."

"I admire them for that."

"So do I. Poor bastards."

"They are setting themselves up for disaster. Without allies, my father will not have the strength to come east and fight their fight for them, and they cannot fight it themselves."

"He will have allies. The Ailo-shut, the Eight Tribes, even many of the Vigilant will join him. Your father's banner has always been a beacon of both prudence and glory."

"A beacon of something and something else, anyway. He is too old now, Hustel, and his victories take the form of successful harvests and full fishing nets."

"He is still Vincent Bleuss."

"Even so, he can't save them all."

"Some will go west. Despite appearances, you really did sell some, maybe more than some, with your eloquence."

"My eloquence loses all its luster the minute the first Wildean child is thrown into a Yanz-bound wagon."

"It will not come to that. We will not allow it."

"No, we won't. But she might."

"Her threats are empty, Suashi."

"Are they? She's long been rumored to be on the primate's leash. And he'd like nothing more than to see civil war tear down the Wilds before his Crabs move in to burn it all down."

"Your father would never fight that fight, and neither would Green Home."

"She's crafty, that one, and not without her devotees."

"The fanatical make excellent devotees."

"Are they able to make excellent recruits, though? Are they enough to make war against the right foe?"

"Let us hope so."

"Let us also hope their sense of self-preservation teaches them which way to face when the trumpets blow and the screaming begins. The Tri is coming, and rumors are they are not coming alone."

"The Forum still believe the Scar will hold Druthec Grehmann at bay. It always has."

"Grehmann's miserly forces are the least of our concerns. Velliok's armies will come by the lake. Bundi al Fruwqa will fall in a day, maybe in only a few hours."

"Undoubtedly."

"And they may find a way to breach the Scar."

"They've had many opportunities to try and many years to come up with new solutions. The Scar remains impassable."

"Perhaps."

She looked at him and then turned away. She knew the odds against their success and that their charade tonight in the glen hadn't been wholly successful. The Triumvirate spies might be fooled, for a time, but they had eyes everywhere and new allies who might not fall for the same timeworn tricks. "I need to leave here, tonight. Now," Suashi said.

"I know."

"Those outside, can you…?"

"I will stay here and talk to myself, loudly. Argue even."

"Finally, an argument with me you might win."

"Or lose, as is needed."

"I will miss you, old man."

"And I you. My highest hopes go with you."

She stood and slung a small pack over her shoulder. He lifted her cup and looked inside, poured himself more water, and set it on the table, his mind suddenly elsewhere.

"When will you go?" she asked.

He lifted the water to his lips but did not drink. "Soon, but not too soon. Appearances and all," he said. He downed the water.

"I will send word for your room to be made ready. My father, too, will make ready your yellowsnap."

"Or something finer, perhaps. Something to celebrate."

"We've won nothing."

"I disagree. We've won something: time."

"This from the man who just declared time is in short supply?"

"A moment can serve as well as a year if it's artfully spent." He stood and slowly walked toward the window. He moved the woven curtain and peeked out into the night. "Who's to say? Maybe we're worrying too much."

"My father will. Have something to say."

"I expect he will. Been a while since *he's* lost an argument, hmm?"

"Too long. He's starting to believe he can't lose."

"I will endeavor to…dissuade him of at least *that* notion."

"Please do."

"Suashi, your deeds will make him understand."

"Easier said."

"I've known him a long time. We must elevate our level of concern the moment your father claims to understand. It usually means he's working an agenda."

"He is. But I believe that in this instance, he knows exactly what we're trying to do. And in his own way, he supports us."

"Which is better than him not supporting us. We take what we can get, eh?"

"I suppose so." She walked toward the table and tested it with her fingers. "They'll try to stop you."

"I know."

"Poor bastards." She hugged him tightly for a moment, then kissed his cheek and looked him in his eyes. "Good-bye."

With that, she leapt up on the table, then up to grab a beam. She swung onto the beam and slipped out a small hole in the roof.

She was gone. He would most likely never see her again, he knew. He wept a few moments at the thought.

"Good-bye, my sweet bear. And good luck." He rubbed his hands on the back of his neck and sat back down. "Find him, Sua. Find the damned Ashorne and bring him back."

Hustel then began a raging argument that carried on for the better part of an hour. The watchers outside were certain he'd won and for a time were certain he'd beaten her with his bare hands. If this was to be his last performance, he was hell-bent on making it a masterpiece.

Paomaintanna was waiting for her by the Elm Bridge. "What did they want?" he asked.

"What we expected," answered Suashi. "And now they've heard what they needed to. Are we clear to go?"

"There are four of them in the brush there on the far side. There are three more on the path up on the hillock."

"Just seven?"

"There may be more. I fell asleep."

"Well, if there are more, they're yours. Perhaps I'll sleep while you handle them."

"You sleep? I thought you decided sleep was for cowards."

They moved toward the bridge entrance and then suddenly ducked down underneath it. A few shadows on the far side of the thin river moved as well; they seemed to split up and head in the direction of both the bridge and the river in equal numbers.

A man with a long knife in his hand and a longbow on his back waded into the water, his eyes darting up and down the bank he could scarcely see.

"If you wish to live, you will not move," commanded Suashi's voice from the shadows.

The man spun to find cover and was promptly downed by a stone to the skull. He fell face first into the river.

"Your friend will drown if none of you assists him," Suashi said from her hiding place.

Someone spoke up in a deep, somewhat rasping voice: "If I help him, you'll kill me too, won't you?"

"You have my word as a daughter of Chrestikos: no one who goes to him will come to harm...unless you refuse to let us pass."

"We have our orders. You understand."

"I do. But I am offering you life for life. By now, my companion could have killed each of you three times without any help from me. Three of you are unconscious, and a fourth is drowning. Help that man now, before I have to do it myself."

"You won't shoot?"

"I have nothing to shoot with."

"You shot him."

"I hit him with a small stone. He'll have a headache, nothing more. If he lives."

"Okay, then."

A man crawled out from behind a small pine grove and scuttled down to the one in the river. He grabbed him by the arm and pulled him free of the water, then turned him over and listened. "He's alive!"

She was suddenly next to him. "Of course. Life for life."

He started and then realized her weapon, if she had one, was sheathed or concealed.

"They…we…had orders to kill you if you tried to leave."

"And now?"

"You've shown me something here, and I won't forget it. This here is my brother."

"And your name, sir?"

"Abour, ma'am." He was a young man, maybe twenty-five, short and bearded and plain but with a quiet strength about him. A true Wildean, probably not native to the glen.

"Abour, I am Suashi. The man not killing your other friends — or are they too brothers? — is Paomaintanna of Green Home. We'll be leaving now."

She placed a hand on his shoulder and turned to go. She got ten feet before she heard him behind her.

"Wait…I would ask you something first."

"Ask away."

"You know…our code…our grandfather, he taught us the words, but most folk don't…"

"'You save one of mine, I save you or one of yours.'"

"Yes."

This was something she had not expected, not here at the edge of the Wilds where the people were the sons and daughters of ruined farmers and escaped slaves and burned-out soldiers who'd never won a war. The code, she was sure, was dead here at the Graviss Glen. Abour was revealing himself. "You are asking to come with us."

"I…yes."

"You owe us nothing. Your brother's life was not in danger."

"It's your right to refuse but mine to follow you as if you hadn't." This man knew the law.

"So it is."

Abour stood and looked at her not with defiance or fear but with a sort of patient stillness. There was something familiar about the set of his mouth.

"We'll be moving quickly. We will not rest till morning, and then only for a short time."

"I understand. I can hold my own in the woods."

"I've no doubt you can. But our journey may hold greater unpleasantness than even these old woods can provide."

Abour nodded.

"Your Hustel's grandson, aren't you? From the Hulder Grove?" she said.

"One of them."

"And that one there?" she gestured at the unconscious man.

"Also one of them."

"He can't come."

"He was never meant to."

"He volunteered to get hit in the head?"

"After a fashion. He volunteered to be the bait."

Suashi went over and knelt by the side of the fallen man. "Strange times we live in. Nothing is what it seems, yet we all want the same thing."

"All true."

"And what did your wily grandfather tell you?"

"He told me to guard your life like it was my own. He told me you wouldn't allow it but that what you would allow wasn't relevant."

"Not relevant? Well, he's probably got the math right," she said, "but his subterfuge needs work."

"Got us through so far."

"You could've just asked."

"You would have said no."

"You're right. Trust Hustel to generate an argument that puts me on the wrong side of honor."

"Not the wrong side if you allow me to join you."

The old man had won their last argument without so much as a chirp from her. She smiled sadly. She looked at his grandson and wondered how much Hustel had told him about her destination and their plan. She decided he probably knew what he had to know, which would be just enough to let him decide in earnest if it was worth his life. The price wasn't likely to end up being less. "Your ruse was your audition."

"Hustel also knew that you would not allow me to come without a show of mind skill, law be damned."

"Your skills are impressive enough. They had better be, if you share our road and purpose. Welcome. Pao!" she called out. "We've some fresh ears for your atrocious chatter. Abour, my deceptive friend, you have not yet heard Paomaintanna's infamous tales of the lower Wilds. When you do, you may come to wish it had been you who'd offered to get hit in the head with a rock."

Chapter 31
"This ain't my first go round
on the Qi Dao Lu."

Place: Somewhere in the middle of the kingdom of Arbana, Arba Environ
Date: Quattrenim 39, AY 998

"These vermin aren't worth a bag of my shit, Vensol."

William stood in the cart alongside one very dark man with only one ear and a small, fat woman who had been smiling broadly ever since her capture.

"Your shit must be very valuable then, friend Banam. These here are from the south, hillworkers and strong, able settlers."

"Hillworkers? Settlers? Ha! These are Tritto shit, these ones. What do you call this here?" The tall, thin slaver slapped the hand of a child who was leaning on the cart's bars. "Are you a hillworker, hmm?"

The child smiled weakly, not understanding but mistaking the man's interest for potential kindness.

"This haul is shit, Vensol. Turn your cart around before I set it afire."

"Come now, surely there is something here that might be of use to you? What about that one, the dark one there? And the one beside him, with the beard?"

"Hm. Okay, perhaps those. And maybe the old man with the mark. Are you a metalsman?"

The old man behind William spoke up. "I've work'd the metals. All my life."

"Can you walk? Can you see?"

"I can do both."

"Hold up your hands. You have not so many fingers. Can you work without those fingers?"

"I can."

"What about you?" Banam said to William roughly. "You a fighter?"

William didn't look at him. He looked away.

Banam poked through the bars of the cart with his stick, jabbing William in his side. William grabbed the stick and yanked it out of his hands.

"Ho! He's got a little spirit. Maybe I'll fuck him later."

"And the dark one?"

"Fine. Him too."

"And these others? Is there nothing you can do with them?"

"I can feed them to my pullers and loaders. I'll pay ten barb for the whole lot."

"Ten barb! They're worth ten times that still!"

"Then those three, eight barb, no more. Take the rest back with you and burn them yourself."

"Eight barb. Done."

A small bag was handed over, and William, along with the two others, was pulled out of the cart.

"I hope you two really can fight," the slaver Banam said to William and the dark man. "You'll be working the Qi Dao Lu, you will, so it's fight or die, all the way from Chralm Doanna to Motatinfo and back." He laughed at them and smacked the old man in the head. "With me, Sir Metalworker. Urj, take care of our new fighting men."

Urj, a giant and an apparent blend of races William could only guess at, emerged from behind a wagon with a huge bone in his left hand and a scimitar as long as a man in his right. "Fighter men?" he said, pointing the bone at William and the other man. "Hahahahahaha...no." He belched, slid the sword through a strap on his back, and ambled away.

The two men followed him, but at a comfortable distance.

An hour later, in what William judged to be late afternoon, they were walking in a caravan. They kept pace alongside a huge, multileveled wagon pulled by what looked to be two enormous, long-necked, bluish-gray dinosaurs. The wagon was chained to the wagon behind it, and that one to the cart behind it, and so forth for almost as far as the eye could see.

The dinosaurs were pulling the entire caravan. They were also talking to one another, but not in any language William could understand.

"That's messed up, huh? What's that, something from *The Flintstones*?"

William turned and stared at the dark man who'd been recruited as a fellow soldier-slave. He'd heard what he'd heard. He was sure of it. He kept walking and didn't turn around again, but after a few minutes turned his head a bit and said flatly, "The dinosaurs on *The Flintstones* never talked."

The dark man laughed out loud and then seemed to think better of it and acted like he was coughing. "That's true, that's true," he said in a kind of hiss, "but they could yabba dabba, and that shit there sounds like yabba dabba to me."

They both chuckled for a moment but went silent when a guard turned his head and snarled at them.

The guard turned back around, ignoring them, and moved up the line to a woman who had bent to pluck up a weed from the side of the road. She had shoved the weed in her mouth and was still trying to chew it as the guard tried to slap it out of her mouth. She spit at him and received a kick for her efforts.

"You don't sound like you're from around here," said William to the black man.

"No, what? Me, I was born right over there by those trees. You?"

"No. Upstate New York."

"New York, New York. I went to a Yankee game once. Played that song about twenty times."

"I was an Orioles fan. Dad was from Maryland."

"Cardinals."

"No shit?"

"No shit. I guess as an Orioles fan, this place here is kind of a step up for you, huh?"

They laughed low again. William unconsciously braced himself for the kick he knew was coming from somewhere.

"Don't worry, they can't hear us if we keep it down. Too much noise from the yabbas and the carts. And they definitely can't understand us."

William wondered at that. He could understand everyone, no matter the race. Something that the Landing Point had done to him.

Not wanting to tempt fate and not necessarily trusting the man, American or not, he kept it toned down for a bit and trudged along in silence.

He was starting to wonder if leaving Cvuklon had been the right move. Maybe he should have talked to the kid, let him know what he was thinking. The Slau might have even helped him get back to the Landing Point.

But no, he'd done what he had to do. The kid clearly had an agenda, marching orders of some kind from someone else, someone he hadn't felt the need to tell William about. No matter what he said and how he seemed, he worked as a slave trafficker with his uncle and was probably looking to sell William to someone in Carthage.

Why all the chicanery then? Why the rhetoric? To get him to cooperate? Hell, Cvuklon could have kept him sedated the whole time with the agilios. No, there was something else up. There was an agenda, but even if it wasn't about selling William's ass to the highest bidder or into some other ghoulish fate, it was still about him, and that he couldn't figure. He was nobody. On Earth, he'd been a father, a husband, a businessman, a taxpayer, an embezzler that one time…but here, nobody.

And yet, somebody wanted him for something.

Why?

And why wouldn't the kid just tell him?

Probably because he didn't know himself.

"Well, for what it's worth, pleased to meet ya," said the man out of the blue.

"Likewise. You're an American?" asked William.

"Yeah. Was. Place called Hilltown, Missouri. Know it?"

William shook his head.

"It's got a few other names. Bellefontaine. Chesterfield. We call it Hilltown. Called it. Don't know what they call it now."

"I've heard of Chesterfield," William said, believing what he said was probably true. And then he added, "You're the first one I've met since I got here."

"First what?"

"American."

"Oh, yeah," said the man. "Probably gonna be the last one, too. I've been here a long time, and you're only my third."

"Where are the other two?"

The man just looked at him and shook his head.

"Died?" asked William.

"Doesn't seem to matter much now, but yeah, they died. Long time ago."

"Sorry to hear it."

The man extended his hand to William. "I'm Joe."

"William."

They walked for a little while longer, though they did it in silence because despite Joe's assurances, their conversation had been drawing attention.

William was hungry. Really hungry, to the point where he felt he might pass out. He assumed every slave on the line was in the same condition. They hadn't been fed since before they'd been sold.

At one point, the wind picked up and began to whip against the caravan. The dust from the road kicked up so badly it became hard to breathe. William tried to cover his mouth with his arm, but the dust was choking him anyway. Joe tapped him on the shoulder and handed him what looked like a long piece of red leather. William could see that Joe had wrapped his own face with a similar piece, even his eyes, so William did the same.

The material was translucent enough to see through, and he could breathe through it as well without getting much dust into his nose and mouth. Joe tapped him again and gave him the thumbs-up. William raised his thumb and said, "Thanks," but the wind was howling now too loudly for him to hear or be heard.

The dust storm continued for another hour, but they marched on. Then, just as the winds were letting up, one of the dinosaurs stumbled and fell face down, dead. Banam and his man Urj poked at it and then stabbed it a few times, but it didn't move.

Banam said something to Urj, who turned to the caravan and yelled, "Make camp."

He strode over to William and Joe and barked, "You two, cut that up for meat. Don't eat any. If I see you eat, I cut you up for meat too." He pulled two stubby-looking knives out of his belt and threw them on the ground. "Move."

They moved. Joe bent down and grabbed the knives, inspecting one and handing the other to William. "These ain't gonna cut into that," Joe said.

Urj just looked at him.

"Guess we'll give it a shot." Joe walked toward the fallen pack animal and stared at it. William joined him.

"Any ideas?" William said, running his finger carefully along his dull blade.

"Dunno. Maybe if we go at its stomach?"

They tried that. Each one stabbed a few times with his pitiful blade, but the creature's skin was impenetrable.

They stepped back and considered what to do, fully aware that Urj was watching and would only wait a moment or two more before expressing his displeasure at their lack of industriousness.

William got an idea, but it was disgusting. Still, it was that or a beating. Or worse. "Maybe…the ass?"

Joe raised his eyebrows. "You think?"

"Gotta be softer, right?"

They started walking to the back of the animal when they heard the ring of a sword being drawn. They turned, expecting the worst, to see Urj raising his massive scimitar over the thing's belly. "Like this, fighter men!"

Urj triumphantly split open the belly with a mighty hack, and then he hacked at the ribs a few times and split open the side. "Now, you cut out all meat." He grabbed a small hunk of what looked like intestines and walked away, gnawing at his take.

"I would have rather hacked open the ass than see that," Joe deadpanned.

"You and me both, Joseph," said William.

A little while later, covered in blood and mucus and the guts of the thing they'd just butchered badly, they sat on the side of the road and watched the guards eating roasted meat while they themselves tried to eat the uncooked skin that had been given to the slaves. The smell of the roasting meat was intoxicating.

Urj, now very drunk, stumbled over to them and pointed. "You two, first watch, back line."

William got up, but Joe remained seated.

"First watch!" Urj belched, glowering.

Joe rose slowly, whether out of exhaustion or anger William couldn't tell, and regarded Urj.

"Now!" growled Urj.

Joe spread his hands out and looked down at the ground. "Forgive this request, but would it be okay if we washed up a bit in that stream down over there? Getting your meat left us a little...messed up," he said without a hint of irony in his voice.

Urj took a look at the place to which Joe had gestured. "Go. Do it. Fast. Then first watch."

The huge guard turned and stumbled back to the roasting fire. His fellows were singing a song about a Wildean woman who had apparently pleasured a whole army. William wasn't impressed by the melody.

"Time to walk around in circles. You know how to shoot a bow?" Joe asked him as he removed his dust mask.

"Not really. Tried it once at a state fair when I was in college."

"Hit anything?"

"The ground. And a bucket of frying grease behind a food stand. Got me thrown out of the fair."

"You were aiming for it?"

"Which?"

"The bucket."

"No."

"It'd be a little better for us if you were aiming for it. You're sure?"

"Yeah."

"Well, it don't matter much. If anything comes at us that's too far away to hit with a sword, it'll probably turn us into pincushions before we get a chance to yell yabba dabba."

"Does that happen often?"

"What, an attack? Let's just say I been doing this kind of work for almost five years — theirs, not ours — different caravans, different highways, and I can count on one hand the number of nights nobody attacked. Usually it's just starving raiders and children, though."

"And when it's not?"

"Well, let's just pray it is, 'cause when those other ones come to play, they play to win. And you didn't hit that grease bucket on purpose."

"Great. It's gonna get real dark out there, I bet. We won't even see 'em coming."

"Speak for yourself. I got some eyes, man, some serious eyes."

"What, you can see in the dark?"

"Kinda, yeah."

"That standard for a kid from Hilltown?"

"Well, I was a black kid in Hilltown, which ain't exactly Saint Louis, so things were different…seeing in the dark came in handy. But I'm playing with you. No, when I first got here, I was grabbed by the military—you know, the Crabs? Anyway, they needed scouts, and so they had my eyes done up. Said I wasn't a good candidate to get crabbed, which made me as happy as a man can get in a place like this. You don't want to be crabbed, ever."

William didn't know what that meant. He thought maybe he didn't want to know. "What did they do to your eyes?"

"Made 'em able to see in the dark, and far, and even in really bright light. Only time I can't see too good is dusk, but even then I can see better than I ever could back home."

"Sounds good to me. You see anything, yell so I can hide," William said.

"They catch you hiding in a fight, they'll feed you to the haulers. Someone comes, you just get mean, wave your sword, and stick close to me. I'll show you how it's done. This ain't my first go round on the Qi Dao Lu."

"The what?"

"The Long Weeping Road, man. The name says it all."

They passed cart after cart of crates and barrels and cages, all chained together like a massive snake, mostly filled with livestock but some with the odd human or humanoid, until they reached the back of the mile-long caravan. William scanned the hills and trees about them.

Joe said, "This isn't exactly an ideal place to stop: the lack of a 'flat periphery' gives all them slippery raiders too many good places to hide."

"How do you know there are raiders?"

"There are always raiders, man," Joe answered, nervously glancing about. "We may be here a day or two, though. Guaranteed. With that yabba dead, they're either gonna have to redistribute that load so one can pull it, or they're gonna have to get themselves another hauler. Now, I don't care how close the place is where they find a replacement or how fast they get to it: haulers are slow-walking mothers, so it'll take some time. So stay frosty, because raiders don't love nothing more than a stuck caravan."

They did a few laps up and down the back quarter of the line. Joe got something in his shoe, so they stopped for a rest.

"So let me ask you: How'd you get caught?" William asked.

"I dunno. Well, yeah, I do: I fell asleep. I'd been fishing on that river, you know the one with the bridge we came over? Yeah, well down a few miles from the bridge, right there on that soft river bank, I found a bend where the fish — something that looked like a cross between a catfish and a frog — were stacked so full you could barely see water. Been going to that spot for months now, just me, ever since I got away from…well, never mind.

"Anyway, that day, I fished, I ate, I drank a bottle of something I didn't have no business drinking, and I napped. Guess their dogs smelled me or smelled all the fish guts or something. I woke up in that cart."

"Bad luck."

"Yeah, well, like I said, I've been doing this for years now, walking the Long Road, as they say, and it ain't so bad. They feed you — sometimes better than dead dino skin — and you get to swing a dull sword and it's good exercise, all this walking."

"But you'd rather be fishing."

"You bet your ass."

They laughed. Joe stood back up, his shoe returned to its rightful place.

"Let's do a few more laps and tell that scimitar dude we had enough," he said.

"Fine with me. You tell him first. He likes you."

"The hell you say."

They walked for another hour. If there were raiders in the hills, they were taking their time making plans. Or maybe, having seen the ferocious duo guarding the back of this particular caravan, they'd decided to just leave.

Joe sat down on the wheel of the last cart. "So let me ask you then: Were you fishing too?"

"Me? No. I was…there was an accident. A big fire, outside a town called Carthage."

"Carthage. I know it. Name's familiar, ain't it?"

"Yeah, pretty funny. They couldn't have a Vegas or Paris or Honolulu. They have a Carthage."

"So they bagged you."

"Yes, they did. I was traveling with someone, a young kid — well, not really a kid: he was a Slau, and…"

"A Slau? Known me some of them. Ugly, ugly, ugly."

"Yeah, well, this kid saved me…got me away from his uncle's caravan and took me to Carthage. Was taking me there, anyway, until they bagged me," William lied. This man didn't need to know he'd volunteered to go with Vensol and his Gumundurs, and he didn't need to know why.

"Why'd the kid save you?"

"Someone told him to. I don't know. He never said, and to tell you the truth, I didn't much care."

"So what happened when you got there?"

"We stayed in some old woman's place for a few weeks, mostly hiding in the cellar. She let us up at night to eat and talk. There was a lot of talk, mostly about nothing, and we played some games I couldn't understand. Something with knucklenbonas…"

"Suns-shone-knucklebones. Played it all the time at the harbor."

"Well, the old lady just called it knucklenbonas. And the Slau said she cheated her ass off."

"Huh. Who around here doesn't?"

"Well, that dead dinosaur, for one. He's probably as honest as a Methodist."

"You got that."

"Anyway, there was a fire one night, and I tried to help this girl…this pregnant girl, she was trapped in an alley…"

"I thought you said you were kept in the house?"

"I was. I was, but when the fire broke out, it was a free-for-all. Cvuklon—"

"Who?"

"The Slau kid…he took off yelling about something…a book he'd lost, though I'd never seen him with a book…and then I went out the kitchen door because the whole place seemed like it was gonna come down. I heard someone screaming in an alley right across from the house, and I went to see if I could help."

"That was your first mistake. In Arba, never go see if you can help. Rule number one."

"I'm starting to understand that. So I see her, and she sees me, and I go in, but something hits me and sends me practically through a wall. When I woke up, I was in chains. You know the rest."

"I guess I do. Sorry it went down like that."

"Yeah. You know what's weird? That woman in the alley…she looked familiar."

"Oh, don't worry about that. There's all kinds of weird déjà vu shit that goes on around here. I see my mother at least twice a year, you know it. You ain't seeing what you think you seeing, so try to put it out your mind."

"It's gonna take a while to get used to this place."

"I wouldn't worry about that either. Something is bound to sit on you before too long and just put you out of your misery."

"That's sweet of you to say."

"I'm just saying, yabba dabbas got to sit down somewhere, and you can't stay awake all the time."

They laughed a bit at that.

"You know, William, I got to tell you: it sure is nice to have someone to talk to again. It's been a long, long time."

William was silent for a moment. He was deciding whether or not he could trust this man. He was an American, sure, and he wasn't wrong about having someone familiar to talk to. But Joe had been here a long time, and he'd probably been through some unimaginably painful shit. Was it even safe to assume he was still sane?

What did it matter? William was going whether Joe was sane or not. And he needed information. "Joe, let me ask you something."

"Shoot."

"If I wanted to get back to the Landing Point from here, what would I have to do?"

"Hahahaha. Is that a trick question?"

"Why do you ask?"

"Because, Billy my friend, if you wanna get back there, all you gotta do is live a while longer."

"I don't understand."

"Where do you think this road leads to, anyway?"

"No kidding?"

"No kidding. But let me ask you a question: Why in the hell would you wanna go back there?"

William didn't answer. He couldn't bring himself to say it out loud.

"You looking for somebody, ain't you?"

Willam just nodded very slowly.

"They ain't gonna be there. No way. I'm sorry to tell you that, I am, but they ain't gonna be there. Only thing's gonna happen if you try to find them is, you gonna die."

"Been there."

"Maybe."

"What? What do you mean? I thought…"

"Billy, you know that old saying about never making an ass of you and me?"

"Yes."

"Assume nothing. Listen, think, listen more, but assume nothing. Because half the shit you hear around here is lies, and the other half is just plain stupid. One thing you gotta know about this place is: nothing makes no sense, so you gotta make your own sense, for you, you hear me?"

William didn't really understand, but he nodded again.

"Good, that's good. Now let's get down to talkin' about the only thing that should matter right here and right now."

"What's that?" William asked.

"How are we gonna get away from this goddamn slave train?"

Chapter 32
"Now I am a dead fat man in the middle of nowhere..."

Place: The Sapphire Forest, in the western part of the kingdom of Xatumka,
Arba Environ
Date: Quattrenim 41, AY 998

Two weeks had passed since they'd left the lake. Now they sat in a clearing at the northern edge of the Sapphire Forest, drinking wine and eating boiled pond fish.

"I suppose you'll tell me when you're ready," said Theodore. He picked another bone from his fish. "Ah, could you please?" He gestured at their small bag of salt, which was sitting by Sh'arnau's foot along with a few other loose sundries.

"Tell you what?" asked Sh'arnau as he stooped and picked up the salt. He pulled the strings tight before he tossed it to Theodore; they didn't have much, and it wouldn't be easy to get more if this spilled. He sensed his hostage — or was it companion? — would be far less manageable without salt for his pond fish, among other things.

"Tell me what the plan is."

"There isn't one. We're safe now. Out of range, I think."

"But as lovely as this forest is, we can't stay here forever."

Sh'arnau looked around him at the broad oak trees, the thickets of wild ivy and bramble bushes, and the stream that wound its way into a nearby series of yellow-gold meadows and shimmering ponds. There were far worse places to spend forever. He'd been to most of them. "No, and we won't. But for now, it's what we've got," he said.

Theodore salted his fish, tasted a bite, then salted it more. "You do realize we have ourselves a bit of a dilemma," he said as he pulled some white flesh off his trout and shook his head with a mumble about too many bones. He examined the flesh, spotted another bone, and threw the fish into the fire. He grabbed another fish and began the process anew. "When all is said and done, all I have to aid me in forming a perspective of my own is your word," he said to Sh'arnau matter-of-factly. "That's a difficult position for a man like me, or, I suspect, pretty much anyone, to be in, wouldn't you agree?"

"I would," the wolf answered, deciding not to comment on the waste of food. He'd heard enough complaining from the scholar, and was now, apparently, in for more.

Theodore paused and seemed to wait for Sh'arnau to elaborate, which he did not.

"Aside from your version of events, I have almost nothing to go on. I have no idea why you pushed me off that walk, if in fact it was you who pushed me. I cannot understand why you would have gone against Grewea and saved me or why he would have wanted you to do exactly that after instructing you to kill me. And I have no idea why you've brought me out into the wilderness. There are plenty of civilized places to hide, and it's not like my portrait is hanging in every one of them."

Theodore paused. After a long moment, his captor responded:

"It's a situation, to be sure."

"I can come up with some working theories, most of them predicated on the assumption that you have lied to me."

Sh'arnau snorted and reached for another piece of fish. He didn't mind the bones.

"For example," Theodore continued, "this might be a simple kidnapping. You've taken me not because someone paid you to but because you know someone will pay to get me back. That theory only goes so far, though, because it doesn't explain why you would bother to make up a whole story about saving me and dragging me away from Hunberg. And it doesn't seem Grewea's style, if in fact he is involved. Given that you're his man, I assume he really is involved."

"This is no kidnapping. I do not kidnap, and I have only ever ransomed one person."

"And?"

"And she died. Horribly."

"At your hands?"

"When I kill, I kill quickly and, if possible, painlessly."

"No need to watch their eyes as they die, and all that?"

"No. Death is a private matter, deserving of brevity if and when dignity isn't possible, and it would be unwise to treat it any other way. What are your other theories?" Sh'arnau asked as he pointedly held up his bare fish skeleton for the other to behold. He chucked the skeleton into the woods.

Theodore ignored the display. He gave the impression of a man who was suddenly deep in thought, or pretending to be deep in thought. Then he rose and began to pace.

"Someone paid you to get me out the way for a while. Someone who wouldn't want my death or at least my disappearance on his conscience...but that doesn't make sense because, well, if it's true, why you? You're the most feared killer on any shore of Lake Iale and everywhere in between. Getting you to grab me, a man who would hardly be in any shape to put up a fight, is like hiring a Challowian to build a child's toy boat. Overkill. Unless...unless they expected there would be resistance. But resistance from whom, if no one else knew what was happening?"

Theodore plopped down, almost out of breath. He looked down at his plate and his two remaining fish. "I can't live on this. Pond trout and water."

Sh'arnau agreed. "I can't either. And your theories are hurting my head."

"Then why can't you give me something, some reason to trust you?"

"Okay, here's something: I haven't killed you."

"And while I find that comforting, really I do, I cannot bear to go on without knowing more of the facts."

"You'll have to, for now, because I don't have any other facts to feed you."

"For now. Okay. So you don't have a plan, and we're here indefinitely. Understood. Let me ask you another question, then. Let's assume your story is true. Why did you save me?"

"I can't answer that."

"Why not? You must have had a reason for going through so much trouble to fake my death. What was that reason?"

"If I knew, I'd tell you. I was sent to kill you. I decided not to."

"Who sent you?"

"We've been over that, no?"

"And why would he want me dead?"

"He didn't tell me."

"He just told you to kill me?"

"Yes."

"Just as he'd told you to do the same with, how many, I wonder, over the years?"

"Many. This was different, though."

"How so?"

"This time, he promised to set me free."

"Free? You mean you were his prisoner?"

"Not prisoner. But I was bound to him…in an old way, and for a very long time."

Theodore sat for a moment and considered this information. "So why now? Why would he set you free now? Just for killing me?"

"No. There was something else," Sh'arnau said. Then he added, perhaps not quickly enough, "I don't know what exactly."

"Interesting," said Theodore with a quizzical look that seemed to say, *I saw that.*

"Maybe, maybe not." Sh'arnau ignored the man's sudden puckish expression. "I've found that trying to decipher Grewea's mind was never worth the time or energy. The answers are locked away within him, for him alone to know."

"So speaks the assassin. But I am an academic, and we live for such mysteries."

"You live *because* of this mystery. Perhaps you should leave it at that."

Sh'arnau got up and went into the forest to relieve himself. He listened carefully to the night sounds. There weren't many; most natural things steered clear of him. Too many years of living and killing had tainted his aura, he supposed, or maybe he just stank. In any case, this forest sounded as it should: there was no reason to suspect they were being watched. And yet there were things about, always, that could watch without raising suspicion. His senses were extraordinary but not infallible.

He heard water and chuckled; at least the stream persisted in its routine despite its veiled fear of Sh'arnau the Unmaker. Water was like that: unafraid, persistent, and in this world, usually nearby. Very much like himself.

The trout were another story. Would they tell their children tales of the Unmaker, the Bane, the Wolf? he wondered. Why should the trout be any different?

Soon, it might not matter if they were, not anymore.

It was almost over for him.

He could scarcely allow himself to believe it.

He went back to the camp to find Theodore reading. He put one more small log on the fire and lay down on the ground.

"That doesn't look too comfortable," said Theodore. "Try my roll," he added, gesturing at his own meagre bedding. "There's room."

"It's fine," Sh'arnau answered. He was mildly impressed by the scholar in the moment. Few had ever willingly thought to invite him into closer proximity. Perhaps Theodore wasn't as much the cowardly nuisance as he'd convinced himself he was.

The moment passed when the scholar started to speak. Again.

"You know, I thought of another question, one I'm sure you won't answer either, but we're alone out here, and I've read this book a hundred times — which by the way, thank you for providing it, though I can't imagine why you had it to provide — so humor my thirst for conversation."

"The book is mine. I've never read it. What's your question?"

"And yet you carry it with you. You're a curious person, to be sure. But as for my question...after your man brought back the viahrta root, you left for a few hours, this despite your insistence that it was in our best interest to move on."

"Yes."

"I know how long it was because I slept, but only fitfully, and when I woke, your men only told me you'd be back but didn't say when. They didn't seem to know and were frightened they'd be left with me to deal with."

"Your point?"

"Where did you go?"

"Hunberg."

"I think I know why. Do I?"

Sh'arnau snorted and rolled over.

"What did he say?"

"Nothing."

"He must have asked about your success."

"He assumes my success and never asks. But to answer your question, he wasn't there."

"He'd gone? I wonder why. And to where?"

"Who knows. I don't think he expected me to come back; he was sincere in his promise to release me, it seems."

"I wonder if he would rescind that offer if he knew what you'd done."

"He knows."

"Can he find us?"

"No, not here. I don't think so. He doesn't come up this way. No one does. No one else."

"Meaning what?"

"I was the only one who would come here. The rest are afraid."

"Superstitious?"

"Perhaps. Many of them assisted in the cleansing. Him included."

"The Malliorelum are no more. There is nothing left for those who exterminated them to be afraid of, except perhaps their own collective guilt."

"As you say. But Grewea doesn't feel guilt or fear. He doesn't come here because he has no reason to."

"Maybe you gave him a reason to."

"Maybe." Sh'arnau rolled over and tried to go to sleep. He found he could not. He lay there with his eyes open and fixed lazily on the forest.

They were out there. Maybe watching, maybe not. There weren't many of them left. He knew they wouldn't come out and challenge him; they'd made that mistake once before. But they were very good with spears, and it was possible they might reach the camp with a lucky throw. If it could be done, they had every reason to try it. The Malliorelum would not have forgotten his role in the purging of their kind.

He wasn't too worried, not about that. He was more than quick enough to move aside, and he was betting they weren't in the habit of coming this far east with any more than a small patrol. All they had left were small patrols, that and the secret of their own fractured perpetuation. Maybe they'd simply let the two of them be because, when all was said and done, it was to him they owed a debt for that perpetuation, and they knew it.

Sh'arnau the Merciful. Alas.

But it wasn't the Malliorelum that were keeping him awake.

There was something else on his mind.

He hadn't told Theodore everything. Grewea hadn't been there, in the city; that much was true. But it wasn't the whole truth. He had left a note explaining to Sh'arnau the conditions for his promised release. The note had been a brief but powerful one:

Find the Sword of Endings. The Timesinger Charlton, on the isle of Pedry, will know where it lies. Do this, and whatever else you've done, I forgive you and free you. Be at peace, my friend.

The night came on more deeply. There were small sounds from the forest: the wings and calls of owls and bats searching for prey, the occasional crack of a branch as a large and otherwise silent deer made its way along the edge and into the meadow. It seemed to Sh'arnau that whatever effect his damaged aura may have had in the daylight did not carry over into the night, and for that he was thankful. He was damned, a thousand times over he was damned, and he knew it, but if there were some things in the world that didn't fear him so much as to completely steer clear of him, he often thought maybe he could endure whatever damnation was waiting for him.

That thought was every time chased away by the weight of his past misdeeds.

He was every bit the monster they thought he was.

For him, there would never be redemption.

Death would have to do.

For a while he sat there, several feet from the dying fire, whittling arrow shafts. They hadn't had to use but two of the arrows he'd brought with him, and one of those was for game — a very large raccoon — but there was always another battle on the horizon. For him, at least. Still, he suspected that somewhere in the cities and the distant farms and fishing villages, battle of the kind he knew and had always known was rare or even nonexistent. Even Yanz and Tritto surely had their moments of something like serenity when hell found its equilibrium and the agony felt a little like peace, he mused.

Somewhere, there was peace.

As his knife slid down the thick birch branch he held tight with his other hand, he was not uncomfortable with the thought of a pending fight.

Sometimes he wished it weren't so, but not tonight, and not for some time.

Theodore stirred in his sleep. He was dreaming. Sh'arnau hadn't dreamt in many, many years. He hardly ever slept. Perhaps after so many centuries of keeping vigils and taking respite on the cold, broken ground of this odd world, he had outgrown the need for it. But watching Theodore, he thought that if he ever had a chance to rest his head with as reconciled a conscience as this one seemed to have, he would sleep for a year or more.

And then Theodore woke up with a start.

"Bad dreams?"

The scholar blinked at him and glanced at the knife in his hand. "Always."

"I'd concluded you were the type of man who usually slept like a lamb in a barn," said Sh'arnau.

"Me? You're joking, I trust. I am not only a student and teacher of the teachings of our Noble Four; I am also, I regret to say, a bureaucrat of the first order and a first-rate son of a bitch."

"You're a Mindman, yes?"

"Yes. Or at least, I was. Now I am a dead fat man in the middle of nowhere, waking up from a dream about falling to see the man who very recently made him fall staring at him with a knife in his hand."

"I am not a man."

"Forgive me. A Thicknomite? A Terendislau? A Mundite? How do you identify yourself?" asked Theodore as he rose from his bedding and starting walking away, looking for a place to pee.

"I'm an intruder. Isn't that what you Arbans prefer to call us all?"

Theodore didn't answer except to grunt. He busily huffed off toward the nearby stream. A half a minute later, he returned to the fire and asked, "Have we any soap?"

"In my bag, on the side. There's some cassia oil. Will that do?"

"Is that what you put in your hair? Forgive me, your...fur?"

"I have to. Without it, I look even more the beast than I do now."

Theodore found the cassia, grabbed it, and held it up. "Quite right. But were it not for this fine supplement, we would all be beasts." He walked a few paces over to the small stream, knelt down, and washed. When he came back, he looked down at Sh'arnau's pile of arrow shafts. "Are we expecting something untoward?"

"Always."

"And I assume you have heads for those?"

Sh'arnau smiled. "Of course, friend Theodore."

"Don't call me that, please."

"What should I call you? Fat Teddy?"

"No, I don't mean...I mean, in Hunberg I was surrounded by

thousands of persons, all of whom wanted something from me, always calling me 'friend Theodore' — and not a one of them my friend. If I recall correctly, it's what your master called me as well, on those rare occasions when he called upon me."

"Count yourself lucky. He called upon me all the time."

"I consider myself quite the man of the world, rarely rattled even in the nastiest of debates. I once made the Mather of Grandhold Exaltus break down and cry. But each time I had a meeting with your boss, I had to stop myself from ripping out my own eyes and flushing out my brain with seawater."

"Good thing you were able to stop yourself. Seawater stings."

"The man unnerved me, what can I say?"

"The man unnerves everyone."

"But not you."

"No.

"Why?"

"It's been a very long time since there was anything he could take from me." Sh'arnau went to his sack and pulled out a small pouch of smoke. He packed a pipe, lit it, and sat there, staring into the fire and puffing.

"There's something you haven't told me about your visit to Hunberg," said Theodore after a while.

"What makes you say that?"

"Grewea Lon never leaves a task incomplete. I knew him well enough to know that. He's a scheming, cold bastard who prides himself on trapping his prey seven different ways."

"So he is."

"And so I deduce that he would never have simply left the city, particularly if he was looking forward to your report of the completed act, regardless of this releasing business."

"And?"

"Are you going to show me the letter, or are we going to pretend whatever was written in it isn't vexing you somehow?"

"How do you know there's a letter?" Sh'arnau asked in a low tone, not at all pleased that Oxenhaft might have been spying on him.

"Deduction. That, and I can read something in your face. I don't know you very well, but it's clear something dreadful is on your mind."

"I'm an assassin. Something dreadful is always on my mind."

"I'm beginning to understand that. I merely suggest to you that I might be able to help."

"You saw me reading the letter."

"I saw you reading the letter." Theodore smiled a broad smile, and then he sat back down on his bedding and started settling in. Sh'arnau watched him for a moment and, with a sigh and a slight growl of discontent, told him what the note had said.

"The old man is insane," Theodore said, sitting back up. "No one, not even him, knows if the Sword ever really existed. I can tell you, the current thinking among my colleagues is that it most certainly did not."

"Grewea would not command it if it were not possible."

"Well, he may believe it's possible, but he's wrong. And who is this Charlton he speaks of? Never heard of the man, and I know all of the wise men of Ashkinda — and the fools, of which there are more than a few — and their scattered and scant subordinates from Pherriuskata to Pebbusku. There is no 'Charlton.'"

Sh'arnau considered what his captive had said. "I've been to Pedry, once or twice, but long ago. Or maybe not so long ago. It is not a memorable place. Nor is it a place for scholars, not even Timesingers."

"No, it isn't," said Theodore, "but that doesn't mean one isn't working there as a dockhand or menial clerk. They do that. Pose as ordinaries and servants so they can steal or otherwise glean information from the unsuspecting. Very unethical. Deplorable, from a scholarly point of view.

"The university man, claiming the high moral ground?"

"Yes, I'm aware of the irony. The question is, is there an unknown Timesinger hiding on Pedry? Seems very unlikely unless maybe he's doing some secret research of some kind. There are no ruins to speak of on that island, no mysterious histories to unearth...the obviously tragic historical instance being the lone exception."

Sh'arnau wasn't sure what he was referring to. Still, a certain keen sense of discomfort momentarily poked at him from somewhere deep. It left him as quickly as it had appeared. Whatever it was, he decided it was of no concern, not to them and not anymore. He focused on what he knew about Pedry and ignored what he didn't want to know. That policy had always served him well. "There are some ruins but no more than on most Lake Isles."

"Anything notable, would you say?" Theodore asked.

"You've probably been there more often than me. What would you say?"

"Nothing comes to mind. There's a wrecked keep or two. An abandoned fort, pre-Pebbuskan, that by now can't be more than a ruined foundation. The place is of no interest to academics. It doesn't even feature a decent inn where one can dine, nor a cloister of any kind for writing. I went there a few times, but most unwillingly, and I can't recall having done either, which for me is nearly a tragedy."

"I wasn't there to dine or write either."

"I suppose not. Why were you there? No, never mind. Please,

don't tell me. I can only imagine."

"As you wish."

Theodore didn't say anything more until dawn, about two hours later. He hadn't gone back to sleep either. He spent most of that time cleaning his shoes, attempting to brush his teeth, reading some of his book, and trying to get the fire started up again. As Trilesti bent herself over the southeast horizon and the first morning shadows sprang up around the camp, he seemed to come to a decision. He rose and walked over to where the Thicknomite sat, waiting, in a sort of half-wolfen trance. "I think I can help you find the Sword."

"How?"

"I'm beginning to understand that you sacrificed a great deal to save my life. I have no idea why you would have done that, and I cannot, knowing what I do about you, say that I trust you as far as I could throw that massive stone on which you're sitting, but the fact remains that you did save my life. If I can help you, I will."

"Well, that's good to hear. Unfortunately, I have to go to Pedry. Unremarkable as it is, Pedry is on the lake. Someone would recognize you."

"Would they?"

"Yes. Without a doubt. And that would not serve."

"I'll have you know I've spent many evenings frolicking about Hunberg, the Lake Isles, and even Pashka; there's no better place in the environ to gamble and dine than Shulito, you know. Given the pressures of life in both university and governance, one must abandon the scholarly robe now and again for a garb more, shall we say, primal?"

"But it's not your garb that concerns me; it's your face."

"Ah, but you see, who would recognize my beautiful face if 'twere buried behind the mysteries of a mask?"

Sh'arnau understood. And he laughed a great, growling laugh that surely reaffirmed for all the creatures of the northern Sapphire Forest it was a good day to remain in hiding.

Theodore Oxenhaft meant to become a Tri lady.

Chapter 33
"These are the friends
I was telling you about…"

Location: The Wilds, the Bamboo, and Ontonu, border town west of the
Scar, Arba Environ
Date: Quattrenim 43, AY 998

Paomaintanna lead them north and east, away from the Graviss Glen and
toward whatever awaited them in Arbana.

They steered clear of the heavily travelled paths and roads, and
before they'd gone too far from the glen, she'd donned a black wig, some
paste that gave her complexion a dark-tan hue, and an Ailo-shut shawl.
Too many people knew her face now, and too many people, even if they
couldn't place her, would recall that Suashi Bleuss travelled with a tall
Ailo-shut tracker. She could not afford for even one word of her true
direction to reach her enemies' spies, or for that matter, her supporters,
most of whom never knew when they were cheek-to-cheek with enemies'
spies.

"You look like my sister," Pao said.

"You don't have a sister."

"You look like my wife."

"Which one?"

"Which was the one with the funny walk?"

She kicked him in the ass for that.

Abour proved to be every bit the Wildean he'd claimed he was. He
had no trouble keeping up and was actually better at catching game than
Pao. He rarely talked, which in this situation was a plus. Eventually,
they'd have to tell him the details of their intended route and the reasons
for the mission overall, but there really wasn't much need for fresh ideas
from a young tracker, and for now he didn't need to know much, so they
didn't tell him anything. Suashi was growing to like the man, but it would
take some time for her to trust him.

*And what about him trusting me? He won't if he knows what's good for
him. I'm almost certain to get him killed.*

She tried to put that thought out of her mind and focus on their
objective, but she found the objective itself wasn't clear enough to shut out
anything at all, let alone the likelihood that she and anyone who walked
with her were probably living on borrowed time.

They walked the old back trails, the kind not even the Vigilant
used in their rounds, the kind that had been abandoned for better trails
over the many years. They were generally overgrown, almost completely

reclaimed by vegetation, or just plain impassable. Even so, they made fairly good time through the forest; they just had to climb and slash a lot more than they were used to.

The season of chairo had not yet begun in earnest, but it would be here quite soon. The nights were very pleasant and cool, and some of the rare species of trees were already starting to show their fine, bright colors. At night, crisp air crept quietly down from the southern winds that pushed and twirled the treetops; it was the kind of air that made for the best, most restful travel sleeping if one had the constitution to endure it.

Suashi chose, each night, to take the first watch just to take in the approaching evening, its sounds, and its smells. The forest had an audible rhythm paced by the whooshing, whispering sounds of the wind through the pines and the scent of earth and life and growing, vibrant things. She told herself it was out of habit that she chose those watches, but part of her recognized the unpleasant possibility that it might be a very long time till she heard those sounds and smelled those scents again.

Nightly also she attempted to perform her rituals, if only to clear her mind, but she found they had the opposite effect. She had never been one to be still for very long, had never mastered meditation in any respect, and even here amid the pleasant forestal tones, safely hidden from dangers in the kind of place that was far more familiar and comforting to her than any hut or bed or keep, it remained true: her head was a swarming mess of thoughts, fears, hunches, and misgivings.

She focused on focusing on nothing.

Some nights it almost worked for a few minutes.

On the fourth afternoon, they came across a group of skeletons down in a small, thickly wooded dell. Closer inspection revealed that they had been two groups, British League and someone else, maybe a handful of early Vigilants.

"These have been here a while," said Pao. "Leaguer idiots."

"What were they?" asked Abour.

"A group of Earthers who bit off more than they could chew. Twice, in fact," answered Pao. "They're gone now."

A day later, they entered the Bamboo. Suashi knew it was frowned upon to say so—so many terrible things had been done here, particularly in the time of Kold—but this was her favorite spot in all the Wilds. She found the bamboo forests to be as quiet as dreams, a place where even her unquiet mind found a certain degree of stillness. They served as a buffer between the edge towns and the Wilds proper, and there was an agreement that neither edgers nor Wildeans should settle there. In some sense, then, the Bamboo was the wildest, purest place in all the Wilds, perhaps in all of Arba.

Pao loved it here too. He never said as much, but his demeanor completely changed in this place. Only in Green Home did he seem as peaceful, although somehow there was almost always something there to trouble him, even if it was simply the understanding that his respite was destined to be broken by his impulse to sojourn. There had been whole years during which he had not seen his home, nor she hers. Such was their calling as sworn protectors of the Wilds; information was what kept their lands safe, and information could not be gleaned by sitting at home with one's bare feet on the warm hearth's stones.

But someday, when this is done, it will be someone else's turn to go out in the world and learn the types of things we've learned, she thought. *Or maybe not. Maybe when this is done, that will be done, too.*

They stopped to rest and to take some food.

"Bamboo makes a fine bow. I had one as a youth, but it was stolen," Abour said.

"Maybe someone ate it," suggested Pao. "You know, bamboo shoots are delicious. My grandmother used to make this soup..."

As the men prepared the meal and chatted about the best use of good bamboo, Suashi wandered off to relieve herself and to grab a moment alone. The forest was almost silent; there wasn't even any birdsong. She walked a bit and came to a small stream and waterfall. There was a slight breeze here, and she unwrapped her hair as she kneeled to the pool under the fall. The icy water felt good on her scalp and neck.

Sitting there, the water dripping down onto her chest and back, she wondered, and not for the first time, if peace was an illusion, a shadow one chased on the chance it might be real but without any real intention of ever catching up to it. She believed the Tellers who spoke of a need to reach but to never attain, for perhaps all that one could truly attain in a mortal life was the chance to end it, and so the game was mastered through the art of graceful failure. But here, in this place, her musings came to a sweet and abrupt halt, for such were the depths of its unassuming and untainted tranquility.

I know nothing.

Perhaps it was the relative youth of the place that made it as it was. The Bamboo had been planted only three hundred years before by the Malliorelum as a gift to their friends in the Wilds. The fast-growing and versatile plants replaced tens of thousands of ancient oak and maple trees that had been chopped or burned down during the various early Arban wars. Now the wars were all but forgotten and the Malliorelum had been purged, but the Bamboo remained to silently signify both, however simply, however inadequately.

However fittingly.

I know nothing.

I am empty, and I know nothing.

A small fish jumped up out of the water and splashed. The noise startled her out of her own thoughts. She looked down and saw dozens of the fish swirling and weaving about. For a moment, their movements looked almost choreographed, almost unnatural, but then she noticed a few random chases and flits that renewed the sense of nature's chaos. She put her hands down in the water and felt the fish rubbing against them as they darted back and forth.

After a time, she made her way back to the men. Whatever they were preparing smelled good. When had they last taken a good meal?

Graviss Glen, probably. *And I didn't eat much then*, she thought. *Probably should have.*

"We should reach Ontonu by evening. Gregor will be there," Pao said.

"Him. Great."

"What's wrong with him?" Abour asked.

"Gregor never bathes," Suashi said, wincing.

"That will make it easier to find him. Did you want to stay in town or camp?" asked Pao.

"Do you think my disguise will hold up?" she asked with a grin.

"Yes. Or no. Either way is fine with me," Pao said. "I need to find some more wild chives." He shuffled off into the dark woods. She heard him humming in the distance.

"I don't understand. Won't our whole mission fall apart if you're recognized?" said Abour. "I mean, doesn't everyone think you're headed back to Chrestikos?"

Suashi gave him a half smile. "Yes, you're completely right: we'd be in a bit of trouble if I were spotted this far east. I think what Pao is saying is, if I am recognized and the mission is betrayed, we don't have to go to Arbana, and he gets to go home to his wives. He likes his wives, most of the time, anyway."

"How many does he have?"

"You know, there are just some things you don't ever ask an Ailo-shut. That's one of them."

"Ah, oh..." Abour stumbled to recover. "Well, if I had a bunch of wives waiting at home for me, I might shout your name out at the top of my lungs in the middle of that town. But I don't, and I've never been to Arbana, so try not to get recognized, please." He dipped a small ladle into his soup pot and held it out for her to taste.

She took the ladle and sampled the soup. It was excellent. "Good stuff, thank you," she said, handing the ladle back to him. "I can't speak to your lack of wives, my friend, but once we reach Arbana and you see it for what it is, you may wish you'd chosen to shout." *Or maybe some slaver will catch us and make us all wish it. Or someone else.* There were many ways to die young in Arbana, or so the saying went.

She left him to wash her hands in the stream. She dunked her hands and then her whole head in the water and felt the rush of the cold.

There was a sound in the forest, something that didn't belong there.

Suashi stood, swung her bow, and drew an arrow in an instant. She notched the arrow and stood there, listening and staring into the dark.

Pao whistled low to her from about twenty feet to her right. He pointed north and shook his head, indicating where it was and that he had no idea what it was.

And then, whatever it was, it was gone.

But someone had been watching them. Or had come close enough to do so. In this place, as a rule, friendly things didn't stay hidden or run when spotted.

They entered Ontonu well before evening. Suashi had insisted on making better time, partly because the peace of the Bamboo birthed or at least gave shelter to the tiniest doubt in her resolve for their mission, but more because it was fairly clear that someone was tracking them.

So onward.

The mission. A burden. A burden to end all burdens, right?

She wanted it all to be done, for Arba to be saved, and to be home again on the shores of the great Decone Ocean, watching her cousins play toss-up in the water and smelling the smart, salty winds that crept down to their coast from as far away as Prement. She wanted to give her father a reason to burn his ships or turn them into floating restaurants.

Maybe I can run one, play a small fiddle after dinner so my guests can dance. Fresh fish, dancing music, and the heads of ten thousand Crabs adorning my walls.

Can you even take the head off a Crab? Is what they have still technically considered a head? Why would anyone use even one to decorate a wall?

Restaurants and fiddles. No heads. And done. Done with it all.

It wasn't to be, not yet, and so she led Pao and Abour at almost a run along the quiet paths that meandered to the Yellow Meadows and their strangely peopled border towns. Ontonu was such a place, a sort of stopping hole that, for many, became a permanent stop. Here one found all kinds: descendants of the tree cutters who'd ruined so much of the Wilds long ago, slaves who'd escaped Yanz or Tritto against impossible odds and had either bought or fought their way over a Scar crossing, merchants whose tolerance for governmental gouging had sent them scurrying from the markets of the Tri, and even fishermen and sailors who'd tired of a life on the lake and had opted for one near a river.

Here and there, Suashi saw a musiker, a magicker, a poemsman, a mercenary, and even one broken Crab, head intact but armor badly cracked. That one seemed barely alive, although with his kind, it was always difficult to be sure. There were Mindless everywhere, but most had attached themselves to parties with the heart to aid and shelter them and the greed to gently — or not so gently, as one beerman with a whip demonstrated — exploit them in all the ways a person with nothing can be exploited. There was always good labor to be done in such a place, and for that the Mindless were well suited.

She walked among them, unrecognized. Her wig itched, and the skin on her face felt dry and tight, but no one gave her a second look. That was as it should be. Ontonu wasn't quite Yanz, not by a long shot, but seeing the filth and desperation of the place gave her an unwelcome jolt of discomfort, and she felt it best to meet their contact and get out with all due haste. With any luck, Gregor would be where he was supposed to be, and they'd be gone within the hour.

"Wife, I want some food. Here's good," barked Pao as he gestured at a small tavern with broken holes for windows. A few persons glanced over at the three of them and saw what they expected to see: a drunken Ailo-shut, treating his wife like a dog and traveling with some skin-wearing Wildean.

They entered the tavern but were immediately confronted by the proprietor. "Oh, no. I don't think so. I don't serve animals in here."

"We don't have any animals with us, my friend," said Abour.

"Don't get smart, Wildean, just get out."

"Hello! Friends, friends. You are late!" came a choked but loud voice from the back corner of the room. "Come, sit, have something to eat! Mr. Balogh, please, say hello to my friends!"

"You...you know these people, Mr. Yount?" asked a confused Balogh.

"Of course, of course! These are the friends I was telling you about," said the smallish man as he rose from his seat. He smiled by widening his thin mouth, but his overbite and sparse gray moustache rendered the gesture somewhat menacing.

Balogh clutched at his own forearms as if he were suddenly chilly. "Well, yes, uh, normally, I don't serve...I mean..."

Yount came closer and put a hand on Balogh's shoulder. "But these are not normal circumstances, are they, sir? Have you not enjoyed the largesse of my purse thus far? Please, man. Enjoy it further, and bring these good people food and drink, as much as they can down!"

Balogh lowered his head and strode to the side of the room and the entrance to his kitchen.

"Come, my friends. Sit a bit and talk with me," said Mr. Yount. He turned and walked toward his little table in the corner, his back to them.

Suashi glanced at Pao, who simply raised his eyebrows in a gesture that meant "why not?"

They did as they were bid. They followed him to his table and sat down.

Suashi studied the man a moment, wondering who he was and how — or if — he knew who they were. He seemed to. Pao sat there, wearing the usual blank expression he used on someone he had no reason to trust, and she knew along with that look, his hand would be grasping the hilt of his knife under the table.

It was more than likely that Mr. Yount would need to be silenced — his kind usually required at least that much — but first, they would listen to what he had to say. She was particularly interested to hear what might have happened to Gregor, so after a moment she asked after him.

"Oh, yes, well, Gregor had business to attend to in Rathweine. You know it? Terrible place, not a decent tavern in the whole town, and everyone looking to cheat you at dice. Haven't been there in years myself, and I can't imagine why anyone would go, but Gregor was quite clear in saying he couldn't delay getting there, so I say, to each his own. Of course, he's no shirker, so he asked me to meet you and deliver…whatever it is he had for you," babbled Yount in a matter-of-fact cadence that was designed to disguise the edginess beneath. Suashi caught it; Pao would have as well.

"Gregor never played dice," said the Ailo-shut.

"On the contrary, he did, and often," Yount corrected him with another small, odd smile. "But as is so often the case with those who are fond of gambling, he did his utmost to hide the fact from those he cared about and those who relied on him."

Balogh brought three plates of sausage and cabbage and a pitcher of dark, thick beer. He set them down with a nervous glance at Yount and then hurried off to get three glasses. No one spoke until he had brought them and left.

Suashi poured the beer and casually said, "You seem to know a lot about Gregor. More than any of us, even."

"No, no, my dear, not a lot, and not more; I just happen to know him in ways unfamiliar to you."

"I see. You understand, of course, that we don't know you, and so we can't and don't trust you," she said, sipping the bitter beer.

"And were I in your shoes, I would feel similarly. I suppose, however, we'll have to work around that problem and make the exchange."

"Exchange?"

"I don't mean to be crass," Yount said as he poked at a sausage, "but Gregor mentioned a payment?"

Suashi looked at him full in the face and then turned her head and gazed out the window. "Of course. But first, tell us, please, how you knew Gregor, and how you came to be here in his stead."

"Well, as I said, he asked me to do him a favor, and so here I am. As for how I know him, well, as you have no doubt discerned, we are both humble practitioners of the same secretive craft. It is not uncommon for those few of us who engage in this type of life to, on occasion, stand in for a fellow practitioner."

"Gregor was a friend of ours. He wouldn't have done what you're suggesting, not without a very good reason."

"Quite right."

"So then tell me, Mr. Yount, before my friend decides to legitimize that dead look in your eyes by cutting your throat, what was that reason?"

"There isn't any need to resort to threats, Suashi Bleuss. I didn't have to be here; in fact, when he first asked me, I refused him. The border towns, on the whole, disgust me." He took a long, slow pull from his beer mug and then wiped his mouth with a soiled napkin. "Your friend Gregor was absolutely certain he was about to be killed. He told me he couldn't risk leading whoever was stalking him to you, and so he asked me to give you this." He pulled a small envelope from his waistcoat pocket and laid it on the table.

Suashi didn't touch the envelope. "You know my name. Why?"

"Gregor trusted me."

"Did he?" *We're in trouble; this one's not even trying to mask his lies, which means he has help.* "Who are you, and what do you want?"

Yount laughed for a moment and smiled another smile, this one more complicated and dark. "Well, I wanted to befriend you, to get you to trust me, and to have you send me back to Chrestikos, a new and valuable friend, so that I might enter your father's household and learn what the old screw's closely guarded plans are." He poured himself another beer, drank down half the glass, and let out a low burp. "Pardon me. In any case, you see the people we have in Vaprosta are less than useless, and Vincent is as closed as a Mariendan Bay clam, with his thoughts and intentions all nestled away in that monstrous large skull. But really, I can find out all I need to know on my own; I'm fairly accomplished at insinuating myself into a situation, if I may say so, so I suppose I really just wanted to see your face when I told you we now know where your precious Ashorne is being kept, and that's tantamount to saying he's already dead."

"You lie."

"Do I?"

"Absolutely."

"My apologies." Quick as a snake, Yount swiped a dagger at her head. She spun away; his blade just missed her eye but did nick her temple and ear. He swung again with a blade in his other hand. She threw herself backward, falling with her chair onto the floor, but the second blade scraped her thigh. She rolled away, heard Pao grunt and Abour cry out in pain, and then sprang to her feet just in time to see a half-dozen Tri blackboots crashing through the tavern door. Yount leapt over the table, past the falling body of Abour, and disappeared into the kitchen. She rose and made to pursue him, but the blackboots were on her, and it was all she could do to avoid the points of their swords.

Pao was by her side in an instant, an ugly gash across his forearm. Blood welled from the cut and flew about as he swung his staff to parry the blows of the blackboots and hold them off.

The blackboots pulled back a moment and then charged as one, their swords pointed right at them. Suashi kicked a table up and over; five swords jabbed into the wood. She kicked the table again, much harder, and threw it back against the assailants as they tried to yank their swords free. Pao was on the sixth one and quickly had his man down with a feint and a smash of the staff's end into his forehead. His bolo came out and, in an instant, three of the remaining five were a tangled mess. He knocked all three unconscious with the staff as Suashi's small hammer rattled against the helm of a fourth. The last blackboot threw his sword at her to cover his hasty exit.

Suashi ran to the kitchen, but there was no sign of Yount. She ran out the back door, into the alley, and out to the street, but the man was gone. This was all planned, and she'd walked right into it.

Back inside, she found Pao looking grievously at Abour's wounds. The Wildean was not breathing, and blood was pouring out of him. "He's done."

Suashi gritted her teeth and turned angrily to face the owner, who had come in to assess the damage and moan at its extent. "You spoke to that man?" she asked.

"What?" stammered the owner.

"You spoke to him, right? What did he say?"

"He said nothing. He liked beer. Showed me lots of barbs."

"What else?"

"He thought Ontonu was a shit hole."

She stood up and grabbed him by the collar. "Nothing about where he was going, where he came from?" She cursed herself for an idiot: a man of Yount's skill was clearly not one to spill his secrets to a moronic tavern owner. But there was nothing else, no way to pursue him.

"He told a few stories. I didn't find them funny, but he didn't seem to care. He laughed a lot at his own wit. Called me Fubb once or twice. I don't know what that means. He drank a lot, but he didn't seem to get drunk."

"How long was he here?"

"At least two hours before you."

"Anything else?"

"Nothing. He said he didn't know why I wasn't laughing, because his stories always had the room falling apart in Martanouk."

"He was from Martanouk?"

"No, I don't think so. But he's spent some time there, I'd wager."

And either he wasn't as savvy as I thought, or he wanted us to go to Martanouk. But why?

Abour was clearly dying. Pao had some healing skills, but he was shaking his head now. "We need to find him."

"We do." Suashi turned to the owner and commanded, "Send someone to fetch a healer. And stay here with our friend until we get back. For your sake, I hope he doesn't die."

"Please, I can't...I don't...this isn't my fault!" the owner whined.

"Maybe it is, and maybe it isn't. But you'll do as I say. Get a healer, and watch him!"

She turned and strode out the front entrance. Pao joined her. Without another word, she went left, he went right.

But they didn't find Yount.

An hour later, they returned to the tavern to find the owner and a small young woman dead next to the place on the floor where they'd left their friend.

Abour was gone. So was Balogh.

"Yount came back. He took him," said Pao, shaking his head.

Both observations were true; there could be no doubt. But why were they true?

Suashi grimaced.

Pao put a hand on her shoulder. "Let's check this rat's nest one more time. See if we can find that owner. And then, when we don't find him or Yount or anything, which I assume we won't, we go to Martanouk to play the next round."

Suashi knew Pao had the right of it but she also knew it would take the whole trip to Martanouk to wrap her head around why.

But she would be ready when they got there, and she'd better get some answers.

Chapter 34
"They'll lead us through if we ask them to."

Location: West side of the Scar, Arba Environ
Date: Dakaj 7, AY 998

Suashi and Paomaintanna road east toward the Scar.

And what will we find when we get there?

A massive, uncrossable, haunted pain in the ass.

I should have listened to my father and stayed home.

She shifted in her saddle and lifted her head. Pao was at least a quarter mile ahead of her now. She'd been lagging, not paying much attention to the particulars of the path, but he seemed sure of where he was going. He always seemed sure.

And why should I have listened to my father? Vincent has no more understanding of what to do than any of us. He builds ships he may never use because the need may come, but if it comes, it'll almost certainly come far too quickly for anyone to make use of them. Why exactly is he building them, then? To give his people something to do? Fishing and gathering seashells isn't enough?

Truly, if the end came, and it might — she had to admit it probably would — what would it matter if one had ships, even if they were lucky enough to board them and set sail? Where would they go? The Prementians had all but said they'd resist a mass migration, and certainly Velliok's indelicate naval orders had done little to change their minds.

And where else but Prement was free of Vo'ix influence? The Takers were everywhere on the OSM. It was a small miracle that they had never simply claimed Arba for their own. Instead, they used it, or used to use it, as a sort of meat locker. They hadn't come in years. Where had they gone? And why?

I have to find the Ashorne, and the Proving has to happen.

However it happens.

So my father builds his ships to go nowhere, and I ride my horse into nowhere.

To each their own.

She rode along the broken shale of this place and thought about her last conversation with the shipbuilder himself, the indomitable Vincent Bleuss.

"I will find him, Father."

"Yes, well, you've said as much before, Sua. But the question remains: How?"

She'd wanted to tell him, to let her father into her world, to let him know she trusted him and loved him and wanted them to be, always, on the same side, working for the same result. She wanted to, but she couldn't.

She said what she could. "Pao's visions will lead us, as before."

"You don't believe that," said Vincent, with the kind of paternal authority that both weakened and stiffened her resolve.

"I have to believe it," she answered firmly.

"It makes no sense, this vision," he huffed at her. "It never has."

She couldn't blame him; she herself had little faith in such things as visions anymore, and declared as much. "It's happened before."

"Once. But Pao is not Maria Xi. No one living is even sure if Maria Xi was Maria Xi."

"Some are sure."

"Yes, some are. Some don't need proof of anything to believe everything. Or to believe whatever parts of everything serve their immediate interests. But this is not simply a matter of faith. Arbana is a rare kind of hell, the kind the occupants of hell itself dread."

"I've been there before. Several times."

"I know, I know. But it's not a place a body should want to visit, not without a plan."

"And yet, that is where he is. Or where he'll be. And we have a plan, you know that."

"So you say, but—"

"Father, we've not only been there before, we've succeeded there before."

"Succeeded? You barely escaped with your lives. Pao's brother was not so fortunate. He was in Pashka, was he not? Pherriuskata is Arbana in a mask and a fine house. One and the same. That city consumed Bealaki. And without him, you are going in blind."

"Not blind. Pao remembers the way and the dangers. And Bealaki is not dead."

"You know this for a certainty?"

"As I told you, he left us to find…something he felt he was missing."

"And what was that? Enslavement? A role in the Mansdrelam Play?"

"He wouldn't say."

"He must have told his brother."

"I doubt it. In any case, Pao hasn't told and no, I've never asked. I'm not sure we needed to know, but I'm reasonably sure I know anyway." She eyeballed her father closely, trying to penetrate his complicated mind, but she could find nothing telling in his expression. "Why are you asking?"

"Because I'm not sure Pao isn't leading you back there just to find him."

"Oh, but he is. Partly. That's how I convinced him to go."

"You made that deal?"

"We did."

"You know about him and deals, yes?"

"He's my friend, so yes, I do. And I remember. But that was your deal with him, not mine. And I know what you believe about him. You've told me often enough."

"And you're going anyway?"

"Yes. Because if we find Bealaki, he'll help us protect the Ashorne."

"How?"

"He has...many friends."

"Friends to him that might or might not be enemies to you. You are aware of his...creative allegiances?"

"Yes."

"Then may I ask you to please be more specific?"

"I would prefer not to."

"Sua...you need to trust me. Especially in this."

She'd decided there was no harm in admitting something to her father that he already knew, as long as she didn't let him know she knew he knew. He might just get a little cocky and let something slip. "I have long suspected Bealaki was involved with the Spectrum," she said, almost whispering.

He raised his eyebrows in faux surprise. "The Spectrum? How could he...?"

"Bealaki is a magicker."

"That much even I suspected."

"Born of the Wilds, but with a color. More than a color."

"I see. So they sought him out. When?"

"When he was a boy. Please, don't ask me more, Father. I've given my word to keep this secret; it might be fatal to him if others — these allies or enemies you alluded to — were to find out."

"They won't find out from me."

No, not unless you decide it's politically expedient to tell them. "I know that, but there are things have been taken from you before, while you slept..." *By a magicker I hired to take things out of your head while you slept.*

"Yes. Yes, of course. Don't tell me; you're right. But let me ask you: How might Bealaki and his dubious friends locate the Ashorne?"

"They have information. They make it their business to know the comings and goings of the Tri. And they will have been watching for the Ashorne in any case."

"Why? They have no faith in the Four."

"No, but they do have a vested interest in survival, and they are almost as renowned for their thoroughness as they are for their secrecy."

"I've had dealings with them in the past," Vincent said, shaking his head.

"In Aethrelius."

"I told you that?"

"Yes. A long time ago."

"I think maybe I've told you too much, little one. Now you tell me something, please: Why can't we just send word to Pao's brother? Why must you go?"

"Only Pao has seen the Ashorne."

"Right, in this alleged vision, yes? But you said he came — or he'll be coming — through the Landing Point. Can't you trace him through those records? For a small bag of Arban fleck, any clerk —"

"We suspect he will not be processed upon entry."

"Someone's going to grab him?"

"Almost certainly."

"He'll likely be killed in that case."

"No, he won't. Or at least, he'll remain alive long enough to reach a town with a theater and a small underground wading pool."

"Pao's dream again. Wading pools and theaters. What play was he watching? *The Fall of the Kis?*" Vincent said, scowling with sarcasm. "Never mind. You say he saw the Ashorne's face?"

"He did."

"Then let him go alone."

"No. I must go with him. Too much depends on finding this man."

"What? What depends on it? The possibility that those old, vague teachings have some specific application in the here and now? That if every man, woman, and child in Arba doesn't figure out exactly how to Prove something to someone at some point immediately following the end of next year, we're all going to die? The whole thing is madness, and the fact that any of it is being taken seriously by the powers that be, this one included, is a testament to our need for serious ideological and practical change. Stay here and help me build a new world, Suashi!"

"The People's Vision denies me that option, Father, and though I have long since come to know I am not the Fourth, that does not relieve of my responsibility to the believers."

"Why not?"

"You know why not." There was a moment of tense silence. She turned to him. "In my place, you would go."

Vincent Bleuss put his hand on his daughter's arm. He took a deep breath and let it out, his head sinking toward his chest. "I know, Sua. I know," he said, looking up into her eyes. "Mad or no, you have a duty to perform, and one that may determine the doom or salvation of us all. Forgive a father for trying to protect his only child."

"There is nothing to forgive. As you would do what I must in my position, so I would do all I could to stop me in yours."

"It makes you wonder."

"What?"

"Your friend had a dream, and so you must leave. I have a daughter and must try to convince her to do otherwise. How much of our lives is really ours to decide? Or is it all decided for us?"

"There is still choice," she assured him. "We can always choose not to try, not to go, not to live."

"True enough, perhaps, for others. They can choose not to. Yet there is something of a Bleuss legacy, or so they tell me, and ours is but to honor it. Or die trying. Die choosing."

"You are still alive."

"As are you," he said as he opened his arms for an embrace.

She hesitated for only a moment as she stood looking at this complicated, strong, loving man who was her father, in name if not in blood.

"And I intend to stay that way, Vincent Bleuss," she said, surrendering to the hug. "I'll see you again."

"I know you will," he answered without a hint of patronization. Whatever else was true of him, she could not deny that he believed in her. That had never changed.

"Will you go to Graviss Glen first?" he asked as he pulled away and reassumed the role of commander.

"If we are to have any hope of success, we must."

"Have a care. That old woman's still strong in the Wildean ways, even if her people have forgotten them."

"I'm counting on it, Father."

They reached the Scar just before sundown.

The endless field of scattered shale on which they'd been riding gave way to a canyon that they could see was at least several miles across and perhaps five hundred feet deep, though it was difficult to tell in this light where the mist-covered bottom really was. A small grove of dying pine trees served as a weak wall between the shale plain and the canyon's edge. And there before them, the ancient narrow stairs that wound down into the Scar itself.

"We should camp here tonight. The horses are tired," Paomaintanna said as he reined in his rust red. They hadn't spoken in over six hours, and Suashi was momentarily startled to hear his voice, so deeply in her thoughts was she wrapped.

"The horses are fine," she said as she urged her mount around the grove and closer to the stairs.

"I'm tired."

"So am I, but if we don't head down now, we'll lose a day."

"Then we lose a day. We've been pressing since we crossed the Meadow. We need to rest. And we need to eat." Pao opened his pack and began to rummage through it. He pulled out a small skillet and a flint. "I've got some cured boar, some illu root, and half-a-dozen mushrooms left."

"I'm not hungry."

"Well, I am."

"Tired. Hungry. Why did I bring you along?" She smiled.

"I'm here to remind you what a human is," he answered. Without waiting for her consent, he dismounted and walked over to the trees. "These horses need water. Why is it so damn dry around here? It was never this dry." He looked around with a disgusted expression and then shrugged and took a swig of water.

She watched him but stayed on her horse. "Pao, we really do need to press on. I know he will be."

He started going through his pack again. "We'll have to sleep sometime, my friend, and so will Yount."

There was sense in what he was saying. They could press on, but the Scar was no place to get sloppy or to be less than oneself. Descending into it even a little impaired might mean never coming out of it. But she said, "How do you know he sleeps? Was he human? He was a little too quick for a human," she asked as she looked around for something with which to make a fire. There wasn't much. The dying pines were still alive, but their branches were hard as stone. "Will these burn?" she asked him as she pulled on a branch fruitlessly.

"No," he said, "but these will." He'd found a few tumbleweeds lodged into the rocks at the cliff's edge.

She made a small fire, and he prepared the light meal.

Going down into the Scar was the only way they could make it into Arbana without being detected or questioned, she knew that. But they had very little water left, and the risks, which they hadn't spoken about at all, were the stuff of legend. Souls taken. Pasts erased. Loved ones with no memory of those who'd dared to enter the Scar.

She decided to eschew any discussion about those legends—she'd had her fill of those—and return to the issue at hand: their pursuit of Yount.

"Is he human, do you think?" she asked again.

"Everything sleeps. Sleeping is good. Don't worry: whatever he is, we'll catch him. We know where he's going, right?"

"Maybe. I don't know. What if something changed? What if they moved him?"

"Who's 'him'? Yount or the Ashorne? We can't worry about the Ashorne right now. But we'll catch Yount, Sua. For now, let's eat, let's sleep. The rest is for tomorrow."

They sat in silence for a bit. The wind was cold, so they huddled together. It was not new for them. "We've lost so much time as it is, with that stupid ruse and those fools in the Meadows," she whispered

"They're not fools. They're sentries, and they're doing what they're supposed to be doing."

"They're supposed to keep strangers out."

"And keep Wildean strays from dying on this" — he waved dismissively at the shale plain — "or from falling into this" — he pointed a disgusted finger at the Scar — "or from being rounded up and dragged to Yanz."

"Do we look like strays?"

"I think the way we look, even the strays would deny any claim to us."

She laughed. He was right. They'd ridden two straight days out of Ontonu, through the Pajisti, over the shale...and they were spent. She didn't want to let it go, though, not when she still felt the burn from the cut on her ear. Yount had taken the tip off, and she hadn't been able to completely staunch the bleeding days later. The scab wouldn't take.

She pictured Abour's writhing body on the floor of that filthy tavern amid the corpses of the blackboots. They might have sent him back to the Wilds, to his grandfather, but Yount had decided to take him for whatever reason. She considered that somehow fortunate; it probably meant Abour was still alive, or would be until Yount figured out he knew next to nothing about her mission. Or maybe he did know something.

In either case, she owed it to Hustel to find him. She had no interest in someday relaying the details of his grandson's death to her old friend. The thought of having to do so filled her with some new mix of rage and sorrow.

Yount was a liar and a spy; she'd seen it, but she hadn't been quick enough, she hadn't reacted to him. It ate at her. She knew why things had happened that way, or thought she knew — Yount had a color and had lulled them with some kind of spell. Or, more likely, he had something borrowed, something perhaps from the old Mer Ponx bastards — but still she blamed herself for her failure to anticipate the attack. He'd been taunting them, spilling details...he expected to kill them all, as if he'd killed like that for a lifetime. Maybe he had.

She was going to make damn sure that lifetime came to an end.

"The horses will be fine," she assured Pao. "There aren't any wolves out here, and they'll get plenty of rest now that their leg of the journey is almost over."

"But it isn't over. Sua, we have to go south. Or north. We can't cross here."

Here it comes. The argument we've been avoiding for days.

"The bridge would be a mistake. Someone will recognize me. There may be more Younts in the towns up there," she said.

"Then we buy a skiff and take the horses around the Maw. We'll need them in Arbana."

"Too risky and too time consuming."

"Risky? You want to go down there and through that" — he pointed east for emphasis — "now, and with the sun setting, and no horses to carry this stuff, and the Maw would be too risky?"

"The goods were a decoy; you know that."

He snorted. "The goods were potential payment in case we needed it. And you know we'll need it."

"Maybe. There are other ways to get along."

"In the Wilds, maybe. I think you've forgotten what things are like in Arbana. Or you're ignoring what common sense should be telling you."

"I haven't forgotten," she said, turning away from him to stare into the Scar's thick mists. "And I don't understand why, if you felt this way about crossing, you led us directly east."

"It looked to me like there was going to be some weather. The Half Road was our best bet for avoiding landslides. Maybe our only bet." He smiled at her.

"And?"

"And I wanted to give you time. You looked like you needed it."

I can't argue with that. Time is definitely something I need: time to think, time to plan, time to sleep and maybe fuck and talk myself out of whatever we think we're doing out here. We haven't even gotten into Arbana, and already one of us has been murdered or worse and someone — maybe many someones by now — probably knows where we are, what we're up to, and why. Time is something I need, but no amount could make a difference now. Now we need to move and stay ahead of whatever's at our backs.

Pao laughed as if he knew what she was thinking. "I know, I know. Dumb idea, wasting time like that. Anyway, here we are, and this at least is true: I cannot find the way through in the dark. No one can."

"We don't have to."

"Suashi..."

"They'll lead us through if we ask them to."

"Or they will lead us to our deaths."

"Or that."

"It's not worth the risk."

"It is if we want to catch up to Yount."

"We don't even know if he knows anything yet or what he's done with Abour. And we have no idea where he'll be."

"He's a drinker. He'll be in a tavern, eventually."

"With a hostage?"

"Maybe. I don't know. What's to stop him from roping and gagging Abour in some woods while he drinks?"

Pao stretched down slowly and grabbed his ankles, then stood up and lifted his hands high, leaning back with his eyes closed. He took a deep breath, and another, and said, "He's not just a drinker, you know. He's something else."

She joined him in the arts. Her body was aching, and some movements were exactly what she needed. And she could see he'd offered to follow her lead in this instance. *He trusts me still. I'll probably never know why.* "Of course he's something else. But he's also a drinker, and he's an arrogant piece of shit. No matter what he is, we can handle him. And he won't expect us to be on him."

"He'll be a hard one to find no matter."

"Well, if we don't find him, we'll never know what he knows or what he is. And Abour will die."

He knows what we have to do, and he's going to do it, but he's scared. I don't blame him. I still have the occasional nightmare about the last time, and that was four years ago.

"If we go down there tonight, *we'll* die. Then who will save Abour?" he asked, pretending once more to be annoyed.

"We've gone through it before, right?" She was arguing with him, but her tone was growing milder. It was her way of signaling that she was willing to concede the argument, and he knew that. For her part, she was just very tired and stressed.

"Yes, we've gone through it, but we had daylight and a map. And luck, lots of luck. And they still almost got us."

"I remember. Let's have a rest and think about this."

Pao paused for a moment. He started walking around and then made his way to the top of the stairs and knelt down in the dirt.

"They came this way. Two men. One of them was either Abour or someone who stole his shoes."

"They went into the Scar?" Suashi said.

"It would seem so."

She smiled to herself. Pao had known exactly which way to go all along.

He came back to her side and plopped down. They sat in silence for a few minutes. He took out his skin of wildwater and offered it to her.

"Thank you," she said, taking a deep, long pull.

"So why did our Mr. Yount decide to go through the Scar? There are no inns down there, no wineries."

"There's no saying he made it through."

But he probably did, the bastard. He had something, something that made him confident enough to take the risk.

"You think he's still in there?" she asked.

"Maybe. No. I don't know."

"Maybe his secrets — and his hostage — die with him."

"Maybe he flew over."

"I doubt it. He hasn't got a full color; he'd have magicked us completely in Ontonu."

"Maybe all he can do is fly." His brother notwithstanding, Pao had never trusted magickers, specifically with regards to what they could and couldn't do.

"You're not serious. How many are able to do that, and how many of them are courageous or cunning enough to try?"

"Probably not too many. But, you know, there are no Visshilla in the Scar."

"There are Visshilla everywhere."

She passed him the bottle, got up, and bent over to stretch her back a bit.

"Okay, he didn't fly," admitted Pao with a smile. "Then we have to assume he went in because he knew he could get through."

"How could he know that?"

"I don't know. Maybe they helped him. Maybe he's got friends down there."

"I doubt it," she said, passing the bottle back to him.

"Why?"

"He doesn't seem at all like their type."

"They have a type?"

"They're dead, so they prefer the dead."

"They're not dead," he said, though he clearly did not believe what he was saying.

"You've seen them?"

"I saw something when we went through. So did you."

"What did you see?" she asked, knowing full well what he'd seen. He'd described it to her at least three dozen times since then. It was his go-to story when he was very drunk.

"It was...almost a man. A gray shape, a thing, there but not entirely there."

"You saw a ghost?"

"I saw something."

They slept. Mostly slept.

In the morning, they tried and failed to urge the horses down the narrow stairs, so they removed what supplies they could, sent the horses back on their way west, and descended into the Scar.

It took them the better part of a very difficult day to descend and to cross it, and by the time they ascended on the other side, both suns were down.

"We're lucky Branaedes is glittering so generously tonight," Pao said as they made their way up the eastern stairs.

"Yes. Lucky," she answered, huffing a bit from the climb. "Still lucky."

She thought about pressing on into the night, but it was too much to attempt after the scramble they'd endured down below. It was time to rest. When they reached the top, they made a small fire, ate a little something, and collapsed on their bedrolls.

As she began to pass out, she heard Pao whisper: "So are we gonna talk about all that?"

She didn't answer. She fell asleep in the hopes that in her dreams she'd be able to steer clear of "all that."

She was wrong. Her dreams offered no respite; she revisited the difficulties they'd endured below. Getting separated. Getting lost, again and again. Almost drowning in a place that held little or no water. Skeletons that seemed to sing and laugh while not moving in any way. A calm discussion with something claiming to be her mother, who she did not remember at all.

"You have a sister. I wonder, will you find her?"

"I have no sister."

"Yes, of course, but will you find her?"

"You are not my mother."

"I am not your mother."

"You are my mother."

"And you are mine."

"And I am yours."

And there was something else, something good, something that had helped them, led them, and from what she could tell, advocated for them in the presence of the lonely, mischievous entities that occupied the Scar.

Liolesca.

Her name was Liolesca. They would not have survived the Scar without her.

An angel?

Maybe so. And while Suashi dreamt, she smiled in her sleep,

knowing that her angel had always been close and always would be.

When she woke, she wept.

There were no angels in Arba, and there never would be.

Chapter 35
"There is nothing here that can kill us.
Except this tavern's fish."

Place: Lake Iale and the island of Pedry, Arba Environ
Date: Dakaj 10, AY 998

The trip to Pedry from the Sapphire Forest's shore was brief and uninteresting.

The winds cooperated, the threat of a wild Dakaj lake storm — despite the incessant mumblings of their attendant sailors — did not materialize, and no one killed anyone.

Conversation between Sh'arnau and Theodore was mostly cursory and guarded. Best to keep Grewea and his myriad spies guessing. And if the crew of their hired schooner wondered at all about the oddly matched passengers, they kept it to themselves.

Sh'arnau had marched them down along the shore, away from the Sapphire Forest and west to the ancient town of Thielbackler — famed as the birthplace of the composer Dubaku, whose music Theodore openly stated, several times, he despised. In Thielbackler, they'd been lucky enough to find a boat that was headed to Pedry on some business or other. Sh'arnau had paid the captain enough for him to eschew taking on any other passengers. It was best for all concerned, the assassin had stated plainly.

The captain agreed without hesitation — or, more accurately, with just enough hesitation to indicate his levels of both terror and assent.

The acquisition of the appropriate dress and mask for Theodore proved far more challenging than the hiring of the boat; in the end, Sh'arnau located a tailor, who seemed almost as old as the town, to rework an existing gown. The mask the Thicknomite simply stole from the unguarded collection of some absent merchant. He'd enjoyed that part; it'd been a long time since his skills had been applied to anything but a grisly outcome, the abduction of the scholar being the lone exception.

Theodore for his part played the role of the chubby Pherriuskatan lady quite well, dipping and murmuring when appropriate. He clearly hadn't been lying about his occasional incognito sojourns. He clucked and sighed and cooed like a true bride of Pashka would and should; whether or not the crew bought it or simply did their best to mind their own business out of fear of Sh'arnau, the Thicknomite couldn't say.

It didn't matter. They got where they were going.

Unfortunately, something else got there too — ahead of them, which was, when all was said and done, lethally confounding. Sh'arnau

vaguely sensed whatever it was but couldn't place its source, so he chose
to proceed, doing so without informing Theodore of the danger, partly
because he did not yet trust him but also because he simply wasn't
interested in hearing the requisite, incessant speculation that would spring
from Sh'arnau's giving voice to the threat.

To Sh'arnau, Pedry appeared not to have changed in the many years since
he'd last seen it. It was still a big island covered in rocks, stumpy trees,
weathered shanties, and seagull shit. Along the road from the dock were
many thin people in weathered clothing, shuffling about from here to there
with no seeming need to do anything or be anywhere. Animals that didn't
seem capable of providing more than an ounce of milk or a mouthful of
meat wandered around also, attended on occasion by a shoeless child or
two. A few old people sat in old chairs in front of old houses that looked
like they would fall if a harsh word were whispered in their direction. The
island on the whole was inhabited by the mumbling denizens of
absentmindedness, sloth, and decay. Theodore seemed to disapprove.

They made their way down what passed as the main
thoroughfare. Sh'arnau noticed some odd looks thrown his way. The fear
he was used to, but here was something a bit different: whispers, knowing
nods, and shaking heads.

There was no way they could have known him; such common folk
had no idea who he was, or if they did, none would expect that the Bane of
the Malliorelum would still be alive today. No, it wasn't him they feared,
not specifically: it was his appearance.

It was his race.

Why would that be?

Their hired schooner was anchored — slightly offshore, no doubt
out of deference to an unspoken sailor's tradition when visiting Pedry —
and awaiting their return. Theodore and Sh'arnau wandered through this
impoverished setting, intent on finding lodging but very much aware of
how odd they must look to these ghostly inhabitants. It had surely been
many years since the last conference of any kind on this island, Theodore
commented, and for good reason: the place was simply not equipped to
host an event attended by real people with real needs and appetites.

"Truth to tell, the last time I was here, it was an outright disaster.
Half the visiting dignitaries, most of whom were not of high birth themselves, wound up leaving early because there wasn't enough to eat. And
there was a storm. It was all quite insufferable. I'll never forget that night,
Four forgive me."

"Why would anyone hold a conference here?"

"Hearts were in the right place. The idea was to renew interest in
the island in the hopes of drawing commerce here. Of course, it was an

unqualified disaster. You see the result about you."

Sh'arnau thought it best to find the inn, ask some questions, eat, and leave. They'd figure out how to find this alleged Timesinger right quick: Where would such a person hide on such a barren island, after all?

Theodore asked questions here and there, but the responses were generally vague or even unintelligible. As near as he could tell, no one had seen or heard of this Charlton person.

The town itself, situated at least fifty feet above lake level, was a sullen place with the unfortunate name of Brownhold — pronounced without the ending "d" by the locals — and it hadn't much in the way of…anything. A tiny church that looked to no longer be in use. A fisherman's supply hut or two. A municipal structure made of brick and what appeared to be shells. And on the town square, such as it was, a small shop attached to a tavern very much in need of some maintenance.

They took a table outside the tavern and ordered fish and beer.

Sh'arnau glanced around the square. There were stone ruins here and there, and a few rows of once fine, now abandoned and dilapidated houses up along the cliffs above the town that suggested Pedry had enjoyed better days. The ruined old fort, the name of which neither of them could determine — the locals just called it "the fort" — hovered on the highest peak.

Considering that Pedry was at least as large and well-situated an island as thriving, rich lake kingdoms like Mariendo, Little Britain, and Nintuktu, Sh'arnau found himself wondering what had happened here to bring this place so low and why the attempt to revive it had failed.

He further wondered what if any role he'd played in Pedry's downfall. He'd forgotten too much and played roles in so many downfalls. "This place is a mess," he said.

"Absolutely. Never recovered," said Theodore. "Where's our fish?"

"Recovered from what?"

Theodore, staring impatiently at the door of the tavern, glanced at him with annoyance. "From the Epidemic, of course. Five hundred years ago. It started here. How do you not know this?"

"The Festofor Epidemic."

"Yes."

"That was here."

"Yes, of course it was here. Where else?"

"Evacuated?"

"Perished, mostly. Those that did evacuate brought that horrific disease to every corner of the lake. Wiped out half of Tritto, killed thousands on Fan Pell, Fan ni Dok, in Quintish, pretty much all the western islands as well. Mariendo and Staidop were hit particularly hard.

Never reached Pherriuskata — there were more than a few blockades along the way — but it did go as far south as the Wilds and even Bno Suj, though I don't think the Slau were as vulnerable."

"Thicknomites were immune."

"Yes," said Theodore. "That's why so many were enlisted in the cleansing and containing effort all over the kingdoms."

"'Enlisted' seems a kind word for what was done."

"So it is," the scholar acknowledged with a small sigh.

"My people were put to some purpose here, weren't they?"

"Yes. But if you've no memory of it, what made you assume so, if I may ask?"

"The people. The way they're looking at me."

"Of course. Yes, your people were instrumental in cleansing many islands, many towns."

"We killed for you."

"Not for me, surely."

"Your government."

"Well, perhaps my ancestors' government. But why are you surprised? Your people did work like that for many governments over many years, did they not? They were the go-to muscle until the Brull made themselves available and the Crabs were…created."

Sh'arnau did not answer.

"In any case, after the disease was finally contained, it took about three hundred years, give or take, for even a few starving fishermen to risk settling on Pedry's poor shores again. The navy and the Juks Xi Ren did their best to discourage it, but they had no interest in actively evicting those who chose to take the risk. Once or twice there were small blockades or sea battles — results of overzealous imaginations, no doubt — but over the years it became clear the Epidemic was a resident of old history."

"A resident that wrecked an island," said Sh'arnau flatly.

"More than that. It redirected the course of history and delayed the formation of the Pebbuskan Alliance for two hundred years. There are those who believe the Gri Na Leus would have been defeated much sooner had there been less of a — shall we say — 'culturally and politically isolationist mentality' here on the lake at that time. A nation of islands combining its might with those who would later form the Quadrate — formidable. Alas, it was not to be. And our fish is…ah. There." He smiled with relief.

An old woman carrying two plates, followed by a somewhat dim-witted–looking young man carrying two pints of ale, approached. She put the plates down in front of them, mumbling to herself in what seemed the typical Pedrian inaudible fashion, and then stepped aside while the young man awkwardly placed the ale on the table, spilling just a bit onto Sh'arnau's fish. The old woman suddenly and viciously slapped her helper across the back of the head and then smiled at the patrons with the few teeth she had. "Yer pardon, please. Ignorant, him." Then she shoved the young man back toward the door, and they were gone.

"This fish is fresh," Theodore said, diving in. "Smells wonderful."

Sh'arnau wasn't so sure, and his sense of smell rarely lied, but he was hungry, so he ate.

They rested a while, and then Theodore set about asking more questions of the locals. Sh'arnau left him to that while he scoured the surroundings for any clues that might lead to the whereabouts or doings of the person they sought. Was there a hut, a room somewhere with a collection of old books, a hidden cave reputed to be occupied by a crazy old hermit?

Pedry was a shunned island, but a very large one. Plenty of excellent hiding places for people who didn't want to be found. Caves, yes. Thick groves of twisted pine. Nests of haphazardly stacked driftwood. There were entire abandoned towns scattered all around its coast and up in its grim, bare hills. If the Timesinger had chosen to hide in one of those, the search could take months, even years. Indeed, a man who knew how to fish and who didn't mind the taste of seagull, a man who could endure countless nights of isolation with nothing but the winds to keep him company—such a man, if healthy, could remain hidden on Pedry for decades.

And if magick were somehow involved...who could say?

The Timesingers were not practitioners of magick, but they had never taken an active role in its purging either. Had the powers-that-be in that centuries-old conflict suspected anything but an ineffective and neutral position from them on that score, they would have long ago been eliminated, Sh'arnau knew. The brutality of the fight over magick had been, even by Arban standards, insanely vicious. Given his own very tentative yet determinative connection to it, he had chosen to steer clear of it whenever possible.

Still, there was something about the current situation that bespoke of magick. Grewea had no compunction about avoiding its use; magick was just a useful tool to him, not a watchword. No doubt he'd played a crucial part in many of the skirmishes and debates that had surrounded the issue over the centuries, but Sh'arnau had never known Grewea to be an aficionado. He had no color of his own, nor did he often associate with any who did. His dealings with the Mer Ponx and the Broken Mind were strategic, not habitual, titles and appearances be damned. And he certainly never went anywhere near the Jamoi, although whatever reasons he had for that choice he never disclosed to or in the presence of his dependable Thicknomite killer.

Perhaps it was because magick was involved that Grewea had

pushed Sh'arnau toward Pedry. Not as a test, per se, but rather as an exercise in being doomed whether one did or didn't. If Sh'arnau failed and died, Grewea would send someone else. If he succeeded and Grewea withdrew his hold, truly allowing Sh'arnau to be free, the result would be the same.

But what result was Grewea aiming for? The Sword of Endings was a myth—an Aethrelean myth, no less. It was, by all accounts, pure nonsense.

Sh'arnau sniffed and examined trails both beaten and untrammeled. He looked for smoke on the horizon that might give away an old man's location; he twitched his ears, listening for anything irregular; he breathed in all the scents, trying to detect something useful amid the lake air and the animal dung and meagre cook fires.

Nothing.

They searched all day and into the night. Sh'arnau, when he returned from following dead ends and climbing down onto vacant, rocky beaches, watched Theodore visit every location in Brownhold at least two or three times. Doors were slammed in his face repeatedly, and one woman threw a handful of goat shit at him for good measure. His face was tight with frustration and indignation, and there was a bit of goat shit stuck in his hair, yet he persisted, and this impressed Sh'arnau. He hadn't expected persistence in a fat, spoiled scholar.

Theodore had belied his expectations several times. Perhaps Fat Teddy was made of sterner stuff than his reputation indicated.

They collected themselves back at the tavern. Seated at the table where they'd survived lunch, Theodore put his feet up on a very suspect and frail stool and tried to rub them.

"No one knows anything about this Charlton," he said with a flustered huff. "Grewea was playing games with you."

"Doubtful. He sent us here for a reason."

"Maybe to die."

"There is nothing here that can kill us. Except this tavern's fish."

"It was terrible, wasn't it?"

They sipped bad beer and decided to stay the night. Theodore hired a boy to take a message to their schooner.

"What did your note say?" Sh'arnau asked.

"I told them to wait and that we'd be back before Ponesta falls tomorrow."

"We're giving up that easily?"

"Unless you want to wander the island looking for this man no one seems to have ever seen or heard of, yes," said Theodore as he flagged down the hostess and ordered another two mugs.

"I do not. But if I don't find him, and if I don't find this Sword, it won't go well for either of us. A lifetime on Pedry will seem kind compared to what will happen."

"Point taken. What do you suggest?"

"Have you any magick?" Sh'arnau asked, staring pointedly at his companion.

"Excuse me?"

"Magick. We're in desperate need of some."

"You do realize you're talking to the Head of Hunberg University, a sworn ally of the Mer Ponx, and a signatory of the Latter Medlite Declaration?"

"I do."

"Then your question offends me, sir." Theodore's earlier indignation returned in full force and then some.

"And?"

"And of course I have access to magick, but not the kind that would help in this situation. Mine is more protective."

"Meaning what?"

"Meaning the Scourge Ravagers protect me from mortal danger."

"Meaning all this time, you knew I wasn't going to kill you?"

"No. I knew that if you tried, you'd have your hands full."

"I did try."

"Apparently not."

Sh'arnau stared at the scholar and realized he was staring at something of a human onion. He laughed aloud.

Theodore, perhaps out of exhaustion or befuddlement or both, joined him. They had a good long laugh, much to the dismay of whoever was in earshot. Seeing the looks on the faces around them, Theodore put on a dumb face and mumbled, "I donna ta know no Chawton but I am fish!"

This sent them both into a frenzy of laughter that almost had Sh'arnau in tears. Several locals ran away in tears as well, and there were children screaming.

After a few minutes, they settled back down. "Where did everyone go?" deadpanned Sh'arnau.

"Probably to the symphony. But let's now get back to our most immediate and pressing problem," said Theodore, wiping his eyes with his handkerchief. "We need to find Charlton. We've searched and we've asked. What else is there left to do?"

"I'm not sure."

"You're the hunter."

"I am. But there are no trails."

"Then we must stay on the island and search. For as long as we have to."

"We may develop habits."

"Mumbling?"

"Stumbling?"

"Throwing goat shit at strangers?"

"Is that a sport? I want to be the champion."

"Done."

They laughed again, but weariness and frustration began to take them both.

Sh'arnau sighed. He knew Theodore was right: staying till they had answers was the practical thing to do. But did they have months or years to search the groves, caves, and dead enclaves for this man? Would Grewea have sent him on such an insanely tedious and obtuse mission? It didn't seem to fit somehow.

They sat awhile, sipping more beer, each brooding in his own particular way. Theodore mumbled to himself here and again. Sh'arnau paid him no mind. His senses were telling him that the longer they stayed on Pedry, the greater were the chances they'd never leave it.

"I think I understand," Theodore said.

"Understand what?"

"Grewea wanted you to come here and search for something he knew you'd never find."

"Why would he do that?"

"He didn't tell you to find Charlton. He told you to find the Sword of Endings."

"But I have to find the Timesinger to do that."

"Not necessarily." Theodore stood up and went into the town square where he could look down at the docks. Sh'arnau followed him, curious to know what he was on to. "I have a suspicion that Timesinger Charlton, whoever he is, will be coming to us."

The schooner was gone. Theodore was gone. The fat professor had fooled him and escaped.

And it wouldn't be long until someone killed him, the fat fool, his misplaced faith in Ravager protection be damned.

Sh'arnau wasn't too concerned. He was somewhat annoyed that he'd let the man get away, but he was more irritated that they hadn't found this Charlton. But he was here or would be, Sh'arnau was now quite certain. The attack was proof of that. Someone wanted to prevent their meeting.

Sitting high up on a wall of the old fort at the midlight, he could see most of the town and the docks. There was no sign of the aggressors;

he'd fought them to a standstill, but it had taken almost everything he had.

He looked down at his legs. They were healing, but much more slowly than they ever had. Perhaps whatever protection his service to Grewea had afforded him all these years was beginning to ebb away. Perhaps death was finally within his grasp. His legs and his left side had been torn wide open in the battle. He could barely lift his left arm, and something was wrong with his eyesight. Why wasn't he healing properly? Had Grewea withdrawn his spells already, only to see him to die here, his mission incomplete?

No, that wasn't it. The magick might have weakened, but it was still present. This had happened before, at least twice, though each time had been several centuries ago. He couldn't remember the exact circumstances. His memory was his worst quality, and quasi-immortality hadn't been accompanied by a concurrently effective capacity for recall. He had, however, perfected the art of forgetting and for living in the present. The ancient religions, he knew, held that ability in high esteem, and yet he'd found no peace through it. He forgot because it was madness to try to remember.

And he would soon forget Theodore. Good riddance.

He leaned against the wall and coughed twice, and then he listened for any sounds the nearly silent attackers might make.

Theodore had fled during the first wave, probably to the boat. He was almost certainly dead. He would have died if he hadn't fled, so vicious and sudden had the attack upon them been.

Sh'arnau found that a little sad. The man was a fool, but a knowledgeable one with a strong mind for many subjects and, more importantly, a sense of humor. He had come to enjoy their discussions. It occurred to him that Theodore had become something like a friend. Hadn't he said as much?

Sh'arnau chuckled at that thought. Friendship was something for children and women and blind holy men, not for assassins whose very souls were held by sinister wizards bent on burning down an entire race. Not for him.

And that was all done in any case. It was time to do what Grewea had asked him to do in the second letter, the one he hadn't discussed with Theodore.

Sh'arnau needed to find Frulla and this Ashorne before the Wildean girl did, and he needed to kill them both. Or not. Maybe he'd make friends with them too, he thought as he rubbed his aching legs. Why stop at one friend when you could have three? He'd need friends if he were going to keep defying Grewea. Maybe Theodore, if he were by some miracle alive and willing, would agree to go lecture Grewea to death.

Right now, Sh'arnau needed to leave this place. To do that, he needed another boat. A boat...and someone to pilot it. It wouldn't be too difficult to find both, he guessed: during the battle, most of the island's people had fled from the town and were now hiding among the docks and the beaches that lined the coves. They had no idea what they were hiding from; if they had, they would have been looking for boats themselves...or swimming out into the lake to take their chances with the fangwhales and grippers.

What were they hiding from? He wasn't sure himself what had attacked him. The creatures were strong, no doubt, and good hunters. Hard to kill. He'd never seen their like before.

How the creatures had tracked them here to this place, Sh'arnau had no idea. The only explanation he could come up with was that Theodore had somehow informed someone of their arrival, someone who'd taken a fatal message back to his people in Xatumka. But that made no sense...unless one considered how Theodore might have escaped creatures that had practically overwhelmed Sh'arnau. The odds against that were staggering...unless the Ravagers had materialized.

He'd seen no evidence of that.

Theodore was up to something.

So they catch him and kill him, and then they'd kill every living thing on this island for having had the gall to...what, share some fruit with him? No. They had better reasons for that. They were looking for something, not just Theodore but something else.

They were looking for Sh'arnau.

But why? And then, why not capture him instead of attacking? Did they know he could not die?

Perhaps they knew what he was after and were hoping he would lead them right to their prize. He did not understand their motives, but he knew there was likely little else on this island that would interest them.

He walked to another cliff wall, this one facing north at the edge of the lake. He peered down and then took a long look left and another right. The drop to the small, rocky beach was at least a hundred feet. He wasn't sure he could climb that given his condition, and besides, he saw no sign of any boats.

What he did see alarmed him, if only for a moment.

More of the creatures were putting in to shore down below, gliding toward the base of the cliff in a long, thin black craft. He looked out into the night but could see no ship. There must be one out there, though, and it had delivered them to this side of the island. Why?

He looked down and saw dozens of the creatures beginning to scale the cliffs.

"Are you mad? Don't let them see you!"

He whirled to see Theodore standing there. "You're still here."

"Yes, of course I'm still here. I left you to get some help. I couldn't exactly carry you, could I? I couldn't find anyone; they must've run to the sea keeps by the beach, as if that will do them any good. Anyway, you seem all right...can you walk?"

"I can."

"How about 'run'?"

"If I must."

"I think you must. As crazed and lethal as you are, I doubt you could beat so many of them, especially in your state."

"Don't doubt it. Know it. I cannot," said Sh'arnau. "What happened to your protection?"

"Apparently, it was revoked. Possibly an effect of my having been declared dead. Possibly something more sinister."

Sh'arnau regarded Theodore with renewed respect. The spirits were no longer guarding him, and he knew it, and still he'd come back to help his abductor.

Theodore chided him, "Stop staring. Come on then, I've got two horses just down the way."

"I cannot ride. Horses detest me."

"No, they detest your smell. I took care of that with a little of this," Theodore said, flashing him a small empty bowl.

"What was in that?" asked Sh'arnau, although his olfactory sense already knew the answer.

"Goat shit. Smeared in on the horses' noses."

"They let you do that?"

"Okay, I had the stable boy do it. For a few coins."

"Smart."

"Thank you."

They shuffled quickly down the winding path to a thicket and a small, dark row of huts. Sh'arnau could hear the nervous breathing of the horses. "They're not happy," he said.

"I think they know those things are coming."

"Knowing won't help them. Or us."

"Quit complaining. Mount the horse!"

"Our boat is gone."

"No, it's not. Get on the damn horse."

They mounted the horses and rode down toward Brownhold as quickly as the steep, broken path would allow. Sh'arnau glanced behind him, but with his usually keen eyesight so hampered, he saw nothing but midlight shadows.

"I can't see," he called to Theodore, but there was no response. The sounds of the wind and the hooves drowned out all others.

They were coming, he knew.
They were not finished with him.
With either of them.

Chapter 36
"He made a small pronouncement."

Place: Narth Downs, Mak, and points south of them, kingdom of Xatumka,
Arba Environ
Date: Angem 1, AY 999

"Listen up."

The sergeant was chewing an apple, spitting chunks of it out as he spoke. A polished maple cudgel hung from his belt; it hadn't any signs of purpose or usage. A small crowd, some on foot, some in small wagons and hay carts, sat silently, listening up.

"We'll be making our way down the East Road to Mak, then south along the river to Quintish. There's been a lot of trouble along there lately, and we'll be wanting to avoid that, so keep your heads down and your mouths shut."

Xian stood next to a small passenger wagon in which were two men who seemed to be merchants, an elderly woman with a Miranquellan sash and a young male attendant, and a man who was apparently a Tri prisoner escort. The escort, a portly, nervous official of some kind named Mr. Geminstra, was a man accustomed to neither travelling nor escorting.

They were gathered on the edge of Narth Downs. The day was overcast with a slight chill, and the soldiers with whom they'd be travelling looked underpaid and underwashed.

Their sergeant stood at the end of the wagon, his eyes mere slits — probably owing to drink, Xian thought — and one hand clamped on its edge as if he meant to somehow shove it and its passengers off the bridge and into the Camedua River. The other hand held what was left of the mangled apple.

"The whole trip should take about nine days if we make good time. Which means it'll take at least two weeks," he said, regarding the apple and then chucking it into the river. At least one horse glanced at him with something like disdain. "We'll reprovision in Mak, but we won't lodge there. I'd like to get this business over and done with. Maelor's Country is a real shit hole, especially these days. Oh, and happy new year. Four's blessings."

The sergeant grinned a little, having offered those last phrases somewhat less than sincerely, and pulled his handsome cudgel off his belt. He twirled it once or twice to show off his obvious prowess, but his audience seemed unmoved.

"Sir," asked the woman with the Miranquellan sash, "are we in any danger from the Northerners?"

The sergeant looked at her with his eyes half closed, shrugged, and walked away.

"Can I take that as a yes?" she called after him, turning to her attendant with a smirk that didn't quite mask her fear and indignation.

Xian said nothing. The Northerners were farmers trying to fight for their rights against the Triumvirate. They'd no reason to attack a few travelers heading south to Lake Iale, even those with a mandatory Tri escort. It was an exaggeration on the part of the sergeant to say that the current conflict ran so far east to Maelor's Country and the Camedua; in truth, most of the fighting had been happening in Eshe, the central part of Xatumka.

The party was likely in no real danger at all. Still, Xian had to admit to having little understanding of the immediate threat the Northerners posed. If he'd had to guess, he'd say: not much of one. If history was in any way instructive, he expected they would be put down. Their crops and home and families would be burned, and the price of wheat, corn, and barley would triple by the harvest time. Again. Thousands would starve, the Tri would go on, and in a decade or two, there'd be another rebellion that would end similarly.

If they had another decade or two, he reminded himself.

They did not.

The current rebellion was, in any case, not so rare a development. Thousands had been starving in Arba for centuries for one reason or another. It was a given that those in charge in Hunberg and Motatinfo and Pashka had never been among them, due in part to their well-honed prowess at eliminating rebellions and neutralizing whatever pesky effects they brought to bear.

Xian climbed into the wagon and took a seat across from Mr. Geminstra. The man looked at him for a moment, plainly puzzling over him—perhaps even recognizing him, although that seemed unlikely--and almost looked about to say something but then thought better of it and looked away.

Back behind the wagon, about twenty yards off, there was a covered cart hanging off the back of a team of twin mules. Iron bars were visible through the tattered cloth.

Xian turned to a soldier who was loading a few crates of foodstuffs and wine onto the already crowded wagon and asked, "Do we also have the pleasure of escorting a prisoner today?"

The soldier didn't stop what he was doing but grunted back his answer: "Some lake lizard. Big shit captain, or so they say. Heard he killed his whole crew."

That was almost certainly a fabrication; Challowians were fiercely loyal to one another and rarely if ever fought among themselves, even when it cost them much not to, as it had several times in history.

"He's going to Pashka?" Xian asked.

"They're throwing him down Bi way, if there's any justice in the world," barked the soldier as he heaved his last crate up. "If I were you, I'd leave it be, old man. Fucking lizards should all of them be burned up anyway," he said bitterly as he strode away.

Xian ignored the hateful remark—in the Tri, prejudice was as omnipresent as air—but was, in spite of himself, fascinated by the situation. He'd never before heard of a Juks Xi Ren being sent to Bi Prison for any reason, but this story of mass murder? Nonsense. Yet somewhere behind the nonsense might be an element of truth. A crew had apparently died, and the captain was being blamed. He resolved to generate a moment during this journey when he might talk to the prisoner.

No time like the present.

He stepped down around the barrels and off the wagon. Approaching the sergeant slowly and agedly so as not to appear as threatening as he was convinced he could still be in a pinch, he asked, "Sir, if you are transporting a Juks Xi Ren, may I inquire: Have you assigned someone to water him?"

The sergeant turned to him lazily and gave him a condescending, almost hostile glare. "Get back on that wagon unless you prefer to walk, old man," he growled.

"Because you know, if you do not water him hourly, he will without doubt die before he reaches wherever it is you're taking him."

The hostile glare turned doubtful. "Is that so?"

"Yes."

The sergeant became at once suspicious and indignant. "Then why the hell wasn't I told about that? Goddammit. Burrowfal, get over here."

A small soldier carrying two huge sacks hurried over, the sacks dragging behind him.

"Does that thing in the cage have to be watered?"

"What, sir?"

"The lizard. Does it have to be watered, or is this old man talking bullshit?"

"Um, I'm not sure, sir."

Xian interjected, "Why don't you have a look at him?"

The sergeant glared again at Xian and then nodded to Burrowfal, who scurried over to the cage cart and pulled the sheet aside.

Inside the cage, Baks Mu sat, stoically, looking very dazed and somewhat shriveled. He wore only his fishskin vest and trousers, and his hands were shackled to the floor.

"He looks fine to me, sir," muttered Burrowfal. "Definitely alive."

"Good enough," agreed the sergeant, his concern quickly fading.

"Alive he may yet be, but he is not fine, Sergeant," said Xian. "Juks Xi Ren require water on their persons to facilitate, among other things, their breathing. They breathe in part through their skin."

"So?"

"So your prisoner is suffocating."

The sergeant looked at Baks Mu, squinted, and then said to a burly soldier on his left, "Mort, put this old man in the cage with the lizard. Give him a bucket of water, and if he says another word, run your sword through his eye."

"I will also need a cloth," said Xian despite the threat to his eye.

The escort, Mr. Geminstra, had approached them and was looking more than a little distressed. "Sergeant, if I may, this man is under my supervision and guidance. I have the papers here that indicate…"

"You want to get in there with him?"

Geminstra stopped, looked down at the ground, and shook his jowly head.

"Get back in the wagon, then. He'll be fine in the cage. Unless the Challowian eats him. Anyone else gets off that wagon, and I'll feed him to the lizard myself!" the sergeant barked as he wheeled away and wiped his hands of the situation.

An hour or so later, the Juks seemed to have to recovered somewhat and was breathing more steadily.

"You could have let me die," said Baks Mu.

"Yes," said Xian, gesturing at the water bucket. He'd been dripping a soaked cloth onto his new cellmate intermittently since the caravan had started moving. "More?"

"Please."

Xian soaked the cloth, squeezed it out a bit, and applied it to the skin of the Juks.

"How do you know it's not my preference to die?"

"I don't. But I wanted to talk to you, to hear your story, before you do," Xian chuckled.

"My story? Who says I've got a story?"

Xian shrugged and returned the cloth to the bucket. "I have a kind of modest expertise in this area. And while almost everyone has a story they want to tell, yours certainly seemed one that needed to be heard."

"So you saved me for the sake of your own entertainment. How kind," said Baks.

"You're welcome."

"Are you going to water me all the way down to Pashka?"

"If you need me to, yes, I will."

"For my entertaining story that needs to be heard?"

"I was joking about that. For all I know, the soldiers have it right and you are just a mass murderer — though your being the first ever among the Juks Xi Ren adds a certain level of intrigue."

"Not the first."

"No? Hmm. I doubt that's true. In fact, I know it's not."

"Know a lot about my people, do you? You a xenofreak, then? Hoping for something extra after your little chore, are you?"

"Ha, no. Thank you, but no. I am not a — xenofreak? — I am a Timesinger."

"No shit?"

"No shit."

"I didn't realize there were any of you left."

"Believe me, most of us don't realize there are any of us left, either."

"Old, huh?"

"It happens to the best of us, I suppose. But not to you without this water," Xian said, dousing the Challowian once more.

"Okay, okay, you've got your tale. Why not? It's not that big a secret. I'm sure everyone in Camedua has a version to tell by now."

"Yours is the only version that interests me."

Baks looked at him, trying to discern the nature of his interest, and decided to take him at his word. "The road is long, and what lies beyond is bound to be tedious. You don't have the keys to these, I'm guessing," he said, holding up his shackled hands.

"Sorry, no."

"I've been wearing shackles for what seems a month now."

"They're afraid of you."

"I got that."

"Have you eaten?"

"Not since last night."

"All I have is bread and cheese. Neither is very good, but you are welcome to half."

"I thought you knew about my kind."

"I do. You can eat bread and cheese. They won't kill you."

"Fish, my friend. Seawood, mollusks, fish — "

"My apologies. These I forgot to pack."

"I won't hold it against you."

"Thank you, Captain...?"

"Not captain. I'm second-in-command. I was...second-in-command."

Xian looked at him and decided he wasn't lying. The others were mistaken. "My name, in case you need it, is Xian."

"Baks Mu."

"A pleasure."

They rode in silence for a while, past some ruined old farms and more than one burned house. Neither commented upon what they saw. Such sights were far too common to make much fuss about, and though neither had been in this part of the world in a long time — in the case of Xian, a very long time — nothing substantial had changed about the manner in which events in the low places of Arba played out. The poor, the uneducated, and the unfortunate, of which the greater portion of the environ's population was ever composed, never stood a chance against the forces that molded and shaped this deeply flawed land.

Xian took note of his own practiced apathy, which for so very long he had not needed to call upon, having spent many years sequestered in a more beautiful and forgiving part of the world. He felt ashamed and also powerless, and he wondered, not for the first time, who if anyone he'd be truly helping by saving these people. It saddened him deeply to even consider for a moment that death might be preferable to the lives they called their own, here in Maelor's Country, or on the cold roads south of Carthage, or in the slave cities of Yanz or Tritto.

He wondered if those whose lives were at stake would agree with that sentiment, but he quickly concluded that such questions were not his to answer. He could only do what he could do. What happened from there was for history to determine.

There came a small group of dappled horses that seemed to be tracking them from a distance; they were probably just hoping to find someone to feed them. Many someones had no doubt died in the recent skirmishes and struggles, though, and the someones' horses would probably wind up roasting over someone else's fire.

Baks Mu moved in his shackles, and the clanking sound stirred Xian from his thoughts.

"You're going to testify, aren't you?" he asked the Challowian.

"How would you know that?'

"Because the Tri doesn't transport prisoners all the way to Pashka just so they can execute them or send them to Bi. Much simpler and less costly to cut off your head in Camedua. You know something, and they want to know what you know."

"They want what they think I know."

"But you're going to disappoint them?"

"Without a doubt."

"Then you are certainly dead."

"As I said."

"But you haven't yet said."

"Hit me with that cloth again, then, and open your ears, Timesinger."

Xian soaked Baks once more and could feel the man's considerable relief. This kind of travel was unthinkably cruel for a creature like this. *Then again, "Unthinkably Cruel" could be Arba's collective motto, couldn't it just?* he thought. "Very well then. Better? Let's have this tale. And please, tell it all, or as much of it as you can, with effort, recall."

"I promise I will."

Baks told his story to Xian. Having told it so often to Pamitter, Shi, and the Brown Men, he was getting rather good at it.

He left out, as he had each time before, his suspicions about what had really happened. He had never seen a Visshilla, but whatever had attacked his men and ship belied everything he knew about the Protectors of the Sky. They were said to be merciless but honorable, unforgiving but wise. The things on *Ho Matsuni* were simply butchers.

Xian sat there and listened quietly, nodding here and there. He asked no questions, but when the tale was finished, he made a small pronouncement:

"They weren't after you. The damage done to your crew and ship was incidental."

"Really? What were they after, then?"

"A passenger."

"There were no passengers."

"Are you sure?"

Baks thought about it a moment. "There were some merchants from Abeilon, now that you mention it, but I knew all three of them. They dealt in beer. Do the Visshilla drink beer?"

"No, but it wasn't the Visshilla who attacked you. And those merchants—I doubt they were who you thought they were. In any case, they had or knew something. The question is, how did the attackers know they were on that ship? What was it they were after?"

"I don't know. I've been asking myself that question since that night, and I cannot come up with a satisfactory answer."

"Have any other Challowian ships been similarly attacked?"

"Not to my knowledge."

"Hmm. Not to mine either."

"Timesingers get reports on the Challowian fleet?"

"Timesingers get reports on everything. All we do is sit around, drink tea and wine, and read."

"Sounds liberating."

"Oh, it is."

"And also brutally boring."

"It's that too, I suppose. But one's perspective on what's boring and what isn't evolves as the decades wax on," Xian confided, chuckling softly.

They both settled back into their own thoughts. The mystery of that night on the ships hadn't been solved; in fact, it had, for both parties, deepened. And yet there now seemed to be a trail to follow, some potential sense to be made of the incident. Baks wondered how the old man had drawn his conclusions even as he grudgingly and silently conceded that they were almost certainly accurate.

Xian wasn't sure what to make of the tale; he knew that Baks had not told all of it, but he intuited, based upon the facts and the circumstances, that it was neither a random or nor an isolated incident. There were forces in play that would be heard from again, and he shivered slightly to consider in what capacity.

They reached Mak in good time, despite the sergeant's pessimism, but did not stop there for the night. After a brief respite during which they re-stocked the necessary food and provisions, they set out again. Clearly the sergeant and his men were far more uncomfortable with this assignment than they'd let on. There'd been occasional riders that had met up with them on the East Road; Xian inferred from the gestures and sullen nods he witnessed that these were reports on troop movements. The Northerners, he further inferred, were giving the Tri military a bit more than it had bargained for, even this far east of Eshe.

Their trip had thus far been uneventful nonetheless.

How long that would remain true, Xian could not say. But there was an unsettling feeling nagging at him, made even more so because he was essentially locked in a cage. Then again, he was sure the Northerners would have no quarrel with him or with the Challowian, for what could either of them, both prisoners of the Tri, at least in appearance, do to offend these angry farmer folk?

Passing by the unremarkable settlement of Mak had not been without some intrigue. One rider, then another, delivered news that the sergeant in his fragile authoritative wisdom decided he could share: there'd been some progress made where the murder of Theodore Oxenhaft of Hunberg was concerned.

The murder had taken place just over three weeks ago; at the time, there were no witnesses and no body. Only a small logbook belonging to Oxenhaft, covered in what appeared to be his blood, had been found at the place of his last sighting. Now it seemed there had been witnesses — a great many, in fact — and even a body. There was no accounting for the discrepancy in the two reports, but there was no discrepancy regarding the simple fact of the great man's death.

The travelers and soldiers received this information from the sergeant and almost immediately began to buzz with one another. Xian listened to their almost-excited tones.

"Given the man's pedigree and political standing, there will be a vigorous investigation and unending debate. This country loves nothing more than to debate unendingly."

"We like a good festival here and there too, madam."

"Oh, to be sure, heads will roll. But will they be the right heads?"

"Who cares, long as there's a festival to mark the moment?"

What wasn't yet clear to any of them, what might never be clear, was who exactly had perpetrated the act. Common wisdom, of which the sergeant was clearly a fan, pointed at the Northerners. "Those shit-shoveling bastards have gone too far," growled the sergeant, to the approval of his men.

Xian dismissed that thought out of hand. The rebellious farmers had nothing to gain from such an act. It was also true that they hadn't the means to commit a murder so artfully in the middle of what was essentially a bastion of Tri power, not without the assassin getting caught or killed.

The murder of Theodore Oxenhaft, the disappearance of the ancient Timesinger Malalji, the destruction of three ships by Visshilla or another airborne race, the murder of a crew with a Challowian being summoned the capital to offer testimony…strange events indeed.

Xian was very much used to demystifying veiled connections. It was a strength of his, without doubt. The vagaries of history required a Timesinger to acquire and nurture this skill, particularly if he wanted to be of any use to the order, and in this regard, Xian was known among his compatriots to be quite useful. One began with the presumption (and oftentimes the presumption alone was sufficient to render a trail viable) that there were no coincidences and that massive historical events and small anomalous occurrences could be counted upon to have a kind of interconnected gravity.

The East Road had been forged alongside the River Camedua. The river had once flowed much more strongly, but over the centuries, various storms and other, not-so-natural occurrences had reduced it to a very feisty brook. One could fish in it, and on a few occasions during a stop Xian attempted to do so at the behest of his new cage mate, but it was impossible to navigate the river with any craft owing to the inconsistency of its depth. Still, it was a comfort, particularly to Baks Mu, to hear its persistent trickle and babble. By his own admission, he had never in his life spent this much time away from the lake or the seas.

Clearly, it was a deeply troubling experience for him. Or rather it should have been, but Xian noticed a certain nonchalant resignation that, if feigned, was feigned expertly. No, the Juks Xi Ren had decided he was going to die, so the method of his inevitable death wasn't a massive concern for him.

Their friendship, as doomed and tentative as each understood it to be, grew as they bumped and crawled down the road in the midst of their caravan. They spoke of Baks's family — though not of his son — and of his home on Lake Iale, which he had not seen in several years. Their journey over the lake from Quintish, if they secured passage on a ship, would take them within fifty miles of Challow's Rock, but of that they did not speak either.

They did revisit the subject of the *Ho Matsuni* once or twice. It was an event that was, for various reasons, never very far from their thoughts.

What was unsaid weighed heavily on the minds of both men.

So they rode in the slow, caged wagon and stared at the complicated landscape, or napped, or spoke. Sometimes, when he'd latched on to a point, Xian's hands gestured as he spoke, as if he were painting a springtime tree and the sky behind it; at other times, his hands were still, kept in front of him as if he were about to play an organ but had forgotten the first notes to his song. Baks's eyes danced about bemusedly but with a telling hint of involuntary alertness. They were eyes that said, "All that has ever gone wrong might go wrong again…and it might go wrong right now."

The Timesinger wondered about his companion's life but limited his questions, preferring to wait for any answers that might be forthcoming. He told Baks about Ashkinda and evenings in the Westview Garden and the quiet yet vigorous debates he and his fellows would have. Where had Samuel le Underrac really come from? Why did Frulla go to Thesseline? What was the Festofor Epidemic: A natural occurrence or an act of war? Was the Gift necessary to the survival of the environ or a political scheme by the Tri to consolidate power?

Baks listened and sometimes laughed but mostly shook his head in either disgust or amazement. The depth and breadth of Arban history was beyond his current scope of concerns, but neither did he bid Xian remain silent.

What Xian did not discuss with Baks Mu was the reason for his current journey. He felt that perhaps he could, and that the Challowian might even offer some insight on the situation, and yet something about Baks's demeanor said that he seemed to have received a full helping of traumatic experiences. It's not easy to tell someone like that you believe the world is coming to an end.

Omissions aside, the tales and conversation passed the time, and Xian noticed the watchful eyes of his new friend becoming a little less alert and the Challowian himself a little less resigned.

The attack came on the sixth night of their journey, just one day after the reprovision at Mak. They had not yet stopped but were instead trying to push through to an alleged military way station forty miles north of Quintish.

They never reached the way station, though they could see it burning in the distance.

The battle, if one could call it that, lasted fifteen minutes at best. Xian and Baks's caged cart was immediately yanked by their panicked pull horses, right over the embankment and into the Camedua. The battle raged above them on the road. The cage itself shattered, but neither of its occupants were hurt. Baks Mu pulled an unconscious Xian away from the shattered wagon and down into the river's paltry thalweg.

For an hour or so, he breathed for both himself and the old Timesinger in the hopes that the attackers would abandon the battle site. When he surfaced, however, he realized immediately his hope was a vain one: someone was looking for them. He could hear the cries of the soldiers as they were pressed most unkindly for information.

This had not been an instance of Northerner aggression. This was something else. Whatever was asking the questions wasn't righteous; it was cruel.

And so Baks Mu the Juks Xi Ren, towing Xi Lo Fui the Timesinger, swam quietly upstream, keeping to the deeper areas of the water, until the scene of the attack was quite distant. Only then did he attempt to rouse his companion.

"We need to have a look," said Xian groggily. He coughed a bit but not loudly.

"That would be ill advised," answered Baks Mu with a scowl. "Whoever they were, they were surely looking for me. Or for you, perhaps?"

"Possibly both. Neither of us is without value. And they will not stop looking. But if my suspicions are correct, they will not look during the day."

"So we wait for Ponesta."

"Yes, I think that's best," said Xian, coughing and looking his age.

"What are we going back for? We should leave here, follow the river."

"We cannot, not yet. There might be others left alive, people who need our help."

Baks shook his head. "That would be a mistake. We have no weapons. And I doubt anyone was left alive, not from how it sounded."

"You might be right. Still, we need information. Who did the killing. Why." Xian tried to move to a dryer spot. "I have to lie down," he said.

Baks supported and guided the old man across to the river bank closest to the road. They sat down on the roots of a massive willow and listened.

"Would the Tri kill its own to get at us?" asked Baks, knowing the answer was yes but wanting also to gauge the posture of the Timesinger. He watched closely.

"Of course. But this was not the Tri, I suspect. Let's rest a few hours."

"I cannot, not with the battle this close. But the water has so refreshed me, it's hardly necessary. I will watch."

"Very well. Wake me when the first sun rises."

There were fewer screams now, but still the danger was present. Baks slid up along the willow and watched and listened as best he could. There was fire and pain and death.

How often, he reflected, had he said that of late?

Chapter 37
"Convince me, then."

Place: Chralm Doanna, westernmost keep in the Great Nation of
Aethrelius, Arba Environ
Date: Angem 2, AY 999

Aethrelius was mobilized.

From every direction, thousands of troops were marching to the capital to aid in the defense of their beloved city.

It would have been an inspiring sight had it not been so tragically futile.

They have no idea what's in store for them. They believe they're going to fight the good fight, to join with their brothers and beat back another invading horde that's made the mistake of believing Aethrelius is a ripe target. They believe they can go to the city, fight for a few days, celebrate for a few more – free beer for every man who took a life! – and go home, unscathed, undaunted, mission fulfilled.

They believe they can win.

It was like that for a day or so on the road: troops marching past, their stern and eager faces proud, their steps sure. They passed Leander's men without acknowledgement, though there were a few curious and sometimes disdainful looks.

On the third day, Heop had given the order to beat down their escort. When that was done, quickly and with only a small amount of bloodshed – one of the Stavers hacked off another's hand with a halberd – what remained of the Fourth Mandate gathered around their commander.

"We have to go back, Captain," said Michael.

"We're not going back," Leander replied, shaking his head. "Men, listen now. If we return to Renikalar, we will find one of two things: either there will be no Renikalar, or Beir will waste five times the number of men he sent this time just to get us to Chralm Doanna."

"But if there's fighting – they've labelled us cowards, sir!" cried Pulami.

Leander grimaced a bit but put a hand on Pulami's shoulder and said, "They can label us whatever they like. Soon, it won't matter. Renikalar will fall, and the country is lost."

He looked around at the faces of the men to gauge their reactions. It was perhaps the saddest moment of his life. *They know it's true. They don't want to believe it, but they know there's no denying it. Aethrelius is gone.*

They stood there for a long minute. The horses whinnied with mild impatience, and the wind moved in the oaks.

Heop broke the silence. "What are your orders, Captain?"

Leander tilted his head a bit and listened to the wind. It was time to tell them what was on his mind, what had been in his mind since he'd seen the burned fields in the north. "We will seek out and find the Sword of Endings. It's apparently our last hope."

No one said a word.

Leander let his plan hang in the air. *I have to assume most of them know what I'm talking about. And I have to assume they'll all believe I've gone insane...*

"Captain, do we...where do we look for that?" asked Pulami.

"In the west," answered Leander. *Somewhere in the west. Somewhere between here and the end of the world.*

"You know where it is, sir?" asked Michael.

"Well, of course he knows where it is. We're not just gonna wander around checking under rocks," yelled Heop as he gave Leander a look that said, *Are we?*

Leander addressed the Stavers. "You men are free to return to the capital if you like. Your other option is to join us. You heard what we're about. Think on it and let me know in ten minutes what you've decided."

He turned to his men and said, "I give you each the same choice. You can return to the capital and try to join whatever fight you find there, or you can remain among us and try to find this thing."

It didn't take ten minutes for anyone to decide anything. The Stavers picked themselves up, took what weapons Michael and Pulami allowed them, and headed east down the road at a less-than-enthusiastic pace. No man of Leander's went with them.

"Very well. Good," said Leander. "Let's eat something, then, and get started. And while we eat, I'll outline the plan."

I'll outline the plan. Yes, that's exactly what I'll do. While we eat? What do I tell them? "My mother kept a diary; I think maybe it's at Chralm Doanna with her cousin, her cousin who hates me because his brother was supposed to marry my wife. He probably burned the book, and he might burn me, even if he hasn't received orders from Beir to do just that."

He chuckled to himself, realizing he was in just the right mood to say exactly that. But his men were in no such mood; they hadn't had visited upon them the gift of giddy, legend-inspired apathy; they were probably not able just yet to avoid imagining the horrible fates of everyone and everything they loved. Too bad for them, really, and he stood there as they made ready the meal and wondered how he might find a way to share his newfound insulation with them.

Am I going mad? Am I just seeing clearly because seeing clearly is the only thing left for me to do? Hunt down the legendary Sword of Endings, a way to reclaim the country or whatever is left of it...is that really the thing to focus on here? If not that, what? What else is left?

Maybe I'll just let old Cedril stab me through the eye, the vengeful bastard.

During the meal, the men were relatively quiet, talking a bit about how this country smelled funny without the sea nearby and how it seemed like the highway and even the few homes one could see scattered about in the distance were pretty much deserted. No one said anything about the Sword; they seemed to understand that their captain would tell them what he intended when he was ready.

When the meal was through, the men waited for a moment before getting up and making ready to travel in order to give him an opportunity to speak.

I've got to say something.

"The Sword of Endings is not a myth. It is a weapon, a very real weapon, that was used not only to defeat the very creatures that have now invaded our Great Nation but also to vanquish the monster history knows as Kold the Creator. And though I do not know where this weapon is, or even what it is, I do know how to find it, and in the name of Frederick and Renik and everything we hold dear, I swear to you, with your help, I will do this thing! And when we find the Sword, we will use it to avenge our country, save our people, and end the life of every Vo'ix on this tortured planet!"

The men cheered and clanged their weapons against their shields. It was what they needed to hear; they'd seen, and heard, enough defeat for a lifetime.

"For now, we head to Chralm Doanna."

Because most of them were on foot and not in the best condition, it took them fourteen days, more than the entire season of Dakaj, to reach Chralm Doanna. They took little notice; the brief month of dark winter wasn't something most Aethreleans cared much about—Dakaj was for the devotees of ONOF and the decadent shits of the west—and yet Leander missed the small ceremony he and his family would have had on the Cliffs, if only for the conversation and closeness. There was also something about the idea of the Proving that had always intrigued him. Given his tendency to eschew mysteries and puzzles and attend instead the persistent challenge of his reality, the fact that he cared at all amused him. Maybe the notion that nothing was inevitable, even the doom of an entire race, appealed to his warrior's spirit.

He and his men arrived at the Gateway to the West on the second of the month of Angem.

Leander wasn't sure how they'd be received. Cedric sa Mino, the

Chralm Doanna commander, was an old friend and, by some reckoning, a relative, but he had a fairly good reason to hold a grudge and had always been a very political animal. He'd always been completely loyal to the Unchained and their initiatives and ideals, and yet he never seemed to entirely embrace them. He had, as he often reminded the Square and anyone else who'd listen, things more pressing than ideals to attend to.

And he was right. His was the business of overseeing commerce and a bustling community of traders and merchants. The Aethrelean economy flowed back and forth through the massive iron gates of Chralm Doanna. The tolls alone were an enormous boon to the government, and the goods that entered came from places as distant as Pebbusku and Miranquella.

Leander had always found it strange that a country surrounded by seas saw very little commerce come and go by ship. He blamed the many mountains of Brull country, Viqual's Teeth, and eastern Pherriuskata, but more so the founders of Aethrelius, who had chosen to forge a single road through them and live a life apart from all else in Arba. How many times and for how many years since the dissolution of the Quadrate had Aethrelius isolated itself, the gates of Chralm Doanna closed hard and fast, no traveler admitted and not a loaf or a basket let pass?

While admirably constant in its vision of what could be, Aethrelius had far too often displayed a woefully self-defeating grasp of what was. Still, despite her endemic contradictions, she'd persisted well enough.

Yes, the embargos and trade cessations had been many. And those were truly the only times when ships mattered. First the smugglers, then the navy built to stop them, then the smugglers and the navy fighting the never-ending fight against the Delariun. And of course, they'd taken their ships past Grellgorot to the Atuut Mountains to fight the Brull when the Triumvirate had entreated them to help in that mess.

But in the end, even after those wars and the tentative opening of the border and the presence of a clear need and demand for more and more of what the West had to offer, commerce had never found its way by water. The Aethrelean Sea, particularly east of Rash al Brek, was merciless. Once, an enterprising group of cloth merchants made a decision to ignore the advice of their compatriots and send a small fleet, laden down with a small fortune's worth of wine, foodstuffs, medicine, and of course the latest Pherriuskatan fashions, bound out of Rash al Brek for Fellow's High. Of thirty ships that started the journey, one made it to the High.

As Leander and his men approached the edge of the mountains and the great keep that guarded the way to the West, something seemed irregular about the place. Chralm Doanna was typically a bustling keep, and the town that adjoined it was dependably lively in almost every season. Yet today, there were very few people about. Today, Chralm

Doanna looked almost abandoned save for the few scouts and guardsmen that came out to greet them.

Cedril sa Mino, first commander of the Doanna, was among them, looking weathered, perhaps even a touch sickly, but proud of gait and firm of eye. "Welcome, Tha'it Dossilea."

"You honor me by the use of that title, Cedril, but I'm afraid it is no longer mine to claim."

"Nonsense, Tha'it. The Stavers have no authority to make such determinations, not in Renikalar and not here."

"Even the people of Chralm Doanna are bound to obey Aethrelean law, my friend."

"And where there is just and untainted Aethrelean law to obey, we have ever been ready to do so. We do not recognize the decisions of an incomplete Square."

"The Square is complete. Forty members sit upon it."

"Begging the Tha'it's pardon, but his math seems in error. Seventeen members sit upon it, while twenty-three rogues and henchmen occupy seats not rightfully or lawfully theirs."

"These are gray times, to be sure," said Leander evenly.

"Not for those who understand the law. Janstrin Beir was once a good man and devoted to principles many have shed dear blood defending, yet I'm afraid his fears and the fears of his equally weak allies have distorted his present views. The actions of the Stavers are discommandmentary. What he has done cannot be allowed to stand."

"And yet stand it must, for now."

"Perhaps. You believe attention must be paid to other, more pressing problems. But when it is over…"

Leander leaned over to Cedril and in a low voice said, "Please, let us speak of these things more privately, my friend. My men are weary from the road and in sore need of sustenance."

Cedril sa Mino glanced at him with an almost nervous look in his eye, but of a moment it was gone, replaced by the familiar keen aspect Leander had always found encouraging. "Of course, of course. The hospitality of Chralm Doanna is yours, good Tha'it. Come."

They entered the courtyard of the keep, and Leander found it also quite inactive. "Where are your people, sa Mino?" he asked, perhaps too bluntly.

"Hmm? Yes, well, with news of the happenings east, many of my men — thousands, to be more accurate — have been called to rally around the capital. The rest are positioned at the guard posts along the pass. We don't want to let the Tri sniff an opportunity and catch us with our pants down, do we?"

"And the people?"

"There's no trade right now, so everyone's hunkering down in the villages and their homes, I suspect. The keep's attendants are inside, preparing for your arrival, but many of the usual suspects are out and about keeping themselves busy, trying not to believe the worst is upon us."

They dismounted and headed inside the first commander's residence. Leander's men made to follow, but he turned to them and said, "Gentlemen, go rest, bathe, and eat. I will join your shortly, and with any luck we can make more sense of this mess we're in."

The men seemed relieved at their orders. They strode toward the main part of the keep, laughing, Heop telling them some kind of lewd joke about a farmer and his stock.

Cedril watched them go for a moment with an almost wistful gaze. "They're good men, your boys."

"The best," agreed Leander. "Always true."

Inside, they sat at a small, round table. Cedril opened a bottle of hard pear rum. He poured, raised his glass, and waited for Leander to toast him.

"To Chralm Doanna," Leander said.

"Yes, yes," said Cedril with a noticeable halfheartedness.

Leander ignored this uncharacteristic lethargy and focused on the discussion at hand. "Cedril, I fear those other, more pressing problems you mentioned have grown beyond any scope we might have earlier imagined they would."

"The invaders?"

"Are not Delariun," Leander said, referring to Aethrelius's old enemy to the east.

"Then who?"

"Aethrelius is under attack from the Vo'ixtavracci."

Cedril's reaction was, to say the least, underplayed. This man had seen it all: years of war against the Brull, campaigns into Delariun and the barren land to its south, the Containment...but despite all that, Leander had expected some stirring in the man. Leave it to the old soldier to keep his cool. And yet, there was indeed something odd about his demeanor, something almost wooden and forced. Stress, no doubt: he'd seen too much.

"You are sure of this? The Great Ships have been seen?" asked Cedril as he poured himself another drink, this one from a different bottle, and gestured to Leander with the bottle — to which Leander nodded yes.

"As of yet, no. But it is the slaughter, there is no mistake. Rockmen have destroyed the Glaring Cliffs and were marching on Renikalar when we left there twenty-one days ago."

Cedril handed the drink to Leander and raised his glass but lowered his eyes. "To the Cliffs, then. They will, as always, rise to keep the vigil. This isn't over."

He hasn't asked about Baeselle or Frainle. He hasn't asked anything.

"No, it isn't over," said Leander. He took a sip of the liquor — a brown, thick whiskey from the lower Midforest — and set down his glass.

"Rockmen! This is grave news you bear, Tha'it," Cedril barked, turning his back and strolling away to the window. "With the Mudarrisi gone, we have no true magick to resist them, and the old ways are all but forgotten, if there were ever really any old ways to begin with. And with Beir in power..."

"Kilenya is gone? When?"

"We received the order over two weeks ago. She left the following morning."

That seemed not to be true. The Mudarrisi might have been ordered out and back to Jamoi, but many of them had been born here, had lived much of their whole lives here. They wouldn't have been so quick to leave, especially not from a place that wasn't a Staver stronghold. And Kilenya was Cedril's niece.

Something was not right.

Leander joined his friend by the window, trying to grasp his game. "Beir is not the issue," Leander said. "Had he or any commander the combined might of all Aethrelius, all Stavers, and all the Unchained, we could not hope to resist the rockmen. And the Vo'ix Slaughter is composed of more than rockmen. They say there are creatures among them the likes of which Arba has never seen."

"Anadal's Point?"

"Destroyed, I am sure. I know only what I learned at Renikalar. Some of it while in prison."

"Prison?"

"Beir."

"I see. And what of Fellow's High? Surely not the Khampier?"

"The High has fallen. The Khampier was under attack and, I fear, is likely also razed by now. The Slaughter comes by land and sea. Our ships have faced them in both north and south, and all who fight, burn. One, *Horizon's Grimace*, commanded by Captain Romer Fed'onai, was rumored to have escaped near Fish's Mouth; there was but a single witness."

"The Khampier, gone..." Cedril almost whispered. "Then nothing stands between the Slaughter and Renikalar. Hy Reac has no defenses to speak of, not in the face of such an enemy."

"Beir had amassed a force thirty thousand strong to defend the city. Those retreating from the Khampier will have joined them. And Beir sent word to all the coastal keeps, but — "

"They will not answer. Stavers or Unchained, they cannot run to the aid of Renikalar and leave their own defenseless."

"They are Aethreleans. They understand their duty. They will bring their people to Beir."

"And by his side, they will all die."

"No. I fear they will not. The Vo'ixtavracci take prisoners."

Cedril's eyes widened with understanding; for a moment, he seemed to tear up. "The Gift," he whispered. "The Taking."

Leander nodded. "If our people are driven to Renik's Holy Keep, there they will stay. Until the Vo'ixtavracci decide otherwise."

"We cannot let that pass. Beir must...does he have the courage?"

"Either way, it means our end."

"Then all is lost," said Cedril vacantly.

"Not all."

"What, the Three Thieves? Those fools haven't the forces or conviction to beat back the Slau, let alone the Slaughter."

"They have the Challowians. They have the ships of the Lake Kingdoms."

"The Challowians are too few," Cedril barked, pouring himself another whiskey and downing it quickly. "And the Lake Kingdoms are nothing more than fat pirates dodging sea twalets and stealing one another's purses."

"The Knights of ONOF are strong," said Leander, watching Cedril. The man's hands were shaking.

"No, they *were* strong. So long has it been since the Three faced a true challenge, they are now a band of ill-tempered drunks and bullies. They cannot help us."

"Still, the Body must know. They must act. Mer Ponx, the Order, even the Spectrum — there must be an answer among them."

Cedril stood up and almost stumbled a few paces from the table. Leander started to rise to help him, but the older man waved him back down into his seat. He steadied himself and looked at the tha'it. "Leander, my dear old friend...the Body does know. Magick will not save us, because neither Body nor Mind will let it."

"You know something," said Leander.

"Only rumors. It was a certainty that the Three would look upon our burgeoning civil conflict with interest, and what they are interested in observing, they are interested in manipulating. But things do not go well for the Thieves."

"We have heard. The unrest in Xatumka. The stirring in the camps. Vincent in Chrestikos and his Wildean daughter...rumored to be the Fourth. The Body cannot have been pleased."

"I have come into some information in these last few days," Cedril said. "I had sent two riders by different paths to deliver it to Renikalar. To our people."

Leander was suddenly on guard. "What did you find?" If there had been messenger riders on the road from Renikalar, he and his men would surely have seen them. There had been none such. And there were no quicker routes to the capital from Chralm Doanna.

"What was expected: treachery," said Cedril coldly.

"The Three backed the Stavers?"

"Worse than that. The Three backed the conflict itself because they knew it would weaken us. I did not understand why they would not have chosen a side, but now that the Vo'ixtavracci have fallen upon us, I do."

"Beir had help at the Square."

"A move of strategy, not of true alliance. They want Aethrelius gone, and with it, Aethrelean ideals. And Aethrelean might."

"They made a pact with the Vo'ixtavracci?"

"Not all of them. Most in the Body are shortsighted and greedy, but they know enough history not to invite a grisly encore."

"The Mind."

"The Mind. Yes. For so long have they lived under our protection, they now believe they can do without us. They made a deal with the Vo'ixtavracci."

"You know this?" Leander asked.

"I suspect it. I did not know with whom the deal was made, or by whom, but I could guess. And now, only a few particulars remain in doubt. They mean to sell us to our ancient enemy and in so doing rid themselves of our ways and our threat."

"The Vo'ixtavracci will not be satisfied with Aethrelius."

"No, they won't," Cedril confirmed. "But I'm sure the offering of such a gem without interference by any of the magickally inclined bought the bargainer, at the very least, time."

"Time for what?"

"I do not know." The old commander came back to his chair and slumped down.

There was something he wasn't saying, but what he had said was more than a little alarming. Still, it was also information Leander might have guessed at. The Tri was without doubt a nest of treachery and idiocy and self-interest. That nation rarely belied its well-earned reputation.

But now was not the time to be concerned with the betrayals and machinations of their former ally. The invasion had changed everything. "Cedril, there is...another answer."

Cedril looked at him and slowly shook his head. "I don't think so. No army, no allies. Our fighting vessels swept aside."

"Yet I believe there is a way."

"Tell me."

"The Sword."

Cedril started, held Leander's eyes for a moment, and then looked away. "The Sword of Endings?" he whispered, his voice raspy.

"The very same," said Leander, rising from his seat. "Forged by Renik, used to defeat Kold the Creator. Then three hundred years ago, Frederick wielded it against the Vo'ixtavracci at the Khampier."

"But no one has held or even seen the Sword since that time. Some even doubt it was real. How do you expect to find it now, after so many years?"

"I have learned of a man, a Timesinger, who has spent a lifetime puzzling over the whereabouts of the Sword."

"As many have, all in vain. Your mother, for one."

"It was she who told me of him."

"Who is this man? What is his name?" Cedril's expression had changed. He now wore the look of an eagerly suspicious man, his eyes wide, his tone urgent. Leander thought to guard his words somewhat, but had he already said too much…and how could he ever say too much to a stalwart man like Cedril sa Mino?

"His name is not important. His work is all that matters to us. I have come to believe he can lead me to the Sword."

"How? Who told you this?"

I just told him it was Theresta. Did he not hear me?

"The one who told me is dead now. But she more than convinced me."

"Convince *me*, then."

"I cannot, except to say I am reasonably certain the Sword can be located, if it still exists. I don't know what to believe, in truth, but I have to try."

"And were you to find the Sword, you would use it to save Aethrelius from certain destruction?"

"For that I fear it may be too late. But I would chase the Vo'ixtavracci back into the sea, and as Frederick once did, I would make them dread a return."

Cedril rose and moved farther away from Leander. "I am sorry, my friend."

"For what?"

"I believe you when you say you might find the Sword. And given time and enough clues, you might."

"But you have doubts?"

"I cannot allow you to pursue even the slightest hope that Aethrelius survives its current unrest."

"What do you mean?"

"I truly am sorry, my tha'it, my friend, but they…they have my wife and sons."

Leander turned toward the door as it banged open and guards entered the room.

"This is as far as your quest for the Sword will take you."

Chapter 38
"You understood the question."

Place: Martanouk, kingdom of Arbana, Arba Environ
Date: Angem 4, AY 999

Suashi entered the common room of the Underhat Low, the busiest tavern in the dead west Arbanan town of Martanouk, and put her hand on the hilt of her longsword. "I'm looking for Thomas Yount."

The room went still.

There were thirteen patrons in all, three of them Triumvirate lowguard and two of them workers; the workers excused themselves immediately. She wasn't concerned about the lowguard; such types rarely stuck their noses into trouble unless there was something to be gained and little to be lost. They leered at her openly for a moment but looked away when her eyes swept over them.

Near the back, in a booth, were two Thicknomites in deep-green cloaks talking to a small, bald Pherriuskatan midmerchant. They wanted nothing to do with her and showed it by continuing their conversation after casting her a brief, contemplative glance.

The five around the table to her left were drunken revelers, probably soldier-slaves and their handler, killing time between loads. They would know, if anyone here did, where Yount was. Two of them stood and grinned at her coldly.

She smiled back and repeated her statement. "I'm looking for Thomas Yount."

"And who's doing the looking?" asked the bigger of the two, sporting an exceedingly ugly, patchwork beard.

"My name is Miss Fifty Barb."

"Is it now?"

"I wouldn't lie to such a big man as yourself. Fifty barb for the whereabouts of Mr. Yount."

"I don't know him. And I can't say as I've ever had a Fifty Barber, but I'd be very happy to try you, Miss Barb," laughed Ugly Beard.

"I expect you would. And ordinarily, I might enjoy that too, but my companion and I, we're in a hurry."

"But you're alone, Miss Barb."

"Am I? That happens so infrequently, I sometimes fail to recognize when it does."

"You chirp prettily."

"So I've been told. And what might you chirp in return, sir?"

The soldier-slaves laughed at her jest, but their eyes didn't fully squint. "You shouldn't be alone, not in a place like this. Hells, not in a town like this, eh, boys?"

"She don't have to be alone, Fubb. She can be with all of us!" chimed in one of Ugly Beard's companions.

"Fubb. Of course. Your companions are as generous and inviting as yourself," Suashi said.

"No, they're not."

"Well, almost so…but tell me, what do you know of Mr. Yount?"

"Let's see the fifty."

Suashi pulled out a small sack and threw it to Fubb. He caught it, pulled it open, and peered in.

"Mr. Yount?" she asked.

"Never heard of him."

"Yes, you have."

"Sorry. Can't recall. Can't say for sure. But I'll tell you what: I'll keep this in case I run across him and have something to tell you down the line."

"Tell me now."

"Enough of this business, Miss Barb. Why don't you come be with us, like ol' Jyte said? Have some fun and forget about this Yount fellow."

"You are heading down a path uncertain."

One of the drunks stood and shuffled over to her. He cupped his ear and leaned in dramatically toward her face. "What was that?"

"I said you're heading down…"

"Hey, she talks like a Wildean. You a Wildean, Miss Barb?"

"I am."

"I heard Wildean women are animals, more as like tear a man to pieces in bed as please him."

"You've got it almost right."

"What part?"

She twitched and swirled. Jyte's cupped hand fell to the floor. She then grabbed a handful of his hair and pulled his face toward her. "We like to tear things to pieces. The bed is optional."

Jyte screamed and rolled to the floor, his hair tearing out in her grip, his new stump spewing blood. Except for Fubb, the others rose awkwardly, clutching at their weapons. Fubb himself sat down with his back to her and said, "You'll regret that before the night's through, Miss Barb. Jyte's my best loader."

"Not anymore."

"No, it would seem not."

"Mr. Yount."

"Still on about Mr. Yount, huh? Well, the fifty and a roll might've bought you something, but this business with Jyte…this means renegotiation."

"No. I have offered a fair price, and you accepted the sack. Under Tri law, you owe me an answer, and a good one."

Fubb turned to regard her, his face reddening. She had him, he knew. The lowguard were watching carefully; they could care less about a loader's severed hand, but it was their job to enforce the Merchant Code. They might not have cared so much about doing their jobs in that moment, but the presence of the midmerchant in the back booth demanded they act according to protocol.

That's if I read the room right. If not, more hands come off.

"He's not here," Fubb said.

"Clearly. More."

"He left last night."

"Where was he headed?"

"He didn't say."

"But you know."

"I can guess."

"Please do."

"He was probably headed to Brestum, on the Chalki al Fabr."

"On his way to Motatinfo?"

"Or the Point."

"What business has he there?"

"Don't know."

She came around and stared him full in the face. He tried to look away, but she grabbed his chin and brought her face inches from his. "Mr. Fubb, the Merchant's Code is quite clear on this point, particularly in Arbana. Were we in Xatumka, we'd be done, but Xatumka is a land of fools. Here I have the right to extract the information I paid for by any means customary to me. You understand?" She released his chin.

He nodded and looked down.

"Mr. Yount?"

"He works for someone in the Mind. He's bragged about it to me once or twice while on the frantish."

"For whom does he work, and in what capacity?"

"He gathers information."

"What kind of information?"

Fubb fiddled with the moneybag and stared at the floor.

"You understood the question."

"Yes."

"Then answer it."

"I…don't know."

"You do. And I know that you do. So answer it or face whatever consequences are permitted me in this district."

"Hanging or the pull," said one of Fubb's associates, a smallish man with a thin black beard and an oversized Pastorine hat missing its feathers.

"Is that right? I hear the pull is almost unthinkably painful. Do you think that's true, Mr. Fubb?"

"Yount's a Redeemer," stammered Fubb.

"He told you this?" Suashi asked, attempting to hide her surprise. This wasn't good news for her and Pao.

"No."

"Then how do you know?"

"I saw his bracelet. Once, while he slept."

"You were lovers."

"No, no…we were…close."

"And he let you see the bracelet."

"No, I…"

"If he is what you say he is, he wouldn't be so sloppy as to let a local lay discern his true nature. He wanted you to know. The question is, why?"

"Can't say. It's never come up before."

"And why would it?"

"It didn't. Never. Not once."

"You're lying."

"Please, my boys…"

"They're not your boys anymore, I expect, but I wouldn't worry about them right now. You've got bigger problems now. The prospect of the pull, for example. Tell me all I want to know, and that prospect vanishes."

"Thomas was working for the duke's lead man himself."

The room went still. The Thicknomites, who had been watching the entertainment with amused interest, suddenly looked less than comfortable.

"And who is that?" she asked, though she knew full well who he was.

"You'll find out, bitch, unless you turn 'round and run back the way you came!" snarled Fubb. "The Scourge ain't got nothin' on this fellow."

Suashi smiled. "Then I shall offer him as warm a welcome as I did your man Jyte, should he come calling." She glanced around the room to gauge the reaction of the onlookers. Maybe this lead man had other spies among them. All were simply sitting there, breath held, watching the drama play itself out. Spies they might be, but not so foolish as to reveal their natures in a moment of amused weakness. She looked back at her quarry. "Keep the bag, Fubb, and tend to your man. It's my pleasure to have met and done business with you."

She turned and left the room.

A minute later, Paomaintanna slipped out from where he'd been watching and exited through the kitchen.

They paused in an alley a few blocks from the Underhat.

"That went better than our last tavern meeting," Pao said. "A chopped-off hand is better than a half-dozen dead."

"For everyone but the man whose hand is chopped off."

"Yount works for the Mind."

"I caught that."

"This means he works for Grewea Lon."

"So it would seem."

"The stakes have just been raised, Sua."

"I don't see how. We set out to find the man who can save the life of every man, woman, and child in this environ. Our goal hasn't changed. If anything, we're closer to picking up the Ashorne's trail."

"Yes, but we're not the only ones on the trail who know a thing or two about seeing a job through."

"I never expected we would be."

"Neither did I, really, but I did expect we might remain… unnoticed for a while longer."

"That was never likely to happen, not after that show in Graviss Glen."

"I thought the show was designed to avert suspicion."

"It was. But we knew there was a chance someone else was watching, someone who wouldn't be fooled. People, all kinds of people with all kinds of interests, have been watching me since I was a child, Pao. *She* made that happen. Why should they stop now? Her mouth is louder than it's ever been."

"Well, they may have watched, but to my recollection, they only tried to kill you twice since I've known you, and one of those attempts was…a mistake."

"A mistake? Please don't start with that again. The Kellotta Men knew exactly what they were doing."

"They were misinformed."

"They were idiots."

"Nice hats, though."

She laughed. "Yes, that's indisputable. The hats were top notch."

"I wonder, do they get buried in those hats? Or do the hats get passed on to another idiot?"

"Only their haberdashers know for sure."

They headed down an alley toward the break in the town wall where they'd entered Martanouk. The night was growing thicker, and most of the houses they passed already had their lights doused. A few dogs growled and barked somewhere in the distance.

Behind them, moving with utter stillness but not so as they wouldn't notice it, a small, strange shape slipped quickly from the shadows and stood watching after them. It stood statue still for a moment and then turned and disappeared into the nearest house.

"Someone is following us," Pao said.

"Yes."

"No one from the tavern could have…"

"Someone did. There was a magicker."

"I felt nothing."

"Stop with that already, Pao. Your magick is as reliable as my Prementian."

"Maybe, but you know the man without the hand will want his day, and he and the magicker…"

"He's nothing to worry about. We'll be long gone before they drink enough to get the nerve up to come after us. And I doubt the magicker was with him."

"Okay, but maybe he was also a friend of Yount's."

She paused a moment and considered. "That's bothering me too."

"Should we ask him?"

"Yes. If nothing else, he'll have more information. But be careful. Some people have real magick, and some of it can burn your face off."

"Not mine. My face is made of stone," he said, putting on a stony expression.

"Quit fooling around. This man could be dangerous."

Pao stopped walking, turned into a smaller alleyway, and hid.

Suashi crept along at a slightly slower pace for a minute or so. She came to the break in the wall and sat down on a large, round stone to wait. She didn't have to wait long.

"Your companion is injured, Herald." It was a woman's voice, about twenty feet from her; the speaker was hiding in the shadow of a darkened house.

"Who speaks?"

"Please listen…"

"You've come to kill us?"

"No. I've come to warn you."

"Warn me about what?"

"The one you seek, the one you have always sought, has been taken."

"I seek no one."

"Please. You are losing time, and I am not your enemy."

"You claim to have killed my friend."

"No, I informed you that he was injured. I did not injure him."

"Where is he?"

"Here, with me."

Suashi rose and walked toward the voice.

"He is your protector?" the voice asked her.

"No. He's my friend," she said. Seeing Pao's limp body on the ground, she quickly knelt and felt around for injuries. "Who did this?"

"Something not of this environ. Something quite dangerous that does not want to be watched, captured, or even noticed. You were mistaken to believe you could trick it."

"We needed information," she said, pressing two fingers onto Pao's neck and putting the other hand on his chest. He was breathing, steadily but slowly.

"It has none to give you, and it speaks no tongue you would understand."

"What did it do to my friend?"

"A toxin, injected into his neck. Not the full dose, I think, but enough to serve as a reminder for the rest of his life."

"Will he awaken?"

"In time. Perhaps a week, or a month. And when he does, he will have...changed."

"How so?"

"Difficult to say. The toxin is...from very far away, and not meant to be used on humans."

Suashi looked up at the shadow for the first time. She could discern a thin form and a slightly misshapen face. "Who are you?"

"I am someone who has...been told to help you."

"Told by whom?"

"Your father."

"My father sent you? But how...where are you from?"

"I am from a place you know as the Garden. But please, hold your questions. We must attend to your friend, and you must hide. Your enemy is still very near."

Suashi didn't know what to make of this creature, but she was fairly sure she wouldn't be able to fight it. It didn't seem to have a form to fight. She didn't trust it; for all she knew, it had done this to Pao and was about to do it to her. "If you're going to help, then help."

"Follow me."

Pao wasn't very heavy, but Suashi was exhausted after the ordeal in the Scar and the run to Martanouk. He was bigger than her too, by just enough to make carrying him very difficult. She gritted her teeth and trudged after the shadow, but she knew that if there really were another attacker out there waiting to strike, she was about as vulnerable as a cat napping in a dog's hut.

The shadow led her to a nearby stable and then into a small tack room adjacent to the larger area. The horses shifted a bit upon their entry but didn't spook, and that boded well. She trusted animals to sense the presence of evil, and usually her trust was well placed.

"Remain here. I will go out and see if the enemy is gone," said the shadow.

Suashi nodded, and the thing left. She stripped Pao's vest and leather off and inspected him more closely. There were no marks, not even one on his neck where he had allegedly been stabbed. There was no evidence of poison; his breathing was deeper now, still steady, and his coloring was good. He looked like he was taking a nap.

She drew her weapon and wondered if it would be any use against their unseen foe. Whatever it was, it had disabled Pao in an instant. Pao was one of the most able warriors she'd ever met, probably the second most cunning Ailo-shut warrior in the Wilds. She'd never even seen him injured, let alone subdued. It was unnerving. If the thing could do that to him, what could it do to her? Her instincts told her to light out immediately, to try to continue the mission on her own, but she couldn't just leave him here to die…or to change, whatever that meant. Besides, without his help, what chance did she have to reach Carthage or to find the Ashorne?

They'd been working as a team for so long; she wasn't able to conceive of going it alone.

After about twenty minutes, the shadow returned. "It's still looking for you. It knows you are in the area."

"How good a tracker is it?"

"Excellent. But it can only track at night. By day, it needs to rest and hide from Ponasa."

"Not Trilesti?"

"No. The Violet One only weakens it. But even weakened, it is formidable."

"If it knows we're here, it will find us before the dawn."

"No, it won't. I have hidden you…in another place. It cannot see you there."

"I don't understand."

"I will try to explain, but not now, please. I am nearly spent from my efforts here and…earlier. I must recede. And you must hide. Please."

"Wait…I need to know. That was you in the Scar, yes? You helped us get through…"

"I did."

"Who are you?"

"I am...I must show you, but not now. I will come back when I can."

"Do you have a name?"

"Liolesca. Now hide and rest awhile. Please."

And that was what Suashi did. Because there was nothing else she could do. Wherever Liolesca had hidden her, she was not able to get back to Martanouk. She was there, in the stable, in Martanouk with Pao, but they were not only hidden there, they were trapped there. And not there. Several people came and went but they couldn't see Suashi and they couldn't see Pao.

Liolesca never came back.

Suashi hid, trapped, in the stable, somewhere else, and watched Pao die.

He didn't die right away. It took many hours. Suashi prayed for her mysterious benefactor to return, but she did not.

Suashi was alone with her friend with no way to help him, no way to leave and get help for him. She was safe but she was helpless, and it was horrifying.

Pao never spoke. He never woke.

Eventually, whatever was trapping and protecting them fell away, and she stood up and went outside. It was night, and it was cold.

She asked a stable boy she'd been watching while she was hidden what day it was. His answer stunned her: Six weeks had passed in the stable. In the other place that wasn't the stable.

She went back inside, hoisted Pao's body over her shoulder, and set about burying her friend in the forest near the edge of the town. The stable boy helped her.

When that was done, she sat down, wept, and tried to decide if she should just go home.

Chapter 39
"May I please see your face?"

Place: House Cruakle, island city of Pashka, kingdom of Pherriuskata,
Arba Environ
Date: Angem 5, AY 999

Petrecia wanted to be anywhere else.

They were attending yet another ball, this one at House Cruakle, in celebration of the fortieth birthday of Gil Cruakle's portly and sluggish son, Avimo.

The Wasi Sagotr Cruakle was the family guild that carefully controlled the banks of Pashka. The Cruakles were also the bitter rivals of the Grehmanns of Motatinfo. By comparison, theirs was a more refined approach to both currency and life; one would never see bags of Simisola and children in cages at their events, but there had nonetheless been countless lives ruined by their subtly carnivorous and usurious practices. Rodolpho himself was rumored to be indebted to them, but that was not surprising. She had determined through observation and inquiry that there were very few of the Wasi Sagotr to whom he was not somehow indebted.

The best part, the only favorable aspect in fact of attending this asinine, stifling party, was that House Cruakle was only a mile or so from Canamow House. It wouldn't be that difficult for her to quietly and quickly vanish and retire to her own rooms. But it was still too early. Rodolpho hadn't yet absorbed enough of Cruakle's wine; he'd notice her absence.

She knew everyone—almost everyone—at the event, masks notwithstanding. She noted (and not for the first time) how completely ridiculous was the Custom of the Mask here in this shitty kingdom that would never be her home. What was the point? Anonymity was moot when one learned to read the curve of a shoulder, the cadence of a voice, the style of the apparently haphazardly selected garments…and the hair. Oh, the insane and embarrassing coifs these people chose. Hair in towers sticking out in every direction. White hair tinged with gold flecks and what looked to be bird droppings of some kind. Hair combed down over the eyes and reaching below the chin. Did these people have mirrors at home? Their looks were unintentionally designed to render any trace of natural beauty irrelevant. It was all laughable and sad at once.

Her own mask, once again the leopard, was giving her trouble. Something was wrong with the strap on the left side. It wasn't loose exactly but it was…itching her. Itching? No, that wasn't it. Tingling.

She made her way to the ladies' chambers to address the problem. Down the stairs and to the left, an attendant told her.

Down the stairs she went, but turning left brought her to a part of the house that looked unoccupied — a series of storerooms and libraries and a bath chamber.

Is this the right hall? she thought, annoyed because she knew it wasn't.

And then her mask fell off.

She was shocked for just a moment…then she laughed. There was no one there to see, but oh, what if there had been? She knelt and scooped the misbehaving mask off the floor with a sigh. Wouldn't that be something? No greater scandal than a lady with her mask off, no.

Pherriuskata was a mandatory, maudlin masquerade if nothing else, and the price of a missing mask, well…few had the capital to both pay for and survive such a thing.

Shame, she thought. *Maybe they'll feed me to something in a cage.*

She held the mask up and looked at it. Why a leopard? They'd been native to her home but were now long extinct, a thing from the past hardly anyone remembered. It was an odd choice, but something about it made her feel like there were still chances available to her…

"And it is a beautiful creature, but nowhere near as beautiful as its bearer."

She started and reflexively slapped the mask back on her face. Turning toward the voice while fumbling with the strap, at first she could not see who had spoken. She got the leopard to stay on, though it still tingled somewhat, and then she spun around to identify whoever had spoken.

A tall, somewhat wiry man, handsome, with a slightly hooked nose and dark-tan complexion, was smiling at her. He held a lute and sported a worn velvet tunic. "Come find me later, and I'll play something for you, my beautiful friend!" he said, bowing slightly.

Before she could think of what to say, he turned and was gone back toward the stairs and the party.

She blinked a few times, astonished, and then once again despite herself, laughed aloud.

Beautiful friend indeed.

The party continued for hours, but it got no more interesting to her than it had been at the start. Rodolpho got soused, as was his habit; she could have slipped away at any time and gone home. She found herself wanting to stay, however. She couldn't understand why.

Or she could, but she fought not to.

At some point, just before the birthday fool was to start his roasting of the guest of honor, she rose from the table, making apologies to a bunch of people who wouldn't have noticed if she lit herself on fire. "I'm going to take some air," she said as she left them.

No one commented; at least, no one commented whilst she was still in earshot.

She made her way around the party, going from room to room, once or twice coming upon persons engaged in intimate activities that were sadly unfamiliar to her at present. And some with which she'd never wished to become familiar, she noted even as she chastised herself for her prudishness. Some people would do anything for a moment's thrill.

Not me.

But what would I do if not anything?

Something?

What am I looking for?

Him, of course. Yet among the more than a thousand guest and servants and entertainers present—a small affair by comparison to other feasts but nonetheless imposing—she could not find him. Perhaps she had imagined their encounter. Perhaps her generally unacknowledged need to refamiliarize herself with the aforementioned activities had conjured him and their shared awkward moment altogether.

She wandered out to the Cruakles' gardens. There were rows and rows of fountains and hedges and statues of dukes and conquerors and Cruakles of the past. After a time, she found herself staring at a statue of Chaq, the two-headed, four-winged eagle of Boi legend.

"He is alone. He should not be."

The tall man with the aquiline nose was at her side, strumming his lute, regarding the statue with a thoughtful expression.

"Perhaps Ald and Teutelin are near but hidden," she said, glancing at him twice and then staring back at Chaq.

"Isn't it always so?" He stepped away and sat on a bench next to a small candlelit fountain. He began to strum a different tune, something familiar to her. And somehow the trickling water seemed to complement the song.

"That is by Cam Tropeo, is it not?" she asked.

"It is. He doesn't like for me to play it, but…well, he's not here."

"You play very it well, sir."

"Thank you. And you are a delightful listener, Madame Celeranet."

"You know my name."

"I've made inquiries."

"You have? Whatever for?"

"Perhaps for the sake of curiosity. And perhaps for...something more."

"Something more?"

He stopped strumming for a moment and gave her a small smile. "Yes."

She looked away and chose a hedge to closely examine. Having satisfied herself as to its qualities, she spoke to him again. "And that would that be?"

"Just something I wanted to ask of you...after seeing you for the first time," he said, resuming his playing.

"And now?"

"Now?"

"Is there still something more...something you wish to ask?"

Dangerous, Petrecia.

"I should tell you 'no.'"

"You could tell me 'no,' but..."

"Yes?"

She abandoned completely her examination of the hedge and spun to face him, recognizing she should have turned more gracefully even as she decided she didn't care. "But if you tell me 'no,' then I wouldn't get to ask you *my* question."

"You have a question for me?" he asked with a sense of play in his voice.

"Perhaps. But now that you've answered 'no,' we shall never know."

"I haven't answered 'no' — I've merely stated that 'no' would be my wisest answer."

"And are you always so wise that you choose only the wisest of answers as a rule?" She took a few steps away from him and found her hand on the clawed foot of Chaq; its timeworn roughness inspired her to recoil, but though she did flinch, her hand remained where it was.

"I confess, no."

"Then why not say 'yes' and tell me about the something more?"

He stopped strumming. "Very well. I believe I have fallen in love with you."

Petrecia stared at him and then looked away. She looked back at him, her eyes betraying a fierce emotion. This man, this singer, was taking liberties. She should be at least as fierce with her retort as with her eyes, but she found herself unable to speak; her studied shock and indignation seemed both to have been quietly overwhelmed by something less familiar.

"You haven't asked me anything," she said softly enough to surprise herself.

"Ah, of course." He rose and stood directly before her, his body only inches from hers. She looked away and then down at the flagstones. He placed a gentle finger under her chin and tilted her head up. "May I please see your face?"

"You...have seen it."

"Only for a moment. And though that moment is dearly burned into my sweetest chamber of memory..."

"Please." She turned her head, leaving his finger in midair.

"I would add to it companions and own the dearest collection of moments to recall upon the waves."

She turned away from him, but slowly, reluctantly, as if she were somehow stuck. Forcing herself to take two steps, and then, after a moment, a third, she kept her back to him and asked, in as nonchalant a voice as she could muster, "The waves? Then you are leaving our Great City?"

"My ship sails tomorrow. Or the next day. Or the next. I am always leaving, Madame Celeranet, Flower of Miranquella, and sometimes I arrive as well. But mostly, I leave."

"It sounds a lonely life."

"It is. It is a lonely, interesting, colorful, merry, troubled life. I have seen more places than anyone I know — I have even seen your home and the wild frantic birds of sweet Mont du Grace — and I have learned more songs than any musiker I ever knew save my own dear grandfather. But also, I have seen our world for what it is, and what it is not...and so I would have those moments of you, if only to defend myself from all that batters and burdens me from without and within."

"Your words themselves are truly those of a poet — or a merchant, perhaps — but I must refuse your request."

"Tell me why."

"I cannot."

"Cannot or will not?" he asked, his voice suddenly more earnest than playful.

"Both. Cannot, and would not if I could."

"Why?"

"I have to go."

"But first tell me why."

"I cannot give you what you ask for."

"But..."

"Law, for one, and honor, for another...and...and I do not know you, sir."

"Petrecia, do you believe I have fallen in love with you?"

"Madame Celeranet, sir."

"Madame Celeranet...Petrecia..."

"I believe you are simply a poemsman and a musiker who has seen what he should not."

"I saw only what you let me."

"My mask came unfastened."

"Yes, it did. And how did that happen?"

"I don't...a broken clip."

"Your words now border on the scandalous. In Pherriuskata, folk are executed for 'broken clips.' You know the story, yes?" he teased her.

"I know the story...of course, but..."

"Then let us be that story, you and I, right now, together!" He laughed and began to dance around her. "Without the execution, of course!"

"Sir, you are ridiculous. Stop dancing. I am no Kwanita, and you are certainly no Gregory."

"Aren't we? Who is to say?" He stared at her evenly, a slight smile on his lips. "I could be a Wildean warrior, and you a fiery Jamoian woman of many colors, no?"

"No!" She was shocked, she was even angry, and she was...something else.

What else, Petrecia?

"No? No, you are right. We are not those two. Or at least, I am not Gregory. My name is Bealaki," he said as he bowed to her and winked. "And I must confess, I've never even been to the Wilds. Even though I've wanted to visit, something about that Cheat—or do you call it 'Scar' in Miranquella?—something about it freezes my feet and fries my typically stalwart resolve! Can you forgive me a small lie?"

She rose and walked away slowly, but not toward the party. In point of fact, she had completely forgotten the way back to the house. She stopped, knowing he had followed her, was right behind her...she could hear his breath.

Why is he so close?

Why is he not closer?

She spoke to him over her shoulder. "I know your name: Bealaki. I made inquiries too, after our first encounter."

"Did you?"

"I asked about the poemsmen, about the one with the jagged scar, and the one with the long white hair—and you."

"I have competition."

"No."

"Then I have won?"

"I mean, no. There is no competition because...there is no prize."

"I disagree."

"Please..."

And then, he was closer to her. "In all my travels throughout Arba, from Ashkinda to Aethrelius to Motatinfo to the Atuuts…in all my life, to be sure, I have beheld no greater prize."

"You've been to the Atuuts?"

"Just the one time. It didn't suit me. I wouldn't go back."

"Never?"

"Unless you asked it of me."

"What? Why would I ask you to…the Atuuts, of all places!"

He reached out and touched her cheek again.

"Please don't."

"Why?"

"Do you know who my husband is?"

"Yes."

"He would kill you. He would kill us both."

"Yes."

"But then why…"

He stopped, looked down, shook his head…and his hair fell off. She gasped despite herself and beheld the soft, curly blond head of hair that was left in place of his disguise. He was alarmingly handsome. It annoyed her to no end. "A wig?" she asked.

"Sometimes. Sometimes a false nose, or an eyepatch, or a limp or missing teeth…"

"Missing teeth? Whatever for?"

"It serves me, usually, to not be me. But right now, here, with you…I am me."

"Well, you who are you, I hope you realize my fool of a husband is going to have us both beaten, just for having this pointless conversation." She prayed she was wrong. There was no one else about, after all…but that guaranteed nothing, not in Pashka.

"Let him beat me, let him kill me, then; if he is so great a fool as to let a woman as beautiful as yourself out of his sight for even a moment, my own death at his hands would outshine his diminishingly ignorant life a thousand times over."

She stared at him. "We cannot."

He reached up to her face and around the back of her neck. "Cannot what?" He unfastened her mask and slowly pulled it away.

"Please…" she said.

The leopard fell to the ground.

"I love you, Petrecia."

And there, in the soft light of the fountains' candles, witnessed by statues of figures no one knew or noticed much anymore, Petrecia and Bealaki kissed for the first time. It was a long, indescribable release of passions neither had ever suspected they had within them.

She pulled away from the kiss reluctantly, and he placed his mouth by her ear, whispering: "Tell me, please. What was your question?"

The next afternoon, she went walking alone in her husband's garden, a garden that was nothing like the one where they'd come together, she and her new friend. Or maybe the gardens were very much alike. She couldn't say.

One garden is just like another, isn't that always true? she thought, even as she admitted it was not always true.

She was thinking, wondering, musing…and trying not to think and wonder and muse. What had she done? Nothing, really. A kiss. And she had allowed him to hold her hand. Or had she? She thought about that word—"allowed." She wasn't sure it applied, for it implied control, and if anything was clear to her now about their encounter, it was that neither of them had had anything resembling control. And she had surely not allowed a kiss and a handholding, or anything more than that, but more had occurred, and she found herself beginning to admit that it had been so unforgettable as to be impossible.

The lovemaking had happened almost as an extension of the conversation, so natural and insular and forbidden. And funny. They had laughed. This man made her laugh like she hadn't in years, not since she was a little girl in Mont du Grace and her uncle Nejima would tell stories of three-legged gremfis and fish with hawk's wings, stealing plums from the castle's orchards…

She and her lover had laughed together. Drunk on the madness of what they'd done, perhaps. She couldn't say.

And then they'd parted, and it was as if the air itself had abandoned her. She wanted him back before he was gone. She laughed softly to herself even now as she noted her burgeoning weakness.

And then she stopped laughing.

No. He was gone, it was done, and she was back in Rodolpho's realm, in his uncomfortably familiar garden, and she had little doubt that both she and this mysterious poemsman would soon be dead. Her husband was far too jealous of his things, and though she was low on the list, she was still very much one of his things.

And yet, she was not afraid. Why should she be?

That was a foolish question. She had every reason to be afraid, and yet in her current state, reason was absent, despite her retaining enough of its echo to note its absence. She found she welcomed it. Reason had never been her ally. Reason had trapped her here, in this life, with that thing she called a husband, surrounded by these people who were living purveyors of self-absorbed idiocy and cruelty. Rodolpho, the elite, the life, the Tri. All shit.

But inescapable shit.

What could she do? Where could she go? Could she leave? Madness. And Bealaki hadn't told her where to find him. He hadn't avoided the subject, either. It just hadn't come up, and she didn't blame him now for the oversight, not at all, no, but the not knowing, the very mystery of him, as unbearably compelling as it was, was maddening enough as well to drive her out of her already fragile and porous mind. She found herself with one single thought, an eye in a storm of unimaginable emotions.

"I don't know who I am," she said aloud.

"But I do, missus, and I've been sent to find you."

She started and shook, having had her private thoughts so abruptly interrupted. There was Hobknot the gardener, an ancient little Arbanan, standing there with a hoe and looking at her with big, desperate eyes. What had he seen? Anything?

I've done nothing to see...have I?

"Everyone's out looking for you, missus."

"Why is that?"

"Lord Canamow. He's in a bad way, you know, yes, so bad a way I'm glad I found you and, you know, not so glad, if you know what I mean," Hobknot said, glancing over his shoulder a few times.

"And does he have every gardener in every garden in Pashka scouring their grounds for me? Did he think to check his own garden before sounding the alarm?"

"I...I don't think so, missus. Just happens I have a cousin that works in the Vinedance Green, you know, and he was talking about it all at the pub before. They been lookin' for you for hours."

Hours? How long have I been gone?

"Good to know a lady can still find some privacy when she wants it. You're not going to tell anyone you found me, are you?" she said, smiling at him and winking.

The little old man smiled back with his several teeth and shook his head. For a moment, they seemed conspirators, which was perhaps what inspired him to offer up his next piece of information.

"You know, missus, I been working in this garden for a bit, but there's another not far from here I've been at for almost my whole life. My dad and his dad too."

"I didn't know that," she said, her mind already focusing on the guff she'd have to take from Rodolpho. She hadn't been gone all that much longer than she typically was. Why was he so anxious to find her that he would raise such a general stink about it? He couldn't have known about Bealaki; she hadn't even known herself that she would meet the man. And no one had seen them together, of that she was reasonably sure.

"I'm speaking of the Baywinders. There's places in that garden, old places, places a woman…and maybe a man…can disappear, if they like."

He knew. Somehow, he knew. This gardener. What was he? A spy, sent to read her thoughts?

Her stomach tightened as she began to understand the power this little old man had over her.

"You saw us." No sense beating around the bush…and yet he couldn't have seen them. He wasn't there at the Cruakle Estate. Or was he? No. "You were at the party?"

"No, missus. And I didn't see nothing." He smiled. "Except a beautiful young lady finding some peace among the greenery and the colors of this wonderful place here."

She looked at him. His expression was familiar but difficult to place at first. Tears welled up in her eyes when she finally put a name to it.

Regardless of how he'd come about his information, and she was now certain he knew her secret, this old man was not her enemy.

Hobknot was simply being kind.

"Thank you, Hobknot," she said, feeling that she should embrace him but deciding against it.

"For what?"

"For your discretion, and for your kindness."

"Missus, I don't much understand what you're going on about, but if you have a few minutes, there's something I'd like to show you, if you please."

She followed him deeper into the garden to a small wooden door in the eastern wall. He opened that door and then led her to a few more gates and doors that looked like they hadn't been opened in centuries. He opened a few she hadn't even recognized as openings at all. They went down and up several winding, vine- and root-covered stairwells, through a long, dark tunnel, and came to a small clearing surrounded by large, irregularly shaped stones.

"And where have you brought me?" she asked, trying to be playful but in fact becoming slightly alarmed.

"To a place hardly anyone still living knows anything about."

"We're in the Baywinders, yes? It seems so…tranquil."

"It is. And it's more than that."

He reached over and touched a tall stone near him. It started to shift with a soft scraping sound. He touched another to its right, and that stone did the same. The two moved farther apart, and then it seemed there was a very narrow stairwell leading up into the trunk of a huge lotus tree and also down below its roots.

"And where do those lead?" she asked, fascinated by even the slightest display of magick.

"To places no one would ever look for you," he said, smiling again.

"Except perhaps for me," said Bealaki at he stepped out of the shadows and took her hand.

She stared at him a moment and turned to ask Hobknot what was going on…but the old man was gone. Bealaki led her to the staircase and then up into the trunk.

"I'm glad you're here," he said, smiling and tugging her hand.

Up they went, to a place among the branches, a room where they could see the sky and the suns and all the city and out at the bay and the mainland.

What an extraordinary tree, she thought to herself.

Over the next few hours, her opinion of the tree only improved.

Chapter 40
Bad riddles at best,
and false guidance at worst…

Place: Carthage, kingdom of Arbana, Arba Environ
Date: Angem 5, AY 999

Because she was still afraid for her life and the life of her child, Ftuu went to Carthage.

She should have been braver, she suspected, but she'd never needed to be brave and so wasn't sure how it should feel. Was there supposed to be an absence of fear altogether, or was bravery marked by having the will to act despite being afraid?

She could not say.

She was an excellent cook, an attentive bedmate, and a fair flutist. But on the road, alone, with murderous creatures tracking her and no sense of how to survive off the land, she was nothing, and she knew it.

And whatever the thing was that had spoken to her and had murdered those thieves, it had not spoken to her again. She had decided it was gone, or a figment of her imagination. Either way, it would be of no help to her, none that she could rely upon anyway. She stayed one night outside of Wukneesh and, despite its pleasant appearance, decided not to risk entering that place. It was not nearly far enough from Tent City to be safe.

She reached Carthage almost three weeks after leaving the City of Tents, and when she got there, she was half-dead from exhaustion and hunger.

Her body had only just begun to show its state, and so she was certain the life inside her was…still alive. There had been many times on the road when she'd been so hungry and tired, she had almost forgotten she was with child.

Because it was not her way to speak, she was unsure of how she might find the inn Dalter had spoken of. She wandered the dusty Carthagian streets for hours. Finally, when she could walk no longer, she sat down on a bench and lowered her head to her chest.

"You can't sleep here," a woman's voice said.

"That's right. Don't fall asleep, young miss," added a second woman.

She looked up to see three old women standing in front of her, tiny things all. They had squinted eyes and few teeth, and they wore matching orange kerchiefs.

"Did she hear you, Bel?"

"She heard me."

"Did you hear her, miss?" asked the one on the right.

"You all right, miss?"

Ftuu looked at the women for a moment and slowly shook her head.

"What's wrong, then? Don't you talk, child?"

She shook her head again.

"Well, where are your people? Or are you alone in the city? It's no good to be alone in the city, any city, even Carthage. It'll be dark soon, and you'll be in a lot of trouble with the Guard if they catch you sleeping here."

"She'll be in worse trouble if someone else catches her sleeping here."

These women meant well, she saw. Maybe they knew where the inn was. She had just decided to risk using her voice and ask when the woman called Bel reached down and gently grabbed her arm. "You come with us, then, child," said Bel.

"Yes, come with us," the others insisted together.

"We can't let you sleep out here tonight. Gonna get cold, it is," clucked Bel.

And they led her away from the bench and down the street. Bel told the other two to introduce themselves, and they did: the one with the dark hair was Hova, the one with the gray hair was Ewa. They were sisters, and Bel was their cousin. Bel was younger than Hova and Ewa, but she was somehow the bossiest of the three and, so it seemed, made the decisions.

The decision now was to get off the streets before nightfall. Something had the women worried, but they only hinted at it and then turned their attentions to how they might convince Hova and Ewa's mother, who was apparently as old as stone, and as easily convinced of a thing, to let Ftuu stay the night.

Ftuu should not have trusted them, she knew, but she'd been running and hiding for so long, it felt good to be in the company of people, any people. They were kindly and fussy and preoccupied with small things. Along the way, they stopped at a market and debated for no less than twenty minutes with a man who was selling onions about the shameful quality of those very onions. They knew people and stopped to chat here and there with them, mostly about whose daughter was marrying whose son, whose home was falling apart because the husband was so lazy, and the shameful quality of onions these days. Bel did most of the talking, and Hova and Ewa did most of the nodding and tsking and agreeing.

Ftuu drew a few curious looks from the people they met, but each time she simply smiled and looked away, largely because she had no idea how to respond to their curiosity. Bel shooed away a few men whose looks were more than curious, except for one who was someone's nephew and a very good catch for a young lady, maybe even one who found herself all alone in and a stranger to Carthage. He parted but not before favoring Ftuu with the gift of some very large carrots.

The suns had mostly faded from the sky and a chill had begun to set in the air by the time they arrived at the home of the mother, who they called Mama Chaudhri. "She doesn't trust strangers, girl, but she loves guests, and so we have to tell her you're a friend and a guest and not a stranger, because you know Mama Chaudhri gets prickly around strangers. And besides, you're no stranger now, are you? Though you haven't told us your name — do you have a name? Can you tell us? No matter. We'll call you…what should we call her, Ewa?"

Inside, the fire was almost too warm, and Ftuu felt a wave of exhaustion overtake her almost instantly. Ewa saw this and responded by leading her to a deep-cushioned chair by the hearth. "You rest now," she said in a soft, melodic voice that surprised Ftuu with its gentleness, for Ewa was a husky, weathered old woman with arms as thick as those of some men Ftuu had known. "You eat later, yes? Rest now."

Ftuu nodded and looked up. There she saw all three women, smiling kindly at her and glancing at one another with looks that reflected equal parts concern and curiosity. Then the small, shriveled woman they called only "Mama Chaudhri" (never just "mama"), ancient but bright of eye, pushed between them, carrying a thick shawl. She placed it over Ftuu's chest and said, "Sleep, sleep."

And Ftuu did.

She stayed with them for weeks. They never asked her to leave; in fact, they seemed very much to want her to stay, and she had nowhere else to go in any case. She'd lost the letter with the inn's name on it and couldn't recall the name of the place no matter how hard she tried. Some days, she would wander around the city, or at least the parts that were near to Mama Chaudhri's house, but no place she saw aroused a memory or connection. And yet there was something, a detail she could almost remember about the place…

She tried to look for the Slau Cvuklon as well, but here in Carthage there were so many Slau. And she'd always found it difficult to distinguish among their strange, somewhat reptilian faces.

The women who'd found her were glad to have her in their home and gladder still to find her an excellent, willing housekeeper and cook. They themselves never admitted to having been married, though Ftuu suspected at least Hova and Bel had. Even so, marriage was never far from their minds. They quite openly began to devise a plan to marry her to Bel's brother's grandson Olafur; he was a woodworker and a scholar both, they bragged, but he was far away at Hunberg studying hard to become a master of something or other, they weren't sure what. His older brothers, Serge and Samual, who were twins, had been taken by the Crabs seven years ago and were probably Crabs themselves now, the women tsked. But Tansy — which is what they'd finally decided to call Ftuu, after Bel's mother's sister who had married and moved away to Pashka when Bel was only eight — Tansy would make Olafur a wonderful wife and also, the Crabs, the women were sure, only took unmarried men into their service. It seemed their single greatest mutual regret in life that they had not married off the twins before the regiment had come to claim them, and they were not about to repeat their mistake with Olafur.

They didn't have much to say about Ftuu's condition, and that condition was becoming more and more evident as the weeks progressed. The sickness and the cramps would come upon her at all hours, not just in the morning. They never asked her about how she got that way or who the father was. What they did do was help her and begin to make preparations to have a baby join the Chaudhri household. They brought her hot or cold towels as the need arose, and Mama Chaudhri in particular began to take a great interest in what Ftuu was eating and drinking. She prepared each week a huge pot of some kind of strong vegetable broth and insisted Ftuu take at least one cup with every meal instead of tea.

Mama Chaudhri had a deep devotion to the Four, particularly to Frulla, who had come from Carthage and was still very much a presence in this city. They honored both Naipek and Tristan and read their Books on the appropriate days, to be sure, but Frulla, they insisted, was unlike the other two in that she hadn't ever died.

"No, she never died, no. Just left us for a bit; went up north for some peace and quiet. She'll be back when we need her, she'll be back," said Mama Chaudhri more than once, and when she did, she almost chanted the words. Ftuu came to hear the phrases like they were a sort of private prayer or incantation.

Each night after the evening meal, Mama Chaudhri would read a passage or even a chapter from the Book of Frulla. She loved particularly the story of how Frulla had created lifewine from a dead vineyard her father had planted before going off to die in the Linosian civil war; she would grow wistful recalling how her own long-dead husband, Jarred, had met his end similarly as a young man recruited to fight for Velliok.

Mama Chaudhri insisted that she read and memorize the Three Prophesies of the Ashorne, and Ftuu, for lack of a substantial objection and because she was beginning to grow quite fond of the old woman, did so.

She read:

Naipek did write: "He will be in shadow, he will embrace the empty, but

*the empty will not love him, he will be lost among us, he will die before he lives,
and the name he will bear is Ashorne."*

*Frulla did write: "He will have no children, he will burn two cities, he
will save a wise child but end a kind one, and the Last Dreamer will find him, and
her he will slay."*

*Tristan did finally say: "He will be a slave, he will be a soldier, he will
crawl and fly, he will make the Fourth, and the Fourth will Prove."*

She did not understand it, but she read it often. She wondered
why the first two prophesies were said to have written while the last, by
Tristan, was remembered only to have been said.

Dalter had taught Ftuu to read some, and at the women's
insistence, she started to take an interest in the Three Books beyond the
Prophesies and fireside tales. She wasn't becoming a believer, she was
sure, but still she could not help but be drawn in by the schemes, the
depth, and the history she found within those hallowed pages. The
women, particularly Bel, seemed pleased that she was such an avid reader
of the Books; she refrained from telling them that to her the least
interesting sections were those that purported to guide one toward a moral
life. She thought the Prophesies were a little foolish: bad riddles at best,
and false guidance at worst. Still, she read and sat and thought, and they
loved her for it.

One afternoon, Bel received a letter from Hunberg telling her
Olafur was very ill and would probably not live. The old women were
beside themselves with worry and grief from then on, and there was little
anyone could say or do that might instill some cheer back into the
household. Even Mama Chaudhri seemed distracted and withdrawn.

To respect their grief, Ftuu began to take longer and longer walks,
staying away for hours at a time. She did not know how to comfort the
women whose emotional state seemed to somehow remind Ftuu that she
might be a guest, but however welcome, she was still also very much a
stranger in their world.

Two weeks after Bel had received her letter, Ftuu went out on one
of her walks and visited a part of the city she had not yet seen, the Lower
Gate District. When she was drawing near to Carthage's south gate, she
saw something that jarred her memory: a small fountain in the middle of a
square. And there, across from the fountain, was the little inn Dalter had
called Ferrela Fout.

Ftuu stopped for a minute and looked at it. It was not the only inn
on the square; in fact, there were at least five others that she could see. She
walked to the closest one, Emer's Rooms, and entered. After securing a
room on the second floor, she put a chair near the window and watched
the square.

And that was all she did for eight days.

She thought about returning to Mama Chaudhri's but chose not to. They'd been kind but now, she knew, it was time for her to do what she'd come to do and then, to move on.

Her meals she had brought to her in her room. She never went out. She did not approach the Fout or Dalter's brother. She did not trust him or believe she would be safe in doing so.

It was easy to do, this sitting in, because her obvious state made it clear that rest was the highest priority, and no one questioned it: not the innkeeper, nor his daughter nor his two young sons.

She didn't know what she was looking for. Nothing, really. She kept an eye out for the fat Slau, but really she was there to get away from all the people. Something had happened to her on the road, something she'd never felt before. At first, she'd found the feeling very disquieting, but then she began to realize it was a feeling she very much enjoyed and had missed for all of her life up to now.

Ftuu now understood that there were certain benefits to privacy and to being left alone.

And so it followed that she understood why, when they'd given her an opportunity to do so, she'd fled the women of the Chaudhri household without so much as a good-bye. She had felt a shift in her then, like the other time before, on the road, and these seemed to reveal to her portions of her soul she'd never seen or felt before.

Her soul. She would never have thought in those terms before reading the Books, and for that she owed the Chaudhri women a debt. Perhaps someday she'd find herself in a position to repay it, but for now she was content to sit in a room where no one knew her and watch. And wait.

While she watched and waited, the thought crept into her head that maybe someone was looking for her after all. It was a strange feeling, both subtle and strong at once. Were they coming, the ones from the City of Tents? Alone with her thoughts, she tried to puzzle together all that had happened. Little of it made sense, even the part when the women had so readily taken her in. She hadn't noticed it then, but poverty was in abundance in this town, and there were broken women, children, and even men wandering all over, begging for food, sleeping anywhere that was dry, and looking generally lost and without prospect. Carthage was a pit. Everyone needed help. So why had Bel, Hova, and Ewa chosen her?

Try as she might to make sense of it, there was nothing for it. She sat and waited and tried not to think too much about her current situation. The baby moved inside her now and again, slight flutters and such designed, she supposed, to inform her that he or she was alive and well and preparing to enter the world in the full glory of nature's intent.

And that nearly scared the life out of her.

She was running out of money; the thieves on the road hadn't had much. The room was nice enough, but to have a baby she would need…more. She would need help. The thought of going to Pir Choss plagued her mind. Could she make it there alone? Could she find someone to take her? Would they take her baby if she got there?

And what of Dalter's brother? Nuadac was a drunk and a fool who'd had three wives, but his current one, according to Dalter, was different: she owned the inn, and her family was all about. Maybe she would help Ftuu. She might give Ftuu some currency she could use to buy passage south.

To where? And why?

She wasn't sure. But something was urging her south. Not the voice, not Alwaud'wah. A need within her, some kind of ache…

She sat one night, likely her last at Emer's Rooms with her purse now almost empty, and thought she might go mad from the debate in her head. She left the room and went into the square. The fountain was lit up with dying candles from some low celebration. A few old drunks lay leaning with their backs on the sitting stones. Ftuu stood and stared at the Fout and wondered.

"Go to them."

"What?" she asked the drunk closest her. He did not answer. He seemed, in point of fact, to be nearly dead. And the voice had been so soft and clear and low, it could only have come from him.

"Go to them, Zeni. They will have what you need."

"Who is that?" she asked aloud.

There was no reply.

But she needed no reply. She knew who it was. Part of her had always known.

Alwaud'wah.

She hurried back to Emer's Rooms, climbed the stairs, and sat down in her chair to peer out the window. There was nothing in the square; even the shapes of the sleeping drunks blended into the nights' shadows, and all but one of the festival candles had winked out.

The next morning she woke and found she had slept in the chair. Then she remembered her walk in the square and the sound of the voice that had spoken to her. She hadn't dreamt it.

Her things were stacked in a little pile on the dresser. She hadn't got much; most of what she'd taken when she fled the City of Tents was gone in one form or fashion. Some things she'd left at Mama Chaudhri's. All she had now was her clothes, her shoes, half a barb and ten — just enough for breakfast, if she ate light, and a few supplies — and a smallwhip she'd taken from the dead thieves.

And my child, she told herself. *I have my child.* Which was very much like having a lot less in some sense, because when the child came, it would need far more from her than she had or could hope to somehow gain.

She gathered her few belongings and headed down the stairs. There, at a small table in the corner of the small parlor, sat Emer the innkeeper and his two sons, quietly sharing a loaf and some buttermilk.

"Will you be leaving us, then?" asked Emer as he glanced down at her midsection.

Ftuu nodded once and tilted her head to indicate that somehow, she had no choice in the matter.

"Please," said Emer, "if you're going to go, let me give you...I have just a few things that might help you."

One of his sons left the room and came back after a moment with a small satchel.

"It's just a blanket and one or two things that might help you. And your baby."

Ftuu took the satchel and stuffed it into her own sparsely filled bag, then smiled at the Emer and his sons. All three of them blushed.

She turned and then headed out the door and into the square.

She didn't look across at the Fout; in her mind, that door was shut to her.

Go to them. They might help you as well.

This time, she was not confused about the voice's origin. It had come from within her.

But she ignored its advice.

It was time to go.

She exited Carthage through the south gate and found her way down the stairs to one of the many quays on the lake the locals called the Lequoia. There, she boarded a small boat headed to the southern shore and the famous road known as the Dropping Trace.

The Trace led to the south and its oncoming winter winds.

The Trace led to Pir Choss and to Slau and to...Jamoi.

She left the city of Carthage behind her, none the richer for having visited.

Or so she tried to tell herself.

In her hurry and her confusion, she almost disregarded what she'd read. But she did not forget it, nor did she forget the kindness the sisters and their mother had shown her, or even the small kindness of Emer.

Chapter 41
"Bear witness,
so you may know his joy!"

Place: Chralm Doanna, westernmost Aethrelius, Arba Environ
Date: Angem 7, AY 999

He was alone, for five days, in his cell.

At first, they fed him but refused to talk to him. He assumed they were waiting to see what the Mind or whoever had Cedril's family wanted done with him. After a few days, they began to starve him and to deny him water. On the fifth morning, they came into his cell while he was still asleep. They beat him soundly, and then two of them placed wood and tar over his cell's single window. When they shut the door and did the same to the peephole, he was left in total darkness.

They'd fed him once each day, and sometimes there was water. Leander was a very strong man; he always had been. He'd rarely been sick in his life. But he imagined that after a few weeks like this, in the dark, he'd begin to fall apart. He might even begin to wish for death, if it came to that.

Death seemed willing to oblige him, as always, but he wasn't ready, not nearly ready.

That thought kept his mind occupied, the thought that had begun as a vague idea way back in his bedchamber in the Glaring Cliffs. She was still with him them, still alive and young and intense. One night, she'd spoken to him.

"Do you remember our wedding day?" she'd asked him.

"I do."

"They called us the Knight and the Witch."

"They still do."

"They call us worse things now."

"So they do."

"What will they call our son, Leander? Do you ever wonder?"

"Our son will be strong and wise, Baeselle. He will light up this world."

She placed her hand over his. "He would have someday carried this country's hopes in his pocket."

"But now…"

"No. There's nothing for that now."

"But you…"

"What about me?"

"You too can light up the world, Lea. You can do it now."

"No."

"Yes."

"Not me."

"If not, then who?"

"Someone else. No one."

"Are you willing to watch it all die?"

"The Stavers will not allow this country to fall into the hands of an enemy. They know we cannot defeat the Vo'ixtavracci divided. We cannot either defeat them united, I think, but together we could try."

"You are sure it is the Vo'ixtavracci?"

"Who else?"

"You have seen them, the great ships that float like islands?"

"No."

"Then how do you know?"

"To the east, Baeselle, there is nothing beyond Delariun but the Vo'ixtavracci Empire. They rule land, sea, and air for as far as it would take a lifetime to travel. And they are many, from many lands...and we are now certain they have claimed Delariun."

"But the great ships..."

"Have not yet come."

"Perhaps...we can only believe that if they haven't come, perhaps a..."

"They will come. And when they do, Aethrelius will fall."

"No."

"Yes. There is nothing left to keep them at bay. If the Mudarrisi are banished—and Beir will see that they are—we won't be able to stop the Vo'ixtavracci from landing, and once they do..."

"Frederick could have stopped them."

"Frederick died many years ago."

"But his Sword—the Sword of Endings—endures."

"Please, do not speak of it. I cannot, not now, not with so much at stake."

"Why?"

"Baeselle, Renik's Mosta Nom was lost after Frederick, if it ever existed at all."

"You don't believe that."

"I do."

"But if it did exist...and you found it...you could turn them back, you could save all Aethrelius, and all Arba as well."

"Do you think I haven't dreamt of this thing you suggest? What Aethrelean man, what Aethrelean child hasn't? A quest to find the Sword!

Heroism, unblemished in its certitude. But my mother was wrong. Her dream was a child's dream, and her search for answers resulted in naught but a wasted life."

"Theresta learned much in her search. And she believed it was your destiny to find the Sword."

"She was mad."

"She was a mother, and a woman with sight."

"No. She was a woman who insanely believed in a quest most men had long since given up on, and rightly so. Quests are for fools."

"We need more than a fool's quest, dear husband. We need salvation."

"Then do not look to a child's dream to provide it. Salvation is a fool's quest when it comes in the form of a dead warrior's mythical weapon."

"Then it is time for dreams to vanquish the sleep-ridden tie that binds them so pointlessly, and sojourn to the waking world, to find fertile grounds upon which salvation needs so dearly to be delivered."

"The poemsmen have nothing over you, Baeselle, but the sentiment must live and die in verse alone, I fear. The dream of the Sword is one the waking must forego."

"Must, or simply will?"

"Either, if it please you."

"What would most please me is you laying claim to the solution the path of the Sword presents us."

"The path is lost. The Sword is lost. If the Vo'ixtavracci are truly coming, we are undone."

"But if you—"

"Speak no more of it. I cannot engage in empty fantasies."

"If not the Sword, my husband, then what? Surrender?"

"The Vo'ixtavracci do not accept surrender."

"Then it is death or enslavement for us all."

"Death. We'll fight them to the last."

"And when will that be? Next week? Tomorrow?"

"I cannot say."

"Or will not say? Do not attempt to spare me the pain of my final moment's knowledge. I welcome death, if death must come, as a true Aethrelean woman."

"I would see you live."

"Without you?"

"If needs be."

"No."

"Yes. You will go to Renikalar with Frainle. You cannot stay here."

"The Glaring Cliffs have been our home for twenty years. I will not leave because an enemy sails toward it."

"Not just an enemy. They are the Last Enemy."

"They aren't gods. They've been defeated before."

"Perhaps. Perhaps they got what they wanted and left on their own."

"You know that isn't true."

"Baeselle, you cannot stay here."

"I will not abandon our home; I will not abandon you. I can wield a sword better than most."

"Swords will not avail us here. We seek only to purchase time with our lives — time to permit all the Cliffs' people to flee. I must lead my men one last time, to Tolii Nus. If you stay here, I will not be able to lead."

"But I will stay, and you will lead, and when you return, I will fight by your side."

"No. Please, Baeselle — "

She turned abruptly and walked away from him. She stood at the window with her back to him and stared at the sea without seeing it. "You want me to leave?"

"Yes."

"Would you pay any price to gain my consent?"

"Name it."

"Stay here and defend this place, if you must. See the proud Cliffs fall. But before it ends, before they come for you, flee…save yourself…and then, for me, for all Aethrelius, do as I ask and seek the Sword."

"Again, the Sword. Why?"

"If you are right and there is nothing we can do to stop the Vo'ixtavracci invaders, then what harm would there be in one captain choosing not to die but instead to pursue his poor, dreaming wife's vision of possible salvation?"

"You are mad. Like Theresta."

"No, I am negotiating. She would have as well, with so much at stake."

"Indeed."

"Then we have a deal? I will flee to whatever safety Renikalar can provide, and you will seek Mosta Nom?"

"You are Theresta in my wife's skin."

"How so?"

"She once tried to bargain me into leaving the Unchained and the military to help her search for the Sword."

"I know. But you never told me: What did she offer?"

"I have forgotten."

"Have you?"

"Yes. In any case, her offer failed to convince me."

She turned and took two steps toward him. "So it would seem. And mine?"

"I cannot abandon my post."

"Then we die together at it."

"No. Our son...he will live."

"You cannot change my mind with less than a solemn vow."

He stood and faced her, then embraced her firmly. The wind slipped through some gap in the thick purple curtains that guarded their bedchamber against the weather of the sea. Leander had neither the time nor the will to debate his wife; there was too much at stake for all of them, and though he would never admit it to her, part of him had always believed, against all sense and logic, and both she and his mother were right about the Sword.

Leander said, "Then I solemnly vow...to do as you ask."

"Yes?"

"I will seek the Sword of Endings, the Sword of Renik, to the ends of Arba and beyond — if you leave and take our son away."

She hadn't left. She hadn't had the chance.

She was dead now. And their son would never be born. No chance for either of them.

He lay in his cell in the dark and anguished over what he might have done differently. The Vo'ixtavracci bombardment had started so suddenly, in the night, with no signs and no warning, or so the few survivors had told him. He could have arranged a ship or a team of horses, and they would have all known where to meet in the event of an attack...

But no. There simply hadn't been time, not the night of the attack. And before then, when there'd been all the time in the world, he'd hesitated, he'd played politics, he'd believed that life would go on as it had, he'd ignored what he knew and played the hopeful fool.

Now, in his thoughts, he watched as the tower that had been their home exploded and the ship that had been their way out burned. He heard the horses he'd never arranged screaming.

He watched knowing his wife, their unborn son, and their young daughter were perishing, over and over, in the flaming bombardment.

Four thousand people had been destroyed in the time it takes to consume a meal.

He waited in the dark and more than once believed he'd died and thought about that night and the fall of the Cliffs.

Why had it happened? What in truth could he have done differently? Could he have swayed the Square, could he have seized control of the government, could he have somehow sniffed out the insane Tri plot to ruin his country and hand it to the monsters?

No. There was nothing he could have done. Every substantial item and avenue had been set against him from the start. The Stavers. The Tri. The Vo'ixtavracci. All in league. And his own ultimately careless party the Unchained, too long in power, too stifled by the constraints of a stagnant ideology and too many years spent unchallenged at home and abroad.

They'd been asleep. But now, he was certain, they were awake. Those that were living, in any case. Awake and screaming.

The Vo'ixtavracci were far too powerful, far too swift, and far too wicked to be defended against. They were mythic in their dominance. They were too strong for any Arban army, or perhaps any army anywhere, to meet on the field of battle. They'd conquered most of the known world and had done so in absolutely merciless fashion.

They'd only been turned back the one time.

He considered that one time and what he knew about Renik, which wasn't much. A good man, a strong man. He'd found the Sword and used it to save his country and his people.

Leander's thoughts began to circle around that Sword.

What was it? Where was it? Had it ever been real? What did he — what could he — believe?

His wife had believed. His mother had believed.

Why? What had they known that he did not? Or was it simply a matter of faith, a matter of something beyond reason and strategy and experience?

He knew now he'd never believed in the Quest. He'd tried to, but he never could.

He'd told his wife a lie to save her life. It wasn't the first he'd told her, but it could have ultimately proven to be somehow forgivable, had she lived. Now, he lived with the knowledge that the last conversation they'd ever shared had ended with an impotent lie.

And then once again, he thought about the Sword.

What if it were true? *Baeselle, what did you know?*

He thought about the fires at the Glaring Cliffs. He remembered the screams, but how could he? He hadn't been there. And yet…he imagined it so fully, so viscerally, that he was convinced he remembered the destruction and the shock of seeing so many die so suddenly and so needlessly. His people. His family. His life.

The Vo'ixtavracci weren't interested in land or even abstract conquest. What they craved was death, the death of every living thing that would not yield to them, and even the deaths of those who might have, were they given the opportunity.

They were evil incarnate. They were monstrous slavers who dined on human flesh, murderers of the young and of the old and of women. They delighted in torture. They ate, and they burned, and they ate again.

And he thought once again about the Sword.

What did it look like? Where would it be? Could it be true, after all, that some Timesinger held the key to its location?

How could he find that person?

And how could he get out of here to do so?

On the evening of the fifth day of his imprisonment, Cedril himself finally came to his cell. He had ten guards with him. Leander sat and watched as four of them took position in the cell between him and the man who had for over twenty years been his friend and ally but now was only another loathsome puppet of the Stavers.

"I need you to come with me," said Cedril flatly.

Leander did not stand. "Where are my men?" he demanded.

Cedril hesitated for just a moment and then answered, "Your men are…here, in the keep, with us."

Why the timidity? Why the lie? "Take me to them," Leander commanded.

"I will. I am. Please…" said Cedril, gesturing toward the open cell door.

Leander nodded and allowed himself to be taken. *Not that I have the strength at present to resist even two men. Cedril had them starving me; was that on Beir's orders as well? Or the Duke's perhaps? Why?*

They ascended the dungeon stairs, climbing for some ten minutes, and finally reached the keep proper. They proceeded down the main way toward the Great Doanna Hall, in which Leander had been betrayed by Cedril only a few days before. They stopped at the door.

"Are you bringing me here to feed me, Cedril, or to somehow remind me of your treachery? I assure you, I have not forgotten, nor will I ever. But I'll accept a good meal if you're offering one."

"I am bringing you here because I was told to."

"I see. And who commands you now, my old friend? Beir? The Mind?"

Cedril was silent. The guards opened the door.

"I asked you a question, sa Mino. Who commands you?"

"We do, Captain Dossilea."

The voice that spoke to him was deep and rich and louder than a voice in a hall as large as this one should have been. Leander saw its owner and trembled for a moment despite himself.

It can't be. Not here…how could they be here?

"Come in, come in! Do not be afraid, good sir, for we have only the purest of intentions here tonight! We welcome you to our dining hall, Tha'it Leander Dossilea! There is most certainly the promise of a good meal, as you say, although I cannot promise you will enjoy it quite as much as my friends and me!"

Leander collected himself and regarded his hosts. There were three of them, two males and a female. They were here in the Great Hall of Chralm Doanna, sitting at a table the size of a small house.

"Captain! Captain, please!" The cries of his men came from within a massive bucket near the far wall, just next to the hall's enormous fireplace. Inside the fireplace was a huge spit on which the Doannans often roasted three or four boar at a time; Leander had been here many times before during Holy Day feasts.

"Ah, how they squeal, the meat! They say, Captain, that squealing, lively meat is best, for it energizes us, clarifies our thoughts, and brings us closer to the Ones Above!" intoned the giant creature, its deep voice shaking the room.

The guards pushed Leander forward toward the table; he noticed they did not follow. Cowardly Doannan bastards.

"Come closer, yes, come near to us. Garkin Frwi is about to eat — he prefers his meat uncooked, the savage — and wishes you to bear witness, so you may know his joy!"

Leander stopped walking and stood still.

"Oh, don't be that way, Captain! Join us!"

The Vo'ixtavracci stood and bent down with what was unthinkable speed for such a huge being. He grabbed Leander by his legs, lifted him, and unceremoniously dumped him onto the middle of the table. "My name, and where are my manners, is Braeru Ketwa. Now sit and bear witness like a gracious guest!"

In front of one of the other Vo'ixtavracci was a large, square plate. On the plate was a naked, unconscious Heop. Both of his legs were broken and angled unnaturally. The Vo'ixtavracci called Garkin picked up a large, two-pronged fork and poked at his "meat." Heop stirred and then slowly began to awaken. He saw what loomed above him and screamed. He tried to move away, but his shattered legs prevented him from being able to crawl, so he simply wriggled.

Leander was nor more than ten feet away from him. Heop turned and saw him, his face a twisted mask of agony and terror, but in his eyes, there was, momentarily, recognition and affection.

And then the fork came down, hard. It stabbed through Heop's midsection and pinned him to the plate. The screams that followed were brief as the man passed out again.

"Screaming meat is better, but either way, as long as it's raw," said Garkin Frwi. He used the edge of the fork to sever Heop's body in half and then scooped up his legs and shoved them in his mouth.

Leander vomited and tried to stumble away.

The Vo'ixtavracci Ketwa caught him and slapped him back

roughly. Leander hit the table so hard he was sure he'd broken several bones.

"Stay, little meat. Watch." Ketwa rose again and walked toward the bucket, needing only two steps to cover the distance. "I prefer, as does Perda Frwi, to cook my meat through," he bellowed.

He reached into the bucket with both hands and drew out Famish and Youssef.

When the meal and the screams were done, Leander lay there on the table with his eyes closed, praying they would kill him quickly. They didn't.

Ketwa poked him in the chest with a long forefinger. "I hope you enjoyed our little dinner party, Tha'it Dossilea. And I hope it goes a long way to discouraging you from any foolish dreams about myths and legends. You know that fucking Sword is surely at the bottom of the sea, don't you?" The Vo'ix smiled at him, bits of flesh still stuck in his teeth, and laughed, spewing some of the flesh back onto the table and onto Leander's face. The other two, the ones called Perda and Garkin, joined in the mirth, each of them spewing and spitting meat about.

Leander sat in a stupor and stared at the remains on his hosts' plates. They were laughing. They'd just eaten his friends and now, they were laughing.

"This was an excellent feast, friend Cedril, though it doesn't compare to the night we had at the Glaring Cliffs. Most of the meat had been roasted by our dear friends' firerocks; we had only to wander and chew."

"You...were at the Cliffs?" Leander rasped.

"Yes, of course, but there is only one thing you should concern yourself with now, my dear Captain, and that is this: even Vo'ixtavracci appetites have their limits. I myself won't eat for several days after this sumptuous feast. And so you get to live for at least that long. Goodnight, Captain."

He pushed Leander off the table and onto the floor. There was a crack as his elbow slammed down.

"I'm sorry about that. Guards, see he gets some lifewine or whatever he needs to heal. Can't have him falling ill. Spoils the meat."

They led him back to his cell and left him there. Someone brought him lifewine, but he knocked the glass over trying to thrash his way to freedom. They left him and locked the cell door. They needn't have. His will to escape, and even to live, was nowhere to be found.

He lay on the floor and wept.

An hour later, Cedril sa Mino came to him.

Leander was still slouched on the floor, his arm throbbing, his mind afire with rage and fear. "What do you want?" he demanded of Cedril.

"I've come to help you," Cedril said, his voice dead except for a slight nasal whine.

"Help me? Help me? You murdering, foul animal! You want to help?"

"Please, listen to me, Leander…"

"Listen to what? The lies and madness of a man who would allow his countrymen to be eaten…who would welcome such creatures into his home and follow their orders—"

Cedril broke down and howled. "I did not welcome them! They arrived a week before you did. I'd been ordered to detain you by the Square, but I'd no intention…I wouldn't have—"

"You let them…my men, you animal! Men you knew, men you fought beside!"

"They did the same to my sons! Last week. And just now, to Gallivette. They ate my wife in front of me! They ate her in front of me, Leander!"

Cedril slipped to the floor, weeping. Leander stood and watched him. He understood then that sa Mino had little choice. His mind was surely gone and had been for some time.

It didn't make him hate the man any less, and it didn't make Leander any less ashamed of his own misplaced hatred.

"They came and they killed and they took Chralm Doanna from me. Their rockmen destroyed my garrison in minutes," Cedril said, his voice trailing off, his eyes distant. "Minutes."

Leander said, "We saw no evidence, no battlefield."

"The fight took place on the shore. What fight there was, anyway. Our citizens were rounded up and put in great pens."

"How many Vo'ixtavracci?"

"Just the three, but three is enough. They move about like storms."

"Where are Michael and Wexshai?" asked Leander, hopeful at least that someone he knew might still be alive. He hadn't seen or heard them in the dining hall.

"Hiding. Down near the southerly stables. My people spotted them on the first night."

"Why did you let them…why didn't you capture them?"

"I thought…the Vo'ixtavracci weren't aware, and I couldn't bring more men, more of…"

"Cedril, why did you not fight them? Why did you not die fighting them?"

"Gallivette. They had Gallivette. And my sons, my beautiful, young boys...Thretei was only seven years old!"

What horror. Aethrelius had a long and brutal history of warfare, it could not be denied, but even among the denizens of the Gri Na Leus and the Linosians, it had always been considered off limits to threaten wives and children. It was not honorable, it was not even sane to do so, and any who did had ever been considered the lowest of the low, worthy of no quarter or consideration.

But to make a man watch while his wife and young sons were consumed...Leander, who could not hide his mind from the memory of his men's eyes and screams as they were eaten, could find nothing in himself by which to place Cedril's pain, no frame of reference by which to empathize.

There was only rage.

"Why are you here now?" he asked calmly. "Have they asked for me again?"

"Asked for you? No, no, they have not. And it wouldn't matter if they had. I am here to set you free, old friend."

"They'll kill you."

"That was always going to happen."

"I think it's happening to everyone in our country, to Aethrelius herself. These are the true Vo'ixtavracci, the things of legend...the Takers, the Eaters, the Ruination," said Leander.

"They are here at Chralm Doanna to close off any escape through the pass. They are here to kill us all."

"I believe it."

"But you, Leander, can you...will you seek the Sword?"

"With all that I have in me. But first, get me out of here and to the Western Road. And have what men of mine remain meet me at the pass."

"The pass is not safe."

"Then where?"

"I have a plan," said Cedril, his eyes shifting downward and then flicking from side to side.

"I would not trust you now if you offered me even a bowl of soup. I would murder you with the spoon, I would bash your face in with the bowl...with my bare fists."

Cedril winced and looked at him. "I know that. I understand that, I do. But I will do all that I can for you. I have to. I have to. I should have done more, I should have warned you, I should have fought and died — but dammit, I didn't!"

He stood there, shaking and weeping and barking out his confession and his shame.

"When I leave here, go to the end of this hall" — Cedril pointed down to the left — "and push at the wall. There is a small tunnel that leads to a larger one, one that goes under the keep, along the canal, and under the town to the sea."

"And the men?"

"I have already sent word. They will enter another tunnel from the stables and find you where the canal empties into the Cjaknok Bay. Some of my men are with them. But take care, my old friend, yes, for I cannot promise these monsters won't be waiting there; they have taken us in full, and their servants are everywhere. The rockmen, and worse…" Cedril slumped down onto the floor, lost once more, done.

Leander stood and, despite himself, touched Cedril's shoulder in a gesture of camaraderie. "And you, my friend? What will you do?" he said quietly.

"Me? Nothing, really, nothing at all. I plan to simply host one final dinner, complete with roasted meat and perhaps the kind of scream we have not yet heard. I plan to see if our guests can survive an entire keep collapsing on them."

"I would like to see that for myself," said Leander as he offered a hand to Cedril to help him up. "For Aethrelius."

Cedril took Leander's hand, stood, and nodded, a dark, defiant look finding its way into his eyes. "You, and I…and your father, and Yallous, the times we had, the battles…yes. For Aethrelius. I wish they were here now. Fighting by our side."

"Good-bye, my friend."

"Good-bye." Cedril then slipped a small book into Leander's hands. "And good hunting, Captain."

Chapter 42
"I must admit, then,
to a certain arousal of curiosity."

Place: The Midforest, Arba Environ
Date: Angem 8, AY 999

The first sun rose, but Baks Mu did not wake the Timesinger. The old man was shivering, trapped in a damp and restless sleep, and did not look ready to face whatever was next.

Instead, the Juks Xi Ren left his companion and made his way through the water and rocks back to the scene of the previous night's massacre.

The smell of burning flesh, that of men and horses both, reached his sensitive nostrils, and he reflexively dipped back below the water for a moment. Coming back up, he adjusted his breathing much more toward his skin's mechanism, an ability he was thankful for on occasions such as these.

He climbed the bank and peeked over at the scene.

Whatever had attacked was long gone. Nothing had been left alive.

The wagons had been flipped and the soldiers and passengers butchered. The elderly woman with the sash and her young companion had had their throats ripped out and were sitting next to each other on the ground like two children sharing a secret. There were pieces of soldiers and horses everywhere. Three soldiers without heads were propped up against a broken wagon. No doubt they'd been the ones without answers.

The sergeant himself leaned against a rotting maple tree, his dull expression frozen in the moment when he'd been run through. He hadn't seen it coming; even a man of his practiced lethargy couldn't have maintained a detached visage in the face of such viciousness. A long, black spike had pinned him to the maple. Baks did not recognize the spike's make.

All the travelers were present and accounted for; none had escaped. None except the man who'd been watching the old man.

"Geminstra is not here," said Xian.

Baks started, not expecting the Timesinger to be awake much less right here beside him. The old man was stealthier than he appeared. Baks squinted at Xian and then surveyed the scene once again. "Perhaps they took him," he said.

"Perhaps. Or perhaps he went with them," Xian answered.

"You know this? Or is it a guess?"

"It's a guess that fits the facts. How he might have signaled them eludes me, but there were ample opportunities along the way."

"Or perhaps whatever did this was able to easily able to track a stinking, slow-moving target to this place."

"That also fits the facts — save for the disappearance of Geminstra."

"Maybe his pieces are scattered," remarked Baks. He thought it likely.

"Maybe," Xian said doubtfully.

"We should leave."

"Agreed."

They spent a few short minutes hurriedly collecting their scant belongings, along with a few minor additions: a soldier's pack that Baks had stuffed with much of the food their escorts had been carrying, a longspear for Baks, and for Xian, the maple cudgel their friend the sergeant had seemed never to wield with any actual purpose.

"We should say a few words, to ease the passing of their souls," said Baks.

"I had thought to say a few words to them. They would not have listened. He would not have listened," Xian said, nodding toward the sergeant.

Baks murmured a quick sea prayer and then turned to Xian and nodded. Time to go. "You expected this," he said.

"You didn't?"

Baks grunted, shrugged, and strode back toward the bank.

Xian gave the site a final glance and followed him. When they got to the bank, Xian said softly, "Wait, please."

Baks stopped and turned to him. "We cannot linger here."

"No, we cannot. But neither can we travel along the river."

"But if we're to get to Quintish without being seen, what other way is there?"

"Through the Midforest."

Baks regarded the old man with distrust and shook his head. "I am not comfortable with that idea."

"I understand. But you know they'll be back. And you know they will assume you, a half-dragon, escaped with me via the best possible route: the river." Xian placed his hand on the Challowian's shoulder. "Please, walk with me while we talk about this."

Baks nodded. The road was no place for them to debate, even in daylight. They had assumed the attackers were nocturnal, but that assumption was only for the sake of convenience. It was at best a guess.

Together they made their way down the riverbank and then to the Camedua's eastern side, Xian hopping from stone to stone, Baks wading through and enjoying, if only briefly, the gifts of the water.

Xian led him up into the edge of what many considered the most dangerous forest in the Triumvirate, if not all of Arba. Baks stopped and put down his pack. He said, "We won't have access to water. Your cloth trick kept me alive, but if we are forced to remain in there for a time, or to fight…"

"There are streams and ponds within the forest, Baks," Xian assured him.

"So I have heard. I've also heard that Deconian females sweat liquid gold, but I have never seen that for myself. There are also many alleged dangers within this forest, dangers that you and I alone would be ill-equipped to contend with if they turned out to be something more than alleged."

"Perhaps so. Yet we were both almost assassinated last night, and we no longer have our Triumvirate companions to, let's be kind, protect us. The river route is not safe."

"On that we agree. They'll be coming," Baks said. He stared eastward toward the gnarled oak trees, the infinite patches of bramble and darkness, and the shadowy groves of thin pines. "You know this way?"

"Yes. I have travelled it many times, though not for several years now."

"And you are sure there is water?"

"I would not condemn you to death this early in our friendship."

"Later, then?"

"Oh, to be sure. But I will kill you with food and wine."

"Poison?"

"No, quite the contrary: excellent, unspoiled foods, so tempting and so plentiful that you would have little choice but to eat and drink yourself to death."

"So you cook too? What other talents do you have?"

"All in good time, Lakeservant."

Baks chuckled and hoisted his pack. "Very well. I accept your invitation, Timesinger."

"It may be a while."

"If we live through this forest and reach Pherriuskata, we will find a house of your order with a large kitchen, and you will make good on your threat."

"My order has but one house."

"Ashkinda."

"Yes. And you are always welcome there."

"I may take you up on that offer. Maybe not today or tomorrow, but the road of life is long, one hopes…"

"And of course you would prefer fish?"

"A safe assumption."

They walked east, Xian leading the way. He laughed suddenly to himself.

"Something is funny?" Baks asked.

Xian shook his head. "Only an old fool's dwindling sense of awareness. I was just now going to tell you why I am traveling to Pashka, but I have had a second thought about the timing. Would you mind if I delayed until we've put some distance between ourselves and the river?"

"I don't mind at all, my friend. If we have breath for tale telling…"

"Then we probably aren't moving fast enough. Understood."

"And if anything else amusing occurs to you, please share it. I could use a laugh. But keep it brief."

Xian led them into the Midforest and away from whatever would surely be pursuing them. They both knew it was probably too late for them and that anything that could tear apart a regiment of Tri soldiers would have them at a severe disadvantage once that pursuit ended successfully. But neither of them was of a mind or nature to acknowledge the overwhelming odds they faced.

They marched together in silence toward whatever awaited.

After several hours, during which time they encountered very little water, they stopped for a rest. Both suns were obscured from their view as they considered the forest's canopy.

"It might rain," Xian said, shrugging slightly.

"How would we know, in this?" Baks said, waving his hand at the seemingly infinite pine trees and rocks and thick oaks and maples. "Do you have any idea where we are?"

"Not really. Do you?" Xian responded as he yanked a loaf from his backpack.

"Not funny."

"But it was brief, no?" Xian smiled, broke off a chunk of the loaf, and offered the rest to his large companion.

Baks held up his hand to refuse the bread. "You promised me water."

"I did."

"And?"

"There used to be water," Xian said with a shrug.

"That won't help me now. And stop being so funny."

"Use the canteens. All of them, if you must. I have some wine."

"The canteens won't last."

"Neither will this bad luck. There will be streams. Trust me."

"If there aren't, neither of us will survive. What good does it do us to die in this nasty place? We should have taken our chances along the river," Baks grumbled.

Xian shook his head. "Had we done so, we'd both be dead already, without a doubt. Perhaps it doesn't matter. It seems reasonable to assume that I may not survive much longer. They'll find me. Not here, not in this place, but as soon as we reach Pashka."

"Why are they looking for you? You know something?"

"Yes, and someone else knows what I know, and apparently now they know that I know it. So Xian hasn't much time, has he?"

"Maybe not. But how do they know so much?" Baks asked.

"Not sure. Magick? Spies? Something else, maybe."

"But you're sure they want you dead."

"Yes. They were not after the sergeant."

"Well, he did have that special cudgel." Baks smirked. "And he was very handsome."

They exchanged a slight grin. Baks dumped a little water on his head and let it trickle down along his body. Xian noted how the pores in his scaled and somewhat amphibious skin seemed almost to drink the water.

Shaking his limbs in an attempt to relax, Baks said, "What you know must be important."

"Yes."

"Very well. Tell me already. But before you do, I must first tell you something, because you may not want to trust me so fully."

"Like I said, I know of your people, Baks Mu. There is nothing you could say to make me trust you any more or less than I am already inclined to."

"I lied to you."

"Except for that."

Baks just looked at the Timesinger, unsure of his meaning.

"Bad joke. Again. Please, continue," said the old man.

Baks looked down the trail and gestured for them to continue their hike, which they then did. "I know who was on my ship, and I know why we were attacked," he said after a time.

"Go on."

"I cannot tell you who it was. I am sorry."

"Did they kill—whoever it was?"

"No. She got away."

"Did she?"

"I was not performing a Felsorad. Or rather, I was not only performing a Felsorad. Nor was I honoring a death. My son lives and is a crewman on the *Wei Viette*."

"You were celebrating his birthday."

"I was."

"And that does not require the full trance of the death ritual."

"You know more about the Juks ways than most."

"Well, as I said, I read a lot. Tell me more, if you wish."

Baks hesitated to consider how much he should reveal. He thought about it and concluded there was no good reason not to trust the Timesinger. Even if the man turned out to be a Triumvirate spy, things couldn't get any worse for the Challowian than being condemned, hunted, and stuck in a forest hundreds of miles from the lake and his kin and their ships. He admitted to himself again that he expected to die somewhere on this journey, as he had expected to die on the deck of the *Ho Matsuni*. So why not just trust the old man?

"We knew the attack was imminent. I helped the person in question escape via yalessi. My boatswain, Pua Ta Dou, went with her."

Xian did not seem surprised. "And you're sure she escaped?"

"Yes. They entered the yalessi and submerged a full half hour before the attack. But I'm not even sure the woman on our ship was the woman they were after. I think she may have been switched out at some point."

"I see," said Xian. "It's all a bit confusing, and suggestive of perhaps the involvement of multiple interests. Surely whoever arranged for her passage could not have been behind the attack."

"I expect not."

"Tell me about the attack, please."

"Not much to tell. They came, they killed. I lit the ship afire and swam away while my captain stayed behind and destroyed what was left of them."

"Fortune allowed you to survive."

"No. Yes. Using the ritual, I hid until they attacked in the hopes I could gain advantage and surprise the attackers. But they were too quick, too brutal. They flew."

"Your crew knew what was coming?"

"They were ready for something. Out on the sea, Juks Xi Ren usually are, and the captain had given the word to be watchful. But what came...no one could have known."

"And now your good fortune has placed you in suspicion."

"Yes."

"The Guild."

"I have been suspended and must now travel to Pashka to give my testimony and request reinstatement."

"You cannot tell them the truth."

"I am aware."

"And yet, given the suspicious circumstances of your survival—compounded by your having survived a second attack on the road—the only thing that might save your life is full disclosure."

"Perhaps. Although now I seem to have you to vouch for me."

"That, my friend, will not help you make your case. I am little liked in the circles to which we contemplate travelling."

"They know you?"

"And I them. But I said, your penchant for miraculous escapes makes you highly suspect. I would, were I you, expect to be transported posthaste to Bi."

"If that is what is meant to be."

"Are you so willing to die?"

"I am, if honor demands it."

"Still, if honor takes you, the mystery will remain unsolved, and the deaths of your crewmates will be rendered meaningless, surely."

"Their deaths *are* meaningless. There is nothing I can do to alter that fact. And with regard to the solving of this great mystery, remind me once more what it is you Timesingers do?"

"Point taken."

They hiked and climbed and wiggled through forest vines and growth for hours. The trail was a trail only in name. It was nearly nightfall when the rains came. They decided to rest a while, maybe even try to sleep.

Baks put the food pack down but not the spear. He stripped off his fishskin vest and his leggings. He let the rain fall down on him, and he moved in a slow, rhythmic dance of sorts, ensuring his whole body would be thoroughly soaked.

Xian walked away to give his new friend some privacy. He pulled out a wide-brimmed hat from his pack and fitted it onto his head. Then he rooted around in the pack and produced a short weed. Looking in toward the forest, he squatted down on a large stone under a wide pine, lit the end of the weed, and took a few short puffs. The frantish cleared his head a bit, but the clarity only served to bring their current troubles into more specific relief.

A while later, Baks walked up, looking relaxed and refreshed, and took a seat on the stone next to him. The rain was still falling, lightly but steadily, and a mist had crept in. "So tell me, finally: Why are you going to Pashka?" he said.

Xian offered the Challowian the weed. Baks declined with a smile. "I cannot. Doesn't sit well with my kind."

Xian tilted his head, blew out some smoke, and said: "I am going to Pashka to address the Body."

"The Body? That information you've almost been killed for must be valuable," said Baks Mu, genuinely surprised. "And here I thought somehow the Body was perhaps behind all these attacks. Obviously I was wrong. Why kill you for it if you're so willing to just tell them?"

"The Body is nothing. They won't think what I've got is valuable. But it's not them who need to hear it."

"Who then?"

"Who else? The Mind. The ever-listening, ever-scheming, perpetually self-defeating Mind."

"Hard to get an audience with them. Impossible, even."

"Unfortunately. And the Body may not even agree to honor my petition."

"No?" Baks leaned back and stretched his long, semireptilian body in several directions at once. "Well, I expect not, unless your petition has bearing on a matter that directly affects their purses...or their recreation or their wars. Their purses, mostly."

"What I know, what I and my kind have learned, will affect all of those things, not directly, but in a nonetheless devastating fashion."

"I must admit, then, to a certain arousal of curiosity."

Xian gave him a small smile, but his eyes were elsewhere. "We've got some time. This storm is just beginning, I'm afraid. But it won't come to full fruition for a while now, I suppose."

"Then in the meantime, while we wait for our doom, let's make camp, brew something hot—tea for you, freiduvi for me—and have your tale. I must warn you, though, my expectations for entertainment are high."

Xian got up and stared out at the forest. "You will be sadly disappointed, Baks Mu. My tale is not entertaining, just daunting, and the near certainty that it will be ignored by the powers-that-be makes for a grim ending indeed."

Baks regarded Xian as he stood there staring off into the rain and the mist. There was no mirth or tale-teller's countenance about him. He looked, if anything, very sad and even a little afraid. He wore the same look he had after the attack by the river.

Xian took off his hat, shook off the raindrops, and put it back on his head. After taking another few puffs of his frantish weed, he began:

"In the spring of 997, a member of my order, a dear friend of mine, received a letter. He only found out who sent it very recently, but at the time he set aside his curiosity about the sender's identity because of the striking nature of the information the letter contained.

"The author claimed that there was something to find—or rather, would be—something essential to the survival of every living thing in Arba, somewhere on the long-deserted northern coast of Abeilon. It wasn't specific about what that was, but there were other references in the letter, references to finds and theories that only those within a very select Timesinger inner circle could know about.

"At first, my friend Wolsa was deeply troubled, because to him, ever watchful and wary regarding the fate of the Timesingers in this world, the letter could only mean that someone had infiltrated our ranks or turned one of our inner circle into a spy or worse. He didn't know who to trust, and so he hid what he'd learned for over a year, all the while contemplating the right course of action and watching for any odd behavior in those near him.

"Life in Ashkinda hummed along at the same meticulously uninspired pace, however, and he almost forgot about the letter and its dour implications. Then one day early this year, during the last of the Iobus rites, another of our order, Hartenow, had a strange meeting by the ocean. He was out walking just after the suns had set, paying little attention, as is common with our kind, to anything outside of his own head, when right before him was a young man in a yellow cloak. His face was mostly covered in an otter's mask, but his smile was visible, and something about that smile made Hartenow comfortable enough to listen to this man, despite his vulnerable circumstances.

"'You must go to Abeilon, to the once-great places by the sea. The fate of all you know depends on it. Please, do not ignore this warning as you ignored our first. Heed me or face the fate of the Thesselines,' said the young man.

"Hartenow asked him his name and where his home was. There was no reply. He invited him back to our keep to lodge and dine and take his respite, for there is nothing near to there for many miles, and darkness was almost upon them. The young man's smile persisted, but he refused the offer and then turned away and walked quickly north along the beach, almost too quickly for a human, which he had appeared to be.

"Hartenow reported this encounter to us immediately upon his return. The seven of us, the Seven Learners, as we are perhaps inaccurately called, were puzzled but not alarmed. We sent a rider to Fort Dilan to ask after and perhaps locate the young man, or to see if there were more of his kind about, but that was fruitless. We debated on and off for a few days about what the message could mean — Abeilon, as you know very well, has been a mostly dead island ever since the F'lonedian Influx and the subsequent migrations and skirmishes.

"There is Braidenosh, of course, but that town is young as towns go, and not of any historical interest. Much as we are renowned for placing excessive food orders in proportion to our numbers — we feel it is best both to be prepared and to eat well when one is preparing — we couldn't imagine any emissary of that seaside place being issued forth to lure one of ours there with a ruse designed to sell us fish or beer. Some of our less impressive wine kegs go there, especially in the month before Dakaj, but those are purchased by the guilds and shipped from our door. Other than that, there was no connection between ourselves and Braidenosh — and certainly none between ourselves — or anything else Arban — and the Thesseline Environ. That place died long ago."

"Intrigued though we were, it seemed best to let the matter drop into the great vat of unanswered puzzlements — as you might expect, we often are driven to places where our curiosity remains woefully unsatisfied — particularly when there were no further reports of contact with the mysterious young man and no further cryptic messages from any source whatsoever involving Braidenosh, Abeilon, or Thesseline. We turned our attention to other matters.

"It was a month later when Wolsa at last broke his silence about the letter. Why he chose that time to do so, he didn't say. He apologized, again and again, and swore he had only the best interests of the order in mind when he'd elected not to reveal either the letter or the misgivings it had authored in him. But the burden had proven too heavy and the mystery too deep even for him, the wisest and most widely read of the Timesingers. He produced the letter.

"We each read it. We read it carefully, slowly, and repeatedly, as is our custom. We read it for riddles, for codes, for subtextual clues. Some believed it was a great hoax, a game being played upon us by some lake lord throwing a party — not an insane notion, if you know about the lords and their parties — but most were sure there was an unmistakable, if obscure, authenticity to it. Its connection to the encounter on the beach was undeniable as well, for to suddenly have two apparently unrelated parties imploring us to explore forgotten portions of Abeilon within the same relatively short time span was too coincidental by half, and the young man in the yellow robe had referred to an earlier warning, after all.

"Someone wanted something from us or was simply warning us, and though it seemed improbable that whatever was at stake could include 'the fate of us all,' we were unwilling to dismiss the warning or the want on the chance that it might."

Baks said, "You went to Abeilon."

"I did not, but four of us — the Learners--along with twelve lesser members of our order, set out within the month, again after much debate."

"What did they find?"

"Nothing, really. They found nothing. It would be more accurate to say that something...or someone...found them."

"The stranger from the beach?"

"No. We still haven't determined who he was. No, this was...someone who claimed to be a member of the once ruling family of Thesseline."

"Thesseline? Not possible. As you said, that place died long ago. It was destroyed. A war, they say."

"So many have long believed. So the Linosians claimed. But

something about their tale never made sense. What kind of a war would eliminate all life in an environ? Even the F'lonedian poisonings left some creatures immune and able to survive. And many years later, a host of Linosians returned there, confident that the poisons would no longer pose a threat."

"Maybe the Thesselines were more efficient at poisoning their environ."

"Leaving none alive, and with none escaping? The Prementula have never reported contact with anyone claiming to be a Thesseline."

"Perhaps they escaped to Namus. Or perhaps they concealed their identities."

"Perhaps, but unlikely. According to the individual who contacted us in Abeilon, he and his wife were the only survivors."

"The Thesseline Environ has been dead for five hundred years."

"Six hundred."

"Six hundred? Then how could any be yet living? We are the longest-lived people we have encountered, in all our travels, in Arba and elsewhere on this world. Even the Malliorelum had shorter lifespans. And the oldest of us wasn't yet two hundred years old when she died."

"True. And yet, this Naightermender, alleged royal of Thesseline, was still with us, still very much alive."

"Did your people also see the wife?"

"Oh yes."

"And she confirms his story?"

"She confirms it and augments it with one of her own."

"Meaning?"

"She has made a claim that in itself will lay the great thinkers and the church of ONOF low."

"Explain."

"Naightermender's wife is...Frulla of Carthage."

Chapter 43
"Your song is a warning.
So was the first, I think."

Place: The Midforest, Arba Environ
Date: Angem 13, AY 999

They hiked for five days, south and east on the Cturrom al Nish road.

Twice the road was completely gone, fallen into massive crevasses of mud, stone, and darkness. The highways, built before the Gri Na Leus conflicts centuries before, were now little more than overgrown, weed-ridden paths. One occasionally came across a worn, irregular stone grouping that might have once been an overpass or building or community; there was no way to tell so many years later. The Boi Na had been a great empire, but there were many places in the environ where it was now not even a memory.

Baks Mu tossed ropes across a crevasse once or twice, creating a sort of bridge that Xian was just barely able to manage. Most times, though, the gaps were far too wide, and they had to climb down and back up to get to the other side. That had taken them the better part of the second, third, and fourth days.

Much to Baks's relief, they came across many deep ponds, trickling streams, and even a small group of waterfalls. Xian was glad for his new friend that the Midforest could provide him with the means to sustain and strengthen himself.

They often spoke at mealtimes but not always. When they did, they found they enjoyed one another's company despite — or perhaps because of — their strange and uncertain circumstances. Baks Mu had a sailor's love of stories, and Xian had many stories to tell as well. And he was a skilled storyteller, when he was in the right mood. Somehow the cover of the forest and the pace of their journey had put him in such a mood; he didn't question it.

Baks, a keen listener, came to suspect that there was something about the Timesinger that desperately yearned for absolution or at least respite, but he seemed resigned to a fate where neither would be forthcoming. Though open and somehow even warm, Xian was also a man with another kind of story, a kind he was not inclined to share.

So then sometimes they ate in silence, but even then it was a comfort to have good company. Both men understood the value of what was by necessity kept locked inside.

On the fifth day, in a wide clearing by the end of a long, thin lake, they were approached by the Tromontius.

"We are not alone, Timesinger," said Baks in a low voice.

"No, I suppose not. But then, I don't think we've been truly alone since we entered this forest."

"True enough, but now, the watchers are much closer. Surely that makes them more of a threat."

"Not necessarily. Some who watch only do so to see, not to threaten," said Xian.

"What if you're wrong?"

Xian shrugged. "Then we should assume as nonthreatening a posture as possible. In this place, we are guests. Or at least, passersby. And I suspect those watching us could have captured or killed us many times over, were that their wish."

Baks snorted and then nodded. "I agree. Would my taking a swim qualify as nonthreatening?"

"To the casual observer unaware of the rejuvenative aspect of a Challowian swim, yes."

"Then let us hope they are casual and unaware. I need to get wet."

Baks Mu set down his packs and his weapons. He removed his cloak but not his fishskin vest, which at times Xian found difficult to distinguish from his actual flesh, and then dove without ceremony into the small lake before them.

When he was gone a few minutes, Xian pulled out his small pipe and played a few notes. He took a drink to wet his whistle and then played a tune in earnest.

Someone was definitely listening.

He let them. Best they should approach in their own time and state their business according to their pleasure. This was their home, and he and the Challowian could not expect to pass through this forest by avoiding or challenging its inhabitants. From what he remembered, there were a great many inhabitants to encounter here, very few of which could be comfortably challenged or easily avoided.

The song he played was a slow, slightly sinister-sounding dirge, one he'd learned from a local musiker many years ago on the island of Little Britain. Whenever he played it, and he would often play it for one person in particular, he couldn't help but consider its cunningly wrought simplicity, its apparently limitless charm. He found the tune enchanting, but he didn't know quite why. As time went by, he'd come to understand the song's true meaning: it was both a warning against boldness practiced without the benefit of wisdom and an anthem for seizing opportunity. He then believed it an ironic match for his own naiveté's evolution toward worldliness as he entered the world to seek adventure and prosperity.

Early on, though, understanding had not been of primary importance. The song was enticing, and it won him a woman.

He chuckled a bit at his own foolish youthful yearning, and it made him fudge a few notes. Listening to his own playing now, he chided himself and his overblown sense of self-awareness, which he admitted had always been as sharp as a pebble. Perhaps the song was just a song.

He liked to believe he'd grown, but somehow he still understood the dirge's message was somehow beyond him in any case.

"That song you play...it reminds me of someone."

The voice came from behind him, in the trees. It sounded somewhat distant, as if it were echoing from a cave or down a mountain, and yet it was not loud or harsh but instead almost like a whisper.

Xian did not turn around. He began to play another verse.

"She was somewhat older than me, smallish, with a dear bright smile and eyes that glittered," the voice said.

Xian stopped playing. "She was your lover?" he asked.

"No. She was my mother. She died in the Yabklunear."

"I am sorry. Did she play?"

"No, she sang. And she had many friends among the Malliorelum. They sang very well."

Malliorelum. It was not a word Xian longed to hear, and yet it was a word that was always on the tip of his tongue.

Xian was just then struck by the memory of a young man he'd once befriended several years before the actions that had so shamed them all. Or him, anyway. When it was done, many were proud of what they'd accomplished: the preservation of the Arban way, the stamping out of a clear and persistent threat to their beliefs, whatever they were. Four knew there were enough medals given out and balls thrown in honor of the rousingly successful massacre.

Many more who had participated in the action had simply let it go, as if they'd burned some old cornhusks in the fireplace and had a nap on the hearth, their dreams as calm as midnight snow in the dead of winter. To them, the genocide was merely necessary and so almost incidental, a thing to be neither regretted nor celebrated.

But not the young man, Xian's friend: he had taken his own life.

And Xian—Timesinger, reader, learner, student—could never recall the young man's name.

Not now, not ever.

"You know of the Malliorelum?" asked the voice behind him.

"Yes. I knew a few in my time." *Knew and helped murder.*

"Unlike them, your time is not yet through, is it? You sing still."

"I hum more often than sing, my friend," said Xian softly, "and I blow a fair tune when there's time, but you're right, I am still here, reverie be damned. Come, sit beside me and tell me more of yourself and your people."

The Tromonti hesitated. "I am not permitted to let you see me."

"Then come sit behind me and rest awhile. Tell me a tale about your own dear mother. I will not look upon you."

"If you think this will be good, Xian...very well."

Xian did not react to the fact that this stranger knew his name. He just played again. He heard nothing from behind him, but then, after a while, the voice spoke and was much nearer.

"You are a Timesinger, yes?"

"Yes. What gave me away?"

"Your eyes. Those who have read and seen and come to understand as much as your kind has often have eyes that hold much depth and blindness."

"Blindness?"

"You have read and seen too much," said the creature as it moved in behind him, trusting him for reasons he couldn't place but was glad for.

"You're not wrong."

"You should stop. Rest. Be."

Xian smiled and thought of Ashkinda. "If only you could see my home, you'd know I do little else but stop and rest," he said.

"Your body rests. Your mind has not ceased travelling for many, many years."

"I hadn't considered that. And I wasn't aware my Timesinger eyes looked any different than anyone else's. Your own must be very sharp to pick up such a subtle variation."

"Sharp eyes, yes, but also a sense of things. So it is with us in our forest. We have a certain sense of things. Living things. We see."

"There is much magick in this place," Xian conceded.

"It was ever so. The magick is within us, and we breathe it in and out with each step. But as with most beautiful things, there is also...danger. Please, finish your song."

Xian did as requested and then played another song, one with a more uplifting tempo, albeit tempered as well with some darker undertones.

"Your song is a warning. So was the first, I think."

It was not, Xian knew. But he had thought it so for so long. Maybe he was wrong. "Your Tromonti senses are reading only me, not the song."

"There were others, Xian, yes? Who heard your song and its warning?"

"Most of those have long since passed from this world."

"By your hand?"

Xian started, a sharp pang suddenly coursing through him. After a moment, he collected himself and considered the Tromonti's question. In his mind, he saw the table, the glittering robe Glea Siven had worn for the occasion. What had they talked about? The wine? The early winter? He couldn't recall, but that robe. She was so beautiful. And his young friend had fallen in love with her.

No. Not the friend.

He himself.

He had loved her.

"Some. Yes, by my hand, some."

They sat in silence for a few minutes, listening to the slight splashes made by Baks Mu's arches and dives.

"I am curious as to how a Timesinger happens to be traveling with a Juks Xi Ren warrior here in our forest. I don't recall ever having seen such a strange pairing."

"We were following the Camedua down toward Quintish and the coast. Our destination, for better or worse, is Pherriuskata."

"But you lost your way."

"Five nights ago, our party was attacked. Only we two survived. After that, I judged the Cturrom to be our best bet."

"Your companion was prisoner of the others you travelled with."

"Yes."

"Was he your prisoner?"

"Not at all."

"And now he is your friend?"

Xian wasn't sure how to answer this. Baks Mu was of a kind that didn't have much use for men or any other race, he believed. And they were wise to steer clear after all that had happened and all that still might. "He's been a pleasure to spend time with."

"I understand."

They sat a while, and Xian played. After a few more songs, the Tromonti, who Xian thought might have gone, spoke again. "Your enemies have followed you."

"You've seen them?"

"Not I, but others of my kind. Attempts were made to discourage them in their pursuit, but in vain."

"That is disappointing. Our enemies are most lethal."

"So we have learned. But we have plans for them that may yet render them…less so."

"Please, don't put your people in danger on our account."

"We have not. We approached them, as I approached you, to satisfy our curiosity and to know them better."

"And?"

"Two of us were injured. Many of theirs burned. Still, they come. They do not die when burned."

"They are not of this place. Of Arba."

"Perhaps."

"What will you do?"

"Our forest holds many dangers, and she protects her own."

"Tell your people to please be very careful."

"I shall. And you be careful as well. The judgment you so fear isn't quite the terror you believe it to be. I see peace ahead for you, Xian Lo."

And then Xian found himself alone. He smiled at the thought of encountering what he knew could only be a Tromontieri, a True Old Spirit of the Woods — although the woods to which they belonged had long since passed from this world.

They were watching him, watching both of them, he and Baks. It was a very reassuring thought that made him feel a little safer, safe enough that he leaned back and gradually drifted off to sleep.

He awoke to find Baks Mu sitting across from him, cross-legged and looking quite peaceful and refreshed. He had no idea how long the Challowian had been in the water, but it must have been several hours because the suns were deep into their evening descent. Here in the forest, under the infinite net of vines and branches and nests and leaves, the darkness had already begun to creep in.

Baks Mu said, "You were sleeping so soundly, I thought it best to leave you be."

"Thank you. I probably shouldn't have, though. We're still being followed."

"Followed?" Baks Mu tensed and made to spring up.

Xian held his hand up and bade him to stay seated. "Don't worry. We're being observed by some members of a very good old race, and I don't believe they'd let harm come to us."

"Which race?"

"The Tromontieri."

"Never heard of them."

"They've been around a long time, perhaps since the beginning of Arba. They used to inhabit the whole of the Midforest and were once dear friends of the Malliorelum, though not so dear that they shared that race's affinity for humans and their ways. Long ago, most of them fell to hardship and disease. It's been said that most of the others left this environ for a better place, though as far as I know, no one ever knew where. Now, in Arba, there are but few, and most of those are likely here in these woods."

"You've met them before."

"In a manner of speaking. I have had the pleasure of their silent, reassuring company several times, especially back when I travelled often throughout the Arban kingdoms. Cturrom Road used to be as serene a path to walk as any in the known world."

"The world has changed. This path is shit."

Xian nodded slightly to concede the point. "True enough. But at least here, there are ponds."

"Yes, there are ponds here. And waterfalls." Baks laughed. "Good stuff."

"Not as bountiful as Iale but not as forbidding as Bi, yes?"

"Agreed, my friend. Maybe we should just live here."

"Yes, maybe," Xian said, half wishing he could do just that. There were worse places in the world, and he'd been headed right for them since he'd left Ashkinda.

Xian consulted a small collection of maps he'd brought with him and determined they might have veered slightly northeast. Lake Iale itself was at least a week away on foot if they headed directly south; with the density and irregularities in this terrain, closer to two weeks was his estimate. And there were the Wasi-Sagotr estates to navigate as they moved south as well.

Baks Mu nodded when given this information but looked hesitant.

"You are having doubts," Xian said.

"Yes."

Xian decided to say what needed to be said. "In truth, there isn't a need for you to accompany me to Pashka. No one would blame you for opting out of an appearance before a gathering of fools who will not listen and who will certainly condemn you to death."

Baks shook his head slightly. "It isn't my way to run. And the Tri, they would find me. Eventually."

"You haven't done anything wrong. Surviving isn't a crime. Being made to pay a debt with your life because someone is unhappy they lost a vessel and their foolish schemes went awry would be. They don't know what actually happened on those ships, and they don't need to know, ever."

The Challowian seemed undecided. Xian saw him struggling. Juks Xi Ren were a proud people who typically chose the high road. That habit got them into trouble when there was no clear high road to choose.

"Honor, I believe, would demand that you help an old man reach the lake. Given that we've quite some time before we get there, why don't you hold off on making any decisions for the time being? If we get to Lake Iale and you want to push on to Pashka, then that path will be there for you. If you choose to jump in the lake and swim all the way to the Challow's Isle, then by all means do so. I will tell them something in the Midforest ate you."

"Something still might. But if it does, you won't be around to tell anyone anything. It'll eat you too."

"Doubtful. I am skin and bones, and I smell. Even a starving Koldian horror would pass on consuming me."

They turned south and eventually found what appeared to be another ancient road heading in approximately the same direction. It was difficult here to see the skies, and so navigation was not, for Baks, as simple a matter as it was on the sea. Twice they seemed to lose their way, but after some small debate and the use of an ancient compass Xian had forgotten he had with him, they were back on track.

Two days after heading south, late in the afternoon, they came to a clearing. "Someone has just been here," Baks said.

"Someone still is," said Mr. Geminstra as he emerged from behind a small grove of pine bushes. "Relieving myself, I'm afraid."

"How have you found us?" Xian asked evenly. He doubted he would be surprised at the answer.

Geminstra approached them with his hands spread open and a matter-of-fact smile on his chubby face. "I never lost you, not really."

"Are you alone?" asked Baks, his eyes flitting about in search of creatures bent on ambush.

"That's not the point," said Geminstra, who stopped and reached into one of his many pockets. He pulled out a small cloth and dabbed at his brow. "But if you must know, no, I am not alone. I suspect few who travel through this abysmal forest ever are."

Baks once again surveyed their surroundings but saw no hint of any others.

"Don't worry, Challowian. They're there."

"I think perhaps a more thorough explanation regarding your presence is in order," said Xian. "Don't you?"

"No. Forgive me if this is too blunt a response, but you're not entitled to an explanation of any kind, thorough or otherwise. I'm here only to make sure you get where you're going. Both of you," said Geminstra as he glanced at Baks meaningfully.

"You've been listening to us."

"Of course."

"What are you?" asked Baks.

"A friend," said Geminstra.

"That seems unlikely," Xian noted.

"If 'friend' makes you uncomfortable, then instead call me...insurance."

Baks was becoming impatient with the conversation. "Who are you working for? The things that attacked the caravan?"

"Noble Four, no! If I were with them, you'd have died back on the road. I led them away, I and my associates, while you stumbled into this forest."

Xian asked quietly, "How did you survive the attack on the road?"

Geminstra shrugged. "I didn't survive it. I anticipated it. I wasn't there."

"Not very effective as insurance, are you?" Xian remarked.

"Who do you think arranged for your little prison cart to tumble over the bank?" came the reply.

"So you saved us?" asked Baks.

"You're welcome," said Geminstra.

Baks strode up to Geminstra and got in his face. "Tell us who you are."

"As I said, you're not entitled to an explanation. But I will at least tell you that our interests for the time being are mutual and aligned. I need you both to reach Pashka."

Xian looked at him for a few moments; then he smiled. "I've been around for a long time, my friend," he said to Geminstra.

"I am aware."

"And having been around that long, I've picked up a few skills along the way, subtle abilities..."

"You are a gray one," Geminstra said, tsking.

"Yes, I am, but the ability to which I refer has little to do with that. No, this is a skill one only develops after being lied to by the most practiced of liars, for decades."

"I assure you—"

"Do not embarrass yourself. I *see* you."

Geminstra sighed and nodded. "Very well," he said. Then he barked a command in a language both Baks and Xian had heard before but never under pleasant circumstances. "But for the record, I have not lied to you. Yet. I really am here to help, in a manner of speaking."

The bushes around them rustled, and then there were seven hulking Brull warriors surrounding them. Gnarled and deformed in the same manner their kind had been since the wars against the Gri Na Leus, they were nonetheless formidable and well armed.

"Impressive," said Xian. "Mercenaries?"

Geminstra chuckled. "We have an arrangement."

Xian nodded, unmoved.

"And I have an arrangement with the ghosts who haunt these woods as well," said Geminstra.

"Of whom do you speak?" asked Baks.

"Let's not play games. We all know who holds the hammer in this place. They're the only reason there's still a thick forest here after all these years, and this despite the ridiculous price of wood. In any case, they've agreed to let us escort you out of here. Some very important people are waiting for you both on Sianthis. Shall we?" Geminstra said, gesturing vaguely south.

There was no way to confirm his story, but the fact of Xian and Baks Mu even being here seemed to at least support a part of it. The Tromontieri had destroyed their pursuers from the road. Why they had done so probably had as much to do with their finickiness about who they allowed into the Midforest as with their civility and kindness — but then why allow even a handful of their northern neighbors in? In almost four hundred years, the Brull had never once tried to come down from their mountains and claim even a little of the forest for themselves, and for that there were clearly undeniable reasons. The Tromontieri were not at all political, but they were ferociously territorial — and their ferocity was the stuff of legend.

Xian had counted on that ferocity when he'd taken them into the forest. And the Tromontieri did not like the Brull, that was a given. But then why had they permitted Geminstra and his Brull?

He sighed. The Tromontieri were territorial, not political. They wouldn't be concerned about poor Xian and Baks once they had passed through the forest, and all Geminstra was looking to do was escort them. One more level of protection, however unnecessary given the powerful vigilance already afforded them, would not make a difference to those Geminstra had inaccurately and disrespectfully called the "ghosts of the forest."

And so they headed south, the ten of them, no doubt under the watchful eye of the ambiguously aligned Tromontieri. The path they now followed, however, was not necessarily the one they would have chosen to follow unencumbered by their current escort. Nonetheless, they were drawing closer to Lake Iale and the island of Sianthis and the great city of Pashka, so not all was lost.

After a time, they broke for what Geminstra glibly called "luncheon."

"We'll be heading through the game land of the Wasi Sagotr Vied-Bronste.
I've arranged for us to spend one night there in the family lodge. Giorgio Vied-Bronste himself will meet us. He's very curious about you two," Geminstra told Baks and Xian with a satisfied expression on his face.

"I thought the lodges were long ago abandoned."

"They were. But a new arrangement with the ghosts allows for a few of them to be used as places of solitude and recreation. Offerings are made, of course."

"And what *does* one offer a ghost in exchange for his acquiescence?"

"I'm quite sure I don't know." He looked at them and smiled. Then he pulled three loaves and a small box stuffed with cured meats and dried fish out of a pack one of the Brull had set on the ground beside him. He proceeded to feast with gusto, only stopping momentarily to offer food and drink to his two guests. They each refused him at first but then thought better of it and ate.

"In any case," said Geminstra as he held out the mustard to Xian, "we should reach that place in maybe two days. That should give you ample time to figure out how you're going to try to escape from us."

Baks chewed a piece of dried fish and then glanced at Geminstra. "I was thinking I'd go with something simple and just stab you in the heart with your own knife."

"And my escort? How would you dispatch them?" Geminstra asked, bemused.

"Brull love the taste of human, no? We'd just hand them the salt and pepper and walk away while they ate you," Baks said, spitting out some bones. "See, simple."

Geminstra abruptly picked up his plate, walked away, and sat down at a comfortable distance.

He finished the rest of his meal in silence but he did not take his eyes off of Baks Mu.

Chapter 44
"I think we have to go look for that fucking Sword, is what I think."

Place: the dead city of Rash al Brek, Arba Environ
Date: Angem AY 999

The irony would not have been lost on him if any opportunity to focus on trivial mental fancies were his to claim.

Still, in some corner of his mind, he could not help but acknowledge it.

They had found themselves, he and the handful of men who had escaped with their lives from what was once the impregnable fortress at Chralm Doanna, in a place known to all as the Dead City of Rash al Brek. There had been a time when its position in Arban history was almost unique. One other city short of unique, rather. In 661 AY, Rash al Brek on the Aethrelean Sea, once considered a sister city to Pashka, had been razed to the ground by the Vo'ixtavracci. Wei Da, a more modest yet fairly important and well-populated town situated directly between Pashka and Rash, was also razed to the ground.

The issue, to Leander's recollection, was that the Quadrate was late with a payment—the very first payment, unfortunately. Fifty thousand slaves were due, and they were due on the morning of Feschille 10, promptly to be delivered at the famous and bustling Rash al Brek port known as the Eastern Eyes.

This delivery was to be the first, and there'd been quite a bit of haggling about who owed what in the deal. Who it was owed to was never in question, but the naïve and the self-centered were not yet overly concerned with what the consequences of not honoring that deal might be. Payment was payment, and lateness was standard in the comings and goings of all business, as was haggling.

The deal itself had been brokered between the members of the fairly young alliance known as the Quadrate—a loose but ambitious association that included Pherriuskata, Arbana, Xatumka, and of course, Aethrelius, which some in mid-Arba then called, with intention to insult no doubt, "Aralis"—and the Vo'ixtavracci Empire, the latter of which had no tolerance for haggling or, as it turned out, lateness.

Thousands burned on that tenth day of Feschille. Thousands more burned two days later at Wei Da. Those who hadn't burned, and they numbered many more than fifty thousand, were taken by the Vo'ix, whose leader infamously intoned to the shocked collection of Quadrate brokers who arrived on Feschille 13 at the Eastern Eyes, forty-seven thousand slaves in tow: "You will give, or we will take."

The Vo'ix took the forty-seven thousand as well and departed, two cities left razed in their wake.

From that event, three overwhelmingly significant developments followed:

In 664, Aethrelius exited the Quadrate, setting up centuries of political discord in the environ.

The Triumvirate was never late with another payment.

Frederick Czackus found the Sword of Endings and used it to repel, at the Khampier, a landing party of Vo'ixtavracci, also in 664.

Leander sat quietly near what had once been a beautiful and vibrant quay and contemplated this last point. Frederick had had the right of it. He'd beaten their monstrous hides back into the sea, and after he had made a deal with the Jamoi, they had never returned — not to Aethrelius in any case.

For their Gift, they had returned regularly, and to this very place.

But for some reason that practice had ended a hundred years ago. And no one knew why.

There were seagulls walking around him and flying near him, almost daring him to reach out and grab or perhaps just pet them. They had no reason to fear him. No one came here anymore. Arbans feared and hated this place where so many had died and where the specter of what had murdered them forever loomed.

Gulls, he thought, were exempt from any contemplation of history. And they were permitted to fly without any fear of retribution by the Visshilla.

Perhaps he'd been born into the wrong race.

He fought against it, but his musings about the birds turned to how most of his homeland had just recently joined Rash al Brek and Wei Da in the annals of history. The Cliffs. The Khampier. Deer Vale. Renikalar. Chralm Doanna. All their people, and all the people in the countryside and on the farms and in the small keeps and taverns and fishing quays and schools.

Gone.

All of them.

Now, in what had been Rash al Brek, there were only seagulls. Millions of them, it seemed. No human society had ever dared build upon this massive gravesite again, but nature had crept back in and given rise to a different kind of life. The rise and dip of the birds as they hunted and bickered and pruned themselves was hypnotic, almost comforting.

Would the gulls claim Aethrelius as well? Would they, biding their time, eventually come to claim all of Arba?

The people in the west, or some of them at least, had for many centuries been quite concerned with the concept of the Proving and the destruction that a failure to Prove would allegedly rain down upon them. Was what had happened to his country, to his people, what they feared? Had they somehow brokered another deal, one that would appease whatever might otherwise orchestrate their doom and bring about the Nulling?

Had they sacrificed Aethrelius to save themselves?

He couldn't say. He knew little of the Noble Four and the Books. He'd read them, years ago, but he'd come to consider them so much nonsense.

But here, now, as he watched the birds and listened to the distant voices of his remaining men trying to make sense of their lives from this day forward, he was not sure.

"Captain, we shouldn't linger here long."

It was Michael. He was still dressed in his squadron armor. He hadn't been captured, he hadn't seen…he hadn't gone into the keep. Leander looked at him and wondered if he were better off for having been spared that experience. *Yes.*

"Where should we go?" Michael asked him.

It was clear from the bright defiance in the young man's eyes that he still believed there was a fight. And maybe there was. No matter how efficient or how hungry the Takers might be, there had to be limits to their abilities.

"They won't kill everyone. Only those they have to," Michael said.

"Agreed," said Wexshai as he strode up to join them. "They'll only kill those they need to. The rest—we know their plans for the rest. And I believe it will take months, maybe years, for them to round up all of our countrymen."

Michael's face darkened. "Then there's time. How do we help our people?"

"We cannot," Leander said.

"We cannot? How can you say that?" said Michael.

"He's right. There is nothing we can do for them. There are eight of us against an army that brushed our entire military aside as if it weren't there," said Wexshai.

"So we do nothing? We run and hide? Nothing?" cried Michael.

Leander shook his head.

"What does that mean? We have to try. We got out, yes?" Michael said as he reached out and clutched Leander's shoulder.

Wexshai put a gentle hand on Michael's arm and shook his head.

Michael let go of Leander and turned away angrily.

"We could try to sneak back into Chralm Doanna and get others out through the tunnels," Michael stammered.

"We could do that. We would die. You know we ourselves barely got out of there alive. We shouldn't have even stopped here for this long. They're looking for us," Wexshai said.

Michael said, "We should try. Die trying, if that's to be our fate."

Leander was barely listening to them. His thoughts had returned to Frederick. *He'd had it. What had he done with it? Why was there no record of it?*

Whatever it was, it had been used before, by Renik, to defeat Kold. And then, in the time of greatest need, Frederick had found it and used it. But why hadn't he kept it? Why wasn't it locked up somewhere under the Square, safely tucked away, ready to be wielded against whatever else might someday threaten their country and people?

The book. He now had his mother's notes, her diary. He hadn't yet had time to open it, but he knew that somehow it would put him on the right path, the path that would deliver the Sword to his hand and enable him to enact revenge.

He'd been a fool for too long. He'd hesitated, he'd delayed, but now, here upon this blackened beach where death had once ruled unquestioningly, he knew what to do.

"Captain, are you even listening?" asked Michael.

"I am, Michael. And I know what you want. I want it too," Leander said. "If we're going to give what's left of our people a chance, we need the Sword."

"The Sword? But where…we have no idea where it is. Or what it is," said Wexshai.

"True enough. But we have a need, do we not? We have a purpose. And for the right man at the right time, a purpose is more than enough," said Leander as he rose.

The seagulls scattered and went back to what they'd been doing all along, what they'd been doing for many decades. Their musical cries accompanied the three men as they walked up the beach to join their brothers.

They hid up in the ruins that night, just as they had the night before. It had taken them two days to reach this place after their flight from Chralm Doanna, and they were certain they'd been followed. There were no fires, and they made quite sure there were routes of escape available should they be spotted. They were fairly close to the edge of the dead city, well within a sprint's reach of the heavily forested Somasindhu Mountains. If necessary, they could hide indefinitely in those mountains or make their way as far north as the Windgiver Sea. At this point, it was difficult to say what would be necessary or which direction they should take. They kept their eyes open and weighed their options, which though few were not without some merit.

They had to remain vigilant, that was certain.

Had Cedril cracked? Had he told his monstrous guests what he'd done, how he'd helped them escape? Perhaps. Leander doubted it, though. If he'd told them anything, he surely had included no details or particulars.

There would be no more betrayals by sa Mino. His mind was gone, possessed by only one thought: the Vo'ix must die.

Leander empathized entirely with his old friend's condition.

He wondered if the man had succeeded in burning down his grand old keep with his guests still in it. Probably not. They were large, but they were quick. And they weren't fools, either. They'd have seen it coming.

No, the greater likelihood was that Cedril's ruse, as well as the tragically late assistance he'd offered to the remaining members of the Fourth Squadron, was easily seen through by the Vo'ix. Leander hoped sincerely that the end had come without delay. No one deserved to die on a plate screaming.

They waited and they talked and they planned. They hadn't much to eat with them. Wexshai came across some dead scouts while ranging ahead a bit into the mountains. Their packs had some cured meat and bread in them. The scouts themselves had been torn to ribbons.

"But not burned," Michael had noted.

"And not eaten," noted Thom, who had also survived along with Bili Hu, Josef, Alain, and Viktor, among others.

They were game for any campaign or fight and did not appear rattled, but Leander could see a difference in them nonetheless. They were scared. And why wouldn't they be, after hearing all they had about the destruction and the cruelty? Still, they hadn't yet seen any of it closely, not since Tolii Nus, and there'd been nothing to see on the island, just black sand and the smoldering former creek.

No, thought Leander, *they are scared but not quite scared enough to burn the fear right out of them.*

He wondered if any of them, Michael and Wexshai included, would be so anxious to do anything but run into the mountains and hide for the rest of their lives if they'd come face-to-face with their enemy.

The suns went down. Nothing arrived to burn the men, rip them to shreds, or eat them.

They ate and talked a while and collectively decided they had no idea where to go.

Leander, who had spent most the meal just listening and thinking, reached into his pocket and withdrew the item he hoped would guide them going forward.

It was time to read Theresta's book.

"What do you mean, it's blank?" Michael exclaimed.

"That old piece of shit. That damned snake!" Alain spat. The others chimed in with curses of their own, knowing Cedril sa Mino had doomed them, and all of Aethrelius, from the grave.

Leander stared at the blank pages of his mother's alleged Sword notes.

He was, to say the least, deeply confused.

The men were huddled around him, a small torch in Josef's hand. They were even more confused than he.

"I don't understand. Did he give you the wrong book? Are you sure your mother ever wrote such a book?" Michael asked.

"She wrote the book," Wexshai said. "I've seen it before, just once, but I saw her with it when I was young. She'd gathered many children together and used it to tell us the legend."

"And it was this book? You remember this cover?" Michael asked.

"I can't be sure. It was a long time ago," Wexshai admitted. He had a curious look on his face as he stared at the book.

"Captain, is this the book? Is this your mother's book?" Michael asked.

"It is," said Leander. "And it isn't."

"What does that mean?" asked Michael.

"Her book was filled with notes, maps, theories," said Leander.

"What happened to it?" Thom asked.

"I think I understand the problem," Wexshai said.

They all turned and looked at him. It was the way he'd spoken that caused them to go silent. His tone had taken on a lyrical yet dark quality, almost like he was uttering an incantation, which perhaps he was. Or more accurately, he was putting himself in the proper state to do so.

Every man but Michael took two steps away from Leander.

They'd all seen Wexshai practice magick before, though not often and not willingly. He did it, when he did it, out of necessity, and rarely amid a crowd of true Aethreleans. They were a people who, although not hateful and suspicious of the Mudarrisi ways as their brethren in the Tri claimed to be, did not embrace the ways of magick despite its obvious and plentiful offerings and advantages. Aethreleans were never born with a color, or so the common wisdom said, and while the Mudarrisi had always been treated — until recent developments — with respect and affection, their ways were regarded as their own and not, as a rule, truly Aethrelean.

Wexshai was something of an exception. His mother was of the Jamoi, and his father Aethrelean. He had a color, and though it was hardly one of note — he had never been invited by his mother's people to come and live among them — he had been schooled by various Mudarrisi since he was a child. It was all something of an open secret and always had been, but there was nothing secret about what was happening now.

There simply wasn't the need for the pretense of a veil any longer.

Leander saw and heard his young soldier and understood.

He placed the book next to him on a large stone and made to move away.

"Stay, Captain," Wexshai murmured in a low and scarcely human voice.

Leander did was he was told.

"Please place your hand on the book," Wexshai continued.

Leander touched the book gently and looked at Wexshai, not sure where this was going but with an inherent sense of faith in the young man.

Wexshai came near but touched neither the book nor Leander.

Several minutes passed. Then several more.

"What do you sense, Wexshai?" asked Alain.

"Be silent. Let him work!" Michael hissed.

A few moments later, it was done. Wexshai sat down, his head lowered, his body slumped.

The men were shifting restlessly.

"Wait. Everyone just wait," Michael commanded.

Leander rose, went to Wexshai and put a hand on his head. The younger man looked up, his face exhausted. "The book isn't blank," Wexshai said. "It's protected."

"What do we do?" asked Leander.

"The spell is strong, very strong. To me, at least. Perhaps someone with more…a Mudarrisi could read it."

"The Mudarrisi are all gone," Michael said. "All gone back to Jamoi."

"So they are," Leander agreed.

For a few minutes, they were all silent. Even with but one small torch flickering among them, Leander could see the fresh doubts in the eyes of his men.

"Two things, gentlemen. First, the book is not our only lead. I have some knowledge that may prove useful. Second, we will find someone to read it for us. We will find someone to remove the spell."

They all looked at him.

"Captain, we can't go to Jamoi. It's too far, and there's no saying they'd even let us in or help us," said Michael. "We need answers now, before it's too late to save our people!"

"They would help us," Wexshai insisted. "The Jamoi would help."

Leander said, "Perhaps they would, Wexshai, but Michael is right: they are too far from here. No, we have need of assistance from elsewhere. Someone closer."

"Who, Captain?" asked Thom.

Leander wasn't sure about his thoughts here, but he knew from the several minor wars he'd fought against them that those who had settled in the northern mountains might just have what it took to put him and his men on the path. If they couldn't read the book, they could certainly point them in the right direction. He was sure of that at least.

What he couldn't know was the answer to the question, would they? They still had every reason to hate the Aethreleans. Or maybe they'd let go of those reasons over the years. Maybe he could bargain with them or capture one and make him help.

He had nothing to bargain with, and capturing a Brull was no easy task. But whatever the angle or method, he had to try.

He looked up and into the eyes of his men. "We need to go to the Atuut Mountains. We need the Brull."

"Are you sure?" Wexshai asked, his tone filled with doubt.

"You know what they can do. You all know."

"They'll murder us all," said Alain. "We cannot trust them!"

The other men agreed.

"You said you had other knowledge. Tell us what that was, Captain," said Michael.

"My mother traveled many times to Oak Harbor, and several times, farther, onto Lake Iale. To Pedry."

"Pedry? Where the Epidemic...?" asked Wexshai.

"Yes, Pedry. But why she did so, she never said, or if she did say, I don't recall."

"So if we go to the Brull...even if they cannot read the book, which is likely, they can use those unnatural sight gifts to give us more detail? Is that what you're thinking?" Wexshai asked. He still sounded doubtful, but the idea of an actionable plan seemed to appeal.

"That's it."

Wexshai stood up. "Then we need to capture a Brull. Asking them for help is suicide."

"Agreed," said Michael. "Captain?"

"Finding one alone won't be easy. They tend to see you coming."

"We'll figure something out, Captain!" cried Thom.

"We'll get it done for you, sir!" added Josef.

"Not for me, men. For Aethrelius," Leander said solemnly.

They kept their voices down, but their passion was unmistakable when all seven of them answered him. "For Aethrelius!"

They left within the hour. Rash al Brek and their homeland were behind them, and ahead, the Atuut Mountains and the quest for the Sword of Endings awaited.

Chapter 45
I am no leader,
and I am no legend.

Place: Vamoul Downs, kingdom of Xatumka, Arba Environ
Date: Angem 31, AY 999

The pass had been taken, the day won.

Frainle, the victorious Aethrelean girl who the people had named "Asima" (something like "good luck charm," or so Stephan had told her), sat on a small dead stump, listening to David and Stephan.

"They want you to lead them. Can you? Will you?" Stephan asked.

Frainle glanced at him and saw the earnestness in his face. "I am not a leader. I am a fool who got lucky reciting something from a book."

"They don't think so. And neither do I," said Stephan. "I think you're someone who knows what to do and how to do it, and in the context of warfare, that's more rare than a smile on a duke's dog."

David waved his hands at her a bit as if to dispel both her doubts and his fears. "Lady, I don't know what you are," he said. "But what I see in the faces of the Northerners now is pride, a sense of defiant dignity and even of hope. Do you know how long it's been since I could see such things in those faces?"

"Their faith in me is misplaced. I am not my father."

"Perhaps not — or perhaps not yet — but you are everything they need you to be today, now."

I am not is what she thought to say, but instead she found herself wondering if she was. What would Shain have done here? What would he have told them? Could he have led them to the Pass, to victory? Could he have protected them? And what would they have named him? Whatever name they gave him, he would have gently told them to lay it aside; his given name would suffice for the task at hand.

She smiled at David and nodded slightly. There was silence for several minutes.

She had no idea why she'd been resisting. Inside her, she could feel a palpable sense of the moment growing, thrusting her toward a role she could now admit she had always craved to assume. In Aethrelius, any such yearnings would always by necessity have been quelled by the realities of her father's timeworn and immutable culture — she was, after all, a woman — but here, in this place, was both opportunity and need. Her womanhood was viewed neither as a weakness nor a sign; it was her prowess and knowledge that led these people to believe in her.

And it made her afraid. She'd wanted and needed to somehow

prove herself, to find some purpose, since Shain had died. But was she too terrified to prove or reach out and claim that purpose as her own? If only she could face herself in battle, beat herself ruthlessly until the truth of her natural desires and talents could assert and establish itself beyond the reach of any eroding reproach.

This was all wrong. She stood to leave

David stood up and made to block her departure. "Then you will not lead us?" he asked, his face a mask of apprehension. "Because if you don't, if you say you can't, I fear we are lost."

"You can lead them," she told him.

"No. I can help them. I can surely convince others to join us if there is anything left to join, but they don't need someone to follow. They need someone to believe in. And that person is you."

"Why? Why is it me?"

"You are an Aethrelean, a Daughter of the Code, a living embodiment of the teachings they came to hold so dear. Your country broke from the Quadrate, defied the Vellioks, and has thrived in its own determined manner."

"We thrive no more. It's all gone now, my country."

"Perhaps it is. But perhaps its lands and peoples were only part of what made it what it was. Perhaps the ideals are what will last, come Caratans or civil wars or even flesh-eating monsters from distant environs. The question is, here and now, will you give these people, these beaten, ruined people upon whom innumerable injustices have been heaped, hope by believing in and acting on those cherished ideals? Because if you won't, they will all die, just like your countrymen, just like your mother and your brother."

"My countrymen's deaths could not have been stopped, not by hope, not by anything."

"Perhaps that's true, perhaps no one could have saved them. But these Xatumkans? You can save them. Just keep doing what you've been doing. You can save them. And you know that."

He turned to leave but stopped and said without turning around: "Please, consider what I've said. Consider the people and what you mean to them," adding, "Asima."

Once he was gone, Stephan stood and walked to her side. He took her hand and smiled, his eyes laughing. "Asima, forgive me, but you look like you want to get back in the Mansdrelam and go back to your burning tombs!"

She smiled back at him through her worries. She wished her mother were her to advise her; she usually had something insightful to offer despite her paradoxically cynical sense of the world. Shain would have been a help too. An immeasurable help because he would have relieved her of this burden that circumstance had laid before her.

What she really wished was that her father could be here, right now, with his Fourth Mandate Squadron. He'd tell these people to go back to their farms, and then he'd go out and beat the pants off their oppressors.

But he wasn't here, nor was her mother or her dead brother. Just her. Her and this wayward warrior and a few hundred tired and terrified country folk.

"What do you think?" she asked Stephan, knowing he wouldn't have an answer for her.

He took her hand, squeezed it a bit, and shook his head. "He isn't wrong. If you won't lead them, they're in trouble."

Then Stephan left her alone to think.

She sat down on her blanket and tried to still her mind. It wouldn't work; she didn't want to be alone, and she didn't want to be the person responsible for the life or death of a people. It was too much.

She wished, not for the first time, she had her sketching materials with her. There were none, so she reached instead for the wine Stephan had left. She poured herself a mug and sipped it, tasting first, then swallowing half of what she'd poured in one gulp.

Why shouldn't I get drunk? she thought. *I'm the embodiment of everything Aethrelean, a genuine savior and soldier, and I know how soldiers drink.*

So she drank for a little while, alone.

And then she decided to lead them.

For the first month, it went just at it had at Calawak Pass. They turned to her for answers, and she provided them. And each time she was amazed at how effective the plans she offered were. Was the enemy that incompetent, or were she and the farmers that lucky?

She presumed the former was not a fact to be relied upon, and the latter…well, everyone's luck ran out eventually. Just ask the dead back at the Cliffs. Just ask her mother and her brother and Eni.

David had left to visit the villages and the counties all throughout Eshe; then he crossed the river and recruited as far east as Debrein. She knew because they'd come to find her, the ones he'd found and told about her victory at the pass.

They were old and young, women and men and children. Some had lost their homes and farms and families and lives; some were just curious or bored. Most weren't fighters by any means, but many were healthy and willing enough to learn.

What did she teach them? Not much. The instruction she left to Stephan and others like Ratner and Gregash, a fierce large man from Carata who'd seen some time in the military. She herself had no real skill in warfare, not in that way. She never fought if it could be helped. But she offered them plans: plans to protect themselves, plans to ambush patrols, plans to liberate a few small towns, plans to save themselves from the hazards of being on the wrong side of the Triumvirate military. And she offered them words: reading to them often from whatever Aethrelean texts were available, telling to them stories of great Aethrelean battles, many of which she couldn't recall the precise details. It didn't matter. Her words inspired them, and her legend grew.

I am no leader, and I am no legend. It should be Shain here, now, helping these people to believe in and fight for their freedom.

But Shain was not here, nor would he have been had the accident not claimed his life. He would have died another time, perhaps at the Cliffs in fire or perhaps many years before that during an equally brutal moment. Shain was gone, and always it would wreck her inside, but she was here, doing her wonderful, empty, rudderless Shain impersonation.

They won little victories here and there, and they suffered very few casualties. Slave labor was being brought in from over Lake Iale to assume the duties of the absent farmers, but more than once those farmers essentially freed them by attacking and dispatching of their military overseers. Not having anywhere to go or a reason not to, most of the slaves joined their cause. By the end of the month, the Northern numbers had swelled well into the thousands.

Their main encampment, though they had moved it frequently to put off spies and scouts, was originally about two miles east of Yi Shu, the first town they had taken back from Tri forces. However, after adding so many to their ranks, they weren't as immediately mobile, so she made the decision to move them from the flat and indefensible meadows of Yi Shu back to the very hills they had so successfully used to their advantage during the retreat to Calawak Pass.

And then they came to her and asked her to help them take Vamoul Downs.

She shouldn't have listened; she shouldn't have answered that call. Everything she knew told her it was the wrong move. But what was their end game, these farmers, these dreamers who thought she was some kind of savior? Sit and farm in peace and hope the Triumvirate would accept their rebellion's success and leave them alone indefinitely? No, there had to be resolution. One side or the other had to lose.

And she'd been lying to herself all along about which side that would be.

Vamoul Downs was a legendary fortress, a place that housed at least five thousand Triumvirate troops, many of them Caratan. In the month since the Calawak Pass, the Northerners had found that many

Caratans, perhaps sensing a turn in the war, had decided to cast aside their Triumvirate yokes and join the righteous fight. She knew that Carata itself, once a proud, prosperous district of the great Boi Na Empire, had a long and sad history of having been suppressed by and incorporated into whatever kingdom had supplanted the Kis: first the Linosians, then Kold, then Makeiron's new Xatumkans, and finally, the Quadrate, or what had been called "the Triumvirate" since the secession of her country in 622. The only thing the Caratans had left was their name and their small city on the plateau, Dwidedi Lok. Now they'd been beaten badly enough by farmers to want to join them. Caratans were like that.

So they had some arguably real soldiers in their ranks, and though they were only Caratans, they were trained and armed. But Vamoul Downs? She wasn't sure. The reasons for taking it were sound: it was where the crux of the forces who were being used against them were quartered. Fort Ram had sent a squadron or two, but they'd stopped short of losing sight of the river. It seemed the governor was content to contain and curtail the Northern activities, never letting them get beyond or to the river, never believing, she was sure, they'd ever try to fight their way south. Word reached them that the military had systematically clamped down on Maelor's Country in the east too, so there would be no more help from that place and no more joyful liberation of slave gangs.

"We cannot stay here. They'll be coming for us, you know, and besides, we've too many mouths to feed and nothing to feed them with," said Ratner.

"I agree. We need to make a move," David said. He'd returned the night before with fresh recruits from the lands southwest of Havenor. "I say we go to the river, to Qays or Shamsi."

"Those towns are guarded by Knights of ONOF. We'll not be able to take them without serious losses," said Gregash. He gnawed on a piece of venison defiantly and stared her in the eye.

He wants me to say something. He wants to go to the Downs, they all do, but they want me to be the one who suggests it and makes it happen.

Very well.

"I know what it is you all think we should do, and I understand why. But I can tell you we don't have to do it. It's not a popular thing to say here, but in the interest of protecting the families we have here in camp, it is worth considering taking everyone and leading them through the Eventuals and into Miranquella."

"Abandon our homes?" cried Ratner.

"Run? Why then did I just spend the last month gathering every able-bodied Northerner and bringing them here to you?" asked David.

"You did not bring them to me. You brought them together to fight a righteous war."

Gregash said, "This is so."

"Then let's fight it!" Ratner shouted.

"But," Frainle continued, "this is not a righteous war we can win."

They all stopped and stared at her.

One of them has to say it too: one of them has to agree with me. The truth is plain as day. The Tri will not allow us to win. Not the governor, and certainly not the duke. And all these people will die if we stay and fight. One of them has to see that, and then the rest will fall in line.

But none did. None except for Stephan, and Stephan, despite all he'd done for them, was still not one of them.

"She's right," Stephan said. "We've beaten them off for a month, true, and we've got an army of sorts with us now, albeit an undertrained and underequipped one. But it won't be enough, not when they decide to take us. And attacking them at Vamoul Downs, and I say this in the full spirit of a man who, like the rest of you, would like nothing better than to burn that shithouse down and all its rats with it, is madness."

"Why? Why is it madness? We've beaten these Caratan slobs so badly half of them have turned around and run back to the Lok or just given up and joined us. No offense," said Ratner, glancing at Gregash, who simply grunted.

David addressed the Caratan directly: "So what of it, Gregash? Can the downs be taken?"

Gregash shook his head slowly and then smiled and pronounced, "Yes! Of course. Any fortress can be taken. But I would not advise it."

"Why not?"

"You know the place is on an island. The lake is small, but you have to cross it."

"What about a siege?"

"Vamoul Downs is well provisioned. At any time, there are maybe five thousand men there. Many mouths, sure, but you'd have to hold the place at least a few weeks before they started feeling it."

"We could do that."

"And if you do, they come out, but they come out fighting. Or maybe they don't wait the few weeks and they come out fighting anyway. Either way, they have more men than we do. More real fighters," he said, looking pointedly at Frainle.

"Doesn't matter. We'll beat them down when they come out, just like we beat them down at the pass and Orlean and a dozen other places. And we've got something they don't, Gregash," said Ratner, moving over behind Frainle and placing his hands on her shoulders. "We've got this one."

They all cheered and called out her name, not the one her parents had given her, but the one they'd seen fit to bestow upon her since the

Pass. "Asima."

She had felt pride when they'd chanted that, a pride she could not resist or understand. She wanted to be that for them, a protector, a savior of sorts, and so she let herself believe she could be that, and she let them lead her where they wanted her to take them.

It was a mistake.

Standing here now, on an oak-covered knoll across the lake from Vamoul Downs, its massive, seemingly impregnable stone walls staring down at her, its single, well-fortified bridge silent and unpassable, "Asima" seemed to her to be something of a curse. It was their third night of siege, and though no one had yet charged across the bridge to challenge or even talk with them, she could sense that something was amiss.

"You look happy," said a slightly mocking voice behind her.

It was Stephan. He'd been out checking the ranks with Ratner.

"Is everyone fed?" she asked, not taking her gaze off the castle before her.

"Everyone is in the process of being fed. Everyone but you. Why don't we remedy that? The Downs will keep until after you've eaten." He put a hand on her shoulder and turned her toward him. "You really should stop worrying. Your plan is a good one."

She looked up into his eyes and saw a plan there too, or thought she did. He'd been sending her mixed signals since they'd been lashed to that tree together, but now wasn't the time for parsing through them. She pulled away and started down toward the command tent and its fire. "Please stay here and keep an eye for me. I'll be back in ten minutes."

Ratner was standing by the fire pit, roasting a small bird on his sword.

"Asima," he said by way of acknowledgment. "Did he bring you up to speed on the new developments?"

"Up to speed? No." She hadn't really given Stephan a chance to say anything. Would it have been any different if she'd just let him kiss her already and be done with it? Would his mind be clear then to focus on the events at hand? Probably not.

"The Caratans — our Caratans — have all moved to the rear, down past the road and toward the edge of the woods."

"Moved? Why? I need to speak to Gregash."

"Gregash is gone."

"Gone? To where?"

"Maybe into the woods, maybe somewhere else. I don't think they were listening to him anyway."

"Who are they listening to?"

"Dunno. But whoever it is moved them back far enough to where if a battle starts, they might get there in time to loot the corpses."

Her thoughts raced wildly. She hadn't been too sure of allowing the Caratans to ally themselves with her people—*her* people?—in the first place. Now this, an apparent act of cowardice in the face of battle. "Do you think they'll run?"

"What, back up to Carata? Wouldn't be surprised. Some of them are probably halfway to the Lok right now, and I'd count Gregash among them, that piece of shit."

"Then why did they come with us at all?"

"Maybe they thought we'd slice 'em up and feed 'em to the Trittoes and Yanzies if they didn't."

Frainle took some meat and dried fruit from a table near the fire and wandered, lost in thought, back up to her knoll. She looked down at the lines of Northerners and ex-slaves that had formed on the north side of the lake and then glanced down at the bridge where her thirty best archers were positioned behind stumps, trees, and piles of dead hay.

Something was wrong.

There were no archers.

Then, from the north, there came the sound of horns. Only they weren't horns; they were seashells, hundreds of conches, being blown.

There was only one army from which such sounds ever emitted.

The Crabs had come for them.

Chapter 46
"Have you forgotten
who gave you that permission?"

Place: Halls of Watlier, island city of Pashka, kingdom of Pherriuskata,
Arba Environ
Date: Angem 32, AY 999

"You shouldn't have come, my old friend," said Duke Velliok without turning to face his visitor. "But I am glad, very glad, to see you again." He waved his hand at the guards; they exited without hesitation. The duke's shadow fell long over his desk and across the floor; it too had waved at the guards, but in less definitive fashion, almost like a school of fish that passes beneath one's eyes in the moonlight.

Xian stood in the doorway. He was certain he should remain where he was until he was invited to move. The doors closed softly behind him. "It was not my preferred course of action, but I am glad to see you, too, Estau."

"Ashkinda is an easy place to live, yes?" asked the duke, ignoring the use of his given name.

"It has been these many years."

"Yes. I imagine so," murmured the duke. "Sianthis is not."

"It never was."

"It's worse now. Too many interests to attend to, too many ambitious little landholders and merchants' sons looking to make names for themselves. I still enjoy the game at its highest levels, but its inevitable low points are enough to make even a saintly duke want to dive off the tower. I have only through the practice of extreme and hard-earned willpower avoided that fate myself."

"As any good ruler would have to, I suppose."

"No doubt, no doubt." The duke turned at last to face Xian but gave him only a passing glance before letting his eyes fall to the brandy bottle that sat on the desk before him. "So what made you come back? If you were so comfortable by the ocean, hiding among your books, why are you here?"

"Comfort is not meant to last," said Xian.

"This I understand all too well." Velliok looked more closely at his old friend. "You appear to have gotten…old."

"Rather say 'older,' if you don't mind."

"I don't mind. I feel as old as you look. But appearances aside, some things about you haven't changed."

"Such as?"

"Back when we were both young, and I daresay something to behold, you never gave answers willingly."

Xian tilted his head and gave a small smile. This was the duke he remembered: willing to be patient, willing to dance the dance...to a point.

"And you still haven't answered my question. Do you think you might?" asked Velliok.

"Of course. The answer is simple: They — and you — need to hear what I have to say."

"Maybe they do, and maybe they don't. The Mind is truly a nest of cold vipers who spend their days and nights deciding how best to eat one another. But either way, it won't go well for you. I cannot protect you in this."

"Estau, I would not ask you to."

"No, I don't suppose you would." The duke relaxed and looked for a chair. Finding one, he sat down and removed his hat. After a long moment, he gestured for Xian to join him, and so he did. "It has been a very, very long time, hasn't it?" the duke said.

"Yes."

Velliok poured a small cognac for himself and then, after a moment's hesitation, another for Xian. He sipped a bit of his own and then set it back down on the table and let out a long, slow sigh. "I need to know why," he said.

"Why?" asked Xian.

"No more games, please. We're too old for games."

"Speak for yourself, my friend," chuckled Xian. "Games are sometimes the only thing that gets me out of bed in the morning."

"Hmm. Yes. Me too. Sadly, though, I always win. My attendants and so-called friends are too frightened of what might happen to them — politically or otherwise — if they defeat me."

Xian heard the warning but ignored it. He wasn't playing a game in any case. "Tell me, if you are ready: What is it you really want to know, Estau? Why did I never tell them what happened, why did I let them exile me, why did I assume responsibility and keep the secret of your involvement?"

The duke regarded the Timesinger evenly for a moment. "Yes," he said. "All that, and whatever else you feel is worth sharing. I'm sure there's more. Much more."

Xian rose slowly and walked over to the window. He stood there a moment, regarding the lights of the city and the Gods' Bay beyond it. It was truly a wonder. Pashka wasn't simply a city, it was a world unto itself: dozens of islands upon which millions lived, worked, and schemed. Out on the water, ships were still coming and going even at this late hour, and music came from every corner of the city as the Vamir festival neared its climax. "In the end, for me, it was never about what you did or didn't do," Xian said.

"No? What was it about, then?" Velliok asked, his voice taking on a slightly snide tone.

"What *I* did...and didn't do."

"You did your duty."

"I did more than that. Far more, and we both know it."

"They were attacking us."

"We were taking their children, their husbands, their parents —"

"What choice did we have?"

"None. We had no choice at all."

"Then why —"

"Because I had given myself over to an authority that created those conditions. I had allowed it to happen."

The duke grunted. "You speak as if you yourself birthed the Tri."

"No, but I did promote it. Unflinchingly. Blindly. I assisted in promoting and ensuring its grotesque perpetuity," said Xian.

"We all did."

"And so each of us has to seek his own answers as to why. We never asked why. I never asked why."

Velliok poured himself another drink and downed it. Then he threw the bottle on the floor. It exploded in a thousand pieces. "I need only one answer!" he shouted as he pointed his finger at Xian. "And so do you. We do what we must, for the good of all."

"Who is playing games now, Estau?"

"I'm not playing a game, my friend."

"Oh, but you are. You play a game of self-deception, you play a game of semantics, you play a game of brutal ethics. Let me ask, for whom is it 'good' that we yielded to the Gift in the first place? Would you describe the conditions at Yanz and Tritto as 'good'?" Xian hesitated just a moment before adding, "Was your father doing something good when he ordered the Action, and we were good for following that order?"

The duke began to laugh out loud. It was not entirely a forced laugh, either: he genuinely seemed to find the situation humorous. "Xian, listen to yourself."

"I have. I have listened very closely to myself for a very long time."

"And what have you heard?"

"I hear, 'You owe, Xian. You owe them everything, and this is not a debt from which you can hide.'"

"Nonsense! What's been has been, and what is, is!"

"Is it? Every one of us made the wrong decision at Quintish. And then in the Midforest. And the Sapphire Forest. And we kept making that decision again and again."

"Not you. You got out," Velliok said.

"Not soon enough."

"As soon as was permitted," Velliok said. "Have you forgotten who gave you that permission?"

"No, I have not. And I remain grateful for what you did and for what you tried to do. I remained grateful even when you tried to have me killed."

"Never."

"Please. I thought we agreed we were too old."

"You were a threat."

"No more?"

"Perhaps. I haven't decided."

"I understand. Either way, I owe."

Velliok gestured to a servant to clean up the shattered bottle. Another servant brought a new bottle and poured another drink. The duke took a sip and said, "If that is what you wish to believe. But tell me then, if that is so, what do I owe?"

"Nothing you are willing to pay, and nothing I am able to pay for you."

"'Nothing' is right. Nothing can bring those people back. Nothing is what would have become of all Arba had we refused the Vo'ixtavracci or listened to the Callunians with their lies and their demands. But the important thing, my friend, is that we are still here. The Gift saved us all, not the Callunian lies: the Gift."

"Not all. It saved you. It saved me. It saved those who own the fields and the palaces and the guilds. It saved generations of privileged mask wearers with no regard for — "

"It saved Theresta as well."

"No. She died."

"Did she? I had heard she lived a long and interesting life."

"You heard wrong," said Xian. "She died during Creli Monshua."

"No, she did not."

"Estau, I watched her die."

"You watched what you were meant to watch and saw what you were meant to see. But Theresta lived."

"I do not believe you."

"No? Well, I suppose it's difficult for you to believe anything a privileged, brutally unethical mask wearer like myself could say to you, but whether you choose to believe it or not, Theresta Dossilea lived. She even returned to Aethrelius one more time, to see her son, as we had agreed."

"And then?"

"Who knows? There were reports of her heading east to seek the Seer of Waln. Someone once told me she'd changed her mind and sailed to Namus to negotiate a peace with the Vo'ixtavracci. And I half believed it. Doesn't it sound like something that crazy witch would do?"

"You have no proof."

"True. You could ask her son, but I doubt he's available."

"Leander is dead?"

"If he isn't, he soon will be. Along with all the other Secessionist traitors."

"What have you done?"

"What needed to be done. We've brokered another deal to keep our large friends happy."

"Again? And have you considered that the price of their happiness might someday increase to the point where your deals are no longer satisfactory to them?"

"Not really. I have thought it through, you see. And the harsh reality is, they could always have taken us. At any time. If it served their interests to do so, they would have. But they haven't."

"Perhaps you've misunderstood the basis for their restraint. Perhaps we are to them not a people to conquer and consume but rather a self-sustaining food source that is best kept functionally deceived and so thriving and self-replicating."

"That's not a new theory. But in the end, what's the difference?" asked the duke. "What would you have us do? Muster a crusade to strike a fatal blow, make war on their home environ? And where is that, exactly? Seems to me they own half the known world. And even if we went completely insane and decided to move against them, we almost certainly wouldn't make it past the Namus Desert, let alone to the heart of their empire. Or have you forgotten that idiot Rosen and his two equally brainless friends?"

"Dov Rosen was a good man. He did not go to make war; he went to find allies."

"Yes, allies who would fight the Vo'ix. And they burned his fleet, drowned his troops, and ate him, or so the story goes."

"I am not suggesting we make war on the Takers."

"What then? Throw books at them? Sue for peace? We have peace. Behold the cow in the pasture: Is there a more peaceful sight than this animal as it grazes lazily under the early morning suns?"

"We could align ourselves with Jamoi," said Xian.

"With Jamoi? I think maybe the ocean air has salted your brains, my old friend. The witches want nothing to do with us, nor we with them. There's too much history there."

Several guards entered the duke's chambers and stood at the ready.

The duke continued, "I think I've decided whether or not you are still a threat, my old friend. Listening to you here today, I am reminded of why I couldn't send you away fast enough those many years ago. It is the sickening, ridiculous cadence of your voice, you see. Forget your pious ideals and your wise insights. I just can't stand to hear your voice. Wherever you came from, if they all speak that way, well, I can tell you I may have one more good genocide left in me, that's certain."

Velliok waved to the guards casually and then lifted the bottle to pour another drink. "And now, sadly, I need you to go. I'd say we'll talk later but…that's unlikely. Good-bye."

The guards grabbed Xian and dragged him from the room.

The meeting with Velliok had been an unqualified disaster. He hadn't even been allowed to say what he'd come to say. And he wasn't going to get what he'd come for.

And now, not only was the Mind not going to listen to him, they were also not going to give him a chance to speak to anyone, ever again. He was quite sure of this. And he was sad to have overestimated the degree to which his old friend might have remained his old friend. The man was mad, fully believing that his old schemes could save this world of theirs.

They hadn't even discussed the Proving.

And now Xian knew they never would.

But they'd taken his scrolls, all that he'd written on the subject, and maybe, just maybe, someone would read them.

Cra Savanie, the ancient statesman, shuffled into the dim antechamber with a servant at his arm for support. When he reached his chair, he whispered a few words to the servant, who nodded and withdrew. Moments later, three Watlier guardsmen entered and took positions behind the two who were already guarding Xian.

Cra Savanie stared for a long moment at Xian; then he cleared his throat and said, "We've decided to reject your evidence and deny you any further right to speak to this august Body and knowing Mind."

"I thought you might."

"Good. Then there are no surprises in store for anyone, and the matter is settled."

"I cannot let this be the end of it."

"We assumed you'd take that position, so you're being offered a choice, though if it were up to me, there would be no choice."

"I understand."

"Do you? You've blasphemed and you've slandered and you've questioned without basis the most sacred beliefs of Pherriuskata and the blessed Triumvirate. I'm quite sure you should be fed to the Reismyl," croaked Savanie.

Xian shook his head. "But there is a basis. The evidence I brought to you is incontrovertible. If we do not find this woman, this true Fourth, and follow the path described by the Abeilon scroll and the Thesselines, the people of Arba will never be able to Prove. We won't even learn how."

"That's enough! I won't stand here and listen to any more of this nonsense about mysterious scrolls and this...this conveniently unknown woman who is allegedly the key to saving us all."

"She is not a complete unknown. We may not know who she is, or where she is, but we are sure we know where she will be and perhaps what she will look like."

"We've read all that in your petition. Sounds like a weak Timesinger story to me. Sounds like the ramblings of an order that never got over being rendered obsolete. And I will not listen to any more of it."

"But you must listen. The fate of Arba will be determined by your actions."

"Nonsense. This hearing is over. You must be make your choice and be gone."

"What choice do you speak of?"

"You can return to Ashkinda and remain there under house arrest until your death, or you can go to Bi Prison. I think you're learned enough to know what that means."

"And the scrolls?"

"Have already been destroyed."

"That was a mistake. Do what you will to me, but the information in the scrolls was critical to the survival of our people."

"No. What is critical to the survival of our people is that the sovereignty of the Triumvirate, led by Duke Velliok of Pherriuskata, continues to bring stalwart order, boundless prosperity, and discreet guidance to its people. The Noble Order of the Four and its promise of salvation are essential and not to be questioned."

"Not even by Frulla herself?"

"Please. Frulla has been dead for centuries, and whoever you think you've found is a fraud."

"You cannot know that if you haven't met with her."

"Yes, we can. We can know it through reason, through experience, and through a determined collective will not to have our vision and future tampered with by a discredited buffoon like yourself."

"You are afraid."

"No, Xian Lo Fui, I am not afraid. I am annoyed. I am annoyed to have had to waste as much of my time and the Mind's time deliberating this idiocy as I have."

"Why don't you speak to her? Go get her and speak to her."

"Oh, we plan to go and get her. But she'll never be allowed to speak, she'll never be allowed to spread more dissent among the followers of ONOF."

"You cannot! Now that you've burned the scrolls, Frulla is a key to our survival."

"Nonsense," said Savanie.

"You are mad."

"I don't believe so. I believe I am perfectly sane, unless you consider how much I indulge my wife in her shopping sprees."

"You will regret what you've done here today."

"Doubtful. Now, I've got a lunch to attend, so if you please: make your choice."

Xian stared at him for just a moment and then smiled. "I choose Bi."

"Bi? Truly?" Savanie was genuinely shocked. "Well, then you are as mad as you claim I am. There are, however, no shopping sprees where you're going. Die well, or die poorly, as the fates demand."

"Welcome to Bi Prison."

The convoy had stopped on the road that ran through the middle of the bog. Xian and Baks Mu, along with several others to whom they were linked by chains, were pushed toward the head of the line.

Baks looked around. There was nothing for miles in any direction but more bog. He was comforted by all the water but wondered where the prison might be. Or maybe there was no Bi Prison after all, and the reason none ever returned from it was that, in truth, all were simply slain out here in the bog and pitched into its dark, thick water.

"Please, please: come forward, that's right. Walk to me."

A small, bent Mundite with a tall, thin slave beside him sat on stool in the middle of the road. He rose as he spoke and gestured for them to come.

"A few informative words. There are no cells here. No windows, no prisoner's yard. No need for such niceties. You will have such food as you can catch in the tunnels. There is of course water in the caverns, but I would not drink long if I were you. There is also no way out.

"Rue, please open the Hole."

The thin slave was holding the end of a muddy rope that ran across the water. He leaned slightly back and braced his legs as he began to pull the rope. There was a small sucking sound, then a stirring of the water. The waters began to churn. Suddenly, the end of a massive wormlike creature broke the surface, rose about ten feet above it, and then fell down and landed just next to the road. Its maw opened slowly, revealing thousands of soft, bent, barblike teeth, then completely to reveal a "hole" of about ten feet in diameter.

"This, gentlemen, represents your passage into the last place you will ever know. The Yrewlak will eat you, one by one, and shit you out. Some of you will not survive the journey. Those of you who do will need a key to remove the shackles."

He threw a key down into the creature's mouth.

"Leave your shackles there, or take them if you please, but remember: they are heavy and they make a lot of noise. Quick and quiet stays alive. Slow and noisy…no.

"So, safe journey, then. Enter."

One man, who wore the braids of a Mariendo statesman, screamed in horror and began to thrash about, trying to find a way out of the chains. The Mundite raised a small hand to signal the battalion of guards. One of them split the thrasher's skull open with a mace.

"It seems perhaps your chances of making it through the Yrewlak have increased. The creature prefers to feast on the dead and excrete the living, though it doesn't necessarily follow any strict rule about all that. I don't know why, nor do I care. But you all should."

He waved them cordially toward the mouth once more.

"Please, enter."

And so they did. One by one, though they were shackled closely together, they entered the mouth and were swallowed. The body of the Mariendon was dragged along and consumed as well. As Baks entered, he reflected on his imminent death. Xian found himself impressed that for some many centuries the Pherriuskatan powers-that-be had concealed the fact that their most notorious prison was no prison at all, but instead a crafty method of execution.

Excretion, indeed.

Perhaps the two of them were better off.

With the Nulling coming and no means of preventing it, a quick, painless death was all anyone could hope for.

Xian fell into darkness and saw, in his mind, Glea Siven's glittering dress.

"What a wonderful garment…" he whispered as he fell.

Chapter 47
And then
she made her choice.

Place: House Canamow, Island City of Pashka, Kingdom of Pherriuskata,
Arba Environ
Date: Angem 38, AY 999

"Ah, there you are, Pet. Come in."

He was sitting alone, having tea in his favorite study. She entered the room, chose a chair that was not near him but was also not close enough to inspire suspicion, and sat down.

"Where have you been? I've had the whole house looking for you."

"I was in the garden."

"Whose garden?"

"The Baywinders." She told him what she had to assume he already knew.

"The Baywinders," he said, rising. "No wonder no one could locate you."

He had a cool, detached expression on his face, but that meant nothing. He had worn a similar expression since the Low Feast, as if something he couldn't quite grasp was occupying most of his intellectual faculties even as it dulled his emotions.

"Do you often go to the Baywinders alone?" he asked as he moved to a spot directly behind her.

"I do not."

"Then why today?"

"Why not today?"

"Indeed. But that's not an answer."

"No? I suppose that's because perhaps I don't understand the question. Or the need for it. I go out."

"Yes, you do. Often. But when do you go out alone? And when do you disappear for hours?"

"It wasn't my intention to disappear. I've had a lot to think about, and the Baywinders has always given me comfort."

"Really? I did not know that," he said.

She heard him pour himself a glass of something, and then he continued in a strange, kind of cooing voice: "Such a lovely garden. And the atrium — astounding. There are so many paths on those grounds, so many grottos and nooks and groves…it's a wonder you didn't get lost!"

"I never go too far in."

"Probably wise. They say untoward things happen there."

"Do they?"

"Yes, they do."

He left her sitting there, alone, to think.

Several weeks went by, during which Petrecia stayed in the house.

Rodolpho stayed close to her, neglecting to go to his usual meetings and trysts and haunts, events that typically occupied the greater portion of his waking hours. He lunched with her, he dined with her, he sat with her and listened to music and entertained a few guests and watched her.

All of which meant one thing: he knew.

And it was only a matter of time till he acted on what he knew.

Or maybe he knew nothing. Maybe it was a slow season in the Body; maybe he'd decided to take some time off to deliberate on whatever it was he'd been presented with by Grewea at the feast. Or maybe the old creature had told him to stay home and away from his duties for some reason. Maybe it was part of a plan. She could only speculate, and her speculations led her to dark and fearful thoughts, so she chose to ignore them as best she could.

She still found time to get away. Market trips and sojourns to fashion shows with Fernanda she knew Rodolpho would never attend, not even in his current state of watchfulness.

She had to be careful. She sometimes sent word, usually through Hobknot and once through Fernanda, that it wasn't safe to meet. Nonetheless, she'd met with her lover half a dozen times, always in the Baywinders. They were safe there, they were secret, even if Rodolpho knew she might go there. The tunnels beneath gave them all the protection they needed from prying eyes and loose tongues.

Or did they? She believed as much, but was she right to do so? Her doubts plagued her. She could not continue this, and she could not stop. She was like a woman falling, reaching for anything to stop her, grasping nothing and knowing all the while it was she who had chosen to jump.

"We cannot meet here, not any longer. He knows."

Bealaki held her and kissed her shoulder and whispered, "He knows nothing."

"You don't...why...we have to be careful."

"We are being careful. This place is hidden. Let's not waste the time we have speaking about the fool you call husband..."

His caresses and kisses quieted her, but the feeling of falling remained.

Rodolpho knew. He must have known. If not, why the questions, why the sudden interest in her movements, her walks in the gardens, and her moods?

He had never cared much about any of those things before. When he wanted her there, he wanted her there, but when he didn't, it was as if she did not exist. And so it had been for years.

She listened to his questions; she tried to read his face even as she did all she could to hide any hint of desperation and deceit in her own. But she was sure of one thing and sure that one thing would be her undoing: she had tells. Everyone had. And while her husband was in no way adept at reading them, he must surely have been aware of them on some level.

Rodolpho's ability to read her wasn't the problem. His ability to delegate was. She fearfully considered this because it was so obvious she wanted to look away from it. But there is was, staring her in the face: he had hired a Truther.

When? She couldn't say, she wasn't sure. Truthers weren't usually human, and she couldn't remember being in the company of Rodolpho and any new nonhumans of late. There were two Slau who visited him semi-regularly on business, but she had known them for years. There was someone else, a buffoon of a man named Goatie or Gostie, who had dined with them once weeks ago, but he didn't seem the type to listen. But wouldn't that be the type one would expect a Truther to be? Someone who hid behind a persona, someone who didn't want to be seen for what he was?

She smiled darkly at the thought. Wasn't that true of all Tri citizens, maybe even all Arbans now, for all she knew? No one wanted to be known or to know. No one cared about religion or the Proving or the perpetual wars or the racism or the slavery or the cruelty…no one cared about anything but their own immediate world: who did they know, who owed them, where was the next party to be held, from where would the next profit or advantage be gleaned, who was fucking whom, who was bound to die because of it?

And what a sad little hypocrite she was after all, preoccupied as she currently was with that last ominous and inevitable point. She too was fucking, and she too would likely die.

Indeed, a Truther in the mix would mean her time here was almost at an end. And before she'd met Bealaki, that thought would have brought her some comfort, however cold. But now…

Now she wanted to run.

Now she wanted to live.

The sea outside her window was calm. Ponasa was gone, and sweet Trilesti was slipping down below the eastern horizon, casting out fading rays of violet and crimson like a child tossing petals for a hero long after the parade has passed by. The familiar colors danced off the water and warmed Petrecia's heart for a moment; she felt as she had when she was a girl and the seas around Mont du Grace held her safely in their comforting embrace.

He opened the door, and it banged against the wall.

Not as hard as before, she told herself. *Perhaps he is growing weary of this game.*

She continued to stare at the lake. She felt his glowering hatred, his need to somehow deliver his feeling of utter betrayal onto her person in some unspeakable physical way, and that was the same as it had been yesterday and the day before and for weeks now.

But something was different.

She waited.

She watched the water.

She would not turn around, not this time.

This time he would have to scream at her back.

And she didn't turn, not even when she heard the unmistakable sound of booted Umeanitur soldiers entering the room. Her mind went blank, and she waited, almost relieved, for some kind of resolution. She wondered where Elzbieta's children were, and if their mother was with them.

But no, she thought as they grabbed her: Elzbieta was long since dead now — he had killed her, she knew — and the children were far away, and none of them were coming back to her. Not now.

It was for the best, really.

"Hold her." The voice was unfamiliar: it was Raxsus, Rodolpho's Mer Ponx. He was in full throat, rasping, wheezing almost, in the throes and possession of some spell.

Rough hands grabbed at her.

"Yes, bind her…and then put her on the table," hissed Raxsus.

The soldiers pulled her off her feet and threw her down onto the table, hurting her arms, her neck and legs. A rope was pulled tightly around her wrists and ankles.

"Her mouth…cover her mouth."

A gag was forced into her mouth and tied hard around her head.

"That doesn't look all that unfamiliar. Are you comfortable, Pet?" she heard Rodolpho ask, his voice dripping with acid. "We want you to be comfortable, of course."

Something was wrong, very wrong. They'd never tied her up before, and he'd never brought his Mer Ponx to her room. Raxsus had watched her for years, and she knew why, but he'd never come near her, had never even spoken to her. He'd never even bothered to hide his disgust toward her. To him, she was a filthy creature of color, nothing more.

And now she knew: they were going to do something terrible. She tried to cry out despite herself. She was coolly surprised at the magnitude of her terror even as she struggled to suppress it.

What would come next she then guessed, though she couldn't believe even in his current mental state Rodolph would allow it. She twisted her head to look back again out the window, but the curtain had fallen, and now all she could see from her position was the dark, rich purple of Trilesti's last farewell.

Raxsus, standing at her head, laid his thin, leathery hands on her cheeks and looked down into her eyes. She'd never seen his face up close. And now he was so very close. His hairless chin looked like a fat, scarred nose from this perspective, his typically grim, downturned lips like a wicked smile.

"Now, Lord Canamow, if you please: you must tell me what you have decided. Is she to forget, become completely empty, a mindless vessel who must and will do as you command, whatever that command may be...or is she to be aware, but silent, trapped within, and yet just as compliant as if she were a Mindless One nearing the end of its unfairly angled time?" The Mer Ponx's words sounded more like a spell already underway than a question to his liege.

"Let me consider a moment, if you please, Raxsus. You say she can be offered the respite of complete numbness, never again to be conscious of herself: all memories gone, all thoughts erased save those I impart upon her?" Rodolpho asked with a tone of feigned ignorance, though he plainly knew the answer.

"That is the most common application of the Breaking magick, by far; it seems both just and merciful."

"And yet, there is the other option. The one you'd no doubt consider unjust and cruel. But let me ask you, Raxsus, where were justice and mercy and their oft-misplaced companions love and fidelity when my dear Petrecia was fucking her unfortunate little musical friend?"

Rodolph must have seen her eyes when he said this.

"Ah, she didn't know. But how could she? Yes, Pet. I found your sweet Wildean. An Ailo-shut, no less. How exotic of you. Bealaki—sounds like a sour dessert I once had on Fan Pell. He made it all the way through the marsh and past—this is almost funny—Bi Prison. Jui here caught up with him just before he entered the Waterfields six nights ago. Don't worry, Pet, and certainly don't cry. The only pain he felt was when the Granderman's wolves tore off his feet."

She gasped, and tears rolled down her face onto the table. She felt something in her—something dead, something cold—taking hold.

Rodolpho leaned down to her face, his breath ripe with yellow chew and wine. "He sang before he died, he did. A song for you. How did it go, Jui?"

One of the soldiers yipped and screamed and yowled, then moaned and cried, and ended his mockery with a high-pitched, malicious chuckle that clearly amused his fellows and her husband.

"Such a sweet, irresistible melody…I can see why you found him so alluring," said Rodolpho, smiling.

The dead cold had just about consumed her. Her body was freezing.

"Lord Canamow, I must insist," Raxsus said. "Her color is manifesting, and I'm not entirely sure we'd be able to manage if—"

"Her color? Please."

"Have you chosen, sir?"

"Of course I have. But don't rush me, Raxsus. I'm speaking to my wife about the dearly complicated affairs of the heart. We must understand, above all else, that these precious pursuits must be given due time and warmth, must they not, Pet?"

She remembered the words as her own. How long ago it seemed she'd found them so wonderfully subtle in their double meaning as she'd cooed them to herself in preparation for her first trip through the Mansdrelam.

And then she remembered: she hadn't been alone. She'd cooed the words to someone else.

Synthyea.

The icy feeling had completely consumed her now. She looked up at her husband. His crazed, eager stare was more than she should be asked to endure, but something inside her felt strong, capable of ripping that eagerness right off his skull.

She tried to find the window with her eyes, but the purple sky was all but black now, and her eyes returned to his with a look of unmatchable defiance.

"Please, my lord. I fear her foulness is stirring."

"Very well. Mustn't keep a magicker waiting. Option Two."

Petrecia felt the sharp pinch of a needle entering her neck.

She closed her eyes.

The room was gone.

She awoke some time later. She had no way to tell when.

She was in a room she'd never been in. It had no windows, only a small bed and two chairs. She was sitting in one of the chairs, unable to move.

Am I paralyzed? Am I dead?

She strained to get up out of the chair, but she had no ability to do so. The ropes they'd bound her with when they'd done whatever it was…they were gone.

The Breaking. That's what they'd called it.

And then she remembered: he was dead.

Her Bealaki was gone.

She felt the impulse to sob but found she could not. A wild panic rose up in her, pushing up, trying to burst out…but it stayed within her. She could not express it. Nor could she make a sound or even breathe deeply. All she could do was move her eyes back and forth and up and down. She was not even sure if she could hear anything; this room was completely silent.

She was completely and utterly paralyzed, trapped within herself.

Hours passed.

She passed out once but couldn't stay asleep. She peed herself. Twice. The room stank of urine, which she took as a good sign because at least she could still smell.

She was very hungry, and her throat was parched.

Several dozen times she rallied herself to try to rise and get out of the room. But she simply could not move at all. She could blink. She could sniff slightly. She could move her eyes up and down and side to side.

And she could wait.

"The nature of this spell, my lord, is that the subject must be kept close to the one to whom she is bound. Not initially, no, but soon thereafter…"

"How close?"

"Within fifty or fewer paces, I should say, particularly in the case of a subject with a color. And I will have to renew the spell weekly for it to remain in effect."

Rodolpho sighed. "So you're saying I need to bring this thing with me wherever I go? Why can't she just stay here while you do your weekly ritual and bind her to me that way?"

"The magick doesn't work that way, my lord."

"Well then, how does it work?"

"As I said—"

"Imagine my shock and dismay at learning that my family's personal Mer Ponx clown does not understand the nature of his very own spells."

"Sir, please. The Medlites' tomes have ever been the subject of our most astute perusal, but—"

"But after centuries, you still don't know what you're doing."

"We…we have only clues, and these we follow with rigid devotion—"

"I doubt any of you has any idea about rigidity, devoted or not,"

Rodolpho said, sighing again. "Very well. Will it follow me around?"

"If you command her to follow, she will. She will do just about anything you command."

"What if I tell her to walk into the lake?"

"That she would not do. The Breaking cannot render the subject suicidal."

"Understood. Get out."

"As you wish."

Rodolpho stood before her with a somewhat simmering expression on his face. "You must be wondering how you got here. You must be wondering how I caught you."

She looked at him and then looked away.

"It's all right, Pet. We humans have naturally curious minds. I'm not above a little curiosity myself. I wonder too."

He slapped her hard across the face, and her head flopped to the side. The room spun before her.

"No, don't you move. Stay completely still!"

He slapped her again; this time, her head remained still. A sharp pain ripped at her neck, and she saw only black.

"Yes, curiosity. For example, I wonder how in the world you ever expected to get away with it. I wonder what it is about me that seems so gullible, so permissive, so trusting that you got this wildly false impression upon which you based so many very bad decisions."

She lifted her head and started to speak.

"Shut up, Pet," he whispered softly. "Never speak again unless I tell you to. Not to anyone, ever. Do you understand?"

She tried to scream at him and found she could not produce even a whisper to match his own. Any words died in her throat.

"In fact, if you try to speak, you will feel a tremendous amount of pain, a searing, burning sensation right behind your eyes. Nod if you understand."

She didn't nod. It enraged him. He slapped her again.

"Why didn't you nod? Answer me."

She hesitated to do so but then attempted to answer. And passed out immediately from the searing pain behind her eyes.

"Wake up!"

She woke up.

"I could have hours of fun doing this, but I've got better things to do. For example, right now I'm leaving you to go fuck Synthyea. You remember her, right? Yes, I see that you do. I expect you'll regret not being more careful around her. I expect you'll come to regret that quite a bit when all is said and done. Now stay awake till I get back and think of all the ways I can hurt you. For now, just for starters, bite down as hard on your tongue as you can. Don't bite it off, right, just hurt yourself. And bleed. Right. That's good. Good night, Pet."

He blew out the candles in the room and left.

The weeks that followed were all like that. He used her. He hurt her. He tormented her. And on occasion, he let her sleep.

She accompanied him to every meeting, every event, every tryst. She watched as he fucked Synthyea again and again and again. They laughed at her and spit on her and threw bedpans at her. Synthyea loved to stab her with sewing needles in ways that wouldn't kill her but were nonetheless agonizing; Rodolpho liked to watch Synthyea do it. Once, they set her hair on fire and made her sit there while her skin burned.

They were insane, but what was she?

She'd spent her life hiding from the truth of the insanity around her. She'd excused it and silently, passively condoned it. She'd benefitted from it too. And now, she was completely and finally in its cruel, chaotic grasp.

Rodolpho let the Umeanitur at her nightly. All of them, and there were at least ten stationed at House Canamow at any given time. He watched that too. He never let them beat her too much — she had to be able to walk, after all, to stick close to him and maintain the spell — but they hurt her plenty in any case.

She wanted to run but couldn't.

She wanted to die but couldn't.

And there was no one coming to help her. Bealaki was dead. Her father was an eternity away. She had no more brothers. She had no friends. Fernanda had abandoned her.

Where, she wondered, was Hobknot?

But then one day Rodolpho led her to Baywinders, to the very tree where she'd once met with Bealaki to make love and sing and laugh.

And there, nailed to the bough, was the rotting corpse of her gardener ally.

Rodolpho made her kiss him, maggots and all.

"See how happy he is to receive your kiss? It's a pity his cock has rotted off; I would've enjoyed seeing what you could do with that!"

Such was her life now.

The price of a few weeks' happiness was an unending nightmare of horror.

She wanted to die but couldn't.

She wanted to live but couldn't.

And he was gone, he was dead, he would never hold her again, so it didn't seem to matter much as the horrible days and the worse nights crept by. They owned her, Rodolpho and his lackeys. She owned nothing. Paraded around, beaten, used, harmed, shit on, thrown into pools with a rope around her neck so they could bob her up and down, and burned when the mood struck them.

Such was her life now.

But in her heart and mind, she remembered him, her poemsman, her musiker, who was so bold, so sweet. And somehow, when no one was watching, she made herself smile.

His song still filled her ears.

Beneath the mask that was her life now, she listened closely and, on good nights, was able to weep to his song.

The room was still. Outside somewhere, perhaps on the boulevard, Petrecia could hear some men singing, but the sounds only lasted a few moments and then faded. They must have moved on. She was glad despite herself that outside there was a world where people could move on.

She began to drift off to sleep, but there was a voice:

"Hello, Trecia."

She heard the voice in her mind and somehow knew it wasn't her imagination. Someone was talking to her, but in her mind. It reminded her of a time, long ago, when she'd heard a voice like this...no, not like this: this very voice.

She did not answer. She listened more closely.

And the voice came again:

"Please don't be alarmed, dear. I don't mean to startle you; far from it. I am here to help you."

"Aunt Hanziella?" Petrecia wondered.

"Yes," came the reply. "It's me."

"You can hear me?"

"Yes, dear, I can. Don't speak, just think, just like you're doing."

"Where are you?" Petrecia asked, her pulse quickening. She had not spoken to anyone, in her mind or otherwise, in a very long time.

"Close. But please don't try to look around for me. You'll only hurt yourself. Stay just as you were and, please, be calm. We don't want anyone to see you...getting excited."

"How...?"

"I am speaking to you as I used to...do you remember? When you were a little girl?"

"I...yes, I remember. We talked in our heads. But that was in my dreams...I always believed you were in my dreams."

"Sometimes it was a dream. I spoke to you sometimes when you were asleep...sometimes when I was very far away."

Petrecia tried to absorb this information but found she could not adequately concentrate on what was being said. She could not think it through. "My husband..." she managed.

"I know, dear. I know all about what's happened. I've been watching. I wasn't here in time to stop him, but I'm here now."

"Can you help me? I want...please just kill me. Find a way to kill me...please!" Petrecia begged.

"No! You need to be calm, Trecia! Do this for me: think of home. Think of Mont du Grace and the beach near your home, think of the waves from the Windgiver Sea and the suns beating down while you played...that's it. Yes."

Petrecia listened and tried to calm herself. She saw the beach in her mind, saw her sister and her mother and Aunt Hanziella.

"Now what's this about killing you? Why would I do a thing like that, Trecia? No, girl: I am here to save you."

"Save me?"

"Yes, dear. More precisely, I am here to offer you a choice."

"Choice? What choice?"

"First things first. How are you...how are you holding up?"

"I...I want to die."

"I know, dear. I know it."

"They raped me."

"Who did, dear?"

"All of them, I think. I don't remember faces. I can't feel much."

"I see. Are you in any pain?"

"Always, yes, I think so...I can't really say. But...the pain in my mind, this prison...that's the horrible, horrible place...I can't think. I can't remember..."

The vision of her home was quickly receding.

"Trecia, breathe. And focus. You can remember. Back in Mont du Grace, on that beach, on that day just before you left to get married...I told you someday you would need me and I would be there for you. Do you remember?"

Petrecia thought for a moment. Yes! The day had been cooler than normal, and overcast. "I remember. I remember being afraid when you said that."

"Well, you now understand why you were afraid. Clearly, that day has come. And as promised, I am here for you. But there's something I want you to think about, something I want you to do for me, if you can."

"The choice."

"Yes. Here it is: be saved, right now, by me, or...stay the way you are and help us bring down the duke. And Rodolpho."

Us? "I don't understand."

"I wouldn't expect you to, not right away, at least."

"You can't save me, Auntie. No one can. Rodolpho's put a Breaking curse on me. I'm nothing more than a living mannequin."

"Oh, that's simply not so: I know for a fact you are quite a bit more than a mannequin. No mannequin on its best day could come close to being a fraction of what you are every second of every blessed day."

"I still don't understand you. I am deeply thankful for your coming! It's been so long since I've spoken to anyone…but it's unbearable, and I fear I've gone mad, and…I want to die. Please…kill me!"

"I understand. But I cannot do what you ask. You know that, don't you?"

Petrecia knew she should understand the choice being offered to her, but she couldn't think, she just couldn't wrap her head around what was being said. Everything she saw in her mind seemed cloudy, every image brought with it a sharp pain that cut through her mind, or was it her heart, or maybe her body itself…

"Tell me what you see, Trecia," Hanziella said patiently.

"I barely remember…oh, Four, Auntie. They killed Bealaki! Rodolpho had him murdered."

There was a long pause from her aunt. Then: "Yes, well. No. My dear, your idiot husband only thinks his men and that hateful hunter murdered your lover. It is not so. In fact, I saw him — broke bread with him — just yesterday."

"What? For true?"

"Bealaki is one of us, Trecia. Bealaki is of the Jamoi Nogo."

"Bealaki is alive?"

"Yes. Oh, I know it's rare indeed to have a male, especially one born outside of Jamonogia, painted with a color — and is he ever painted, my dear — but it is so. He's as much his color as you are yours. He never told you, mostly because we wouldn't allow him to. Partly because he didn't want to scare you away. He really is in love with you."

"I know that now. I've wept for so long now…we could have —"

"The role he plays for us was far too important to compromise, even for love. Though that's pretty much over and done with now. Can't blame love, though, if only out of principle. We blame madness — Rodolpho's — instead."

"Over and done…you're sure Bealaki is alive?"

"Yes, of course."

"And Elzbieta and the children?"

Hanziella paused once more, this time for more than a few moments. "The children Rodolpho has sent away, dear, to some relative in the Measured Fields. They'll do fine there, I'm sure. The Second Wife, though…do you not recall?"

"Has something happened to her?"

"We're not sure. We think she might have gotten out. Her cousin—"

"The Dervinth."

"It seems he might have helped her. We're just not sure," Aunt Hanziella said.

"But she's alive?"

"Maybe. Maybe not. We'll keep looking if you'd like us to." She paused for a moment before resuming. "And now let's talk about your choice."

Hours after her aunt had gone, Petrecia was struggling with the offer she'd been made.

She was still having trouble focusing, having trouble breathing, having trouble understanding whether or not she'd gone completely insane. Were her thoughts her own? Had her aunt truly visited her?

Was Bealaki alive?

She wanted to do what was right; she wanted to be Noble and true. Yes. It was best for everyone that she opt to work for the Jamoi, wasn't it? To help bring down the Mind and the duke and her insane husband and all the rest, all of them.

But she was afraid. Since the night of the Breaking spell, Rodolpho had her raped a hundred times. More. He had allowed others to do things to her, things she couldn't remember clearly, but she could feel them, she did feel them, over and over, every moment, every time she closed her eyes or heard the sound of a door or boots or men's voices. She was sure that these experiences had robbed her of sanity, and she could not trust herself to do anything but flee.

Then came the sound of the key in the door to her room.

The door opened. Rodolpho entered, slammed the door, and stood behind her.

She could smell his sour Mariendan cologne and hear the slight wheeze in his breath. He thought he was being clever, but she knew exactly where he was. And it didn't help her at all; the blow was still coming, and it was a blow against which she couldn't even brace.

"Ah, there you are, Pet. On the floor, then."

He pushed her; she fell face down. The room was carpeted; he'd had the carpet put in after she'd gone down a few times, hit her head, and almost lost consciousness. He liked her to be awake and aware.

He flipped her over and sat on her stomach, grinning hatefully. "Oh, Pet, don't look so frightened. You know how this is going to go. Is it so bad? Have I really hurt you, even once? I mean, I'm sure I've hurt your feelings, but after all, you hurt mine first. Isn't that so?"

He smacked her once with each hand.

"See, now. That stung, I'm sure, but did it hurt? Now this, this will hurt...and you'll be able to tell the difference."

He punched her hard in the center of her chest. She coughed as hot tears sprang from her eyes; she almost blacked out as her breath left her.

"See the difference? Yes?" he said, laughing and grinning even more wildly.

I should be numb to this by now; I should feel nothing, she thought.

"Here, try this" — he punched her left breast — "and this!" He punched her right breast.

The pain was excruciating, and she passed out.

"WAKE UP!" he screamed.

And she did, for the spell would not even allow her body to protect itself by passing out. Not just she, but her body independent of her will and mind had to obey his every utterance.

He started to beat her again, at first viciously, but then less so, till finally he was doing nothing but pushing his body against hers. She realized after a while that he was trying to have sex, not with her but somehow, anyway, perhaps even despite her or despite himself. He was weeping.

He left her sometime in the night, and when he did, he made a terrible mistake. He forgot to tell her to be still and not think. And being how and who she was, she could willfully ignore any orders she hadn't received. For the first time in what felt like forever, her will was her own, and her thoughts were her own.

She stood up and went to the window.

She stared out at the lights of Sianthis Island. She stood there for a long time.

And then she made her choice.

Chapter 48
"I very much wish to find this Wildean magicker child who you say does not exist."

Place: somewhere in the southern portion of the kingdom of Pherriuskata,
Arba Environ
Date: Angem 43, AY 999

"You know of the Broken Mind, F'nios?"

"I know what any child knows: they were an order of magickers bent on controlling or destroying all life in this environ. And they're all dead and buried."

Grewea sat on a stone bench and gazed out at the small brook and the marshy wetlands beyond it. He thought back to a time when this brook was something more than a mere decorative tributary of the Vinatuat River, the marsh was a breeding ground for the finest horses ever raised in Arba. What a people those early Pherrius had been: the best of the Boi Na, the products of the Golden Age, here to rule and better the world for all eternity…all gone now, gone these many centuries. *Dead and buried*, as poor F'nios, standing here in his cracked leather and his weathered, sweat-stained hood had intoned.

"That's all true. Somewhat true, at least. You know your history," Grewea said.

"And?"

"And did you know they almost succeeded in doing just that — destroying all life in this environ? Did you further know, F'nios, that according to our best reports of the time, the Broken Mind, through their sinister efforts and allegiances, wiped out nearly one-third of the Arban population when all was said and done?"

"I've read that, yes. I had hoped the writer was exaggerating. How would such a thing even have been possible?"

"It was no exaggeration. You would be shocked, my good man, to learn how vast are the possibilities of this world, particularly where death is involved."

"I don't doubt it. I'll pass on that, if you don't mind. But why the history lesson, Grewea? Either way, all that's done with, and don't we have important matters to discuss?"

Grewea rose and stretched from side to side. His wild mane of gray-and-black hair flopped in front his eyes, and he leaned back to get it under control; then he placed a small gray skullcap upon it to help it settle. Why did his hair still grow so after so long? "Those matters can wait," he said. "I have something else in mind for this meeting."

"I see. Tell me then, what preoccupies you?" F'nios said. He was making an extra effort to listen attentively, Grewea noticed, which was a good thing. Given his people's failure in Hunberg with Sh'arnau, it was in his best interest to do so. Grewea didn't bother explaining to F'nios that his people had failed in exactly the manner Grewea had expected them to. The plan, such as it was, was stumbling forward, and for that, if nothing else, Grewea was grateful.

Grewea asked, "Your people have long believed in industry, economy, and learning, yes?"

"Of course," F'nios said. He seemed to be caught between expressing pride and practicing humility, and this caused him to cough a few times.

Grewea waited until the coughing ended. "And because you believe so fully in these things—industry, economy, and learning—your laws forbid the practice or learning of magick, isn't that right?"

"You know it is."

"Hmm. Yes, well, tell me—what do you do when a child is born with a color?"

"We rarely encounter such a situation."

"But when you do?"

"It has long been our practice to offer such children, if they survived, to the Spectrum."

"Even the males?"

"There have been no males. Not in over three hundred years, leastwise."

"Really? Not one?"

"Not that I've heard."

"I have heard differently."

"You've heard wrong. To my knowledge, only eleven children with a color have been born since the time of Graviss the Grim. All were female. Seven were slain by their people. One disappeared, into the Scar it was said, so it almost certainly died too. And the remaining three were given to the Spectrum."

"In exchange for what?"

"I couldn't say. It was all long ago. Livestock, I expect, or tools."

"Or political power?"

"Perhaps. I don't see how, but I wouldn't rule it out."

"Neither would I, but it's not a germane point in the here and now. We'll come back to that topic if we need to, but I'm more interested in the male child."

"There was never any such child."

"F'nios, you seem a practical man not given to any particular ideological delusions, if my sources are to be believed."

"Your description is fair."

"And you have served three Belolli warmasters and two Underrun lords, have you not?"

"I am fortunate to have had a role to fill."

"And you did not fill that role by taking unwarranted risks, I am sure."

"True. I have always been careful."

"With your selections and allegiances?"

"Aye, with those, and with my life. Careful," said F'nios, who seemed to be growing more anxious with each of Grewea's questions. *He doesn't know where I'm going with this, nor should he, the buffoon.* Resourcefulness was often the first quality to be sacrificed at the altar of loyalty, for only the truly courageous and individualistic were apt to be able to think for themselves.

He found himself missing Sh'arnau, or at least, the tool that was Sh'arnau. The creature himself had never made good company, but his efficacy and efficiency had ever been beyond any reproach. Grewea wondered if Sh'arnau was still alive, and if so, how far along he'd come in completing the near-impossible task Grewea had set him to.

"Careful. Why yes, of course. But also quietly open to possibilities, yes?"

"Yes."

"Then given the virtually limitless opportunities your service to me represents for you, why do you lie to me now?"

F'nios, typically unshakable, blanched. "I am not lying," he huffed. "There was never a male magicker born among us."

"My sources, who you acknowledge were accurate in their description of you, say otherwise," Grewea replied.

"They're wrong! About the child? They are wrong. I have no reason to lie, Grewea."

"Such was the case I was making: no reason to lie, indeed. And every reason not to, I would add. And so I believe you. And yet, there is this lingering question…"

"I don't myself know what it is you refer to. I can, however, make inquiries."

"Yes."

"I will go back to the Wilds and make inquiries…on your behalf."

"No, not on my behalf — on your own. I very much wish to find this Wildean magicker child who you say does not exist. He would not be a child any longer, of course, and he may not even know of his own abilities, though I doubt very much that's true. He is very important to me, and were you to be the one to help me locate him, I think I might find a place for you here, in Pherriuskata. You seem to be wearing out your welcome in the Wilds, and the accommodations here are far superior in any case."

F'nios seemed to understand that his life would not end here and now, and his face began to regain its natural hue. "I would be most grateful."

"I expect you would be."

"May I ask, why the urgency? You need this child — this man — for something?"

"Something, yes. Quite possibly, everything. The one we seek might very well be the key to finally ridding ourselves of the Broken Mind."

"But I thought we agreed that the Broken Mind are long dead."

"Would that that were true. And would that our agreeing that it was true would render it so. Alas, we haven't such power, but once, near to this very spot where we now sit, there were men who did. Well, not men, but they did sit here. The wonders they wrought, the glory they brought, as the song goes."

F'nios looked confused, and in his confusion, once more, afraid.

Grewea ignored this and strode toward the brook. He waved his fingers toward it, and a small stream of water rose into the air and came to him. He leaned in, took a sip, and then turned to F'nios and indicated that he, too, could take a drink if he liked. The Wildean, his eyebrows furrowed, declined by shaking his head twice. He added, "No, thank you," after a moment.

Grewea turned back toward his bench. The water stream fell to the ground. He sat down again, wiped his mouth gently with his sleeve, and sighed.

"The Broken Mind is, it saddens and annoys me to say, very much alive, and though they've been of use to me these last few years, they are nonetheless a serious threat to every living creature in this environ. Again."

F'nios's expression indicated he wasn't following.

"*You* need to find the Wildean magicker boy, F'nios."

"You're saying you need my help specifically to find him? Or am I simply one of many possible sources?"

"Ordinarily, though also impudent, your second question would be prudent, even indicative of standard practice. Who among us isn't better served by plentiful and reliable sources of information and action? But alas, in this instance, you are my only lead, my only resource."

"How so?"

"You have a unique connection to the one I seek. You knew him, in fact."

"I don't follow."

"The boy — the man — is the one who killed your wife."

"What?"

"Twenty-four years ago, your wife was killed in her sleep. Isn't that so?"

"Yes."

"It was this magicker, the very one I am seeking, who did the killing. He took her from you."

"That was never proven."

"But the boy disappeared?"

"Yes. That very night. We assumed he'd been murdered by the very same killer who —"

"He was not. He lives, and he was the killer."

"Why? Why would a boy of eight —"

"I cannot say."

"How do you know this?"

"For that answer, I refer you back to your recent second guess. My sources in most matters are plentiful."

"But they cannot help you now."

"They might, eventually, be able to put me on the right path. After all, they led me to you and to this bit of personal history you never saw fit to share with me. But for some reason, that was where the trail ended."

"To learn of…to find him, after all this time…I would be most grateful."

"Of course.

"And I will be most helpful."

"Yes, you will. Tell me, because my sources cannot confirm this…what was the boy's name?"

"His name was Bealaki."

Grewea ate in silence.

He sat alone in his mountain keep on the windy, ice-covered pass and ate eggs and drank a very old vintage of what long ago was called *shivik* or soul water.

Frulla had discovered nothing, he chuckled. Nothing he hadn't put there for her to discover, in any case.

He came here, to the Waln Environ, six thousand years ago, when he needed to think and when he needed to rest. Given what was happening back there, in the future in Arba, he was very much in need of doing both at this time.

A Yalkonba came with more of the *shivik* and a basket of the strange, hard biscuits these people seemed to favor. He'd had enough to eat, but out of politeness, he took a biscuit. The water he gratefully accepted. He knew his tired body wouldn't get by on just the one bottle he'd already finished.

Why not just leave them? he thought. *Why not just stay here and die?*

The Yalkonba, a tall, very hairy cross between a bear and an ape, sat next to him. It was looking at him with a somewhat curious expression on its face. Its eyes were soft and somewhat glassy, not in any way unkind.

"Don't look at me like that. Please," Grewea said. "I've done what you've asked. Everything you asked. And I know you've given me more than I ever wanted or needed. You helped me save them. I know this."

The Yalkonba just continued to look at him.

"It's the math…all this math. You understand, yes?" Grewea said softly, feeling himself drift off. "I was never very good at it…"

Chapter 49
Alwaud'wah knew.

Place: Along the Trace between the kingdom of Arbana and the Slau lands,
Arba Environ
Date: Naipekan 5, AY 999

She washed her face and hands in a near-freezing stream off the road.

She then made the mistake of trying to wash her hair.

The suns had gone down, and it was getting cold. Autumn was harsher now that she'd travelled south. Her clothing was scarcely adequate. And she was afraid to risk a fire after what had happened to those thieves all those nights ago.

The chassariete was asleep inside her, or so she wanted to believe. Or maybe it was simply watching and waiting for another opportunity to assert itself. She didn't want that. She wanted it to stay asleep. What it did when it was awake was, to say the least, unpleasant. And it terrified her. It hadn't killed but the one time, but that was more than enough.

She had no towel or cloth to dry herself with, and the air was chilly enough that she feared she might take ill if she didn't dry off. She tried to use her light cloak, but it did little to help. The wind through her damp hair was brutal. *What a fool*, she thought. *I've proven once more I don't belong out here.* She pictured the fire in Mama Chaudhri's home.

And then she heard them.

There were men back by her belongings.

She hadn't much — just what Emer had kindly given her and what she'd carried from the Tent City: a small blanket, some food, her clothes, a tiny flask of lifewine. And now there were men, poking around her camp.

How had they found her things? She'd built no fire. She'd made no sounds.

They were laughing and singing. Then their voices trailed off.

She scurried up from the river and saw that they'd taken everything.

She did not despair. She sat for a moment and thought.

And then she followed them.

"You cannot enter this place."

She'd found their lair. It was a cave, perhaps an old mine, with a thick iron gate over the front of it and a single sentry sitting there, humming to himself and paying the night and the woman in front of him next to no mind. He'd barely looked at her when she'd approached. It was not how men typically reacted when they saw her.

"Are you deaf? Go away."

She stared at him and then gestured to get past him to the gate.

He stood up slowly and chuckled, blocking her path. "That anxious for business, are you? Okay, let's get this done then, girl," he said, reaching out with both hands for her breasts.

She didn't hesitate. She lashed out at his face with her smallwhip. It cut him across the forehead, blood immediately gushing, and he howled, falling to the ground and groping at the wound.

She darted past him and pulled at the gate. It was not locked. She opened it, just enough to pass through, and entered. A tunnel sloped downward straight ahead of her. A single candle was lit on a table far down that way, and from what she could see, the table was surrounded by sacks, barrels, and chests.

My things are there, she thought. *My things, and more.*

On her left there was a long hall; someone had a nice fire going down at the end of it. The fire reminded her abruptly of how cold she was; her hair was still damp from the river. She shivered for a moment but stilled herself. The fire crackled, and she could smell meat roasting. Her stomach clenched from hunger.

Several men were laughing and arguing down there, not at all concerned that anyone, let alone a pregnant invader armed only with a smallwhip, might be among them.

She ignored her shivers and hunger and looked down the sloped tunnel. The dim light from the candle did nothing to reveal the tunnel itself. That was pitch black, and there were no sounds.

She made herself listen more closely.

No, there didn't seem to be anyone else down there, but something about the tunnel seemed wrong. She made herself very still. It was not her way to be this careful, but somehow she knew she should. She heard more laughter from the men down the hall. The smell of their fire and food and the snap and crackle of their wood popping and burning was almost too much to bear.

And then she heard him: someone else, down in the tunnel, breathing softly, waiting. He too knew someone was coming, and he was quiet, very quiet, though clearly not as quiet as he believed himself to be. He was poised to strike at her, somewhere just about twenty paces down. He was not like the others, the drunken lout she had beaten or the laughing morons by their nice fire. He was more careful, more lethal; he had purpose.

She understood this somehow. And she also understood that his purpose, in this moment, was to kill her.

She did not give him the chance. She took a slow breath, then another, and called to Alwaud'wah.

He came. *Yes.*

Help me…I need to go down there…and someone…help me.

What shall I do?

She considered the question, but only for an instant. *Whatever is necessary.*

It is done.

She understood with absolute certainty that the chassariete would dispatch the waiting man.

How she knew that, and why she was suddenly so comfortable with that, she could not say.

She realized as she sat and waited for the inevitable that this thing, this spirit that had attached itself to her, was not only ruthless but also unstoppable. It killed with lightning-quick impunity, and its unquestioning compliance with regard to her requests for protection, along with its merciless brutality, had invaded her thoughts and lingered among them, ever threatening to block out all else…even concern for the life inside her.

And that she could not permit.

Alwaud'wah would need to go. She needed to make it go. But how would she do that? She had no idea how it had come to serve her in the first place. She knew about it only as much as it had told her. And it hadn't told her much.

Still, she needed food. She needed to get her things back: they were all she had in the world, and she had a long road ahead of her. It wasn't fair that these thieving bastards had a full larder and warm clothes and a fire and her things behind that gate, while she stood in the cold begging for something to eat just to keep herself and her baby alive. And if they were wicked enough to deny someone needing help in the cold the smallest of favors, punishment should be the natural result.

There were cries and shouts of surprise from down the hall and tunnel both, all at once. Then, seconds later, no sound but that of the crackling wood and something dripping.

The chassariete was there again. *It is done.*

He is…dead?

They are dead.

All of them? Why?

It was necessary.

She tried not to let it sense the revulsion she felt. She knew, however, she would fail to do so. *Go now,* she told it.

You are sure?

Yes.

Zeni…

Yes?

You need not fear for your child. I will not allow it to be harmed. I will always do what is necessary.

And then it was gone, though she could sense that it had not gone far. It never would.

So it knew about her baby. What had made her expect it would not? It knew her thoughts, responded to her feelings. It was always near, somehow, like a terrible shadow, waiting for an opportunity to destroy in her defense, whether she willed it or not. The thieves on the Road had come upon her in her sleep, and Alwaud'wah had slain them without her knowledge.

It had a will of its own.

So far, it had only served to protect her, but she could not afford to believe she had any real control in this situation. The chassariete would make its own judgments and choices, of that she was sure. And this realization did not cause her to fear. The only relevant question in her mind then was: Could she trust it?

She had no answer for that question.

The baby stirred within her, turning and kicking for the briefest of moments, and then settled back down and was still but for a barely discernible flutter. She placed a hand on her belly to still her son. Or her daughter. She wasn't sure; she had no feeling either way what the baby would be.

But Alwaud'wah knew. It knew that and more. She couldn't keep it from knowing, and she found herself admitting that she didn't want to.

She needed the chassariete. For now, at least.

All her life, a slave. All her life, she'd watched other slaves, those few friends she'd made, even in the end her kind and loving benefactor, a man who'd never beaten her, never used or raped her — she'd watched them all sold, murdered, starved, burned. And never had it been within her power to save them, to help them. She admitted now what she'd fiercely denied for as long as she'd drawn breath: that she'd been powerless to protect and help herself.

Not anymore.

But why?

What had changed?

She walked down the hall toward the fire. There were at least five bodies there, but she barely glanced at them. Greedy cowards, stealing from starving pregnant women. She grabbed some bread and a hunk of roasted meat and three bottles the labels of which she couldn't read and shoved them all in her bag. She also grabbed a thick blanket from a bunk and then turned and headed back toward the tunnel.

The candle on the table was still burning. She could hear something — and then she saw him. Her would-be assassin was embedded in the wall, somehow still alive, looking at her with eyes that were almost lifeless.

She looked down, saw her small satchel on a pile of sacks, and snatched it up. Then she ran up the tunnel back toward the gate.

But when she gained the outside, she stopped and grimaced.

"Where am I going?" she asked aloud. "The night is freezing cold, I am heavy with child, and yet I run out blindly, like some foolish mouse who's snatched scraps from a floor."

She barely noticed that she had, quite uncharacteristically, spoken, though the sound of her own voice was somewhat disorienting, so long had it been since she'd heard it.

You cannot stay here.

"Why?"

More will come.

"Then you'll kill them too."

To that, there was no reply. She took that to mean he would go along with her impulse. She would stay here; maybe she would stay as long as was necessary to have this child and see to its young needs.

"Get rid of all those bodies, please, and then seal the gate shut."

I will do it.

And it would. The chassariete would make this place safe for her and her child. Cost? She wasn't worried about any cost. She would think on it and decide what to do later. For now, she was tired of running, tired of fretting, tired of starving. She would stay here. She would rely upon her ally, answers or not.

She stayed there. For weeks. And others did come, but after the first few nights, during which Alwaud'wah dispatched at least a dozen aggressors and chased off two dozen more, most came not to fight.

No, those who came were mostly Slau or Arbanan merchants looking to trade for food or goods. She had claimed for herself, it seemed, a very well-situated trading post on a very well-traveled road.

At first, she turned the visitors away, locking the gate and ignoring their pleas for conversation, commerce, and exchange. They stayed for a night or two anyway, so used to doing so on their regular route were they. She took to hiding in the shadows just inside the gate, listening to their talk, their music, their laughter. It all reminded her — *they* reminded her — of her home, of Tent City, and the easy life she'd had there. She'd never been hungry or cold or lonely, and she'd rarely felt truly afraid.

What a fool she'd been, taking it all for granted.

And yet now she felt somehow more alive than ever she had. Her old life was gone, and all she could think of was giving birth and protecting her baby. And with all she'd found here — a cavern full of food, blankets, water, weapons, and even three small chests containing currency of all kinds—she could do that, she was sure. If she could survive the giving birth part, if she could do that on her own…

She was quite sure her protector could do nothing to help her with that particular challenge.

But the life she had now, and the choices it required of her, were hers and hers alone.

"Come on out, Lady with the Killing Ghost!"

It was late one night, and she had fallen asleep in her usual perch just inside the gate. The cry woke her.

"Come on, talk to us! But please, leave your Ghost inside! Give him some wine!"

"Why do you assume my Ghost is male?" she asked, speaking again and finding she enjoyed it. And she had no fear, not behind her gate and with her protector's vigilance.

"Ha-ha! She speaks! Who said she never spoke?"

"We mean you no harm, Lady. Please tell the Ghost. We only want to buy some furs. It's cold out here."

She glanced outside and saw two young humans, boys really, one very skinny and one stout and muscular. Both wore simple, somewhat jolly expressions on their faces and seemed a little drunk.

Ftuu left the gate and went down into the tunnel. When she returned three minutes later, they were still there, arguing clumsily. "See, I told you we should have left her alone," said the stout one.

"She's got to talk to someone," answered the skinny one.

"She doesn't talk to anyone."

"She talked to us."

"Shut up, Mulp. Think about it, would you? She probably went to get her Ghost. Now we're dead."

"Why would she kill us? We've done nothing to deserve that."

"We annoyed her. And she's a witch. Isn't that enough?"

"You haven't annoyed me," Ftuu interrupted them. "And I only left to fetch what you asked for. You do look cold."

She pushed a few large furs through the bars and dropped them to the ground.

The boys gaped at her, stunned and blushing. Not with the lust men usually looked at her with, but with something more like…wonder. She blushed in return.

"Um, oh, they…um…they didn't say you were so…so…"

"So, um, Lady, so…"

"Yes, I mean, I'm sorry, yes…"

"Do you want those?"

The boys blinked at her, not understanding. She smiled and nodded at the furs.

Glancing at each other, they seemed to decide to ignore their shame and take what was offered. They hurried over to the bars and scooped up the furs. They each slipped into one and draped another over their shoulders.

"Oh, thank you, thank you, Lady. This is…oh, I feel better already," said the stout one.

"How does it look?" asked the skinny one, apparently named Mulp.

She regarded them for a moment and burst out laughing. They both looked like overstuffed beavers, with their faces barely poking out through the enormous furs. They turned to face each other so they could get a better look. And they burst out laughing too. "Thank you so much, Lady!"

"I…I don't mean to laugh at you," she said, still laughing.

"It's okay; people laugh at us all the time," said the skinny one. "By the way, his name is Jerad. I'm Mulp."

She did not give her name but did smile. It was pleasant to laugh again. And it was surprising, after so long, to talk again. Why had she done that? She couldn't say, but she didn't mind.

Mulp decided they looked beavers too, but Jerad was sure they looked more like hedgehogs.

"Beavers are fatter," insisted Mulp.

"But hedgehogs are smarter," Jerad corrected him.

"No, they're not! Beavers build things," laughed Mulp.

"So do hedgehogs. Whole cities, underground."

Ftuu decided that these boys could probably argue about anything and said so.

"You're right, miss — madam? — absolutely. We're brothers, twins actually. Couldn't tell by looking at us," said Mulp.

"Why are you here?" she asked them.

"You mean, here as in why did we make camp here or here as in at your gate?"

"This place on the road. Of all places."

"Well, I'm sure you know, up till recently, this place was run by the Gumundurs."

"Bunch of bastards," added Jerad.

"No doubt about it," agreed Mulp. "Anyway, everyone stops here on the way to Slau and back."

"Mostly Slau," said Jerad.

"Right, mostly them. Sometimes Arbanan caravans will meet up with the Slau right here, make their trades, camp a few nights, and head back up north."

"Good place to stop. Even better now that that the famous Lady with the Killing Ghost has kicked out the Gumundurs."

"Famous?" she asked hesitantly.

"Sure, everyone's heard about you! Gumundurs are shitting their drawers all the way from here to Tent City!"

She'd been thinking of late that she might have made a grave error stopping here and making this her place of sanctuary. Now she knew she had.

"Um, Lady…can we…can we see it?" asked Mulp.

She looked at them both, confused for a moment. Perhaps she had misjudged them.

"Your Ghost."

"Ah," she said. "No, that wouldn't be a good idea."

"Sorry to offend," said Mulp, clearly let down.

"No offense. But I think—no, I know—I like you two hedgehog brothers. You seem good people. And my…Ghost, he doesn't come around to greet good people. Only bad ones."

Jerad coughed. "Um, well, then we thank you for not bringing him around. Don't we, Mulp?"

"In any case, I have to rest," said Ftuu. "Please, build yourselves a fire. Tell the good people, if there are any other out there, they don't have to be afraid."

"Well, they're merchants, so they ain't no good and they're afraid of everything, but we'll pass along your message!" said Jerad.

"And thank you, Lady, for these furs! We'll leave them here for you in the morning!"

"You can take them. They are a gift," she said.

"Um…well, thank you, but we can't," said Mulp.

"What he means is, if someone sees us wearing these, they'll probably cave our heads in and take them. Or take them and then cave our heads in," Jerad clarified.

"Ah. Well, be warm for at least tonight then. Good night."

"Good night, Lady," they said as one.

She smiled; it was the first true hint they'd offered that they were really twins. Something about that seemed somehow very familiar, and it made her heart hurt.

She went down into the tunnel to the room she'd made her own. It wasn't as warm as the big room in the hall where she'd seen and heard the men and smelled their fire, but there was still an air of death in there, so she steered clear. She'd had the chassariete remove the man from the wall in her room, though it was unable, she assumed, to remove that image from her memory. Or was it?

She thought of the hedgehog brothers in their furs and was glad to have something with which to replace that ugly image. They were funny, those two. And she envied them their freedom, their life…and their companionship.

She was lonely, very lonely. Even an evening with nasty Hara back in Tent City would be better than what she faced every day since her flight from Dalter Bubussa's tent.

Maybe she would ask the brothers to stay. They were harmless and they seemed kind.

That would be a mistake.

And there he was. Watching.

Why?

Your baby must be kept safe. As must you.

Those boys pose no threat.

They are an unknown. Have I not protected you thus far?

You have. And I thank you. But…

You are lonely.

He heard me. Does he hear my every thought?

Yes.

Your loneliness is nothing compared with your purpose.

And what is that? What is my purpose?

Do you not yet know?

She had to admit she did not. She only had a vague suspicion that she did, in fact, have a purpose, and that was new to her, because in her prior life she'd had none.

And her life had been unquestionably better because of it.

I'm going to ask them to stay. If they're here tomorrow.

They will not be.

How do you know that?

He did not answer. He was gone.

No! She jumped up from her bedding and ran up the hall. When she got to the gate, she looked out and saw two piles of fur lying next to a small fire. She quickly unlocked the gate and rushed out to them.

One of them stirred. It was Jerad.

"Lady? What…"

"Shhhhh. Get up. Come inside. Please."

"But why…"

"You're in danger."

Jerad rolled over and grabbed his brother. "Mulp, up, we hafta go!"

Mulp grunted and did not move.

"Mulp! Now!" cried Ftuu, shaking him.

"What...what's wrong?" Mulp asked as he sat up. "Lady?"

"Inside, with me. Now."

They rose, collected their packs, and followed her into the mine. She led them to the left and down the hall.

"A fire pit. Nice!" sad Mulp sleepily. "And look at all this food!"

"Listen to me, you two, please, and then answer me one question," she said.

They both stared at her blankly, waiting.

"Can I trust you?" She moved her cloak slightly to reveal her state.

"You're...you're with child?" Jerad said, more stating than asking.

"I am. Please answer my question."

Mulp shook himself a bit, trying to wake himself up more fully. "Yes, Lady, you can trust us. What do you need from us?"

"Nothing. Right now, you need something from me."

"What?"

"My trust. Because if I don't believe I can trust you, really believe it, you will both die tonight, and there won't be anything I can do to stop it."

Chapter 50
He thought to play the angle,
maybe only out of pure instinct or habit...

Place: Island city of Pashka, kingdom of Pherriuskata, Arba Environ
Date: Naipekan 16, AY 999

"Your uncle has written you, Goslangios. He wants you to come to Motatinfo and help him with the business. Otherwise, he says, he'll have to disown you."

Gossie stopping picking at his plate and laughed. "Klav has been disowning me since I was able to walk."

His legs were still killing him from romps up in the mountains and back down south again. Bavish had promised a calm pace on the journey southward, but Gossie had discovered that among the Brull, calm was a matter of one's perspective. Tough lot, them. And then a little respite in Vied-Bronste and, ultimately, the most portentous and insidious meeting he'd ever had in his life.

Was it even his life anymore?

"But that's a lot of money to be disowned from," said his lifelong friend and lifelong albatross, the admittedly unfortunate yet somehow wildly blessed Blane Shimizu.

"I've never seen a black barb of it."

"Sure, not yet, but the old man can't live forever."

"He might. He has some very strange friends."

"So do you," said Blane with a roguish grin. "The difference is, yours know where all the pretty girls rest their heads."

"Mine should know that, having a massive family interest in the flow of pleasure slaves."

"That's an unfair label, cousin!" cried Blane. "Those women—and men—who serve us come of their own free will, and they keep most of their earnings."

"After they buy themselves back from you, which few do while they still have teeth and hair. And you're being awful cavalier with the term 'free will,' aren't you?"

"How so?"

"You're implying that the choice between staying in Tritto and serving in the sex houses is...a choice?"

"Not implying: stating. Some people rather enjoy the challenge of a life in the Miserable Muds," Blane said.

"Really? Name one."

Blane took the opportunity to finish his mug, stab some more meat off the tray adjoining their table, and smile thoughtfully, as if there were truly a name that had come to him and it was up to his dear cousin to guess it.

Gossie grunted and went back to his thoughts, trying to ignore the sharp pains he was feeling. He didn't like this job; he knew all the players, but something about the setup made him uneasy. Or maybe he was just still shaken from the way his last job had gone down.

After the Midforest and the Brull, he'd given up on trying to hook up with his hired abductors. Instead, he'd made a beeline to the Vied-Bronste estate with the intention of grabbing a ship and sailing down to Little Britain or the Pyrontals to rest himself for about a century. His only hesitation was: he wasn't sure he was in the clear vis-à-vis his Cameduan entanglements, and he had a very clear idea how those who'd pursued him treated seagoing vessels. Still, the farther away he got, the better. He wondered if he could run a game in Vaprosta…

Once at Vied-Bronste, he'd sent word to his people about what he was up to and what they should do with the woman. He'd sat and pretended to listen to his Vied pals whine about market prices while drinking their wine and eating their food. But his mind was focused on a few very specific topics…

Anyone who'd been after him for money — T&G, the Siddiquis — would have either given up by now or contented themselves with waiting for his inevitable reappearance in Camedua. They all assumed that, somehow, he'd make good eventually; they always made a big show about punishing, pursuing, demanding, and threatening, but it was all standard pretense to the next big deal, a way of gaining leverage at the table. He owed them, was all. This was how the game was played.

But those others weren't playing a game and weren't interested in money. Rot and musk and requirements…they wanted something. Information, yes. And her. They wanted her, and somehow they believed he'd been involved in abducting the old woman…from himself? It wasn't a scheme that was beyond him, to be sure, but he'd have to have a reason, or lots of round shiny reasons, to bother with something like that. And when would he have had the opportunity to grab her? When they or whatever they'd sent were tearing apart the crews of those ships? He was good, but he wasn't that good.

Or so he pretended to the world at large. And, to sell it just right, to himself.

In fact, he was exactly that good; he now had the alleged Frulla holed up in a small keep ten miles east of this very spot, in another part of this enormous and soulless city. Or so his associates had hinted to him. He'd told them to be vague.

Did his pursuers know that? They couldn't, could they?

He'd concluded, as he made his way south along the Midforest border with his Brull escort, that they suspected he really didn't know anything, and that they were more interested in probing for clues and eliminating the players out a sense of alien thoroughness or something. Not so unusual. But the methods of these things: awful. Brutal.

He'd heard things he could not unhear.

News out of Camedua hinted that Shen's had burned to the ground shortly after Gossie's flight. Poor Shen. Had his sons and wife perished? Probably. They never left that place and would have died fighting the flames, he'd no doubt. His old pal Smythe had disappeared completely. And at least three dozen persons he didn't know had been butchered in a single night — the same night as the fire — in different parts of the city.

Brutal.

But he wasn't as frightened as he was curious.

Who were these creatures, and why did they want Frulla?

To shut her up? To sell her themselves to the ONOF idiots? To send her quietly back to Thesseline, never to be heard from again?

And then there was the whole business of the sarcophagus, which he'd very much tried, in vain, to banish from his thoughts since the night it had all happened. The only thing he wanted more than to know was to have never seen or heard or been present in the first place.

Frulla and an ancient living mummy from the Boi Na.

Puzzles at every turn.

It was almost enough to inspire him to read a Book.

Almost.

Blane threw a biscuit at him. "Is anyone awake over there?"

Gossie picked up the biscuit and took a huge bite. "This is pretty good. Needs honey, though."

"I'm concerned. This isn't like you at all."

"Honey on a biscuit? True enough. But I'm in the mood for something sweet..."

"Not the honey. No. This...this brooding, or whatever it is you're doing, is nothing like you, is my meaning."

"Sure it is. And don't throw things at me, particularly not food."

"I won't if you agree to go and see your uncle."

"We're still on that? Nice try, but I'm not concerned, except about the absence of honey or a server to bring me any, and...I am not going to see that rat."

Gossie slugged down the rest of his pint and signaled the inattentive server, who was busy flirting with two Mariendan maids, for another. He poked at the burned flesh on his plate and sighed, and then he stabbed it with his fork and popped a bite into his mouth. There were three young women in matching blue farthingales hurrying by, and he found himself wishing he knew where they were going.

"Why since you were able to walk?" asked Blane.

"What?"

"You said he's been disowning you since you were able to walk."

"Because the first direction I picked took me as far from him as my limited gait would allow."

Blane nodded knowingly. "Still, you must admit, he's been most generous to your family."

"Generosity is overrated, Blane. Klav never gave a gift the value of which he didn't expect to triple upon expected and inevitable payment of the debt."

"Gift or debt?"

"What?"

"You said both. Gift or debt?"

"With him, there is no difference. Payment is always due."

The server came with four more ales, and Blane reached into his purse.

"No, my friend, this is with me," belched Gossie as he tossed a thick coin onto the waiter's tray. "And thanks, we're fine without the honey," he sniped at the waiter, immediately feeling petty for having done so.

They sat and drank and took in the crowd. What lives these people had, these Pherriuskatan merchants and dignitaries and peddlers and military so-and-sos. *Extraordinary*, he thought. *Give me a second life to join them in their blissful ignorance.*

"Your mother loved him," Blane said, poking the bear.

"On the contrary, my mother despised him."

"She married him."

"What choice did she have? He held the deed to her lands and her ancestral home. He'd sold two of her sons into the Monshua War and condemned a third to the service of the Guild. She had nothing."

"But she did love him."

"That woman was incapable of seeing the bad in anyone."

"She loved you too."

"I rest my case."

They were seated at an outdoor table next to a small cafe in the shopping district, their favorite for reasons unrelated to the menu. The Rosen Square, the envy of every Arban would-be buyer with or without two barb to rub together, sprawled out before them, stuffed with merchants selling only the finest garments, goods, and foodstuffs. Quality moved here and there, surrounded by flocks of servants, leadfolk, and porters. There were hundreds of colored pennants flapping gently in the steady lake breeze.

One cared more for the colors than the signals; so it was and had been for a very long time in the Tri. There was really only one banner that mattered here, and all the birds, fish, beasts, and dye couldn't change that. But the flapping colors certainly added to the look of the thing.

Gossie had selected their table near the corner so they could watch both the north and east streets for their target. So far, there'd been no sign, and that troubled Gossie, because they'd been sitting there for over two hours, and the target was late, very late.

Blane said, "So let me ask you: If Klav is such a horror, why don't we just get rid of him and take as much of his money as we can get our hands on?"

"You know why."

"I know what you believe, sure, but he's not untouchable or even all that powerful."

"Yes, he is. There are things here you aren't seeing, or at least, things you aren't willing to admit."

"The Ill Return?"

"His doing."

"Nonsense. That was never proven; in fact, as far as I know, you're the only one who ever made the connection."

"He was in Phrattington when it happened."

"It happened in Hyu."

"Exactly."

"We've been over this. That he'd cancelled a meeting in Hyu means nothing. The man has ten thousand business interests, more than a fair share of them in Phrattington."

"But on that day, he was supposed to be in Hyu."

"And you know this how? The shoemaker?"

"Yes."

"The man's a moron."

"No, the man's a genius who does a very good job at pretending to be a moron."

"If he never comes out of character, even when he's alone, he's a de facto moron."

"Untrue. He's an artisan."

"With shoes, yes. Otherwise, he's a moron. And his word is your only proof."

"Your trouble, Blane, my good Xatumkan dust mongoose, is that you lack a subtle sense of deduction. A series of related coincidences renders the concept of coincidence moot. One must pluck the truth from the nest of misdirection as a snake plucks a chicken."

"Snakes don't pluck chickens."

"Yes, they do. They pluck them by squeezing them until the feathers pop out."

"What? No, just no! But while we're arguing snake policy or lack thereof regarding alleged chicken plucking, I'd like you consider another theory altogether, if you can cram one into your paranoid head."

"I always leave room in here for the stupidity of another," said Gossie, tapping the top of his head. "Humor is the source of long life."

"I think you're unwilling to rob ol' Klav because you do, in point of fact, love him."

Gossie stood up. "There you go. You've unveiled me, you puzzlemaster, you boundless mind...you've teased up truth and put the lie to my earlier accusation. You are indeed a fine and subtle deductionist."

"I've hit a nerve."

"No, you've hit a dead end," Gossie said.

"You love the man."

"But you do not, so if you want to rob this beloved, coincidentally charmed, impotently and imminently pluckable grand old chicken, be my guest. Hold your snappy retort for another time, though...I think I see your man."

There he was. Rodolpho Canamow. He was being trailed by a horde of sycophants and bootlickers, as his kind often was, but what caught Gossie's eye was the woman who walked behind them. She was, or more accurately seemed to have been at some point, beautiful, and yet now there was a horrifying weariness, almost an emptiness, about her. His first thought was that he was seeing a ghost.

Petrecia Celeranet.

"She's seen better days, hmm?" said Blane from behind him.

"Who?"

"That's his wife, no?"

"Is it?"

"You've been away awhile. Big scandal. He caught her having an affair. Put her in the grips."

"The what?"

"The Breaking spell."

"That's against the law, no?"

"Oh, yes, you're right. And how rare it is that we see one of these Body men breaking one of their own laws."

Gossie watched her go by. She stumbled a bit as she walked. Her dress was filthy. Her hair was unwashed. But for her piercing, staring eyes that were without doubt locked on the back of her oppressor's neck, she might have been a stray resident of Yanz.

His new employer hadn't told him about the spell. It was unpleasant to behold, but still he watched. Blane had been hired to keep track of Canamow — Gossie had seen to that so he'd have a reason to take his pal along — but Gossie was there for an entirely different reason. Weeks ago, he'd been given a new assignment. And a new life, of sorts...

"Your name is...Goslangios Mhetlonac, yes?"

"You already know what my name is. Why ask?"

"Would you believe it if I told you I simply like to be thorough?"

"Absolutely. And so why don't you be thorough about fucking yourself, my friend?"

There was no reply.

Gossie was seated at a table in a small dark room. His hands were no longer bound, but he was in no condition to attempt an escape. His head ached like a ship had dropped anchor on it. Perhaps his situation would be a bit less sticky if one had.

They'd been after him. He'd never really lost them, he knew that now. He wouldn't have survived an hour in the Midforest before they'd've descended on him, and he'd had no more twigs or twine. The Brull had saved him, or at least spared him temporarily, for a price: his services, though for the love of the Four, he had no true understanding of what services he'd actually provided. And they had done so at someone's instruction.

That someone was now standing behind him, questioning him. He was alive, but beyond that Gossie wasn't sure if his situation had vastly improved.

There was a small candle flickering on the table that contended quite poorly with the dark in the room, almost as if it had been instructed somehow to keep its light to itself. The shadows did not dance on the walls despite the flickering. It was all very disorienting. Gossie kept blinking.

The voice behind him spoke again. "Your father was a soldier, is that true?"

"Again, you know the answer."

"My friend, I have known the answer to almost every question I have asked for the last six hundred years. That doesn't mean I don't enjoy hearing the lies that come out of my victims' mouths."

"I'm not your victim. I'm your cohort," said Gossie. He needed to spin some kind of conversation with whoever this was; how else would he form a plan to extract himself from this oddly lit chamber?

"Interesting. My cohort, you say? And how might you have reached that conclusion?"

"You need me. Either that, or maybe you need something from me."

"Do I?"

"I assume so, yes — or you wouldn't have saved me from…well, you wouldn't have kept me alive."

His captor sat down at the table directly across from him, and just like that, Gossie's hopes for even a fledgling plan disintegrated.

"Hmm, well, you might be right," said Grewea Lon. "There's always a chance you're spot on with that desperate assessment. But then again, maybe I don't need you, or maybe I don't need you in the way you think I do. Maybe you're this morning's entertainment. Maybe you're a mere exercise for me, a petty, desperate thing here to keep my wits — and claws — a bit sharper."

There he was, in the flesh, his famous disheveled hair and pale-blue eyes just a few feet away. His decaying robes were gray and brown with a hint here and there of gold and maroon, reminding Gossie somewhat of the man who'd emerged from the sarcophagus. Grewea smelled of the land, perhaps even of the grave, and he moved in a manner that Gossie's eyes could somehow not track: now slow, now quick, now frozen, now vibrant and present.

Gossie knew the game was probably up, but being who he was, he thought he'd play till the last die was cast and the last coin lost. He chuckled. "You're just screwing with me, then? Killing time between killing kings?"

Grewea seemed unmoved by the chuckle. "Perhaps I am."

"No chance." Again, he thought to play the angle, maybe only out of pure instinct or habit, but still…even Grewea Lon had needs, he imagined. "You need something, maybe something I know or something I have. I haven't quite figured it out yet, but this isn't just some cat-and-mouse shit, that I'll tell you for free. And if you say it is, you're a liar."

That might have been a step too bold, Gossie.

"Am I? I suppose I am. Among other things, of course. I am a liar. *The* Liar, one might go so far to say if one were inclined toward the theatrical, and yet I am so much more, wouldn't you agree?"

"We both know what you are." Gossie sighed, starting to accept that he had no cards, no coin, and no hope. He was a dead man.

"Well, one of us does, anyway. But I'm not interested today in the daunting insights you might heap upon me should I afford you the opportunity. I must say, you had a very auspicious start up there in the Atuut, to be sure. Impressive."

"That was your show?"

"Yes, it was my show."

"I don't suppose I get to ask…"

"No."

Suddenly, life. A chance. "What is it you want?"

"This has very little to do with what I want. Almost nothing I do does, I'm afraid to admit. However, I do have a simple request to make of you: I might want you to work for me."

"Might?"

"I am still deciding. Perhaps you have already performed your best, first, and last service for me. It's difficult to be sure," Grewea said, his face a mockingly exaggerated portrayal of doubt and consternation.

He does want something, and his is the name Bavish wouldn't speak.

Gossie had no idea what was happening — a sensation he was becoming accustomed to — but yes, life was making a comeback, right here, right now. "Work for you doing what?"

"Following someone. In a sense."

"Who?"

"A friend. Of mine, not yours. A future friend."

"Who?"

"The wife of a man whose activities require subtle supervision."

"Why not just watch the man?"

"The wife is…also in need of supervision."

Gossie glanced into Grewea's eyes. Nothing. Those eyes were deep and ancient and gave him nothing. They seemed instead to take, but what it was they took, he could not say.

It was pretty much what he'd expected from eyes such as those, but it was almost always worth it to glance in any case. To the right observer, even nothing can sometimes offer something.

Not in this case. Grewea's eyes were like two bottomless holes, and Gossie got the sensation that a fall into their secrets would never, ever end.

"Looking for something? Have a care. Far greater men than you have made the attempt," said Grewea with what seemed to be a smile.

"Forgive me for saying so, but you're not all you think you are, Grewea."

"Now what did I tell you about offering insights?"

Gossie looked away and reminded himself once again that he was almost certainly dead; he might have a chance of selecting how and when, but even that was a reach.

He knew next to nothing about what this creature really wanted from him. He decided to simply listen, and given that he had no other moves to make, he told himself halfheartedly that it was a considerably wise course of action. There was no way out of this except to play along and hope for an opportunity. And to knock it off with the smartass quips. "Tell me more," said Gossie. He noted he was damn lucky, given who he was talking to, to have anything to play along with.

"I want her watched, I want to know who she makes contact with. And though it will likely be impossible for you to come by this information

— and I hope you won't take that as a slight against your obviously considerable skills — I want to know what she learns."

"What she learns? How could I know that without asking her?"

"Do what you do. Assess the situations she finds herself in, and fill in the blanks as best you can. Trust yourself, Mr. Mhetlonac."

Those four words were more than a tad ominous, but Gossie knew how to comport himself in dark moments. Or he hoped he did. He looked Grewea full in the face. "And what do I get if I do this for you?"

"Nothing. Everything. What do you want?"

"I want you to let me go and forget you ever met me."

Grewea didn't smile. "Impossible, I'm afraid. Once, many centuries ago, I forgot something, something very important, and many, many people — more than you can imagine, more than anyone should have to imagine — died quite horribly and without warning. As you might expect, I made it my business from that day on to never, ever again forget anything."

"Your head must be a crowded place," said Gossie.

"It would be if it were as limited and blunted as say, your own, but as you have no doubt guessed, I am not exactly human. While that comes with quite a bit of baggage, it also comes with a few fascinating and useful rewards."

"The six-hundred-year comment gave you away."

"I must endeavor to be more guarded."

"Might have a less chilling effect if you did."

They sat in silence for a moment.

"So what do I get if I do this?" Gossie asked again.

"You get...another assignment."

And there it was.

Grewea was looking lazily but nonetheless closely at Gossie. His eyes were watery, almost murky, but at the same time, bright. Gossie stared down at the table, doing his best impression of a beaten man. It wasn't much of a reach.

"Where is this woman you want me to watch? For my...first assignment?"

"Right here in our beloved Pherriuskata. Down in Pashka, to be precise. It won't take very long. I don't expect her to live beyond the month."

Gossie didn't bite on that. "Why me? You have other spies."

"Why not you? Are you not up for the challenge? Can I not trust you to bring me the information I need?"

Gossie sighed. There was no way out of this. While he was watching whoever it was, Grewea would have ten others watching him.

He'd heard all about how this creature worked. And once you were in, you were never out. His life, he admitted sadly, had truly ended when he'd entered the Midforest.

"What's the woman's name, praytell?" he asked Grewea.

"Her name is Petrecia Celeranet. She is the wife of a slithering shit of a politician named Rodolpho Canamow. A friend of mine, one might say. But now I'm wondering: Is 'friend' the right word here? Perhaps there is another, something more suitable."

"Should I make contact with her?" asked Gossie, ignoring the digression.

"At present, that would be...impossible. For you, in any case. But no, keep your distance. Learn what you can. And then, when you're through with that, if you've done well, another assignment."

Another assignment. And then another. And another. "I figure I owe you just the one."

"You are mistaken. You owe me...everything."

"How's that?"

"Do you know who was pursuing you in the Midforest? Who followed you up into the mountains and then back down again? And do you know why?"

Gossie just stared at him.

"Not ready to share?"

There was no reason to tell Grewea what he probably already knew. And if there was a slim chance he didn't know about Frulla...well, that was Gossie's card to play, and he'd hold it a while longer.

"They would not have killed you, of course, but they might have delivered you to someone who would slowly eat you. Or worse. After you'd confessed to everything you ever knew, everything you'd ever done, and even things you never knew and hadn't done."

"The Vo'ix."

"Indeed. Or someone just as awful, or someone worse."

Someone like you, Gossie thought. He momentarily pictured the old man trying to chew off his arm.

Grewea smiled but seemed to drift off, his face becoming almost reflective. "There are many odd and mysterious pieces to our current puzzle here in Arba, and many puzzlers vying for power, position, and whatever else such beings crave. And despite what they say about me, I really don't know everything, so we'll just have to see how it all unfolds."

Gossie couldn't wrap his head around this one. The Vo'ixtavracci were not the sort of nightmare he involved himself in or even allowed himself to consider. And hadn't they been gone for over a century? What was Grewea on about?

"I can see you have doubts. No matter. Let's stick to the matter at hand."

"Petrecia Celeranet. In Pashka. Follow, don't contact. Report."

"Yes. And then…" Grewea hadn't delivered the worst news. He was clearly somewhat anxious to do so, though: his countenance betrayed a hint of what looked like excitement.

"Someone else then, right? Who?" asked Gossie.

"We'll get to that."

"Okay. Where? Pashka?"

"Bi Prison."

Gossie started. He quickly composed himself, but Grewea was chuckling at him with amusement. "This alarms you?" said Grewea, not bothering to suppress his grin.

"Alarms me? Hells yes. Surely you're joking."

"I am not."

Gossie sat for a moment, stunned and even a little bit afraid. "No one comes out of there," he said, almost whispering.

"Completely correct."

"How would I?"

"Who says you'd be coming out?"

"If you want to know what I learn, then I'm assuming…I expect you have a way for me to get you the information."

"Of course."

"And so a way to get me out of there."

"Of that, we cannot be sure, can we? I suppose a greater degree of certainty might by crafted or gained as a direct function of the quality of your information."

"You're not giving me much incentive," Gossie snarled.

The old man sighed and shook his head. "Incorrect. I'm giving you all the incentive a man like you needs. A chance to do what he does best in defense of his very life, free of charge. An opportunity to fight for his life."

"Won't be much of a life if you leave me in there."

"Won't be any life at all if you refuse this offer."

Gossie, more out of a need to stretch and center himself than to get at Grewea Lon, stood. He tried to see another angle. He told himself he could overwhelm this old devil and make a run for some other environ or some other planet…and then he sat down and smiled sadly. He had no choice but to go along with what this creature was asking.

"Take your time, Mr. Mhetlonac," said Grewea.

The spying was the easy part; that he did in his sleep. Far more challenging would be escaping from the most formidable prison in all of Arba. Could it be done? Had anyone ever done it?

"You will naturally be concerning yourself with the math of the problem I have presented you, trying to decipher a way to cheat both death and myself—and contrary to popular opinion, there is a distinction between us, the Reaper and me. But let me assure you: the only way you will ever emerge from Bi Prison as something other than a digested meal will be with my assistance."

"I suppose you're right."

"Suppositions are irrelevant. I state only fact here."

"Facts are curious things, though. The way they reflect the light, the weight of them when measured in certain varied contexts..."

"Ha, very good, Mr. Mhetlonac, very good. But I knew the great and venerable Oxenhaft, and believe you me: the man shit more out of his mouth than his ass. Now, what is your answer?"

"I have little choice. I'm at your service."

"Was there ever any doubt?"

Chapter 51
Gossie had every intention
of bucking the trend...

Place: Island city of Pashka, kingdom of Pherriuskata, Arba Environ
Date: Naipekan 27, AY 999

"You're not going to get what you came for. It isn't here."

Gossie ignored the ugly man he'd tied to a chair and continued to rifle through his drawers.

"Did you hear me?" snarled the man, his face contorting in such a way as to render him even uglier. His nose appeared to have been chewed by something, and his eyes were not level with one another. "It isn't here."

"What isn't here?" Gossie asked as he dumped the contents of two drawers on the floor.

"Whatever you're looking for. And can you please try not to make such a mess?" the man said as if he were talking to a servant and not someone who'd clubbed him over the head and bound him up like a bundle of Wildean sausage.

"You've no idea what I'm looking for."

"No? Very well. Then by all means, don't let me interfere with your search. When you come to your senses and are ready to negotiate, I'll be sitting right here in my Bunabwai chair."

"You do that."

"Tell me, thief, do you know how a man comes to be able to afford a Bunabwai?"

"I don't know. Maybe he sells his mother."

"My mother wasn't worth one leg of this chair."

"His sisters as well, then."

"Never had any. Would've been an only child if mother hadn't given birth to that rat of a brother," said the bound man, trying very hard to show he was enraged. Trying too hard.

"Sorry you missed out. We only children are special in ways you can't imagine," said Gossie as he ran his hand along a high shelf.

"My brother died within a week of being born and robbed me of my chance, the rat."

"I feel your agony. Take comfort in knowing that if I don't find what I'm looking for, your opportunity to complain to him face-to-face will not be far off." Gossie rifled through a stack of papers he'd found on the shelf. He had to make this a good show, and so he tried to assume the visage of someone who wasn't about to laugh his ass off...or lead a man into a situation he would likely not survive.

"You're no assassin."

Gossie looked wounded. "Don't I look the part? No? Well, the joke's on you. In fact, I'm an elite assassin. I'm an Essential."

"No, you're not."

"I am."

"If you're one of Patrick's crew, I'll eat this chair."

"Tell me, does a Bunabwai taste better than, say, a common stool?"

"Of course. This chair is probably tastier than any meal you've ever eaten."

Gossie stopped sifting through the man's junk for a moment. He turned to stare him full in the face. "I have eaten at the finest tables in Arba, good man, and I've never spotted Bunabwai on any of them. Though I once had a braised dish of lobster and engoon on Bunabwai that was worth eating ten chairs to sample."

"They let you onto Bunabwai? How'd you manage that?"

"Someone owed me a favor he didn't know he owed me. That happens a lot. It might be happening now, for all you know." Gossie gave up plowing through the debris and leaned against the ugly man's desk, which was also ugly, a beaten pine thing that didn't quite match the highly regarded chair. He'd found nothing so far, but then, he wasn't really supposed to find anything, was he? Still, there might have been something, a little side benefit or two. There usually was. Not today. He farted loudly in disapproval.

Ugly screwed up his nose and gasped, "Show a little mercy, will you?

"Mercy's not on the menu today," said Gossie.

"Are you quite through?"

"Almost. I could go faster if you would shut up about your stupid chair."

"Faster than leaning there huffing like a mule that's been led up a cliff?"

"I have a septum issue."

"Looks like you have other issues as well."

"You're one to talk. Is that how you were born, or did you have that done by the Pir Choss surgeons?" Gossie said.

"What's that?"

"Never mind. Just shut your trap for a bit and let me do my work."

"I'm trying to distract you. Stalling, so to speak."

"Really? I hadn't noticed. I'm new at all this, you see."

"Seems to me maybe you are. Otherwise, you'd be negotiating."

"Did it ever occur to you, my misshapen friend, that it is I who am stalling?"

"What? Nonsense. Why would you be doing that?"

"We're waiting for someone."

"Who?"

"A friend."

"But then why are you…you've dumped every drawer on the floor and emptied all three closets — "

"I was hoping to find something else, something unrelated to this meeting."

"What?" asked Ugly.

"Doesn't matter. It isn't here."

"Perhaps it is, and you just haven't found it."

"Perhaps, but I doubt it. I'm fairly thorough when it comes to this kind of work."

"Untie me, tell me what you're looking for, and I'll find it for you."

"Can't do it."

"Why not?"

"My friend would be very unhappy if I were to let you go. But it makes no matter. Once our meeting is through, I'll look again, just to be certain."

"And where will I be?"

"Here, I would guess, but in no condition to object."

"You're no killer."

"So you've said. And it's true; I'd much rather dine, steal, or gamble than take a man's life. Pardon the pun, but it's ugly business and rarely as profitable as it is costly, if you take my meaning. My friend, however, takes a different view. He has no reservations about pushing folk into early meetings with their maker."

Ugly shifted uncomfortably in his beloved chair and closed his eyes for a moment, showing what Gossie concluded was uncommon calm for a person facing such a situation. *People never fail to surprise me*, he thought.

"How much do you want?" asked Ugly.

"I can't."

"Please…"

"Well, I…let me see. What were you talking about before, when you were so smugly insisting 'it' wasn't here?"

Ugly hesitated. "I…can't tell you. That's too high a price. Name something else."

"I haven't actually named anything. Nor have you."

"As I said…I can't."

"That's unfortunate. We haven't much time, sir. My friend is late, in fact. I can't imagine what's keeping him."

"Fine, fine. I'll tell you. It's a Boi Na crown. But I'll have to take you to it."

"Will you? Why?"

"It's too difficult to describe where it is, and I've memorized the ways around all the locks and traps."

"Tell me anyway."

"It wouldn't do any good. They know me there; they don't know you. They won't let you in."

"Who are 'they'? Yours or someone else's?"

"Never mind. Just untie me, and let's get moving before this friend of yours shows up."

Gossie hesitated and then undid the ropes that bound Ugly to his beloved chair even as he left the man's hands tied behind his back.

Ugly stood and gave him a grunt and a once-over. "You ain't much to behold," he said.

"Says the man who clearly has an aversion to mirrors."

"I know you, don't I?"

Gossie had anticipated this but ignored the question. "My friend will have to be disappointed for the nonce, but remember…he knows where you work and where you live. Maybe this crown you claim you have will change his mind about offing you."

"Oh, I think he'll be very pleased, as will you."

"Then lead on, my handsome friend."

And out they went into the night.

It was a bold and perhaps not-entirely-thought-through plan, but at least now, he would find out where ugly old Harald Nettans kept the good stuff. With any luck, the thing Gossie was really after would be there. Of course, none of that would matter if Nettans succeeded in killing him, which he certainly intended to do somewhere along the way. He'd done it to at least three other thieves Gossie knew of, good men all. Presumably each had made it to the infamous Nettans vault; none, however, had made it out, so the presumption was nine-tenths imaginative gossip. The only clues as to their fates were their bodies, always found in the same place: behind the Payer's Public House in the Believers Quarter, and always in more than one piece. Ten pieces, to be precise.

Gossie had every intention of bucking the trend and making it out intact. He was counting on not only his wits but also his "friend" to make that happen.

As he followed Nettans down the stairs and out the back of the building, he mused on the fact that Nettans had never once alluded to his connection to a very powerful, very dangerous family.

Most men in his situation would have dropped names like a tree drops acorns, but not this one. Though his cousin was the wife of Benjamin Menniki, who himself was the son of the great Unther Menniki, the King of All Wheat and Meat, Nettans played the game tightly, holding his cards choke tight against his skinny chest.

There could only be one reason for this: he fearlessly relished ensnaring would-be thieves. His household guard had been two sleepy Slau, which was tantamount to no guard at all. No, this one wanted to get caught and wanted to lead his prey to the vault. God only knew what waited there for Gossie. Perhaps there really was a Boi Na crown. But even if there was, it was doubtful he'd get a glimpse of it, the success or failure of his real mission notwithstanding.

And what was his "real mission" anyway?

They made their way through a few dark avenues and alleys, up several staircases and down several more. They encountered not a single soul, nor did they speak.

Gossie wondered just how savvy Nettans believed himself to be and tried to contrast that with his own impression, which was that the man was an obvious imbecile. Or at least, he was woefully overconfident. He never once feigned an attempt to escape, he didn't gibber in the hopes of distracting, and he asked no probing questions. Labyrinthine though their route might seem, there was little or no hesitation in Nettans's manner: he was leading Gossie directly to a specific place.

Very much unlike a man who wanted to protect the whereabouts of and possessions in a secret vault.

The ambush, Gossie assumed, would likely occur at the place itself. He chuckled when their late-night journey took a turn that led them right into the Believers Quarter, raucous laughter and haphazard music emanating from the infamous pub somewhere up ahead. Could his man really be that lazy and careless to dispatch prey so close to his vault, wherever that was, and then just dump the bodies within sniffing distance? What an arrogant prick.

An arrogant prick who had no idea what was coming.

Hells, Gossie had no idea what was coming. And he preferred it that way, as long as it came in time to save his skin. He had no intention of sticking with this plan, even if it was his own plan, if it meant getting strangled, stabbed, or otherwise maimed and dumped behind a pub.

Nettans turned a corner into a wide alley. The buildings on each side were abandoned, boarded up, and fire damaged. There were wrecked barrels, crates, beams, and debris piled high all about them.

"We've arrived, have we?" asked Gossie.

"You could say that," said Nettans with a smile. "I'll need my hands to open the locks."

"No doubt, no doubt. But I have other plans for you. And if you want to live, you'll do things my way."

Three figures wielding clubs emerged from behind a pile of wreckage.

Nettans tsked. "Your way? I don't think so, chum. Or should I call you Fundra?"

"Well, it is my name, as far as you know, so sure, why not? These fellows are with you?"

"They are. My sons. I'm afraid you won't have time to become pals with them."

"No? Do tell."

"They are about to beat you to death with those clubs they're carrying."

"Those are clubs? Hells, seeing as they're your sons, I assumed those shadowy members were their very own cocks, being held out proudly for Daddy's new pal to behold," Gossie said matter-of-factly.

Nettans scowled. The sons seemed to take that as their cue. They advanced as one, smelling of ale and sweat and sour food.

Gossie braced himself, wondering if his "friend" had all along simply intended him to die. There was a bright flash, and he involuntarily closed his eyes.

When he opened them, there were no more sons, just three char marks on the pavement. The air smelled of burned flesh and was thick with dark smoke. Harald Nettans was standing exactly where he'd been, and though his mouth was wide open, he emitted no sounds and was completely still.

"So this is the fool who has what we want?"

Gossie didn't recognize the voice, but he knew who'd sent the speaker. He nodded and then squinted, trying to make out who he was talking to. "You're a little late to the party, hmm? My poor brains were about to be jellied," Gossie said.

"Your safety isn't my concern. He wants something this man has," said the aforementioned speaker, a tall, wiry man in a light brown cloak and a gray bowler who now stepped into view. "And I'm to retrieve it." He turned to Nettans and, after a long look, addressed him. "Where is this vault of yours? Open it."

Nettans stood, frozen, staring at the char marks in mute horror.

"Come on, I haven't got all night," said Gray Bowler.

Nettans started shaking with rage and then braced himself as if he were going to charge at the man who'd just incinerated his sons.

Gossie stepped between them and put his hands on Harald's chest. "I wouldn't," he said. "Trust me on this, Harald, particularly if you still have any children left you'd like to see tomorrow."

Harald stopped, coughed once, and then sank to his knees and began to weep. "My boys...my sons...you burned my boys," he sobbed.

Gossie turned to Gray Bowler and shook his head. "Was all that necessary? Haven't you a spell or whatever that just knocks people out?"

"Wasn't it you who characterized this person as a remorseless and prolific murderer? Or did I misunderstand?"

Gossie turned and looked at the pathetic figure of the once-overconfident Harald Nettans. "He looks pretty remorseful now."

"You can go, Fundra. Go back and watch the wife."

Damn. He had been very curious to get a glimpse at whatever was in the vault. "You're sure? I could certainly assist with —"

"Go."

"And what would I be watching her for? Do you know?"

"With our employer, no one ever really 'knows.' One does as one is told. You'd do well to remember that, especially now."

"Why especially now?"

"There's been a setback of late. A complication."

"Do tell."

"A longtime employee has...broken ranks."

Then it was true, what he'd heard. Sh'arnau the Ancient Slayer had skipped.

"I'll do my utmost not to upset the apple cart. Off I go then, to watch the silent wife."

It wasn't such a terrible gig anyway. He got to sit or slink around eating, sipping, and taking in the air. He'd had worse assignments. And as if to remind him that the worst possible assignment was still pending, Gray Bowler turned his back on him and muttered, "There are no apples in Bi. Only discarded cores."

Gossie answered him only briefly as he started back toward the city proper. "As you say."

But his curt and obedient reply did not reflect his true demeanor. He'd been called upon to do something horrendous — and even if it had been done to a terrible man, it was not within the range of what Gossie would ever consider less than horrendous — and he had no understanding as to why. Couldn't they have just grabbed Nettans and made him lead them to the vault? Why had they needed him to be involved?

He didn't like working for Grewea Lon, not at all. He was fond of knowing why he was doing what he was doing...and also very fond of profiting from it. He often found his work thrilling and challenging and invigorating as well, though the incidents in Camedua and the Midforest had borne out his suspicion that age was indeed catching up with him.

Here, there was no profit, no thrill, no invigoration. And the only challenge was to stay alive long enough to get himself out from under Grewea's thumb.

Sh'arnau had apparently done just that. Of course, if the rumors were true, Sh'arnau had worked for several centuries for Grewea Lon before figuring out how to extract himself from his situation. Maybe he'd just waited Lon out.

Gossie didn't have centuries to wait.

He had to find another way. His way.

And he needed very much not to go to Bi Prison. Despite its thrills and invigorating challenges, Arba was without doubt a dangerous and shitty place to live, and Gossie was fully qualified to say so, having worked and lived in so many of its corners. But the shittiest, most horrifying corner of all was Bi Prison. He'd never been—and it was redundant to say so, to his mind, because no one had ever escaped or been released from that place. The only reason anyone knew anything about what went on there was the Low Workers, a mixed-race group of vicious enforcers who doled out punishment and oversaw the delivery of foodstuffs and water. The Low Workers had plenty to say, probably much of it complete horseshit, except that their tales were too consistent to be entirely fabricated.

Bi Prison was hell.

And he'd be damned if he was going to go there, Lon or no Lon.

Or so he told himself as he strode back to the small inn where he'd been sheltering these past few days. He argued back and forth about the merits of running, the merits of offing himself, the merits of a life in Bi—of that last, there were none, though for a man of his considerable talents and ego, Bi represented a kind of terrible mystery, the allure of which was difficult to deny. It scared him, and that alone was worth serious contemplation, because he'd long since stopped being truly afraid of anything.

Why is that? he asked himself as he arrived at the inn and took a place at the bar. The place had a reputation that was equaled only by perhaps the legends of old—the wrath of the shitwings, the appetites of the Vo'ix, the enormous abominations of Kold the Creator—but these were all just stories that drunks, acolytes, and mothers related for various self-serving reasons.

Bi was real. Bi was an underground labyrinth inhabited by the thousands of wretched souls who had been banished to its confines to confront their inescapable fates. Political prisoners, warriors whose sides had lost, thieves, rapists, persons from undesirable races who had somehow offended, and worst of all, *things.*

It was the things, he admitted as he gulped down his first mead and waved a hand for another, that scared the shit out of him.

What were they? Creatures from ages long past. Monsters captured in or near the Garden. Monsters captured when they'd strayed too far north. Hideous, lethal visitors from other environs. All of the above.

Perhaps they were just stories. Perhaps the worst thing about Bi would be the air, the stinking, unbreathably infected cavern air that sucked the life out of all who pulled it in. Or so it was said.

That was the problem, in a nutshell: one couldn't be sure, not about any of it.

He ordered some meat and cheese and tried to put the idea of the prison out of his mind.

Instead, he focused on what he could do to avoid going there.

A fat old woman brought him his meat and cheese and another flagon of mead. She smiled at him with missing teeth, but her eyes were cold and observant.

"Many thanks," said Gossie. He stabbed a chunk of the shriveled meat, popped it in his mouth and made an exaggerated show out of his enjoyment of it. "Excellent!"

The woman snorted at him and left.

He gnawed at the terrible meal and continued his contemplation.

Grewea had in his employ strange magickers like Gray Bowler who could snap their fingers and incinerate men whole. He had the ears of Duke Velliok and the Mind. Most of the Wasi Sagotr, Gossie knew from having had peripheral — and some not so peripheral, God help him — dealings with them, were at his beck and call. And until recently, he'd had the deadliest creature in all of Arba, Sh'arnau the Thicknomite, killing for him.

Gossie had no doubt there were others — other servants, other contacts, perhaps whole races who owed Grewea Lon all, just like he'd been told he did. Lon's people were everywhere. Perhaps everyone in Arba was in some way one of Lon's people, whether they knew it or not.

Was there a way out of this?

Gossie chewed his inedible meat and concluded there was not.

Unless he were dead.

And he smiled then, for he'd been dead before. Four or five times, if memory served.

He picked up a piece of cheese, surmised it to be no worse than the meat, and began to author a plan.

Chapter 52
"What kind of man were you, Billy?"

Place: north of the Qi Dao Lu, kingdom of Arbana, Arba Environ
Date: unknown

They were running through an apple orchard in the middle of the night, trying to find a place to hide.

"The kind of guy who didn't like to have conversations when he was running for his life," answered William as he panted.

Joe pointed at a small dip in the orchard. When they got closer to it, they saw it was a pond.

"Can we hide in that?"

"Probably won't do no good. They won't smell us in the water, but they'll smell us right up to the edge," Joe answered. "But I need a drink."

"You buying? I like Jameson's, neat, rocks back."

"From your mouth to God's ears, Billy boy!"

They both got down on their bellies and scooped water into their mouths. It tasted a little foul to William, but he was parched and didn't care.

"This is some good shit. Like somebody's toilet water," joked Joe.

William nodded in the dark, stopped drinking, and sat up. "What'll they do if they catch us?"

"Depends. If they think we're worth somethin', they'll just hurt us a bit and chase us back to the line. If they don't, they'll beat us to death and probably place bets on whose head comes off sooner."

"So it's heads for us, right?"

"Most definitely. We ain't worth shit to them. 'Specially a newbie like you."

"I suggest we keep running," William said, standing up.

Joe took one more drink, splashed some water on the back of his neck and head, and then popped up to his feet. "Let's go. And don't think I forgot about how you didn't answer my question."

"What question?"

William had been with the caravan for about a month, never getting anywhere near the Landing Point during that time. Contrary to what Joe had told him, Banam and the people who held his chain were more interested in visiting Yanz, the worker slave city, this time of year. Joe hadn't known that.

Or maybe he had. Maybe he was trying to save William's life. He certainly knew much more about how to survive in this place than William did. And he'd saved his ass more than once during the regular raids the caravan endured.

William had gotten by well enough with Joe's help, but all he could think about, night and day, was finding his family. He'd told Joe the story, in bits and pieces, of what had happened to him, but Joe couldn't make heads or tails out of it.

"Nothing like that happened to me. I was just walking home from a date. Cecelia Tremont. Beautiful girl from the West Indies. Man, she was somethin' else. I was gonna call her as soon as I was in my door even though I'd just left her ten minutes before. But I never made it home."

"Did you go through the Landing Point?"

"All of us do."

"And the Reismyl?"

"No, man, not me. Somebody bought me or something, me and a few others, and we never had to do any of that. You?"

"Yup. Yes. Uh-huh," William said, trying desperately not to think about what had happened down in the Reismyl's maze.

"Sorry to hear that. But there's a silver lining there, you know. Probably nothing worse is gonna happen up here than what happened there."

"Probably?"

"Maybe."

They'd laughed at that.

They did all their patrols and chores together. They talked a lot. Joe talked more than William, who heard all about Joe's sister, Jackie, who was three years older and a singer. She'd gone off to New Orleans when Joe was fourteen, and she'd never come back. He talked about the times they had in the summer in Missouri, playing and hiding and fishing and singing, and about how their dad was a military guy who'd lost his leg and his soul fighting in a desert somewhere. He was pretty sure Jackie had left because of him, but his story pretty much ended there, or rather it looped back to when his mama was alive and daddy wasn't there and they'd just sing and laugh at night and tell stories with the neighbors and just live. Joe missed his mama and Jackie a lot, but he never seemed sad about them—it was more like he was still living those very same times, inside.

William was pretty sure that was the only real reason Joe hadn't gone off the deep end in this hellish place.

They were on patrol once more, this time in a forested part of the Wei Lo Da. Joe tapped William on the shoulder. "Did you hear that?" Joe asked.

"Hear what?"

"That quiet."

"Yes?"

Joe was staring out into the trees and nodding. "They're coming."

"Who's coming?"

"I don't know, but there's an awful lot of them."

"So we're screwed."

"No, man, we ain't screwed: this is our chance. Forest, lotsa trees, a big fight, mayhem everywhere. We ain't gonna get a better chance."

William stared into the trees too. "I don't see anything. You're sure about this?"

"How many battles I been through? Yeah, I'm sure. Get ready."

"Ready how?"

Joe looked around and down and up. "Let's climb up in them trees there."

And that's what they did. The battle started about ten minutes later. The assailants came from everywhere: not the typical raiding party, not by a long shot. When it looked clear and there didn't seem to be anyone near their hiding spot, they dropped down from the trees and ran north.

Twenty minutes later, they emerged from the forest into a meadow. They heard shouts in the distance behind them. William was sure one of them had come from Urj, which made him run all the faster. They crossed the meadow, hopped a small fence, and ran through several small farms before coming to the apple orchard.

After the stop at the pond, they started jogging north again. "Do you have any idea where we are?" William panted.

"Not really. Maybe. Never done much exploring in these parts, you know."

"We better come up with a destination or at least a plan."

"We got a destination, and it's the same as the plan: we're going as far away from them behind us as our legs can take us."

"They'll catch up. Some of them aren't human, and they don't get tired. Plus, the smell."

"You sayin' we should go back?"

"I'm saying we need a destination. Or a plan. Or both."

They walked north for days. A farmer, a tall, middle-aged man with a short black beard, spotted them sitting in his field one afternoon and asked them if they were slaves on the run. They didn't see any point in denying it.

"Well, you can hide here as long as you like. I got work for you in the barn, and if anyone comes looking, I've got all these dogs around that'll give you a heads-up so you can get in the cellars underneath."

"Those fools who are following us, they don't care about dogs or cellars," said Joe.

"We don't want to put you and your family in danger, sir," added William. "We'll just rest awhile and go."

The farmer shook his head. "You keep heading north from here, you'll definitely get caught. Maybe not by the ones chasing you, but there's plenty more like them in every direction. No, you take my advice and lie low awhile — a week or two. If you still want to go after that, I think I know someone who can help you."

It was a generous offer, and William was relieved to accept it, but Joe had a very wary look in his eye.

The farmer led them to the barn. "I'll see about getting you something to eat. And maybe some clothes. I can't have you holding weapons around my children."

"We're not giving them up," Joe said evenly.

"Not asking you to. Just rest them over there by the wall, please. They'll be there if you need them, but you won't. Please."

William and Joe did what was asked. They leaned their dull shortswords against the wall. Then they sat down on the hay bales about ten feet from the wall, Joe never taking his eye off his weapon.

"Thanks much. Boy's afraid of men with weapons. Can't think why," said the farmer as he left them.

When he was gone, William said, "Who would have imagined it? A civil human being in Arba."

"Listen, we can't trust this dude," said Joe.

"What? Why?"

"Nobody does nothing for nobody on this planet unless they're gettin' something back."

"He seems all right."

"He seems very willing to help us."

"So what's the problem?"

"The problem is, he's too willing. If you found two bums in your field, would your first move be to offer them food, jobs, and shelter?"

William replied, "I never had a field...but I see your point. I guess I'm just too damn tired not to trust somebody."

"Thinkin' like that will get you killed. And me with you."

"So what do we do?"

"We do what we do: we wait for the right moment, and then we run."

The farmer and his young son brought them a meal and sat with them while they ate. "You came from the Qi Dao Lu, didn't you?" the farmer asked.

Neither William nor Joe answered him.

"Had an uncle who got caught up in that once. Long time ago. Wound up dying in Tritto."

They sat in silence for a while after the meal. The boy took the plates and cups and left them. The farmer took a small pipe out, filled it, and lit up. "I know you men have no reason to trust me. If I were you and I'd been where you've been, I wouldn't trust me either. But when I say you're not going to make it very far if you leave here, you should consider the possibility I might be telling you the truth. Frankly, I'm amazed you made it this far. Lotsa eyes in this part of the world. All kinds of eyes."

Joe didn't say anything. He just levelled a very cool gaze at the farmer.

William didn't know what to think, but it seemed to him that on the whole, this man didn't want anything from them, and he'd at least fed them.

"We appreciate the food and the rest, sir, we really do, but we don't know you, and you're right, where we've just come from…not a place that inspires trust. But you seem a decent man."

"How much did you get for us?" said Joe.

William glanced at him warily. "Joe, I don't think he…"

The farmer chuckled. "Nothing. I didn't get a thing for you."

"But you told someone we're here?" demanded Joe.

"Yes, I did."

William turned angrily to the farmer. "So the meal was what, just to keep us here?"

"The meal was because you looked hungry. And judging by how much you ate, I was right about that, no?" said the farmer as he puffed his pipe.

"How many are coming?" asked Joe. "And where are our weapons?"

The farmer shook his head. "You don't want to fight them. And they're not coming here to fight you, but if there is a fight, you don't stand much of a chance."

"Sonuvabitch!" William barked. Then to Joe he said, "We gotta go."

"I wouldn't do that," said the farmer calmly. "They'll be here any moment."

There was the sound of horse hooves and whinnying. Whoever the farmer had summoned was already here.

It was too late to run.

"Cobo Dau! Where are you hiding my new recruits?" came a firm baritone voice.

"In the barn," the farmer answered.

Neither Joe nor William moved at first. William looked at the spot where they'd left their swords. They were gone. He spotted some farming tools, just rakes and shovels, along the same wall. He grabbed two shovels and handed one to Joe. They each got into a fighter's stance.

There were at least ten armed men just outside the entrance to the barn. A broad man wearing chain mail and a black-and-gray helm entered; his gray whiskers made his face appear old, but he carried himself like a young bull. "Cobo!" the man cried, slapping the farmer on the back.

"Gorthau."

"What have you got for me?"

"Two from the Wei."

"Really? Made it pretty far north, you boys did. Congratulations. You fed them?"

"I did."

"Gave them the work-in-the-barn story?"

"Word for word."

"Good man, Cobo, good man!" said Gorthau. "You can go."

Cobo the farmer nodded and exited the barn.

"Have a seat, boys, and let me lay out the situation for you," said Gorthau.

"I'll stand," said Joe, clutching his shovel and glancing toward the door.

"Suit yourself. I'm sitting. Been riding eight hours a day for what seems like months, and my ass needs a rest." Gorthau sat down and took off his helm. "Damn thing barely fits me anymore," he said as he removed his gloves and set them on the bale beside him. "Okay, then." Gorthau looked from William to Joe and back to William. "You look like reasonable men to me, so I'm going to speak to you like a reasonable man."

"Or you could skip all that and just tell us what you want. Or let us go," said Joe. He was clearly very angry and more than a little scared.

"I could do that, but that wouldn't help me, and it wouldn't help you."

"You're interested in helping us? Why?"

"I am, and as for why, that requires you to sit down, be calm, and listen."

Seeing that they had no choice — they couldn't fight their way out, nor could they run away from men on horseback — William and Joe reluctantly sat down.

"Thank you. Once again: here's what I have. I'd like you to join us."

"Who is 'us'?" asked Joe.

"'Us' is me and my fellows and our commander and whoever else is inclined to join."

"Pardon me, but are you...what, some kind of volleyball team? Basketball?" asked William.

"We are not a team of ballplayers, no, and thank you for confirming that you at least are an Entrant. Cobo wasn't sure. Congratulations on making it past the Reismyl and living this long. You must be a resourceful man."

"I have my moments," William said.

"No doubt, no doubt. Well, the fact that you're an Entrant means you're familiar with a concept called 'freedom,' yes? Civil liberties and the like?"

"Sounds vaguely familiar."

"Excellent. Well, the purpose behind our movement — really, James the Dervinth's movement — is to free Arbana."

"Free it from what?" asked Joe.

"How best to answer that question? Let me see," said Gorthau. "The Grehmanns. The Triumvirate. The slave traders and the Van Underracs and the Vortmers and whoever else holds the many peoples of Arbana under a boot."

Joe started laughing.

Gorthau started laughing with him. "Good stuff, no?"

Joe stopped laughing. "Mister, you must be out of your damn mind! You want to do all that, beat down all those people and ring the bell of freedom, but you're here in a barn recruiting two half-starved Entrants like us?"

"Don't sell yourself short, young man! You don't look more than a third starved to me, and Entrants who aren't Mindless, well, they tend to know things, don't they, that we poor Arbans don't?"

William, not wanting to give too much credence to this man's quixotic gibberish and feeling a bit overwhelmed — his customary emotional state since he'd arrived here from the asylum — blurted out, "Hey, I've got a question: why do you call your country 'Arbana' and your environ 'Arba'? Doesn't that get a little confusing? I mean, is there also a city named 'Arbanana' somewhere around here?"

Gorthau burst out laughing again. "Yes! Yes, there is. Arbanana, or 'Our Banana' as many of us who hold it dear refer to it, is located not ten leagues from here!"

"I guess it's not possible for you to have no bananas there, huh?"

Gorthau stopped laughing, put on a very serious face, and answered solemnly: "Yes."

Whereupon all three of them burst out laughing. William was sure he'd lost his mind, but it felt great to laugh his ass off. Tears were streaming down his face.

Joe shook his head, still cackling, and sighed. "Y'all are crazy.

Talkin' 'bout bananas."

They sat there for a minute or two, recovering from the laughter.

Gorthau cleared his throat and said, "Thank you for that. One needs to be reminded about the comical futility of our quest, to be sure. But we're going to start a war, just like our brothers and sisters up in Maelor's Country, and we're going to change things in this land. Count on it."

He was no longer laughing. He wasn't arrogant, but William could tell that this was a man who believed what he was saying.

"I was looking for my wife. My children," William said. "Can you help me?"

"He thinks they came through the Landing Point," Joe said to Gorthau, shrugging.

Gorthau rose and put a hand on William's shoulder. "I will try to help you find them. And even if we do not, I can make you a promise: no one who ever comes through there again will suffer the way you and countless others have."

"Can I use it to go back?"

Gorthau looked at him quizzically and then seemed to be working something out in his mind for a moment. "I can't answer that question, but I'll introduce you to someone who might be able to. Will you join me?"

"We need to keep moving," said Joe.

"I will. I'll join you," said William. "I'll fight to get you what you want if you help me…to find them."

"You have my promise, my thanks, and my sword. Welcome to the Dervinthian Brigade."

They stayed the night in a tent that was erected in Cobo's yard. The soldiers shared whiskey with them and gave them black-and-silver capes with the promise of full armor to come once they returned to Dervinth Keep.

Joe was mostly silent. He looked tired and scared. It was clear he didn't trust the men they'd allied themselves with.

"You're pissed at me," said William when they got a moment alone.

"No, man, I ain't pissed at you," said Joe. "I understand why you did what you did."

"They seem like good men."

"They might be. I dunno."

"You thinking about ditching them?"

"You know I am."

"I wish you wouldn't."

"I know. And I wish you'd forget these fools and come with me."

"Come with you where?"

"Wherever. A quiet place somewhere where we could fish and tell stories and not have to swing a sword or run for our lives every five minutes."

"Is there a place like that on this whole planet? And if there is, could we ever get there?"

"I dunno. I do know your family ain't at the Landing Point. Only thing worse than not finding them there is finding out they were there."

"You're probably right."

"I am right. A kid, down there with that Reismyl? You seen that thing, right?"

"Don't."

"You told me they died, all of them, before you were ever brought here. Why would they be here now?"

"I'm here."

"Different story. Listen to me: your best bet, my man, is to find out who those two dudes were who made you that offer. You want answers? That's the first one to get. Who brought you here and why. Never heard of anyone, ever, being given the choice to come here. And that kid, that Slau, where was he taking you? To who? You need answers, I get it, but they ain't coming to you at the Landing Point. And they ain't coming to you in the middle of a battlefield surrounded by thousands of Motatinfo men and Crabs and Tris with battle-axes and crossbows...nossir, you're making the wrong move here."

"These people are fighting for freedom. From, among other things, slavery. I've heard about Yanz and Tritto. Whole cities, filled with starving, sickly slaves nobody even wants."

"You're gonna tell me about slavery? Please. I grew up hearing all about that shit. I seen the Klan burn down two churches near my cousin's home, I seen race riots, Rodney King bullshit here and there, all my life I seen it. And let me tell you what I learned: stay the fuck away. Keep moving and don't trust them when they ask you to join 'cause they'll push you right in front of them when the bullets fly."

"I'm sorry you feel that way."

"Don't be. I'm alive today because I feel this way."

"Joe, you're a good man. A strong man. And you're the only friend I've got here. So if you want to go, I'm coming with you. But after all that we've been through...can I just ask you, please, to stick around a little while longer, just to find out more, just to see if sticking around might be worth it?"

William didn't want to beg Joe, but at that moment, he felt like whatever small amount of sanity remained to him he had because of Joe. Joe had done more than help keep him alive all this time: Joe had kept him from going mad.

Joe looked at him a long time without saying anything. When he finally spoke, all he said was: "Do you think they'll give us horses? I used to love riding horses."

The Appendices
(such as they are)

Glossary

(caveat emptor; some narrators are...unreliable)

A

Abeilon
island north of Arba

Abour
Hustel's grandson, a Wildean

Abraham Inek Moto II
architect and city planner of Castle Moto

Abtrinora
the prior name of Aethrelius

Aethrelean Sea
see map

Aethrelean Trueknight
a knight who has seen a vision of the sword Mosta Nom

Aethrelius
see map

agilios powder
a sedative administered in various ways, often to Entrants and slaves

Aidan Dossilea
Leander's grandfather

Aidan's Square
main public square in the center of Renikalar

Ailo-shut
Native Americans who inhabit Five's Wilds; Green Home, name means "New Beginning"

Akanouava
Ailo-shut leader

Alain
soldier of the Fourth Mandate Squadron

Ald
old man of Arban legend who's role in the legend is forever changed by the teller of the tale (see Chaq, Teutelin)

Allan Gentry
see William chapters

Alms Camps
government camps for the poor

Almstans
the ranks of the poor

Alukko Dwivedi
boy in Vaprosta who works in father's tavern

Alwaud'wah
name of the chassariete

Anadal's Point	fortress in northern Aethrelius on the coast
Anastasia Eleonadera	ruler of Carthage
Ancient Secrets	a collective truth essential to the Proving
Andre	baron of something or other
Anhariq Measured Fields	district; Pherriuskatan region
ONOF	premiere Arban religion; based of the appearance of four noble saviors
Arba	the 15th Environ; primarily sylvan, some mountains, lakes, plains
Arbana	see map
Arithicus	a kobold wizard from Waln Environ (see Quivix)
Aschare	see text
Ashkinda	Timesinger community in the northwest of Arba
Ashorne	according to ONOF, person who will usher in the Fourth
Asima	name the Northerners give to Frainle; loosely means "good luck charm"
Attana	a Visshilla, the one who found William after the cliff
Attard, Julian Cmdr	commander of the 3rd Caratan Army in Xatumka (Vamoul Downs)
Atuuts	mountains north of Midforest, east of Camedua

B

Baeselle Dossilea	Leander's wife
Baks Mu	lead character

Balkac Grehmann

King of Motatinfo and Governor of Arbana

Balogh

owner of a tavern in Ontonu

Bamboo, the

an enormous grove of bamboo trees in the eastern region of Five's Wilds

Banam

see William slave chapter

Banterkam

Aethrelean town near Renikalar

barb

one "gold piece" in Arba; minted in Castle Moto, made of something less than gold

Barli

a thief who harasses Ftuu on the road...and pays the price

Bas al Lowen

former district on the coast of Aethrelius

Battreshean Road

Renikalar to the Glaring Cliffs

Bausa

Opell's wife

Bavish

Brull pack leader north of the Midforest

baybish morning glories

a common flower of Pherriuskata

Baywinders

large garden in Pashkaka on Sianthis

Bealaki

lover of Petrecia, Pao's cousin, Spectrum magicker

Beene Street Facility

Camedua headquarters of Trades & Guilds

Beir Province

province in Aethrelius

Bel Miccalef

Carthage

Believer's Quarter

region in Pashkaka

Bellindor Highway

road leading from Renikalar to Chralm Doanna

Belolli Warmasters

F'nios served them, see Grewea chap bk 1

Benjamin Feespeaker

Aethrelean historical figure

Bents, the

a fishing village in southern Xatumka

Beriq Shudan	head of mosque in Castle Moto
Bi Prison	Massive and inescapable prison in the Marsh of Night
Biblists	outlaws who believe in Christianity, Judaism, and Islam
Bigs, the	governing board of the slaver traders in Arbana
Bikita Badhru	town in Xatumka
Bili Hu	soldier of the Fourth Mandate Squadron
Bjarni Malalji	timesinger who lives in Xatumka
Blackbear Road	road from Camedua to Narth Downs
Blackboots	local enforcers in service to the Triumvirate
Blane	gossie's companion from Northern Xatumka
Blutkirche	large Christian monastery near Fort Camedua
B'mai	visits William in his sister's backyard. What is he?
Bno Suj	Slau capital on the 43rd parallel
Body, the	lesser ruling congress of Tri
Boi Na	the first Arban Empire beg 102; defeated by Linosians 427
Boinage	ninth month in the Arban calendar
Bon People	Kabbie-na folk (Garden)
Bovellius Schau	tristain dictated his Book to this scholar
Braeru Ketwa	Vo'ixtavrac on Chralm Doanna
Braidenosh	town in the north, see Xian chapters
Branaedes	the moon of the OSM, also known as "the Silver Giver"

Braun
> servant in the Canamow
> househould

Breaking, the
> spell used to silence and control
> Pherriuskatan women

Breeding Houses
> places where native Arban men
> mate with enslaved females
> from Earth

Brestum
> town in western Arbana

British League
> a failed union of former subjects
> of the British Empire who found
> each other in Arba

Broken Flats
> nw area of Xatumka

Broken Mind
> see Order of the Broken Mind

Brownhold
> town on Pedry Island

Brownmen
> Arba's judiciary system;
> traveling judges

Brull, the
> remnants of Gri Na Leus
> invaders who regrouped in and
> held the north

Bubussa, Dalter
> Ftuu's owner and lover

Bulin Arc
> haunted ancient fortress in Lake
> Iale

Bunabwai
> a forest in the Namus environ

Bundi al Fruwqa
> settlement on the Lake shore
> northern Wilds

Burden, the
> what the Wildeans call the duty
> to find the Ashorne and make
> whole the teachings of the Four

Burrowfal
> a Tri footsoldier

Bvay
> province in Aethrelius

C

Calawak Pass
> mid Xatumka, see Frainle
> chapters

Callunia (8)
> original Environ of the
> Malliorelum

Cam Tropeo	a legendary Arban musician
Capt Fedonai	Aethreliean sea captain who survived Vo'ixtavraci invasion
Carata Chasm	northern Xatumka
Caratans	Tri soldiers from the Carata region of Xatumka
Carlo Leotrada	shipbuilder of Oak Harbor; business rival of the Half-dragons
Carmen the Yeti	William's friend on Earth
Carthage	city in central Arba; home to mundane colleges; city where they make most Lifewine
Carthagian Defenders	Rangers who defend Carthage
cartileggi beans	what Opell farms: but what are they?
Carvers	Trelk van Underrac's special forces
cassia oil	an oil used for grooming and ablutions
Cecelia Tremont	former romantic partner of Joe
Cedril sa Mino	Chralm Doanna commander
Celenya	Rodolpho's Second Wife
Cewra Bno	Slau city on the southern end of the Teeth
Chab's Inlet	south mid Arbana
Chaem Dossilea	King as of 968, son is Leander Dossilea
Chairo	autumn in Arba
Chalki al Fabr	body of water or river, Brestum
Challowian smooth armor	a light armor made of fish skin; favored by the Juks Xi Ren
Challowians	colloquial name for the Juks Xi Ren

Challow's Isle

island home of the half-dragons; located in eastern part of Lake Iale

Chalp

town in Aethrelius

Chappy

Stephan former sponsor

Chaq

an eagle with two heads and four wings of legend

Charge of Elering

a spiritual, mandatory visionquest the origins of which lie outside Arba

Charlton

a supposed Timesinger who allegedly lives on Pedry

Chaschei

saves Leander near the Garden

chassariete

see Ftuu chapters

Cheat, the

what Arbanans call the canyon between Wilds and Arbana

Chief of the Caucus

elected leader of the Aethrelean government

Chiella Windmother

title of the leader of the Jamoi

Chinunam Plains

farmland and towns to the immediate west of Renikalar

Chisek

island in the city of Pashkaka

Chop Point

island on the Lake

Choss

the lesser kingdom in which Palace Pir Choss and its medical facilities are located

Chralm Doanna

westernmost Aethrelius

Chrestikos

country founded by Vincent Bleuss on the western shore of the Wilds

Church of ONOF

the chief religion in Arba; tenets revolved around the Noble Four: Naipek, Frulla, Tristan, and the Fourth

Cjaknok Bay

just north of Chralm Doanna; portion of Aethrelean Sea

Clara Pyan-wu	the Aschare
Cliff's Awake	Leander's schooner
Clipal Debine	north of Hunberg
Cobo Dau	Farmer in Arbana who works with the Dervinthian Brigade
Core of the Mind	chairman of the Mind governing body
Cornus Wie	Aethrelean architect; designed the Square
Countess Cha Rettinbotter	a figure from a common comical Arban tale
Cra Savanie	current Core of the Mind
Crabs	Triumvirate soldiers who are bonded to their exoskeleltal armor
Creli Monshua	an Aethrelean military action in which Leander and Yallous participated
Cronelle	winter in Arba
crowderfish	fish found in Arba
Cruakle D'io	Midforest south merchant house districts
Cturrom al Nish	ancient roads in the Midforest
Custom of the Mask	cultural mores that govern the ornate covering of faces, particularly female
Cvuklon	lead character
Czackus Hall	location of the Aethrelean Square

D

Daetel	summer in Arba
Dagi Point	island in western part of Lake Iale
Dakaj	the brief month of dark winter: last season of the Arban year

Dalivia Island

island surrendered to Tri by Miranquella

Dalleo Winds

town in Xatumka; Theresta was born there

Dalter Bubussa

slave trader in the Camp and elsewhere, Ftuu's master and lover

Dammish

dark winter: last season of the Arban year

David Abadjide

commander in Northerners' army

Debrein

town in Xatumka

Decone

another environ west of Arba

Deepening Shadow

area of the Wilds where Bleuss established his kingdom

Deer Vale

province in Aethrelius

Del Miask Quay

wharf in Pashka

Delariun

enemies of the Aethreleans from the next Environ east

Demarr

fighter with the Northerners

Derric

a henchman/ hireling of Sh'arnau

Dervinth Keep

home of James the Dervinth and headquarters for his Brigade

Dervinthian Brigade

group of soldiers who oppose the rule of the Tri

Distrel Muertiva

commander in the Tri army

Doanna Pass

part of the Western Road (Qi) that leads through the mountains from Chralm to Tri

Dov Rosen

explorer who went to Prement and Namus; killed by Voix

Dropping Trace

road from Carthage south to Slau land past Viqual's Teeth

Druthec Grehmann

Son of the Lord of Motatinfo (Balkac Grehmann), Mind member

Dubaku	composer from the town of Thielbackler
Duhnx, Hanziella	Petrecia's aunt in the Spectrum
Duhnx, Jakob	Petrecia's uncle, a Master Jeweller and businessman
Dwivedi's	tavern in Vaprosta
Dwuan Lior	birthplace of Renik, dead city located between Carthage and the Chralm Doanna gates
Dying Plains of Xatumka	region that produces wine

E

Eeyora	steed of Cvuklon, named by William
Eight Tribes	in the Wilds, there are eight primary tribes who consult together to keep peace and counsel
El Malo	lake iale
Elean Val	ship sunk with Ho Matshuni
Elm Bridge	near the Graviss Glen
Elzbieta	Rodolpho's second wife; from Aethrelius (Hy Reac); distance cousin of James the Dervinth,
Emer's Inn	Carthage
Enimuat	Spectrum student, Frainle's friend
Entrant	a human brought by the OSM to Arba through the Landing Point
Erris Tarbiz	dead Arban nation
Eshe	town in Xatumka
Esut	guard at the Landing Point
Eve of Proving	last night of Dakaj
Evenhash	Evenhash makes a man as strong as iron

Eventuals

mountains between western Xatumka and Miranquella. Few paths.

Ewa

Ftuu in Carthage

F

Faler Mussan

former ruler of Pherriuskata and the name of the tower

Famish

soldier of the Fourth Mandate Squadron

Fan Ni Dok

southern Lake Iale "the Devil's Basket" (lotsa prostitution here)

Fan Pell

island in southeastern lake iale

Fashionable Citizens

name for the wealthy elite of the Tri

Fedonai, Romer

Captain of the Horizon's Grimace

Fellow's High

minor fortress in Aethrelius

Fellows Seas and Lake

shipping Guild major one in ARBA

Felsorad

Challowian ritual honoring birthdays

Fernanda Ji Norva

Petrecia's friend, wedded to George Ji Norva, Body Member

Ferrela Fout

small inn in Carthage

Fester Quay

quay/ neighborhood in Hunberg

Festofor Epidemic

massive lethal epidemic that originated on Pedry Isle

Fifth Rendlet

minor government official on Sianthis

Final Court

of the Brownmen, located in Carthage

First of Hunberg

the chosen leader of the Hun Kingdom

First Table

in the Aethrelean Square, the closest table(s) to the center of the room, signify rank

Fish's Mouth	large bay on the east coast of Aethrelius
Five's Wilds	Coniferous forest west of the Lake Iale in Central Western Arba
Fleck	Arban slang for money
Fleguriod	Tri presence in Arbana; calvary & infantry
F'lonedia	environ north of Arba, nuked or poisoned at some point resulting in migration
F'lonedian Influx	invasion by the occupants of the F'lonedia environ
F'nios	wily Wildean enlisted by Grewea to assist in locating Bealaki
Foam March	province in Aethrelius
Foplu	Gumunder bandit
Fort Camedua	one of three Forts in Hun kingdom built to defend against the Gri Na Leus
Fort Dilan	one of three Forts in Hun kingdom built to defend against the Gri Na Leus
Fort Ram	one of three Forts in Hun kingdom built to defend against the Gri Na Leus
Forum, the	loose group of Wildean leaders
Four Towers	Seat of Kold the Creator's power: located in Kold's Garden; heavily guarded; believed destroyed 539
Fourth Mandate Squadron	Leander's command/troops
Fra Chiang of the MP	old title for a magical practitioner in Xatumka
Frainle Natchalef Dossilea	main character
Frantish	Arban marijuana

Frederick Czackus

Aethrelean leader who found Mosta Nom and used it against the Voix in 664

Fredobbil, Graig

Aethrelean at Glaring Cliffs who supports Stavers

Freedom Prayer, the

Aethrelean prayer

Free Land Act

964: Almstans permitted to go to Northern Xatumka to claim land; most slaughtered/ captured by Brull Atuut (expected by Council)

Free Men Gate

gate leading out of Renikalar's west side

freiduvi

Challowian tea

Freme

island in the Aethrelean Sea that is known for its fruits and sweet wines

frenecoots

large hairless pack lizards

Frulla of Carthage

Carthagian member of the Body

Ftuu

main character

Fubb

Suashi in tavern

G

Gallivette

wife of Cedril sa Mino

Garden of Waiting

garden in Hunberg

Garkin Frwi

Vo'ixtavraci at Chralm Doanna

Geer, the

race who had Arba before the humans...they didn't prove. Grewea is one?

Geminstra

see Suashi storyline

Glaring Cliffs

northernmost Aethrelius

Glea Siven

leader of the Malliorelum murdered at table by Max

Glinbe-satyr

White satyrs of Saiblinor. Some can regenerate . In service to Pir Choss.

Gods Bay	bay at Pashkaka the origin and intent of which are obscure
Golden Age of Thiote	time of discovery, invention, and technology in the Boi Na Empire (see Timesinger History)
Gorthau	character in William's storyline; Grandeis Hold chapter
Gossie Fundra	Goslangios Mhetlonac
Graan al Soix	from Underrun (same as Fnios)
graffal	narcotic ones smokes; mostly from the Wilds
Grand Market	massive shopping district in Pashkaka on Sianthis
Grandeis Pil	31st Grandeis of Pashka; assasinated by High Chaos in 922 for an undisclosed reason
Granderman	a hunter/sheriff who hunts down those who escape on their way to Bi Prison
Graviss Glen	the pre-eminent central public meeting place of Five's Wilds
Graviss the Grim	founder of Wildean culture
Great Doanna Hall	chamber at Chralm Doanna
Great Takers, the	Vo'ixtavracci
Greater Bay	province in Aethrelius
Green Home	main settlement of the former Native Americans in Five's Wilds (nw)
Gregash	Caratan soldier who joins the Northerners
Gregor	Suashi's contact in Ontonu
Grellgorot	huge island north of Aethrelius
gremfi	a small pack animal
Gretus	Saiblinoran who tends the wild deer at the Glaring Cliffs
greunes	illegal smoke, like opium

Grewea Lon	lead character
Grey Bowler	see Gossie chapters
Gri Na Leus	invaders from the F'lonedian Environ (9); came in 613; defeated in 622 by future Quadrate; Brull are their descendants
Grivtel	Cvuklon's uncle, a Slau slaver
Gumundurs	thief gang in east Arbana
Gupta	chieftain who renounced his humanity and embraced his Arbanan nature

H

Hallowed Undertaking	Aethrelean history
Hara	Ftuu's fellow slave in the Camp
Harald Nettans	Master thief in Pashkaka
Harbinger of Maja's Dying Dance	song by the conductor Dubaku
Hartenow	Timesinger
Hasalk	cvuklon's cousin
hassie	cvuklon story
Hatitorp Manhoui	Quintian, spy used by Grewea Lon
Havenor	town in Xatumka
Helter Holding	prison in Camedua where Brown Men hold Baks Mu
Heop	Leander's second in command, rank = Markon
Herald (Suashi)	obscure name for a person who will find the Ashorne, mentioned in Bk of Naipek and Tristan
Herald Makeiron	Rise of Xatumka; First King: Herald Makeiron 555
Herdas	leader of the Northerners

High Chaos

Empty Riddler order of assassins, subsect of them is Patrick's Essentials

High Feast of Trantuse

one of the many seasonal feasts in the Tri; this one has a high and low version; the distinction has social implications

High Visshilla Pass.   northern xatumka

Highnight District

poor district in Hunberg, nicknamed "Reveler's Delight"

Hills of Wild Winter   in Thicknom; battles

Hilltown

town in Missouri where Joe Wheatle was raised and lived before

Hneock   Cvuklon's dead brother

Ho Matsuni   Baks Mu's ship

Hobknot   Canamow gardener

Holy Three in Delariun

battle in which Leander participate

holymen   ONOF scholars/leaders

Hookel gang

group of bandits with whom Gossie long ago did regular business

Horizon's Grimace   Fedonai's ship

Hova   Ftuu in Carthage

Hua Tsetang   mother of all Jamoi, born in Yanz (called Madeira di Betrio) in 237

Hulder Grove

settlement in the Wilds, home of Hustel

Hunberg

city on the north shore of Lake Iale

Hustel of Red Hill

Suashi's mentor and friend, resident of Graviss Glen

Hy Reac

bureaucratic district between the Khampier and Aethreliuis

Hyu   town in Arbana

I

Ignataus blood
: a drink favored by Pherriuskatan elite

Ill Return, the
: involving Klav Fundra

illu root
: a root that tastes like ginger and carrot; hard, durable, nutritious, favored by Wildeans

Iobus rites
: ceremony that occurs at the beginning of the year

J

Jaik
: male servant of Canamow

James the Dervinth
: leader of a rebellion in Arbana

Jamestone Quay
: quay in Camedua

Jamoi/ Jamonogia
: southeastern Arba, see Loretta's Journal

Janstrin Beir
: Leader of the Stavers, nominal head of Aethrelean govt

Jarred Chaudhri
: dead husband of Mama Chaudhri

Javier Rabishol
: Staver commander at Tolii Nus

Jemein the Reader
: Timesinger of Pashkaka

Jensenom
: province in Aethrelius

Jerad
: befriends Ftuu

Jipper
: leader of the slaves of Yanz and Tritto

Joe Wheatle
: soldier slave buddy of William's

Jolais
: James the Dervinth's sister

Jorge Celeranet
: Mont du Grace leader

Josef
: soldier in Fourth Mandate Squadron

Joyeux
: city in Aethrelius

Jui
: Rodolpho's enforcer

Juks Xi Ren

the Dragonmen who came from the K'nevar Environ centuries ago. Masters of the waters and water vessels. Reptilian humanoids

Justella

Ftuu's fellow slave in the Camp

Jyte

thug in Martanouk tavern

K

K'nevar

original home of Juks Xi Ren

Kalawatiem

strange race of nursemaids who moan...benevolent or evil?

Kalor Bromata

11th Prime of Carthage; arrived here via ship on a mission of exploration 603

Kalor Subramaniam

Eleventh Prime of Carthage

Kelgale

second largest island in the city of Pashkaka, houses most of the foreign dignitaries and races

Kellotta Men

Pao and Suashi

Kesel

Rabishol's civil recorder

Ketnice Arotrhis

arbiter from Renikalar

Khampier, the

stronghold in aethrelius on west coast

Ki Ang

First Emperor of the Boi Empire

Ki Dertali

fourth emperor of Boi Na Empire 207--256 (Golden Age of Thiote)

Ki Naipek

Second Emperor of the Boi Empire: younger half-brother of Ki Ang

Killinad Furain

rep from Greater Bay, Aethrelius, Unchained

Kisstari

lake iale

Klav Ouram

gossie's uncle

knucklenbonas

a game that is played by tossing
handbones and trying to form
patterns with them

Kold's Garden

SW region of Arba, deserted but
for the remaining creatures
created by Kold

K'olowinyad the
Creator

Wizard/Scientist who bred and
created monstrous species;
blocked OSM's nulling
technology; murdered tens of
thousands

Krendor Book D'io

Midforest south merchant house
districts

Krumerizon

the intelligence division of the
Vo'ix. Horrible creatures whose
psionic abilities stretch across
miles

K'tain the Burned

went to Prement with Dov
Rosen and Juks Xi Ren in 680

Kwanita and Gregory

a romantic Pherriuskatan story
about a broken clip (Petrecia)

L

Lady of Umda

attendee at the Low Trantuse
Feast

Laen Shi

Juks Xi Ren counsel at
Camedua, naval advocate

Lake Iale

large central lake, freshwater,
around which most human
culture in Arba was originally
formed

Lake of the True

large saltwater lake on the
shores of which Renikalar was
founded

Lake Servants

loose association of skilled
sailors and fisherman; Lake Iale,
a few near Lake Pimenchan

Landing Point

location towards where the Entrants have been pulled since the beginning of Arba. No Entrant has ever appeared anywhere else

Last Dance

the ceremonial and dramatic end to feasts; always varies depening on venue

Last Dreamer

a minor figure in the Book of Tristan; someone who will help the Herald find the Ashorne

last Quadrate Armada

sailed from Hunberg during the Lake Wars; lost at sea

Latter Medlite Declaration

pertaining to magick and its regulation

Latter Medlite University

For dabblers and minor practitioners; new students are accepted on the first of each of the five seasons. Only gifted students on Dammish. Located in Hunberg

Leander Dossilea

lead character

Lequoia Lake

second largest lake in Arba

Leroux

of Carthage

Li Poam Tascut

Challowian naval command

Liam

among the Juks Xi Ren, a loose family association to which much loyalty is owed

Lifewine

created by Frulla of Carthage in 793; certain rejuvenative properties

Lingler Forest, the

province in Aethrelius

Linosian Horde

invaders from Uo 321, defeated Boi Na, comprising six new races

Liolesca

Suashi: a spirit of sorts, chaotic neutral??

Little Britain	lake island first settled by British ex pats
Lixue	sugar merchant in Vaprosta
Lok, the	sub-region of Carata
Long Cold Arm of Motatinfo	name for Druthec
Loos	pre-eminent Medlite, uncle of Kai Ang
Lore of the Strangers	book about the legends and knowledge of races from outside Arba
Low Feast of Trantuse	see High Feast of Trantuse
Lower Gates	southern part of Carthage along the Lequoia Lake shore
Loxo	race of toll collectors and highwaymen: they watch the roads and profit from doing so
Luven tobacco	an illegal form of smoke, see Sharnau 1st chapter
Lyknore	soldier of the Fourth Mandate Squadron

M

Ma Shi Luang	elemental wizard who visited genocide upon several races, including the Halfdragons
Maelor's Country	eastern region of Xatumka, mostly farmlands
Mak	town in eastern Xatumka
Malliorelum	formerly of Callunia; wiped out by Velliok Action
Malliorelum's Bane	a name for Sharnau based upon his actions against the Malliorelum
Mama Chaudhri	Carthage; see Ftuu storyline
Manafla	Thicknomy drink

Mandate, the
Aethralean imperative to disseminate certain values

Mannler
hand at Glaring Cliffs

Mansdrelam Man
attends to the Mansdrelam device and the queue that leads to it

Mansdrelam Play
term for the lethal transport ritual

Mansions of Devotion
halls of decadence and indulgence for the Tri Elite

Marcin Tumus Velliok
father of Estau, author of the Velliok Action

Maria Xi
sculptor of Watersea; creator of Our Noble Four

Mariendo
western Lake Iale

Mariendo Compact, the
a collection of stories about the Lake and its peoples

Mark Oanime of Bas al Lowen
Aethrelean leader who gave Tolii Nus to the Saiblinorans

Markonite Two
a rank just below Markon in the Aethrelean military

Markus Crimusi
Mont du Grace commander

Marlon
fighter with the Northerners

Marsh of Night
in lower Pherriuskata; several hundred square miles of marsh; Bi prison

Martanouk
Suashi?

Mather of Grandhold Exaltus
a dignitary Theodore once made cry

Mattan
south shore of Xatumka

Maxonu Szetakas
King of Xatumka

Medlites
early magick users in Boi Na

Menniki D'io
Midforest south

Menniki, Benjamin
son of Unther Menniki

Menniki, Unther
powerful merchant whose family controls the wheat and meat in Arba

Menwaut island

famine and rebellion leading to Yallous' Act

Mer Ponx

descendant body of the Medlites; watchdogs for magick abuse; pikers in magick

Merchant Code

loose business rules of the Tri

mettlebrack

a crustacean sea animal; similar to a lobster or crab but meatier

mevatua

means "boat" or "ship" in Juks

Michael Pulami

Leander's third in command

Michelle

William's sister

Midforest

large forest to the east of Xatumka; southern portion divided into large estates

midlight

time when both suns finish descending for the day

Midpath

town between the Khampier and Renikalar

Mindless One

an Entrant whose mind does not survive the trip from Earth

Minister Pou'esi

a member of the Staver party, a functionary in Czackus Hall

Minkel

nickname for spring in Arba (and for the country)

Miranquella

kingdom on coast of Northern Xatumka; also, spring in Arba

Misle

Cougar Man at Landing Point: what race

Molish

town on the shore of the Lake

Moloa Boulevard

district in Pashkaka where one finds the pleasure houses

Monshua War

see Leander chapters

Mont du Grace

small peninsula stewardship in the upper NW of Arba; Petrecia was born and raised there

Moresso

ship sunk with Ho Matshuni

Mosta Nom

the legendary Sword of Endings

Motatinfo

in Arbana, home of the powerful Grehmann family

Mudarrisi

magickers who assist in the protection of Aethrelius

Mulp

young traveller who meets Ftuu

Murel

Malliorel

Mushon Smythe

merchant boss in Camedua

Musiker

a professional musician in Arba, usually makes a living playing at feasts

Musilia

Yallous' lover of twenty years

N

Naightermender

alleged royal of Thesseline and Frulla's husband

Naipek

1st of the Noble Four, once ruler of Boi Na

Naipek Sound

body of water that surrounds Pashkaka

Namus

Environ northeast of Arba; mostly deserts and mountains, original land of the Brull (Gri Na Leus)

Narth Downs

large town south of Camedua in Xatumka

Naruless

creature in Bi Prison

Nejima Celeranet

Petrecia's uncle (father's brother)

Nettan's vault

the legendary vault of Harald Nettan, thief king of Pashkaka

Nintuktu

lake iale

Noble Four

Naipek, Frulla, Tristan and...

noble home

household devoted to the Four

Northern Plains

northern xatumka

Northerners

farmers and homesteaders in Xatumka who rebel against the Tri

Nuadac Bubussa	Dalter's brother who lives in Carthage
Nulling, the	what happens to a people if they fail to Prove
Number Four	the 4th revival from drunkeness at a feast; considered taboo

O

Oak Harbor	eastern shore of the Lake
Olafur Miccalef	Carthage student in Hunberg
Olin's Keep	main town and castle of the Deer Vale
Oliver Woods	in Northern Xatumka
Onotu	where Suashi finds Yount
Order of the Broken Mind	defunct rogue organization of magickers who disappeared centuries ago
Orferio the Wicked	two tailed cat/demon of Arban legend
Orlean	town in Xatumka
OS Maeketel	planet on which are located 84 Environs or habitats for various abducted races
Other Sea	the name people who are not from Carthage often derisively call Lake Lequoia
Our Noble Order of Four	ONOF, the primary religion of the Arban environ; based on the teachings of Naipek, Frulla, and Tristan and the phenomena of the Proving
Overbaron Covo di Rienta	leader of the barons; main palace in Quintish

P

Paomaintanna
Suashi's companion, brother of Bealaki

Pashka
the Bright City, capital of the Triumvirate and of Pherriuskata, home to the elite of Arba

Pastori
island(s) on Lake Iale

Patrick's Essentials
association of Arban assassins

Payer's Public House
a tavern in the Believer's Quarter in Pashkaka

Pebbuska
island(s) on Lake Iale

Pebbusku Alliance
a loose alliance of the western islands of Lake Iale

Pedram
Sharnau's henchman at the Riles

Pedry island
an island on Lake Iale where there was once a terribl epidemic (Festofor)

Pella
Strak's helper at the Landing Point

Pengyou Ren
samurai monks who are a subsect of the Happy Magick Temple

Peod Barrens
site of an alleged murder of two Unchained by Stavers

People's Vision, the
pertaining to Suashi Dao

Perda Frwi
Vo'ixtavracci at Chralm Doanna

Pesil Acu
beings who enforce the will of OS Maeketel' they are not organic

Petrecia Celeranet
born in Miranquella, married to Rodolpho Canamow.

Pfadic Vortmer
Overseer of Tritto

Pherriuskata
kingdom in mid Arba, member nation of the Tri

Phlobalor
animal; resembling a cross between a pig and a dog

Phrattington
town on the shore of the Lake

Piell
plateau on which the Glaring Cliffs Keep was constructed

Pimenchan Lake
lake in Carthage bordering on the north side of Viqual's Teeth

Pine Point
island on the Lake

Pintavot
river through Yanz to Chab's Inlet

Pir Choss
community in Viqual's Teeth where advanced medicine is practiced

Pir Choss
innovator, doctor, Renaissance Man, immortal (a Master?)

Plaetithon's
disease that Theodore Oxenhaft has (sexual)

Poemsman
Arban storyteller

P'olif D'io
Midforest south merchant house districts

Ponasa
larger of two suns that OSM orbits

Popov, Marcin
member of the Mind, the barons' representative in that chamber

Po's Cup
Po's Cup is a flower from the hills of eastern Arba

Pravaronq
merchant guild island in Pashka; much of the commerce of the known world flows through here

Prementia
NW of ARBA

Primate, the
head of ONOF church

Pu'arinya, the
seer of the Graviss Glen

Pumcat
lizard like race who live in southern Arba

Pwaklon
enemy of the Vo'ix

Pyrontals, the
islands on the Lake

Q

Q'errash	Islamic settlement near Salora Falls
Qa Meistler	Architect of the Secret City
Qi Dao Lu	the long weeping road, from Chralm Doanna to Yanz and Tritto
Quality Steps	in Hunberg
Quattrenim	see calendar
Quintish	town on the shore of the Lake
Quintish viahrta	herb that tamps down symptoms of Derrithon's disease

R

Rabishol	Staver, Marshall, cousin of Beir, at Tolii Nus
Raja's Wall	in Hunberg
Ranthe	fourth largest island in the City of Pashkaka
Rash al Brek	dead coastal city where the Gift was given
Rathweine	town near the Scar on the Wildean side
Ratner	fighter with the Northerners
Ravagers, Scourge	spirits that protect and kill via magick
Raxsus	Canamow Mer Ponx
Redeemers, the	Triumvirate spies
Reestenfal	Pherriuskata. Petrecia
Reismyl	the Landing Point dungeon's primary inhabitant
Rel Nafan	the Keeper of the Boats on the island
Rendlet	title in Pherriuskatan/Tri gov't
Renik	founder of Aethrelius
Renikalar	capital of Aethrelius

Retractor, the

a book about the need to reject the cultures and history of Earth

Reveller's Delight

district in Hunberg

Reyna, the

Janstrin Beir's mother in Deer Vale

Riles, the

small settlement on the northern shore of Lake Iale in Xatumka

River Camedua

shallow river that runs from Lake Iale to Camedua

Rodolpho Canamow

husband of Petrecia and Body member

Rosen Square

of Pashka, town center

Rouks pullers

kind of small dinosaur used to haul loads on the Arban roads

Row of Plenty

merchants bazaar in Pashka

Rules of Watlier

a protocol for conducting a meeting

S

Sad Singers of Calmy

singing group, typically perform at Low Feasts

Sadneesh

physician at the Glaring Cliffs

Saiblinor

island off of Aethrelius; once the site of a war between two...

Samual Miccalef

Carthage Crab

Samuel Le Underrac

Founding of Carthage

sandpiggy

slang name for a Brull

Sapphire Forest

former home of the Callunians/Malliorelum

Scar, the

what Wildeans call the huge canyon to the East

Scattered Islands, the

archipelago in Delariun Environ

Schau Edicts of Elevation

Decide

Schmidt's

tavern in Vaprosta

Scourge Ravagers
creatures who sense and control the use or abuse of magick in Arba

Sea of aethrelius
waters north of the Aethrelean peninsula

Seaguard
name for the naval force of the Juks Xi Ren

Seastinoa
Brull Atuut information broker and...

Secessionists
slang Tri term for the Aethreleans

Seer's Walk
walk along a high wall near the Hunberg University

Serge Miccalef
Carthage Crab

Sergeant, the
in charge of escorting Baks and Xian to Pashkaka

Seuvel
Decide

Seven Learners
seven higher ups in the Timesingers

Seventh Westerly Inn
inn at the edge of the Vostloki district in Hunbger

Shain Dossilea
Leander's dead son

Sharnau
indentured Thicknomite who serves Grewea

Sheel, the
another name for the Triumvirate Body

Shen the innkeeper
Gossie's associate who owns an inn in Camedua

Shilah Takacs
Stephan's uncle on Kisstarae

Shitwings
slang for the Visshilla

Shulito
third largest island of Pashkaka, home of the Believers' Quarter

Sianthis
largest island of the city of Pashkaka, seat of the Tri gov't, the Trink, and the elite

Siddiquis
merchant family in Camedua

Simisola

finest narcotic in all of OSM, harvested from the Ma'erya environ, very expensive (Pet Low Feast)

Simon Rurstmeyer

Governor of the West (Xatumka)

Sincere, the

small town where Sh'arnau's men hang out and hide

Sinhag

Gumundur henchman

Six Shields

fortresses in the north and west of aethrelius that were constructed to fend off a Gri Na Leus invasion

Slau

amphibian humanoids who have travelled for centuries from environ to environ

slow riders

soldiers and attendants who travel with slave caravans but often stay indefinitely in Tent City

slyweed

Frantish product cureall, poison to some...

Sniffer

boy in Arbana; see Suashi

Sokanon

a small but busy port city on the north shore of Arbana

Somasindhu Mountains

mountain range north of Rash al Brek and Wei Da

Songs of Adornment

legendary Pherriuskatan fashion and masking rules

Soham

Northerner

Southern Road

Carthage to Wukneesh to Tent City

Spectrum

the intelligence division of the Jamoi; they search for women with color to save and/or recruit them; they also train magickers

Square, the

Aethrelean Congress

Staidop

island on the Lake

Stavers	political party of Aethrelius; opposed by Unchained
Stephan Takacs	mercenary soldier
Stestipha	province in Aethrelius
Stestipha Containment	fatal incident in Stestipha
Strak	Landing Point broker
Stranger's Road	southern road to Slau land
Strevkla	dead brother of Cvuklon
Strun Hao	deckhand on the *Ho Matsuni*
Suashi Bleuss	lead character
Summering Markets	a gathering of merchants in lower Pherriuskata in the summer
Sunray	Fraine's sailboat
Swinler House	brewery in Camedua
Sxa	Malliorel
Sylvester Gentry	William's son
Synthyea	Petrecia's servant woman

T

Tadills	Slau community
Tahmores	Alex Furain, battle
Takers	the Vo'ix
Talking Man Pass	in southern Arba near Slau country
Tamios Frendami	Th'ait, Staver, oversaw massacre at Menwaut
Tansy	name the Chaudhri women give to Ftuu
Tassa Celeranet	Petrecia's younger sister
Tent City	massive collection of tents and caravans that moves around within a limited range in eastern Arbana; focused on goods, slaves, and livestock

Teren Sound

see map

Terwam

an archaic lesser title in
Aethrelean non-military society

Teutelin

a half devil, half woman of
legend; associate with Ald, Chaq

The Sergeant

in charge of escorting Baks and
Xian to Pashkaka

Thelevin Crossing

somewhere in Arbana not too
far from Opell farm

Theodore Oxenhaft

descendant of Tristan; ONOF
scholar

Theresta Dossilea

Leander's mother; Mosta Nom
scholar; born in Dalleo Winds

Thesseline

environ north of Arba and
Flonedia

Thicknom red dust

a kind of snuff from Thicknomy

Thicknomy

mid south peninsula peopled by
sharnau

Thiecla Vortmer

Overseer of Yanz

Thielbackler

just west of the Sapphire on the
Lake shore, birthplace of
composer Dubaku

Thimi

merchant in southern Xat

Thiote

a philosophy of peace and
progress during the Gold Age of
the Boi Na Empire

third great race

Visshilla

Thom

soldier of the Fourth Mandate
Squadron

Thomas Yount

Assassin

Three Prophesies

of the Ashorne

Thrsea Machaul

Fra Lwang of the Mer Ponx,
member of the Mind

Thusear

nursemaid at the Glaring Cliffs

Thusollus

re Sharnau, may have had
Hatitorp followed "Lord
Thusollus"

Tiasmic Order	order of ancient masters
Tiero	town in Xatumka
Timesingers	Arban order of historians
Timesinger Charlton	see Sharnau/Theodore mission to Pedry
Tolii Nus	small island off Aethrelius (NE)
Tower of Faler Mussan	the Duke's tower overlooking all of Pashkaka
Trades and Guilds	administrative division of merchants
Trantuse	a lesser God associated with the color Orange. ONOF permits a lesser pantheon.
Trearlinket	vicious predator mammal
Trebi Cann	The Knower, refers to poems
Trelesti	the smaller of two suns that OSM orbits
Trelk van Underrac	Mind member from Arbana, military leader
Tret	Sharnau's henchman at the Riles
Trink, the	military training facility in Pashkaka on the western side of Sianthis
Tristan Oxenhaft	3rd of the Noble Four
Tritto	Alms Camp west of Moto: a true and massive slum marred by disease and crime
Tromontlus	race that lives in midforest
Twelfth Delariun Empire	the final empire of the piscine Delariuns, brought low by the Vo'ix and to some degree the Aethreleans
Twine of C'nai	magickal device that captures and ensnares
Two Brothers and their Son	Aethrelean legend

Tyun   Malliorel

U

Umda   province in Pherriuskata

Umeanitur
                             soldier thugs who serve various
                             Pashkakan Elite and merchants;
                             particular to a Lord, etc.

Unchained   Leander's political party

Underhat Low   tavern in Martanouk

Underrun
                             a place where warlords rule
                             somewhere near the Kold
                             Garden (F'nios)

Underwalk   Arban Council's intelligence
                             arm

Unji Maiter
                             Boss of the Creek, Tolii Nus
                             Saiblinor

Unwalien   name for sect of Slau

Uo
                             21st Environ; destroyed by
                             nukes in 461

Urj
                             slave guard on the Long
                             Weeping Road

Utla
                             visits William in his sister's
                             backyard. What is he?

V

Vaces
                             a thieving merchant of Xatumka
                             (see Hatitorp Manhoui)

Valdinedon
                             capital of the Jamonogia; plateau
                             city overlooking great plains

vamana bird   extinct Arban songbird

Vamir festival
                             festival in Pashka, decide, Xian
                             late chapters

Vamoul Downs
                             Triumvirate forces in central
                             Xatumka

Van Underrac

Vaprosta
                             capital of Chrestikos, on the
                             West coast of the Wilds

Velliok Action	re Xian
Velliok, Duke Estau	Duke of the Triumvirate
Venla	Leander's aunt
Vensol	Gumundur leader
Veter Iocole	merchant in Camedua; associate of Gossie Fundra
viahrta root	a root that can allay the symptoms Plaetithon's disease
Viemenburg	on the edge of the Midforest, S-E Xatumka
Vied-Bronste D'io	land owned by that House on the northeastern shore of Iale.
Vied-Bronste, Giorgio	merchant elite of House V-B
Vigilant, the	ranger protectors of the Wilds, assembled from/of all Eight Tribes
Viktor	soldier of the Fourth Mandate Squadron
Vinatuat River	river in the Carthage region of Arbana
Vincent Bleuss	Chrestikos leader and former Aethrelean commander
Violet Halls	meeting place of the Mind
Viqual's Teeth	Mountain range that runs n-s and borders Carthage on the south and Jamoi in the north
Visshilla	race of harpy warriors in the far northwest of the Arba Environ; once decimated parts of Hun
Vod Pamitter	Guild official in Camedua
Vo'ixtavracci	deadly meat-eating giants who have conquered over half of the OSM's southern hemisphere
Vortimer	Pad Vortimer of the Brown Men
Vostliki district	power district in Hunbger

W

Wanda Gentry — William's wife

Wasi Sagotr — term for a "house" or agnate

Wasi Sagotr Andre — Wine & Beer, Quintish

Wasi Sagotr Cam Tropeo — Music, Pashka

Wasi Sagotr Chestrele — BOATS/SHIPS, Hunberg

Wasi Sagotr Cruakle — Banking, Pashka

Wasi Sagotr Duhnx — Jewelry, Moto

Wasi Sagotr Hastern — Garment, Pashka

Wasi Sagotr Ilda — Glazier, Pottery, Pashka

Wasi Sagotr Joseph — Horses, Arbana

Wasi Sagotr Krendor Book — Bows, Ji

Wasi Sagotr Krendor Book — Woodcraft, Hunberg; mechanisms Carthage

Wasi Sagotr Menniki — Meats, Wheat

Wasi Sagotr Moto — Banking, Moto

Wasi Sagotr P'olif — postal system

Wasi Sagotr Swinler — Fish/ shipping, People's Isle

Wasi Sagotr Vied-Bronste — Armor and Weapons, Moto

Waterfields — agricultural district in midsouthern Pherriuskata.

Watersea — name of Hunberg before the Fall of the Boi Na Empire

Watlier, the — halls where the Body meets

Wauni — the southern shore district of Xatumka

Well's Time — a ship of the Fourth Mandate Squadron

Weru — Velliok's servant

Wesse — guard in Grivtel's caravan

Western Road — what the Aethreleans call the Long Weeping Road; Chralm Doanna to Tritto/Yanz

Western Tower	one of the Pherriuskatan palace towers
Westview Gardens	gardens in Ashkinda
Wevelor's Finest	a type of alcholic beverage very expensive
Wexshai	an Aethrelean citizen born of the marriage between a Mudarris and an Aethrelean warrior.
Whestibird	night songbird (cross between crow and hawk)
Wildberry District	neighborhood in Graviss Glen
Wildean Hadj	what Aethreleans call Vincent's march to the west
William Gentry	lead character
William's father	self-explanatory (Allan?)
Windgiver Sea	sea north of Arba
Wintering, the	a tradition of slavers and merchants during the winter: they travel , they gather at varied locations
wobo bear	koala-like creature native to Miranquella
Wolsa Vettunik	Timesinger leader
Wrangun	Thicknomy capital city
Wukneesh	Arbanan town, south of Tent City, west of Carthage

X

X'uks Ji Ren	half-dragons
Xa'yru	Geer name for the Masters. It means "shit."
Xatumka	nation of the Tri
Xereshon	see Sh'arnau
Xian	character
Xian Lo Fui	lead character

Y

Yabklunear
historical event that affected the Tromontius adversely

Yaderfa
Xian's dead friend

Yalessi
small Juks Xi vessel

Yallous, Sebastien
Leander's former commander

Yancy Gentry
William's daughter

Yanz
Alms Camp southwest of Oak Harbor on Lake Iale: a true and massive slum marred by disease and crime

yellow chew
an opium like narcotic native to the Marsh of Night

Yellow Meadows
region east of the Wilds and west of the Scar

Yi Shu
town in Xatumka

Yount, Thomas
see Suashi storyline

Youssef
soldier of the Fourth Mandate Squadron

Yrewlak
worm who is the entrance to Bi

Yulim
suits that hold water like a skin around their bodies (Juks Xi Ren)

Z

Zac
a boy who died long ago

Zara Sparth
character

Zarc of Jibba, Lord
character

Zeni
Ftuu's name as a child

Earth year	Arban year	Timesinger History of Arba
466	1	arrival of humans in the Arban Environ of the OSM
502	23	First sighting of the Visshilla
535	44	Founding of Pash
567	65	Founding of Watersea (later rebuilt as Hunberg)
570	67	Dema Gupta famously declares "I am not a human, I am an Arban!" rejecting Earth and its peoples
591	80	Medlites discover magic
653	120	Asians and Aztecs form Boi Na Empire; first ruler: Ki Ang.
721	164	Death of Ki Ang; ascension of Ki Naipek
742	177	Graviss the Grim and his five sons enter the Wilds
742	177	Ki Naipek formalizes Landing Point choice procedure
752	184	Naipek has the First Dream of Ashorne
779	201	Naipek finishes the Book of Naipek; dies same year
	188 -276	Golden Age of Thiote: advances in the arts, music, medicine, technology
799	214	Maria Xi sculpts Our Noble Four (currently in grotto in the center of the Pash Duchy)
799	214	Founding of Carthage by Samuel Le Underrac
807	219	Ailo-shut Pilgrimage; settling of Green Home
	d	arrival of the Juks Xi Ren
835	237	Birth of Hua Tsetang
	237-280	Rise of the Jamoi and Spectrum
837	238	beginning of Salora Locks construction
896	276	The Burning of the Medlaton
	270 - 280	Jamoiuian War on the Medlites

961	318	Minor Nulling by the Pesil Acu
966	321	The Fall of Boi Na (defeated by the Linosian Horde of Uo Environ (21)); incursion of 6 new races
975	327	Birth of Frulla
	321-355	Rise of the Terendislau (Linosian occupants, ruling class warrior Slau)
1009	349	Frulla has the Second Dream of Ashorne
1019	355	Civil war among the Linosians (Terendislau vs all comers) begins
1023	358	Frulla of Carthage creates Lifewine
1041	369	Linosian Civil War ends, Arba fractured, many Slau leave
1055	378	BOOK OF FRULLA IS COMPLETED
1059	381	Frulla of Carthage travels to Thesseline
1128	425	the Great Nulling by the Pesil Acu
1164	448	Ascension of K'olowinyad the Creator (geneticist who found a way to block Pesil Acu
1167	450	Birth of Renik of Dwuan Lior
1187	463	Poisoning of the F'lonedian Environ (9); massive influx of Mundites (Gnolls) and Pumcat (Lizardmen)
	461 - 488	The Festofor Epidemic
	475-499	war against Kold
1212	479	forging of Mosta Nom (the Sword of Endings)
1243	499	Fall of the Four Towers and the disappearance of Kold
1257	508	founding of Aethrelius and Renikalar by Renik
1297	534	Castle Moto (designed by Abraham Inek Moto II) completed
1330	555	Rise of Xatumka; First King: Herald Makeiron
1363	576	attempted crusade to eliminate Biblists

1366	578	Declaration of independent Pash Duchy by Duke Arin Sheel
	601- 606	refortification of Forts Dilan, Camedua, and Ram by Xatumka
1420	613	Coming of the Gri Na Leus
1422	614	First Treaty between Xatumka and Aethrelius
	613 - 617	Construction of Forts Trigolor, Masset, and Gupra San, of the Six Shields
1434	622	Defeat of Gri Na Leus by the combined armies of Aethrelius, Pash, Xatumka, and Arbana; Gr Na Leus retreat north and form country (Brull)
1436	623	Formation of the Quadrate (Aethrelius, Xatumka, Pash, Arbana)
1455	635	Formation of the Pebbuskan Alliance (Lake Iale)
1495	661	Coming of the Vo'ixtavracci, destruction of Rash al Brek and Wei Da
1500	664	formalization of Yanz and Tritto
1500	664	Rise of Frederick Czackus; Mosta Nom rediscovered and used against the Vo'ixtavracci, Aethrelius secedes from the Quadrate
1525	680	Dov Rosen, K'tain the Burned, and the Juks Xi Ren go to Prement
1542	691	Ascension of Kalor , Eleventh Prime of Carthage
1568	708	assasination of Grandeis Pil of Pash by High Chaos
	655-657	French war with Spanish
1565	706	Max is crowned King of Xatumka
1573	711	Birth of Tristan Oxenhaft
1573	711	Broken Flats
1573	711	Carata Chasm
1575	712	Formation of the Triumvirate
1582	717	Triumvirate members sign the Fan Pell Act
1584	718	Tristan has the Third Dream of Ashorne

1629	747	End of Naipekan syphoning at Landing Point
1635	751	British attempt to conquer Mindatatta
1637	752	Tristan dictates the Book of Tristan to Bovellius Schau
1710	799	Death of Tristan Oxenhaft
1729	811	Arrival of Pir Choss
	820 - 823	Saiblinor Aralian War
1749	824	Thicknomite/Slau Wars begin
1765	834	British attempt to conquer Mindatatta
1771	838	(refer to the Ashkinda Papers)
1788	849	Desecration of Northern Xatumka by Brull
1811	864	Free Land Act northern Xatumka farmers
1831	877	Destruction of Uo Environ in civil war (nuclear weapon)
1841	883	Wildean Accords
1888	913	A ship crashes in Viqual's Teeth after firing on Carthage; searches come up empty…
1902	922	Grandeis Braima Pil assassinated by Patrick's Essentials
1940	947	Xian Lo born
1944	949	coming of the Callunians
1965	963	The Velliok Action
1969	965	Leander born
1970	966	Birth of Theodore Oxenhaft
1987	977	Creli Monshua
1990	979	Vincent Bleuss of Aethrelius begins his journey to Chrestikos
1993	981	Stestipha Containment
2000	985	Birth of Suashi
2003	987	birth of Frainle
2020	998	arrival of William
2023	1000	the Proving

ARBAN CALENDAR

MONTHS	1	2	3	4	5	6	7	8	9	10	11
Angem	a	n	fe	m	fr	t	u	c	b	q	d
Naipekan	a	n	fe	m	fr	t	u	c	b	q	d
Feschille	a	n	fe	m	fr	t	u	c	b	q	d
Mua'al Yi	a	n	fe	m	fr	t	u	c	b	q	d
Frullan	a	n	fe	m	fr	t	u	c	b	q	d
Thiotean	a	n	fe	m	fr	t	u	c	b	q	d
Underracs	a	n	fe	m	fr	t	u	c	b	q	d
Ceou	a	n	fe	m	fr	t	u	c	b	q	d
Boinage	a	n	fe	m	fr	t	u	c	b	q	d
Quattrenim	a	n	fe	m	fr	t	u	c	b	q	d
Proving (Dakaj)	a	n	fe	m	fr	t	u	c	b	q	

	12	13	14	15	16	17	18	19	20	21	22
Angem	a	n	fe	m	fr	t	u	c	b	q	d
Naipekan	a	n	fe	m	fr	t	u	c	b	q	d
Feschille	a	n	fe	m	fr	t	u	c	b	q	d
Mua'al Yi	a	n	fe	m	fr	t	u	c	b	q	d
Frullan	a	n	fe	m	fr	t	u	c	b	q	d
Thiotean	a	n	fe	m	fr	t	u	c	b	q	d
Underracs	a	n	fe	m	fr	t	u	c	b	q	d
Ceou	a	n	fe	m	fr	t	u	c	b	q	d
Boinage	a	n	fe	m	fr	t	u	c	b	q	d
Quattrenim	a	n	fe	m	fr	t	u	c	b	q	d
Proving (Dakaj)											

	23	24	25	26	27	28	29	30	31	32	33
Angem	a	n	fe	m	fr	t	U	c	b	q	d
Naipekan	a	n	fe	m	fr	t	U	c	b	q	d
Feschille	a	n	fe	m	fr	t	U	c	b	q	d
Mua'al Yi	a	n	fe	m	fr	t	U	c	b	q	d
Frullan	a	n	fe	m	fr	t	U	c	b	q	d
Thiotean	a	n	fe	m	fr	t	U	c	b	q	d
Underracs	a	n	fe	m	fr	t	U	c	b	q	d
Ceou	a	n	fe	m	fr	t	U	c	b	q	d
Boinage	a	n	fe	m	fr	t	U	c	b	q	d
Quattrenim	a	n	fe	m	fr	t	U	c	b	q	d
Proving (Dakaj)											

	34	35	36	37	38	39	40	41	42	43	44
Angem	a	n	fe	m	fr	t	U	c	b	q	d
Naipekan	a	n	fe	m	fr	t	U	c	b	q	d
Feschille	a	n	fe	m	fr	t	U	c	b	q	d
Mua'al Yi	a	n	fe	m	fr	t	U	c	b	q	d
Frullan	a	n	fe	m	fr	t	U	c	b	q	d
Thiotean	a	n	fe	m	fr	t	U	c	b	q	d
Underracs	a	n	fe	m	fr	t	U	c	b	q	d
Ceou	a	n	fe	m	fr	t	U	c	b	q	d
Boinage	a	n	fe	m	fr	t	U	c	b	q	d
Quattrenim	a	n	fe	m	fr	t	U	c	b	q	d
Proving (Dakaj)											

Note: There are ten months of 44 days each. The 11th month, Dakaj, has only ten days. Each week is 11 days long.

The names of the days are taken from the names of the months.

Thus "Angem" becomes (or begets) "Angta", "Naipekan" becomes "Naipta", and so on.

One solar day lasts approximately thirty-one Earth hours.

So there's extra time for napping or windsurfing or...reading.

LORETTA'S JOURNAL

Dearest Brianna,

I miss you. My God, I miss you. And I'm sorry I left you, and that you probably never knew why, or how, or anything about it, any of it. How could you?

I've wanted to write you for so long now, and I even tried a few times, but I knew doing so would break me and leave me broken for weeks, or months, or years on end. And in this place, one cannot afford to be in such a state. This place eats the broken.

I shouldn't complain, not anymore. I've found a home. A family, even, if you can believe that.

A long way from Chippenham and Mother's garden. "Loretta, don't stomp on the stalks!"

You remember that, how she would howl at me from the kitchen window? You do. And I remember too. I do. I've forgotten so much, I'm sure, and I'm starting to forget whatever was left, I can tell, but that I remember. Mother at the kitchen window. You and I in the garden, me stomping, you watching me and shaking your head and giggling and making that "shame on you!" face whenever you heard Mother...that happened, right? Please tell me that isn't something I just dreamt up...

It happened. Chippenham. You. Me.

We were real.

But it's been a very long time, and I am truly starting to forget. And I have one of the many diseases that runs rampant in this place. I have for many years, but now it's in the final stages, and I haven't much time to live or to remember. It robs the mind, you see. Renders it unreliable.

I fight it. I try to fight it. Forgetting. It seems odd that in a world so filled with visceral danger, it's such a subtle danger that most threatens me now. Odd and somehow comforting. I don't know why. Maybe forgetting makes me nostalgic. One isn't allowed to forget the visceral dangers. Not here.

I know that it's because I'm starting to forget that I wanted to finally sit down and write to you.

There are things I need to tell you, things I need to say, before I die.

Things it thrills me to imagine you reading. Is "thrills" the right word here?

I couldn't say. I feel something, and it isn't fear, and it isn't sadness. You decide.

Over the years, I took notes, and I kept them hidden, not because it would have meant my immediate and painful death to have them discovered but because they were mine, mine alone — my thoughts. I can't tell you how much it means to have something of your own to hold on to in a place like Arba. I wrote the journal with you in mind. One does need an audience after all, and there was a time when you were my first and best reader, and I yours. Your essay on *Middlemarch*, your romantic attachment to poor Lydgate…and my horribly morbid obsession with Yeats's Theosophical dalliances. I'm going to share my journal with you, as intended. I put it together so that maybe one day you or someone like you — smart, brave, shrewd — might find it and make some sense out of this place. Perhaps there's a chance you might even find a way to…no. No. That was a ridiculous thought, and I'm sorry. For all of this. I know you'll never really read them, these notes. How could you? You're impossibly far away, at the very least. Or perhaps not. No one knows. And you must never come here, even if it ever became possible. Never. You must promise me.

But I pray that you're happy, that you found a life back on Earth like I never did. A husband, maybe? Children? I hope so. I had a husband here, for a short time, and I can tell you I was never happier, not in either place, than I was with him. His name was Atiq. He made shoes.

He died, I think. I never knew. He's gone, long ago, in any case. Taken.

Brianna! Oh, my dearest, my sweet sister…I am crying now. Foolish, I know, after all this time.

Why should any of this matter? Oh, but it does. It matters. It does.

Were we ever close, you and I? After I moved to the States…we barely spoke, we barely wrote. But know that I write to you now for no other reason than to say I love you, and I always have. And I miss you, and I don't care about what's possible and how far away from one another we find ourselves today.

I love you.

Nothing will change that.

I'm sorry I left you.

And I'm very sorry we'll never see each other again.

Hunberg, Underracs 27, 984

An Informal Reflection

L. T.

I was brought to this place, to this world, almost twenty years ago. Twenty of their years, not ours. I don't know how many of our years it's been. This planet revolves around its suns — it has two of them — in an irregular orbit. They say one Arban year is the equivalent of one and a half years on Earth. Maybe they're right. I don't know.

There's that phrase. The reason why I'm writing this journal. "I don't know." And that's the thing about this place that almost drove me mad when I got here. It wasn't the alien races, the lack of a humanity among the many kinds of humans that live here, the endless violence, the diseases, the prevalence of slavery, or the largely absent fixtures of medicine, education, employment, transportation — oh, they have versions of all those things in Arba, to be sure, but access to them is the prevalent issue — that almost broke me.

No, instead, it was simply not knowing.

Anything.

The first question was: Why was I brought here?

The second was: Why am I still alive?

For as long as I've studied this place, I have to acknowledge that I've never been able to find satisfactory answers to either question. Never. And I don't expect I ever will.

There's plenty of empty speculation by both those that are new to this place and those who are native — and believe me, there's a sharp distinction between the two, highlighted first and foremost by the absolute certainty that I will be killed if anyone ever reads this, simply because I had the effrontery to use the forbidden word "HUMAN." These people have rejected Earth. They despise it.

And I don't know why that is. I suppose it has something to do with some socio-psychological need to render themselves distinct and independent of their home species and world.

As if being on an entirely different planet in what appears to the eye to be an entirely different galaxy shouldn't sufficiently handle that concern.

But now that I've confessed my ignorance and frustration both, where should I let this journal take me? Should I admit that I'm done with this place and, at the same time, that I've come to love it? What should I tell you, who will never read what I write here? Like all writing, I suppose, the journal is as much for me as for you. More so than most, given the obvious disconnect between writer and reader. Still, there are things I need to say, things I need to get straight. Things I would want to say to someone but most especially to you. I'll write it then, to you, to everyone, to no one, but write it I will, and when I'm done, I hope they find it and do what they do.

So let me state for the record, in the style of a poor scholar who a lifetime ago hoped to be widely read but knew she never would be – no one reads academic papers, God knows – who I am and what I believe has happened to me. Some of it you know. Most of it, no. Let me tell you about this place and what I have learned.

I have learned so very much…

My name is…or was…Loretta Tunbridge. I was born in 1966 in an English town called Chippenham in Wiltshire. I taught history, first in England and later, after I was married to a man who later tried to have me murdered (or did have me murdered – I'm a little unsure, as I indicated),

in the States, at the University of Maine in Orono. I was happy there. We never had children, but I had students and friends and fellow faculty. He was there too, was George Pole, my husband whose name I never took…perhaps that's why he tried to have me killed. Do you suppose? In any case, we lived there, and I taught history, mostly that of early Greece and Rome.

It was in the early autumn of 1995 that George did what he did. He said he was doing it because he loved me and couldn't stand to see me in the arms of another man, but given that there was no other man and he had never given me any but the faintest indications that he even knew what love was, I've come to assume he murdered me because he was insane and deeply resented my position at the university. When I was just twenty-seven, you see, they'd awarded me tenure. George was a thrice-failed businessman, almost ten years my senior, who'd overseen the financial fall of a textile importer in New York, a wine distributor in England, and finally, an electronics shop in Orono, the town in which he'd been born and might very well still live today.

I suppose he hated the security, however small and incidental, my life afforded me. Hated it enough to kill me, though I have to admit I was naïve and even a bit in love and so I never saw any of that coming. I wonder if it would have made a difference if I had.

Perhaps not. I was never very good at believing bad things could happen. When Father got sick. When Mother got sick and took her own life. When Jody's two brothers — dear Kenneth and James — when they died in the Gulf War. Do you remember how we cried? Two silly girls who'd gone out one time to the cinema with two boys they'd never seen before and would never see again.

In any case, I wouldn't have left George because I would never have allowed myself to fear him.

It wouldn't have occurred to me to do so.

Odd thought, that, because for so long here, I've been afraid of everything.

I know he tried to kill me, I know that. But if he succeeded, then that would make Arba…the afterlife, or some such thing.

It is not.

I did not die.

My best guess is that I was taken just at the moment of my death.

Taken and brought here.

The prevailing theory used to be that only those who take their own lives are brought here, but few believe that anymore. Too many stories don't match the theory, I suppose. And maybe it was true at the beginning, but it seems it's no longer the case. The taking seems arbitrary at best.

Does it matter? Maybe to someone, but ours is not to reason why, not here.

Here are the facts as I understand them:

About fourteen hundred years ago, whatever brings humans to this place began plucking individuals from Earth — every country, region, continent, and island — and bringing them here.
Back then, thousands were brought. These days, very few. A dozen or two per year at best.

And every single human who's ever come here arrived at the very center of the Environ, a place called "The Landing Point." It has other, more colorful names, as you would expect. It is not a pleasant place, though its unpleasantness doesn't in the least compare to what awaits most of its guests down the road.

Many who come are what the natives call "Mindless" — and as the name implies, these people aren't much good to themselves or anyone else. Perhaps it's something about the journey from our planet to this one that robs them of their sanity and faculties. It's safe to say that some, for whatever reason, are better equipped to come through than others. Why, one can only guess.

Given that one hardly ever learns much about the Mindless before they are shunted off to Yanz, Tritto, or worse places and destinies, if one can believe that "worse places and destinies" than those twin cities of cruelty and suffering exist, it is very difficult to determine what the actual difference between those who become Mindless and those who don't might be.

I suppose in that respect, I was lucky. In other respects as well, for I was sold almost immediately to a cartel of slavers who dealt exclusively with Xatumkan businesses, and, thank the heavens, the University. I endured my share of beatings and was raped at least three times that I can remember, but ultimately I found myself in the service of scholars, in the great northern city of Hunberg on Lake Iale.

All of that bears explaining, and I'll explain if time allows. But allow me first to say that I believe I am only alive today because of my initial luck. Imagine leaving a university on Earth, in an abrupt and homicidally handicapped manner as I did, and finding oneself God knows where on the other side of the universe...at another university. The power of tenure at work, hmm? I hope wherever George is, he somehow is compelled to stick that in his pipe, or wherever else one sticks difficult truths.

In any case: a bit of geography. Arba is a continent, at the center of which there is a massive lake called "Iale." I intend to include a map of the place, or perhaps several, to help guide you.

I have access to maps here. Access on the sly, in truth, though I doubt anyone would mind if they caught me looking at them. Most people here are preoccupied with far more important things than an old woman staring at some maps.

There are four major kingdoms in Arba, three of which (Xatumka in the north, Arbana in the south, and Pashka in the east) belong to a kind of collective government: the Triumvirate.

The fourth used to be allied with the others but broke away many years ago. That's Aethrelius.

It's the most honorable of the four, or at least it claims to be. I myself have never been, but knowing the Tri as I do, I can't imagine a country that decided to take its leave of the Three Thieves can be all bad. I know they don't treat women as anything less than men; many are warriors and some are in government.

I also know they don't keep slaves. Many years ago, there were incidents of alleged genocide — a race called the Saiblinorans, who look very much like little people with goat heads, occupied what is now Aethrelius. There isn't any true written history outside of Aethrelius, however, and the Saiblinorans, who still occupy a large island to the south of that kingdom, are a people who rely largely on the oral tradition to pass on their history and culture.

That's most of what I know about Aethrelius.

I know a great deal more about the Triumvirate. Its past is rich and bloody and quite complicated, and I won't endeavor here to present an exhaustive perusal — I've chores and a life to lead and frankly, so much of what I could say would be horrible and speculative.

I'll give you my impression.

Next time.

Hunberg, Underracs 40, 984
So I promised you an impression of the Triumvirate, the government that rules over the better part of the Arban Environ.

The seat of the Tri is situated on the island city of Pashka, at the far eastern end of Lake Iale.

There are several islands there, all in very close proximity to one another, and in turn all very close to mainland Pherriuskata. Sianthis is the most important of the islands, and it's there that we find the Violet Halls, the ducal palace, the Faler Musan, the dreaded Trink — the home of the Tri's military — and most of the residences of both Mind and Body members.

The Body is something of a loose ruling body; its members range in number from year to year, but always it includes several hundred representatives from all over the realm.

The real power, however, rests with the Mind and the duke. The Mind consists of anywhere between six and thirteen members, depending I suppose on how keen the stronger members are on eliminating the excess baggage among them. Typically members of the Mind will hail from the most powerful enclaves in the nation: the rulers of Arbana, Xatumka, and Pherriuskata, and then also various representatives of the magick and academic communities. The merchants have traditionally chosen one voice to represent them, the exception being the Druthecs — they deal mostly in gold, gems, and slaves; they tend to speak for themselves.

The Mind is overseen by one member, the Core. Some say the Core rules, not the duke. I doubt the duke would agree, but somehow it seems it could be true, depending on who the Core is at any given time.

It's a country, it functions — however brutally — and it's not all that dissimilar from how things used to work, or perhaps still do, on Earth.

I suppose I've given you the impression that life on Arba is quite terrible and inferior to life on Earth. But I'm doing Arba a disservice if I have. It isn't that simple.

Naturally, there are some distinct differences. Here there is very little technology as we on Earth understood that notion. And I believe it's by design. And I also believe it's not necessarily to the detriment of the people here.

Here, we have magick.

We also have the collective fusion of dozens of culture not only from different environs on this world but also from other worlds. Every race here was brought from somewhere else.

Humans here — Arbans — are just as violent and conflicted and enigmatic in their behavior as they are on Earth. There is beauty, there is music, there is art, there is joy — these people have festivals for everything, very much like the old Romans. Always a party. For example, here in Hunberg, there is a holiday declared if it stops raining. Imagine that. Imagine if we'd had that in England.

Doesn't do much for the work ethic, but in general there is a sense of being truly engaged and directly appraised of what one's life entails and what it doesn't. I've seen very little evidence of neurosis, and suicides are unheard of. The practice of psychology never took hold here; I'm guessing that was a result of there being no need. Which is not to say there is no mental anguish among the people. There is. Stressors here are persistent and visceral. But death and the possibility of violence are almost factored in to the point where the overarching zeitgeist-ridden angst we came to accept as a given on twentieth-century Earth is virtually nonexistent here. One persists, one endures, one lives and dies in Arba. What one does not do is worry oneself into a tizzy or an early grave.

I have come to believe that, in that at least, Arba is Earth's superior. But if that's true, it's a superiority born of an artificially induced related phenomenon.

Technology doesn't factor in here because it's not allowed to. The OSM simply will not let it take root, and the penalties for pushing the point are severe and immediate.

And I think I know why. It's actually quite a common assumption in these parts. Simply put, technological advancement results in societal benefits but most often at a terrible price. That price is the advancement of the art of war.

Here, war has advanced no further than perhaps the period of Earth's late Renaissance.

Gunpowder is not permitted. Bioweapons are not permitted. Nuclear weapons are not a reality here.

Without those things, killing on a mass scale is impossible.

There are no Hiroshimas, not in Arba.

On the other hand, there are pockets of this place where electricity and advanced medical treatment, as well as sophisticated means of transportation and communication and the production of food, clothes, and goods are all rather enviable, even by Earth's standards. It's said that in the time of the great Boi Na Empire, during what is called the "Golden Age of Thiote," this world far surpassed Earth, parts of which were at the time stuck in or just emerging from the Dark Ages.

The rules about technology are enforced by what appear to be large metallic beings. Arbans have long since named them the Pesil Acu, or perhaps that's what they call themselves. I've only ever seen one from a distance. Come here and try to construct a bomb or a gun and you'll see one up close, I'm sure.

So why the control? As I said, the prevailing theory is that the planet, or whoever runs it, brought us here for a reason, and it would run very much counter to that reason to grant us the ability to destroy ourselves. As I mentioned and will mention again, there is genocide here, and there is war, but this requires enormous efforts, time, and resources.

No one pushes a button to resolve a problem.

Hunberg, Ceou 1, 984

I realize, having reread these notes, that my good intentions have been rendered irrelevant by my increasing mental incompetence. I never used to have this problem, not back on Earth when I was teaching leastwise. I was structured in my approach to a given subject and disciplined (if not devoted) in the creation of whichever work product I was about.

Now I find it difficult to remember to eat.

It may sound here as if what I'm suffering from is Alzheimer's. If only that were true.

I won't describe the physical symptoms of my ailment except to say that one's bones literally begin to erode as the disease worsens. One becomes something of a sack of sand, from all that I hear.

But I'm not there yet, and today is a good day.

And I promised some facts.

The name of this planet is the OS Maeketel.

It revolves around two suns: Trilesti, the smaller star that somehow casts off a violet light, and Ponasa, which seems more like our Earth's sun. They rise and set at different times, and the effect, particularly at twilight, is difficult to quantify. Some have called it an "ominous serenity," perhaps owing to the fact that so many untoward occurrences take place at night.

Like Earth, the OSM has one moon: Branaedes, or the Silver Giver. This moon actually glitters. It's assumed that it has exposed deposits of rare metals all over its surface. The light, at certain times of the month, is a wonder to behold. And it goes without saying that there are festivals devoted to Branaedes.

The Arban Environ, like all the others — there are forty-two in the southern hemisphere where we are — is seventeen hundred miles wide east to west and just slightly smaller north to south.

The other environs, to name a few notables, include Prement, Decone, Uo, Fl'onedia, Callunia, Thesseline, Waln, K'nevar, Delariun, Ma'erya, Namus, Daldor, and the dreaded Vo'ixtavracci. Some are wastelands, some are mostly oceans. Arbans do not travel to any of them, with the exception of perhaps Prement, a somewhat tropical land inhabited by an insectoid race.

An Arban year is 450 days long. Ten months of forty-four days, with an additional ten-day period at the end of the year called Dakaj, or the Proving. A week lasts eleven days. There are no "weekends" as we understand them. The days themselves are the approximate Earth equivalent of thirty-one hours long.

I'm used to that now, but it took years to adjust, I can tell you.

The months and days are named for various historical figures and events. The days take their names from the months by adding a suffix to the month's prefix. Thus, Angem becomes Angta, Naipekan becomes Naipta, and so on.

There are four seasons, as on Earth, and the climate, running from cold in the south to warmer on the northern shore, is quite comfortable. The seasons are chairo (autumn), cronelle (winter), miranquella (spring, and also the name of a beautiful little kingdom in the northwest), and daetel (summer).

I'm sure I've said enough about all that, and I've wasted too much time whining about my old bones as well, so for now, I sign off.

Hunberg, Ceou 4, 984

Today, I'm going to write about magick. It's something we didn't have on Earth, not really.

I'm not sure why we have it here. Maybe it's another control created by the OSM. Difficult to say. It is, nonetheless, present, and so a discussion worth having.

The Medlites were a group of learned men to whom the secret of magick was given. Most assume it was the OSM who gave them the secret, but no one knows for sure. The Medlites guarded the secret tightly throughout their two-hundred-year existence.

Magick came about in the eightieth year of humanity in Arba. The Boi Na alliances were just beginning to enter the stage of "proto-empire." Ang, who would later become the first Ki, was nephew to Loos, the preeminent Medlite. Ang commissioned the building of a small university, the Medlonat, where the science and practice of magick were to be studied.

What the Medlites learned early on was that not every human could practice magick. Only about twenty percent of those born in the environ had the ability. For those who came through the Landing Point, the percentage was much lower, maybe four percent. There seemed to be no clear pattern; the ability was present in persons of all creeds, races, and ages. Gender made a difference: only one in three hundred males had abilities, but one in ten females were blessed, some extremely so. Also, the ability as it manifested in males was trivial, unpredictable, and even painful. Males needed to study, as in the case of the Medlites, in order to master any magick at all. Females simply had abilities, and any attempt to enhance or alter them through formal study had no effect.

The female magick, which once in a great while would manifest in males as well, seemed to be tied not only to seasons but also to hues.

Intensity of abilities varied greatly, with most able to perform acts from time to time, many with greater frequency, and far fewer at will. These abilities, detected in women, were cause for alarm throughout much of Arba. Men feared these women and the lack of male control these abilities implied.

Magick by women was subsequently forbidden by Ki Ang, and Loos and the Medlites dedicated themselves not only to the capture and study of magickal women but also to their extermination.

The Jamodaemonogial War

In the year 237, during the reign of Ki Dertali, a woman was born in what is now Yanz but was then called Madeira di Betrio. This woman, Hua Tsetang, was born with more of a magickal gift than any on record before or since. There was, unknown to the Empire, a small renegade group of women magickers who called themselves the Jamoi. They operated largely in Watersea and some of the more populated islands of the lake.

Their self-ascribed purpose was to find gifted young women and save them from the Medlites. They found Hua first. They nurtured her and taught her. They were discovered and mostly destroyed, but some, including Hua, escaped to what is now Jamodaemonogo in the far southeast of Arba.

They covertly established a small colony where women of all kinds, magickal or not, could seek refuge from the Medlites, the Empire, and a male-dominated world where females had few if any prospects.

A Medlite practice arose whereby magickally gifted women were bred to men with abilities. The sons were kept alive and found to have notably higher magickal ratios.
The daughters were slain or experimented on by the Medlites.

Years later, Hua Tsetang, now the leader of a much-grown and prospering Jamoian colony, led an organized but clandestine campaign of lethal revenge on the Medlites. It took ten years, but they succeeded in eliminating nearly every single Medlite. The Medlonat in Watersea itself was burned.

The women returned to their country and were not heard from again for many years.

However, the policy of identifying and eliminating female magickers was quietly perpetuated by the Empire.

Women throughout Arba assisted in the secreting of their magickal sisters to Jamodaemonogo.

After the fall of the Empire and the crumbling of the ill-fated Linosian occupation, an organization known as the Spectrum arose. It was essentially a Jamoian intelligence agency operating throughout Arba. No one dared challenge it, for the magick displayed by its members was impressive. To this day, magickal women, if they can find the Spectrum, are invited to find a home in Jamodaemonogo.

The Scourge Ravagers

Part of the secret of magick the Medlites never revealed was the existence of the Scourge Ravagers. The use of male magick taps into an energy that attracts the attention of a terrible lifeform, possibly previous occupants of Arba or perhaps natives to the OSM, that devours the users of male magick. This festering, gnashing collective only pursues those who use their powers often enough and with enough intensity to be notice and located.

Somehow, the Jamoi have found a way to banish the Scourge from their lands, but in all other places in Arba, they roam freely and hungrily. They serve, at a price, the Mind and the duke.

They do not bother with minor magickers, but they immolate those who practice regularly or in the extreme.

Magick in the Tri today

Mer Ponx is a toothless, latter-day incarnation of the Medlites. They perform minor services for the various powers-that-be, often being employed in Houses. They are really more of a scholarly organization in this day of today, although the quality of their scholarship is forever scoffed at by the great minds here in Hunberg and, I suspect, other notable universities. They are humored, at best, but to what end I cannot say. Perhaps those in charge feel it's best to keep an eye on magick, however it manifests (or doesn't). Certainly the Jamoi and Spectrum are feared and hated, and it's likely one feels safer when protected by, at least, those who claim to understand magickal tenets. I cannot say.

Other races and magick:

For some undisclosed reason, perhaps a reason that died with the Medlites, no other races — those who came from other environs — can use magick in Arba. The Malliorelum claimed to have possessed the abilities while they dwelt in Callunia, but they did not have them here in Arba. Alas, the question there will never be answered, as all the Malliorelum were wiped out by Duke Velliok and the Triumvirate.

The Slau and the Brull have minor powers of telepathy and clairvoyance, it is said.

And the Geer, who allegedly occupied this environ before the humans came but disappeared before their Proving, were also so gifted, but that is merely conjecture. No written records survive.

Hunberg, Ceou 42, 984

I haven't written of late, and I'm sorry for that. Old Fratta has forbidden it. She wants me to rest.

But rest won't help this condition, and Fratta is about as vigilant as a bushel of turnips, so I'm going to try to finish if I can.

There is so much more to say about this place. I wish I had the time. Its history is vast and rich. Its culture is complex, infused with alien influences as well as those of every culture Earth ever had. There are languages, but the planet somehow helps with the Babel effect, and most everyone can be understood by everyone else, unless they choose not to be.

And that describes the place as well as anything: its capacity for perpetually expressing the paradoxical bond between shared and productive commonality and its limitless and incendiary capacity for discord. It functions. Who can say why? Certainly, the presence of referees in the form of the Pesil Acu can account for some of it, but I think perhaps it's the knowledge that each being here is, for better or worse, a part of this place. There is no going back, and most people were born here anyway, so for them, there is no "back" to speak of. One makes do.

Isn't that universally true?

There have been wars, massive wars, throughout Arban history, and slaughter. Suffering, murder, pain—all abound here. Several dozen regimes have risen and fallen. Something always rises to replace what has fallen.

The human race continues. Its nature remains the same. It rails against itself and yet, above all, stands the drive to perpetuate, to survive, and even to make whole.

It demands of us that we build even as we raze, that we love even as we kill. Growth is a constant. And the human race—the Arbans—are still here.

And along those lines, I find that before I end this journal, as inadequate as it is, I must highlight one topic among the many: The Proving.

It is said that each race that is brought here gets exactly one thousand years to prove...something. What that something is, no one can say. But the rule is immutable, or so I have read.

In just under sixteen years, the Arban environ will have to figure it out or be wiped clean. The trouble is, as with Christ on the Cross, just about no one really believes that anymore.

There have been three prophets, all of whom predicted the coming of a Fourth, a kind of savior.

Naipek, Frulla, and Tristan Oxenhaft all wrote verses that are now canonized as the teachings of the Noble Four. The major religion here, in fact the only legal religion, is ONOF — Our Noble Four.

There are churches and clergy and such that blend the philosophies and precepts of Earth's forbidden religions, but any adherence to the religion itself by the people at large is largely ceremonial and superfluous. No one believes the world will end. Another parallel to Earth's people, to be sure. However, Earth's people cannot logically infer the presence of at least some kind of intelligence behind its design and fate. Here on Arba, it's a given that someone made this place, someone brought us here, and someone enforces restrictions. Who that might be is anyone's guess, but there is further proof of its existence and its intentions vis-à-vis the Proving in the stories of other races who've fled their own environs to come here.

It's been centuries since that last happened, and it's my assumption that what lessons Arbans might have truly learned have been lost to the apathy and shrunken memory of history.

No one is concerned, not really. Perhaps some in Five's Wilds, but motivations and truth are difficult to discern. Safe to say that the Proving is regarded as something of a fairy tale. Ironic in this place, which itself would be the stuff of fairy tales back on Earth…

I hope it is all an empty legend. The people here deserve a chance to find themselves, to become something more than they are. But if that happens, or if Arba does die, I will not be here to see it.

I'm afraid I've run out of time, you see.

Even now, I can feel my arms failing, and it's been some time since I was able to walk.

Brianna, I'm sorry, and I miss you and always have.

I hope to see you wherever…just not here.

Never here.

The Arban Tales
will continue in 2020…

(assuming the Vo'ix don't make
sandwiches of the lot of us first).